Delafield Public Library
Delafield, WI 53018

ALSO BY PHILIP CAPUTO

A Rumor of War

Horn of Africa

DelCorso's Gallery

Indian Country

Means of Escape

Equation for Evil

Exiles

The Voyage

The Voyage

BY

PHILIP CAPUTO

ALFRED A. KNOPF

NEW YORK

1999

Delafield Public Library
Delafield, WI 53018

THIS IS A BORZOI BOOK
PUBLISHED BY ALFRED A. KNOPF, INC.

Copyright © 1999 by Philip Caputo

All rights reserved under International and Pan-American Copyright Conventions.
Published in the United States by Alfred A. Knopf, Inc., New York,
and simultaneously in Canada by Random House of Canada Limited, Toronto.
Distributed by Random House, Inc., New York.

www.randomhouse.com

Knopf, Borzoi Books, and the colophon are registered
trademarks of Random House, Inc.

Library of Congress Cataloging-in-Publication Data
Caputo, Philip.
The voyage / by Philip Caputo.—1st ed.
p.   c.m
ISBN 0-679-45039-4 (alk. paper)
I. Title.
PS3553.A625V69   1999
813'.54—dc21   99-23568
CIP

Manufactured in the United States of America
First Edition

FOR JOHN PEYTON WARE

Born June 20, 1921. Crossed the bar, March 30, 1999.

All the tempestuous passions of mankind's young days, the love of loot and the love of glory, the love of adventure and the love of danger, with the great love of the unknown and vast dreams of dominion and power, have passed like images reflected from a mirror, leaving no record upon the mysterious face of the sea. Impenetrable and heartless, the sea has given nothing of itself to the suitors for its precarious favours. Unlike the earth, it cannot be subjugated at any cost of patience and toil. For all its fascination that has lured so many to a violent death, its immensity has never been loved as the mountains, the plains, the desert itself, have been loved.

JOSEPH CONRAD

Part One

THE BAYS OF MAINE

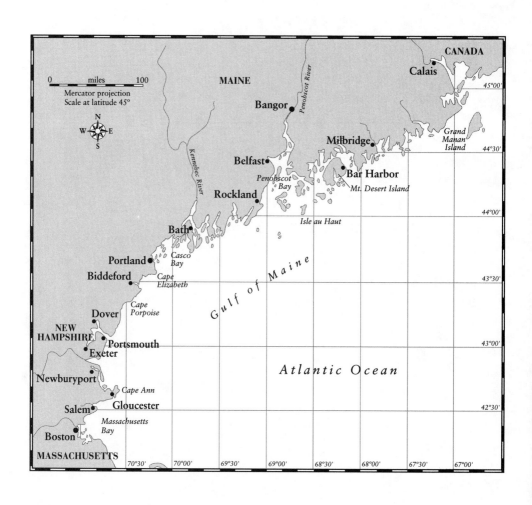

CANADA

Calais

MAINE

45°00'

Bangor

Penobscot River

Milbridge

Grand
Manan
Island

44°30'

Belfast

Bar Harbor

Penobscot
Bay

Mt. Desert Island

Rockland

44°00'

Isle au Haut

Bath

Casco
Bay

Gulf of Maine

Portland

Biddeford

Cape
Elizabeth

43°30'

Cape
Porpoise

Dover

NEW
HAMPSHIRE

Portsmouth

43°00'

Exeter

Newburyport

Atlantic Ocean

Cape Ann

Salem

Gloucester

42°30'

Boston

Massachusetts
Bay

MASSACHUSETTS

70°30'   70°00'   69°30'   69°00'   68°30'   68°00'   67°30'   67°00'

0   miles   100

Mercator projection
Scale at latitude 45°

N
W   E
S

Kennebec River

1

THE SEA was gray that morning, and as smooth as the surface of an eye. Eastward, the edge of the earth had been brought miles closer to shore by a fog that had drifted in during the night as far as the mouth of the bay. There it stopped, neither advancing nor retreating, and the out islands and all that lay around them and beyond them were held in a windowless dungeon of vapor. From the dock in front of his family's house on the mainland, Nathaniel could not see even a suggestion of the islands' spruce steeples; nor of the granite plinths and ledges that usually showed through the trees. Forest and rock seemed to have been dissolved, made one with the mist that also cloaked the lighthouses and the tall crucifixes of the stone drogers, waiting at anchor or at the quarry wharves for the fog to lift and a fair wind to bear them down the long roads of the ocean to Boston, with paving blocks or a carved hero's pedestal, to Charleston with Corinthian pillars to glorify a city hall, to New York with polished slabs to face the new buildings rising into the skies of the new century. He knew the ships were there because he heard their bells, clanging five seconds each minute to mark their anchorages. Other sounds were mixed in with the bells, and he listened like a blind man at a discordant symphony, identifying each thing and its location by the noise it made. That shrill piping—the steam ferry that serviced the islands. That sad, lost bleat—a doryman cranking his handheld horn. That di-tonal moan far off—a lighthouse . . .

He thought it curious how the fog held in one place, as if an invisible wall were blocking it from coming ashore. Over his head was a cloudless sky and sunlight, out there murk. The division between the realms of the clear and the obscured was as sharp as the bifurcation in a half-moon, and he wondered what caused it. A sudden change in water temperature? In air temperature? In both? It was hard to tell the difference between air and water, what with the two elements merging seamlessly into the whiteness that erased the horizon, and the sky the same color as the dead calm sea. His father's two-masted schooner, moored offshore near an exposed ledge, made a vivid, perfect copy of itself in the polished plane of water, only upside down. Nathaniel pulled his oilskin from his seabag, folded it to make a cushion, then squatted, braced his elbows inside his spread knees, and turned himself and the world topsy-turvy. Now the sea became the heavens and the heavens a waveless sea, while the schooner and the ledge and the cormorants perched atop the ledge appeared as reflections of their reflections. Topsy-turvy he and the world remained, until the illusion was spoiled by two harbor seals that surfaced astern of the schooner and sent ripples shoreward in sleek undulations, like the luffing of a satin sail. The reflections of rock, birds, and boat swayed and shuddered, testifying to what was object and what was image, to what was sky and what was ocean. Gravity, that most unambiguous of the world's forces, also would not be deceived; blood rushed to Nathaniel's head and told him which way was up.

He lowered his legs slowly and stood and laid his hand against a piling to steady himself. The water below, with the reflections of snail-encrusted pilings angling off into the depths, wasn't gray, as in the distance, but adamant green, and as cold as it looked. Cold enough even in early summer to kill a man in no more than fifteen or twenty minutes. His father, that nearly infallible authority on all things maritime, had seen it happen years ago, when a sailor on his ship fell from a yardarm and was plucked out less than a quarter of an hour later, bluefaced and as dead as Julius Caesar. Nathaniel watched the seals swimming along in their blubbery insulation, dark heads throwing off sparkles of pearlescent light. Then, in a synchronized arching of glossy backs, they dove out of sight. He put the oilskin back into the seabag, which had his first name inked on it to distinguish it from his brothers', and sat down and dropped it into the dory. She was twelve feet long, with white lapstrake, and her rail, oars, and thwarts gleamed under new coats of varnish.

The dock shook. He turned to see his father, face darkened by the shadow of a wide-brimmed straw hat, carrying a crate of dry stores. His shirtsleeves were rolled up to the elbows and his muscles, straining under freckled skin covered by fine, cinnamon hairs, still had the look of knotted whips. A young man's muscles. But was a young man's strength still in them? There was more gray than ginger in his beard, and half the hair under that hat was gone now. Closer to a grandfather than to a father in age—fifty-six this year, Nathaniel thought, and got to his feet and went to take the crate. Cyrus waved him off with a movement of his head and carried it the rest of the way, setting it down alongside the piling to which the dory's painter was tied with a bowline.

"What were you doing?" he said. He was breathing hard, as if he had run down from the house, and Nathaniel saw that his face had not been darkened by the hat brim but by the color that rose in it from an excess of sun or exertion, or whenever he was angry: the color of an earthenware platter, a shade so close to his beard's, before it had begun turning silver, that the distinction between flesh and hair had been hard to see from far away.

"Putting my personals aboard, sir."

"Looked to me like you were standing on your head."

There was a faint note of disapproval in his father's voice, and Nathaniel felt himself blush.

"Oh, that. Just an exercise. A friend of mine at school told me that he'd read that the Hindoos of India stand on their heads all the time and that it's very good for you."

Cyrus stared critically with his good eye, frosty as winter seasmoke, while the left eye, its stilled pupil cocked off-center, seemed to stare over Nathaniel's right shoulder. It was always disconcerting, this being looked at directly and indirectly at the same time.

"If the way those Hindoos live is an example, don't reckon putting your head where your feet oughtta be is of any benefit."

"No, sir."

He had wanted to say, What do you know about the way Hindoos live? You've never been to India, because he now could look straight into Cyrus's sighted eye, as well as wear his shirts, and the parity in stature and bulk had opened up the possibility that he might be his father's match in other ways. Sometimes, he imagined himself challenging the old man to wrestle, or to put on the gloves and go a round or two—fantasies both thrilling and frightening that had begun to grow in him in the past year, right along with the whiskers sprouting from his chin and upper lip, and with the new inches in his height and the new muscle slabbed onto his ribs and shoulders, beard and inches wondrous gifts from nature, while the weight was more the fruit of his own husbandry: He exercised with the dumbbells ordered from the Sears Roebuck catalog last Christmas, played football and boxed at Andover because he'd read that boxing and football had transformed the vice president from a sickly kid into the hero who led the charge up San Juan Hill. Not that Nathaniel had ever been sickly or a weakling; he was in training for the moment, which he was sure awaited him somewhere in the future, when he would be called upon to lead a charge in war. Or to rescue people from a burning building. Or to capture a gang of Chinese bandits, as Frank Merriwell had done in the last issue of *Tip Top Weekly*. When the moment came, he wanted to make sure he was fit and tough and equal to the task.

"Intend to stand there all day?"

"Sir?"

Cyrus dropped his gaze to the crate wherein sacks of flour and coffee lay atop tins of beef, pears, and beans. Nathaniel eased down the ladder into the dory. The thwart, wet with dew, chilled his bare feet, and he felt a residual tackiness in the coats of spar varnish. He reached up and took the crate and stowed it forward.

"Y'know, we ought to build a floating dock like the Williamses," he said. "Then we could step into this dory, no matter what the tide. It would make things a lot easier."

"Reckon it might. But I never have believed that easier is necessarily better. 'We glory in tribulations also, knowing that tribulation worketh patience, and patience experience, and experience, hope.'"

"Romans?"

"Five, three through five. In the original, 'experience' would have meant 'character.' Therefore, it is through tribulation . . ."

"Yes, sir, I understand," said Nathaniel, meaning that he understood his father's interpretation; he did not understand how a floating dock could spare him tribulation sufficient to be harmful to his character.

"Those stores there and whatever your brothers bring down will be the last of it. Bottom of the incoming in . . ." Cyrus withdrew from the pocket of his canvas trousers the tarnished watch he'd used to time his logs when he was wrecking in the Florida Keys. "About an hour." A quick glance seaward, as if he did not entirely trust the timepiece and was compelled to check the tide to verify that it and the instrument were in agreement.

"We should catch the start of the ebb," said Nathaniel. "Need some wind, though."

"Wind there'll be," the father forecast, and with such confidence that the son expected the first puff to spring up that very moment.

"Eliot and I were talking. We seem to be taking a lot more than usual." Nathaniel motioned at the crate. "Enough to last the four of us a lot longer than a week or ten days."

"That's what you figure, is it?" his father said, and then nothing more. He stood sidelit by the sun, legs spread, hands under his braces and resting on his chest.

"Mind me asking if you're planning a longer cruise than usual?"

"And if I am?"

Nathaniel rose on tiptoe and, ignoring the ladder, threw his forearms onto the dock and heaved himself back up in a single, fluid movement.

"With Mother not feeling well, we thought . . ."

"Your mother's fine."

"Yes, sir. But she's been gone two weeks."

"Told you and your brothers that I got a wire from Dr. Matthews, didn't I ? Nothing serious."

"So we'll be cruising longer than a week, then? That's all right with us."

"It's all right with you three," said Cyrus, with a derisive huff. "It had better be all right. I'm going to get Eliot and Drew to shake a leg. Sure you've got all your personals?"

"Yes. How about your seabag? I could bring it down for you."

"Won't be necessary, Nat."

He watched his father go up toward the house, walking as if he were carrying a seabag: a heaviness in his old nimble sailorman's gait, a slump to his shoulders—too slight to be noticed by those who didn't know him well, but obvious to those who did. These changes in stride and posture, like his short-windedness, had come about very recently, appearing simultaneously with changes in his manner: an air of distant preoccupation, pensive silences at the dinner table, and something else that had come to share tenancy with the ferocity that was the hallmark of his temperament. Nathaniel could not give a name to it. A melancholy? A somberness? Maybe there was no single word for that hint of something autumnal, like the first yellowing of September leaves. He acted like a man with a broken heart, sometimes. Not that Nathaniel knew much about broken hearts, beyond what he had read in novels, beyond the disturbing ache that afflicted his own heart whenever he saw Constance Williams in her new Gibson girl hairstyle and the lace-collared blouses that she now filled out in a womanly way. He couldn't imagine his father with a broken heart, in any case—there were people who would question if the man had one to break.

He sat down to wait and gazed at the schooner, and she affected him the way a beautiful building or landscape affects a lover of architecture or art. There was nothing fancy or exotic about her; her lines were elegant simplicity itself. She was sturdy enough for blue water work, yet she was agile and quick in stays, for a full-keeled vessel, and she gave an impression of lightness and buoyancy, as if she were ribbed with the airy bones of a gull or frigate bird. She had been christened *Double Eagle* the year before Nathaniel was born. Built in the Story shipyards in Essex as a miniature Gloucesterman, she was forty-six feet overall, thirty-eight on the waterline, and as swift as a vessel that length could be: last year, homeward bound from Canada in a gale, she had topped nine knots. Even at rest, she seemed to be in motion. Nathaniel loved her dark green hull, accented by white sheerstrake, sweeping back like a giant egret feather from the gilded ivy carved in her bow; loved as well the Euclidian shapes her stays and shrouds drew against the sky, the symmetry of her Sitka masts, varnished to a glossy butternut.

This year, she sparkled as perhaps she hadn't since her launching. At the end of May, with the boys out of school and the family settled into the Maine house for the summer, Cyrus decreed that *Double Eagle* was to be overhauled, stem to stern, topmasts to keel. He set Nathaniel and his brothers to work in Potter's boatyard in Blue Hill harbor, where the schooner had been hauled for the winter. They scraped, sanded, and repainted her bottom with two coats of red copper. They recaulked her seams, their ears plugged with cotton against the mallets' thuds, because they didn't want their hearing damaged, like the professional caulkers down in the Essex yards—men who could not answer to their own names except when shouted to from a yard or two away. When the caulking was done, the brothers examined the standing rigging and the running gear, and long-spliced new line into worn spots in the main and main-peak halyards, burned Irish pennants off the jib and staysail sheets, and coated whipping thread in candlewax and finished the sheets' bitter ends with sailmaker's whips. They found too much white powder on the anchor cable, bought a new one at Potter's chandlery, charging it off to their father's account, and then shackled it to the chain. They spread the sails on the ground—all seven plus a spare jib—and inspected each for mildew and frayed stitching, ever mindful of the admonition Cyrus had driven home to them over and over: "A sailor can no more hide his sins from the sea than a killer can hide the stain of murder from God. You cut corners, leave something done halfway to right, say to yourselves, 'Ah, that's good enough,' and the sea will find you out, boys, and she'll be a different god from the God of our fathers, because she'll show no mercy, nor forgiveness either."

Each day's work began about an hour after breakfast, when Tom Dailey dropped them off at the yard with their lunch buckets, and ended around four in the afternoon, when Dailey returned with the wagon to drive them back to Mingulay in time to wash up for dinner, promptly, unfailingly served at six. Their father had given them a list of tasks, written in his crabbed hand on three ruled sheets of paper, and they checked off each item methodically. Was the rudder sound? The steering cables? Were there signs of rot above or below decks? They did not find any and hadn't expected to: *Double Eagle* had been framed in white oak and her hull planked in Dade County pine, brought all the way up from Florida—a wood as rot-resistant as steel and almost as hard, so hard it sometimes bent nails and broke drill bits.

Cosmetics came last. She was given a fresh coat of paint, her brass was polished, and Cyrus, who came by to inspect, wasn't satisfied until he could see himself in the binnacle well enough to shave. They put her in the water the following day. After a winter on the alien land, she rumbled down the launching ramp as if rushing into the old familiar embrace of the everlasting sea. She sat at her berth for a day and a night, to give her planks time to swell and make her seams watertight. Next morning, the boys bent her sails and brought her home. The trip of some ten miles barely qualified as a day sail, much less as a voyage, but it was the first time they had been allowed to handle the vessel without their father's supervision. He had put Nathaniel in command, which was only fitting, in Nathaniel's opinion. The honor and the responsibility were in keeping with his nascent beard, his five feet, eleven inches, and one hundred and seventy pounds. He thought he proved himself worthy of his commission, bringing *Double Eagle* back without incident, making the mooring on the first try and with such style that even the sarcastic Eliot tipped his cap and said, "Handsomely done, Nat. Handsomely."

Nathaniel heard a screen door slam. Turning, he watched his father and brothers come trooping down the long easy slope of the lawn, the great house behind them dormered and verandaed, the ostentation of its size softened by the rusticity of its plain cedar shake shingles and unembellished posts and balcony rails: altogether, it was a cottage blown up to the scale of a mansion.

Eliot led the way onto the dock, pushing the seabags, supplies, and his guitar in a cart; behind him was Drew, clutching Trajan to his chest, and behind Drew the old man, with two leather chart cases tucked under an arm, walking still with a burdened gait and shoulders slumped, but his gaze fixed straight ahead, grim and intransigent. He was carrying himself like a mourner at a funeral, thought Nathaniel, but that eye was the eye of a man going into a fight.

Drew grabbed the gunnysack from the cart and, with a practiced movement, slipped Trajan into it and quickly pulled the drawstrings tight. The cat squirmed a little, then lay so still that you would not have known a living thing was inside. Passing him to his eldest brother, Drew piped, "Here's a cat *in* the bag" in a voice that didn't know if its owner was a boy or a man. Poor Drew. He was trying hard to sound brave and cheerful, but his look betrayed him. Prone to two kinds of seasickness— the one in his mind and the other in his belly—he looked forward to their father's annual cruise as a condemned man would to his own hanging. Poor *little* Drew, who hadn't sprouted yet and was short, even for thirteen.

Nathaniel stowed Trajan under the forepeak, then took the guitar, a bag of stove coals, and a can of kerosene for the running lights from Eliot, who was dressed in dark green trousers held up with light green braces over a collarless red shirt like the top to a pair of long johns. His faded blue fisherman's cap completed the outfit.

Then Nathaniel, with a smirk: "Put something yellow on and you'd look like a box of crayons."

Silent, Eliot pitched his and Drew's seabags into the dory. Nathaniel laid them between the middle and bow thwarts, then looked up.

"Dad's?"

"It's not on the boat already?" asked Eliot.

Nathaniel shook his head, and then they all three turned to Cyrus, who offered no explanation, but only signaled for the two younger boys to get aboard.

They squeezed in forward, side-by-side, their feet on the seabags, Eliot holding the guitar in his lap, while their father climbed in and took his usual place in the stern.

"Cast off," he said.

Eliot hesitated.

"Father, I don't understand why you're . . ."

"Cast off."

"Yes, sir."

Eliot stood and untied the painter. Nathaniel began to row. He watched the blades make small whirlpools in the smooth water. Far out, the fog still dungeoned the small islands in the mouth of the bay: Great Gott, Black, Placentia, and Swans; it smothered almost all of Mount Desert except for the three summits, which rose above it as if they were islands themselves in a sea of mist. A ship's bell rang, a lighthouse horn groaned again. With one of the chart cases, Cyrus started to beat a slow rhythm on the gunwale . . . thump . . . thump . . . thump . . . and then sang out,

Heave to your oars boys, let her go boys . . .

The first line to the ancient chantey the four always sang at the beginning of each summer voyage. His sons were supposed to answer with the following line, but they couldn't get into the spirit of the thing, baffled and disconcerted as they were by his mood and by his refusal to explain why he was embarking without oilskins, seaboots, or anything but the clothes on his back. They wanted to ask if he'd put his dunnage aboard *Double Eagle* earlier, but they knew better than to speak to him now. With his temperament unpredictable as the sea he loved, serene in the morning and in the afternoon black as a line squall, he had never been easy to live with; but he had become nearly intolerable in the past few days, ever since the big argument with their half brother, who had shown up unexpectedly from New York. They had been at the boatyard when Lockwood arrived (it was like him to appear and disappear on a moment's notice) and did not witness the argument. Dailey told them about it when he came by to pick them up at the end of the day, and all he said was that it had been a nasty one, very nasty, and advised them to stay out of their father's way when they got home.

They needed no more warning than that, so when they returned and saw their father sitting alone at the head of the table in Mingulay's vast and lugubrious dining room, poking at his food, his sloping forehead ribbed as if he were concentrating upon some difficult problem, they went to the kitchen and ate with the help. They were permitted to join him for dinner the next evening, but he was in the same incommunicative mood; likewise the following evening and the one after, Nathaniel sitting on one side of him, Eliot and Drew on the other, and all three afraid to speak unless and until their father did, and since he did not, meals passed as wordlessly as those in a Trappist monastery. No, not like that; a monastic silence was meditative and serene, or so Nathaniel imagined, whereas the silence in the dining room crackled with tension. A disquieting quiet that had a weight and a tangibility and a smell like ozone. At first, the boys made the natural assumption—Lockwood was in another financial mess, and their father was trying to figure out what to do about it. But he had dealt with their half brother's money problems before without acting as he was now, so they began to wonder if he was worried about their mother's health (the exact nature of the ailment that had taken her back to Boston was being kept secret); however, the happy prognosis from Dr. Matthews, delivered recently, had failed to return him to normal. In fact, he seemed to get worse. An obscure anger brindled his gray brooding. His quick temper had made him famous, or infamous, among the Maine islanders—the Italian stonemasons in the Black Island quarry called him *Capitano Furioso*—but this anger of recent days was different; it was silent and oppressive and made sons and staff alike as uneasy as a ship's crew on a greasy sea when the glass was falling. If he didn't snap out of it, this cruise was going to be downright awful.

He beat the gunwale harder and sang out again, louder . . . *Heave to your oars boys, let her go boys* . . . in a voice that drew its power from years of shouting commands into nor'easters and tropical storms. No question now, the boys had better respond, and they did—a baritone, a tenor, and something between a tenor and a soprano, two voices off key and one on, Eliot's.

> SONS: *Swing her head round, now all together . . .*
> FATHER: *Heave to your oars boys, let her go boys . . .*
> SONS: *Riding homeward to Mingulay . . .*

The tune came from the Outer Hebrides, as did the man who had taught it to Cyrus: his maternal grandfather, Alexander Wallace. Its haunting melody rose and fell like slow ocean swells, and Nathaniel's oars fell into the rhythm, brass tholepins squealing in brass locks and the blades dipping to the thump . . . thump . . . thump of the chart case on the gunwale.

> FATHER: *Wives are waitin' by the shore boys . . .*
> SONS: *They've been waitin' since break o' day-o . . .*

Nathaniel had never seen even a picture of the Outer Hebrides, wasn't sure where they were exactly, except off the coast of Scotland; yet those lyrics always evoked in his mind an image so clear it was as if he had been there, maybe in another life: weatherworn women in dark homespun looking seaward from a bleak headland, their expressions revealing hearts poised between dread and hope. He rowed on, looking straight into his father's face, trying to understand the puzzling message of anger and sorrow written there.

> FATHER: *They are waitin' for their loved ones . . .*
> SONS: *As the sun sets on Mingulay . . .*

Their voices carried over the bay for a short distance, heard only by themselves and the cormorants congregated on the ledge, black wings outspread to dry. Nathaniel never liked the sight of those birds, so ominously plumed; sometimes he imagined them to be the reincarnate souls of sailors' widows, waiting, like the wives in the song, for ghosts to come home.

He shipped one oar, back-paddled with the other, and turned the dory broadside to *Double Eagle*. Eliot stood in the bow, reached up, and made them fast to a midship cleat; then he climbed aboard the schooner, Drew following. Nathaniel tossed the seabags to them, passed up the supplies and stores and the sack containing Trajan; then, with his shoes laced around his neck, he stretched a leg over the space between the two vessels. As he went to spring off his back leg, the dory swung out unexpectedly, widening the gap, and he found himself momentarily spread-eagled unevenly over the water, the toes of his back foot just touching the thwart while his left foot, higher up, clung to the schooner. He would have been dunked if he hadn't grabbed the main shroud and pulled himself to safety at the last second, but the violence of the movement caused the knot in his laces to slip and both shoes to fall in. They drifted on the tide, an arm's length from the dory. His father only had to reach out to retrieve them, but all he did was stand and stare perplexed, as if the two objects floating by were some species of seabird or fish he had never seen before. Nathaniel leapt back into the smaller boat, rocking it and upsetting Cyrus's balance. For one perilous instant, it looked as if he would go overboard, but with a flailing of his arms, he managed to throw himself forward onto the bow thwart.

No wrath or sadness on his face now; nor color, either. If Cyrus had no fear of being on the water in any condition, be it doldrums or bare poles hurricane, he had a terror of being *in* it, for like many old-time sailors, he'd never learned to swim.

Nathaniel had meanwhile grabbed an oar. Leaning far over the transom, he slipped the blade under one shoe and scooped it up. Its mate floated out of reach and sank before he had time to cast off and pull after it—the only shoes he had for the trip besides his seaboots, which were hot and clumsy and of no use except on deck in foul weather.

The cold was a shock. Forcing his muscles to move, he swam to where he thought the shoe had sunk, and dove into what appeared to his burning eyes as a fathomless pit of greenish black. Ten feet below, he struck a barrier of very frigid water that was more than shocking; it bearhugged his chest and drove icy nails into his temples. He shot to the surface, got his wind, and stroked back to the dory. Kneeling for a lower center of gravity, his father grabbed the back of his collar with one hand and the seat of his pants with the other, and hauled him aboard. One question settled—a young man's strength *was* still in those arms, in those wide shoulders.

He expected to be chastised, but the old man said nothing, nothing at all.

"Deedle deedle dumpling, my son John . . ." Eliot, capering on deck, sang in a nasal, mock-childish voice. "One shoe off and one shoe on . . ."

"Aw, shut your godda—"

"*Nathaniel . . .*"

"Yes, sir." Cyrus tolerated and, on rare occasions used, most forms of bad language, but he forbade a certain four-letter word and the taking of the Lord's name in vain.

For his sins, Nathaniel was not allowed to change into dry clothes until he had stowed food, coal, and kerosene in their proper places—*and* his brothers' seabags in one of the berths forward. This last task, he thought, dragging the bags down the companionway into the main cabin and through the passage to the forward cabin, exceeded legitimate penance and was meant to humiliate him.

There were two berths in the forward cabin, one on each side and each with two bunks. The port berth was just aft the head and often caught the stench from there, so in the spirit of brotherly love, he chose it for Eliot and Drew. Stepping across the passageway, he entered his— an enclosure about six and a half feet long by six high by four wide, and half the four taken up by the bunks, bolted one over the other to the side of the ship. The cramped space reminded him of one of Dr. Johnson's comments: Being aboard a ship was like being in jail, with the added possibility of drowning. Nathaniel didn't agree with the jail part. To sail the broad ocean was purest freedom, and he liked the confined quarters of a vessel, the snug feeling they gave when you were battened down in safe harbor during a blow.

He tossed his seabag on the lower bunk, undressed, and toweled himself dry, kneading his new muscles just so he could feel them, hard and supple beneath skin that tingled from saltwater and his vigorous rubbing. Likewise, he delighted in the caress of dry drawers, trousers, and shirt. Carrying his wet clothes and the surviving shoe, he passed through the main cabin again, pleased that he now had to duck to avoid the brass gimbal lamp hanging from the center beam. Trajan, orange as a yam, had been liberated and had found a cozy spot to nap on a cushion.

Before going on deck, Nathaniel decided to peek into his father's stateroom, behind the main companionway. He quietly opened the lou-vered door to the sanctum sanctorum. It was spacious for a vessel *Double Eagle*'s size, running the width of the ship, and it had the amenities of a room in a house without sacrificing nautical practicalities. Its teak wainscoting was burnished to the sheen of rubbed leather, its double bunk had lockers built into it. A small desk was bolted to the cabin sole. There was a bookshelf containing tide tables and the almanacs used for taking sights, and over the desk, a dramatic painting of the old man's wrecking schooner, the rakish, white-hulled *Main Chance,* under full press on an ill-tempered sea. What Nathaniel was looking for was the old man's dunnage. He didn't see any. Maybe it was already stowed in the lockers, but opening them would be too great a violation of privacy.

"Ah, my good man. Trust you folded my shirts properly and laid out my dinner jacket. Mrs. Astor will be dining with me tonight."

This from Eliot, leaning against the wheelbox as Nathaniel came up the companion.

"No dinner jacket. Used your shirts to wipe the head."

He spread his clothes on the main cabin top to dry, weighting his shirt down with the shoe against an unexpected breeze.

Cyrus, meanwhile, trooped the boat, his discriminating eye tracing every inch of the standing rigging and the sheets and halyards, belayed in figure eights around the pins in the pinracks. He spun sheaves to make sure they were turning freely in the lignum vitae blocks, plucked stays to test their tautness, checked the hatches battened over the two cabin sky-lights, then went below, by way of the forward cabin. The boys heard him down there, opening and closing lockers and drawers and storage compartments, rattling about to see if everything that should be on board was on board: the coal and lamp fuel Nathaniel had just stowed away, the foodstuffs he and his brothers had brought on board yester-day, and a roster of other items, from marlinespikes, spare blocks, and spare battens to sailmaker's twine; tar, oakum, chronometer, sextant, parallel rules, main anchor, kedge, sea anchor, fresh water butts, kegs of shark oil for use as storm oil, light lists, pilot books, fishing tackle, and a shotgun for shooting game, in case they got stranded and needed fresh meat. Not a likely possibility, but Cyrus prepared for a cruise among Maine's bays and islands no less thoroughly than if he were crossing the Atlantic. Good sailors were pessimists by nature, he often said; they expected the unexpected and provided for the worst, which was sure to come, if not today, then tomorrow, if not tomorrow, then the day after. Small things—say, a sewing palm, needle, and canvas patches for repair-ing torn sails—could spell the difference between a pleasant voyage and a miserable one, even in extreme circumstance between life and death. At sea, the little kingdoms that were vessels really could be lost for want of a nail.

He returned to the afterdeck with a tin of salt cod and a pilot cracker. *Double Eagle*'s tender, slung from the taffrail davit, received his inspection, and then Nathaniel was given the same critical scrutiny, from tousled black hair to bare feet.

Then Cyrus, pointing at the shoe on the cabin top: "What're you planning to do with that?"

"Don't rightly know, sir. Figured since I went through so much trouble to save it, I might as well keep it."

His father lowered his gaze, appeared to be reading the label on the tin. POSEIDON BRAND SEAFOODS, GLOUCESTER, MASS. FINEST QUALITY, it said, alongside a picture of the god of the sea, trident in hand.

"Can't think of too many things more useless than one shoe for a man who still has two feet," Cyrus said.

Was that just an observation? Or did it mean that Nathaniel was supposed to deep-six the shoe?

"No, sir. Don't suppose there is."

"Had shipmates on the *Brooklyn* that wasn't true of, after Mobile Bay. One shoe did them just fine and there was the gunner's mate—"

"Yes, sir. Tim Lockwood. You've—"

Nathaniel fell silent, having received a sleety stare for interrupting.

"Tim wouldn't have needed even the one if he'd lived," Cyrus resumed.

"Yes, sir. We know. You—"

"Watched him die. Watched the light go out of his eyes, same as you would see it go out of a lamp." With a jackknife, he pried the key on the tin's cover, fit the slot into the tip of the metal band, and opened the container, releasing an oily smell. "Tim was on the table next to me, down in sick bay. Sick bay"—a low, bitter snort—"Slaughterhouse is what it was. Yes, an abattoir of human flesh."

"The *Brooklyn* took sixty hits"—Nathaniel, to show he knew the facts about the battle, and also to forestall a repetition of the same old war story.

"Fifty-nine," Drew corrected.

Cyrus fastidiously broke the pilot cracker into four equal parts, laid a piece of cod on each, and passed out three.

"If there was more of us on board, reckon you'd have to perform a miracle of loaves and fishes—should say, crackers and fishes," said Eliot, his attempt to change the mood falling flat because it verged on the impious. He paused and put on a serious expression—never an easy thing for him.

"So did you find everything shipshape, Father? Squared away and all Gloucester fashion?"

Cyrus chewed, swallowed, cleaned his teeth with the tip of his tongue. Rising, he stood with one hand resting on the gallows frame in which the main boom was crutched, and then asked Eliot back:

"Shipshape, you say?" He removed his hat to wipe the sweatband, even though it wasn't a hot morning, and the exposure of his partly bald skull, the gray hairs on his temples showing bright silver in the unsparing sunlight, seemed to age him a decade in a twinkling. "Things are not shipshape, but they will be," he muttered, almost inaudibly, and spit over the taffrail.

There he remained for a time, showing his sons his back, while he looked at the dock and at the green plain of Mingulay's lawn rising gently from the seawall toward the house, beneath whose roof half a dozen families could have lived comfortably, beneath whose roof that many families, and possibly more, were going to live, in summers yet to come: all the sons and daughters who would be begotten by those begotten by those begotten by him. So he had told Nathaniel, Eliot, and Drew; so he would tell anyone who asked why he had built so big a house for only himself, his wife, and three children. Not for them alone, he would say, but for those generations of Braithwaites whom he would never see, whose Christian names he never would know.

He hardly stirred, there in the stern of his beloved schooner, contemplating his beloved house, his air as it was at dinner: remote, dark, preoccupied, and a little frightening. After several minutes, he took something from his pocket—it might have been a matchstick—and dropped it overboard. Behind his back, the boys signed their bewilderment to one another with cocks of their heads, squints, and shrugs.

"Slack tide. Ebb soon," they heard him murmur. He put his hat back on and turned to them, the brim pulled low, as if to eclipse his expression. Still, they could see the change in him: the furrows ironed out of his forehead, his shoulders squared, as if he'd resolved whatever problem he'd been puzzling over these many days. He pulled out his wallet and gave each of them a ten-dollar bill and a quick handshake with a kind of reluctant ceremoniousness, like a general required to give medals to soldiers who don't deserve them. He drew back a step or two and said:

"You boys are to leave as soon as I'm off this boat. You are *not* to show your faces until September. That money should last. If it doesn't, don't ask for more, because you won't get it. Understood?"

They said nothing.

"I'll repeat. You are to set sail on this tide and not show your faces until school starts in the fall."

He wasn't smiling, his voice was stern and crisp, as when he ordered a sail trimmed or a change of tack.

"Nat's the eldest, so he'll be in charge. Eliot, Drew, you are to listen to him just as you would to me. Is that understood?"

They all three nodded, feigning comprehension. He had never given them anything without their earning it twice over, and now, for no reason they could think of, he was giving not merely the run of the ship but the very ship itself, with a summer's freedom thrown into the bargain. Yet, it was his manner that bemused them most. His mien, his tone of voice, were not those of a father bestowing a reward but of a judge pronouncing sentence, and for Drew, that's what three months at sea would be.

"Father, I can't," he pleaded. "I'll be sick the whole time."

For a moment—and this was something the boys perceived as much with their hearts as with their eyes—Cyrus softened a little; his body inclined, almost imperceptibly, toward his youngest son, his hand started to reach out, as if to touch Drew. The moment passed, he dropped his hand and moved forward to the main shrouds.

"Don't get any ideas about sailing to Boston to see your mother," he said. "I will be there, and I meant what I said about not seeing your faces. Won't do you any good to come ashore here, either, in case you get a notion to spend a foul night cozy in your beds. Nobody'll be here. Not me, not Moira, not Gideon or Mrs. Carter or Dailey. As of today, Mingulay's closed up for the season. The boat's your home now. There's worse. Anything not understood?"

"No, sir," said Nathaniel, though in fact he understood nothing.

"All right, then." He grasped a shroud, and swung himself down into the dory. "Cast me off, Nat."

"Where are you going?"

Before he could answer, Eliot butted in:

"Where are *we* supposed to go?"

"Boston excepted, wherever the wind and your inclinations take you. Don't much care."

"You don't much *care*?" Eliot sounded a little indignant and a little fearful. Nathaniel, too, was troubled by the cold sincerity of those last three words.

"One of you cast me off."

Eliot uncleated the painter and tossed it into the dory. Their father began to pull away, stroke after stroke. With a panicky look, Drew grabbed a shroud and leaned out over the water. Nathaniel thought he was going to dive in and swim after the boat.

"Father?" Drew called. "Father!"

He did not say anything. He rowed.

"Father! Why are you leaving us?"

He laughed then; the only laugh they had heard from him in weeks, and it was as brief as it was bitter.

"It's a new century, boys. Yes, indeed, a brand-new century," he shouted, and rowed on, and all they heard then was the squeak of the pins in the oarlocks.

2

THE VOYAGE might not have begun that way for Nathaniel, Eliot, and Andrew, but it could have. Telling what could have happened is the best Sybil Braithwaite can do. She will never be able to say "This is how it was" with the historian's or biographer's confidence; there isn't a soul left for her to interview. The people who took part in her story are dust, their memories sucked with their lives into the boundless abyss of the past. Nor is there a wealth of written records, so Sybil has had to fill in the vast empty spaces in the chronicle by making things up, big things as well as little things, like the way the weather was on a given day, how the sky looked, what people said, did, thought, and felt; the clothes they wore. In this way, she has tried to recapture the tenor of a vanished time, to reanimate extinguished lives, and reconstruct what happened that summer ninety-seven years ago. She hopes that her version of events, its archipelagos of fact, connected by long bridges of fiction, is truthful. Imagination, she will tell you (as she's told me), is not an unreliable sextant, if you're trying to get a fix on the truth. And in matters relating to her family's history, she can be very imaginative, possessing a gift (so she claims) that is the opposite of prophesy: on the scantiest evidence—an entry in a diary, an old photograph, a few lines from a letter—she can *see* things that occurred long before she was born; she hears people, decades in their graves, speaking again, and all with such clarity that she does not seem to be imagining but remembering. She relies on her instincts to tell her if what she imagines (or remembers) is true—not necessarily factual but true. It somehow has to feel right.

The story came to her almost as a rumor, whispered across the decades and arriving in her ear while she was packing to leave New England for good. She heard it from her mother, who had driven over from Brookline to help her sort through her things but didn't do much except to drink Diet Cokes and chain-smoke and talk about whatever came into her head, darting from topic to topic with such speed that Sybil could no more track the conversation than follow the flight of a hummingbird. Catherine was suffering another attack of what she called "nerves," either because she had taken herself off lithium (once again) or because her only living daughter was moving across the country to a desert backwater twenty miles off the nearest paved road. When not occupied with a cigarette or a Coke can, her fingers curled her hair, dyed to its original carbon black above its gray roots, or swept across her forehead with hard, sharp strokes, as if she were trying to rub off her freckles—those fossil marks of youth that had acquired the liverish appearance of age spots. After half an hour of seamless improvisational chatter, she paused to rest her emphysemic lungs and fidgety hands. It was then that something (a random connection of manic synapses?) summoned the tale from her memory. Its telling took no more than five or six minutes, her raspy voice and spooky narrative style—Catherine had been raised in New Orleans on legends of Confederate ghosts and bayou witches—making the whole thing sound like sinister gossip best told sotto voce. She finished abruptly, and without stopping for a breath, said she had got the story some years ago from Emily Williams, whose word she trusted, because Emily's family had been friends with the Braithwaites for so long they were practically relatives. And that was all. She did not volunteer why she had kept the episode to herself until now; when Sybil began to ask the obvious questions, she uttered a litany of "I don't know"s in a tone of bemused surprise, as if she had never considered those questions herself, then stopped the interrogation with a swatting motion. She'd told as much as she knew, she protested, exactly as she'd heard it from Emily—well, as exactly as memory allowed—and had never thought, much less tried, to find out more. Sybil said she found such lack of curiosity not in keeping with her mother's inquisitive nature. Catherine drawled teasingly:

"Daughter, one thing I learned in nearly fifty years of marriage is that when it comes to your late father's family history, some things do not bear looking into too closely."

The story was like a page torn out of a missing diary. It had a gap in its middle, its beginning suggested an earlier beginning, its ending left the listener suspended, waiting for more. Sybil could only guess at the events that had gone before and come after, could only imagine the larger, longer narrative of which the tale seemed a surviving fragment. But her imagination deserted her; she was too distracted by the clutter of packing boxes, clothes, china, crystal—the detritus of a marriage whose failure she neither regretted nor celebrated, but greeted with a kind of relief. Yet, the tale skipped around the edges of her thoughts all that week, pestered and puzzled her, so a couple of days before the movers were to arrive, she phoned her cousinuncle Myles and asked to see him, the author of an unfinished family history, *The Braithwaite Gathering*. He had become something like the Lakota shamans who kept winter count—a living repository of tribal memory. For Sybil had often thought the Braithwaites were more a tribe than a family, and more than a tribe, a consanguineous commonwealth of patriarchs and matriarchs, aunts, uncles, first, second, and third cousins. They didn't have an army, constitution, or formal borders, but they possessed most of the other attributes of a state. They had their own capital at Mingulay (to which Braithwaites still made yearly pilgrimages to renew blood ties and remind themselves of who they were), their own pantheon of heroes, and their own national epic presenting their best image of themselves: They were courageous, perservering, sober, industrious; they made sacrifices on the altar of principle, above all they *served*—their country, their Protestant God, and the cause of improving humanity. A portion of their saga was contained in books; the rest was oral: stories passed from generation to generation, along with the sets of engraved silverware, the antique vases and furniture, the books and jewelry and paintings. And those narrative heirlooms, remarkably, had changed as little as their physical counterparts over the decades; they were sacred myths, not to be revised carelessly nor allowed to undergo the mutations stories usually do in telling and retelling. Sybil had heard them all her life, and had taken their moral lessons so much to heart that when, as a child, she'd been told to blow out her birthday candles and make a wish, she'd repressed her desires for a new toy or dress or some other girlish frivolity and wished instead for world peace, racial justice, the brotherhood of man. How could she do otherwise, descendant that she was of Silas Braithwaite, the clipper captain who'd stood on deck for forty-eight hours in a gale, refusing to rest or eat until his ship and crew were safely through the storm; of a Connecticut headmaster who had left his green campus to help establish a school in Tombstone, when the Earp brothers were teaching different lessons with six-guns; of Theophilus Braithwaite, a fervent abolitionist who had defied the Fugitive Slave Act and turned his house into a way station on the Underground Railroad; and of Theophilus's son, Cyrus, who had rejected the chance to have someone go to war in his place? She had not listened to those tales so much as she'd absorbed them into her flesh and marrow, breathed them in and breathed life into them, until the events became as events she had lived through herself, and the ghosts of her forebears as real as people she had known. No likeness of the clipper captain existed, yet she had seen him, long-jawed, long-nosed, bushy-browed, bearing the wind's wet lash with a martyr's forbearance (and perhaps, too, with the martyr's exultation in suffering), and that same inner eye had shown her the runaway slaves huddled in the abolitionist's cellar, hungry and shivering in the alien New England cold, waiting for final deliverance to Canada, frightened still of the catcher's hounds whose baying must have been grooved into their very eardrums.

Myles told her to come on up after lunch. She left her house in Chestnut Hill at one, and was in Gloucester an hour and a half later. It was a dull November afternoon, a stagnant overcast veiling the sky and a flawed breeze blowing fitfully up the harbor, its surface ruffled in places, and in other places as slick as an oyster bar exposed at low tide. Main Street was sparsely trafficked, now that tourist season was over, and the wharves were crowded with idle draggers, raised outriggers resembling construction cranes, with long-liners and whale-watching boats tied up for the winter, humpbacks and fins having departed Stellwagen Bank weeks ago to breed in warmer seas. From Main, Sybil turned onto the road to Eastern Point, passing turreted mansions, and then saw Myles's house, more modest than its neighbors but still substantial, its peeling window frames white against the weathered shingles' brown, its dark green front door peeling also, and the brass knocker in the shape of an anchor, with the name BRAITHWAITE etched almost invisibly on the shank, tarnished to the color of old mustard.

Corinne answered—Corinne, more massive than ever, smiling as she always did, with her lips only. She raised her flour-dusted hands and arms as explanation and apology for not embracing Sybil, said, "The liberry," and then returned to the kitchen, her ponderous hips switching under polyester pants stretched to their limit. Sybil hung her coat on the clothes tree in the entry hall and crossed the living room toward Myles's study, almost tiptoeing so as not to disturb the dead stale immutable quiet of that house. If it hadn't been for the grandfather clock, ticking in the hall, she would have thought that time itself had been suspended within those walls. The scent she remembered from her girlhood—of roses a day or two past their prime—still permeated the rooms; the same four-masted schooner stood becalmed on the mantelpiece, in air so static that the dust motes glimmering in the dim window light appeared frozen in space, like atoms at absolute zero, and the maroon Persian carpets she had walked on as a child lay under overstuffed chairs and heavy walnut tables occupying the very places they had thirty years ago, the impressions their round, clawed, or square feet had made in the fabric now worn almost through to the oak floors. To Sybil's mind, the whole place, right down to the kitchen in which Corinne was baking, amid an anti-quarium of obsolete appliances, possessed the haunted inertness of a period stage set left with every prop in place long after the play was over.

No, not a thing had changed under that roof except the people who had lived there, and of them, only Corinne and Myles remained, and he didn't look as though he would remain much longer. He was sitting in his motorized wheelchair, facing the double door to his study, the once dense cumulus atop his head thinned into fine white strands like the mares' tails that foretell unsettled weather, his torso emaciated, his skin translucent, revealing a system of blue veins and capillaries in his hands and temples. A catheter tube wormed out from under the blanket spread across his lap, against the chill infiltrating through the windows. He had been a collegiate oarsman, a wartime captain of a PT boat, a peacetime minister whose voice had never needed a microphone but had carried from pulpit to rearmost pew on its own power, and now he looked not fragile, but as if the *idea* of fragility had assumed human form, to warn of the collapse that awaits the most robust of men, if they live long enough. There was only his voice to remind Sybil of the man she had known, booming out a homily or scripture from the elevated pulpit that made him look twice his six feet four. No clergyman in Massachusetts, maybe in all Christendom, could say "God" quite the way Myles could, drawing the first consonant and the vowel into a long rising sonorous note that sounded as if it came from the organ in the choir loft, then adding a syllable to the last consonant with a loud aspiration: *GowwWWWDuh*. Listening to that *GowwWWWDuh* echo inside First Congregational, the ten-year-old Sybil used to think that the Almighty Himself was uttering His own name—*that* voice, which neither begged nor commanded but seized your attention, had not been enfeebled, and was the voice she heard now, greeting her, telling her to take a seat, and after she had (in the leather wing chair that used to be his favorite roost), inquiring about her mother's health and her own. She said they both were fine (lying somewhat about her mother, who would need an oxygen bottle soon), then asked how he was feeling. How did she suppose? Myles answered, irritably and with a jerk of his head. First stomach can-cer, and that no sooner conquered than a stroke crippled him. He was a dead man from the waist down and well on his way toward becoming one from the waist up.

"You're not dying just yet, Cousinuncle," she said, thinking how silly she sounded, addressing him at thirty-eight the way she had as a child.

"Of course I am! So are you, for that matter. I'm just a good ways further down the pike. State your business, Sybil. When you're in the shape I'm in, you don't have the time or patience for idle chitchat."

"It's about him."

Her line of sight rose toward the portrait of her great-grandfather hanging over the fireplace, he in a nautical cap and coat that bore none of the showy braid and brass of the yachtsman he became later in his life but was the plain uniform of the working sea captain he had been when the portrait was painted. He looked to be in his mid-thirties, with a beard the color of brick dust and the neck and shoulders of a man capable of giving you as much trouble as you could ask for, and maybe some that you hadn't yet thought of. The knuckles of his raw, brown hands rested on a quarterdeck's rail and his eyes were of a shade and chill opacity that always reminded Sybil of seasmoke. The artist hadn't depicted them according to the conventions of the day, fixed on a far-off horizon, but glaring sidelong and slightly downward with contempt and rebuke, as if Cyrus had been captured at the moment he'd noticed a shirking sailor on the deck below. The angle of his glance was such that it seemed to meet Sybil's; and so vividly had his expression been rendered that she could put herself in the goldbricking sailor's shoes as he looked up at his captain, from whom he could surely expect more justice than mercy.

"What about him?" asked Myles.

And she told him she had heard that Cyrus, one summer morning in the century's infancy, banished his three teenage sons to sea, cast them out onto the broad ocean in a sailboat, warning them not to show their faces again until September, giving them less explanation than a tyrant would have offered prisoners condemned to a convict island; that is to say, no explanation whatsoever. They weighed anchor, and except for a letter Eliot had written to their mother, there was no word from or about them until August, when a cable from the U.S. Legation in Havana was delivered to Cyrus. There the tale got murky. Sybil's mother had only vague knowledge about what the telegram said, something to the effect that his sons were stranded in Cuba without a dime or a vessel, something about a dreadful storm, a shipwreck, injuries, and an urgent plea to Cyrus to wire money for passage home. But Cyrus responded to it with a silence as complete and inexplicable as the silence of God when He chooses not to answer the most desperate petition.

"Okay, Sybil, what are these theatrics?" Myles grumbled, in interruption. "Don't presume on the Deity."

"I'm not presuming, just telling it the way Mama told it."

"Your mother's a wonderful woman, but you know her penchant for histrionics. They're all that way down in Uncle Remusland. 'The silence of God' . . . Really . . ."

All right, forget Catherine's figures of speech, Sybil continued. The fact was, Cyrus did not answer the cable, and that was as much as she had been told.

Myles turned toward the middle of the three windows, set like triptych panels in the bayed wall of the study, his gaze wandering outside to land on something far away, beyond the dull lawn whereon oak leaves flew, settled, and flew again, beyond the tin-colored harbor intermittently rippled by the fluky wind that set the leaves in motion.

"Our family's full of these misty yarns, what's so special about this one?"

"Why would a man toss his sons onto a small boat? . . ."

"If it was *Double Eagle,* it wasn't all that small," Myles said, and gave her dimensions and said there was an old photograph of her, somewhere in an album.

With a nod, Sybil acknowledged this information, or lack of it, then acknowledged with her voice that the vessel was bigger than she had thought; nevertheless, forty-six feet wasn't much on the open ocean, which made her wonder why Cyrus would put his sons aboard and tell them to get lost for three months. She didn't know what he had in mind, but her mother had said a banishment, a term of exile. . . .

"Sounds like your mother and her Uncle Remusland bombast. Ha! I can hear her now." Myles, turning his head part way to look at Sybil askance, raised his voice two octaves and put on a Southern drawl thick as buttermilk: "They wuh ba-yanushed, they wuh eggzahled." His hand, with its serpentry of bloodless vessels, stiffly fluttered at the bookcases flanking the door. "The left one, bottom shelf. See those albums? Top one on the stack. Open it."

She got out of the chair. Its pages aged to a khaki color, curled at the edges, and barely held together by half-rotted cloth bindings, the album had the delicate, decayed look of a medieval manuscript. She opened it carefully, afraid it would fall apart in her hands, and saw pasted to the inside of the front cover a photograph of Theodore Roosevelt that had been cut out of the frontispiece of a book. Scowling from behind his trademark glasses, firm lips partly hidden by his walrus mustache, bull terrier's head thrust a little forward, as if he were about to charge straight out of the confining oval frame an artist had drawn around him, T.R. looked to be at the pinnacle of his ostentatious virility. Beneath the photo, clutched in the talons of an American eagle, was a scroll bearing a quotation, which Myles asked Sybil to read aloud. She raised the album closer to her eyes to see the small print.

" ' "No nation facing the unhealthy softening and relaxation of fiber which tend to accompany civilization can afford to neglect anything that will develop hardihood, resolution, and the scorn of discomfort and danger." From *The Wilderness Hunter,* by Theodore Roosevelt.' "

He gestured to her to return the scrapbook to its place. She sat again in the wing chair, its leather, too long without saddlesoap or mink oil, stiff and dry and mazed with creases, like the mummified hide of an extinct beast.

"Cyrus met Roosevelt one time and was a great admirer and held him up as a model to his boys," Myles said. "Want to know my opinion, a man like him, a self-made man, was thinking about that unhealthy softening, that relaxation of fiber."

Sybil replied that that possibility had occurred to her: a family-style Outward Bound trip to make men of boys. But you did not have to give the matter an abundance of second thought to question Cyrus's judgment and sense of paternal responsibility. Here was a man on the most intimate terms with the perils of the sea, and those perils in 1901 double or triple what they were today, what with weather forecasting about as accurate as astrology, and no such thing as marine radios, not to mention the electronic gewgaws that made modern navigation only a little trickier than driving a freeway. So, to put a sixteen-year-old in command of a small craft crewed by a fifteen-year-old and a thirteen-year-old, and then to leave them stranded in Cuba . . .

"Ah, sterner times, sterner people, used to taking chances, taking their knocks. No big deal for three strong boys to be on their own at sea. And they were Braithwaites to the marrow. Learned how to hand, reef, and steer before they'd learned to tie their shoes."

"All right, I'll give you that. They could handle themselves and they had a great adventure. If I had an experience like that . . . Well, think about my grandfather. He was always writing stories for sailing magazines. . . ."

"For *Yachting,* yeah."

"But he never wrote about that. Or said a thing. If ever there was a story to tell your grandchildren, that was it, but Grandpa never spoke a word about it to me or my brother or Hilary, never to my father, not as far as I know. I was wondering if he ever mentioned it to you."

Myles shook his head.

"So tell me one thing—why did he never talk about it?"

He began to shrug and then stopped the movement halfway, his wide but thin-fleshed shoulders hunched against the white stalk of his neck to give him the crouched crabbed look of a night heron at rest—a pose he held for several moments, while the dust-moted silence of the house thickened and closed around them and made the air feel viscous. During that brief interlude, she tried to pick out what it was outside that continued to hold Myles's attention, but all she saw were the leaves like shreds of paper bags and the gray harbor and, through the right window of the bayed alcove, Ten Pound Island, with its squat lighthouse and girdle of lobster buoys.

"And then there was their mother," she said into the quietness. "I guess she kept mum, too. So it was the three of them."

"She never said much in any case. Strange woman. She originally came from down there in Uncle Remusland, too, y'know."

"Charleston, wasn't it?"

"Beaufort."

"All right, so we have the three of them, not saying a word. . . ."

"Somebody must have said something to somebody. Otherwise, where did Emily Williams get this story?"

"Any guesses?" Sybil asked.

With a whirring of the wheelchair's electric motor, he turned around to look at her with a direct and appraising squint.

"Y'know, of all the young people in our family, you've always been the one who seemed to have a sense of connection with the past. Always were more interested in our history than my daughter was, or your brother, and I appreciate that."

She offered that it wasn't an interest she'd developed, a sense of connection she'd cultivated, but a kind of natural inclination; it was as if nature, having denied her all hope of mothering descendants (at least by natural methods), had granted her the company of antecedents, the past instead of the future, ghosts in place of children.

"Well, that's a Gothic way to put it," said Myles. "But poking around in family history can be a Gothic enterprise sometimes. Not always the fun people think it is. Ha! Found a colorful horse thief! Ha! Found out Granma had an affair with an Italian opera singer! Nope, not always amusing."

"Myles?"

"A lesson I learned in that little project of mine. Doesn't look like I'll ever finish it, now. Not sure if I regret that or I'm glad of it. Y'see, it wasn't a hobby, like a lot of people in the family thought. The old monkey climbing around in his family tree, looking for colorful horse thieves because he's lost his wife and his daughter hardly speaks to him and he has to do *something* to keep busy, or he'll go off the deep end, mourning his losses. That what you supposed, Sybil?"

She had, but did not say so with word or gesture. The clock in the entry hall struck once: half past the hour. Only three-thirty, yet the sky was edging toward dusk, and out there somewhere, far beyond the long rocky thrust of the Dog Bar breakwater and the outermost bell buoys, a tide of darkness waited to roll ashore. This was the worst time of year in New England, this somber intermission between the last flickering of birch and maple and the novelty of the first snowfall. It was all too easy, in the gloom of the abbreviated days, to dwell on your losses and to feel old griefs you had thought were blunted sting you again, keen as ever. And beyond the grieving, there was the remembering of a lost happiness, and beyond the remembering, the longing to recover the unrecoverable. She was glad she was leaving, turning her back on all of it: the dead dark Novembers and the memories and the grieving and the granite coasts her family had clung to for three and a half centuries.

"What did you mean, 'not always amusing'?" she asked.

Frowning for a moment, he contemplated his fingers, spread out on the blanket like four white pencils. "I want you to know something. My daughter is ashamed of our family. She *hates* it and everything we've ever stood for. Allyson's never made a secret about that, but I'm proud to bear the name, proud of some of the things we Braithwaites have done."

"Yes, Cousinuncle."

She listened as his voice grew more liturgical, falling naturally into a sermon's cadences: a sermon she had heard from him so many times it had committed itself to her memory.

Because we Braithwaites, like most families of ancient lineage, whose ways and opinions had once been templates for the nation, whose sovereignty was once unquestioned, have become mere shades of what we once were—clinging, as the followers of outmoded creeds will cling, to old rites and ceremonies, as much for the sake of ceremony as to keep at least a whisper of life in the traditions that were foundation and buttress to our hegemony. But we are no longer seen as models of order, wisdom, probity, and conduct. It has been decades since we were the only possible candidates to captain industries or to manage affairs of state in peace and war. We haven't suffered any terrible fall from grace,

attended by the noise of crashing temples, but have quietly slipped into
irrelevancy: the families of great achievement and renown—those Sar-
gents and Saltonstalls, those Cabots who spoke only to Lodges who
spoke only to God—as well as families of lesser fame and modest
accomplishments, like ours, or families of no particular fame and
accomplishment whatever. We are no longer objects of envy but of
curiosity. A kind of quaintness overcomes us, and the only models we
provide today are for fashion moguls seeking to create nostalgic images
of patrician charm. Yet we still lay claim to a few things, beyond those
rites, ceremonies, traditions: some money—although that treasury gets
drawn down with each generation—and our family seats that have been
with us for five or eight or a dozen generations, and our family plots
wherein progenitors lie beneath leaning headstones, with their epitaphs
and dates and Old Testament names worn almost to illegibility. Yes, we
have our ancestors, and one another, and those give us something pos-
sessed by few others in this nation of isolates who are lucky if they can
name their grandparents: We know who we are because we know from
whom we come. Thus are we bound to one another, living to the living,
and the living to the venerated dead by our blood, our histories, and our
legacies. And that coherence vouchsafes us, still and despite all the
changes, our sense of a natural sovereignty. So, to despise that blood, to
be ashamed of that heritage is to undermine our own legitimacy at a
time when that has been undermined quite enough by events. Let us take
pride in what we were if we can't in what we are.

And now the voice in her ear overcame the one in her memory.

"I think of my own father, reviled, practically branded a traitor by
his own friends, and why?"

"Because he went to work for Franklin Roosevelt."

"Those blockheads couldn't see that they would have ended up like
Russian aristocracy, if it wasn't for Roosevelt. FDR saved this country
from revolution in the Depression! Not my opinion, the history books
will tell you that."

"I know."

"And for that he was ostracized by those morons with their yachts
and polo ponies. They wouldn't even speak to my father for years, just
for signing on as a dollar-a-year man for the NRA, and I don't mean the
National Rifle—"

"The National Recovery Act, I know."

"And why?"

"Because he thought it was the right thing to do," she replied. They
were into a kind of catechism.

"The right thing," said Myles. "That was his inheritance to me, not money or old furniture or this house, but knowing what the *right* thing was. After I was pulled out of the water that day in 'forty-four . . .'"

She nodded to tell him that he needn't go on because she knew that story as well. He skipped to its conclusion.

"My vocation truly was that. God had spared me for a reason. *Called* me to be His witness and preach His word, and I answered, and I like to think I made some little difference, so it was and still is and always will be a mystery to me how and why I fathered a . . ." Myles's hands fluttered, then dropped back into the gutter the sagging blanket made between his immobile legs. "There hasn't been a day in the past twenty years that I haven't asked myself what Cassie and I had done wrong as parents, what we might have said, or had failed to say, to cause. . . . Ah! . . ."

"You were fine parents," she assured him. "Anyway, I thought you and Allyson . . . Since you got sick . . . That you and she patched things up."

"No peace treaty. An uneasy armistice. We're correct with each other, but when she does speak to me, somehow I can still feel that loathing, that repudiation, and I'll just bet it crackles and bristles in her when she lectures her classes about whatever hateful *ism* might be in fashion at the moment. Just about everybody in her generation got over that after Vietnam, but not my Allyson. She started off hating our family, ended up hating the whole country."

"Maybe you shouldn't talk about all this. It's upsetting you."

"I am quite all right, thank you," he murmured, and Sybil couldn't look any longer at his face and the sorrows scribed there, over and through the lines harrowed by his illnesses and his years. Instead, she looked outside again, at the stump, nearly as big around as a card table, of the white oak felled in the big nor'easter, that maelstrom the papers and TV called the "storm of the century." She remembered playing under the oak with her second cousin, the quietly determined little girl who would become so noisily determined later on, who would set out to cut herself off from her parents and all she came from, succeeding beyond her own expectations. The tree was supposed to have been two hundred years old and had looked as though it would stand for another two centuries, but, like Myles himself, it testified to the vulnerability that lurks within the apparently invulnerable. Maybe a hidden rot had set in, some covert fungus that had opened a crack deep within its core: The first full gust from the nor'easter snapped it as easily as a man snaps a straw between his fingers.

Delafield Public Library
Delafield, WI 53018

"What would have happened if there hadn't been that war? Can't help wondering sometimes how things might have turned out if that war and that whole awful time never happened."

Then Sybil, with a roll of her eyes toward the ceiling: "Why is it that everybody over a certain age is always blaming the sixties for whatever seems screwed up in their lives?"

"Maybe because a lot of us remember what it was like not to live in a moral slum. Everything I've ever held dear is gone—self-restraint, civility and grace and taste and a certain agreement on the limits of conduct. You were too young to remember. . . ."

"Not at all," she interrupted. "Not in the least."

"I meant too young to know, to feel. . . . What's the word I want? *Assaulted.* Assaulted by events from the outside. By history, an ugly history. Turn on the radio, there it was. The TV, there it was. Open the paper, there it was. Try to have a civil dinner conversation at home, there it was. Lord, that one summer we all got together up at Mingulay. When was that? 'Sixty-seven, 'sixty-eight? Allyson teaming up with your cousin Warren, your father and I and Jason on the other side, and all of us screaming at each other. Thought it was going to come to blows right then. All that public history just barged into our private one and warped and exaggerated everything and—" He stopped in midsentence, then added in a lower tone: "Ever since then, it seems that things haven't been quite right in our family. I'm not talking about only the miseries I guess every family's going through these days. The plague of divorces . . ." Both hands raised—a plea to her that he meant no criticism of her decision. "Or the screwed-up child here or there. Or the odd case of addiction. It's that we don't take the joy in one another that we used to. Oh, we still get together and exchange all those long Christmas letters, but something's missing. Is it joy? Love? Or are the joy and the love missing because of something deeper missing? Some fundamental belief in ourselves, perhaps?"

"Myles, as far as I'm concerned, things haven't been right since Hilary died. Twenty-nine years ago, this past Labor Day. Twenty-nine years, two months, and nine days."

"You never have gotten over it, have you?"

She was silent for a while, thinking, She would have been forty-nine this year. Hard to picture the golden girl as a middle-aged woman.

"No, I guess I haven't," she answered finally. "And what happened to her didn't have a thing to do with the sixties or the war. It had everything to do with my father and—"

The clock tolled four and there was a light tap on the door: Maria, the live-in nurse's aide who saw to Myles's needs and soothed his pains and put up with his spells of irascibility like a tolerant wife.

"Time for your checkup."

Bearing stethoscope, blood pressure gauge, and a vinyl bag containing a clean catheter and plastic bladder, she slipped into the room, her child-sized sneakers making a mousy squeal. She was a Filipina only a couple of inches taller on her feet than her patient was sitting down, but she had a stature and a presence vouchsafed by her strict air of competent authority.

"Take your medications at three?" she asked, with a kind of gentle severity, and set her things on the window seat, beside a tray upon which a phalanx of squat brown prescription bottles guarded a plastic water pitcher.

"Which one?"

"Blood thinner."

"Forgot."

"You must take it, Mr. Myles, or you'll go back to the hospital. I can't watch you every second."

"Ah, what's the point? What *is* the point?"

Maria opened one of the bottles and filled a glass from the pitcher, the point so obvious to her that Myles's question wasn't worth answering.

"My father was seventy-six years old and lathering up to shave, and dead when he hit the floor," he said after gulping the pill down. "Nowadays, EMS would be over in minutes and put those awful clappers on his chest and get his old ticker running again. Then tubes up his backside, in his nose, his mouth and there we are, a miracle of modern medicine, a living corpse, until someone has the decency to pull all that stuff out of him."

"Cooking lady wants to know, two for supper or one?"

With a look, Myles asked Sybil if she would like to stay, but he wasn't asking really, he was imploring. She hesitated, thinking, Maybe he has nothing to tell me, only wants company at the dinner table. Almost eighty now and alone, except for Maria and Corinne . . . She nodded.

"Two," he told Maria. "Don't see the point of my eating, either. Used to worry about my weight, and now, ha! Got a golf ball for a belly."

Maria slipped the stethoscope over her neck, then opened Myles's flannel shirt, exposing a sternum ribbed and ridged and cobwebbed with dry gray hairs.

"Everybody talks about how lucky we are today, but my father was the lucky one. People don't really *live* longer now, they just take longer to die."

"Stop talking. I can't hear," Maria instructed, stressing the prohibition with a wag of a finger.

Brows knit pensively, she placed the stethoscope on Myles's chest and bent her head to listen. Then, after making a note on his chart, she rolled up one of his sleeves, and applied a blood pressure band. Sybil, assuming that his catheter was to be changed next and that he did not want her to watch that (she knew she didn't want to), stood to leave until the exam was over.

"Where're you going?"

"Thought you'd want some privacy."

He snorted. "I have had a hundred enemas, been radiated, and invaded, prodded, and penetrated in every damned orifice for nearly two years. Privacy is a luxury the sick learn to live without. Stick around."

She really did not want to see that artificial bladder pulled out from under his blanket, so she rose, and with her back to him, pretended to browse through the bookcases. His was the library of a man who had devoted his life to God and the sea (and who knew but that the two had become one to his mind). Alongside prep-school Shakespeares and Latin grammars from the 1920s, with their red and brown leather spines and look of no-nonsense scholarship, were Myles's texts from Yale Divinity School, theological and philosophical works with weighty titles, various editions of the Bible. Books on maritime subjects crammed the other shelves, beginning with the volumes that composed his secular gospels: *Piloting Seamanship and Small Boat Handling, Celestial Navigation, The American Coast Pilot,* and the *Eldridge's Tide and Pilot Book.* Below that were the albums and scrapbooks and genealogies he had been using for his research, those stacked as bookends against a small grove of family trees and several memoirs and biographies that accomplished Braithwaites (a surgeon, a foreign service officer, the founder of a textile firm) or their children had privately published to provide future generations with testimonies of exemplary lives.

"Everything A-OK!" said Maria, pulling off her latex gloves, which she dropped into the vinyl bag with the used bladder, filled with a pink-tinged, golden fluid. "You be sure to ring me if you need me." She went out with a bounce of her jet-black ponytail.

"Is she here twenty-four hours a day?"

"No. Another one comes on at five. Night shift. Gives me baths.

Hefts me into and out of the tub like a baby in a bassinet. Black lady as big as Corinne, only taller and younger."

"Mama thinks you ought to go into that home she found for you right away, not wait until the house sells. You'd have more company."

"Sitting around with a lot of other shriveled-up people, waiting for the grim reaper express to pull into the station, is not my idea of company. It's my wish—should say my hope—that I'll die in this house before it sells. Speaking of your mother, she told me that you'll be leaving soon, now that the divorce is—"

"Next week," Sybil interrupted.

"Arizona, she said."

"Yes."

"Don't think of people your age going to Arizona, although I suppose they do. Think of people closer to my age, coots and codgers hitting drives over the bones of dead Apaches."

"It's not golf-course Arizona."

"What Arizona is it?"

"Cowboy Arizona, I guess. The San Rafael Valley. I bought a piece of a ranch. I'm going to raise horses. Quarter horses, reining horses, maybe show horses. I'm not real sure, but horses."

"Yeah. Think Catherine mentioned that. Well, you always were a fine rider, always seemed more at home in the saddle than on a boat, like most of the rest of us."

"I hate it," she said, gesturing out the window, and Myles did not ask her what, because he knew. Sybil wasn't sure if he knew the why: that she was fleeing to the desert because she wanted and required a climate, a landscape, an atmosphere as different from New England as she could find without leaving the United States (though she would almost be leaving it; she could see Mexico from her new living room); wanted and required distance from the sea—a distance not geographical (she would be farther from saltwater if she were to move to Kansas) but psychological in nature. The southwestern borderland, scoured by arid winds swooping down from mountains trod and named by Spanish Jesuits a full century before her forebears set foot on their pilgrim shore, was the diametric opposite of the sea and seemed, to Sybil, to deny even the possibility of ocean. The meadows of sere grama grass and the dusty arroyos, bristling with cholla and agave, almost persuaded her that this planet was as dry as Mars, as they allowed her almost to forget the days she'd cruised the Maine and Massachusetts coasts, or the nights foghorns and bell buoys sang her to sleep, or the dawns when squabbling gulls roused her from her bed in the capital of her family-nation, whose halls she walked, past the closed doors of still-sleeping relatives, past the ancestors glowering with cracked-oil eyes, austere, righteous, and a little crazed by the flawed optics that had made them see witches in their neighbors' faces and hell's fiends embodied in the Indians skulking in the unredeemed forests (which those Puritans had redeemed with a fear-born zeal more enduring in its effects than the greed-born zeal of the Castilians who'd plundered the desert seeking a nonexistent El Dorado), and stepped out onto the veranda to feel her child's heart quickened by the scent of tidewrack and by the sight of the great ocean—the same scent and sight that today froze the woman's heart with hatred, even as the woman's mind told her that it was as pointless to hate the sea as to despise a star, the heart hating it, nonetheless, because her sister had been lost to it, and when she cried out, "Why?" its answer was ever the hiss of broken wave sliding back to breaking wave.

"You might miss it, y'know," Myles said.

"Don't think so."

"How about your mother? How's she taking this move of yours?"

"Manic. The way she usually gets before a big change in her life."

"She's had enough of those. You've been a great help to her, but there'll be only Jason nearby to look after her after you're gone. Devoted son never has been his best role." Then he said, without a word of transition: "Original sin."

"Myles?"

"The old monkey wasn't climbing in the family tree looking for colorful horse thieves, but for original sin. Not the original Original Sin, but our family's own. And maybe there's been several. More than one Adam and Eve taking a bite of the apple."

With a movement of her head, she signaled her confusion.

"An explanation for the string of misfortunes we've suffered since your sister's death. Seems to me we've had more than our share," he answered.

"Wait a minute. . . ."

"We are each one of us a bundle of his ancestors. Been reading about all those ribbons of DNA, literally billions of miles of them in each one of us, coiling back through the generations. You, me, your brother, Allyson, we are what our ancestors have made of us, virtues and vices, warts, sins, and all. Yes, I believe therein lies a scientific explanation for what the scriptures mean by the sins of the fathers. Sin can be an inherited trait, so to speak, right along with certain talents, complexion, color of hair or eye."

"Will you please wait a minute? You can't really believe that. . . ."

"I'm a clergyman. Why not?"

She argued that she had seen the most recent membership list sent out by the Mingulay Club: two-hundred-and-fifty-odd names. Two-hundred-and-fifty-odd living descendants of their clan's first immigrants, Joshua Caleb Braithwaite and his wife, Sarah. Among so many people, over a span of thirty years, the law of averages, not Divine displeasure, decreed that there were bound to be misfortunes, and who could say what was the fair share?

"I'm not saying we're like the Kennedys. Don't have the glamour and the money and the power, for one thing. Nor the sex drive, thank God. But . . ."

Now he spoke about the family's other history, the one Catherine had alluded to—the chronicle of things that didn't bear looking into too closely. He'd intended, he said, to include as much of it in *The Braithwaite Gathering* as could be verified and had gone to near and distant relatives, tracking down rumors, asking for letters and diaries sequestered in attic trunks; if they had no documentary evidence, he asked for verbal accounts of misdeeds and moral failings they might have heard about from parents or grandparents, or had witnessed, or possibly even committed themselves. A few balked, considering his enterprise a violation of their privacy. As for the rest of his kinsmen, he'd relied on his reputation for integrity and on his clerical vocation to win their trust and overcome the reserve ingrained in their Yankee natures. More than mere reserve, it was a reticence that made it almost impossible for most Braithwaites to be candid about the family's dark side, even when they wanted to be. It was as if a Board of Censors sat within their heads, ruling on which episodes were suitable for broadcast, which were too sordid or subversive of the family's collective self-image ever to be aired. Oh, its standards were not inflexible, he discovered. Had a ratings system, of sorts, that made allowances for changing moral standards. The kinds of wrongdoing that acquire a patina of roguish charm with time, for example, were upgraded from R to PG. And so—Myles grinned tightly—he had learned that the legendary clipper captain, Silas Braithwaite, had been running opium into a Chinese port when he encountered the typhoon; but that was in 1847, and his dope smuggling, seen now through a softening haze of high-seas adventure in the great days of sail, was readily admitted to by his great-great-grandchildren. The Connecticut headmaster, for another example, hadn't gone to the Arizona Territory only to spread the blossoms of the New England flowering among outlaws and Indians; he was on the run, dismissed from his post because he had, well, put it like this, Sybil, *conceived a passion* for one of his male students and attempted to express it physically.

"You're kidding!" She was enjoying this tabloid history. "So his descendants outed that skeleton."

"Yeah, you could say that," replied Myles. And why not, what with a couple of current relatives out of *their* closets and welcomed with their lovers at family reunions and holiday gatherings. No, those mossy scandals had not been his quest, but the expurgated chapters about which only vague hearsay existed. Buzzes in the air, half-known tales borne on the currents of time, about instances of gross fraud and greed, acts of violence and cruelty that Braithwaites had inflicted, not only on other people, but even on their own and maybe especially on their own.

He stopped there. Sybil, making a scooping movement with her hand, urged him to continue. Myles turned his palms upward, as if to deliver a pastoral blessing. Nothing more to tell. He hadn't confirmed the rumors or denied them; his inquiries had been cut short by his infirmities.

"But cruelty, you said. On their own kind, you said. So Cyrus, maybe . . ."

"I wouldn't want you to get like Allyson. I wouldn't want you to hate our family."

The darkness from the sea had come ashore now, dragging a thin fog with it. He motioned to her to turn on the lights, which she did. The wall sconces' faint, counterfeit flames deepened the shadows in his sockets, the hollows in his cheeks, and she seemed to see a blurred image of his skull, as in an X-ray negative, when she sat down again.

"Myles, are you saying that there's something in the story that might give me a reason to?"

Again, with a hunch of his shoulders, he struck the pose of the crouched heron.

"Wouldn't know. This is the first I heard of it. Thought I indicated that earlier."

"You're sure?"

"You questioning my honesty or my memory?"

"Neither," she answered, embarrassment warming her cheeks. "It's just that you didn't act like it was the first time you heard it."

"And how the hell was I supposed to act?"

"Curious, surprised, I guess."

"Surprised, you guess. If you gave things a little thought, you'd realize that I'm not easily surprised by anything." His voice rattled with cold contempt, and she remembered something Allyson had told her when they were in high school. *He can make you feel so small, sometimes, like you're worthless and stupid.* "Some mildewed tale that you got from your mother, who got it from Emily Williams, who got it from who knows where and who's been dead these past five years—it would take a lot more than that to surprise me."

Corinne rapped on the door once, and loudly, and stuck her head inside the room to declare that dinner was ready. Myles did not acknowledge her. He stared at Sybil, seeming to take her measure; then he gestured with trembly hand at the scrapbooks and albums and genealogies, with their cracked spines and titles stamped in faded gold.

"You can start there. Good a place as any to find a lead. More stuff upstairs. And still more up at Mingulay. In the loft of the storage shed. You can look there, too. Let me know. I'll call the caretaker, tell him to open it up for you. Cart the lot out to Arizona with you."

"*What?* Myles, all this, the work you put it into it . . ."

"Ah! It would take twice as many years as I've got left to go through it all. Go ahead, cart it off with you."

He wants to know, and me to find out for him, she thought, and then a fuller understanding fell on her in a flood of startling light. No, more than just this one episode. He wants me to finish it for him, all of it, *The Braithwaite Gathering.* Maybe to look for the sin, maybe because we are all of us bundles of our ancestors, bound to them, they to us, by the long chains of our genes. They, too, are part of our gathering. To look back to them is to look toward our own futures. Blood is destiny. We can change our fates if we are wise enough and strong enough, but before the wisdom, before the strength, there must come knowledge of the blood and all that is in it, the poisoned and the pure.

Corinne, cupping her ear: "Myles, did you hear me? I *said* supper's ready."

"Yes, yes, yes, I heard you," He whipped his chair into a sharp right turn and said, "C'mon, Cousinniece, I'll tell you what I know about Cyrus at dinner. You'll need to know about him before you start. A hard man, hard as a white oak plank."

3

NATHANIEL KEPT *Double Eagle's* log up to date from the very first day. Sybil shows it to me: a blue bound book about eight by eleven inches, smelling of mold and mildew, the cover water-stained, and the stiff pages stained as well, with brownish spots that make some of the entries illegible or nearly so. But the first one is not. I can see it plainly in the desert light pouring down on the interior courtyard of Sybil's house, so far from the sea. Nathaniel's handwriting—graceful strokes of a young man trained in the old school of penmanship—is easily read. *11 June 1901: At 8 a.m. today Nathaniel Braithwaite placed in command of this vessel until Sept. On board as crew: Eliot Braithwaite, Andrew Braithwaite* is how the first entry begins. The next sentences are equally terse: *Cast off from Mingulay at ten a.m. Very light airs. All sails set. SW by ½ W. Destination unknown at present.*

I am struck by that starkly evocative phrase, *Destination unknown at present,* but Sybil remarks that she is more intrigued by the time lag. It should not have taken them two hours to hoist sail and cast off. There might have been a number of explanations for their lingering—maybe they cooked a hearty breakfast for themselves, maybe they were waiting for a wind. But Sybil imagines a different reason: They must have felt more orphaned than liberated, abandoned to their own devices, which would have seemed in woefully short supply.

She has looked back through time and seen the three dumbfounded boys standing at the schooner's rail. . . .

They watched their father tie up the dory and then climb out and carry the oars into the boathouse; watched him go up the lawn, the yellow crown of his hat growing smaller and smaller. They waited for a farewell wave, a parting glance, but he just walked away, as if they were gone already, and passed under the veranda. A second later, a sound like a dry twig cracking carried over the water, and they knew it was the screen door with the broken spring that Gideon Carter had not got around to fixing: the screen door, slamming shut behind their father.

They looked at one another.

"What do you think he meant? 'It's a new century'?" Eliot asked Nathaniel, as if his older brother possessed some special insight into their father's thinking.

"I don't know. He's been saying that for the past year."

To us, thought Nathaniel. To his friends. To anyone willing to listen, and to a few who weren't willing but did anyway, compelled by the fierce monocular stare, the conviction in that top o' the yardarm voice. *It's a new century, and the man who misses this ship isn't going to be left ashore, he will be drowned in its wake.*

"But he didn't say it like he usually does"—Drew, with a creased brow. "He usually sounds like he's happy that it's a new century but now he sounds like he's mad about it."

"We *know* it's a new century," Eliot persisted. "It's been a new century for the past eighteen months. What does it being a new century have to do with this?" He cocked his cleft chin and pointed vaguely around the boat, not to indicate it but their peculiar situation.

"You'd have to ask him," Nathaniel said.

For a long while, they stared dumbly at the house and at the empty lawn fenced by spruce and hemlock woods, vestige of the wilderness whose gloom had extended down to the shore in the forgotten time, before some now forgotten settler had cleared it for a sheep pasture, his holy work of domestication not advanced until Cyrus bought the pasture from the settlers' impoverished descendants, built a house on it, and planted grass and flower gardens.

Moira, her stout figure recognizable, even across a hundred and fifty yards of land and water, appeared in the doorway on the second-floor balcony. She paused there briefly before pulling the French doors behind her, while someone else on the floor above—probably one of the town girls who helped her dust and sweep during Mingulay's summer occupations—drew the shutters on a dormer window. Then another was shuttered, and another, and, Jesus, Eliot said, in a kind of vexed wonderment, he was really doing it, closing the place up.

Borne by the ebb, bits of weed and flotsam bobbed past *Double Eagle*. The cormorants, their feathers dried, departed the ledge, on whose face a foot of wet rock was now exposed and divided from the dry top by a line as definite as a bootstripe. When the birds left, their wings made a hard wet slapping noise; but once airborne, they flew silently, flew fast and low, with their long necks extended. *Double Eagle* swung on her mooring lines and put her nose into the current. Still, the boys did not make a move, except to go to the bow and watch the house from there. They watched with mute expectancy but without knowing what they expected. A fluky breeze sprang up, scaled the bay here and there, and then died. The sun was halfway toward its zenith, but did not burn off the fog. Islands and ships were as shrouded as before in a mist that emitted the same sounds as before, as if some freakish storm cloud, filled with hoots and whistles instead of thunderclaps, had fallen to earth.

Drawn by a pair of black geldings, the family carriage rolled up the drive from the carriage house, and the boys saw Dailey rein up and hop off the driver's seat and go inside the main house. He emerged a few minutes later, his long frame canted sideways by the weight of the trunk he carried in one hand. Their father followed him out. He had changed clothes, his white linen suit and summer boater plainly visible in the sunlight. Nathaniel went below and fetched the binoculars, a heavy brass pair, seven-by-fifties, and observed a distant pantomime: the old man gesturing to Moira and she bobbing her head in time to his wagging finger (Nathaniel almost could hear her brogue: "Yes, sorr, very well, sorr, Ai'll see that it's done, sorr"). Gideon Carter appeared, was also given some last-minute instructions, and then walked away toward the tool-shed at the edge of the woods. Dailey returned to his perch, took up the reins—Dailey in top hat, white scarf, and gloves, as if he were on a Sunday drive in Boston Common. Cyrus climbed in and settled into the back seat. The geldings started off at a walk, but hadn't gone five yards before they were halted. Nathaniel watched his father stand up in the carriage, look toward the boat, and then swat the air several times with his hat.

"The old man's seen that we haven't weighed anchor," he reported. "And he's signaling us to get a move on."

"Reckon we'd better, then?" said Eliot.

Their father dismounted and came striding toward the land's edge, his head lowered slightly, not like a man's lowered in thought but like a bull's, and they went at their tasks as if they were fleeing an attack of cannibal islanders. Eliot and Nathaniel leapt to the pinrack, uncoiled the main sheet and halyard, and hauled away, the bamboo hoops squeaking up the mast. As Nathaniel went to the wheel, Eliot hopped forward, hoisted the jib, and then tugged on the bowlines, pulling the schooner toward the mooring post to put slack in the lines and make it easier for Drew to cast off. Drew reached out, shook the lines from the notched bracket on the post, and called out, "She's away!"

Nathaniel spun the wheel, the main formed a shallow arc, and *Double Eagle* fell off to a broad reach, barely moving in the listless morning air. Glancing astern, he saw their father at the end of the dock, one hand on his hip, the other pointing. He looked a little comical in that pose, like a character in a melodrama. But Nathaniel realized that this is what he and his brothers had been waiting for: their fear of him to overcome their fear of launching out into the unknown.

For the next ten minutes, they were busy setting the foresail and the topsails. They had done this many times in the past, but were rusty after a year ashore, lacked the liveliness and crack they attained at the end of a summer's racing season. When all canvas was set and trimmed, Nathaniel came about and sailed by Mingulay for a last look. The carriage was gone and their father with it. The flag had been lowered from the staff near the corner of the south wing, as if Mingulay were a ship that had struck her colors. Except for the solitary figure of Gideon Carter, winching the dory up the rollers of the launching ramp, there wasn't a sign of life. He looked up, and the boys waved at him, but he did not wave back. The house passed slowly by: the long tawny rectangle of its shingled face, windows and dormers darkened behind seagreen shutters; then it fell abaft their beam, and after they rounded a headland, out of sight.

Double Eagle's hull whispered through the water. There were few sounds beyond that: the flap of a languid sail, the far-off choral of fog-bound ships. Once a crow's call, harsh and forlorn, reached them from deep inside the woods, crowding a stretch of shore that looked as unpeopled and wild as all the coast had been in the forgotten time.

"You're in charge. Commissioned by *Capitano Furioso* himself. The crew awaits your orders," Eliot said, and imitated the two-tone pipe of a bosun's whistle when Nathaniel did not respond. "Wherever the wind and our inclinations take us, the old man said. Not much wind today, so what are the captain's inclinations?"

"What are yours?"

"To figure out a course, which means we've got to figure out a destination, which means we've got to have a plan of one kind or another, unless it's the captain's wish to sail in circles till the fall."

Nathaniel pondered for a while.

"We could do just that. Not round and round, but from one end to the other," he said, meaning Blue Hill and Penobscot Bays. He had made his first voyage through those waters when he was only fourteen months old. He knew the passages like Casco and Mount Desert Narrows, the beacons and bell buoys, the inlets and river mouths. The shapes and names of the islands (English names, French names, the few Indian names that, by virtue of their quaintness or beauty or resistance to translation, had survived the eponymous zeal of European explorers and Yankee coastermen) were as familiar to him as the houses on his block in Boston and the names of the families who lived in them, and most of the bays' covert treacheries—the shoals and hull-crushing ledges—were sounded and marked in his memory and in that part of his memory that was no longer memory but instinct.

"We know all sorts of people. . . ." he continued, and ticked off the names of other Boston families who rusticated in Maine: the Barnetts in Bar Harbor, the Woodsons in Camden, the Williamses in North Haven, and the Thorps, the Warrens, the Peabodys. "They'd be sure to give us a corking good feed or two. That would help us stretch the food and the thirty bucks."

"Mooch off them is what you're saying, Nat."

"I wouldn't put it that way."

"Put it however you want, mooching is what it would be."

"We could take them sailing, maybe on picnics. They'd supply the food, we'd supply the boat," Nathaniel offered.

"All right, sounds like as good an idea as any, except for North Haven and the Williamses," said Eliot. "We go there and me and Drew, we'll spend all our time twiddling our thumbs like chumps, while you go play Froggie goes a-courtin' with Constance."

"I think we should go back and talk to Mr. Carter," Drew suggested tentatively, unsure if he was permitted to take part in the decision making. "Maybe he could find a boardinghouse for us in town. And maybe he knows what's wrong and could tell us. Because there's something wrong, and if it's with Mother, I think we should know about it, whether Father wants to keep it from us or not. I'll bet that's why he told us we couldn't see her."

Nathaniel regarded his youngest brother. Hair hued like terra cotta, pale complexion that turned rutilant in the sun, small nose between cloudy gray eyes—of the three, Drew bore the closest resemblance to their father. Not as close a resemblance as did the older half brother, whom they saw only once a year at most, the mystery man born of a mystery woman who had surrendered her life giving him his, she whose name was never spoken, as if she had never lived at all. Lockwood (so Cyrus had christened him in homage to his dead shipmate) looked so much like the old man that when the two stood side by side, it was as if Cyrus were accompanied by his reincarnated youth, Lockwood by his not-yet-incarnate middle age.

"We're not spending the summer in some boardinghouse in Blue Hill, or anywhere," Nathaniel declared with finality. "And about Mother—I asked him about her earlier and he said she's fine. He wouldn't lie to us about a thing like that. Anyway, think back to when she left. She didn't look sick the least little bit."

Looked glowing and even glamorous that morning, Nathaniel remembered. Tall and straight in a burgundy traveling dress, her black hair upswept beneath a velvet hat as feathered as an Indian's war bonnet.

"Some kind of female problem," was all Cyrus had told them about her illness the night before. Women had to be allowed their privacy about such matters. He reminded his sons that their mother would turn forty later in the year, and when women got to be middle-aged . . . Well, now, he would not get into that. . . .

Complete silence would have been better than that fumbling explanation. "Female problem" added to the mystery that was disease all the mystery that was woman. Nathaniel could hardly sleep that night, trying to place where on his mother's anatomy the problem existed. Soon, his brain was alight with shameful images he had glimpsed in contraband bootlegged into the dormitory by his classmates, everything from French postcards to "marriage" manuals to anatomical drawings doctors' sons had torn from their fathers' medical texts. He recollected the time, last year in the Marlborough Street town house, when he had come upon the maid washing bloody underclothes in boiling water and vinegar in the cellar laundry room. Turning toward him, her long Celtic face half lit by the gasflame flickering under the copper tub, Moira asked what did he think he was staring at? He answered that he didn't know, as she picked up a shift speckled with scarlet stains and tossed it into the tub like a murderess getting rid of evidence, except she wasn't furtive about it. "Well, I'll tell you, then," she said. "You're lookin' at what you came from, and what all of us came from. You're lookin', lad, at the dark powers of Mother Nature herself. And you're lookin' at God's own curse on woman for temptin' Adam."

The dark powers of Mother Nature herself, yes, and all contained within that alluring, terrifying entity, that vessel of the fecund unknowable, a woman's body. His own mother's body.

The day she returned to Boston (and she hadn't been at Mingulay a week before she came down with the unidentified ailment), she smiled when she kissed her sons goodbye, but it was a forced uncertain smile, and she seemed to drink in their faces with her glance, as if—Nathaniel was alarmed by this thought—she might not see them again for a long time. She turned abruptly, taking the arm Cyrus offered to help her into the carriage; but then she held still, one foot on the running board, the other on the ground, as if she were pausing to make sure she had not forgotten something. Or was she too weak to mount into the seat? "Liza, I still think I should go with you, at least as far as the train station," Nathaniel heard his father say, with the tenderness he showed no one but her (as if his allotment of it was so meager he could expend it on no more than one person). She shook her head, the movement followed by a quick squaring of her back and shoulders, like a soldier snapping to attention; then she hiked her skirt with a single, violent tug and climbed into the seat. Her gloved hands were clasped tightly in her lap, and the tilt of her chin reminded Nathaniel, at first glance, of a photograph he'd seen of the vice president's beautiful and arrogant daughter, Alice. But, on second glance, he realized that his mother's posture did not communicate haughtiness but rather a kind of martial resolve. "All right, Tom," she said to Dailey. He clicked his tongue and gave the reins a shake, and she did not once look back toward her husband and sons, as the matched horses trotted off down the drive.

"Nat's right, it doesn't have anything to do with Mother," said Eliot. "Why would he tell us to get lost for a summer if she was that sick? Maybe it's some big business deal he's working on." He paused and looked puzzled by his own comment. "But then, why would he tell us to get lost if it was a business deal? Could be there's another strike in the works. Hey! I'll bet that's what's been eating him. I heard Moira and Mrs. Carter in the kitchen a while back, whispering something about a strike. Moira's sweet on one of those Irish quarrymen and she probably got wind of it from him. Sure. Maybe the old man's gone off to get some Pinkertons so he won't have to face the strikers all alone, like the last time. He broke 'em, but it might not be so easy if there's a next time. So maybe he doesn't want us around if things blow up."

"Maybe." Instinctively, Nathaniel's eyes rose to check the set of the sails. Directly over the mainmast, in the clean heart of the sky, a small cloud sailed solitary, strayed from the fleet of stratocumulus gathering over the horizon. Possibly, they would bring the wind his father had forecast. "Y'know, there was nothing easy about breaking that last strike," he added, in an afterthought. "Wasn't easy on the old man and wasn't easy for the strikers. Can't say I blame 'em, and I wouldn't blame 'em if they did strike again."

Eliot gave him a look of amazement.

"You wouldn't say that if he was on board. You wouldn't even dare to think it."

"Well, he's not, so I'm thinking it, I'm saying it," Nathaniel declared, and though his seditious remark had been spoken without the least risk of consequence, he felt a surge of masculine pride and independence merely for voicing it. "They put in ten hours a day, six days a week," he went on. "They get blown up by dynamite and get crushed to death when a derrick boom busts with ten tons of rock swinging from it. Their families hardly have a pot to pee in or a window to throw it out of. I saw how they live over on Black Island. All they wanted was a nine-hour day and time and a half for the tenth hour. Hell, if it was you, you'd strike, too."

Eliot did not reply, deferring to his older brother's authority to declaim on the rights of labor. Last year, after the summer cruise was over, Cyrus had put Nathaniel to work in the Black Island quarries to begin learning, from the ground up, the business he was destined to inherit. He'd endured the dust and noise, and suffered cheerfully the practical jokes and sullen resentment workingmen reserve for the boss's son (the jokes more barbed, the resentment more bitter in his case, for only a year had passed since the strike) while he drilled split and plug holes in the raw blocks at the standard rate of half a cent per hole per day, and not with the pneumatic tools issued to the veterans but with a hand drill and a six-pound maul.

The plan had been for him to return to the quarries this summer, after the cruise, and again next summer. Then, after he finished at Andover, he would go on to Yale or Harvard and work in the offices during vacations to learn the arts of managing men and accounts. An apprenticeship alongside his father would follow college graduation, and at some time in the distant future, he would become president of the Cape Ann and Bay Island Granite Company. Presumably, he would be agreeably married to a suitable woman by that time and have a son of his own to groom for future responsibilities. Every mark was there, as clear as the marks plotted on a chart; so clear that sometimes Nathaniel felt as if he had already made the voyage and was looking back on it, full of years and respectability. In those moments, the sense of inevitability and predictability pressed against his ribs like a steel corset.

But now this . . . This strange and unlooked-for rupture in the way things were supposed to unfold. Stranger still, he didn't know how he felt about it, or how he should feel. He yearned for life to be as it had been only yesterday, because right now he couldn't even guess, much less predict, where they were going to spend tonight. Yet, he could not deny that the not knowing stirred a peculiar and foreign excitement that drew its poignancy from fear. He heard Eliot murmur:

"Maybe we should go on strike ourselves."

"How can a man's kids go on strike?" asked Drew.

"They can't. That's the point. So we're worse off than those quarry hands."

"Go to work in a quarry for a day and you'll change that ditty," said Nathaniel, remembering the pits whose sheer sides, fissured and sharp-edged, resembled ancient walls under excavation, or maybe the foundation for the Tower of Babel, considering the garbled tongues spoken there amid the clamor of air hammers and steam drills: the Yankees' down-easter drawls mingling dissonantly with Gaelic, Italian, and the cryptic singsong of Finnish. Whatever their native language, all spoke the common vernacular of the quarryman—the wheeze that came from breathing silicate dust ten hours a day, six days a week, year upon year.

"Listen to the great workingman, salt of the earth, himself." Eliot stretched out his sturdy legs and for a moment took a profound interest in bending his big toes—remarkably flexible digits that he was able to move as if they were thumbs, that is, independently of the smaller toes. With them, he could pick up small objects like a pencil or a jackknife, even a drinking cup if the handle was wide enough. "If he'd just been a little bit nice this morning. Slapped us on the back, told us to have a fine time and to send postals and to wire him if we got in a fix. But it was just that . . ." His voice dropped an octave. "'Don't want to see your faces till September . . .' It was like he . . . You know . . ."

"Yeah, yeah, it was," Drew said.

"I must've missed something. Like what?"

Drew only answered, "You know, Nat," and then gave a quick shrug, while his lower lip curled over the upper. Looking at him, Nathaniel felt his jaw tighten of its own will.

"Like *what*, little man?"

"Like he said he didn't want to see us till the fall only because he didn't have the nerve to tell us the truth. That he doesn't give a darn if he sees us again ever."

There was a long silence before Nathaniel said:

"Boy, you talk about things that wouldn't be said if he was on board."

"I've said it when he was. Sort of."

Nathaniel assumed he was referring to last year, on the homeward leg from Halifax, Cyrus driving *Double Eagle* hard in a doublereef sou'wester and shouting exultantly above the wind and the thrum of rigging taut as fiddle strings. *Ah, she's got a bone in her teeth now, don't she, boys?* Drew wasn't there to hear him; he lay below, fighting nausea brought on as much by terror of the advancing waves as he was by the motion of the boat. *We should be hove to in a wind like this,* he groaned, when Nathaniel came down off watch in drippings oilers. *He's trying to drown us, Nat.* And then Nathaniel, laughing: *Well, if that's true, then he's trying to commit suicide, too.*

"You didn't say it where he could hear it, and anyway, you didn't mean it."

Drew cocked his jaw defiantly.

"No, not drown us really. I meant that he didn't give a da—a darn about us. He didn't then, doesn't now."

"Maybe he doesn't give a damn about *you,* because you're such a goddamned little lamb about things," Nathaniel said.

Now Drew displayed one of the mannerisms he found unendurable: looked at him the way Trajan did when the cat wanted to be petted, except that plaintiveness in Drew's eyes somehow invited a slap, a kick, a wounding word.

"Eliot and I had to stand our tricks in thirty knots of wind, but not you. Lubbing it down below, and you weren't seasick, little brother, you had a brown streak in your drawers. Or maybe yellow's the right color."

"And the ocean waves do roll, and the stormy winds do blow, blow, blow," Eliot sang out suddenly, loudly. *"And we pore sailors a skippin' at the tops while the landlubbers lie down below.* C'mon, Nat. Don't start with him."

"And it was Dad who let you get away with it," Nathaniel carried on. "I told him you ought to do your turn, but he said to leave you be on account of—"

"Jiminy, Nat. Stay off him."

"On account of I don't have a sailor's heart," Drew said. "I heard him. 'Leave him be. Andrew is a smart boy, he may even be brilliant, but he's missing something. He lacks a sailor's heart.' That's what he said. I remember every word because I've got a photographic memory."

Then Nathaniel: "And a pretty picture that Kodak takes. In Dad's book, someone who doesn't have a sailor's heart might as well wear petticoats and put his hair in curls."

Eliot moved his hands in silent applause, after Drew fled below decks to sulk and nurse his cuts.

"Well *done.* Very captainlike of you."

"There's just something about him sometimes. I don't know. I . . ."

Nathaniel couldn't express it. He hated weakness, and hated it because he feared it, and feared it as he would the whooping cough or polio or diphtheria or any other contagion.

"We've got to get along, big brother. This isn't that big a boat. You were in the wrong and you know I'm right."

A noisy splash not five yards to port startled them. They jerked their heads around to see an osprey, its white breast almost perpendicular to the water, its mottled brown wings beating furiously as it fought for altitude, the fat herring in its talons gleaming in the sunlight like a small silver ingot.

Bending down, Nathaniel shouted through the cabin hatchway:

"Hey, Drew! On deck! You're more likely to get seasick down there."

"I'm playing with the cat," came the reedy voice from below. "He's my friend."

"He won't be if you puke all over him. I hurt your feelings and I am sorry. Kindly accept the captain's apologies and c'mon up."

"You didn't hurt my feelings and you're no captain. You're just a big fat jerk."

Nathaniel put a fist over his mouth and blew through it and then struck himself hard in the chest.

"Yaaaarrgh! An arrow to my heart!"

"You don't have one. You're just like him."

"Now there's another thing you wouldn't say if he was here."

"He'd think it was a compliment. Anyway, Mother says the same thing about him."

Nathaniel and Eliot looked at each other.

"*What?*" Nathaniel said. "When did she ever say he was heartless?"

Drew climbed part way up the companionway and stood on a step, his face boxed by the hatchway.

"Last month, when Lockwood was visiting in Boston," he declared, referring to another of their half brother's mysterious appearances. "She said it to him. I heard her."

"She couldn't have. The way he treats her, like a princess, she could never."

Nathaniel was pleased with himself for calling his brother's attention to this aspect of their father's nature. It seemed to compensate for the criticism of his labor practices. Not that he was romantic, like the men breathlessly described in the magazines Mother kept around the house (and that Nathaniel sometimes surreptitiously delved into, hoping to pick up a few tips on courtship, or maybe an insight into the fecund unknowable, woman, but always finding the most awful, treacly mush. . . . *Her brief passionate love dream was forever put aside! Never a word had come from Stelvio since the witching night on the Grand Canal in Venice . . .*). Cyrus's displays of affection always were respectful and restrained—a kiss on the forehead, a pat on the back of Mother's hand. He never spoke a harsh word to her, none that Nathaniel and his brothers had heard. He sat her at the dinner table with formal courtliness, offered his arm when they came down a staircase together, as if he were escorting her at a ball. Women had to be treated that way, he had counseled Nathaniel only this past year, in a man-to-man talk. Female delicacy was a fact of nature. Women dwelled in a kingdom of illusions, or at least in a realm so far removed from the one inhabited by men as to seem illusory, but it was a realm men were sworn to protect and keep inviolate, if for no other reason than that it provided them with a refuge from the gritty struggles of running the real world.

"They were in the sitting room, just like that time a couple of years ago. The doors were closed and I couldn't hear real well," Drew recounted. "I couldn't hear Lockwood at all. He was talking real low, mumbling like he had his face in his hands when he was talking. Mother said, 'Lockwood, please. It will be taken care of, I assure you it will.' "

"I've heard this one before"—Eliot, skewing his lips and nodding—"Old Lock wanted Mother to help him get out of whatever fix he's in. Just like the other times."

"Dunno," Drew answered. "All I heard from him was that mutter-mumble and then Mother saying, 'You must get hold of yourself and not worry. You know how your father is about some things—so thick bullets would bounce off him. He is the *Monitor* and the *Merrimac* of men, a human ironclad, and my dear Lockwood, you can thank God for that.' "

Mah deah Lockwood . . . Nathaniel, ambushed by a pang of longing, momentarily lost the trend of Drew's report. Of all the things he and his brothers missed about her, they missed her voice the most. How her lilting drawl seemed to summon breezes from her native city, breathing moistness into the crisp rooms of the Marlborough Street house, warmth into the perpetual autumn of Mingulay's cavernous spaces; how her speech, festooned with rhetorical excesses learned from the Dixie preachers and stump orators she'd listened to from birth to the day in her eighteenth year when Dad carried her northward in his ship, made a luxuriant counterpoint to his utilitarian barks. "There is poetry enough in the Psalms for anyone, all the rest is superfluity," he liked to say, for in his opinion language was not a source of delight but a tool to impart moral lessons or to convey the information required to run a ship, a business, a household, a government.

"Well, it doesn't sound to me like she meant the old man is heartless," Eliot was saying to Drew.

"Sure she did. That he's so thick-skinned he doesn't feel things like a normal man would."

Recovered now from the insult, Drew came out on deck and sat down.

"The way you put it, sounds to me like she was saying he was *thickheaded*. You'd have to be an idiot to say that he's thickheaded. We'd be poor instead of rich if he was. You must've heard wrong."

"I remember every word, Eliot. I've got a photographic memory."

"I was talking about your hearing, not your memory."

"And did you hear, Mr. Eavesdropper, what kind of fix Lockwood's in? See, if you knew that, then we could figure out what's bothering the old man."

Then Drew, shaking his head: "Moira caught me listening in and pulled me away, right by the ear." By way of demonstration, Drew pinched his earlobe and winced. "Just when I heard Mother get kind of mad at Lockwood and tell him he was insane. 'You have got to calm yourself. Why, I believe you have lost your mind to say such a thing as that.' That's what she said. I heard—"

"We know. Every word because you have a photographic memory," Eliot said. "You're pinching, Captain, O Captain."

He motioned at the jib, which had begun to shiver. The wrinkled canvas scolded Nathaniel for paying more attention to the conversation than to his steering. He jogged the wheel, falling off half a point until the sail set properly.

"All right, listen, crew—North Haven will be our harbor for tonight," he announced, glancing sidelong at Eliot, daring him to object or make a wisecrack about Constance Williams.

4

THE PROMISED WIND was delivered. It blew lightly at first, with just enough strength to texture the slick bay waters, now gone from pearl gray to cobalt blue. Clouds ambled across a luminous sky. In a quarter of an hour, the breeze freshened. *Double Eagle* leapt forward, joyful to be liberated from sluggish airs. She began to heel, showing her windward bootstripe as reluctantly as a modest woman showing her ankle. She was a ship to keep her trim, thanks to the three and a half tons of lead in her keel and to the quality that could not be measured or weighed. "Stiff as a high-church Episcopalian," was how Dad described her, meaning she was too poised and balanced and proud to allow her lee rail to go under in anything less than a half gale. The wind brisked up to fifteen knots. Topsails were doused, and the schooner cracked along, starch in her backstay and in all her rigging, her jaws flashing and flinging spray that struck Nathaniel's face like bits of crystal. He could feel the resistance on her rudder as he held the wheel firmly a few degrees to leeward, fighting her tendency to turn to windward. She was generally docile in light airs, but when the wind blew over fifteen, she became a little less compliant and a little more renitent to the helmsman's pressure to keep her on course. Her firm weather helm wasn't a defect; it was a sign that she had spirit.

They clipped past Naskeag Point and Hog and Harbor Islands, bearing south by west for Stinson's Neck and Deer Island Thorofare beyond. The wind had no effect on the fogbank, no more than it would have had on a stone wall. Inshore, the waters were coming alive with ships, vessels of all kinds departing their harbors, fog or no: kilnwooders and limers with white-powdered hulls, gilded steam yachts trailing sooty pennants, and a three-masted coasterman, westering across Jericho Bay. Looking at her, her jibs three crescent moons, Nathaniel felt all the old feelings stir in his chest.

There wasn't a sailing vessel that he did not love. One might be so beautiful that it made your heart swell and another might be uglier than murder, but so long as a vessel drew its power from God's own wind, it bore the same relation to steamships as man did to the great apes (if Mr. Darwin was right—and his biology teacher had declared Mr. Darwin to be right, inspiring the Reverend Harwood, school chaplain, to deliver several sermons in rebuttal). With ships, however, evolution was reversed, the inferior species coming *after* the superior; for the grandest liners launched by White Star and Cunard, belching smoke like locomotives, were never anything more than agglomerations of steel, rivets, and brass: feats of engineering testifying to human cleverness. But a barque or four-master, or a common sloop for that matter, testified to something higher in the human spirit, to skill and craftsmanship, and beyond skill and craftsmanship, to that love of beauty which produces art. And, in the very finest ships and yachts, there was more even than art. Between the laying of such a vessel's keel and the moment she slipped down a launching ramp to receive her baptism, she was transubstantiated from man-made to living thing. It was as if the men who designed and built her somehow endowed her with aspects of themselves, their various traits seeping with their sweat into her ribs and knees and bowels, uniting there to form a single temperament, a single character that was hers alone. There was no way to scientifically explain the phenomenon, just like there was no way to scientifically prove that he, or any human being, had a soul; yet he knew that he had one, and the faculty that told him so was the same that told him that sailing ships were living beings, while steamers, no matter how impressive in size or might, could never be anything other than as dead as the iron they were made of.

Drew hopped onto the cabin top and sat with one arm crooked around the Charley Noble, as if it were an old friend. He was gazing westward at the green land, and beginning to look a little green himself.

"How about you take the helm?" Nathaniel said to him. Andrew liked to steer. When his own hands were on the wheel, he was less prone to seasickness. "I've got to go below and look at the charts. South by half west."

"South by half west, all mine," Drew said. "Wouldn't it be simpler just to say two hundred and twenty-five degrees?"

"Yeah. But it's more nautical to box the compass, and now that I'm skipper, I've got to sound damned nautical."

Nathaniel squeezed into the navigation station, a grandiose name for the little alcove wedged between the galley and the dining area in the main cabin. He opened the cylindrical cases and laid the charts flat on the canted table, weighting them with tide and pilot books to press the curl out of their edges. Looking for the chart to East Penobscot Bay, he was surprised to find that the old man had included charts for the entire eastern seaboard, forty-one altogether. That could have been another example of his thoroughness, but the wide stiff sheets marked with soundings of coasts Nathaniel had never seen, and with lines of latitude and longitude scribed over waters he did not know, seemed to contain a hidden message. Somehow, merely by touching the charts, he sensed why they had been sent away. He could feel it in his fingertips, as though their father's purpose was imbued in the ink that colored the land buff and the shoal water pale blue and the ocean depths white.

Opening a drawer under the chart table for the parallel rule and dividers, he got another surprise, and to his mind, it confirmed the message. He pulled the teakwood box out of the drawer and opened it. Inside, nestled in green billiard felt, was the Plath sextant. He hadn't seen it yesterday. Had the old man put it on board last night? It was German-made, and as beautiful an instrument as ever had been fashioned by man's hand, possessing a harmony of form and purpose: the aesthetics of precision. "A fine sextant is a *moral* object," Cyrus had lectured once. "It will never lie to a sailor, so long as he uses it properly." And the Plath indeed looked honest and reliable, as certain men looked honest and reliable; it demanded, by its very appearance, to be used properly, the arrangement of its calibrated brass arc with ivory scale, its solid-brass frame and mirrors and sighting scope communicating a kind of rectitude, an intolerance of sloppiness and approximation. The instrument had shot its last sight on Cyrus's last voyage as a working sea captain in 1879, and had for as long as Nathaniel remembered occupied a place of honorable retirement in his father's study. He never took it on the summer cruises; a sextant wasn't necessary for those tame voyages, which seldom took them out of sight of land. The cheap instrument he brought along was mostly used by the boys to practice their celestial navigation. Why would he have given them the Plath if he did not expect them to sail beyond the furthest reach of the brightest beacons? He wanted to make sure they never got lost, and he'd entrusted them with the possession he prized more than *Double Eagle* herself. The schooner could be replaced; not so the sextant. IN GRATITUDE. *ANNISQUAM*. DRY TORTUGAS, FLORIDA. MARCH 10, 1879, read the engraved plate fixed to the inside of the box's cover.

He returned the Plath to the drawer and gazed around the cabin, all paneled in pine and the dining table pine also, and the sun through the skylight adding polish to the varnished wood that, with the cast-iron galley stove, bestowed the snug look and feel of a backwoods hunting cabin. She's mine, he thought. A fluttering came to his sternum, which he touched with a forefinger and felt an artery squirming just beneath his skin. *Double Eagle* was his. For only three months, really a little less than that, yet, by Christ, *his* to sail wherever he pleased, when he pleased. The tiny serpent rose into his windpipe, coiled itself in the hollow beneath his Adam's apple, and stole part of each breath he drew.

He spread the chart of East Penobscot Bay, placed one end of the parallel rule on the boat's present position, drew a line lightly in pencil through the Deer Island Thorofare, and then another line, bearing a little more westerly, into the Fox Islands Thorofare between Vinalhaven and North Haven. He walked the lower arm of the rule down to the Compass Rose and noted the bearings (in case the fog rolled in and he could not navigate by landmarks), then spread the dividers on the mileage scale and measured the distance along his two lines. Navigation was not his long suit. Nothing having to do with mathematics was his long suit. He had barely passed geometry last year. He was competent enough at this sort of thing—dead reckoning—but the calculations and plotting demanded by celestial navigation backlashed his brain. Last year, practicing on the cruise to Nova Scotia, he had placed *Double Eagle* near Salt Lake City, and Eliot had remarked, "Well, at least there's water there."

Now Eliot came down, and as the boat rolled a little, grabbed the companionway and swung himself around to avoid banging into a bulkhead. None of them had their sea legs yet; no matter how many times you had sailed, it always took a couple of days, after a long spell ashore, to get used to the tight quarters and constant motion of a vessel. Nathaniel looked at his middle brother and cocked his head toward the hatchway above.

"He's doing finely. Dead on course, eyes on the horizon, and not a drop of vomit. Aren't you hungry? You're always hungry, Nat, and I'm so hungry that if I was a goddamned beaver, I'd eat that goddamned table."

"Your mouth sure gets free when the old man's not around."

"Corned beef hash and scrambled eggs and sea biscuit. How does that sound?"

Nathaniel nodded, and Eliot went to the galley and scooped coals into the stove, adding a few strips of cedar wood to sweeten the acrid smell of the coals. He lit a fire while Nathaniel sat staring at the chart, which he had folded in half to conceal the buff-colored parts and the crowded numbers and fathom lines near shore. Before him now was a swath of white, a vacant dreamscape. He fiddled with the rule, twirled the dividers, pretending he was a clipper captain laying a course for Hong Kong or Shanghai, like Dad's uncle Silas, who had rounded the Horn, carrying forty-niners to the California goldfields before he sailed on to China.

"I figure we're a little under twenty miles from North Haven," he said.

Eliot dumped two cans of corned beef hash into the skillet with the eggs and stirred them together, the smell causing Nathaniel's appetite to wake up with a growl.

"We'll be a little bit in the lee when we go through the thorofares, so we'll lose some wind and speed. But if we can average five knots, we'll get there before dark. Maybe on time for supper."

"We can start mooching."

"All right, if you've got to call it that . . ." Nathaniel did not finish the sentence, his glance falling onto the chart again, roving over the white expanses that bled off to the edges of the page. "I was thinking, I've been thinking," he began, and then hesitated, because he wasn't sure what he was thinking or, rather, how to express it.

Eliot dipped the water tank, opened the top plate to the stove, and doused the fire. Leaving the skillet with Drew's portion on the stove, he filled two blue enamel plates with the rest and set them on the table. He and Nathaniel ate as adolescent boys eat when out from under parental supervision, that is, with all the decorum of lions on a fresh kill, their heads bowed over the plates as though their mother's frequent admonishments at the dinner table—*Food to mouth, boys, not mouth to food . . . Boys? . . . Boys!*—had been as seed sown upon rock. Trajan, the closest thing there was on board to a lion, showed better manners, rubbing first Nathaniel's, then Eliot's legs to gain their attention, and then waiting politely on his haunches for them to give him a couple of spoonfuls.

"So what were you thinking?" asked Eliot after the meal—its consumption took no more than three or four minutes.

"Remember when we were little and Father taught us to swim?"

"I get cold thinking about it. But I sure wouldn't call it teaching. Told us to strip to our drawers and threw us in. Maine water in early June, and he threw us in and told us to swim."

"Right. And we did, didn't we?"

"Sort of"—Eliot, clawing at the air to mime a desperate dog paddle.

"It was sink or swim and we swam and I was thinking this is like that."

"We're sinking and going to have to swim for it?"

"It would be a bully thing, middle brother, if you took some things seriously, once in a while."

"You're so serious about everything that I figure someone has to make up for it."

Nathaniel spread his hands on the table and studied them for a moment, observing how the light through the skylight brought out the copper tint in his skin—the legacy, which he shared with Eliot, of a (possibly mythological) Creek princess in their mother's ancestry.

"We're being tested," he said. "I mean, we're supposed to test ourselves."

"For anything in particular?"

"Not *for* anything. We're supposed to put ourselves *to* a test. I think that's what this is all about."

"Of what, Nat?" Eliot, his voice rising in impatience, tweaked the bill of his fisherman's cap.

"Our characters, I reckon. To see what we're made of."

"My character's fine. I like my character. I think it's a bully character. Why should I have to test it? And about what I'm made of . . ." He pulled the skin on the back of his hand, tapped two knuckles together, a hollow knock of bone on bone. "I'm made of that, and so are you, and what is there to find out that we don't know?"

"Don't play dumb. What we're made of in the parts you can't see. I was thinking, the old man was only three years older than me when he got wounded, and then . . . then there's this. . . ." Nathaniel rose and pulled the box with the sextant from out of the drawer. The schooner lurched; he lurched with it and fell back into his seat. "He saved a whole bunch of people—"

Eliot, cutting him off with a wave: "I know the story, what there is of it to know."

"We've got something to live up to, and this . . . Being out here on our own . . ."

He was stopped by Eliot's expression: a mixture of curiosity and wariness.

"What's the matter?"

"You make me nervous sometimes, Nat. You make a lot of people nervous. You know that, don't you?"

He shrugged, although he knew that he did, and he basked in his reputation for being unpredictable and daring. He would do risky things on impulse, mostly because they were risky. Four years ago, on a schoolboy's dare, he had climbed the wall of a three-story building. He became known among his classmates at Boston Latin as the Human Fly, although his ascent had not been quite as gravity-defying as a fly's: He'd scaled the building at its corner, using the protruding corner blocks for handholds and toeholds. He hadn't been frightened for a second, a lack of fear due more to a lack of awareness than to bravery. Arms and legs moving involuntarily, he had been in an almost trancelike state, as unconscious of danger as a sleepwalker climbing a tree in the middle of the night.

"Well, you do, and you're making me nervous, because I can tell there's something bubbling in that brain of yours." Eliot slid out from behind the table to fill a plate for Drew from the skillet—"Before it gets cold and ends up tasting what it looks like," he said.

"There's nothing bubbling," Nathaniel protested, following his middle brother outside. "I was just wondering if maybe Dad expects us to make a real voyage of it."

Eliot handed the plate to Drew and took the wheel. Drew returned to his perch beside the Charley Noble, from which a ribbon of smoke trailed into the air.

"Hell, in three months we could sail clear across to England and back if we wanted to."

Although he wasn't looking at them but at the red buoy, marking one side of the entrance to Deer Island Thorofare, Nathaniel sensed his brothers' alarm.

"Said we could, not that we will," he added, to reassure them.

"Bubble, bubble," Eliot said, and then turned to Drew. "Big brother changed his mind about why the old man told us to get lost. Now it doesn't have anything to do with whatever fix Lockwood's in. It's to test our characters. Don't feel my character needs testing, how about yours?"

Drew, wary of saying anything that might invite an attack, motioned noncommittally. Nathaniel kept his eye on the buoy and on the surf foaming around the ledges and rocks guarding the islets of Merchant's Row.

"Bear off some," he told Eliot. "I want to stay well clear of that stuff."

Eliot turned to port a little while Nathaniel went forward to ease sheets. When he returned aft, his brothers were deep into speculation about what Lockwood's current trouble could be. Nathaniel did not join in. It was a waste of time, making suppositions about the enigma who shared half their blood, he of an age so much greater than theirs that they had called him "Uncle Lockwood" when they were small, though he had not seemed any more their uncle than their brother; had not and did not seem any kin at all, but like an old family friend who dropped by now and then to renew acquaintances. He never gave his half brothers any reason to feel otherwise. He was too distant, too close-mouthed, and his gestures of affection—the pats on the head and cheek he gave them when they were young, the handshakes or claps on the shoulder when they grew older—possessed, at times, the awkwardness of someone to whom such expressions did not come naturally, at other times the rote quality of the obligatory, like the kisses campaigning politicians planted on babies. The boys would have concluded that he did not like them very much, if it weren't for the moments when they sensed, as children are apt to sense such things, a kind of bridled love in his restrained touches, a heart prohibited from showing all that it held.

Once, Drew asked him point-blank why he wasn't fond of them. Drew could be like that—come right out with whatever was on his mind. Lockwood gave him a perplexed look, his face flushing as Dad's did when Dad got mad, and said that he was fond of them, more than they would ever know. If he acted standoffish, it was because it was difficult for him to . . . And then he paused, and then he added, "Difficult to come here, but I think I should . . . every now and then. . . ." He broke off, looking sad at the same time that he looked angry.

Drew still wasn't satisfied. Why was it so difficult to come home? he asked. Lockwood laughed caustically and replied, "You sure don't see when somebody wants to change the subject, do you, kid?" All right, he could explain his manner this way—he was a seaman. He had practically been raised and schooled at sea, going at age twelve as both son and cabin boy to their father, and he'd learned then that seamen had to guard one another from one another's personalities. The only way to keep a happy and disciplined ship, because the biggest vessels got to be right small places on long voyages. If you disliked a shipmate, you could not let on that you did or you would disrupt the smooth running of the ship. If you were sad, or afraid, or lonesome, you kept it to yourself, lest your sadness, fear, or lonesomeness spread to the rest of the crew. You learned to keep yourself under wraps. It was a sacrifice you made to the ship, because that's all that really counted: the ship. Maybe after a while that keeping yourself under wraps got to be habit, whether you were ashore or at sea, and maybe after another while, the habit became second nature. He hoped that would suffice as explanation and reassurance that he cared a lot for his half brothers and wasn't the least bit standoff-ish, even if it seemed that way.

"Whatever pickle jar Lockwood's got himself into, you can bet the old man will pull him out," Eliot was saying now. "When you think about it, he sure does treat old Lock better than us. Hell, you don't have to think about it, even."

Nathaniel, leaning toward the port rail to make sure that a big yawl bearing down on them was going to yield right of way, said nothing, though he remembered vividly all the times the old man had rushed out the front door to pump Lockwood's hand almost before he had a chance to pay his cab fare. Slapped his back and called him "old bucko" and nicknames like that, bestowing love with such generosity that the change from his usual emotional stinginess was like a metamorphosis. The curious thing was that Lockwood never responded in kind, as reserved toward Dad as he was toward his half brothers. He would draw back from the hearty welcomes, as if he found them a little offensive, and get all starchy and offer some stilted greeting like "Good day, Father. You're in good health, I trust?" And that's how he would be throughout his stay—never disrespectful but always at an arm's length, as if the gift of paternal love was not important. That puzzled Nathaniel and made him resentful, for the same reason that a hungry man resents someone who rejects a banquet.

Maybe, he offered, in their father's defense (but knowing he was expressing a hope as well), Dad did not hold a deeper affection for his firstborn but a different kind of affection, of one old shipmate for another, rather than of father toward son.

"Yeah, maybe," said Eliot, his glance under the cropped bill of his cap moving restlessly to check on traffic, for they were nearing Stonington and all about them were fishing smacks and dories and lobster sloops—lean utilitarian little vessels sailed by lean utilitarian men. "But if any one of us got into pickles, he'd tell us to get lost. Look at this, now. We didn't even get into a pickle and he's told us to get lost. Do you reckon if one of us had a business that went broke, he'd find a job for us?"

"I think the old man would stand by us. Anyhow, Dailey said that it was quite a fight, so maybe Lock isn't his favorite anymore. Hasn't been since he went bust."

The yawl yielded, her crew paying out sheets and her booms swinging to leeward as she fell off. She looked to be a good fifty feet on deck, and her black hull was trimmed in gold. Someone at her rail was looking at *Double Eagle* through binoculars. The man appeared to be waving at them, but when Nathaniel raised his binoculars to see who it was, the man turned to face his mates. The yawl dashed away, her name and port of call—BLACK WATCH—NEW YORK—blazed in gold across her mahogany transom: a rusticator's yacht, but a rusticator with a touch of the pirate or smuggler in him, for with her dark hull and superb lines, *Black Watch* had a buccaneering look.

"I think Dad treats Lockwood like he does because he hardly ever sees him and he sees us all the time," Drew said, eager to make himself part of the conversation. "Familiarity breeds contempt. I read that in a book."

Eliot asked what book that might be.

"Dunno. A book somewhere."

"Shakespeare. It's from Shakespeare." Nathaniel was gratified to best his kid brother in the knowledge department. "But you don't need a book to know that. The trouble with you, Drew, is that you study on things and study on them, and what you end up learning isn't anything you couldn't've learned just by looking around you instead of in some damned book."

"Nat . . . Na-aaat . . ." Eliot, chiding in a singsong. "You're doing it again."

He did not say anything, recalling what Lockwood had told them about protecting your shipmates from yourself.

LOCKWOOD HAD lived with Mother and Dad in New England until a few weeks after Nathaniel was born, and then, frustrating Dad's hopes to make him a partner in the granite business, went under sail on coasters between Canada and the Gulf of Mexico. When he saw the steel and rivets of the coming age, he switched to steamers that took him to the farthest corners of the earth, from which he would return six months or a year later and pay one of his brief calls on the family before departing to pick up another ship. Eliot dubbed him "the Magi" for the gifts he always bore on his visits, each wrapped in brown paper with a name on it and the occasion on which it was to be presented, Christmas or a birthday. There were silks and perfumes for Mother, Arab daggers and African spears for the boys, barbaric tribal masks for Dad's study, and sometimes he gave Dad a box of cigars for immediate consumption, and the two of them would smoke and drink whiskeys after dinner.

If he was a remote figure to the boys, he was also fabulous, a transmundane phantom of the sea, face browned by exotic suns that had etched spidery lines into the corners of his eyes, and his whole person wreathed in the scent, in the romance of fabled ports like Maricaibo and Jakarta and Dakar. The stories he told about those places and about the things that happened at sea were his most valuable gifts. He loosened up when he spun yarns, and the yarns brightened the drab Boston days, bringing to the common world of school and home a vicarious one of adventure and the uncommon. Nathaniel envied him his sailor's life, as he also envied the youth Lockwood had lived, sailing with Dad in the wild old wrecking days on the Florida reefs—a youth painted in bold hues beside which his, Nathaniel's, seemed a pallid watercolor.

Three years ago, a letter from Lockwood, addressed to "the Braithwaite Family" and bearing a Florida postmark, was delivered to the Marlborough Street house. He seldom wrote on his travels; getting mail from him was something of an event, and Dad usually read his letters aloud at the dinner table. Dad was away, dealing with some machinery breakdown in one of his Cape Ann quarries, when the letter from Florida arrived, so the reading of it fell to Mother. Lockwood wrote that he was quitting the sea. His intention in joining the merchant service had not been to rove but to build up a nest egg doing the one thing he did best. He had not wasted his money on the temptations that usually separated sailors from their pay and had saved a considerable sum. Now, he wanted to make his mark, to become like Father, a man of substance. He and a partner, a Virginian named Taliaferro, had bought out a sponging business from a Greek fellow, whose name he could not pronounce, much less spell. They now owned four vessels, complete with crew and divers, and a warehouse. Lockwood had invested all his savings in the partnership, but the sponge industry was booming in Tampa, and he was confident his investment would be recouped within a year and doubled or tripled the year after.

Mother laid the letter flat on the table and said, with brittle laughter, "A man of substance!" as if she found that phrase ridiculous when applied to Lockwood. (And there was something insubstantial about him. His personality lacked a certain definiteness. It was hard to picture him, the wraith who drifted into and out of the family's lives, solidly moored to the concrete world of commerce.) "A man of substance!" Mother repeated. "Like his father. And all from sponges. From sponges!" And again, the frangible laugh that expressed contempt and mockery and pity all at once, the laugh fracturing as a glass or china cup might fracture, as she slapped her palm on the letter and called Lockwood a "goddammed fool." Her cheeks colored immediately and, looking at her sons as if she had temporarily forgotten their presence, she apologized. Boys their age—of any age—should never hear their mother use such language. . . . It was just that Lockwood . . . that Lockwood . . . She could not find whatever words she was groping for, scooped up the letter, and suddenly left the dining room, just as Moira entered from the kitchen to clear the soup bowls. "Will you not be having anything else, ma'am?" she asked, but Mother didn't answer, and Moira, leaning on the serving cart, watched her mistress pass through the double doors into the hall, her back straight, her shoulders squared, as though she were marching in a parade.

She wasn't easily upset—no, that wasn't it—she wasn't a woman who easily *showed* that she was upset. She, too, knew how to keep herself under wraps. She was the daughter of a quick-tempered and violent people possessed of a pride as fierce as it was fragile, but she could have given tutorials on self-control to the pinched, arid matrons of Back Bay, those heiresses to the puritan tradition who, in her opinion, were able to contain their passions for the simple reason that they didn't have any. But she brimmed with emotions that were always threatening to get out of hand, pitting her will against her heart. The will usually won. She seldom allowed her voice, her expressions, or her eyes, opaque as chips of anthracite, to betray her feelings. She lived according to a code of gracious speech and impeccable manners that (Nathaniel's father had told him) Southern women seemed to absorb into their very beings from the moment they drew breath, a code that northern females could no more hope to learn than they could the intricate rituals governing a Chinese court. But there was this as well: In Mother, the code was buttressed and undergirded by a girlhood endured rather than lived amid the ruins of a civilization (one that had earned its ruin, in Dad's opinion) whose broken temples had collapsed on innocent and guilty alike. She had been one of the innocents, not a year old when robbed of her father by a Yankee minié ball at Antietam, of her mother by consumption some five years later, raised by her mother's younger sister, also widowed by the war (but indirectly—Aunt Judith's husband died of cholera), the two women living with several other females bereft of husbands and fathers in a Beaufort boardinghouse that was, for all practical purposes, a secular convent. The aunt, who at twenty-five had been mistress of a modest-sized plantation, went to work in a textile mill acquired (confiscated really) by a New York man during Reconstruction; Mother, who would have been the daughter of a rich cotton broker but for that minié ball, became a seamstress at fourteen, after she had acquired the rudiments of an education. Working every day but Sunday, aunt and niece earned just enough for their room and meager board. The specter of hunger hovered constantly—not the tummy rumble of a missed meal or two but the hunger that gnaws at the soul as much as at the belly. They feared, as well, falling further than they already had down the social ladder, at the bottom of which lay the realm inhabited by the people collectively known as "white trash." The fear was greater in Aunt Judith because she remembered what it was like to live prosperously, graciously, securely; but she had filled Mother's head with so many stories of the antebellum Eden that in time Mother felt its loss almost as acutely and became no less ashamed of being poor, no less afraid of growing poorer.

She was to this day not fond of her aunt, rarely spoke of her, and never wrote to her: a pretentious woman, she said, who despite her poverty had kept a colored maid, whom she ordered about, for no more recompense than a pallet on the floor, as if slavery had not been abolished. Mother had learned to read and write in school; Aunt Judith taught her the ancient social graces, which in their straitened circumstances seemed as pointless as bustles on a draft horse. (Those were Mother's words, "pointless as bustles on a draft horse.") But if there was a point to her aunt's lessons in how to curtsy, in how to make pleasant conversation and season it lightly with French phrases, in how to dance and hold a fan and know the difference between one style of furniture and another, it was to brighten Mother's chances of marrying well someday—if not well enough to reclaim the place that should have been hers by birthright, then at least well enough to get out of poverty and stay out. A pretty slim hope in a town where most of the eligible bachelors went about with at least one shirtsleeve or one trouser leg flapping in the breeze and lived off inadequate pensions, or the charity of neighbors, or whatever coin they could pick up at odd jobs. All the while, both women were constrained to preserve their honor, that glorious and undefiled Southern womanhood many a rebel boy had believed to be a cause as worthy of his life as state's rights or the right of white man to enslave black. The danger to Aunt Judith's was not too great; she was over forty and her good looks had been worn away by loss and toil. But Mother had to guard herself constantly against predatory carpetbaggers, against the sailors and riffraff who came into Beaufort from Port Royal, and against her own yearnings for a man's arms, her own exhaustion and loneliness and fear that made her vulnerable to the illusory offers of protection and support that unscrupulous males presented from time to time, hoping to bribe their way into a young woman's bed. The female who was not an iron mistress of her emotions and a shrewd judge of character could end up with child and without a husband and a roof over her head, or, what was just as bad, with a roof she had unwisely covenanted to share with some brute fonder of whiskey than of work.

When Mother finally did meet the man she wished to marry, the courtship was so swift as to seem almost an abduction, albeit an abduction she eagerly surrendered to, because life with her aunt in the secular convent had become intolerable. She had to run away, pledging herself to Dad in a secret ceremony presided over by another sea captain: Marrying a Yankee sailor who had borne arms against the Confederacy was not her Aunt Judith's idea of marrying well, and she never forgave Mother for that betrayal. The only thing worse, in her view of things, would have been for her niece to wed a Negro.

Nathaniel had recently pried these details out of his mother—she was averse to talking about her history—and he had wanted to ask how his father squared them with his assertions of feminine delicacy and his claim that women dwelled in a world of illusions, but the old man did not like to be contradicted or to have his own contradictions pointed out to him. Mother's autobiography, however, had given Nathaniel an insight into her character that he had previously lacked. Now he understood her inscrutability, why it was often so difficult to tell what she was thinking or feeling. The only way to read her heart, if not her mind, was to watch what she did with her body, for her will spoke through it; the emotion that gripped her at any given moment never gave direct evidence of itself but was seen in the outward manifestations of the effort to suppress it. If her jaw stiffened, its muscles corded like the muscles in Dailey's forearms when he drove the team at a fast clip, she was reining in an anger. If she was frightened or apprehensive, her back and shoulders straightened into a soldierly brace, as they had the morning she left to see the doctor, as they had when she left the dining room with Lockwood's letter in her hand.

Nathaniel assumed she had called him a fool for giving up the one thing he knew best for something he could not do well at all. The following spring, when the boys were home for Easter vacation, a telegram from Tampa was delivered to the house, heralding Lockwood's imminent arrival. He showed up three days later, looking agitated and even a little disreputable, his jaw unshaven, his suit of tropical linen rumpled (he'd obviously slept in it on the train, unable to afford a private sleeping compartment). By design or accident, his arrival was timed for the middle of the day, when Father was sure to be at work. For the better part of that wet, windy April afternoon, he and Mother were locked away in her sitting room, talking in undertones. Tea was brought in, tea brought out. Nathaniel and his brothers, confined indoors because of the weather, asked Moira if she had heard what was going on. She replied that she was not a spy, thank you very much, and even if she were, she could not report on business problems because she did not understand them. So it was a business problem, which should have been their father's domain. And then the phantom left, having spoken barely a word of greeting or parting to his half brothers. Mother gave him an umbrella so he didn't catch a death, and after she had showed him out, stood leaning against the door and let out a long sigh, as if she had at last gotten rid of an annoying and persistent salesman.

After dinner, another hushed conference was held, this one between her and Dad in the study. Nathaniel and his brothers were in the next room, in the parlor, reading magazines or working jigsaw puzzles, as they listened through the walls for intelligence from the adult world, the world that existed right alongside theirs and yet was a terra incognita, full of mysteries. They heard almost nothing at first, the conversation was so muted. There was something about losses, capitalization, a loan; then they heard a thump—a hand or book slammed against a desk—and their father's voice rising:

CYRUS: *What he's asking is for me to be a third partner, that's the effect of it, and I don't see myself as a sponger. He should liquidate and take his medicine. Be a good lesson. I'll bring him up here, bring him in with me. . . .*

ELIZABETH: *Don't do that! It's best for him to stay right where he is!*

CYRUS: *It's what I wanted in the first place. To bring him in, show him the ropes. He's got no head for business, but I could put one on his shoulders, if anybody can.*

ELIZABETH: *I don't doubt that you could, darling, but it wouldn't be best for him.*

(There was a long pause.)

CYRUS: *I think you mean best for* you, *Liza. You wouldn't want him around here.*

ELIZABETH: *Why, Cyrus, what a thing to say. . . .*

CYRUS: *You used to like him, but after . . . I don't know. . . .* (He cleared his throat loudly, and the boys could picture the movements that usually accompanied the guttural rumble—his fingers plucking at his collar, his head shaking once or twice.) *Years ago, when he got the notion to leave, you were the one who encouraged him.*

ELIZABETH: *I don't recall encouraging him.*

CYRUS: *You don't make him feel welcome. He doesn't see us but once a year, if that, and you don't seem very happy to see him. He never stays but two, three days, and you don't seem sad to see him leave. Relieved, I would say.*

ELIZABETH: *I am standing here, interceding for him, even when I agree with you about his business sense. Doesn't that prove that I care about him?*

CYRUS: *It's only because this business he's gotten into will keep him down there in Florida.*

ELIZABETH: *Oh, Cy, you're reproaching me.* (There was another long silence, and the boys imagined they heard the noiseless noise of silk brushing their mother's legs as she crossed the room to straighten their father's tie or touch his cheek.) *I am asking you to help him out just this one time. I will never ask it of you again, I vow it. And if there's a next time, Lockwood can plead his own case. Please, darling?*

CYRUS: *I'll consider it. I don't want to go throwing good money after bad, and I'll need some time to consider it.*

(There was the click of the study door opening, and Nathaniel and Eliot dropped their eyes to their issues of *Tip Top Weekly*, while Drew feigned interest in his puzzle, all three aware of who had won.)

Everything the old man had said about Mother's attitude toward Lockwood was true, which made his confiding in her rather than in Dad all the more perplexing. She didn't treat him like the wicked stepmother in fairy tales; she was unfailingly courteous, but there was a kind of forced correctness, an artificiality and a tension in her manner whenever he was around. Not too long ago, Nathaniel had mentioned this to Constance and speculated about what caused her to be that way. Constance was almost a year older, and very smart, and Nathaniel often sought her opinion on matters that puzzled him. Sitting in that prim, grown-up way of hers, her hands clasped in her lap, she thought for a while—Constance was like that, thoughtful, and did not just say things for the sake of saying them, like a lot of girls. She: Lockwood is living proof that your father was once in love with another woman, you silly. Your mother is a wee bit jealous, I'd expect. Then he: But Lockwood's mother died in childbirth. She's been dead for years. How could my mother be jealous of a dead woman? Then Constance, with the strained patience of a teacher tutoring a dunce in simple arithmetic: Your mother wants to believe what every woman wants to believe of the man she's married to—that he *never* loved anyone but her. But she can't believe that, and all she has to do is look at Lockwood to see why she can't.

Dad's rescue of Gulf Shores Industries was only temporary, and the scene that had taken place in Boston was re-enacted the following year, with minor alterations in two of the dramatic unities: The time was mid-summer, the setting was Mingulay; the characters were the same, and so was the action. The telegram from Tampa, then Lockwood himself, once again bleary-eyed and stubble-jawed and wearing the very same rumpled linen suit. (Though he himself had changed, looking more than ever like Father: His waist and jowls had thickened—physically, anyway, he was become more substantial—and he had grown a beard.) Another hushed conference with Mother, but on this occasion, Lockwood did not leave immediately afterward. The boys guessed she had stuck to her pledge to make him plead his own case, which is what he did that night in the library. She went with him, maybe to lend moral support, maybe to keep a lid on Father's temper. He wasn't likely to lose it with Lockwood, but he might, under these circumstances, and she would not want any unseemly shouting, not in that house where sound carried easily through unplastered walls made only of board-and-batten nailed to studs. And so it was three of them alone, the original family circle, that ring of intertwined lives from which the three brothers were locked out, literally by the library doors, metaphorically by the accident of their births, which had barred them from sharing in the history parents and half brother had lived together, beginning with the sea captain's wooing of the virgin seamstress from her widowed aunt.

The boys were in their rooms upstairs, fresh from their baths, for the next day was Sunday and they had to be scrubbed and in their best for church. Like stagehands at a play, they caught only fragments of the actors' dialogue, their father's and Lockwood's voices borne through the halls, up through the floorboards, Father speaking in his Yankee burr, all rounded *r*'s and broad *a*'s, Lockwood in his strange Florida Keys accent, cracker twang set to the meter of the West Indies. *Rivals undercutting the markets . . . Profits insufficient to meet maintenance costs of the vessels . . . Second mortgage . . . Liquidation . . . That's what you should do, at least keep creditors off. . . . Declare bankruptcy, Father? . . . Exactly what I'm saying . . .* Then their mother interjecting with the only words she uttered that night: *Oh, Cy, that is so drastic, it would be a disgrace! . . . Not as much of a disgrace as getting hauled into court for . . . No! Once and once only . . . Good money after bad . . .*

In the early morning hours, something Nathaniel had eaten decided to disagree with him violently. Lighting a candle, he padded downstairs to the earth closet in the cellar (the miracles of electricity and plumbing, fully installed in the Boston town house, had not yet come to Mingulay). Returning to his room, he passed the library, saw a lamp burning, and Lockwood seated at the desk, his back to the door. The desk was covered with papers, but he wasn't working, only leaning back in the chair, smoking a cigarette and nipping from a glass and staring out the casement windows toward the black water beyond the long slant of lawn. He slugged back half of what was in the glass—dark rum or whiskey—and muttered, "Son of a bitch, liquidation . . ." Raising the glass, he made a toast, "So here's to liquidating," and then drank off the rest. He looked so lonely and forlorn that Nathaniel wondered if he ought to speak to him for a while, keep him company, but while he debated whether to announce his presence, Lockwood did a strange thing, the strangest thing Nathaniel had ever seen anyone do. He climbed up on the chair and stood none too steadily, unbuttoned his fly, and commenced to piss on the papers, a great long splashy horsepiss it was, too, his pizzle with its hood of a foreskin moving back and forth across the desk like he was putting out a fire, one of his eyes squinting against the smoke from the cigarette clamped between his teeth.

The scene played itself back in Nathaniel's mind all through services the next morning, all through the ride back to Mingulay from Blue Hill, and it spoiled the fairness of the morning, soured the sweet breath of the spruce woods that crowded the road on both sides. He felt like a witness to a shameful crime, but something—he didn't know what—restrained him from reporting it; and the keeping it to himself made him feel less like a witness and more like an accessory. It was close to noon by the time the family got back, and Lockwood was still in bed, to Nathaniel's deep irritation. This was the summer of his introduction into the world of work, Sundays were his one day off from the quarry, and it struck him as a gross injustice that he had been required to get up at seven and go to church, while the half brother who had gotten himself drunk and done that disgusting thing was allowed to sleep in. He had a good mind to rat on him.

He and Eliot and Drew spent the afternoon fishing in the dory, taking turns at the oars as they trolled a bay. They had caught only a few small mackerel, until Drew landed a monster bluefish of twelve pounds or more. When they got back, their father was sitting far up the lawn in an Adirondack chair, a boater pulled low over his eyes. Drew ran toward him, dragging his prize by the stringer looped through its gills and mouth. "Dad, look what I caught, lookit!" he shouted. "Did it all by himself, too!" hollered Eliot, he and Nathaniel striding behind. Dad rose and started toward them, and then doffed the hat and called out, "Surprise!"

They stopped short when they saw the full head of hair without a strand of gray in it.

"Lockwood!" said Drew. "From back there, you . . ."

"'Mazing, isn't it?" A crooked grin appeared in the ruddy beard, and the cheeks above it ruddy also. "But I can do better, sure, a lot better," Lockwood said, just as Mother, in her white muslin morning dress, came out of the house and held the door open for Moira, wheeling a tea cart. "Now you watch this." Lockwood half closed one eye and cocked his head a little to one side to make the opposite eye look askance, miming Dad's peculiar glance. He took a step toward Drew, stumbled, and caught his balance. "Fine fish you caught there, son. Fine fish. Like the cut of your jib, boy"—mimicking, almost flawlessly, their father's clipped accent.

Drew and Eliot laughed; it wasn't only rare for Lockwood to clown around with them, it was unprecedented. Nathaniel managed only a flickering smile, for as Lockwood came nearer, he realized what had ruddied his complexion and caused the change from his usual aloofness, and that faint whiskey reek also brought back the picture from the night before.

"Well, how was that, boys?"

"Pretty good," Eliot replied. "Think you can do the story about Mobile Bay?"

"Lockwood, dear," Mother called. "We'll be having tea now."

He spun on his heel, faced her.

"In a moment, my dear Mrs. Braithwaite." (He always addressed her that way.) "Y'see, looks like I'm a victim of mistaken identity, and I am trying to live up to it."

She stepped off the veranda and pointed her sun parasol, Nathaniel struck by how like a goddess she looked in the moment she moved out of shade into light, how like a white-robed goddess, pointing a sacred sword.

"Gracious! Look at that fish! Who caught that?"

Drew answered that he had.

"Why, darling, good for you. It is a leviathan!"

She told him to take it immediately around back to the kitchen and give it to Mrs. Carter to put on ice, before it spoiled in the heat. Drew started, but Lockwood laid a hand against his chest.

"Hold on, lad, you are about to hear the tale of how the *Brooklyn* led Farragut's fleet into Mobile Bay, under a storm, by God, *a storm* of shot and shell. . . ."

"But—" Drew motioned at the bluefish, its thick flanks speckled with blades of grass.

"You must do as Father says first. . . ."

"Now, Lockwood . . ."

He ignored her, and walked off a few yards with Father's rolling gait, his chin tucked in like a boxer's.

"*Brooklyn* was a twenty-eight and two thousand ton, Captain Alden in command. . . ."

"She was twenty-four guns," Drew corrected, and Lockwood turned on him in an impersonation of Cyrus in a fit of temper. "Are you disputing me? Were you at Mobile Bay, boy? Were you there when the order came down to trice up, secure all sulufer—I mean to say, all su-*per*-fluous spars and rigging? Eh? Were you?"

It was wicked fun to see the ruler of all their lives parodied; at the same time, there was something alarming about it.

"First thing, you'd see the puff of smoke, way upon the distant ramparts of Fort Morgan." Pointing seaward, Lockwood widened his eyes in mock terror. "And then you would see the shot itself, why, it looked like one of the titans of old had thrown a giant baseball . . . straight at you, at *you*." Leaning forward, he thrust his face into Drew's, and grabbed him by both shoulders. Drew wrinkled his nose, squirmed to get free.

"C'mon, lemme go. . . . You smell funny."

"Smell of *fear,* bucko . . ."

"Lockwood, I think that's about enough. . . ." Mother, standing with her feet spread, her parasol braced across her legs just above her knees, and her jaw muscles tightening. "Come and have your tea. I do believe you could use it."

". . . because if you were a green sailor like I was then, you were sure that giant ball was going to hit you right between your sidelights, and it howling and shrieking like ten devils straight from hell. And you know what you wanted to do, then? This, this . . ." Lockwood flung himself to his knees and, with a jerk that bent Drew's back, pulled him closer. "Fall down and pray! That's what!"

"Lockwood!" Mother took a step. He had gone too deeply into his role, and the fun had gone out of the masquerade. "You're frightening him!"

"Just joking around," he said, returning to his own voice. "Right, Drew? A little joke? But tell me something, if the old man, God forbid, went to his glory today, d'you think I'd make a good subsh—substitute? What d'you say, li'l brother? Would I?" He pinched Drew's cheeks hard. "C'mon, what d'you say, could I fill in for your daddy and my daddy?"

He tugged Drew's head right and then left, and Drew, with a flinch and a quick look at Mother, hollered, "Ow!" and she, her self-

containment breached by the one thing sure to breach it—any threat to
her precious ones—closed the distance between herself and the threat in
two or three long strides, raised the parasol by its pointed end, and
smacked the side of the handle into the side of Lockwood's head as hard
as she could. Nathaniel winced with sympathetic pain; the force of the
blow, the ferocity of the attack, seemed way out of proportion to whatever harm was being done.

Lockwood let go of Drew, one hand covering his cheek. In the same
moment, Mother, now that she'd subdued the threat, had to punish it for
being a threat and for making her lose her composure; quickly reversing
her grip, she jabbed the parasol's spike end into Lockwood's ribs as he
was getting to his feet. He looked down at his shirt, as if expecting to see
blood, and then stood with one palm aside his face, the other on his ribs.

"Holy cow! I was only joking around. . . ."

"You keep your hands off him, and you watch what you say, Lockwood Braithwaite!"

Strands of black hair had fallen across her forehead, a tendril
tumbled alongside an ear. Nathaniel never had seen her looking so wild,
so fierce, quite ungoddesslike now, and he felt the same vicarious shame
as he had watching Lockwood last night, the shame then not so much in
seeing his half brother's private parts but in seeing a previously private
aspect of his personality suddenly revealed, and the shame now in
beholding a heretofore hidden aspect of his mother's character: the violence bequeathed by her ancestors, for when she'd swung the parasol
into Lockwood's cheek, Nathaniel had seen, with imagination's eye, her
father or grandfather raising a whip over a black back. For the first time
ever, he was afraid of her.

"I didn't hurt him," Lockwood pleaded.

"You've been indulging yourself, haven't you?" She brushed locks of
undone hair, but they fell back across her forehead, and she swatted at
them as she would at a mosquito. "Since last night, I believe. Isn't that
right? Moira tells me she found you in the library this morning, dead
asleep on the desk, and—disgusting . . . And all on a Sunday morning,
too."

Lockwood said nothing, glanced over his shoulder at Moira, who
suddenly found a reason to go back into the house. Nathaniel felt a little
relieved—now he wasn't sole possessor of the secret: knowledge of what
Lockwood had done—that, too, must have been behind the whack
Mother had delivered with such inspiration.

"I apologize, Mrs. Braithwaite. I . . . Well, now, don't reckon there's
much I can say about that."

"Most certainly not."

Lockwood, wrestling his lips into a weak smile, rubbing his cheek, where a welt shaped like one end of a parenthesis had risen: "Making up for lost time, I suppose. All those years at sea, when the boys were in port, me staying aboard or going to museums like a damned tourist, and for what? Not a damn thing, might as well have blown every dime and dollar. So reckon I was indulging. A sailor's pleasures . . ."

"I believe I heard the word 'damn' twice, and it is still Sunday," she said, tightly. "And as for last night . . . do you consider *that* a sailor's pleasure?"

"No . . ." He paused, and the smile dissolved, and he looked at Mother in a way that made Nathaniel uneasy, though if someone had asked what there was in the look to arouse uneasiness, he could not have answered.

"If you expect to come under this roof again . . . If you act the way you—" Faltering, she seemed to come back to herself, and making a turn toward Drew, told him to bring his fish to Mrs. Carter right away.

"And you boys," she said to Nathaniel and Eliot, "I am so sorry you had to witness such unpleasantness. . . ."

"And all on a Sunday afternoon, too," Lockwood interjected, but she was in command of herself once more and paid no regard to the interruption.

"But it's all over. Go find something to occupy yourselves. Lockwood and I will be having tea now. We have some things to discuss."

Going into the house, Nathaniel and Eliot heard her say, "If ever you act like this again, I promise you . . ." The door shut behind them and they did not hear what promise she made but knew they were glad she wasn't making it to them.

The swift collapse of Gulf Shore Industries convinced Dad that even he could not put a businessman's head on Lockwood's shoulders. From his wrecking days, he knew the president of Merritt, Chapman and Scott—it was a big marine salvage and insurance firm in New York City—and persuaded him to find a place for Lockwood, who was now an investigator in the claims department. That sounded like an important job, and maybe it was, but he was doing none too well—so the boys had gleaned from scraps of parental conversation. There was a limit to how much Dad was willing to do for his firstborn. Having found him a job, he'd refused to help him pay off his creditors, not because he was miserly but because he possessed a sense of justice rove into the fibers of his puritan soul, and that sense had been tautened and strengthened by his years at sea—a court that did not hear appeals. Justice demanded that Lockwood suffer the consequences of his misbegotten business venture, as a captain who carried too much sail in a high wind, or who failed to exercise sufficient vigilance in uncertain waters, had to suffer the penalties meted out by the sea. The details of the bankruptcy were beyond Nathaniel's ken, but it appeared that a court had ordered Lockwood's salary to be garnished—a few dollars here, a few more there, morsels to appease his creditors' appetites and keep him out of jail. His partner, the Virginian named Taliaferro, had disappeared.

"OKAY, if you're so smart, what part of Shakespeare does that come from?" Drew was asking. "'Familiarity breeds contempt.'"

"I don't know, but I know it's from Shakespeare somewhere," Nathaniel answered sourly.

They stopped talking for a while and sailed on past Stonington, its clapboard and shingle houses climbing, in whites and grays, a steep hill reefed with granite ledges.

"Y'know, we come from a kind of strange family," Eliot commented, with a thoughtful frown. "Maybe everybody's family is strange, when you get right down to it, but ours is pretty strange. We've got a half brother we don't know much about, and we've never known our grandparents on either side."

"Mother's parents died way before we were born, so how are we supposed to know them?" asked Drew, annoyed that his brother hadn't grasped a fact so obvious. "And Grandpa Theo and Grandma Ada were gone when we were all real little. They were old when Dad was born."

"Right. And when he went to their funerals, it was the first time he'd seen them since he was a young man."

"The old man was supposed to have had a big fight with everybody back during the war. Or right after. He was on the outs with them. You know that as well as I do, Eliot."

Nathaniel gave a conclusive nod, as if he'd settled the question about their family's strangeness.

He was looking at the town and the harbor, ringed by fish houses and chandleries, when he became aware of a presence behind him; turning, he saw *Black Watch* off *Double Eagle*'s quarter and closing fast, under full press and all in a froth and a fury. *Double Eagle* was ambling along; the archipelago of Merchant's Row isles, as he had figured it would, blocked much of the southwest wind, but, absorbed in conversation and in thoughts about his family, he had not bothered to reset topsails. Soon, the yawl was abeam, and not more than twenty yards away, stealing from *Double Eagle* what wind the land had not already taken. There were four men on deck, the helmsman and two others looking ahead for oncoming vessels, while the fourth, a tall, heavyset man, waved with both arms to get *Double Eagle*'s attention. Nathaniel waved back to tell him he had it. The man hailed them through a brass trumpet: Where were they headed? Nathaniel told him. The man whipped out a bright red bandanna and fluttered it in farewell, giving it one last dismissive flip that communicated ridicule and challenge at the same time.

This is what we need, Nathaniel thought as *Black Watch* drew away. It was what he and his little crew needed to get their minds off family gossip and their present homelessness; it was what they needed to start functioning as a team.

"Gimme the wheel," he snapped to Eliot. "You and Drew break out those topsails and run 'em up. Those lubbers"—jerking his head at the yawl, its transom already some twenty yards away—"want a race, so let's give 'em one."

5

WHAT IF they're not going to North Haven? Suppose they're bound for Camden, Portland, Madagascar? Do we race them anyway and forget North Haven? Where's the finish, and who's to say who wins? Scampering over the decks, wet and cool beneath his bare feet, Eliot concluded that the race was a figment of his older brother's imagination, or, better yet, a product of that busy factory, his overly competitive nature. Nat was never satisfied unless he was in a match, a scrimmage, a scuffle, a race, and if one didn't exist, he would invent one. That fellow on the yawl had only been taunting them, not challenging them. But in the interests of keeping a happy ship, Eliot submitted himself to Nat's fantasy. With Drew, he wrestled the topsails out of the bags and ran them up.

"Picked up a knot!" shouted Nat. "Did you feel her? Like a horse kicked into a trot. They'll be eating our wake, and right quick!"

If Lockwood and Drew looked most like the old man on the outside, Nat was his twin on the inside. How many times, on the summer cruises, had Father spotted another yacht away off somewhere and gone straight toward her, promising to give her a run for her money, show her and her crew how a real vessel manned by real sailors could crack on? Had to win. Had to find something to run against, or be up against, and win. Made his living that way once. When the lookouts on Key West rang bells and shouted from towers, "Wreck ashore!" it was a footrace of skippers and crews to their vessels, and then a sailing race, a regular right smart regatta, Dad had said, sloops and schooners dueling, in barbarous seas and winds, to be first to the wreck and claim rights as salvage master, and the prize not a silver cup to sit gleaming in a trophy case but ten or twenty or thirty thousand dollars in saved cargo and whatever treasure awaited you in heaven for saving lives. Must have gotten into his blood, Eliot reckoned, so he just couldn't stand fair winds and quiet seas, in any sense of the word; hell, he probably had a fine time, facing down the strikers in the Black Island pits two years ago, just him and his manager, the big Swede called Pedersen, against more than one hundred angry men armed with clubs and implements of their trade.

"Hey! I'll do that," he said to Drew, who had suddenly leapt onto the bowsprit.

Straddling it, and it pitching in the chop, Drew inched forward to unfurl the jib topsail.

"L'il brother, you don't have to prove anything to him."

"You can give me a hand, if you want."

Eliot swung on behind him, warning him to hang on tight should the sail, once the jackropes were untied, flap out of control, warning him also not to look down at the waves—a sure way to turn his complexion the same color as the water. They got the ties undone and, as the sail unfurled, a part of it dropped down, forming a kind of hammock a foot or two below their dangling feet, the concavity becoming convex when an eddy of wind got under it and made it flog the air like a maddened ghost. Startled, Drew jerked away from the cracking canvas, shouted, "Whoaaa!" and came close to rolling off into the boil of bow wash; but Eliot held him by the back of his waistband and steadied him in his seat. They slid backward on the bowsprit and set the rebellious sail. As soon as it filled, Eliot felt the sensation Nat had described a few moments before—of *Double Eagle* surging forward like the thoroughbred she was. No trot now, but a strong steady canter.

He looked at Drew, who managed a small, victorious smile, but his eyes had become a little rheumy and his face a little tinged, whether from the pitching or the near dunking, Eliot couldn't tell.

"Well, you know what to do," he said.

"Go astern, stand at the rail, look at the horizon, and if I have to puke, puke to leeward."

They sailed past the thorofare light, rising white and tall out of granite, wind-scoured of all green things, save scattered spruces, and into the blue space of Penobscot Bay. There, the smoky sou'wester struck them full force: over fifteen, rising toward twenty knots, and the fog rising also in the afternoon sun to be shredded like rotted cotton by the wind, whose pressure on the sails made the weather-side rigging hum. The woollies overhead were stampeding eastward, and *Double Eagle* was heeled well over, the two younger brothers clinging to the weather rail, their weight lending the ballast some little help.

Black Watch was a good two hundred yards ahead, and maybe two points off *Double Eagle*'s port bow, the vessels on parallel courses.

"I'm going to drive her hard, till we pass those yawl bums," Nathaniel said.

"How do you know they're racing us?" asked Eliot. "Maybe they're only—"

"What the hell do you think all that hankie-waving back there was about?"

But, Eliot argued, *Black Watch* had a huge head start and a couple, three feet more than *Double Eagle* on the waterline. Plus, he added, *plus,* the wind was forward, and the yawl could sail faster close to the wind than their gaff-rigged schooner.

"Look at the clouds, Eliot! Look at the seas! Wind's veering southwest to south. We'll be on a beam reach right quick, and there's nothing but a steamer can whip a Gloucester schooner on a beam reach."

He was focused now, he was pure concentration, all distraction distilled right out of him by the desire, the need, to win. Eliot had seen him get this way at Andover, on the football field, in the boxing ring. Nat wasn't a stylish fighter, like Bob Fitzsimmons, but he would win on intentness alone, his eyes fixed on his opponent in a way that reminded you of Trajan's eyes when he was poised to spring on vole or mouse.

"You and Drew get the fisherman's staysail, have it ready to send aloft," he said.

"The staysail!"—Eliot, incredulous, no, outraged. "Big brother, if we crowd on any more sail, if we fly a goddammed shirt right now, we'll bust a topmast, for sure."

"It's not for now. It's for just in case. You just have it ready and haul it up when I give the say-so. Get to it!"

I have got to be a little daft myself to be going along with this, thought Eliot, crouched low in the fo'c'sle, coaxing the staysail out of the saillocker, while the ship slammed up and down. The deck jumped under him, he cracked his head against the locker's hatch frame and, cursing Nat and himself and the lumpy seas, dragged the sail through the passage and back on deck. Sure enough, the wind had veered; almost due south now, barreling through the gap between Vinalhaven and Isle Au Haut and straight up the bay.

Drew wasn't much help rigging the staysail. Looked very peaked, and as if he wouldn't have minded being tossed overboard if that gave him relief from his tumbling guts, the feeling that his skull was a soup tureen, sloshing back and forth. Nothing worse than seasickness, Eliot recalled from the few times it had gripped him. Made you feel as if you had never been well in your life and never would be again. With wind and tide running against each other, the seas were confused: a range of colliding mounds. The boat banged into a big one, slewed off to leeward, and a sheet of cold, salty spray drenched Eliot and Drew as they worked amidships. There, they left the staysail loosely furled and went aft.

"Sorry for the dousing," said Nat, without looking at them. "Lousy chop."

But one, Eliot realized, that was working to *Double Eagle*'s advantage. In the short, steep seas, some defect in *Black Watch*'s steering system or sail trim was causing her to swing, as much as a couple of points in either direction. Like a drunk determined to get where he was going, she lurched, first to starboard, then to port, while she labored to go forward. *Double Eagle* was designed for work like this, and though she yawed a bit now and again, she mostly brushed the conical waves aside and rode quite finely through all that mixed-up water, drawing behind her a roiling line of foam as straight as could be hoped for, in such conditions. She rode in a way to make the gulls weep—that's what the old man would say when she cracked along. "D'you see how she rides, boys? Oh, she rides so that the gulls weep in shame!"

Black Watch's lead was halved and halved again. If *Double Eagle* wasn't going as fast as she had on the mad run back from Halifax last year, she was damn close. Eight knots and some. The two vessels, one green as the Maine forests, the other black as a cormorant's wing, lunged across the bay while scudding clouds caused the sun to flicker and flash, like a warship's signal lamp, but without the regularity. Eliot, trimming the sails with Drew—Drew pluckily trying to do his part—began to feel that both crews had become mere observers; it was as though the boats were racing themselves. *Double Eagle* was owned by a man who loved triumph and detested defeat, and that love, that loathing, were in her now, impregnated into her very wood, mystical as that might sound. She had heart, she had sand, and she had speed on this point of sail, and all those qualities, as much as the lumpy seas that made the yawl slew back and forth, appeared to wear *Black Watch* down, to sap her spirit.

Less than fifty yards separated *Double Eagle*'s bow from the yawl's stern, when they entered the wide mouth of the Fox Islands Thorofare. It was a question of tactics now. One of *Black Watch*'s crew stood at her stern rail, watching to see if Nat would make the expected move—cross the yawl's wake and then pass her on her weather side, blanketing her wind. *Black Watch* would then be slowed down, and so lose a lot of ground, while her opponent, bearing off, would streak away. The danger to *Double Eagle* would be this: To slip across the yawl's stern, she would have to point closer to the wind, losing her advantage in speed for a critical thirty seconds or so.

"All right, brothers, we'll give it a try, but be ready to fall off if I give the say-so."

Helm up, *Double Eagle* pointed higher, then came close hauled, her fleetness going right out of her, like a runner who's lost his breath. Eliot and Drew, leaning against the fierce pressure on the sheets, pulled the sails in, while Nat, crouched behind the wheel, watched the yawl, the seas, and the streaming telltales with a naturalist's attentiveness. Quickly, *Black Watch* pointed up to block the passing maneuver; to complete it, *Double Eagle* would have to sail even farther to windward, but she could not. Any more and she would be pinching, which would slow her down further.

"Just what I figured they'd do," said Nat. "We'll bear off and take 'em on the other side. Ease sheets and get ready to set the staysail."

He spun the helm down, and the schooner lunged forward, so near to dead astern of *Black Watch,* she must have looked under tow from a distance. Bearing off some more, she put a few more yards in her pocket, and a few more, until her bow was almost abeam of the yawl's mainmast, and there was so little space between the two hulls that if *Black Watch*'s main boom were to suddenly swing to leeward, it would sweep *Double Eagle*'s decks like a sickle.

"Ready!" Nathaniel hollered. "We'll need the extra drive of that staysail in half a second!"

The boats were now abeam of each other, plunging, rearing neck and neck, snorting bow spray. *Black Watch*'s sails seemed to rise off the port side like a great cliff of canvas, a cliff that left *Double Eagle* starved for wind—Eliot could almost feel her lungs sucking as she began to lose some ground, a foot or two at a time. Abeam, then abaft abeam, and then Nat fairly screamed:

"Now! Heave! Heave away!"

Eliot and Drew heaved on the staysail halyards, hand over hand. As they were trimming, Drew vomited in two or three noisy spasms, let the line go, and fell on his ass. Eliot hopped backward to take up the sudden slack, slipped in the mixture of vomit and seawater, and fell beside his younger brother, the sheet flying from his hands to flail the air like a huge, mad, writhing serpent, while the sail slapped aloft.

Jumping to his feet, Eliot snatched the line and hauled—and felt nothing move. He looked up.

"It's fouled, Nat! Fouled!"

"Well, by Christ, unfoul it! We'll be looking at their arse again in a second and it's a sight I'm sick of seeing!"

God Almighty, he even sounded like the old man now. Eliot ran to leeward and jerked the sheet, ran to weather, gave it another jerk, freeing it, but lost his footing on the wet deck a second time, banged his head against the rail hard enough to see a bright flash. An odd question shot through his mind as he sat: How many times did Jesus fall carrying his cross? And though he could not see them, he imagined that *Black Watch*'s crew were laughing at the circus on *Double Eagle*'s deck, yes, laughing, jeering, as the Pharisees, or Sadducees, or whoever had laughed and jeered Our Lord as he carried his cross. Eliot got up, shook his fist at the yawl, and hollered, "I am the risen Christ!" Then, his mind clearing, he grabbed the line again and set the sail.

Looking forward, he fully expected to see the yawl making for the horizon, but saw that she wasn't but fifteen, twenty yards ahead. Yards that *Double Eagle* made up swiftly, the big fisherman's staysail powering her on as Nat laid the schooner off fifteen degrees to get up enough steam to help drive her through the yawl's wind shadow. She was abeam *Black Watch* for the second time, slowing as she passed through the yawl's lee, but still driving, all grit and perseverance now, and if the rival crew had been laughing at the carnival of mishaps, they weren't laughing now. The schooner's bowsprit stabbed past the yawl.

"We've got 'em! We've got 'em now!" Every fiber in Nat's body was taut as the rigging, his face glowed with an exultation that was, well, damn near religious. Then, with a quick look at his opponent, he let out a yell.

"It's Will! It's Will at their helm!"

Eliot looked. Yes, it was Will, and looking oh so nautical in white yachtsman's cap and dark turtleneck sweater.

"Say, Will! Will Terhune!" Nat hailed, daring to let go the helm with one hand while he cupped the other alongside his mouth. "Got you now! Say, Will!"

Double Eagle's stern soon swept past *Black Watch*'s bow, and with a clear wind, she sprang away. Eliot dashed forward and doused the staysail; if it stayed up, it could blow out.

"Now watch this," he said to Drew, realizing from the breathlessness in his voice that he had become caught up in the contest, that the lust for triumph was in him, too, just a little more hidden. "Look at the yawl's sails . . . luffing. . . . She's losing way. . . . Will's trying to point her up, but he can't, on account of our sails are deflecting the wind into the backs of hers. We're backwinding her. . . . We're in the safe leeward position, because when you're there, it's darn near impossible for the boat behind you to pass you. . . . See?"

"Bye . . . bye, bye, Will. . . ." Nat, looking astern, waved prissily.

"Only one thing he can do," Eliot said, resuming his commentary. "Wait till we're far enough ahead not to backwind him anymore and then bear off . . . And there he goes. . . ."

Will's crew gave chase, but on this point of sail, *Double Eagle* was the faster vessel, and if the wind did not swing forward and no dumb mistakes were made, the race was over.

With the tension released, Nat broke into a grin, which exploded into a hoarse laugh. And what was so funny? asked Eliot.

"You . . . falling on your arse twice . . . And then, when you got up, the way you shook your fist . . ." Nat choked, wiped his eyes. "When you yelled, 'I am the risen Christ!' Oh, I hope Will heard that. That was so rich. I *am* the risen Christ!"

The wind dropped, as it usually did late on summer afternoons. Under her cloud of canvas, *Double Eagle* pranced into North Haven harbor. The lowering sun burnished the waters, but the light did not seem to be shining on them but through them from below, as if gold were being minted down there, in some undersea alchemist's forge. Around here, thought Nathaniel, even the water looked like a million bucks. Vinalhaven, so near that you could row to it across the thorofare, was an island of quarrymen, lobstermen, fishermen, and schoonermen, a place so rough and salty one breath of its air could make your nostrils rust; on North Haven, elegant gardens bloomed around rambling houses (their owners called them "cottages," with a certain snooty understatement) where Philadelphia lawyers, New York industrialists, and Boston textile merchants parked wives and children for the summer, while they stayed in the cities, making the money that bought the houses and the yachts, great and small, crowding the harbor whose surface now glowed with that golden fire.

The Braithwaites belonged in North Haven's social circle (closer to the rim than to the center; they were barons, as opposed to dukes and princes, of America's mercantile aristocracy), but Nathaniel liked to think of himself as an outsider—rougher and tougher, in spirit more one with the people of Vinalhaven, he who had breathed quarry dust and grown calluses last year. Flush with victory, he put on a show for the piazza-chair loafers of this prosperous port. Weaving between the anchored vessels, he bore straight for the Camden steam ferry disembarking passengers at the terminal, just to scare them a little bit, wheeled about, and strutted past the casino, which wasn't a gambling den but a yacht club with a sober face of brown shingles and white-trimmed windows. He waved at a pretty girl standing on the wharf and then headed straight for *Black Watch,* which was coming in to anchor. Having failed to get a rise out of the ferry passengers, he hoped to scare Will and his crew. Some twenty yards short of the yawl, he told Eliot and Drew to get set to drop the anchor; then he spun the wheel and rounded up, *Double Eagle* pirouetting before she stopped dead. Eliot paid out the anchor rode, gave it a tug to make sure it was fast, then snubbed it off to the samson post.

From the yawl, only fifty feet away, came a slow applause. Will stood leaning against the mizzenmast, his hat off, and his hair the color of a hayrick.

"My compliments to your father," he hailed. " 'Some right gud skipperin' thar', as these down-east peasants would say. The losers invite you and yours aboard for a drink. There's some Cuban rum for your old man, sodee pops for the chill-runs. Whenever you're ready."

Nathaniel tossed him a salute and murmured, "Wait till he finds out."

They first got their ship to look respectable, beginning with the scrubbing of the deck. The main and foresail were laced with jack ropes, and Nathaniel liked how they looked, sandwiched between booms and gaffs in folds as sharp as those in a concertina. The whole ship shimmered in a halo of buttery light. *Mine,* he thought again, and with such an upwelling of prideful possession that he wondered—his mind hastening ahead three months—how he could bear to give her up when the time came.

Two to three strong pulls on the tender's oars brought the victors alongside *Black Watch.* Will took the painter and tied the tender off to the stern.

"Captain Cyrus won't be joining us?"

"Nope," said Nathaniel, shaking hands.

"He's been known to take a drink, now and then. Too young a crowd for him?"

This with a motion at his friends, all college men like himself.

"The old man isn't aboard," Nathaniel said, and looked into the face that appeared to have been assembled by a God unable to decide if He had wanted to make it handsome or ugly. From a distance of ten or fifteen feet, it was good-looking, in a spare, angular sort of way; closer, you noticed that the chin sheered to a point, the nose was a little crooked, like a prizefighter's, the mouth had a cant that made Will look as if he were perpetually sneering—at life, at you—and the lips were thicker than they should have been, considering the leanness of his other features; a thickness that suggested an unhealthy sensuality.

"You don't mean to tell me that *we* lost to you three?" he asked, as if some law of the universe had been overturned.

"That's the size of it."

Fishing a package of Duke's out of his trouser pocket, offering one to Nat, who shook his head.

"They cut your wind," he said.

"Stunt your growth, too. If I didn't smoke, I would now be a giant instead of a mere six feet." Tilting his head backward, exhaling, pursed lips compressing the smoke into a slender funnel. "You certainly cut ours, and on the leeward side. Nasty."

With a glance, Will appeared to beg forgiveness from his college chums. Maybe he had bragged to them about his prowess. Like Nathaniel, he had been racing since childhood, first in dinghies, then in small sloops; he had crewed on many larger vessels and had been navigator in the Newport to Bermuda race last year, Portland to Gloucester the year before.

"Clever, Natters. Being a gentleman and gracious in defeat, I'll offer you the hootch that would have gone to your old man, since you were skipper and all." Turning to one of the others, a short fellow strongly built, like a middleweight wrestler: "Van Slyck, you're designated steward for this voyage. Our grog ration, if you please, and sodee pops for the young 'uns."

Nathaniel's one experience with alcohol had been at Andover this past spring: two swigs from a pint of whiskey smuggled into the dormitory by a senior down the hall. Two swigs were all he could take, the first scalding his throat, the second making him feel as if someone had snipped a vital nerve to his brain. Now, in the cockpit of *Black Watch*, in the company of two Yale men (Will and Tony Burton, whose father owned the yawl and who had commissioned his son and friends to deliver it from New York to North Haven) and two Dartmouth men (the sawed-off muscleman whom the others called Van Slyck, without making it clear if that was one name or two, and Herb Wheeler, a slender junior who liked to sit holding an unlit pipe in his mouth and look on in grave silence, giving the impression that he was a man of few words and profound intelligence), Nathaniel hoped he would not choke, gag, or otherwise betray himself as an innocent when it came to liquor. Will had served him a cocktail called a Cuba Libre, composed of white rum and Coca-Cola garnished with a slice of lime.

"I whipped this up for you because I know Colonel Roosevelt is your hero."

"Does he drink Cuba Libres?"

And Will answered that he didn't know what Colonel Roosevelt drank, or if he drank at all, though he assumed he did, given his reputation as a man among men; no, he had mixed the cocktail because it had been invented to mark the liberation of Cuba during the recent war in which Colonel Roosevelt had served so gallantly.

"Actually, Will, I think it was invented before that, in 'ninety-five, I think, when the Cubans rose up," said Burton, a young man who managed to look old. At twenty or twenty-one, he had achieved a middle-aged portliness. He wore thick, black-rimmed glasses, behind which blue eyes sparkled ambiguously with a merriment that looked as if it could turn malicious in an instant. His throat bulged like a mating bullfrog's, his cheeks were slabs of sleek pink flesh, and the overall impression of a well-fed, mature prosperousness was heightened by the cigar he puffed and waved around in the air, like an apprentice plutocrat practicing for the day when he would command a railroad, a steel mill, a brokerage house. Turning to Nathaniel, he said, "Your hero, huh? My father thinks he's a damn cowboy."

"Natters even tried to join the Rough Riders, did you know that?" Will said, Nathaniel wishing he would stop using that ridiculous nickname.

"How could we know it, since we didn't know him until twenty minutes ago?" Van Slyck remarked. Then to Nathaniel: "Weren't you a shade on the young side?"

"I was tall for my age." He looked at Burton, Van Slyck, and Wheeler to gauge if they esteemed him for what he'd done—tried to do, rather—or if they thought he was a little touched. "It was in May, around a month after war got declared. I'd just graduated from Boston Latin."

"What? Did you figure graduating from Boston Latin would have impressed Colonel Roosevelt?"—Burton, tauntingly.

Nathaniel shook his head. Wheeler, tapping the bowl of his pipe against his shoe, although it contained no tobacco, gazed at him with thoughtful curiosity.

"Last thing I'd ever want to do is see the elephant, at any age," he said. "What was the idea?"

"His father," Will said, answering for him. "Mr. Braithwaite saw the elephant in the Civil War, and the elephant took one of his eyes for seeing it too close."

"You must mean his grandfather," Burton said.

"No, my father," said Nathaniel.

"And you wished to follow in the old man's footsteps, right, Natters? Be a war hero?"

Was that it, then? Maybe. But Nathaniel's memory told him it had been something else: the buds on the trees and the scent of the spring air and the headlines screaming WAR!, trumpeting DEWEY TRIUMPHS AT MANILA! that stirred in him an unbearable restlessness and discontent with Back Bay Boston—Back Bay not as a neighborhood but as a way of being—the restlessness and unhappiness impelling him to filch a dollar from his mother's household petty cash and buy trolley fare to Cambridge. He had read in a newspaper that Sanders, the great Harvard quarterback, had joined the Rough Riders, and figured there must be a recruiting post on the Harvard campus. There wasn't, but a policeman directed him to a U.S. Army recruiting station a few blocks away. There, he found himself swearing to a formidable sergeant wearing mustaches twirled and waxed into arrowtips that he was a crack shot and crack rider and seventeen years old, a claim the skeptical sergeant asked to see confirmed with a birth certificate or some other form of documentation. A page from a family Bible would do. Nathaniel's mind struggled to produce a plausible reason why he had nothing to verify his age. He became acutely aware of everything around him—the sergeant's hard and penetrating stare, which seemed capable of laying a man's soul bare, of the crowd of volunteers, who also seemed to be staring at him, waiting for his answer. He felt guilty, all of a sudden, guilty of stealing, of running away from home, of lying, and guilt robbed his voice of all conviction when he blurted out that he did not have a birth certificate or page from a family Bible because he was an orphan with no knowledge of his parents or his exact date of birth. "That bein' the case, boy-o, how in blazes do y'know yer seventeen?" asked the sergeant, and everything unraveled from there. He soon confessed to his true age, identity, and address. An hour later, after the new recruits were sworn in, the sergeant escorted him to a trolley stop and gave him a nickel for the fare. "Courtesy o' the U.S. Army, for showin' the right spirit," he said. "Come see us again in three, four years and we'll put you in blue."

"Lucky thing you weren't taken," Burton said. "My father knows Ham Fish's father, and Ham left his bones in Cuba. Darned shame. He was a first-rate oarsman at Columbia. Helluva polo player, too."

Wheeler rattled the pipe stem against his teeth, looked off toward the sunset splashing garish colors over North Haven Island. Lamps were being lit in the casino, and a band or gramophone was playing a waltz.

"It's ironic, isn't it?" said Wheeler. "The Spaniards discovered the Americas, yet it was we Americans who expelled them from the Americas."

Will said he failed to see the irony in that.

"There's a lesson in it."

"I also fail to see the lesson"—Will, sweeping a comb through his hair. He was very vain about his hair, the thickest hair Nathaniel had ever seen. "Y'know, Herbie, that's just the sort of non sequitur I've come to expect from Dartmouth men."

"Mmmmmm," replied Herb Wheeler, with a secret smile, as if he found Will's failure to see irony and lesson amusing. "You Elis."

"Will's no longer an Eli, as we all do know," Van Slyck said. "So maybe he'll be a Dartmouth man soon, if they let such a rotter in."

Nathaniel looked at Will.

"The president of Yale College has seen fit to request that I not reappear for my third year in the fall."

Will lit another cigarette and smiled furtively.

"Did you *fail*?" Nathaniel asked.

"It was a question of his conduct," Burton explained. "A scandal not meant for young ears."

"Oh, they're not that young, Tony. Expect they know babies don't come from storks, and if they don't, they ought to. It was this way, Natters. A freshman down the hall had not been properly raised. His father failed to give him two dollars and send him to a proper establishment when he reached eighteen. He seemed distressed by his innocent condition, so I decided to act, so to speak, in loco parentis, and brought him to a place I know near the port in New Haven. Madame Zygote or Zagreb, some foreign name like that. It was our misfortune to be in this establishment when the town fathers, in one of those spasms of civic virtue for which Connecticut is famous, had instructed the police to raid houses of ill repute. Election next year, you know. Wanted to look good to the voters. The young man in question was in the midst of his introduction to manhood when the cops arrived. Arrested everyone, ladies and customers alike. Made the local yellow press. The reporter found it irresistible that two Yale men had got caught in the sordid business, and played up that angle. Next day, after I bailed us out, the ex-virgin and I were called in by the dean, whereupon the ex-virgin, seeking to save his own unworthy skin, ratted on me and then some. Said I'd not only given him the money but more or less dragooned him into going to Madame Zygote's or Zagreb's. The dean went to the president. I was already on thin ice for a previous offense—won't go into that now—and the president wrote me a letter, stating that I could finish out the term, but please do not return for the next."

Drew was leaning far forward, his arms folded across his stomach, as if he were still seasick.

"I don't understand," he said.

"Told you they were too young," said Burton. Then Eliot to his younger brother:

"Will took this freshman kid to a *whore*house. Whorehouses are against the law. They got caught there and arrested and so he got kicked out of Yale, Will did, and just in case you don't know what a whorehouse is, li'l brother, it's a place where women get paid to fuck men."

"Eliot!" Drew's hands shot to his ears. "I'm going to tell Father that you cursed."

"'Fuck' is not a curse word, it's a vulgarity"—Will in an instructional tone. "Calling upon the Almighty to damn someone, as in 'goddamn you,' is cursing." He looked at Nathaniel. "Natters, you're not shocked, are you?"

Wishing to appear worldly and sophisticated, Nathaniel motioned that he wasn't. But he was distracted by the picture that flooded his imagination after Will finished his story. He saw one of Madam Zygote's or Zagreb's whores, lying on her side on a divan covered in the skins of wild beasts. Broad hips, lavish breasts, fleshy thighs culminating in a humid triangle of pubic hairs, and all upon a bed of zebra stripes and leopard spots, like the woman in one of the French postcards smuggled into his dormitory last year. But the face he now saw in his mind wasn't that woman's face; it was the face of Will's cousin, Constance. Her face, grafted onto the alluring body of the woman in the postcard. He had never thought of Constance that way, because he wasn't supposed to, because, with her body always locked, throat to ankle, in a vault of cotton, silk, wool, and corsets, he could no more imagine what she looked like underneath than he could her rib cage or spinal column. Now this image, bursting into his brain from out of nowhere, and with it, desire and heat, and with those, shame.

"My mother *was* shocked, was she ever," Will was saying. "*El presidente* sent a copy of my expulsion to my parents. My dad told me she fainted, *fainted* when she read the words 'moral turpitude.' Would've thought I'd gone on a rampage of rape. Dad was upset, but what really got him mad was that I had made Mummy faint. But what could he do? Put me over his knee and paddle me? Put me to work instead, which was worse. Clerking for one of his law partners. I foresaw my summer, wasted inside a stuffy cubicle, no windows, lots of case law and dusty codes. Then Tony telephoned me. Would I crew for him? And here I am. I believe I have run away from home. Nineteen going on twenty may be too old to run away from home, but, better late than never, I suppose. . . ."

"We don't have a home, either," Drew blurted earnestly. "We're orphans. Kind of. For a while."

Herb Wheeler crossed his legs, jabbed his pipe at Drew, like a lecturing professor.

"How do you get to be a sort of orphan for a while? The state of orphanhood is like pregnancy"—now mimicking a minstrel's dialect—"you either is or you ain't."

"He means we got kicked out of the house for the summer," said Eliot, with a scowl. He didn't like any of these high-flown college men, Will least of all. He had never understood why Nat was always so impressed by him. "Our old man told us he doesn't want to see our faces again till September. That's how come we're here now."

Will asked what they had done.

"Nothing," Drew replied. "It's a new century."

Then Burton, leaning his bulk against the wheel: "You don't say? A remarkable observation for one so young. Out of the mouths of babes, eh?"

Eliot wanted to punch his fat face.

"It's what our father told us this morning when we asked him why we were getting kicked out. He said, 'It's a new century,' and that's all."

"Which certainly marks Captain Cyrus as a master of the obvious," Will said. "If you were chucked out, what are you doing with his yacht? What's going on here, Natters?"

And as the long twilight of the northern summer settled in and the wind died off to a breath and the harbor became a black mirror reflecting anchor lights and the lights from the casino, Nathaniel told them the story.

"I'd hardly call that getting kicked out," Burton declared, when he was done. "If it is, I wish my old man would kick me out. I'd take this"—he slapped the wheel—"well, now, where would I take her? Rio. Sure. I'd sail to Rio and dance all night with dusky females with low morals."

"You wouldn't be able to walk them home, much less dance with them all night, you walrus," Will said, and lighted his third cigarette of the hour, the match's flare in the deepening dusk briefly lending a sinister cast to his face. "What do you plan to do, Natters?"

"Don't have a plan just yet."

"And what brings you here? Going to chase my cousin? It's hopeless, y'know. Connie's an older woman."

"Ah, c'mon. I was born March of 'eighty-five, and she was born May of 'eighty-four."

It seemed to him that Will was being awfully flippant about his feelings, telling him it was hopeless.

"A difference like that might not make a difference in ten years, but right now, she's interested in fellows their age." Will indicated his companions with a sweeping motion of his arm, as if he were introducing a stage act. "On the other hand, Tony would be too fat for her, and Van Slyck too short, and Herbie too bookish, so, who knows, maybe you've got a prayer, after all."

The waltz music drifted over the water; couples were dancing on the pavilion under lantern light, and from ashore came the pitchy scent of smudge pots smoking to keep mosquitos at bay. Nathaniel pictured himself dancing with Constance, holding her tight and close, kissing her the way a man on the cover of Mother's most recent *Ladies Home Journal* was kissing a woman in a satin dress, with authority and passion.

"I'll tell you what—there's a regular *harim* staying under Auntie Battleship's roof, right now," said Will. "Cousin Connie and three of her friends, Cousin Johanna and two of hers. We're all having a picnic tomorrow, with Frances Parkman and her mother joining us from Pulpit Harbor. We're short on males. C'mon along."

Nathaniel nodded, but explained that he was missing a shoe, a deficiency that Will waved off; among him and his three friends, there had to be an extra pair Nathaniel's size. He snubbed the cigarette and looked at the three brothers.

"Y'know, it's interesting that you and I should find ourselves in a similar situation. In the same boat?" he said.

6

HE SLEPT LATE, luxuriating in his father's stateroom, which he'd appropriated, now that he was acting captain. Harbor water lapped the hull; through the open porthole came the raucous cries of seagulls arguing over which one had feeding rights to a crab or mussel. Wonderful sounds to wake up to—water, gulls, the creak of anchor cable swinging with the tide—and he missed them terribly when he was at Andover and jangled awake by his Westclox alarm. The biology teacher who affirmed the rightness of Darwin's theory, he remembered, had also told the class that the salinity of human blood was identical to seawater's. Nathaniel liked to think that the atoms in every man's veins yearned to rejoin those in the sea, that all men were orphans separated from what Dad, in one of his rare flights into poetic imagery, called "our great blue mother." Maybe the yearning was stronger in his, Nathaniel's, blood than in most others'. He suffered when he was too far from the sea—and to a degree directly proportional to the distance. Each year at Andover, almost a full day's ride from the coast, he grew restless and then morose after the novelty of a new term wore off. By December, his interior sky matched the one outdoors, and there was no medicine or liquor that could blow the clouds away like the scent of saltmarsh at low tide, or a bell buoy's peal, or the sight of a three-master sailing full and by. Three years ago, while walking him to the trolley stop, the recruiting sergeant told him about fighting Apaches out in Arizona. He spoke longingly of the West and urged Nathaniel to head that way when he was old enough. The frontier was a thing of the past, but there was still room among the red deserts and dun plains and shining mountains two miles high for a man to grow or roam in, as he saw fit. Was there as much room as on the ocean? Nathaniel had asked, and the sergeant answered, No, not as much room as that; if it was ocean he sought, he would have to go all the way west, to the coasts of California, Oregon, Washington. Okay, then it would be California or Oregon or Washington, if it was to be west at all, for he could not conceive of living hundreds of miles inland, never to look upon or touch the great blue mother's breast. It would be like an exile to an alien country, and if ever he was to find himself stuck in such a place with no chance of escape, well, he reckoned he would just have to shoot himself.

He got up, padded down the passageway to the head, lifted the wooden seat, and pissed into the lead drainpipe fitted through the planking.

Eliot and Drew were still asleep. He saw no reason to wake them, and fired up the stove, filled the big blue enameled coffeepot with water, and set it on the iron plate. Throwing on his trousers, he went outside to have a look at the day. There was no wind to speak of, and no fog, and a thin haze was drawn across the sky. A world of metals: the harbor and thorofare sheets of hammered pewter spread between the islands; the sun reflected in the water a band of polished brass, while the sun itself shone through the haze as a dull copper disc.

And to this metallurgical composition, Gertrude Williams added bronze. Nathaniel recognized her as she stood in the bow of the casino's steam launch, her pose reminding him of the illustration in his American history book—Washington crossing the Delaware. Mrs. Williams would have been recognizable from a mile off—every inch of five feet ten and every pound of one hundred eighty, with an enormous bosom that made her appear less, rather than more, womanly, because it had a quality of masculine aggression. Now her light auburn hair, piled high, gleamed in the sunlight like a bronze helmet; her ocher-colored blouse, its puffy sleeves exaggerating the breadth of her shoulders, its front stretched taut by the buttress of flesh beneath, might have been a bronze breastplate; and her matching parasol, held high over her head and at a slight angle, was as a bronze shield raised against arrows raining down from some tower or battlement. Several more women sat on the thwarts behind her. Raising the binoculars, he counted nine altogether, including Gertrude, and he allowed the glasses to linger on Constance, all in white, laughing at something one of her friends had said, one hand held atop her little straw hat against the breeze stirred by the launch's movement. Beside her was her younger sister, Johanna, and then came Amy Thorp, Antonia Codman, Marianne Gordon, Frances Parkman and her mother Hannah, and a girl Nathaniel had met last year but whose name he couldn't recall—everyone called her "Bunny" and she was some relation to Longfellow, a granddaughter or grandniece. There were only two men aboard—Will and the launch pilot—and they looked among that dense lamination of females like captives snatched in an amazon raid.

In the summer, North Haven was mostly ruled by women—except on those occasional weekends or holidays when steamers brought the menfolk up from the mainland cities—and Gertrude Williams was the uncoronated queen of the island's feminocracy. Not all women liked her, but none could deny her. She was too bold to be denied. She spoke out as freely as a man on things only men were supposed to speak about, like war and politics, and what was more, she got away with it. She was a suffragette, and had gotten herself arrested in the '92 elections for storming a polling station with a dozen other emancipationists demanding ballots. But the boldest thing she had done, the thing that made some men a little afraid of her and most women admire her, was to divorce, very publicly divorce the very tall, very good-looking, and very prominent Dr. Gilcrest Williams, a specialist in diseases of the nose and throat, whose list of patients, it was said, could have substituted for the Boston Social Register and whose roster of female conquests was equally impressive—for its length. The case made the papers for a couple of weeks, scandal added to scandal, Gertrude having hired private detectives to track down as many of her husband's paramours as could be found; seven altogether were hauled into divorce court to testify and make her case overwhelming, and the yellow press had a banner day when one of the women turned out to be a patient of the esteemed doctor.

So Gertrude Williams became a free woman, a martyr and heroine to others of her sex. But not to all. A few of her friends shunned her afterward because they thought she'd aired far too much dirty linen far too publicly. She hadn't divorced the doctor, she had gone to war with him, destroyed him by destroying his reputation, its destruction precipitating the ruin of his practice. In the end, he fled to Chicago, where morals were less stringent and no one had heard of him. Gertrude had run him out of town on a rail, but her own reputation as dutiful and loving wife had suffered: Dr. Williams's lawyer argued that Gertrude had denied his client his conjugal rights after the birth of their third child, giving her love to social causes (conditions in the slums, the plight of immigrants, woman's suffrage) instead of to him. That's what the lawyer said, but it cut no ice with the judge.

For a while, Mother had been among those who severed friendship with Gertrude Williams. She was angry because of the curiosity the scandal had awakened in her two eldest children (Drew was eight at the time, too young to be interested in adult intrigue). But a year after the scandal became history, the Williamses suffered a tragedy that drew Mother back: Tad Williams, Constance and Johanna's older brother, a strange kid still in grammar school at sixteen, quiet and gloomy and fat—all he ever seemed to do was eat—had found his father's old revolver in the attic of the Williamses' town house on Commonwealth Avenue. He didn't check to see if it was loaded before he started playing with it. The maid heard the shot, and found him up there, dead from a bullet in his chest.

After the funeral, Gertrude Williams was unable to leave her room or sometimes even to get out of bed. Mother laid her grievances aside and began to visit her several times a week, bringing her cakes and pies she had baked. By the following summer, Gertrude was almost back to her old self, protesting the Spanish-American War (Dad thought she was being unpatriotic, if not downright treasonous, and Nathaniel agreed. How could anyone claim that the Rough Riders' charge had been anything but the most glorious thing ever?); giving dinner parties attended by university presidents, famous professors, playwrights, and novelists; and dashing off to her suffragette meetings. When she installed herself in North Haven for the season, she gathered about her all the ladies who found her fascinating.

Mother did, and, Nathaniel suspected, that fascination, as much as pity for Tad's death, had drawn her back into Gertrude's circle. She became one of Gertrude's closest friends, which was funny, he thought, because the two weren't at all alike. Physically, Mother looked almost childlike beside Gertrude. Mother spoke softly and moved slowly and graciously; Gertrude barked in unadorned, telegraphic phrases, and she liked to tear along, whether it was across a room or down a street, pitched slightly forward at the waist, her great bosom thrust out in front, her whole body like a White Star liner under a full head of steam. And where she was full of unconventional ideas, Mother, for all her beauty and charm, was as ordinary as a Sunday drive, voicing ordinary opinions and making ordinary conversation. The two or three times Nathaniel had been trapped in the house when she had her Back Bay friends over for tea, he thought their talk passed beyond the merely dull into the paralyzingly boring. In such company, she seemed to lose her touch for the embellished phrase, the quirky metaphor. *How do you find the weather today, Mrs. Farnsworth? Don't you think it unseasonably hot? . . . Oh, yes, Elizabeth, it is unpropitious for May. . . . And yet, isn't every season subject to variation. . . .* She kept on her desk in the sitting room the most recent edition of a manual her aunt Judith had presented to her when she was sixteen—*Manners, Culture, and Dress of the Best*

American Society—a kind of pilot book for navigating tricky social waters. A lot of that stuff came naturally to her, but she still consulted the book whenever she was stumped about the proper way to do something or say something. And yet, she did not want to be conventional. Nathaniel sensed that somehow. Maybe it was the way she blew out her cheeks and muttered to herself, "Thank God!" when tea time was over and the Back Bay ladies had gone home. Maybe it was the way her personality changed when she was around Gertrude Williams, laughing louder than she usually did, moving about not with her usual stately languor but with a certain briskness, asking Gertrude, eager as a schoolgirl, what she should be reading (and Gertrude replying, "Can tell what you shouldn't be reading—that stuff and nonsense in *Ladies Home Journal*. Try some Ibsen, Liza, or George Bernard Shaw—*there's* a first rate mind").

The old man could not abide Gertrude (nor she him). To his mind, she was born with a strike against her: She was a Quaker, and Quakers had peculiar notions. He agreed with some of her notions, at least those not Quaker in origin. Woman's suffrage, for example; if Negroes had the right to vote, then so should women. But Gertrude went too far. She always went too far. She had gone too far in her divorce suit, she went too far in this business of female emancipation, advocating that women had a right to hold jobs as well as to vote, and she went much too far, speaking out on the right of working men to form unions. That rankled Dad the most. The rights of labor would be safeguarded by men like him, he fulminated, slamming fist into palm; by good Christian men to whom God in His Infinite Wisdom had entrusted control of the nation's capital, and not by socialists and agitators. Certainly not by the likes of Gertrude Williams, whose chief transgression, in his eyes, was to vocally support the quarrymen during the big strike of '99. He prized loyalty above all things: loyalty to country, to God and family, to shipmates and friends. How could Gertrude claim to be Mother's friend and then write letters to the editors of the Camden and Portland newspapers, declaring that the men employed by her friend's husband had a *right* to walk off their jobs, a *right* to overtime, a *right* to unionize? She had stabbed him in the back, betrayed him and all those men to whom God in His Infinite Wisdom had entrusted, et cetera.

The launch, its short stack smoking, its single piston banging with monotonous rhythm, chugged toward *Double Eagle*. Nathaniel went below, into a main cabin redolent with the aroma of coffee, roused Eliot and Drew, and while they heaved out of their bunks, gave his hair a quick brushing and put on a shirt. When he returned to the deck, the launch pilot, a boy not much older than himself, swung the tiller hard over and eased alongside.

"Good morning, Nathaniel."

"Morning, Mrs. Williams," he answered, and extended a hand to help her aboard.

"No need of that. Got my health skirt on, health corset, too." Gertrude slapped her midriff with a fishwife's gusto, and Constance chided, "Mother!"

Gertrude Williams grabbed a stanchion, stretched out a leg, showing a flicker of petticoat, and hauled herself on board. Will handed her parasol to her, then passed a wicker picnic hamper to Nathaniel.

"We're going to Camden first, my aunt has some business there," he said, smoothing his mussed hair with both hands. "Then we'll all have a fine time—suitably chaperoned, of course."

"Hello, Natty, and bye for now." Constance, with a coy smile, raised her palm and curled her fingers in a coy wave. "See you there."

And the launch swung away, the two captured males in the stern and the eight females, four on the starboard seat, four on the port, sitting with knee mortared to knee, shoulder to shoulder—two solid fronts of sisterhood. In a few seconds, they were alongside *Black Watch,* Nathaniel watching with helpless jealousy as Van Slyck, the squat powerhouse, reached down, grasped Constance's hands, and seemed to lift her as if she were as light as her cotton skirt. One by one, he helped the others board. Soon, it looked like a seagoing cotillion over there, the female phalanx broken, Will and his friends moving about with the confidence of college men, showing the girls where to sit, spreading cushions for them to sit on, and Nathaniel's jealousy flamed when he saw Constance wedged between Van Slyck and Tony Burton. She took off her hat and fluffed her chestnut hair, and her laugh came ringing over the moat dividing him from her.

"You should strive to make your feelings less obvious," said Mrs. Williams from behind him. "You are gawking, Nathaniel, positively gawking."

He turned to look at her. She had seated herself on the after deck, her furled parasol across her knees.

"I was thinking that it's mighty crowded over there. We could've taken three or four."

"You were thinking that she will have her head turned by those Yale and Dartmouth boys. I assure you, that won't happen. Constance's head is not a doorknob."

"Yes, ma'am."

"I have seen to that. She is going to college next year and get a real education, and not the useless fluff dished out by finishing schools. She will do that before she does anything else, and if I ever see her head getting turned by *anyone*"—she stressed the last word—"I shall grab her by her pretty ears and turn it back the other way."

"Yes, ma'am."

"She's over there with the others because I intend to have a word with you and your brothers in private. Where are they, anyhow?"

"Below. Getting dressed, I reckon."

"It's nearly ten. You run a leisurely ship, Nathaniel. Tell them to get on with it so we can heave-ho, or whatever it is you nautical people say, and be on our way."

"There's no wind yet, Mrs. Williams."

"I am expected in Camden at twelve-thirty."

"Yes, ma'am, but we'll need wind to get there."

Just then, there came from *Black Watch* sounds of the new century: a loud pop, and another, then a cough followed by a sputtering. An exhaust pipe near the bottom of her transom ejected puffs of blue-gray smoke, a noxious smell drifted into Nathaniel's nostrils.

"So I take it that this boat does not have one of those?"

He shook his head and watched the yawl, her propeller roiling water at her stern, slip into the thorofare without a ribbon of canvas set—a vessel liberated from the tyrannical whims of the wind.

"I would have thought your father would have installed one of those noisy things. Fancies himself a man of progress, doesn't he?"

More than fancied himself, Nathaniel replied; he believed in progress as a creed second only to his Congregational faith, except when it came to *Double Eagle*. There, he was as sentimental and tradition-bound as all those vanishing sons of sail who thought that putting means of mechanical propulsion into a sloop, yawl, schooner, or ketch was akin to installing a craps table in a church. *I'll not have any damned hunk of iron in her, never,* Father had said just this month, when the manager of Potter's boatyard tried to sell him a kerosene engine. *Do not ever make such a suggestion to me again, sir.*

"And what am I to do now?" asked Mrs. Williams, vexed, indignant. "Sit here and wait for this wind of yours?"

"It's not mine, but you will have to wait for it. Not for long. South-westerlies spring up in the middle of the morning, usually." He underscored the forecast with an optimistic smile, and then, because it seemed the grown-up thing to do, offered her a cup of coffee while she waited.

"I'll take tea, if you have it. Coffee is bad for the nerves. Shouldn't be drinking it at your age, Nathaniel. Your hands will be shaking like an old man's by the time you're twenty."

Despite the warning, he poured himself a cup after he went below to put the teakettle on. Eliot and Drew were dressed, but lounging in their bunks, Eliot tuning his guitar, Drew reading a magazine, while Trajan lapped a saucer of condensed milk. Nathaniel told them to be sociable, go above and greet their guest; and when they were done being sociable, they could help him get ready to make sail. They were to ferry Mrs. Williams to Camden before going on the picnic.

"We'll need a bigger boat to ferry her," Eliot quipped, and Nathaniel clamped a hand over his mouth.

"Here you are, a mug up, like the Gloucester fishermen say."

"'As,' Nathaniel," Gertrude Williams corrected, taking the cup. "What are they teaching for grammar at Andover these days? 'As' the Gloucester fishermen say. Sit down, the three of you. Sit, sit"—motioning with her chin. "Might as well have my word with you while we attend on this wind. My nephew has told me about your situation. Is it true?"

Eliot and Nathaniel looked at each other, Drew at them both, and they nodded almost in unison.

"And your father's reason for doing this—That is to say, when you asked him his reason, all he said was that it's a new century?" She ended the question on a note of incredulity.

"That's the size of it," Eliot answered. "But we can't figure out what he meant."

"I'm not surprised. Who could figure out such a riddle?" She raised the cup to her lips with both hands. "Has your father been himself lately?"

Again, they traded glances, Eliot's and Drew's conferring upon Nathaniel the decision to answer or not. He confined his reply to a tentative shrug.

"I see. Very well, I won't ask for the details. It is your family, after all."

"First off, we thought it was our mother, that he was worried about her," Eliot said. "She's in Boston right now. She's been sick."

"Yes, I know. I got a letter from her day before yesterday."

"You did?"

"Why so surprised, Eliot? Liza and I are thick as thieves, you know that."

"What did she say? Is she all right?"—Drew, leaning forward eagerly. "Father said he'd got a wire from Dr. Matthews that she was all right, but we weren't sure if . . . We didn't know if maybe he was holding something back from us."

Gertrude graced him with a maternal smile, tousled his hair.

"Your mother would be pleased to see how concerned you are, Andrew. Your father wasn't holding anything back. She is recovering nicely, and she told me that she feels terribly guilty, not having written to you boys. She simply wasn't up to it. She promises to send you a good long letter very soon. Why I imagine it's in the mails this very moment. Did I hear you say that Dr. Matthews sent the telegram? Has Dr. Matthews seen her?"

The question puzzled all three. Nathaniel replied that Dr. Matthews was their family doctor, who else would have seen her?

And that appeared to puzzle Mrs. Williams; she frowned and rubbed the crease between her eyebrows with her thumb.

"Your mother was being treated by a different doctor, a specialist. . . ." She hesitated. "Have you boys been told anything about her condition?"

"That it's some kind of—a sort of—a female problem"—Eliot, ill at ease about speaking this way to a woman. "That's all Father would say about it. That's all he knew."

Mrs. Williams studied him for a moment or two with a slightly sidelong look, and then, her bronze brows lifting, she asked:

"And you're quite sure about that?"

"It's what he said. A female problem. Do you know what it is?"

"If your mother considered it too personal to tell her own husband, she certainly wouldn't have told me. Does she know about this peculiar decision of your father's? I can't imagine she would agree with it, or that she'd be anything but upset."

"If Father went to Boston yesterday, then I reckon he'll tell her," Eliot said.

"Whatever do you mean, *if* he went to Boston? He's not here, at Mingulay?"

"No, ma'am. Closed it up. And then he left, with his trunk all packed. He told us we could go wherever we wanted except back home to Boston, because he just might be there and he didn't want to see our faces."

"Will did not mention that to me."

"On account of we didn't mention it to Will."

"This is becoming odder and odder." She stood as if jerked to her feet by a string, and then looked at each of them, her head inclined a little to one side while a zephyr played with the tips of her hair. "I must say you three are your father's sons. In a tough spot, but just brimming with sangfroid."

"With what?" asked Eliot.

"You've been chucked out without explanation, your only home for the time being is a boat, you've barely enough money to last you, your father has gone off to you-know-not-where, while your mother is on her sickbed two hundred miles away, probably without the faintest idea of where you are or what's gone on, and here you three sit, not the least bit upset that I can see, as if all this were perfectly normal. I assure you it is not. It is not the way a normal family behaves."

"We were thinking that yesterday, Mrs. Williams. We're kind of a strange family."

"Oh, Eliot!" She turned, as if to walk away, then seemed to remember that she was on a boat, and turned back again.

Eliot squirmed. He did not know what *sangfroid* meant, but he was pretty sure that Mrs. Williams hadn't intended a compliment. Like there was something wrong with him and his brothers for not being as upset as in her opinion they should be. Not that he had thought for a minute of the past twenty-four hours that things were normal.

"We figure there's not much we can do about it," he said, defensively. "It's a bully boat, we've got plenty of food aboard, and so we'll make the best of it."

"There's my meaning exactly, very coolheaded customers, you three."

Nathaniel, watching another zephyr raise a serpentine of ruffled water on the harbor, said that the sou'wester was aborning. They could weigh anchor now.

"Weigh away, then, but before you do, listen carefully to me." (He, bristling at her bossy tone, felt a pang of understanding for Dr. Williams.) "I have to go to the telegraph office when my business is concluded. You will come with me and wire your mother and tell her where you are and that you are well, and you will explain, as briefly as you can, that your father has evicted you. Yes, that's the word for it. *Evicted*."

"Yes, ma'am."

With their passenger seated once again, they headed slowly through the narrowest part of the thorofare. Once through the passage, they hauled on the wind, passing Dogfish Ledge and the thorofare light, where they bore off on a broad reach for Camden. At noon, a little more than an hour after they'd started, they dropped the hook in the inner harbor, amid a forest of stacks and masts branched with spars and yardarms. Wharves and fish houses formed a bracelet of wood and shingle around the harbor. Camden town lay beyond, the clean white bayonets of its church steeples pinning a cloud-tiled sky, and the Camden Hills rose at the far horizon, their rocks blue with distance, as though a part of the heavens had become solid and tangible.

Nathaniel, wearing his borrowed shoes, rowed Gertrude Williams to the wharf—*Double Eagle*'s tender was too small for her to sit comfortably with his brothers aboard—and after she left instructions to meet her at the telegraph office at one sharp, he rowed back to fetch Eliot and Drew. *Black Watch* lay at anchor across the harbor, the girls gathered in the stern—the long dresses of white and brown, the bright straw hats. It would be fine to join them, he thought, finer still to talk to Constance, instead of going to the telegraph office. But he supposed Mrs. Williams was right, they ought to let their mother know where they were and what was going on. Trouble was, he wasn't completely sure himself what was going on. A suspicion plucked at the edges of his mind that Mrs. Williams knew more about their mother's condition than she had let on. Why had Mother written to her before she'd written to her own husband and sons? And why had the old man left in such a rush? The disquiet grew, and he rowed his brothers ashore without talking. He felt that the three of them were actors in a strange kind of play, one in which they were not allowed to hear the other characters' dialogue or observe their actions, save for a murmur now and then, or a shadowy movement dimly seen, like a ship approaching through a fog.

The telegraph office was in a cottage next to the post office downtown. There they waited, under a snapping Stars and Stripes, under the wires that tethered Camden to the outside world. They had bought ice creams at a store up the street, inhaling rather than eating them because they hadn't eaten breakfast. Still hungry, they depleted their account another fifteen cents and bought three more cones, which they were now devouring while they waited beneath the flag, beneath the wires vibrating in the wind.

Finally, Gertrude Williams hove into view, her majestic prow seeming to cleave through the other pedestrians. Saying, "Let us proceed," she steamed into the office, snatched some forms from a tray and a couple of pencils, and, crouching over the counter, began to write.

"I must send mine first. We have similar missions. I am informing my brother of his son's whereabouts. Will swears he told his father that he was coming here, but I don't believe much of anything Will says." Glancing at Nathaniel, she pushed a pencil and one of the blank sheets at him. "Get on with it. Just remember that brevity is the soul of wit, and when one is sending wire, it's cheaper, too."

"Dearest Mother," he began. "We are OK stop." That sounded dumb, he crossed it out. "Today finds us in good health stop." No. Way too stilted and wordy. Mrs. Williams, meanwhile, handed her message to the telegraph operator, a scrawny man with the dour look of a failed preacher. Returning to the counter, she cast a dismayed look at Nathaniel as he stood chewing the end of his pencil.

"You are writing a telegram, not immortal poetry," she snapped. "And take that out of your mouth. Don't they teach germ theory at Andover? Here. Give that to me."

Half a minute later, she presented her composition to the boys for their approval, then passed it to the operator, who, tucking up his gartered sleeves, began to tap the key. When he was done, she paid him, clearing her throat and giving a quick, conclusive nod, the economical gesture expressing a sense of satisfaction with herself and with the situation she had begun to rectify. She had done her duty to her friend, and beyond her friend, to the cause of domestic order in general.

Outside, she stepped into the street, raised a hand to halt an oncoming wagon, and then strode across.

"You see, boys, this is what we get for things being as they are," she declared, as they returned to the harbor. "These patriarchs, these grand poobahs, these tin-pot tyrants ordering everyone about at their whim, doing as they please with their workers and their wives and children. I am no doubt speaking out of turn, but then, I always speak out of turn, since as a woman I am not supposed to speak about anything of consequence. I consider it unconscionable for your father to have taken the actions he has without a single word to your mother, as if you weren't her children, too, as if she should have no say in the matter, and she down there in Boston, recovering from an operation. . . ."

She had gotten herself so exercised about their tyrannical father that she had made a slip. The boys knew it by the way she tried to muffle the last word, but they said nothing. It was only when he was alone with her in the tender that Nathaniel got up the nerve to ask how she knew their mother had had an operation, and what kind of operation was it?

Mrs. Williams opened her parasol against the sun's glare.

"She told me so in her letter, and she asked me to keep it to myself, but I've gone and spilled the beans, haven't I? I believe in candor, therefore, I'll be candid with you. It's called a 'hysterectomy.'"

He mouthed the foreign word, tried to get his tongue around it, and his mind as well, for it had an ominous sound.

"Now, now, Nathaniel," she said, noticing the look on his face. "Doctors have been performing it for, oh, nearly twenty years now. It's practically routine. You see, your mother had—I shall call it a growth—a growth on her uterus." Beads of sweat suddenly appeared on her upper lip. "Ah, it appears I am not as comfortable with candor as I wish to be. To remove this growth, the doctors had to—oh, it was benign, it was not a cancer, I assure you. Still, the doctors had to also remove the organ this growth was attached to. It means your mother cannot bear any more children, which is not a tragedy at her age, and her with three fine sons already."

He looked over his shoulder to make sure his way was clear.

"Father said something about that, about her turning forty this year."

"Said what about her turning forty?"

"He didn't finish, but I guess it had something to do with what's wrong with her."

"I have told you, there is nothing wrong with her. Not anymore. She wrote to me that she's been up and about, taking some of Worden's nerve pills, is all, but we all take those."

"Mrs. Williams, could we see this letter?"

He backed an oar to swing the tender alongside, waited a couple of seconds for her answer, and when it was not forthcoming, clambered up on deck and lowered a short Jacob's ladder for her.

"I am afraid that won't be possible," she replied finally. "There are private woman-to-woman things in it, and besides, one does not read another's mail, does one?"

"No, ma'am, reckon one doesn't."

She smoothed her dress and squinted against the bright water.

"However, I would like you and your brothers to come to dinner tonight. Afterward, I can read you excerpts. Then you'll see that she's quite all right. Is that fair, Nathaniel?"

He nodded.

"Now fetch Eliot and Andrew, and then we'll join the others and enjoy God's gift of this splendid afternoon."

7

WHICH THEY DID. There is no photograph of that day in her albums, but it's easy enough for Sybil to picture the yachting party picnicking on an island in the harbor: seven girls and seven boys laughing, talking, eating sandwiches, drinking Coca-Cola and ginger ale, and all full of youth and health and simmering hormones, which their watchful chaperons insured would not come to a boil. She can see them gathered for dinner that evening in the big yellow house with the rose arbor out back and broad veranda in front, where Dr. Williams once sat on summer evenings, taking a holiday from his patients and sexual exertions. So it went for the next three days. Nathaniel chronicled the social events in his logbook—a round of day sails, another picnic, a tennis match, a dance at the casino, an afternoon of poetry readings. His accounts were mere bulletins, stripped of mood and emotion, yet Sybil claims she can sense, between the lines, his growing impatience with these genteel pursuits and pleasant diversions of the haute WASP, circa 1901.

On the afternoon of the fourth day in North Haven, a message from Gertrude Williams was delivered to *Double Eagle* by the launch pilot: A telegram for Nathaniel and his brothers had come to her house via the morning ferry from Camden. She believed it was from their mother, and would they kindly stop by to pick it up?

The maid, a rawboned German woman, admitted the boys into the house in which no man had dwelled for five years. She led them to the drawing room, where Gertrude was holding court, surrounded by her daughters and their friends and a couple of matrons from town. So large an assemblage in one average-sized room created a sense of feminine solidarity almost palpable, and when the maid knocked, ten pairs of female eyes turned as one toward the doorway where the three young males stood. Nathaniel could not say they were glaring, but their looks were not welcoming, as if he and his brothers had intruded on a sorority as hermetic and cabalistic in its way as Free Masonry.

"*There* you are," said Gertrude Williams and, turning in a rustle of chiffon and taffeta, towed them outside to the veranda. Motioning with her head, she bid them sit in the wicker chairs, plucked from her skirt pocket a yellow envelope bearing Western Union's stamp, and handed it to Nathaniel.

He read the telegram and passed it to Eliot and Drew.

"And what does she have to say?"—Gertrude, cocking her head slightly and leaning forward, as if putting her ear to a door.

"One doesn't read another's telegrams, does one?"

Nathaniel couldn't help himself, but he sought to soften the cheekiness of the remark with a broad smile. His mother always said he had a winning smile, a smile to melt man's or woman's heart, but it did not have that effect on Mrs. Williams.

"I didn't ask to read it, did I, Nathaniel?" she said coldly. "I asked what was her news. If you don't wish to tell me, the polite way to do that is to simply say that it's private. And you would do well to remember that I am forty-four and you sixteen."

"Yes, ma'am. I'm sorry, ma'am. She told us she loves us and that we should stay put, and to tell you she's grateful to you for looking after us."

"And nothing about your father?"

He shook his head.

"Perhaps whatever's going on is too complicated to explain in a wire." She fingered her broach. "Now, listen to me, boys. Constance's and Johanna's friends will be leaving in a couple of days. Until then, you will of course have to stay on your boat, but afterward, you and your mother will be most welcome to stay with us. I am going to ask Liza to come up as soon as she feels fit. I have plenty of room, and the air here will be ever so much better for her. You can stay for the rest of the summer, if you wish, though I hope to see this confusion with your father straightened out before then, and the five of you back together again."

They thanked her, and she acknowledged their thanks with that quick self-satisfied nod of hers, and then pulled a five-dollar bill from her pocket and gave it to Nathaniel. She was having special guests for dinner that night—the president of Harvard and his wife and their houseguest, a distinguished professor from the University of Chicago—and she wanted the boys to pick up twenty lobsters to save her cook the time and trouble.

Nathaniel nodded and asked if he'd heard right: *twenty?*

"You three, my daughters and their friends, Will and his friends make fourteen, Hannah and I sixteen, my guests nineteen, leaving one of the critters for insurance," she said. "Bring the lobsters back right away, no detours or tarrying. I want 'em alive and kicking—and a dollar in change. Don't let that skinflint down-easter charge you more than twenty cents apiece."

Down the white street they went on their errand, the gravel of stone and crushed shellfish crunching underfoot, and the trees casting long afternoon shadows over the great houses and the gardens, vibrant with iris and zinnia and wild rose. Drew whistled tunelessly to himself.

"Reckon you're happy now, little man," said Nathaniel. The whistling irritated him. "Got a fixed roof over your head again and, pretty soon, Mummy in the room down the hall."

"Stop calling me 'little man.' "

"He'll stop when you stop letting him know it bothers you"—Eliot, exasperated.

"Aren't you happy that Mother's all right?" asked Drew, as they took a zigzag staircase down a rocky drop-off to the shorefront.

"Sure."

"And I'd figure you to be extra happy about living in the same house with Constance." Drew tossed a nasal mockery into *Constance*. "Now you two can practice being married."

"Better not let Mrs. Williams hear you say that."

"What do you mean?"

Nathaniel did not answer, suddenly distracted by a return of the alluring, frightening image: Constance's head grafted onto the French woman's naked body, the divan covered with the stripes and spots of slain beasts.

"What's wrong with what I said?" Drew asked.

"For a genius, you're an idiot, sometimes," Nathaniel said, and then led the way down the shorefront road.

The lobsterman's shack was a gray shingle box perched on the end of a wharf near the ferry dock. The lobsters, thousands of them, it looked like, were held alive in two cars—huge, submerged crates connected by block and tackle to booms, protruding from one side of the shack. The man who ran the place not only was a skinflint, he looked like one, as if his penurious soul had affected his flesh, paring it to the minimum required to cover his bones.

"Mrs. Williams told us twenty cents, not a penny more," Nathaniel said, when the man declared that the price was thirty cents per lobster.

"Maakit price. Thuddy cents," was all the man would say, his speech stripped of excesses like articles and verbs. He was sitting on a wooden stool behind a counter. In the back were stacked lobster traps resembling miniature Indian longhouses, piles of spindle-shaped pots painted white and green, and coils of pot warp smelling of the copper solvent into which they had been recently dipped against rot.

"Excuse me, sir," Nathaniel said. "Mrs. Williams wants twenty lobsters and she gave us five dollars and expects a dollar change."

Moving his lips, which were as scant as the rest of him, the man looked toward the cobwebbed rafters.

"What she 'spects and what she kin git be two differint things. Five bucks'll buy ye sixteen an' two-thuds lobstuhs. I'll make it seventeen. Want twenny, ye be a dolluh shawt."

And then he pulled up the drawbridge and withdrew into the castle of his impervious stinginess. On the wharf outside, the boys were debating which would be easier and quicker—to ask Gertrude Williams for the extra dollar or to row back to the boat and take it from their stash (now reduced to twenty-nine dollars and thirty cents, thanks to their fondness for ice cream)—when Nathaniel noticed a Friendship sloop moored to a float below. Two men in oilskin overalls were scooping lobsters from the sloop's live well into a trap door in the top of one of the cars.

"Hey, if you're selling, I'm buying, if the price is right," Nathaniel called down.

The older of the two looked up. He had close-cropped, gray hair and jug-handle ears.

"Whachye consider a right price?"

"Twenty cents each."

"Haow many?"

"An even score."

"What's the trouble? George ain't in a mood ta baagin?"

"If you're talking about the tightwad inside, he sure ain't."

"That tightwad be my brother, but reckon we kin do business."

He waved Nathaniel down the gangway.

"George, he's a daisy, ain't he? Chaages ye yachtsmen on this side a kinder tax," said the fisherman. "Jus' on account of ye kin 'ford it."

Catching the faint burr of contempt in the man's voice, Nathaniel said he was not a yachtsman.

"Coulda foolt me. C'mon aboard. Pick the ones ye like."

It was a combination of things—the bad fit of the borrowed shoes (they were Tony Burton's and a size too large), the Rockland ferry announcing its imminent departure with a shrill, unexpected blast of its steam whistle, and the sloop's deck, wet and slimy from the menhaden oil leaking from a bait bucket—that caused Nathaniel to slip and fall as a vaudeville clown falls, both feet flying out from under him, his arms flailing. He landed on his back on a trap, and felt the lathes crack under his weight. He lay for a few moments between the halves of the broken trap, staring at the sky and the sloop's boom. The fishermen's faces appeared above him. Must be father and son, he thought, because the younger had the same jug-handle ears.

"Be ye hurt?" asked the older man.

He shook his head, then tried to stand, but he couldn't move. Wedged tightly, he was, for all practical purposes, attached to the trap, or it to him, and it weighed at least thirty pounds, being made of oak, with five or six housebricks in its floor to anchor it to the seabottom.

"Biggest 'un we ever caught, Dad," the younger one said, and both broke into laughter as they pried the lathes from around his back and ribs.

The son took Nathaniel's hands in his (they were solid with calluses, their grip so strong they seemed capable of crushing a lobster's shell with one squeeze) and pulled him to his feet.

Standing, he tried to recover his dignity, but that was impossible, in the gusts of humiliating laughter.

"Lordy, reckon ye yachtsmen ain't usta the deck of a workin' boat," said the father.

With his whole being, Nathaniel wanted to say that he wasn't used to sloppy captains who allowed fish oil to spill on their decks, but his better judgment was in full operating order, for a change.

Kneeling over the live well, he gazed down into a nightmare of twitching feelers and claws and cold, beady, lifeless eyes—how could anything so ugly taste so fine? he wondered. His hand sheathed in canvas nippers, he snatched a lobster by its carapace and dropped it into a big mesh sack held open by the younger fisherman. He went for another, but was a little off his aim and felt the claws prick him, even through the gloves. "Gotta watch 'em, they take yer finger fer dinnah, grab ye by the balls, ye be singin' like a girl," said the young one merrily.

With the twenty stuffed into two sacks, Nathaniel handed the five-dollar bill to the older man, who gave it a snap and then slipped it into his pocket. When it did not appear forthcoming, he asked for the change. The fisherman's glance fell on the broken lobster trap.

"Figger fifty cents fer materials, fifty more fer my labor, buildin' it," he declared.

"Wait a minute. I didn't break it on purpose."

"Still be broke, and 'twasn't me fell on it, 'twasn't Toby. 'Twas ye."

It wasn't his money, Nathaniel protested. He was running an errand. He had to bring back a dollar in change. The fisherman paused, contemplated his slippery deck briefly, and then gave Nathaniel a choice: He could go up to the shack, where there were lathes and ribs, hammer and nails, and the two-chambered nets that made a trap a trap, and build one to replace the one he'd broken. Did he know how to build a trap? He did not. Don't teach that in school, do they? All right, the old man said, and squeezed Nathaniel's biceps and shoulders and pronounced him strong enough. Had fifteen, sixteen traps left in his string; if Nathaniel pulled them for him, he would consider the dollar debt paid off. Besides, his son Toby had been pullin' all mornin' and could use a rest.

"How long will that take?"—Nathaniel, peevishly.

"Got somewheres ta go?"

"Matter of fact, I do. I'm expected at dinner. To eat one of these."

"Traps is set close in, won't take more'n two, three haours."

Nathaniel said the man had a deal, waved his brothers down to the sloop, gave them the lobsters with instructions to bring them to Mrs. Williams right away—no detours or tarrying.

He was impressed by how beautifully the little Friendship sailed, and how skillfully the fisherman—his name was Isaiah Kent—handled her, threading a path through the vessels crowding the thorofare, then ghosting along the north shore of Vinalhaven, where his traps were set. The sloop did not go to wind'ard very smartly, Isaiah said, without apology, she was made to be sailed off the wind, and built for work such as this: well-balanced, her mast stepped forward so she could sail well on the main alone, her deep draft and full keel giving her the stability of a vessel half again as big (she was thirty feet on deck).

The shoreline resembled some Yankee farmer's stone fence, only it was much higher than any fence, and the stones were as big as wagons, big as houses, some of them, and reefs and ledges jutted from the shore and showed through the water a fathom or two below, tresses of olive-green seaweed trailing in the current. Isaiah Kent approached the first of his white and green pots and, swinging the tiller hard over, rounded up, and let the main go, the sloop holding as if she were moored. Toby leaned over the leeward side, snatched the warp with a boathook, and then hauled, while his father told Nathaniel that leeward was the side you pulled from. Weren't no trick to it, all it took was a strong back and a feeble mind, ain't that right, Toby, ain't that you, son, strong back, feeble mind? Sure is, Dad, Toby grunted, with good humor, the muscles in his forearms twisting like hawsers as, leaning backward, he pulled, hand over hand. With one powerful heave, he brought the dripping trap aboard, flipped opened the little door on the side, and pulled out two lobsters and dumped them in the live well. That done, he opened the bait bucket, tossed in a stinking mixture of menhaden and ground-up flounder, and heaved the trap back overboard, Nathaniel watching the warp plunge away into the jade-green depths and the pot skim along the surface until, the trap hitting bottom, it stopped abruptly.

"See wheah he put the bait?" said Isaiah. "Call that the kitchen. Lobstuh walks in, eats his fill, but can't git back out, so he goes for'ard, into the second part, that's the pahluh. Figgers he kin escape that way, but he can't on account of the funnel shape of the net. There he stays, till we come along, and put him on his way to gittin' et himself. That is the way o' the world, ayup, way o' the world."

And now that he'd been shown how it was done, Isaiah added, Nathaniel would pull the remaining traps himself.

He was shocked by how heavy the first trap felt. Hauling the thing up against the resistance of five or six fathoms of water tripled its weight, maybe quadrupled it. He huffed and grunted, and the warp scraped against the gunwale.

"Heh, heh," chortled the old man. "Now ye be learnin' the value of a lobstuh, ain't ye, young yachtsman?"

At last, the big trap surfaced. He reached down and yanked it aboard with both hands, recalling that Toby had done it with one. Thus, another lesson learned: There was a difference between muscles gained by lifting dumbbells and playing football, and muscles gained this way. There were no lobsters inside, only three huge crabs. He asked what he should do with them.

"Take 'em out and I'll show ye," said Isaiah Kent, and when the crabs were on deck, he smashed them to bits with a club and tossed the bits into the bucket.

"Inny sumbitch steals my bait gits to be bait," he said.

They rounded up on the next pot, about fifty yards downshore, and, again, the shocking resistance, the weight, and the old man cackling "heh, heh" while Nathaniel huffed and grunted. The second trap was a harder pull than the first, and the reason was revealed when it surfaced: full as a jail cell on Saturday night. One of the lobsters looked big enough to eat a small dog.

"Ayup, second lesson in learnin' why lobstuhs ain't free. Ho! Was a time not so long ago when they wasn't wuth a fart in a gale, on account of ye could walk out inta the eel grass at low tide and pluck 'em off the rocks. Stealin' candy from a baby, but no more, no more." Isaiah began to tap his foot loudly. "We'll try to make it light work fer ye," he said, and then sang out in a voice that creaked like rigging:

> Goin' back to Weldon, to Weldon, to Weldon,
> Goin' back to We-el-duh-unnn . . .

And then Toby joining in on the last line . . .

> To git a job in the Weldon yards . . .

Nathaniel recognized the chantey, had heard it once in Gloucester, an old net-hauling song from the Grand Banks.

> Cap'n if you fire me, fire me, fire me,
> Cap'n if you fire me-eee . . .
> Got to fire my buddy too . . .

The song somehow did make the work easier. By the fifth pot, he was into the rhythm of it, and even managed to sing along himself as he pulled:

> Don't want a woman, a woman, a woman . . .
> Don't want a wooomaaan . . .
> With hair like a horse's mane . . .
> Goin' back to Weldon, to Weldon, to Weldon . . .

And by the time he had hauled half the string, he was actually enjoying himself—the good strain on his muscles and the smell of his sweat in the warm sun. He shared in the disappointment when a trap came up empty, in the joy when it broke surface, packed with the blue-black critters, and when another sloop passed near and her crew waved, he joined Isaiah and Toby in waving back, feeling himself to have been pledged to a kind of fraternity. Something like letdown came over him when the last trap was rebaited and tossed overboard.

"Yer debt's paid," Isaiah said. "Where d'ye want to be dropped?"

"My boat. My brothers and I are living on a boat."

"Yer yacht, ye mean?"

"All right, yeah, my yacht, my goddammed yacht, and make it quick. J. P. Morgan is aboard, waiting for me to smoke a cigar with him, after we've had our caviar."

Isaiah Kent laughed.

"Okay. Bein' a yachtsman, ye can help me bring her in. Toby's got a back like ironwood, and the boy knaows where lobstuhs er gone ta be 'fore they do, but he can't sail a boat anymore'n he kin fly a balloon to Rio de Janeiro. Got us a good wind, and here's what we're gone to do. Fall off till the tops'ls fill, and we'll tear inta harbor at an outrageous rate. When we git near onto the midchannel buoy, we'll douse the jib tops'l and keep on goin' under main, maintop, and stays'l, which be right civilized sails, don't need much tendin'. Later on, we'll douse the maintop and the stays'l, and come up to yer yacht on the main alone, and dependin' on how out of control we be at the time, we'll either put a hole in her or we'll ease up on her so soft that if there be a raw egg between yer vessel and mine, it won't break."

And that was exactly how the return trip went. Though an egg might have broken, it would not have broken much, so sweetly did the sloop's gunwale kiss *Double Eagle*'s. He shook hands with the two men—Isaiah's grip was as crushing as his son's—and hopped aboard the schooner, feeling happy and sad at the same time.

"Right smart-lookin' vessel," said the old man. "'Pears to be modeled after one o' Burgess's designs. Like the old *Fredonia*."

"How did you know?"

"Partly, it's that clipper bow ye got, mostly, it's on account of I sailed on the *Fredonia*'s sister ship, back when I worked the Grand Banks. The *Nellie Dixon*."

Then Toby shoved them off, and Isaiah pointed up and commenced to sail away.

"Done all right, young yachtsman," he called over his shoulder. "Ye kin pull traps fer me anytime ye be bored or in need of a dolluh, though I don't reckon that's a need ye got."

Goin' back to Weldon, to Weldon, to Weldon . . .

LEATHER-VOICED Isaiah Kent sang the chantey all through the soup course (chilled cucumber) and the salad course, and now, into the main course, he was singing still in Nathaniel's inner ear, as the voices from all around the table jostled in his outer ear: At one end, Tony Burton and

Will bantered with President Eliot about the relative merits of the Yale and Harvard football squads; at the opposite end, Gertrude Williams, with earnest mien, listened to Professor Davenport discourse on his field, a new science called eugenics; in the center, directly across from Nathaniel, Van Slyck strained to sound interested in Mrs. Eliot's review of a dramatization she had seen of *Hiawatha;* beside them, looking beautiful in a pearl choker and a lilac dress falling in cascades of filmy chiffon, Constance was telling Herb Wheeler about a Williams ancestor captured by Mohawks in colonial days; and on Nathaniel's right side, Antonia Codman was delivering a monologue on the dinner. What did you think of the soup, Nat? I thought it excellent, although I prefer vichyssoise for a chilled soup. . . . He wasn't just bored, he was stunningly bored, and could not understand why Antonia preferred to talk about the food rather than eat it. Most of her lobster was untouched, and he, ravenous, was sorely tempted to spear it with his fork and transfer it to his plate.

> *Oh, Cap'n's got a Luger, got a Luger, got a Luuugerrr,*
> *And the mate's got an owl's head . . .*

His experience had made him the center of attention before dinner. Gertrude Williams gave him a smothering embrace for going to such lengths on her behalf, he really shouldn't have, she'd said, and then sermonized with the fervor of a Cotton Mather against the parsimoniousness of down-easters, who could squeeze a dollar so hard it made the eagle scream. Constance and Antonia pressed him for details about what it was like to spend an entire afternoon in the company of lobstermen. The girls spoke as if they thought lobstermen were not men who fished for lobsters but a breed of hybridized and possibly dangerous beings. Combed, scrubbed, wearing his cleanest pair of duck trousers, a tie, and his Andover jacket (Father always made him and his brothers pack jackets and ties on the summer cruises, in case they took dinner in a yacht club), he answered that he'd had a fine time and that the lobstermen were fine fellows who had taught him a few things, chiefly how much a lobster was actually worth.

The poems came afterward, when the dinner party filed into the dining room. Each of the seven young ladies had written a poem about each of the seven young men, and their verses were folded up and put beside the soup plates instead of place cards. That made the tedious business of finding your seat something of a game (the adults were exempted from the nonsense). The poem about Nathaniel involved a play on words, something about Natty looking natty. He recognized Constance's hand-writing, and while a small part of him was pleased that she had chosen him as the subject of her composition, the greater part was annoyed and irritated. He wished that instead of combed and scrubbed and looking natty in his Andover jacket, he had shown up exactly as he had come off Isaiah Kent's sloop—in his soiled jersey, cologned in sweat and the reek of the bait bucket. The smell of someone who had done a man's work, and compared to that work, all the chatter and the poems seemed trivial. He was, besides, disappointed in Constance; he liked to think of her as too serious and intelligent to idle away an entire afternoon writing dog-gerel while people like Isaiah and Toby sweated their hearts out to put bread on the table.

Such was his judgment before the meal began; now it was softened by the way she looked in the manteled glow of the gas-jet chandelier. She had short eyelashes, which gave her an expression of a perpetual, mild astonishment, as though she found every moment of life a surprise; her mouth was ever so slightly downturned, which moderated that look of wonder with a hint of melancholy; and her throat in its pearl choker and her lovely head poised under the graceful sweep of her Gibson girl pom-padour all but shattered his heart. At first, he had been disappointed not to have been seated next to her; now he decided to be flattered: Gertrude Williams was keeping him away from her daughter because she knew that he was the most dangerous of all the young men there, was the one most likely to turn Constance's head.

But when dinner was over and they gathered in the music room, Nathaniel got in only one dance with her. He had been to dancing class—Mother insisted on it—but he, who was nimble on the football field and quick on his feet in the ring and on the tennis court, never quite got the hang of the two-step or the waltz. He moved around woodenly and was in a way relieved when Herb Wheeler cut in. Tony Burton was next, and Nathaniel watched him twirling her around to "Hello Central, Give Me Heaven," then that other new song, "In the Good Old Sum-mertime." Soon, all the disks had been played and everyone got tired of turning the Victrola crank to keep the music from sounding like it was being played underwater. Constance asked Van Slyck if he would sing that jolly Dartmouth song. He agreed and sat at the piano, the crowd gathering around him.

VAN SLYCK: *Oh, Eleazar Wheelock was a very pious man,*
He went into the wilderness to teach the In-dye-an.
With a Gradus ad Parnassum, a Bible and a drum . . .

ALL: *And five hundred gallons of New England rum!*
VAN SLYCK: *Eleazar and the big chief harangued and gesticulated,*
              They founded Dartmouth College,
              And the big chief matriculated.
              Eleazar was the faculty and the whole curriculum . . .
ALL: *Was five hundred gallons of New England rum!*

Part Two

SOUTHERN CROSS

Gulf of Mexico

Florida Bay

Cudjoe Key
Sugar Loaf Key
Snipe Keys

Big Torch Key
Big Pine Key
Vaca Key

Grassy
Key
Long Key
Duck Key

24°40'

Dry Tortugas

*Rebecca
Shoal*

*The
Quicksands*

Marquesas
Keys

Boca Grande Channel

**Key
West**

Boca
Chica
Key

Hawk Channel

Bahía Honda Key
Ramrod Key
Summerland Key
Saddlebunch Keys

Florida Keys

24°20'

Straits of Florida

N
W E
S

24°00'

0   miles   30

Mercator projection
Scale at latitude 22°

82°30'   82°00'   81°30'   81°00'

8

LOG: *16 June. At anchor, North Haven. Comes foggy in the a.m., clearing by noon. SW 15 kts. 30.02 steady. 72 degree F. Took morning ferry to Camden with Will, Will to pick up money wired by his father for train ticket or steamer passage to Boston. Dirigo, square-rigger built in Bath in '94, moored in Camden harbor, taking on lumber for Galveston, rebuilding after big hurricane last year. Chief mate allowed us aboard to look her over. A fine ship. Will and I climbed to top of mainmast. A bully view! Returned to Double Eagle, resolved to sail to Key West. Will to be our navigator. Shaped our course. After some argument with crew, we agreed to shove off with tomorrow's tide.*

Those are the bare bones, written by Nathaniel, in thin brown ink, and this the flesh his descendant has stretched over them:

" '. . . I CANNOT REST from travel; I will drink / Life to the lees. . . .' "
Poised shoeless on the footrope of steel-hulled *Dirigo's* highest yardarm, his chest against the spar and one hand clutching a gasket of the furled royal, Nathaniel imagined himself a soaring gull that, blessed with human voice, uttered not screeches or squeals but Tennyson's verses from aloft.

" '. . . All times I have enjoyed / Greatly, have suffered greatly, both with those / That loved me, and alone; on shore and when / Through scudding drifts the rainy Hyades / Vexed the dim sea. I am become a name. . . .' "

Will, lacking the nerve to follow him out onto the yard, clung to the web of ratlines and tarred shrouds at the mast, and called out the next lines.

"'For always roaming with hungry heart / Much have I seen and known—cities of men / And manners, climates, councils, governments . . .'"

Then Nathaniel, feeling his own nerve slip a little as he looked straight down to the deck one hundred and fifty feet below, marveling at the courage of the sailors who scampered out here, surefooted as squirrels, to shorten sail, not when the ship sat stable as a building but rolled in seas that pitched the spars' ends toward the wavetops. . . .

"'. . . Gleams that untraveled world whose margin fades / Forever and forever when I move / How dull it is to pause, to make an end / To rust unburnished, not to shine in use!'"

"Natters—back to terra firma?"

"No! Incognita! Think what it would be like to sail a ship like this, all around the world."

The lofty view of Camden, reduced to the dimensions of a scale-model town, of the quay upon whose stones and bricks lilliputian stevedores scurried amid wagons, handcarts, barrels, casks, and crates cluttered like toys in a messy playroom, of the bay and the islands and the sea beyond, beguiled him. His horizons were the horizons of the osprey or the tern; he saw sails the earthbound could not, the leaning black columns of a steamer miles out.

"I could stay up here all day," he shouted, then, pointing at the town: "'There lies the port; the vessel puffs her sail. . . .'" Like a windvane, his finger swung eastward. "'There gloom the dark, broad seas . . .'"

"And there"—Will, pointing below—"lies the deck, where I'm headed. Think I'm afraid of heights. Join me before you slip and turn yourself into a splat of birdshit."

Nathaniel sidled along the footrope, reached out to snatch a shroud, and, swinging onto the ratlines, followed Will down to the maintop. Will found the platform, a mere forty or fifty feet up, a less vertiginous perch, and paused there for a smoke.

"You're really addicted to those things," Nathaniel said.

"You must have at least one vice, if for no other reason than to provide a background against which your virtues shine all the brighter."

They sat against the mast, Will puffing on the Duke's until there was barely enough left to hold between his yellowed fingers. He snubbed it out and, figuring the chief mate would give him fifty lashes for tossing the butt on deck, put it in his shirt pocket.

"Don't much fancy going back to Boston," he said. "Every day with my nose buried in the Statutes of the Commonwealth of Massachusetts?"

"What would your old man do if you stayed here?"

"Disinherit me, swear out a warrant for my arrest, possibly send a squad of thugs to kidnap me and drag me back in irons. Can't stay, anyhow. Tony's father is coming up day after tomorrow to take command of his new yacht, with a new, paid, professional crew. Will has lost his berth aboard *Black Watch,* leaving Aunty Battlewagon's house as the only reasonable alternative. No, thank you. Too many women. Aunty would count for two or three all by herself. Reminds me of something I read in *Scribner's* a while back, to the effect that feminine companionship gets to be mentally enervating after a while. Find that to be true?"

"Wouldn't know," answered Nathaniel, sullenly. "Connie hasn't given me much in the way of feminine companionship for me to find out. Too busy figuring which one of your college chums she wants to charm. The hell with women. *Scribner's* was right about them. Mentally inebriating."

"Enervating. Your Latin is better than your English, though I suppose women can be inebriating, too." Will regarded him with a puckish expression. "The cure for mental enervation is to be among one's fellows, roughing it in the open air. 'The long day wanes, the slow moon climbs; the deep / Moans round with many voices; Come my friends, / 'Tis not too late to seek a newer world . . .' Your turn."

" 'Push off, and sitting well in order smite / The sounding furrows; for my purpose holds to sail beyond the sunset, and the baths / Of all the western stars, until I die . . .' Jesus, Will, I love that one best of all, 'Beyond the sunset and the baths of all the western stars.' "

And so they continued, answering one another like priests reading a doxology until, both bellowing the final line—"to strive, to seek, to find, and not to yield"—they had infected themselves with seafever, kindled the fire that had sped young men a half century before to try their luck and test their strength in the goldfields of the West, that had shanghaied them out from under comfortable roofs to stand the trials of rounding the Horn in clipper ships: the romance and glamour of youth, and the recklessness of youth, for whom life can hold no terrors; the flame that consumes caution, blinds young men to foresight, if they have foresight to begin with, and sends them beyond the horizon to unlock what secrets may be hidden there, to behold what beauty may be lying there, to triumph over what ordeals may be waiting for them there, and the prize of that victory (never a doubt in youth's mind that the outcome will be anything but victorious) neither glory nor renown, nor knowledge but the thing that glory, renown, or knowledge symbolize: the stature to stand with men and look them level in the eye and say, We have been somewhere and seen and done and learned and are no longer boys.

"What the hell are we doing, hanging around here with all these piazza-chair loafers," Nathaniel declared, suddenly.

A blackbacked gull, swooping through the rigging, passed so close they could see the vermilion ring around its eye, the orange spot on its beak.

"Go. That's what I would do, if I were in your spot." Will's whole countenance, losing its usual expression of bored worldliness, shone with enthusiasm. "If you don't, ten, twenty years from now, you'll be slaving away and you'll look back on this chance and you'll say, 'I wish I'd done that,' and I think those are the saddest words in the English language. Lord, go. *Go*."

"But where?"

They debated the merits and demerits of possible destinations and directions. North had the prevailing winds to recommend it, but Nathaniel wasn't inclined to revisit the Canadian maritimes, which were too much like Maine. Will spoke of Bermuda or the Azores—names to quicken the wanderer's blood. Southward lay the West Indies, the Florida Keys, the Tropic of Cancer, also names that beckoned, particularly to Nathaniel. But to sail south would be to beat all the way, and, in the Florida Straits, they would have the Gulf Stream, as well as the wind, on their nose.

"Unless you tuck in close to the Florida reef," he said, sliding one hand past the other. "There's a southwesterly counter-current that hugs the reef. Ships use it when they're westering to the Gulf of Mexico. That's what my father told me. It's one of the reasons there's so many wrecks down there. Ships get into that current, and then something goes wrong. Bang! On the rocks."

"Bowditch mentions that current, I think," Will said.

"Hey! You lads! Guided tour is over! Lower yourselves away, 'cause we're to start loadin' soon!"

It was their host, the chief mate, calling from the foot of the mainmast and pointing at the quay, where the stevedores were hooking a bundle of lumber to the crane of a steam derrick.

The discussion continued on the ferry, over the thud of the great brass-plated engine, the slosh and grind of the sidewheel turning. They talked while ships passed them and they passed ships—a mackerel schooner with seabirds hovering over it as though tethered to the ship with kite strings; a stone drogher looking like a granite ledge that had detached itself from land, sprouted sails, and put to sea, for she was sunk almost to her scuppers by the giant blocks stacked on her decks. The voyage remained a dream; yet the more they talked about it, the more it felt inevitable to Nathaniel; the more he felt his inclinations turning toward the latitudes he had heard so much about, where seas broke green on coral reefs and mangrove isles wavered like mirages on the hot tidal flats. And there his compass settled, without his willing it. He had always been curious to see the waters and the places where his father and half brother had sailed and lived; lived a life so different from the one he and Eliot and Drew had known that it seemed mythical to them, a shimmering legend out of a lost time. So the Florida Keys and Tropic of Cancer it would be, despite contrary winds, adverse currents, and the threat of hurricanes. No, not *despite. Because* of. How much more admirable a feat of seamanship it would be to skipper *Double Eagle* there and back, in the face of such obstacles and hazards. His thoughts lunging ahead to the fall, he saw his father greeting him as he once greeted Lockwood when Lockwood returned from the sea, and the picture had the glory of a hope fulfilled.

He slapped the deck rail and declared his decision to Will, who said, "A man who makes up his mind in a hurry. It's inspiring."

"But I'd feel a lot better about it," Nathaniel started to say, then paused. He had to put this the right way. "You're supposed to be a pretty good navigator, aren't you? Right handy with a sextant?"

"I have to be honest with you, Natters. I'm one of the best."

"Why not throw in with us, then? The hell with Boston and law clerking."

Will thought for about fifteen seconds.

"I can make up my mind, too. You've got a callow crew and you'll need someone with my maturity and wisdom to keep you out of trouble."

When they returned to *Double Eagle,* they immediately announced their plans to Eliot and Drew, who were speechless at first, and then began to argue against making such a long and dangerous trip. Their mother had told them to stay put, they said, and she probably would accept Mrs. Williams's invitation and would be looking forward to seeing them soon. Didn't they owe it to her to obey her wishes? Annoyed by their timidity, Nathaniel told them they were free to stay in North Haven with all the other piazza-chair loafers, if that's what they wanted. He and Will were capable of sailing the schooner by themselves, though it would be bully to have two extra hands to share watches.

"Jiminy, Nat, can't we have a little time to think about it?"

"Yeah. A little is all."

He and Will broke out the charts. The charts! There was a thrilling tension in them, a kind of tug-o'-war between science and poetry, exactitude and romance. The strange names of ports and shoals, headlands and capes stirred the mariner's dreams, luring him to come and see, while the lines of latitude and longitude, the Compass Rose, the soundings whose numbers cluttered the blue of inshore waters, cautioned him to pay attention to stern realities like depth and bearing, lest his dreams lead him into trouble. As Will, with dividers and parallel rules, began to plot a course, Nathaniel traced with his eyes the capricious meanderings of the coastline, his imagination roving over seas stormy and calm to Nantucket, to the Chesapeake, the Outer Banks, the Georgia sea islands, and down the long linear plunge of the Florida peninsula to the Keys, their broken arc westering to their end at the Dry Tortugas. How that name sang to him. Even on paper, the Tortugas looked lonesome—a few punctuation marks clumped in the white reaches of the Gulf of Mexico. And somewhere off those desolate islands lay the ship whose salvaging had been his father's biggest failure, possibly his only one, though there had been a lot of people who considered it anything but a failure. . . .

He took the sextant out of the drawer under the chart table, opened the case, and again read the engraved plate: IN GRATITUDE. *ANNISQUAM*. DRY TORTUGAS, FLORIDA. MARCH 10, 1879. Will looked up from his work and, with a gesture, asked Nathaniel what was in the case.

"A Plath," he said, removing the instrument.

"See it?"

Handling the sextant as if it were a precious jewel, Will pointed it at the skylight and moved the indicator on the arc back and forth and declared it a beauty. The Germans were said to be a very precise people. Passing the Plath back to Nathaniel, he noticed the inscription and asked who was grateful to whom for what.

"The passengers and crew, for their lives," Nathaniel replied, with a theatrical lowering of his voice. "The *Annisquam* foundered in a westerly gale, and Dad saved everybody aboard, a hundred and one altogether."

"Do I get to hear more?"

"Don't know much more," Nathaniel answered, and explained that his father had spoken of the incident only once, and very briefly, a reticence due partly to his Yankee taciturnity, mostly to his distaste for admitting defeat. He had not brought up the ship's most valuable cargo, and one of his divers had gone blind searching the wreck while his chief diver, a Bahamian called Artemis Lowe, had lost sight in one eye. On top of all that, Dad had gotten into a big fight with another wrecker who had tried to salvage the ship; they ended up in court, and the judge revoked Dad's wrecker's license.

"It's the whole reason he left Florida and came back north. Losing his license."

"Wait a minute," Will said. "He rescued a hundred and one people, they gave him this to show their thanks, but he lost his license? There's a few big holes in that sea story that need filling."

"Yeah. But you won't get them filled by Dad. And Lockwood never said much about it, either. He was just a kid then, but he saw most of it happen."

"What was this valuable cargo?"

"Candlesticks."

"Candlesticks?"

"Special kind of candlesticks. Great big ones. Seven of them. They were supposed to be about four feet long, maybe five, and solid gold. The *Annisquam* was a fast packet out of Boston, and she was bound for Corpus Christi with some ordinary stuff, and then to Vera Cruz. The candlesticks were for the Catholic cathedral there. They were supposed to be delivered in time for Easter. "

"Paschal candles," said Will.

"That's what you call them?"

"Yup. How much were they supposed to be worth?"

Nathaniel shrugged. "Dad nor Lockwood never said, but you got to figure a whole lot."

Will resumed his plotting, drawing rhumb lines on the charts, but Nathaniel did not help him, his thoughts too unsettled for such exacting work. Then, looking through a porthole, he saw in a moment a purpose for the voyage. The clarity of it, the rightness of it, flooded his mind like a revelation. He called to Eliot and Drew, who were on deck, presumably doing their thinking, to come below. He had something to say; and he said it, driving his words fast and hard, speaking (he thought) like a captain, not a sixteen-year-old kid.

"Well, what's your answer? Are you with me on this, or what?" he asked, when he was done, so persuaded by his own enthusiasm that he couldn't imagine them responding in the negative. But they did not respond at all. Will spoke instead.

"It'll give us something to aim for, I suppose," he said, shrugging casually. A difference of three years is a very big difference in adolescence, and Will did not wish to appear that he was taking orders from one younger than he. "Of course, it will be impossible, maybe even silly, but it might be amusing to try."

"It ain't just silly, it's nutty," Eliot remarked, while his already low estimation of Will fell another notch. Their eldest member should be talking sense to Nat instead of encouraging his screwy scheme. "Dad was a professional with a professional crew, and he couldn't find that stuff, but you think we can? Nat, we don't even know where that wreck is."

"There's bound to be folks in Key West who do."

"It went down more than twenty years ago! There's probably nothing left to her, and that stuff is all a pile of rust by now."

"Gold doesn't rust, you know that." This from Drew, sitting on the top rung of the companionway with Trajan in his lap.

"Are you saying you go along with this idea?"

"What if we did it, Eliot? Found the stuff and brought it up?"

"I reckon we'd be rich."

"We'd have done something the old man couldn't do. Something he won't be able to criticize us for or take away from us. Right, Nat? Isn't that why you got this idea?"

"I don't think about why I do things," replied Nathaniel, who possessed in full the Anglo-Saxon male's love of activity and disdain for introspection. And yet, he knew his brothers shared his longing, knew that they wanted what he did—maybe not as deeply, yet they did want it. And he played on that, exhorting them, inspiring them with the vision that had inspired him—of the welcome that would be theirs when they returned.

"Imagine it, the Dry Tortugas," he carried on. "It's just a short sail to Havana from there. We could send the old man postals from Cuba! Imagine how that will bowl him over, when he sees that we made it to a foreign country, not a fake foreign country like Canada but a real one."

"I like the Havana part, Natters." A look of merriment brightened Will's face. "I speak Spanish. Took it for my foreign language requirement, since it's so much easier than French. There are said to be sporting women in Havana who do things these dried-up figs of Yankee women couldn't imagine doing, and wouldn't do if they could."

"What . . . what sort of things?" Drew asked, in a voice suggesting that he wasn't sure if he wanted to hear the answer.

"Not for innocent ears." Will rifled through the charts. "Looks like we don't have any for Cuba," he said. "We'll have to pick some up on the way down."

"So do you make it three, little brother?" Nathaniel asked.

"Gee, Nat, I don't know. . . . What about Mother?"

"Oh, Mother. Mother, Mother," said Nathaniel wearily. "We'll send her a telegram. Tell her where we're going. That'll be a job for you and Eliot. Take the ferry to Camden this afternoon while Will and I work out the course. So what it'll be? No sense in thinking about it, you either go or you don't."

"Oh, all right . . . sure," answered Drew, after a long pause.

Then Nathaniel turned to the last holdout.

"Three lunatics against one sane man." Eliot shook his head, not in the negative but in disbelief at himself. "I can't let three lunatics go off on their own. It would be on my conscience."

And so they resolved to leave on the next morning's tide, the three brothers together, children of the sea in quest of a father's love, never knowing that love was the last thing they could expect from him. . . .

9

NONE OF THEM got to sleep till after midnight, and they were all awake an hour before dawn. Nathaniel was the first out of his bunk. Yawning, stretching, shaking life into his brain, he lit the lamp in the main cabin, and saw Will stretched out on the cabin sole without pillow or blanket. Late yesterday, he had said so long to his friends on the yawl and transferred himself and his belongings to *Double Eagle*. He had gone to bed in the starboard berth forward, and now he was sprawled on the cabin sole, eyes wide open, and Nathaniel asked what he was doing there.

"Must've been walking in my sleep. Forgot to warn you. The last year or so, I've started to sleepwalk."

"Oh. Thought maybe you didn't find your quarters to your liking."

"The bunk did leave something to be desired, compared to the one I had," Will said, cheerfully. He stood up in his drawers and massaged his scalp and scratched his ribs. "What the hell have you got for a mattress and springs on this ship? Felt like I was in a hayloft."

Nathaniel told him that in a way he had been; the mattresses on *Double Eagle* were made of horse breakfasts: gunny sacks filled with straw and sewn together with twine; and there were no springs in the bunks, only oak slats.

"Papa's way of making sure you don't get soft?"

"Nope. Yacht mattresses don't dry quickly if they get wet and then they mildew. Straw gets wet, you replace it. Springs rust, oak doesn't. Hey, Drew, Eliot. Up and at 'em. We'll want to make sail on this tide."

The two younger boys tumbled out and shuffled into the cabin. Eliot kindled a fire in the stove and made coffee and fried a pound of bacon in the heavy iron skillet. The stove made the cabin stuffy, so Drew opened a couple of portholes, and then everyone crowded around the folding table and ate and washed breakfast down with mugs of the scalding coffee Will dubbed "Lazarus brew"—strong enough to raise the dead.

"I don't feel raised, just yet," Eliot said. "I was awake half the night, thinking."

"Me, too," said Drew. "Gee, but it's an awful long way. That's what I was thinking. How it's an awful long way."

Nathaniel blew out the lamp, for morning twilight had begun to pour through the portholes in beams like the beams from an electric torch, except they were dull silver instead of white.

"Feet getting cold, little man?"

"No! I was figuring that if we sailed east as far as we're going south, we'd be halfway across the Atlantic."

"Just about on the money," said Will, going to the charts, now blackened with rhumb lines and compass bearings. "Thirteen hundred and seventy-five nautical miles, as the crow flies, but since we're not crows, figure our distance over water will be sixteen hundred." With the point of a pencil, he tracked the rhumbs, which would be used only as reference points, not as course bearings. Measuring the shortest distance between Nantucket Shoals and Miami, one line shot straight down the middle of the Gulf Stream, and they could not buck that current for so great a distance and hope to reach Key West before Thanksgiving. Will had explained that to them yesterday, and how they would sail inside the Stream, coasting down in a series of long tacks, Nantucket southwestward to a point off Norfolk, then due south to Cape Hatteras, that dread necropolis of luckless ships, and from there southwestward again to Daytona Beach, Daytona to Miami, and then a westering leg of some one hundred fifty miles to Key West. "There'll be times, I figure," Will continued, "when the wind will be blowing straight into this boat's nostrils. If we're lucky, we'll average four knots and make it in three weeks, but I wouldn't count on less than a month."

"Exactly what I figured." Nathaniel, squaring his shoulders, wished to remind all that he was the captain. "But coming back, we'll have the Stream astern and winds abaft, and then you watch this schooner fly. We might set a record. I'm going to like that, getting way out there in that Gulf Stream."

With a couple of looks, he told Eliot and Drew to clear and scrub the dishes and the skillet. Will stood, gave the lamp a push to make it swing on the gimbal, and watched it settle back to its original position, steady as a lamp in a room ashore.

"Could be awhile before we even get out of this harbor," he said, then went above with Nathaniel to look for auguries of a breeze.

None. A gray sky arched over a still sea, the horizon invisible so that the islands eastward looked like greenish clouds hovering in space. The trees, the boats anchored in the harbor, the gulls roosting on a mud flat—the whole scene was as motionless as a painting. Half an hour passed. A golden shimmer appeared where the horizon was supposed to be, then a red sun pushed up, like the head of some fiery infant bulging out of the gray sea's womb—water giving birth to its opposite element. Two hours went by, and still no wind came. The harbor could have been mistaken for a huge iron plate, if not for the rising fish that dimpled its surface. Another hour, and the boats began to swing on their rodes; the tide was turning, the tide Nathaniel had hoped to ride out to sea. Looking around for a ruffle on the water, he saw smoke coiling from a stovepipe on a—could it be called a ship? A hogged, shallow-draft, bargelike thing with a shanty on its deck and sides that looked as if they'd forgotten the last time they felt a paintbrush or scraper. Two crooked masts, the boom on the foremast yoked high up so it could swing over the shanty, and furled sails resembling heaps of soiled laundry completed the picture of a floating slum. It was moored to the same wharf where the brothers Kent had their lobster shack, and a big sign was hung over the gunwale amidships. Nathaniel read it through the binoculars—MERCHANDISE FOR THE ROLLING DEEP—BOOTS & SHOES REPAIRED & FOR SALE—NICHOLAS CUDLIP, COBBLER & PROP.—and remembered that he'd returned Tony Burton's shoes yesterday.

Eliot remained aboard *Double Eagle*—"to guard against pirates," he quipped—while Nathaniel rowed the tender to the trading schooner with Will and Drew.

Nicholas Cudlip was a stubby man with the quick, appraising eyes of a pawnbroker and small ears, from which so much hair sprouted it was a wonder he could hear anything softer than a gunshot. He said he was surprised, pleasantly so, to find business so early in the morning; surprised, truth to tell, to find any business at all.

"Was makin' fer Stonin'ton when I got caught by thet fog las' night," he said. "Put in heah to wait it out. Didn't reckon to make a sale heah 'mongst the folks of riches and leisure. C'mon aboard, and tell me what I kin do feryuh."

And after he was told, he led them down a companion into a hold musty and dim in the pale light struggling through skylights fogged by dirt and dried saltwater. As Will rummaged among the grocery shelves in the aft end (having provided *Double Eagle* with an extra mouth, he wished to chip in for the food to feed it), Nathaniel went to the cobbler's shop forward, where some two dozen pairs of shoes were piled any which way under a workbench. Eventually, he found a pair of brown high-tops that fit him. Cudlip started at four dollars—the price for a new pair of dress shoes. Wiser now in the ways of haggling with down-easters, Nathaniel whittled him down to a dollar-fifty. After Will paid for the tins of beef and salt pork (out of what was to have been his fare for passage to Boston), he asked the trader if he had any charts for sale.

"Do. 'T'would help if yuh told me what paat o' the ocean yuh want chaats fer."

"Cuba," Will answered.

"Cuber? We-ell naow, don't git much call fer chaats o' Cuber," said Cudlip. He stiffly climbed out of the hold, bringing his customers into the cluttered shanty that was both his home and a sundries store. Moving behind a counter, he opened a cabinet, pulled out a stack of charts three inches thick, and thumbed through them, mumbling to himself, "Cuber, Cuber. Heah yuh be."

He removed from the pile a chart of the Florida Straits showing the port of Havana and a sliver of the island's north coast. Will scowled.

"This says it was drawn up in 1868."

"Don't reckon Cuber's moved any since then. Best I kin do. Be one thin dime, if yuh want it."

Will gave him a five-dollar bill, and Cudlip asked if he had anything smaller because he couldn't make the change.

"One of you Braithwaites have a dime on him?" asked Will.

Nathaniel did, and plunked it on the counter, and Cudlip eyed him thoughtfully.

"Heard someone say Braithwaite. Any chance yuh be kin to Cap'n Cy Braithwaite?"

"We're his sons, two of 'em"—Nathaniel, jerking a thumb at Drew. "You know our dad?"

"Heard of him, tradin' amongst these gunkholes like I do. Quarriers say he's a right haad man, but he's supposedta have been a right smart sailor in his day. So are yuh young fellers plannin' to sail all the way ta Cuber?"

"Key West and maybe Cuba from there," answered Will, rolling up the chart.

"Ain't the best time o' year ta be headin' that way."

"We'll do all right"—Nathaniel, a little pompously. "'Look unto the rock whence ye are hewn, and to the quarry whence ye are digged.' Isaiah."

"Studyin' ta be a preachah?"

"I'm saying we're our father's sons, my brothers and me."

"Yuh'll needta be, yuh git in a hurricane. Got three pieces o' advice, an' yuh take 'em from an old-time sailorman. Keep yer hawsers free fer runnin', yer eyes on the weathah, an' remember that any idjit kin crack it on but the wise man knaowsta shorten sail on time." With a flicker of a wink, Cudlip reached under the counter and came up with a pencil, a pad of paper, and a tin of Copenhagen. "Heah's another piece o' advice. Write daown the name o' yer vessel, the date, and ta wheah she's bound an' wrap the tabaccer in it an' bring it ta Aunt Sophronia o'er ta Isle Au Haut," he said, pronouncing the island's name *Eye'llaholt*. "Phrony be partial ta tabaccer. She'll take care o' yuh." When none of them made a move, but only stared, as if he had begun to speak in tongues, he asked in a scandalized tone, "Yuh ain't never heard o' Aunt Phrony?"

They all three shook their heads.

"We-ell. She brings good luck ta sailormen and fishermen who show her propah respect. Y'see, she knaows the secrets o' the seas, she has command o'er wind and weathah, so it's a good idear ta fix things right with her before yuh git under way. She won't do nuthin' bad if yuh don't, she ain't no witch, but she won't do nuthin fer yuh, either, just leave yuh ta the mercy o' the sea, which in my experience ain't inclined to show much." He nudged the items across the counter. "Tabaccer's free. Wouldn't think o' chaagin' a pinny fer a offerin' ta Aunt Phrony."

Shrugging, rolling his eyes covertly at Will, Nathaniel figured it would be diplomatic to humor this superstitious seagoing peddler with the gray tufts in his ears. He wrote "*Double Eagle*—Key West / Cuba—June 17," tore the page from the pad, and wrapped it around the tin.

"You're not really going to do that, are you, Nat?"—Drew, sounding indignant. "Isle Au Haut's way out of our way for one thing, and for another, this stuff is the craziest stuff I ever heard."

"*What* did yuh say, son?" asked Cudlip, a bit indignant himself. "*Crazy*, yuh say?"

"He didn't mean anything by it," Nathaniel pleaded, angry at his kid brother's lack of tact. "C'mon, let's go, Drew."

"Hang on, I wanter heah what this young 'un thinks is crazy abaout what I said."

"Nature controls the wind and the weather, or maybe God does." Drew looked directly at Cudlip. "Not some Aunt Phrony."

"We-ell, it could be Phrony's got her a telegraph or telephone wire strung 'tween her place an' heaven, caaz everytime but one I seen ta it things was fixed right with her, an' the one time I didn't, we lost three men in the most godawful gale yuh kin think of."

"I don't mean to scoff you, mister, but there are a lot of things that cause gales and winds." Drew, to Nathaniel's consternation, insisted on pressing his point. "Like if you've got a seabreeze at night, that's because the land is cooling off faster than the water, and the air over the land rises and draws in the air from the sea. That's how science explains it. Science explains a lot of things, and one day it will explain everything."

"Ain't yuh the little Mister Smartypants."

"The family genius," said Nathaniel, laying a hand on his kid brother's shoulder. "Stop arguing with the man. Like the saying goes, time and tide don't wait."

"Yuh three are gone ta wait, caaz I got somethin' ta say that bears listenin'." Cudlip slipped around the counter and, his arms spread wide, fluttered his fingers to summon them closer. "The young signtist best listen real good. Long time ago, before I was the businessman I am naow, I was bosun's mate on a trip from Bahstun ta British Honduras ta pick up a load o' mahogany wood. Had us some payin' passengers, an' one was a signtist, studied trees an' plants an' such things in the tropics. Smack dab the middle o' the Gulf o' Mexico, we hit that gale I told yuh abaout. Likes o' which I'd never seen afore, ain't since, and hope ta never see agin. Ran with it two whole days on bare sticks, an' lost one anyways, the foremast." The trader dropped his voice once again to a confidential whisper, while the zephyrs played coolly through his window. "When that storm was at its wust, I was goin' b'low ta take my turn at the pumps. Passed the signtist's cabin, and theah he were, daown on his knees, prayin' like a man who's been told on good authority that the world's comin' ta an end in five minutes. His sci-ince weren't no good ta him then. 'Oh, Lord, I beseech you, make these winds abate,' he were sayin' words like that. When I come up from my trick, pretty much feelin' like I was climbin' a mountain in a earthquake, I seen that he were still prayin', but it still weren't doin' him no good, caaz there ain't no kinder god at sea when the wind blows that haad. That ain't blasphemin', boys. God excuses himself from the premises, an' I knaow that ta be true by the sound the winds makes when it gits ta blowin' a hunnert knots. In case yuh never heah it yerselves, an' I sure hope yuh don't, I'll tell you what it sounds like. Like the lamentations spoke of in the Good Book. The lamentations that'll rise up from the earth from all the souls o' the damned when they find out they're damned on the Day o' Judgment. Yuh don't' heah it with yer ears. Yuh heah it heah fust. . . ."

His hand dropped to cup his crotch. "An' it spreads from theah ta the rest o' yer body an' turns yer bones ta molasses an' gits past yer bones inta yer soul till yuh feel like one o' the damned yerself, an' all yer sci-incin' ain't gone ta do yuh no good then, nor yer prayin' neither. That was the trip when none aboard, includin' me, fixed things right with Aunt Phrony, an' we lost three men o'erboard and our foremast, too, an' we limped inta Nerlins in Luzeanna, forgit British Honduras, an' ever since then gunkholin' 'mongst these bays and islands is as far ta sea as I'm goin'. Naow yuh take my advice and bring that tabaccer ta her. I'll draw yuh a map."

It was dumb, Drew was saying, from his usual perch atop the cabin, it was worse than dumb to sail twelve miles east when their intended course was south, and for no better reason than to make an offering to some hag who claimed to be sovereign of wind and weather. Steering in a freshening nor'wester—an autumn wind—Nathaniel told him, "Oh, pipe down, you're making too much of it," then looked across the bay, sparkling like a jeweled robe of royal blue, toward the heights that gave Isle Au Haut its name. Yes, he had at first taken the tobacco from Cudlip with no intention of using it for the purposes prescribed, but the trader's yarn had piqued his curiosity about the old legend. Anyway, what harm was there in seeking a little extra good luck? Dad was a rational man and a Christian, yet even he, in accordance with ancient customs, had nailed a horseshoe open end up to the tip of *Double Eagle*'s bowsprit, and a gold coin to the foot of her mainmast.

They dropped anchor in the cove marked on Cudlip's map and rowed ashore, passing a shack resting precariously on canted pilings that rose almost as high as telegraph poles against the big Maine tides, the shambles of a pier behind the shack leading in waves like swells on the sea to a boatyard where two ship's carpenters up on a scaffold were planking the frame of a half-finished hull. The workmen lowered their mallets to watch the four boys beach the tender, and when they saw the strangers start toward the road that punched into the woods, each brought a finger to the bill of his cap and nodded solemnly, as if to say that he knew the purpose of the visit, and acknowledged its rightness and its gravity.

The road, covered with bootprints, ran straight as a corridor through the spruce and hemlock and ended half a mile later in a clearing fenced by what looked like untrimmed hedges but were really the fragments of an old stone wall overgrown with ivy. At the far side, an old barn leaned to one side and a house with paneless windows stood—just barely—under a roof bowed in the middle. Between the two, the remains of a wagon sat on its hubs and axles. Over this scene of dereliction, a pair of crows wheeled, the only signs of sentient life; yet a well-trodden path beat through the high weeds toward the house. Nathaniel followed it, with the note and the Copenhagen in his trouser pocket, Will and his brothers behind in Indian file, all four proceeding warily, like a delegation of nervous petitioners approaching the castle of a moody queen.

The house must have been abandoned decades ago. Its front steps were decomposed into spongy masses that retained the shape of steps without the solidity, its doorless doorway opened darkly into an interior vacant of everything except a few rotted timbers and dust and dirt inches thick. Behind the house, the remnants of a fence enclosed a field littered with rubbish, some of which appeared to be of recent origin.

"That old fart tricked us," Drew said, and looked accusingly at his eldest brother.

"Seems so," said Will. "That looks like the town dump."

Still, because the path led there, they went to have a look, and were surprised to discover freshly cut firewood stacked alongside the decayed fence, Will muttering "Well, holy mackerel and everything other kind of fish, too" when they read a note someone had tacked to a log: "For Aunt Frony. Stay warm this wintir. *Jean Frances*. Grand Banks. May 25, 1901."

They fanned out across the cluttered ground, truly a field of rags and bones: a frayed sweater here, a knit cap there, a pair of ladies shoes, other stuff too rotted or rusted to identify, and sometimes, peeking shyly through the green tares, a gravestone that had been set flat into the ground, with an inscription trod and weathered to near illegibility. "In loving memory . . ." read one fragment. Further on, another—"Ebenezer Reed, Born November 19th, 1731, brother of . . ." and then nothing but marks as indecipherable as glyphs in a Babylonian tablet. A cemetery and a rubbish heap, but the rubbish wasn't rubbish: Scattered everywhere were scraps of paper pinned by rocks so they wouldn't blow away, or by corroded tins of snuff and chewing tobacco. The scraps bore messages, but like the markers' inscriptions, they had borne too much insult from sun, rain, or frost to be read. Except for two discovered by Eliot, one tied around a metal box of Twining's tea, the other wrapping a container like the one in Nathaniel's pocket. The first was from a ship called the *Reuben Phillips*, departed for Charleston just this past April 9th. "For Aunt Phrony. Grant safe passage to *Golden Rocket*," read the second. "Bound for Caracas, May 6, 1901."

"Ain't this just something?"—Eliot, hands on his hips, gazing in wonder at the offerings. "Ain't this just the weirdest something you ever saw?"

"Hey, have a look at this, if you think that's something," called Will, who was a little ahead, flattening a clump of tall weeds around a quartet of tombstones. They had been put upright in the ground, and though they now tottered one way or the other, the names and dates and sentiments carved into the slate could be read if you looked closely.

The first said:

"To the memory of Capt. Uriah Reed, born Devon, England, 1727. Reported lost at sea off the coast of Georgia. September 17, 1769. Erected by his loving wife, Sophronia Reed."

And the next:

"Nathan Reed. Beloved son of Uriah and Sophronia. Born April 14, 1757. Drowned off Eastern Head. June 9, 1768."

Then the third, another chapter in a mournful tale:

"Alden Reed. Beloved son of Uriah and Sophronia. Born Oct. 12, 1754. Died at sea in an engagement with the British off South Carolina. May 16, 1777."

And finally, the one before which the gifts and petitions from schoonermen and fishermen and every other kind of mariner lay at their thickest, the tablet leaning forward as if it were bowed by the losses suffered by the woman whose grave it marked:

"Sophronia Reed. Devoted wife of Uriah. Beloved mother of Alden, Nathan, Abigail, and Susan. Born Devon, England, 1731. Died Isle Au Haut, Maine. February 11, 1833. 'Death is a debt to Nature due / Which I have paid & so must you.' "

"Jiminy. A hundred and two!" said Eliot. "Didn't think anybody but Methuselah lived that long."

The stones and the story they told with such stark brevity induced silence in Nathaniel. He felt something like awe, a sense that here in this lonely place resided a mystery as beyond sounding as the deepest part of the sea that had robbed this woman of husband and sons.

"Well, I sure don't get why everybody comes to her for good luck," Drew remarked, scratching the side of his head. He motioned at the other tombstones. "Sure didn't do her own kin much good, did she?"

It was like hearing a blasphemy uttered in a church, and Nathaniel turned on him angrily.

"Shut up! Don't you get it?"

He stood for a moment, reflecting, and then lay *Double Eagle*'s offering atop the others and said:

"Okay. It's done. Let's go."

As *Double Eagle* sailed out of the cove, each of the carpenters raised an arm high and waved a stately farewell. Nathaniel waved back, but the men did not return to work; they continued to watch the schooner's departure, as if to take their eyes off her before she was out of sight would be to violate some code or protocol; and all the while, they swung their arms to and fro with a slow, grave motion that signaled more than mere goodbye but brotherhood, as well. Maybe, thought Nathaniel, they went as ship's carpenters on long voyages when there were no jobs for them ashore, and were saluting fellow seamen.

The schooner cleared the headland at the mouth of the cove, and immediately heeled in the gathering norther. Spinning the helm down, Nathaniel called to ease sheets, lined up his wake with Isle Au Haut light, and put the beacon on Saddleback Ledge off his starboard bow. *Double Eagle* bore off south by west. Will lashed the Bliss patent log near a corner of the stern rail, to keep the log line clear of the tender davit, then flung the finned torpedo astern, the line coming taut and the torpedo diving into the wake, where it sent back a trail of bubbles like pale green smoke.

"Six and a half," he said, looking at the speed indicator.

Nathaniel thought they could do better in a wind like this (it seemed Aunt Phrony had blessed them already, giving them a brisk nor'wester in the middle of June) and told his brothers to let out the sails a little more. The boat picked up a fraction of a knot. The breeze was holding steady at fifteen, and there was some discussion, as they clipped past the Saddleback beacon, about whether to set topsails. The discussion went on among the four, and within Nathaniel himself, for there was a duality in his nature that the sea brought out. His conservative voices argued that it was better to err on the side of caution, while his daredevils prodded him to clap on all the canvas the craft could bear. The result of both the external and the internal deliberations was a nice parliamentary compromise: the jib topsail only.

Saying that he needed the exercise, Will went forward, set and trimmed the sail, and came back again to read the log: seven and a quarter. Westward, beyond the Brimstone Islands, Vinalhaven showed varying shades of green as sunlight and cloud shadow played over its forests. It looked much closer than five miles away, the nor'wester having scoured all summer haze from the sky. A thought of Constance, there in the big yellow house across the thorofare from Vinalhaven, ghosted through Nathaniel's mind. His expression must have betrayed him (he did not have his mother's or half brother's talent for masking emotion;

every passing mood registered immediately on his face), because Eliot slapped him on the back and said, "This trip was your idea, big brother, so cheer up and forget her."

Eliot hopped below and brought up his guitar.

After strumming a few bars to let everyone know the tune, he sang out, with a revision of one of the female names in the actual lyrics:

> *Sing so long to Connie and so long to Sue,*
> *Way you Rio!*
> *And you who are listening, sing so long to you,*
> *For we're bound to the Rio Grande.*

It was a fine, lively, capstan chantey, a tune of departure, and Eliot's voice did it justice. They sang the chorus together, pronouncing "Rio" in the old down-east sailor's way, *Rye-o.*

> *And away Rio. Way you Rio!*
> *Sing fare ye well my bonny young girls,*
> *For we're bound to the Rio Grande.*

His fingers moving skillfully over strings and frets, Eliot led them into the next verse, which he'd also revised to suit local geography:

> *Oh, you North Haven ladies, we will let you know,*
> *Way you Rio!*
> *We're bound to the south'ard, O Lord let her go,*
> *For we're bound to the Rio Grande.*

And the chorus again, sung heartily into the wind and to the fitting accompaniment of crackling bow spray:

> *And away Rio. Way you Rio!*
> *Sing fare ye well my bonny young girls,*
> *For we're bound to the Rio Grande.*

Vinalhaven slipped past their starboard quarter, and they gained on tiny Matinicus, lying low in the distance, passed it, and reached for the open Gulf of Maine. The mainland heights fell farther and farther away, until they could see no land anywhere, nor beacons either, only the great unbroken circle of the sea. Sparkling with spray, the bowsprit pointed bravely southward. Will grinned like a thief who's made off with the diamonds.

"Looks like we are really doing it, Natters."

"Sure are," said Nathaniel, and, glancing astern, was pleased to note the straightness of the glittering furrow *Double Eagle* ploughed across the blue-green plain.

10

THEY HAD LEFT at half past noon, and when the sun set nine hours later, the log was still reading seven and a quarter knots. Will reckoned the distance and plotted their position: a little north of forty-three degrees north latitude, on about the same parallel as Kittery. They could not see Kittery; it lay farther west of *Double Eagle* than she was south of Isle Au Haut, about seventy nautical miles. This fact was announced by Drew, who was honing his navigational skills under Will's tutelage. He then declared a corollary fact, much as a character in a fairy tale would declare entrance into the domain of an ogre: "We've never been this far off shore," he said, meaning himself and his brothers. "We were never more than fifty miles out when we were coming back from Nova Scotia."

The distance should not have made any difference; fifty miles, seventy, or a thousand—it was all the same to Drew if he could not see land. But he was something of a paradox, a boy who loved and even worshiped cold dry facts, mathematical facts particularly; yet he was cursed with the imagination of an excitable poet. To his mind, those extra twenty miles became something more than a statistic; they were the measure of how far he had been cut off from all that was familiar, exiled to a void without reference points, a kind of Sahara constantly in motion. As he looked at the restless immensity, its blue shading toward black in the looming twilight, his pallor grew more sallow and he found that he was having difficulty breathing. These same symptoms had appeared on the trip back from Canada, and he applied the remedy that had worked then; focusing on a point at his feet, he avoided looking out, in much for the same reason that someone phobic about heights avoids looking down from a ladder or the edge of a cliff. Will told him that holding his eyes on the deck instead of on the horizon would only make him queasier. Nathaniel set Will straight: Drew's malady wasn't *that* kind of seasickness, it was *this* kind, he said, pointing at his temple. It made Drew sick to be out of sight of land.

"We haven't seen land for the past few hours," Will remarked, perplexed. He had never heard of such a thing. "Why now, all of a sudden?"

It came on in spells, Nathaniel explained. The best cure for it was a good blow. That was what happened last year, crossing the mouth of the Bay of Fundy; *Double Eagle* was struck by a pretty good blow, and Drew got physically sick and forgot all about being sick the other way. Will wasn't pleased to hear this. Drew was his watch mate. Would he be expected to man the wheel by himself throughout every four-hour trick?

"Don't worry," Drew said. He resented hearing himself spoken about as if he weren't there. "It just makes me kind of nervous, and anyway, it goes away after a while." Raising his head, he forced himself to look toward the eastern horizon. "There. See. Doesn't bother me. I'm okay now."

NATHANIEL AND ELIOT took half-hour turns at the wheel. While one tended the helm, the other kept lookout for approaching ships. They marveled at the steadiness of the wind; it blew as smoothly as oil flowed, with barely a hole, header, or lift in it, and the schooner needed so little steering that she seemed to be racing down an invisible track grooved into the sea by a benevolent spirit. The spirit of Aunt Phrony? They spoke about her for a while, asking themselves how and when the superstition got started and if there could be anything to it. If there wasn't, then why, Nathaniel wondered aloud, had belief in her guardian powers persisted right down to this day? It was a matter of raw luck—that was Eliot's opinion. There must have been a lot of sailors who'd done everything right by her but never made it back home. The ones who had probably went around telling everybody that they owed their lives to Aunt Phrony, and everybody believed them.

"Maybe"—Nathaniel, after a short silence. "Still and all, when we were there, by her grave? I kind of felt like something was there. It was like what you feel in a church. You know that feeling?"

"Bored?" Eliot asked. "That's the only feeling I get in church."

"And never anything else?"

"Nope."

Nathaniel looked at him, long enough to put a kink in the fine, ruled line of phosphorescence trailing astern. The sails luffed, telling him that he had veered off course. He tweaked the helm and brought her back on.

"But you believe in it, don't you?" he inquired, tentatively. He and Eliot generally stayed off the topic of religion.

"Honest truth?"

"Honest truth."

"Honest truth is that what makes sense to me is something I read in this book my roommate showed me last term. The idea is that God is like an engineer," Eliot said. "He built the universe, but once he got it to running right, he left it alone to build something else, maybe another universe. He comes back every now and then to tinker with it, maybe to fix a planet or star that's a little off kilter. He checks the dials to make sure the steam and the oil pressure's at the right level. Stuff like that. The big stuff. He doesn't think about or care about every last little screw and bolt and nut in the thing. He doesn't sit up there, listening to you and me every time we pray for something, like a new bicycle for Christmas, and He isn't taking notes every time you or me does something wrong."

"Boy, I bet the Sky Pilot would have your hide for saying that," Nathaniel said, in a reference to the school chaplain.

"Let him. Look at all that up there. . . ." Eliot's hand swept the sky, so filled with stars that it was in places more white than black. "That's a lot to look after, even if you're God. Do you reckon He's all worried whether you get a new bike, or that He takes notes every time you think about Constance and start playing with Fivefinger Mary?"

That caused Nathaniel to put another curl in the schooner's wake.

"I don't do that!"

"Oh, sure, you don't."

"I mean, I don't think about Constance and do that."

"Whoever you think about, God isn't writing it down and telling the devil to get a room ready for you in hell. He's too busy with more important stuff."

Nathaniel mulled over this notion for a time and decided he couldn't accept it. He much preferred the idea that he and all mankind were under the eye of heaven, but he didn't want to argue the point.

"Well, as long as you think that God exists, I guess that's the important thing," he said, and with that they stopped talking. The sea at night sometimes turns sailors into chatterboxes—the sound of the human voice can be comforting in all that vastness—but there always comes the moment when it commands silence, commands that it be listened to, as it sighs and breathes and rolls on, more indifferent to the fates of those who pass over its skin than the God of whom Eliot had spoken.

They sailed on, and doused the binnacle lamp and steered by the stars. Nathaniel found that he could hold course by keeping Spica in Virgo, between the mainmast and the shroud on the starboard side. It pleased him to not rely on an instrument for direction, and it exhilarated him to know that he was farther offshore than he had ever been. He only wished he were even farther, away out where the great ships went on their errands of war and commerce. With Will along to help with navigation, he was sure he could handle most anything the ocean had a mind to throw his way. His belief in a just and caring God—a belief as yet untried by a loved one's death, by crippling disease, by crushing failure, by hunger, poverty, or by any of the countless ordeals and afflictions employed by the eye of heaven to test one's faith—was the mother of his belief in himself, another faith that had yet to be tried. The spell of self-doubt that nagged him after his father had put him in charge of the ship and his brothers was too minor to count as a trial, and he was fully recovered from it now, restored to the Nathaniel who was captain of the boxing team and the junior varsity football squad, the Nathaniel who had won so many ribbons in sailboat races that he regarded it as an upset in the natural order of things when he didn't take first place. Of the three kinds of confidence—that of experience, of stupidity, and of ignorance—his was the third, which is to say that it was the confidence of a strong, healthy, athletic, good-looking son of a prosperous family, whose experience of life was confined to Back Bay Boston, summer resorts, and a prep-school campus. He suffered from the delusion of immortality common to all young people (except those who have lost it in wars or disasters), but the congenial circumstances of his life had also put a blind spot in his imagination. He could not conceive of anything bad happening to him, simply because nothing ever had. There was, however, a bright patch in his otherwise unenlightened state. Ignorance, in contrast to stupidity, is not invincible; it can be overcome by education.

"WHAT I DID when we went off this morning was take three point bearings." Will, sitting at the chart table, assumed a professorial air as he instructed Drew in the finer points of celestial navigation. He pointed at his plotting sheet, held down at three of its corners by the Nautical Almanac, the Reduction Tables, and the latest edition of Bowditch's

Practical Navigator, and at the fourth by his own sextant, a handsome Hughes with an ebony-wood frame. "I crossed Polaris for the latitude and got the longitude from Arcturus and Capella, and that gave us a good fix. Why, old Nat couldn't have done better, himself—not our Nat, this Nat," he said, rapping the *Practical Navigator* with his knuckles. "This Nat once sailed straight into Salem harbor in a dungeon of fog *three days* after he'd taken his last sights. That's how confident he was. And now I'll show you how confident I am of my accuracy. I will show you, pretty darn close to the yard, where we were as of four this morning. We were right here." He laid his palm flat on the chart, covering about a hundred square miles of the Gulf of Maine. Drew's expression, one of sober attentiveness, did not change, nor did his gaze lift from the chart and the plotting sheet scribed with the lines representing the intersection of the pole star with Arcturus and Capella. "I made a joke," Will said. "You're supposed to laugh. Smile, anyway."

"Kid brother is as brainy as they make 'em, but there's some things he don't get," remarked Eliot, who was at the dining table, writing a letter to their mother, timing the strokes of his pen to the slow, lazy roll of the boat.

"That's the kind of wiseacre thing I'd expect from Nat," Drew said. "How could you tell what the joke was, anyhow? You couldn't see what he did."

"I was making a general observation."

"Well, I got the joke. I just didn't think it was funny."

"I'll try to do better next time," Will said. He picked up the parallel rule and a pencil and marked a little X on the chart. "Since we are being so damned serious, that's where we were as of four this morning. So, if we'd had to find safe harbor, what would we have done?"

Drew peered over his shoulder.

"Hauled on the wind for Gloucester."

"But on what course?" Will joined Gloucester to the X with one arm of the rule, walked the other to the Compass Rose, and, squinting, read off the bearing. "Two fifty-one. What d'you say?"

"I'd say two fifty-one was wrong. That's the reading off the outer scale, the true north scale. You steer by the inner scale, the magnetic north scale. Two sixty-six, because the declination is fifteen degrees west. That's kid stuff. My dad taught me that last year. Were you trying to trick me?"

"Merely testing the level of your aptitude." Will lightly penciled a line across some seventy miles of water. "So, if we had been blinded by fog and for any reason had to put into Gloucester, we could have done so, just as confidently as Nathaniel Bowditch put into Salem in days of yore. A good Christian who takes good sights has no fear of fog. Next kid-stuff question. Why did I shoot those stars at four instead of at two or three?"

The rising sun reddened the rocks of Paradise Cliffs, and Thacher's Island, with its twin lighthouses, looked like a picture Drew had seen in a book of a Muhammadan mosque. . . . Eastern Point appeared, its light flashing welcome, welcome, welcome in the dawn. . . . Passing Ten Pound Island, *Double Eagle* slipped into the inner harbor and toward the forest of masts rising above the wharves. . . . Drew stepped off the boat onto land, blessed, motionless land. . . .

"Still with me?" asked Will.

"What?"

"Why did I take my sights at four this morning instead of at two or three?"

"Because a sextant measures the angle between a heavenly body and the horizon," he answered, parroting his father's lesson, word for word. "It had to be light enough for you to see the horizon."

"Thus endeth the kid stuff. Now you're going to take a sun sight and we'll figure out where we are at this moment."

"We can see where we are," said Eliot, looking up from his letter.

"It's for purposes of instruction," Will informed him, and took his sextant on deck, where Nathaniel stood at the wheel, yawning.

"Don't think we've gone half a mile since that breeze quit," he said, motioning at the dark wall of Siasconset Head in the distance.

He had been looking at it from the same angle for almost an hour now, and was growing irritated as well as bored. *Double Eagle* had logged an astonishing one hundred and seventy-four miles in her first twenty-four hours, inspiring Nathaniel to make some optimistic mental calculations—at that rate, they would get to Key West in nine more days. As if to rebuke him for such presumptuousness, the wind stopped, and the schooner began to wallow, on long, gentle swells, across the mouth of Nantucket Sound.

"My opinion, the god of the wind is about to change his mind," Will said, going to the mainmast with the sextant. "We'll get a breeze presently, and it'll be right where it should be this time of year—in our faces." Kneeling on both knees, he then turned to Drew. "All right, my budding Magellan. Kneel like I am and spread 'em, you'll be steadier that way. Yonder is the sun, yonder the horizon. Give it a try."

Drew looped the lanyard around his wrist, put his eye to the sighting scope, and aimed the sextant at the sun—and was baffled when it failed to appear. He swung the instrument back and forth, up and down, and suddenly it was there, its glare subdued and its color changed by the filter on the horizon mirror, so that it appeared in the scope like the dim, greenish sun of some alien world.

"Now move the arm till the bottom of the sun touches the horizon. We'll use the lower limb for this sight," said Will, patiently. "Soon as it touches, you say 'mark.' Okay?"

For some reason, the arm would not move. Drew pushed the knob a little harder, at the same instant that the boat lurched. He watched the green orb plummet and disappear, as if some invisible hand had snatched it from the sky.

"I sunk it, Will."

"No, you didn't. Who do you think you are? The Almighty? Try it again."

On his fourth attempt, the sun, or, rather, its reflection in the split mirror, swung down to within an inch of the horizon. He made a slight adjustment and called out, "Mark!" when it appeared to float on the surface of the sea.

Will glanced at his watch.

"Call it eleven minutes, thirty seconds past two," he said. "What's the sextant read?"

Turning the instrument on its side, Drew squinted at the ivory scale on the arm.

"Sixty-eight . . . no . . . sixty-nine degrees."

"Okay. Now it's below to do the computations. That's the hard part."

Drew did not move. Looking through the sighting scope again, he savored practicing his new skill, and the feeling of power it gave him to control the movements of the sun. With a touch of his finger, he made it set; another touch and it rose. He bounced it on the horizon like a ball until Will scolded him. A sextant wasn't a toy.

"Figure out where we're at?" asked Eliot as they spread plotting sheets, the chart, rule, and dividers on the dining table. "Bet I can without a sextant." Eyes closed, hands folded on his chest, he rocked back and forth and chanted, "Abracadabra, mooktar kazaam. Tell me, O genie, where in the hell I am." He popped his eyes open, shook his head, as one coming out of a trance. "The genie has spoken. About ten miles north northeast of Nantucket. Is that close, Will?"

Will, a look of tried forbearance on his long face, suggested that he go up and keep lookout for Nathaniel. There were a great many vessels about.

"Aye-aye, second in command." Eliot gave an exaggerated salute. "Maybe there's a sense of humor above decks."

"And now that we are free of distraction, we shall see how much Papa taught you," Will said to Drew. "When you took the sight, the sun was ninety degrees over a certain point on the earth at that moment. That's called its geographic position. Everything we use in navigation— sun, moon, stars, planets—has a geographic position, and we can look it up in here." He motioned at the thick, formidable-looking *Nautical Almanac*. "Got that? You'd better, because what we do with the sextant is plot where we are in relation to that heavenly body's position over the earth. And it's real important, I would say very, no, critically important that you note the time of your sight as exact as you can. And why?"

"Because the sun and planets and stuff are all moving."

"How fast?" asked Will. "If, say, you shot your sight, and then took four seconds to tie your shoe before you noted the time, how far would the sun have moved?"

"Pretty far, I'd reckon."

"Give you a hint. The earth rotates on its axis at nine hundred miles per hour."

Drew bowed his head, struggling to recall his father's lectures of a year ago. The solution came to him when he stopped working for it, came to him, as solutions to mathematical problems often did, in a burst more like a revelation than an answer arrived at step by laborious step.

"One mile," he replied, and Will's approving nod warmed him inside—the same feeling he got when his teacher at Boston Latin congratulated him for solving equations, or when the minister at Sunday school applauded him for reciting the books of the Bible first in alphabetical order, Acts to Zephaniah, and then chronologically, Genesis to Revelations. He could not box or play football the way Nat did, nor row like Eliot, who was a star on the Andover crew, and so he craved and delighted in the rewards his mind won for him.

"A mile," said Will. "That's how far we'd be off if we dawdled four seconds before noting the time. Now, a mile won't make much difference if you're not going far, but sail far enough long enough on a mistake like that and you'll end up in Africa, when you thought you were going to Ireland. Thus endeth that lesson."

They went on to others as the schooner rose and fell on the long swells, and the sails hung listless as parlor drapes and the booms swung with the creaky, banging racket that is the sound of a becalmed vessel. To find one's actual position, Will lectured, you must first plot an assumed position, that is, where you think you are. Generally, the assumed position is taken from dead reckoning. You then make six visits to the *Nautical Almanac* and three to the Reduction Tables, and after doing twenty-one computations, plot your line of position by comparing the sextant reading at the time of the sight to the assumed position's sextant reading.

Will led his pupil through the painstaking process, and the experience was like being in a dark room divided by numerous curtains of diminishing thickness. At first, all was opaque; then the first curtain rose and he saw a faint, faint light. Up went the next curtain, and the light grew a little brighter. He grappled with Greenwich hour angle, which was the same as a heavenly body's longitude, and with local hour angle; with declination, dip corrections, refraction corrections, and other mysteries. He concentrated mightily and felt that his brain would suffer muscle strain in its efforts to lift all the curtains and bring the mysteries into the full radiance of comprehension.

Nat struck out at whatever or whoever frightened or threatened or confused him—in the gale last year, he had yelled at the wind—and Eliot joked or sang his way through the dark and scary places; Drew subdued his terrors with his reason, confined the powers of the unknown within a corral of knowledge. Once, when he was nine, an awesome thunderstorm had driven him to hide under the bed, where he lay quivering alongside Trajan. He felt so foolish, finding refuge with a frightened cat, that he went to the library the next day and began to study up on thunderstorms. He versed himself in the formation of cumulonimbus, on the causes of atmospheric instability, on updrafts and convection currents. Now, when a bad storm struck, he would tell himself that what looked like a blazing, jagged arm intent on his destruction was nothing more than the separation of an electrical charge caused by the interaction of water and ice crystals in the storm cloud; he would mutter to himself, with each ear-splitting, window-rattling crash, "That is only the sound of a shock wave caused by the extreme heating and expansion of the air as the lightning channel passes through it." He would utter such phrases over and over, in much the same way as an Amazonian shaman, cowering in his hut while heaven roars and blazes, utters incantations to quiet the wrath of his pagan gods. Drew's scientific chants did not prevent his heart from leaping when lightning flashed, nor his body from flinching when thunder cracked, but they did give him mastery over his fears. He no longer hid under the bed with Trajan. That was the difference between being a human and a cat.

Yesterday, after the last glimmer of land vanished, vanished, in his recollection, as if the entire continent had been nothing more than a mirage, he was sorry he had allowed himself to be bullied and shamed into going on this voyage. He had been afraid of what his brothers would think of him if he'd stayed behind, of what his father would think, and most of all, of what he would think of himself—fears that seemed trivial compared to the anxiety the featureless sea later awakened in him. No trees, hills, and headlands to give you at least a hint of where you were. When you were far out upon it, every part of the ocean looked like every other part; although your wake or the dial on a log said that you were moving, you did not seem to be going anywhere but floating on a monotonous circle of infinite dimensions, its horizons ever receding and never reached. But he now saw in this art of celestial navigation the means to conquer his terror of that emptiness. If he could master the sextant and the bewildering tables, if he could build a bridge from the sea to the heavens, then he need never again feel lost and disoriented out here. The sun, the stars, and the planets would be his trees, hills, and headlands.

The computations were as simple as Will had promised—sixth grade stuff—but following the steps in the procedure was tedious. Finally, Drew set down his pencil and let out a breath, pretty much feeling the way he did after a tough examination.

"What do you come up with?" asked Will, combing his hair with his fingers.

Shyly, he pushed the piece of paper, blackened with numbers, across the table.

"Last year, with our dad? Nat put us in Salt Lake City," he said, hoping to deflect criticism in case he had made an error.

"And how did you do?"

"I didn't get as far as doing all this. Dad thought it was too complicated for me, on account of I was only twelve."

Will studied the figures for a while, plotted the fix on the chart, and, after pausing to light a cigarette, declared that Drew had not done badly for a novice.

"I didn't?"

"You got us a lot closer than Salt Lake City. Rhode Island—Providence, to be exact. About eighty miles from where we now sit. Show you your mistakes," he said, and turned the page of calculations around so Drew could read them. "Right here, you forgot to note if the declination was plus or minus, that's a pretty common error, and here, in these two places, you did the addition as if there are one hundred minutes in a degree. You forgot that there are only sixty minutes, and that's a common error, too. Thirty minutes and forty minutes don't make seventy minutes, they make one degree, ten minutes."

He could not believe he had made such a fundamental mistake. He had been so careful! A troubling thought came to him. He had shot the sight and done all the computations in a dead calm; how could he possibly manage it in a heavy sea, with the sextant bouncing and *Almanac* and tables and charts sliding all over the place?

THE WIND came up as it had quit, with no forewarning, dragging a great gray train of squalls up from the south. The clouds were full of heavy drops that pelted *Double Eagle*'s decks with a sound like falling gravel. Close-hauled, with topsails doused and reefs in her fore and main, she labored against the wind and rising seas. There was nothing of her usual elegance in her efforts as she battered her way through an endless succession of iron-colored ridges. Ahead, and a few points off to starboard, Nantucket showed through the rain as a brown, indistinct shape with a quality of desolation about it. A pod of whales appeared, the spray from their blowholes like smoke. One dove, its tail five yards from tip to tip straight up; a minute later, it breached, forty feet and God-knew-how-many tons clearing the water, the stove bolts in its head identifying it as a humpback. It hung in the air for a moment and then struck with an explosion such as might be made by a shell from a battleship's biggest gun.

On the dogwatch, with Will steering, the schooner was able to hold her course in the channel that led through the Nantucket shoals. But the wind crept forward, forcing her close to the island. Several times in the next half hour, he tried to coax *Double Eagle* to windward, but she would have none of it, and little by little, she was headed out of the channel into the ground swells that heaved over the shoals. This was one time that Drew was not comforted by proximity to land. Buttoned up in his oilers, rain dripping from his sou'wester's bill, he watched the tide rips, leaping in standing waves peaked as witches' hats, and imagined the submerged hazards passing under the keel. And not very far under, either, said Will. Three fathoms was the average depth on the shoals, and in places it was only two at low tide, and the tide was now getting right close to dead low, and with the schooner drawing seven feet, things could get interesting. Stomping the deck three times, he summoned Nathaniel from his dry slumbers. When he appeared, his oilskin jacket draped over his shoulders like a cape, Will recommended that they come about, run back up the channel, and go around the other side of Nantucket, through Nantucket Sound. The waters there were tricky, Will said, but he knew them pretty well, and the seas were bound to be quieter in Nantucket's lee. Maybe by the time they rounded the island, the wind would have turned more favorable, and they could get back on course.

And so they tacked and reached westward across the Sound, then beat through Muskeget Channel between Nantucket and Martha's Vineyard, and by the following noon, under a sky still dreary and with a Force 6 wind still blowing on their nose, they were forty miles closer to the mainland but not much further south from where they had started. To make any southing at all, *Double Eagle* had to be tacked and tacked again, her course a series of zigzags over a sea the color of pea soup. Wearied by the constant back and forth, they surrendered to the wind and went eastward on a reach, into the open sea, but the waves out there ran very high and Drew got sick, and so they changed direction, heading inshore, where they sailed into a thick, a very thick thick. It was as if *Double Eagle* were inside a cloud of clammy gray wool. They could see only a few yards, except in the moments when the cloud thinned, offering a slightly longer view of, say, fifty yards. The view was always of the same thing: waves surging like liquid granite.

"Wind hasn't quit"—Nathaniel, narrowing his eyes, craning his neck, as if he could see through the mist by sheer muscular effort. "Can't ever understand how you can have high wind and fog at the same time. You'd think . . ."

"Wind doesn't have anything to do with it," Drew said. "What causes fog is—"

"I don't give a damn what causes it. Fog is fog, all right, little brother? Means you can't see a damn thing like rocks and shoals and other ships. What difference does it make what causes it?"

Drew considered it best not to reply and went below to rest.

Nathaniel began to ring the bell to warn approaching vessels of *Double Eagle*'s presence. An hour later, he heard the metallic banging, rhythmic as a drumbeat, of a big ship's engines. The fog toyed with the sound; it seemed very close one moment; five seconds later, he could barely hear it, only to have it resume, louder than before. When a shape appeared through the murk, indistinct, huge, and horrifyingly near, he remembered every sea legend he had heard: those tales of steamers putting into port with the masts and rigging of small craft dangling from their hawsepipes, of fog-blinded liners cleaving Grand Banks schooners in half. He yanked the bell frantically, though he was sure no one aboard the ship could hear it over the throb of the engines, magnified by an atmosphere neither liquid nor gas, but something in between. Then it came to him that the vessel wasn't bearing down on them, but passing alongside, although very close. He watched it sail by, a looming shadow high as a building, majestic, menacing, its stern churning a wake that rolled *Double Eagle* sharply while the seas pitched her up and down. A few seconds after the steamer passed, her foghorn tardily let out a blast.

11

SIX HOURS LATER, Will shook him out of dreamless unconsciousness, and he was back on deck. The fog still lay upon the surface of the sea and a heavy dew dripped from the rigging. The masthead and stern lamps had been lit and the sidelights cast diffused auras of red and green. Under the binnacle light, the compass card showed they were still bearing almost due west. Will said that best as he could reckon, they were outside Rhode Island Sound, somewhere between Block Island and Martha's Vineyard.

"Keep a sharp eye out, because I'm not real sure exactly where. . . . Jesus Christ, what's that?"

He pointed alongside, at a luminous oblong shape far below the surface. It rose rapidly out of the depths, growing larger and brighter. Its ascent stopped a fathom or two down, and it was longer than the boat, a size that instilled, rather than fear, the static wonderment people feel when looking at a high mountain. It swam alongside for several minutes, gliding silently under the black waves; then, with a sweep of its huge tail—Will and Nathaniel could make out the luminescent flukes—the sea monster sounded, grew smaller and smaller, and then was gone.

"Well, that'll be one to tell around the old hearth this winter," said Will. "Must have been another humpback, and a grandaddy, too. Not sure I can turn in now, wondering if he's got a chum nearby with a less friendly disposition."

But he went to bed anyway, and Nathaniel and Eliot were only fifteen minutes into their watch when they shouted, "Breakers!" Will hurried up the companionway, in time to see the fog shred momentarily, giving them a glimpse, in gauzy moonlight, of seas crashing on rocks beneath a bluff a quarter of a mile dead ahead. While Will took the helm, the Braithwaites manned the sheets. "Ready about! Hard aaah-leeee!" Will's voice hit a hysterical pitch. Sails snapped, lines flew, and he spun the helm down hard, the schooner pivoting on her keel to slide into a trough broadside. Finally, she began to sail away from danger, fighting for every yard of sea room, her weather rail riding high and her crew standing on the slanted deck like climbers on a hillside. Rounding the point, they saw a lighthouse high up the bluff, its beacon sabering through the fog. A check of the charts, and Will announced that the light marked Montauk Point.

"Montauk!" hollered Nathaniel. "Christ, Will, we're thirty miles west of where you thought. We damned near cracked into the whole United States of America!"

Apologizing as humbly as he could, but without undue compromise of his dignity, Will admitted his error, pleading that fog and exhaustion had caused it.

The fog lifted with the dawn, but the wind held tenaciously from the south. Figuring it was the remnant of a tropical storm that might take a couple of days to blow through, Will suggested they either tuck into some nice little hole somewhere and wait it out, or set a course for New York City through Long Island Sound. At the mention of New York, Drew and Eliot perked up, but Nathaniel wriggled a finger in his ear to pretend that he hadn't heard correctly.

"We don't have to be in Key West on a certain date, do we?" asked Will rhetorically. "So, instead of sitting idle in some gunkhole or beating our brains out, let's keep this wind on our beam and have us a damn fine sail through the Sound. A side trip to New York City. A corking good meal somewhere, a hot bath . . ."

"And one of your whorehouses, I'll bet."

"The possibility occurred to me."

"Sounds like a fine idea," said Eliot.

"A whorehouse? You've never been to one, and if you were in one you wouldn't know what to do if they gave you a diagram and a set of directions."

"I meant, New York sounds like a good idea," Eliot said to Nathaniel. "Besides, I've got to mail my letter somewhere."

"Go all the way to New York, a hundred damn miles, to mail a letter?"

"Well, we owe Mother a letter. We owe it to her to let her know more than what we said in the telegram." He paused. "And come to think of it, we could look up Lockwood in New York. Maybe he knows what's going on with the old man. Maybe we could find out if we were right about him being in a pickle and all."

Nathaniel could feel his crew's desires as an almost palpable pressure. Already, they needed a rest from the sea. He foresaw mutinous emotions arising if he did not accommodate them.

"Ain't this bully?" he said, sharply. "I got grief for going twelve miles out of the way and now everybody wants to go a hundred. For a hot bath and to mail a letter. Like we're nothing but a bunch of sea-going tourists."

"When you think about it, that's exactly what we are," Will said.

They went in past Gardiner's Island, and then between Plum Island and Orient Point, and reached toward the Connecticut shore, a gentle shore where the rocks looked smaller and less forbidding than in Massachusetts or Maine, and salt meadows cut into shady summer woods surrounding white towns like Mystic and Stonington and Essex. Cruising past the mouth of the Connecticut River, they picked up a passenger, a chestnut-banded kingfisher that landed on their taffrail and rode with them till sunset, when it took off and winged shoreward, into a marsh among whose spartina plains great egrets stalked like predacious angels. By late afternoon, after passing stone lighthouses rising from shoals and isolated rocks (the keepers and their families sometimes waving at them from the towers), they were trolling strips of pork rind behind the boat, along the Norwalk islands. They caught two fair-sized bluefish, and off the Sheffield Light, passed a fisherman who asked where they were bound. They told him and he spat a stream of tobacco juice over the side, but it wasn't clear if he was just cleaning his mouth or commenting on their chances of ever reaching Key West. "Watch out for Hell Gate when you're passin' through New York," he called from his little sloop. "Don't try and sail against that current. Rocks enough there to make a nation of striped bass happy. Wait for the ebb and ride it through and hang on tight."

They dropped the hook and stayed the night, because they didn't want to tackle the Gate in darkness, and were under way again a little after sunrise. The Sound began to narrow and finally reduced itself to the East River. The tide was already on the ebb, spilling westward with concentrated force through the necks and around islands toward New York Bay; it was as if the great city, still unseen by *Double Eagle*'s crew, were drawing all that water into itself. Borne by the current, they sailed past the farms and villages of the Bronx, following the waterway in its sharp hook southward. The river contracted, the current accelerated, and, ripping between lumber yards and low ranges of coal mountains rising over banks solid with iron barges moored end to end, carried the schooner by Wards Island and into Hell Gate—a confusion of cross currents, eddies, and back eddies that Nathaniel could not make sense of. Shunted this way and that by buildings—buildings that looked welded together—the wind had become as chaotic as the current, and it failed altogether when *Double Eagle* was about halfway through the Gate. She lost steerageway, was embraced by an eddy, and waltzed around, narrowly missing a fishmonger's boat steaming upriver. Nathaniel spun the wheel to counteract the turning motion, but then a back eddy, aided by a fluky gust, twirled her in the opposite direction and toward the eastern bank. "Fend off!" he hollered. "For Christ's sake . . ." He did not finish, as the bow struck a barge tied to a wharf. There was a sound like a starter's pistol, and he was sure the jibboom had cracked; but it was only a boathook, which had split in two when Will piked it against the barge to fend off. Now *Double Eagle* careened downriver, stern-first, at the speed of the current, about four knots. Fighting to wrench her head round, feeling four or five separate forces tearing at her rudder simultaneously, he remembered a story Lockwood had told about their father— how in Nova Scotia he had docked, *docked,* a vessel three times as big in a current stronger than this. He was sure that the bargemen were laughing or shaking their heads in disgust at his display of contemptible seamanship. Then his crew did a fine, smart thing: Running forward, they freed the sheets to jib and jib topsail and muscled both sails to the opposite side. Backwinded, the sails forced the schooner's bow around; and as she arced through the wind's eye, Nathaniel brought the helm down hard and she sailed smartly out of the Gate, a vessel again and not some piece of flotsam, plaything of a capricious river.

"Reckon we just learned how Hell Gate got its name," said Eliot, skipping aft, one hand clutching the lifeline.

The tide hurried them down into the clattering heart of the city, a world as alien to *Double Eagle* as the sky is to a fish or the seabottom to a bird; a world of stone, brick, and iron, where fumes rose white and black from stacks and chimneys to tint the heavens brown. The river had taken on the color of molasses, and some of its consistency, and was spanned toward its lower end by the soaring, moiled geometry of the Brooklyn Bridge. Passing under it in both directions were vessels of every conceivable size and type: graceful fore and afters; lumpy colliers; obsolete barkentines under tow by smoke-belching tugs; down-easters with topmasts struck to allow them to clear the bridges; banana boats and ferries teeming with what looked like the populations of small towns. Each one of the ships was making a noise, and while the individual hoots, whistles, or horn blasts meant something, their combined effect was unintelligible. Mingled into the cacophony, or rather, underlying it, was a sound composed of many sounds, yet greater than the sum of its acoustic parts: a low incessant roar, like surf. It was coming from the city, and in a moment, Nathaniel realized it *was* the city, vast, rumbling, busy.

"Jesus, Boston seems like a hick town compared to this."

"Natters, Boston *is* a hick town compared to this," said Will, looking toward it with an anticipatory glow on his face. "Every chance I got at Yale, I was on a ferry or a train for here."

The river pinched itself into a channel barely five hundred yards wide, between Brooklyn (recently incorporated into the city, Will declared, in the voice of a traveler's guide) and the South Street seaport—rank upon rank of wide wharves heaped with cargo, covered with wagons, crawling with men. Ships were docked at every wharf, and the smokestacks and masts formed a gallery miles long. Will, scanning the waterfront with the binoculars, said he was looking for the boatyard where the yawl owned by Tony Burton's father had undergone its final fitting out. They could rent dock space there overnight.

Following his gaze, Nathaniel saw a strange sight: a locomotive pulling a line of passenger cars over rooftops.

"If I didn't know better, I'd call that a flying train," he said.

"Those are the elevated lines of the Manhattan Railway Company," Will said, with careful enunciation, as if speaking to a savage unfamiliar with modern innovations. "Something else New York has that Boston doesn't."

Watching it chuff past flagpoles and steeples, his eyes reaching to the escarpments of buildings beyond, Nathaniel thought of Maine, and how the hamlets there were dominated by the surrounding forests, how even in certain parts of Boston he could imagine what the city looked like when it was a colonial outpost on the edge of a wilderness. New York did not allow any such fanciful pictures; here, nature had not been conquered but annihilated, and yet here the hand of man had fashioned something equal to a natural wonder in its capacity to make you feel insignificant.

The boatyard was near Pier 22, toward the lower end of South Street and in the shadow of the bridge that dwarfed everything. The yard manager, a stubby Scot too recently emigrated to have lost his burr, offered dockage at the rate of a nickel per foot per day. Will paid the fee, since coming to New York had been his idea, and *Double Eagle* was shoe-horned between a lighter and a canal barge bedecked with laundry.

Relieved to be off the river and its scary traffic, Nathaniel stretched out on the cabin top and stared at the hazy sky.

"Kinda late to bring this up, but we don't know where Lockwood lives," he said to Eliot. "Any idea how we're going to find him in this anthill of people?"

"Gleason's Boarding House, number fourteen James Slip, wherever that is."

This from Drew. Crooking his neck, Nathaniel looked at him quizzically.

"I saw it on a letter Mother sent him last Christmas," Drew said, to explain how he had learned the address.

"You're in luck, James Slip is just up the pike aways," said Will. "And there's a first-rate public bath at the corner of Franklin. The water steams, the tubs are copper, and the towels thick as carpets."

As they walked up South Street, New York assaulted their senses with a directness and a zeal unfelt on the river—their sense of smell particularly. Wagons and carts were parked all along the quay by the Fulton Market, hundreds more jostled down the street. The eye-watering stench of manure, compounded with the stink of sewage and of dead fish, oysters, and clams streaming out of the packing houses, was so thick it was almost tangible. Their ears took a beating, too. A piledriver banged, an elevated train screeched as it swung its cars around a curve; a freighter, moored alongside a warehouse bearing the name THE STANDARD FRUIT COMPANY, let out a shrill blast that drowned out a dark-haired man cursing in Italian at the stevedores loading a big banana wagon. Nathaniel noticed that most of the ships were steamers; only in a few places did he see spars and masts and bowsprits, thrusting outward with the anachronistic gallantry of cavalry lances. Powered vessels, after all, transformed delivery dates from hopes into promises.

Will blazed a trail through swarms of derby hats and walrus mustaches (the seaport was a domain exclusively masculine). He had mastered the New York way of walking, which seemed to consist of making abrupt adjustments in your pace and quick turns of your shoulders to avoid crashing into other pedestrians while simultaneously preventing them from knocking you into a lamppost, a wagon, or some other large obstacle, such as the rotting horse carcass that lay at the intersection of South and James Slip.

Gleason's Boarding House, its sign affirming that it welcomed seamen, was two blocks up on James, in a redbrick building nestled between establishments that fulfilled two of the sailor's primary needs— a sea biscuit factory and a liquor wholesaler. Its colonial windows and white shutters gave it a homey appearance. Nathaniel, recalling the whispers about Lockwood's financial straits, had expected something seedier.

The woman who answered the door told them that she did not have any vacancies before they had a chance to speak.

"We don't want a room," Nathaniel said, or rather stammered because the woman, auburn-haired, about thirty-five, wearing a striped dress that pinched her waist to next to nothing, was distractingly beautiful. "Uh, we're looking for someone who lives here? Lockwood Braithwaite?"

"And who's calling?"

"We're his brothers"—he gestured at Eliot and Drew—"and this is our friend Will. We've just sailed down from Maine and thought we'd stop by to say hello."

"Brothers? He never mentioned that he had any brothers," she said, with a skeptical arch of her brows.

"Well, we are. I'm Nat, the middle one's Eliot, the young 'un's Andrew. Are you the owner?"

"I am Mrs. Gleason. Now that I look, I can see the resemblance. In him, anyhow. Andrew, is it?" She motioned to them to come inside. They entered a hall where a tall clock ticked and the walls smelled of fresh paint. "You see, Lockwood isn't in. I haven't seen him since yesterday morning. Pardon me, young man, but where and how were you raised?"

The question was directed at Will, who was at a loss for an answer.

"It is courteous, in the presence of a lady, to ask her permission to smoke"—eyeing the cigarette Will was about to light.

"Sorry. Forgot my manners at sea. May I smoke?"

"No. Go outside, if you must, and why are you staring at me like that?"

"Your beauty is arresting, ma'am," replied Will, without missing a step.

"You don't look Irish but you must have some Irish in you to speak such blarney. I daresay I'm almost old enough to be your mother." She patted the sides of her pompadour, though not a hair was out of place. "Lockwood does travel quite a lot, the business he's in. I'll be sure to tell him you called when he comes back. Or you can leave a note, if you wish." This with a motion at the basket of mail on the table beside the clock. Then, contriving a frown of earnest concern: "There isn't bad news, I hope."

"No. Like I said, just stopped by to say hello." Nathaniel paused. "How come you asked that?"

"Oh, something seems to have been weighing on his mind the past few days. Possibly it's a business problem? He's in marine insurance, I think?"

"Yes, ma'am. He's with Merrill, Chapman and Scott."

"That's the firm," she answered over the bonging of the clock. It was four p.m.

"Is it near here?" asked Nathaniel.

Shrugging, she answered that she thought it was across town, on the Hudson River waterfront. The elevated railway line ran that way. They could ask the conductor or a policeman for the company's address.

"You know, I find it so peculiar that Lockwood never mentioned you," she went on, opening the door for them. "My husband and I make it a point to invite our long-term boarders for Sunday dinner, and Lockwood told us quite a lot about himself and about his, I should say *your*, father. But he never spoke a word that he had three younger brothers."

Nathaniel didn't like the inference, and he said, curtly: "We're not that close."

They rode crosstown on the flying train, glimpsing half-lit hovels through grimed windows opened against the heat. The streets below were canals of caps and bonnets bobbing, surging around pushcarts and horsecarts, into and out of shops shadowed by awnings. Eliot felt as if he were riding a magic carpet over an alien island with the population density of a termite mound. Nathaniel yearned to be at sea again, far from the tyranny of people and pavement. Looking through the smoke vented by numberless stacks, toward the steel bones of new buildings rising in the distance, Drew was thrilled. The scene reminded him of a fanciful picture he'd seen in a book of mountains thrusting up through the steam of a young earth. A new century, all right, and this New York City looked like its cradle. His father's words came back to him, not as he had uttered them two weeks ago, bitterly and coldly, but full of the excitement that had been in his voice last year, when he was showing newspaper and magazine articles about the World Wide Exposition in Paris to their Marlborough Street neighbor, Tom Willoughby. The future revealed, a future free from war because people would be too prosperous and enlightened to fight. They would get from one place to another on moving sidewalks, or by automobile, and speak across oceans by telephone; an electrified future when all the world would dance, as the Exposition's visitors had, to a waltz of the lights. But Mr. Willoughby, a heathen when it came to progress, preferred his sidewalks stationary and the clop of horses' hooves to the rattle of automobiles. He declined a chance to invest with Dad in a telephone company, because he thought the telephone was a novelty people would soon tire of. "After all, Cy, how many people would wish to speak to each other through a wire?" Dad had reported, mimicking and exaggerating the way Willoughby pronounced "wire" in his plummy Brahmin accent: *why-ah*. The penalty for his backwardness was to miss out on the profits reaped by a jump in the phone company's stock, while his family paid by leading a life fast becoming as quaint as hoop skirts. They still communicated by note and messenger, and read by gaslight; the Braithwaites telephoned, and their house, electrified late last fall, blazed like a birthday cake at night.

And now, amid the stink and enthralling bustle of New York, Drew recalled last Christmas, when Nat and Eliot came home for the holiday and ran with him from room to room, pushing buttons to witness the miracle of light that neither smoked nor smelled nor guttered, that required for its ignition no match or fire but was summoned instantaneously with the tip of your finger. After illuminating every room except those on the servants' floor, the boys stood outside in the snow to behold the effect. The house looked as merry as the season, each window a beacon shaming the dull archaic glow in the Willoughbys' windows. The dazzling rectangles in front of them burned with the hope and promise of that future their father had spoken of, and it seemed at that moment to belong to them alone—a possession less sure at the moment, with their lives thrown into such uncertainty.

Eliot mailed his letter in the great, domed post office on Park Row, and then the four walked to Merrill, Chapman and Scott's offices, in a squat granite building a block inland from the Hudson. There, a dour man, who sat behind a smoked-glass partition with the words CLAIMS INVESTIGATIONS painted on it in black letters, said that Lockwood had not been in all day, and, no, he could not say where he was, but if he didn't show up for work tomorrow, he would be looking for a new job. The man took out his pocket watch and told them the offices were about to close, and indeed, the lady type writers were rising from their desks and covering their machines, while clerks and underwriters were turning off the banks of green-shaded lamps on their desks.

"Reckon he'll get fired?" asked Eliot, when they were outside, walking past a row of brass foundries and machine shops. "What do you think, Nat?"

"Hey, I was right there alongside you, so why should I know any more than you do?"

"He's in a pickle, just like we figured. That's what all this has got to be about, somehow or other."

Nathaniel was silent for a time, feeling as he had before: that he and his brothers were acting in a play without knowing what the play was about or what the other characters were saying or doing. The difference now was that he didn't care what the play was about; he intended to create his own action.

"Let's forget about Lockwood," he said finally. "I'll bet we haven't seen him to talk to him more than ten times in our wholes lives, so let's forget about him and get back to the boat."

"Wonderful suggestion. Thought I was going to spend my entire time in New York listening to you three talk about family matters." Will abruptly angled across the street to where a line of oyster barges were moored, and walked up to a stand beneath whose festive umbrella a man was selling the shellfish for two cents each. A sign tacked to a post said the ice water was free. Will bought half a dozen, tipped the half shells over his mouth, and let the slimy gray meat slide into his mouth.

"Gathering strength for tonight's entertainment," he remarked, swallowing the last one. "These things increase one's sexual powers. Half a dozen oysters transforms you into a tireless engine of lust. Care to join me?"

The Braithwaites did not answer because they didn't know if he meant to join him in eating oysters, or in the entertainment he had planned, or in both. He bought half a dozen more and offered two to each of them.

"I don't feel any different," said Eliot as they approached the elevated train station. A boy at the newsstand by the platform's steps held up a *New York World* and cried, "Cocaine fiends on the rise in the city! Read it here!"

"Me, neither," Nathaniel said.

"They don't work like that, you chumps." Will shook his head in dismay. "They don't arouse desire, they give you the strength to carry on after desire has been aroused, say by some good-looking, skillful whore. You can fuck her all night."

At the forbidden word, Drew clamped his hands over his ears.

The flying train sped them back to the East Side, where in the public bathhouse on Franklin Street they scrubbed off a varnish of dried sweat and saltwater. They changed into clean clothes on the boat, fed Trajan, and then, after singing a few bars of "There'll Be a Hot Time in the Old Town Tonight," Will offered to treat them to dinner.

They found a place that called itself the German Lager Bier Haus. It was lit up with electric lights in the city dusk, and a sign over the door promised free lunch and schooner of beer to seamen and dockworkers. A great number of both were inside, standing at a long bar under a tent of smoke, hawking into spittoons, some laughing and telling tales, some getting themselves drunk with a methodical seriousness. Bursts of strange languages punctuated the flow of English—American English and English English, English touched by Irish brogue and the lilting accents of the West Indies, for in this waterfront bar, as aboard ship, a rough democracy prevailed and white men stood shoulder to shoulder with black.

The boys found an empty table. A waiter with a bushy blond mustache gave them menus, which turned out to be a formality, because only one dish was being served that evening—fried fish and potatoes for seventy-five cents. Will asked if the offer of free lunch and a schooner applied to dinner as well. The waiter replied, "No free dinner, want free beer, you ask bartender, maybe he giff you one."

Shouldering through the patrons, Will and Nathaniel posed the question to the bartender, a jowly man sporting a Vandyke beard. He shook his head, telling them to come by tomorrow noon, if it was a free schooner they wanted. Then, squinting at them, he added that the offer was extended only to sailors and stevedores.

"What do you suppose we are, lubbers?" said Nathaniel, in an offended tone. "I just skippered a fore-and-after down from Maine, and this man's my navigator, and we're Florida bound from here."

"Look a shade young to be a skipper," the bartender remarked, with a crooked grin. "Shade young to be drinking beer, come to think of it."

He walked away to take care of another customer.

"Now there goes a man with a fine eye for judgin' men."

The comment, made with a trace of brogue, came from a man standing beside Will. He looked to be about twenty-five and was of middling height, but his back was broad and his fingers thick as cigars. A black, sweat-stained derby was cocked over a scarred eyebrow.

"Wouldn't you say so, Jim?" he asked an older companion. "Wouldn't you say George has a fine eye for sizin' a man up? He can tell a fraud from the real thing with just one look, wouldn't you say?"

The older man said nothing, took a sip of his beer, and licked the foam from his lip.

"Are you talking about me?"—Nathaniel, a sudden thrumming in his chest.

"Hell, no, I was talkin' about George," said the young man in the derby hat. "I don't know you from a load o' horseshit. It's George with the fine eye for judgin' men. For an example, George could look at a chump like you and he'd know straightaway that you ain't no kinda a sailor, much less a skipper." Reaching past Will, he poked Nathaniel where the thrumming was. "And lookin' at ya meself, I'd hafta say George is right. You ain't no skipper, but a lyin' son of a bitch."

The older man said, "Ah, c'mon, Mike, don't start. He's just a boy," while Will, tugging at Nathaniel's sleeve, pulled him back to the table.

"What's the matter with him?" Sitting down, Nathaniel was baffled by the man's animosity.

"He's a roughneck and drunk. Just ignore him," Will counseled.

That proved a little difficult, for the man called Mike had turned to put his back to the bar and stare at Nathaniel with a malicious grin. The waiter brought their dinners, but Nathaniel couldn't eat, not with the roughneck glaring at him with savage merriment. Then, slamming his stein down on the bar, Mike launched himself across the floor and stood with feet planted wide in front of the boys' table.

"Any lyin' son of a bitch comes in here don't get to leave without fightin' me first," he said, in a loud voice that caused several patrons at the bar to turn and look. "That's a rule o' the house in this place. So put 'em up, Captain, or I'll bust you up where you sit."

"My friend wasn't lying," said Will, oh so reasonably. "He really did captain a boat down from Maine. Also, he's only sixteen, so you won't prove much by busting him up."

"How about you, boy-o? How old're you?" the man said, then pivoted and threw a short, crisp right hand that, if he'd thrown it sober, would have caught Will flush on the jaw and knocked him cold. Even so, the glancing blow snapped Will's head back.

With both fists held at chest level, the man named Mike stepped back to give himself room to swing, in case Will came at him; but Will wasn't about to do any such thing. All he could do was to sit, stunned, while his mouth gushed blood.

Mike turned to Nathaniel, and with a backward wave, challenged him to come on and fight. He couldn't move. He had felt fear before his Andover boxing matches, but that fear had been stimulating, a spur to action. What he felt now was a primal, paralyzing terror, as if he were facing a wild animal. The bartender appeared a second later, wielding what looked like a policeman's nightstick. From behind, he rapped it twice on Mike's shoulder.

"There'll be none of your nonsense here tonight, Downey! Take it outside!"

Nathaniel's relief lasted for as long as it took for Mike Downey to whirl and drop the bartender to his knees with two quick punches to the belly. The nightstick clattered to the floor, wood on tile. Someone yelled, "Fight! Downey's got a fight again!" The crowd apparently was well choreographed; they cleared away from the bar in seconds, the men forming a kind of arena, with themselves on three sides, the bar on the fourth. Two big customers also blockaded the door.

"C'mon, Captain, c'mon, you lyin' son of a bitch!" snarled Downey, from a few feet away.

And still, Nathaniel could not move. In the next instant, Downey sprang and yanked him from his chair with horrifying ease. His knees buckled, he staggered backward. He'd been hit hard in the chest. He hadn't seen the punch coming, hadn't felt it as pain, only as a sudden weakness in his legs. Someone grabbed him from behind and stopped him from falling. A voice shouted in his ear, "Fight him, kid, or he'll beat you to a pulp just for exercise." He was shoved back out into the middle of the circle, his feet slipping on the tiles. Downey crouched, fists rolling, derby hat off, reddened eyes narrowed. Nathaniel put up his hands, conscious only of the malevolent figure in front of him, and of the singular, petrifying realization that he wasn't in a fight, he was in mortal combat. He thought he was going to vomit.

Downey rushed him, fists pumping, and in that sliver of time, Nathaniel's training took over. Sidestepping, he slipped most of the flurry. One punch grazed his temple, with enough force to cause what sounded like a dull explosion inside his skull. Clearing his head, he sidestepped another rush, and this time wasn't touched. Carried forward by his own momentum, Downey stumbled into the crowd, the drunk and half-drunk men cheering, cursing, shouting encouragement, most to Downey, but some to Nathaniel.

The wild man spun and came on, throwing a looping right that Nathaniel parried with his left and countered with a right of his own. It cracked Downey in the ear. He'd thrown his first punch and he'd connected! Now his body, released from the manacles of fear, began to move with fluid speed, even with grace. A wondrous clarity came to his mind. He was able to think tactically. His bull-shouldered opponent was by far the stronger, and he didn't seem to mind getting hit, if that's what he had to do to get in his licks. But he was also drunk, disadvantaged in reach, and he had no art, no real skill. If the taller Nathaniel could keep him off with his longer arms, he could whip him. *I can whip him.* The words forked through his brain. When Downey made another rush, he circled left, popped him between the eyes with two straight jabs, and stopped the charge. Two more jabs, the first missing, the second drawing blood from Downey's nose. The sight of it inspired a brutal joy in Nathaniel, a feeling he'd never had before, had never suspected was in him. Stepping in, he drove a short, chopping right into the man's forehead. The punch sent a bolt of pain up his arm, but it also pulled Downey out of his crouch, straightened him right up, like he'd been jerked by a string. Nathaniel flicked another jab, Downey threw up his hands to protect his face, exposing his midsection. Spotting the opening, Nathaniel lowered his left shoulder, as his coach had taught, and pumped a hook to the ribs. The shorter man winced, dropped his guard, and Nathaniel winged a second hook to the temple, feeling a hot, electrical jolt in his knuckles. He ignored it, watched Downey stagger sideways into the bar, and then, all art forgotten in the killer's heat to finish his man, he waded in, arms windmilling, throwing punches from all directions. Only two landed, but they were enough. Downey slumped against the bar, it holding him up for a moment before he dropped to all fours, shaking his head and dripping blood and vomiting the beer in his belly. Nathaniel stepped back, keeping his hands up; both throbbed from their fractures. He wanted to say, "Had enough?" but his lungs burned, as though he'd been fighting for hours, yet the brawl couldn't have lasted a full regulation round. One of the spectators yelled, "Hey, that kid is scienced!" and another cried out, "You'd best finish him, boy-o!" Nathaniel gasped, "He is finished."

But he wasn't. From his hands and knees, Downey flung himself forward, rammed his head into Nathaniel's gut, and then butted his jaw. His brain reeled, he tasted blood as he was grabbed in a crushing bear hug and wrestled to the floor. Locking both arms into an arm bar, Downey pressed down on his throat. All Nathaniel could see was the other man's bruised face, twisted in rage, and above it the pressed-tin ceiling and the electric lights and smoke swirling in the lights. The forearm was like a steel rod pressing against his windpipe. He gagged, went limp, and fought to keep from blacking out. Then he could breathe again. The face above him was crazed by rivulets of blood that spread like cracks in a windowpane, and he watched Downey's eyes roll back in his head, the instant before he tumbled sideways and lay still on the floor. Standing over him was Drew, little Drew, wearing an eerie look of cold, controlled ferocity that reminded Nathaniel of their mother the day she struck Lockwood with her parasol. Drew had used a deadlier weapon—the bartender's club.

"Are you all right, Nat?" he asked, with no more emotion than if Nathaniel merely had taken a bad fall.

He regained his wind and got to his feet. Spitting blood—the head butt had cut his tongue—he stared, first at the motionless Mike Downey and then at Drew. He was speechless, and so was the crowd, their amazed silence finally broken by a voice that cried out, "Did you see it? The little lad flat cracked Mikey's head open. Did you see it?" A man Nathaniel recognized as Downey's drinking companion knelt down, turned his unconscious friend onto his back, and put an ear to his chest. Looking up, he fixed on Drew a puzzled frown, as if he were confronted by some great riddle.

"Mike's still with us," he muttered. "You're a daisy, lad. Could've killed him, y'know that?"

"I meant to," Drew said.

"Can't think of anyone who needs killing more." It was the bartender, rubbing his midsection. "Let's have that stick, young man." He extended a hand, and Drew gave him the club. "Best that you four clear out, before some of Mike's chums decide to even the score. Dinner's on the house."

"That's only fair, mister," said Drew. "We hardly got to eat any of it."

12

THROUGH ISLETS of electric lamp light, through channels of darkness between, they made their way back to the boat, Will with a napkin pressed to his mouth—there would be no entertainment for him tonight—Nathaniel hawking up pinkish phlegm, no one speaking. The thunder of the great city was subdued now, but not altogether silenced. Cabs rattled on the brick pavement, an elevated train rumbled in the distance. The four boys hurried on with the wary silence of a patrol in enemy territory. They reached the wharf and at last came to *Double Eagle,* and how welcome she looked.

Below, Eliot lit the lamp and broke out the medicine chest for cotton swabs, bandages, iodine. He daubed Will's swollen lips, and filled a pan from the water tank and chipped ice off the block in the ice chest and put the ice in the water so Nathaniel could soak his fractured knuckles. Still, no one spoke. They could find no reason to boast about their triumph; it had been too close a thing, won at too high a cost. In Nathaniel's mind, the whole episode didn't seem like something that had happened to him, but to a character in some terrible fantasy. To walk into a place expecting to eat dinner and, in minutes, find himself fighting for his life, with a stranger who hated him for no reason, was beyond his understanding of how the world was supposed to work. Nor could he quite grasp the reality of what Drew had done. His kid brother had a capacity for swift and ruthless action—that was something else he never could have predicted. Now, breaking the silence, he thanked him.

Drew, slumped on the settee behind the galley table, shrugged diffidently and said, "You're my brother."

"Weren't you scared?"

"No." Drew hesitated, thinking that his answer needed some elaboration, lest it sound like boasting. "I didn't feel anything. The club was right there at my feet and I picked it up and hit him with it and I didn't think about it. If I'd thought about it for half a second, I wouldn't have done it, but it was like blinking your eyes when somebody pokes a finger at them."

"Did you mean what you said? That you meant to kill him?"

"He was trying to kill you."

"Maybe."

"He was." Drew looked up at the skylight contemplatively. It framed a constellation, maybe Cassiopeia. He wasn't sure, because the stars were dimmed by city lights and haze. "You should have done what that guy said."

"What guy?"

"The guy behind me, the guy who told you to finish him."

"But he looked finished. I'd busted his nose. . . ."

"You should've kicked him in the face, hard as you could. He would've been finished then."

"Hey, little brother, I wasn't taught to kick a man who's down, and neither were you."

A ship's whistle sounded out on the river. Mooring lines creaked and *Double Eagle* rocked gently, as the wake rolled ashore.

"Trouble with you, Nat, is that you think everything's a sport and everyone's a sportsman."

Nathaniel felt a little annoyed. Drew had done a fine thing, but that didn't entitle him to make such judgments.

"I didn't think there was a damn thing sporty about it. I knew the guy was playing for keeps. Still and all, I was taught to fight fair. Know what gets me, more than anything? I can't figure out what I did to make him so mad at me that he wanted to beat my head in."

Drew lowered his gaze. Nat didn't get it, he thought. Nat never would. Nat the sportsman, fighting fair. Having been bullied and threatened so many times, having suffered taunts from classmates only because he was smaller, it was easier for Drew than for his brothers to understand the moral of tonight's story.

"There's a meanness in some people, a real big meanness, and it's just there," he said. "They don't need a reason."

In gray light, while cloud fleets sped over the city, they rode the ebb downriver and, catching a whole-sail sou'wester, beat into New York Bay, nicking past Ellis Island and the Statue of Liberty, stone torch raised against a sky darkened by blast furnaces flaring from the marshes on the Jersey shore. The flashes came unexpectedly and without pattern, so that it looked as though patches of air were spontaneously catching fire.

Down through the Narrows to the Lower Bay, where the wind hauled to the west, allowing them to reach for open sea, *Double Eagle*, lunging not through the waves but over them, a creature neither of air nor water but belonging to both, like a storm petrel or flying fish. Astern, they watched as the city fell away until nothing could be seen of it save the long reefs of smoke above it, incarnadined by the sunrise, and then the smoke sunk below the horizon. Eliot went below to cook breakfast, singing the sentiments of the entire crew.

This New York town ain't no town for me,
Away Rio!
I'm packin' my bags and goin' to sea,
For we're bound to the Rio Grande.

They ate on deck, with sparks from the Charley Noble flying leeward. Nathaniel used his fingers to scoop up the hash because he could not grasp a utensil. Will managed to eat by passing the fork between his bruised lips and swallowing whole. He couldn't smoke afterward, which made him irritable, and when he tried to speak, he sounded as if part of his tongue had been cut out. It frustrated him to be so conversationally impaired, so he went below to read a book. Drew joined him, bent on solving the mysteries of the *Nautical Almanac* and the Tables.

On deck Nathaniel and Eliot watched long white beaches pass to starboard. Through the binoculars, they made out swarms of bathers and umbrellas on the shoreline—this summer was almost as hot as last year's, and that had been the hottest anyone could remember. When they were off Sandy Hook, their gazes were seized by a full-rigged ship, making ready to cast off her towline. She had a black hull trimmed in white, and ornate ivy decorated her stern, and under the ivy were her name and home port—SLEIBRECHT—BREMEN. Officers were shouting guttural commands, the strains of some Teutonic halyard chant drifted over the water as her sails tumbled from the yards in cascades of patched canvas dyed the color of burned butter by the early sunlight. The tow cable was dropped, the tug saluted the moment with a whistle blast, and the ship gathered way and ran to eastward, drawing a silver wake on the sea's slate.

"Ain't that the grandest sight there is?" said Nathaniel, a little sadly, because somewhere ahead in this new century, it would be a sight existing only in the memories of aging sailors.

They plunged on, bearing south by east, hoping to cross the line of their original course at a point off Delaware Bay. Because Nathaniel could not get his fingers around the wheel, Eliot steered the whole watch. He talked about the brawl, how astonished he had been to see Drew pick up the nightstick and crack that ruffian's skull. Goes to show you, he said, that one of their father's favorite aphorisms was true: Adversity does not create character, it reveals it. These praises began to pluck on Nathaniel's nerves; he wasn't entirely sure that Drew had been brave, a doubt he now expressed aloud.

"I can't believe you said that"—Eliot, pursing his brows.

"I'm not saying he wasn't . . ." Nathaniel started, and began again. "Well, to be brave, you've got to be scared first. That's what bravery is. Overcoming fear. But I believed Drew when he said that he wasn't scared, that it was just like reflex. Don't you think it's kinda strange for a thirteen-year-old kid, in a situation like that, not to be scared?"

"You don't want to give him credit. On account of you can't admit that he did ten times, oh hell, a hundred times more for you than you ever did for him, and you know what I mean."

. . . That afternoon in the dining hall at Boston Latin, when Drew was in fifth grade, Nathaniel in eighth. Already burdened with a reputation as a brain and teacher's pet, Drew was sitting by himself, his nose buried in a book, as usual. One of Nathaniel's classmates looked at him with a nasty grin—"This is the lunchroom, not the library, you're supposed to be eating, not reading." Drew did not say anything or raise his eyes from the book. The boy pelted him with an orange peel—"Eat that!" Drew kept reading. Another boy threw a peel, and a third said, "Ah, he doesn't want oranges, he wants apples 'cause he's a bookworm and worms like apples and he's an apple polisher, besides," then winged an apple core like a baseball, narrowly missing. Drew did nothing to protect himself except to guard the sides of his head with his hands, his passivity raising the flame of the older boys' cruelty, as an underdog's cowering only excites the fury of the pack attacking it. Finally, under an ever harder rain of rinds and cores and harsh laughter, Drew ran out in tears. Nathaniel had not joined in the torment, but he wound up with his three classmates in the headmaster's office, their backsides bared to receive a paddling. His friends got three whacks each, and he got one extra for his failure to display the protectiveness expected of a big brother. "What kind of a coward are you?" said the headmaster. "To allow that kind of thing to go on without even trying to stop it?" It wasn't cowardice—Nathaniel was taller and heavier than any of the boys, and a better fighter. He could have taken them all at once, if he had to. No, it wasn't cowardice, but something darker and more odious and he didn't have a name for it.

"See, Drew's got sand, more sand than you or the old man ever give him credit for, and now you want to take that away from him," Eliot was saying.

"I'm not trying to take anything away from him," Nathaniel protested.

"Sure you are. You don't want to give him credit, because if you do, you won't be able to bully him when he gets seasick or doesn't set a sail to your liking."

Sorry that he had brought up this subject, Nathaniel said nothing, though he knew that Eliot had a point: Everything in his relations with his kid brother had changed. He would have to treat Drew as an equal, and that would feel unnatural. Still, he had seen what he had seen and heard what he had heard. That dead blank look in Drew's eyes, the flatness in his voice when he'd said, answering Mike Downey's sidekick, "I meant to." There had been something so . . . so . . . He groped for a word and found *rational*. So rational about Drew. A rationality that suggested a streak of cold-bloodedness.

With an old issue of *Tip Top Weekly* folded in his back pocket, he went forward to sit against the foremast and read.

> . . . *Preparations were being made for the mile run. . . . Then, at the last moment before the men were called to the mark, a great mad roar went up from the Yale stand. "Merriwell! Merriwell! Merriwell!" Frank Merriwell was seen running across the field. . . .*

His gaze wandered, falling on a sentence here . . . *He shot off the mark with Dalton of Columbia at his shoulder* . . . and a sentence there . . . *Every muscle of his splendid frame was tense, every nerve was strained* . . . and finally left the page altogether. It was one of those rare afternoons that are a sailor's delight: clouds like brush strokes, a moderate seaway rolling in a moderate breeze, shearwaters skimming the tops of sculpted waves. A school of dolphin appeared, and played around the schooner for a quarter of an hour, diving under her, streaking across her bow like green torpedoes, breaching to make acrobatic leaps, arched backs sleek and sparkling. When they swam away, Nathaniel returned to the artificial entertainment of his magazine. . . .

> . . . *for Merriwell had won at the last moment, and Yale was in the lead. . . . Men hugged each other, pounded each other,*

danced and shrieked and also died with joy. . . . "Merriwell!"
roared the throng. . . .

Oh, come on. The crowd didn't die with joy, he thought, and tossed
the dog-eared magazine overboard, fed up for the time being with Merriwell! Merriwell! He of the splendid frame and never-sullied virtue,
who always won at the last moment, always outwitted Chinese bandits
and got the drop on Texas rustlers. But Merriwell! Merriwell! had never
run into a thug like Mike Downey.

Looking out again, past the easy lift and dip of the jibboom,
Nathaniel projected onto the real ocean the one represented on the
charts, and he came to a conclusion: Mike Downey had wanted to beat
him up because he didn't believe he was a real captain, and he didn't
believe me, thought Nathaniel, because I haven't taken charge. I don't
act like a skipper, don't sound like one. So when Will and Drew tumbled
out to stand their trick, he declared to his crew, in a tone that left no
room for argument, "We aren't making any more detours, everyone got
that? We're going to drive straight to Key West fast as we can push this
boat."

And then the ancient ritual of watch-change was observed. Eliot,
keeping hands on the helm, stepped aside to give his relief room to pass.

"South by a quarter east," he said.

"South by a quarter east. All mine," Will replied, and took the
wheel.

AND WATCH followed watch, the days divided not by intervals of light
and darkness but by four-hour increments of time. They were sailors
again, as attuned to moonrise and moonset as to dawn and dusk, accustomed to being sound asleep at noon and fully awake while night skies
wheeled above them. The wind swung from southwest to southeast and
back to southwest, and for the better part of their second day out of
New York, it headed them inshore, close enough to give them a glimpse
of the land around Chesapeake Bay, wreathed in bluish mist. There was
no wind all the following day, *Double Eagle* lying nearly dead in water
that, creased by errant zephyrs or subsurface currents, resembled the
hide of a great blue beast, vast as all the world. She lay becalmed that
night. Will and Drew listened to the slat of sails, watched shooting stars,
and, at ten o'clock, saw something red on the horizon. The port sidelight
of a ship, Drew ventured, but changed his mind when the red glow grew

larger: It looked as though the ship were on fire. The light rose, bigger and bigger, a blazing balloon that he and Will finally recognized as the moon.

In the morning, the tender was lowered away, a towline bent to the samson post. As the strongest of the four, Nathaniel tried to row the schooner out of the doldrums, but she was a heavy craft and the tender's oars too short to give any leverage. His sore hands aching, he quit after twenty minutes, having moved *Double Eagle* barely a hundred yards.

Sunset. Cumulus towering in the south, their tops spreading into anvils edged in a gold incandescence. Lightning trembled in the clouds, and the wind, yearned for in the morning, came on with the venom of an answered prayer. They sailed into the heart of a squall, main furled and foresail double-reefed, and when they sailed out of it, it was as though they had passed through a door from a tumultuous room into a serene one. The seas laid down, stars glittered like crystal rivets, and far behind the wake, the army of flickering clouds retreated to fading drum rolls of thunder.

Drew practiced with the sextant until he could take sights almost as fast as Will, and he eventually became quicker at the computations. He studied the constellations, observing how their positions changed as the latitude dropped. His faithful landmark, or skymark, was the summer triangle—Vega in Lyra, Deneb in the Northern Cross, and Altair in Aquila. On clear nights, his terror of open ocean diminished, and he felt himself one with the ancient mariners who had neither compass nor sextant nor even astrolabe but found their way by their knowledge of the skies.

The patent log's torpedo swam in the wake, recording their speed and distance with such fidelity that they acquired an affection for the darting metal tube. It became a kind of mascot, and to honor its logging the miles of their exodus, they dubbed it "Little Israel." When seaweed fouled it, they hauled it in, cleared it, and returned it to the water, giving it tender pats and instructing it to go back to work. Once, on Nathaniel and Eliot's watch, a huge swordfish, mistaking the log for prey, swatted it with its bill to kill it; when it continued to swim, the swordfish charged, its entire body turning iridescent blue. For a moment, Little Israel's life appeared to be over, but *Double Eagle*, brisking along at six knots, yanked it out of the swordfish's mouth. A second later, the fish shot out of the water straight as a rocket, its blue flanks striped with lavender, shuddering and throwing off spray. At the top of its leap, it arced over and returned to the water headfirst. The two brothers looked at each other as if they had seen a hallucination. The creature had not looked like the swordfish in New England; its bill was shorter, its colors more vibrant. Drew had brought along an illustrated book of saltwater fishes, which they consulted, and identified the creature as *makaira nigricans,* a blue marlin. The book said blue marlin were habituated to semitropical waters, and Will speculated that the one Nathaniel and Eliot had seen had been following a tributary of the Gulf Stream, a theory supported by the color of the sea, a rich royal blue rather than green, and by the flying fish that could be seen skipping the surface like silver stones.

Gulf Stream! The mighty river in the ocean. Nathaniel knew, from reading the positions recorded daily in the logbook, that *Double Eagle* was now approaching the 35th parallel and the Hatteras Banks; but to see evidence of their southing in the ocean's tint, to feel it in the ever-warming air, thrilled him more than any number in a logbook possibly could.

They had little wind the last two days of June, and Diamond Shoals lay flat and serene, with only the masts and stacks of wrecked ships to testify that they were among the most dangerous waters on the East Coast.

A full sail easterly came on July 1. Viewing himself, like most adolescents, as the center of the universe, and believing in a deity that took a personal interest in him, whether to aid or hinder him, Nathaniel was convinced that the favorable wind was a reward for his enduring the extremes of line squalls and dead calms. On a beam reach, her canvas without a wrinkle in it, *Double Eagle* logged one hundred and eighty-two miles from midnight of the first to midnight of the second, the farthest she had ever gone in one day. The next twenty-four hours saw her better that by four miles, and her crew celebrated the record and the beginning of Independence Day by firing four shots from the L. C. Smith twelve-gauge. Eliot marched around the ship, tooting "Stars and Stripes Forever" through a rolled-up magazine. The dead reckoning was checked against Will's star fix, which put them at a latitude and longitude about one hundred and twenty miles east of Savannah, Georgia. The wind holding, they would be off Jacksonville by noon; the wind still holding, they would sight the Florida shore by the following midnight. None of them dared say this, but they all thought it, and the thought was sufficient for the sea gods to punish them. Within an hour, the wind dropped to five knots; by dawn, it turned south and fell to under five, and *Double Eagle*, with topsails set, loafed along at two.

Nathaniel was dozing on the cabintop when Will's cry from below—
"Port the helm!"—startled him awake. He was down the companionway in two steps, and found Will trying to shove his head through a
porthole, yelling, "Breakers dead ahead! Port the helm!" From above,
Eliot shouted, "What the hell's he talking about? There's no breakers
inside of a hundred miles!"

"He's sleepwalking again," Nathaniel called back, and shook Will
into consciousness.

"Bad dream, sorry for the false alarm, Natters," he said, when his
head cleared.

"What are we going to have to do? Tie you to your bunk when
you're off watch?"

Nathaniel felt strangely overstrung and irritable, which he ascribed
to the uncommon heat. The air had a thickness suggesting an imminent
change of state from gaseous to gelatinous. Trajan, who had dozed for a
good part of the trip, paced nervously.

"Feels like the hinges of hell," Nathaniel said, pulling at his sweat-
spotted jersey.

Will wiped dampness from his upper lip and lit a cigarette; then, as
the boat rose and fell with a long, slow ponderous motion, his body
tensed and he cocked his head aside, as though listening for a faint noise.
Going to a porthole, he said, "Those are damn big swells. When did they
start coming in?"

"Maybe half an hour ago. What's the matter?"

Will did not say anything, peeked at the barometer, and then
checked the last reading in the logbook.

"Dropped a tenth since Drew and I went off watch," he said, and
quickly went on deck.

All around, high broad ridges heaved and dropped with a grave
motion, like the chests of sleeping giants. The swells were rolling up
from the south, where an eerie, milky white haze hung just above the
horizon; the sky directly overhead was clear, except for one or two high,
wispy cirrus. A solitary shearwater, now white, now brown, wheeled
fine on the bow; otherwise, there wasn't a living thing in sight, nor a
smokestack, nor a sail. Ships had been sighted nearly every day, but now
the little schooner appeared to be alone on the vast, the isolating sea.

After taking a good look around, Will dropped down the companionway, returning ten minutes later, holding a sheet of paper with calculations written on it.

"Bring her west by quarter north," he said to Eliot, speaking calmly
but with an undertone of urgency. "Nat, you and Drew better make sure

our lines are free for reefing or dousing, whatever we have to do. Better have storm oil handy, too. Then we should all turn to and lash and batten whatever needs to be. Storm hatches on the skylights."

Saying, "West by quarter north, aye," Eliot started to bear off. Nathaniel grabbed the wheel and stopped him from making the course change.

"What do you think you're doing?" he said to Will. "I don't remember any change-of-command ceremony."

"There's a daisy of a storm brewing somewhere to the southard. Very probably a hurricane, and very probably headed in one of two directions—west or north. West, we should be okay, north, we'll want to be in Savannah when it hits, nice and snug."

"Savannah! Thought I said no more detours."

"This isn't tourism. This is running for safe harbor."

"Just how do you know it's a hurricane? Some little bird tweet in your ear?"

"Didn't that salty old man of yours teach you anything about tropical cyclones? No? I will. Those"—Will motioned at the swells—"and the fall in the barometer are my little birds. Could be a hurricane, maybe not, but I damn well don't want to be out here when we find out. The *Practical Navigator*—you'd do well to read it, Natters—calculates that a cyclone tracks at between ten and twenty knots, and the swells advancing out away from its center travel at between twenty-five and thirty-five. Judging from the size of these, I'd guess that blow is three hundred miles from us. If it is heading our way, we've got around thirty hours to get out of its way. Savannah is closest."

The display of seamanlike knowledge inflamed Nathaniel's irritability: His friend was making him look stupid! Nevertheless, he hesitated.

"Are you captain now? All right, *Captain* Terhune, how far is Jacksonville? At least, that's south and not west."

"Didn't plot it, but . . ."

"Then it's Jacksonville. I aim to get to Florida. Make it south by half-west, Eliot."

Though Eliot's inclination was to side with Will in this case, he repeated the second course change and ported the helm. Feeling that his command of the vessel had been restored, Nathaniel ran to the pinrack to trim the sails. Will took advantage of his momentary absence, shoved Eliot aside, and seized the helm.

"Ease those sheets, Natters! We're bearing off hard to starboard," he called, and turned *Double Eagle* again to westward.

"You're getting another busted lip!"

Leaving sheets to fly, Nathaniel hurried aft, feeling murderous. He grabbed Will's hands to pry his fingers from the wheel. That failing, he took half a step backward to punch him, but the boat rolled heavily, making him miss. Thrown sideways by a swell at the same time, he latched onto Will's sleeve, pulling him down on top of him. Drew, awakened by the rumpus, thrust his head out of the main cabin hatch to be presented with an odd sight: Will and his brother wrestling on deck and no one at the helm. It was holding steady, as if in the hands of some invisible pilot, but he knew that situation couldn't last, rushed out, took the wheel, and called, "What's the course!" Forward, belaying the loose sheets, Eliot shouted back, "West by quarter north! We're running for Savannah! Storm coming!"

Nathaniel heard that. His whole damn crew was against him. Though he had Will pinned, he felt the fight and anger go out of him, like water from a punctured balloon.

"All right, you win," he said, getting up.

"Win? *Win?* Oh, for God's sake, Natters."

"Quit using that goddamned nickname. I hate it."

"But I've always called you Natters." Will glanced at the sea, then back at him. "Don't you see, Nat? By running west, we'll be on a reach and go faster. Running south for Jacksonville, the wind will be in our faces, and if that storm is bearing north, we'd run right into it."

Of course he saw, now. Self-pity shrouded him. He was trying so hard! He was the one who lay awake on his off-hours, listening through the normal groans, creaks, and thuds of the ship for the groan, creak, or thud that wasn't normal. Was the one who checked the bilges to make sure the seams were tight, who walked the deck looking for frays in the lines, who insured that the logbook was kept up to date. He was trying so hard to complete the task his father had set for him, or that he had set for himself, or that they had both set together in a kind of partnership. Now there was a hurricane lurking out there somewhere, and he wasn't sure what to do, because he wasn't sure what the storm intended to do. Gazing southward, over the ominous swells, he could sense its presence, and it became a living thing to him: inscrutable, prowling the seas for prey.

13

FOR MOST OF the morning, *Double Eagle* labored up and down the ever moving hills. Clumps of sargussum weed, carried northward from their native waters, continually fouled the log. When clear, it registered a speed of three knots; only with the greatest luck would they reach Savannah in thirty hours or less. Turning to Nathaniel, Will said that since he was the most religious, it was up to him to pray that the blow head westward, or if it must come north, that its center pass well out to sea; then, at worst, *Double Eagle* would only have to contend with the weaker winds at its edges.

Light, capricious airs played about the vessel from all directions. The phrase "dirty weather" took on a literal meaning, as the murk on the southern rim of the world grew darker and climbed higher; it was as though an unseen hand were drawing over the sky a blanket of soiled wool. High cirrus, speckled and feathery, coiled up from the clouds and spread directly overhead. The sun shone through them as a brassy wreck, and the mounting swells assumed a leaden color.

"'Mackerel skies and mares' tails, tall-masted ships lower their sails.'" Will murmured the old sailor's axiom. "What do you think, Natters?"

All he thought was the advice Cudlip had given: *Any idiot can crack it on, but it's the wise man knows to shorten sail on time.* But what did "on time" mean, in this case? If they shortened sail now, their progress would be slowed to less than a crawl; if they did not, and the first blast caught them with too great a press of canvas, they could be knocked down or dismasted. But he could not allow himself to appear indecisive, and so he said, with contrived firmness, "We'll reef when we have to, not a minute before."

They had to soon enough. At midday, the wind rose to twenty knots, topsails were lowered, and *Double Eagle* was cracking along at seven knots; the vessel herself seemed desperate to reach safety. Late afternoon, an unbroken dome of gray above, and far to the southeast, black plumes looming—smoke from a forest fire where no forest was. The storm was coming on. No swells now, but seas, right mean seas tumbling and surging, driven by a wind piping to thirty knots . . . main and foresail double-reefed . . . to thirty-five . . . main and fore shortened to the third reef point, jib reduced to a truncated triangle . . . nightfall, and forty plus . . . the last of the two big sails was doused, and only a staysail flying for steerageway. Nathaniel and Eliot, standing tiptoe on a cabin top glistening from spray as though newly varnished, flaked the sails with jackropes; Will stood to the helm, the froth flung back from the bow, crackling against his oilskin jacket; Drew, hopelessly seasick, had been sent below. Coming from due south, the waves struck *Double Eagle* on the beam—an endless pack of hounds tearing at her flank. She fought them off gallantly, but she was heeling thirty degrees at times, and one of the seas boarding her nearly sent Nathaniel and Eliot somersaulting over the main boom. The flaking done, they slithered aft on bellies and elbows, waited till the boat was between rolls, then got to their feet.

Will bent his head to Nathaniel's ear and shouted that he figured they had at least thirty miles more to go, and then he spoke the words he did not want to speak and that his listeners did not want to hear: "We aren't going to make it!" They could not stay on this tack any longer; *Double Eagle* could be rolled onto her beam ends. Of the two alternative choices—run with the seas or set the sea anchor and ride it out—the second seemed the wisest.

"We're damned lucky!" he hollered.

Though the two Braithwaites indeed felt fortunate to still be on board, they thought Will's assertion needed some supporting evidence. With a jerk of his chin, he indicated the sooty pall to the southeast.

"That's the heart of it way out there! Been keeping my eye on it! Tracking north by northeast, staying out to sea! We're catching the edges! Or they're catching us! Shouldn't get any worse!"

Which is bad enough, Nathaniel thought, wrestling with the hatch cover to go below for the sea anchor. Had to be blowing fifty now, a Force 10 gale. Inside, after he slammed the hatch shut, the wind's shriek and the roar of breaking seas were muffled, but a scene of disarray greeted him: Drawers and lockers were open; gear was strewn over the floor; pots, pans, and broken crockery littered the galley, where cabinet doors, their brass hooks popped loose, whipped back and forth on their hinges.

Staggering forward, he passed Drew's berth and saw him lying on his side, knees pulled into his chest.

"You all right?"

"Sure not. I'm trying, Nat. . . ."

"Yeah, I know," Nathaniel said, indulgently. Yet beneath his indulgence of Drew's condition lay a peculiar satisfaction. Not that a bout of seasickness nullified Drew's heroics in New York, but it was a sign that the old kid brother had not completely vanished, the kid brother whose weakness provided foil to Nathaniel's strengths.

"Think you could secure things down here?" he said. "The locker doors in the galley are going to get torn off if they're not lashed shut quick."

Drew sat up and stumbled toward the galley.

The howling outside seemed twice as loud, after the relative peacefulness inside. Will's forecast notwithstanding, the weather had gotten worse. A savage squall spawned by the distant center of the hurricane—a storm within a storm—bore down. The winds accelerated, the skies collapsed in a deluge of slicing rain, lightning spiked, the vertical streaks throwing out jagged branches, and the flashes showed spindrift twirling on the faces of broken, wandering seas sixteen feet high.

Below decks, in the swaying light of the gimbal lamp, Drew battled to stop from vomiting while he braced himself against the rolls and lashed the cabinet doors. A bolt of lightning struck very close to starboard—the cabin lit up for an instant with a bluish fire, and he felt rather than heard the blast; felt it get inside him and rattle his bones. A few seconds later, another hit on the opposite side, and he began to mutter his chants—"It's only the separation of an electrical charge caused by . . . It's only the sound of the shock wave caused by . . ." but they failed to overcome the feeling, in the core of his heart, that the heavens were hurling thunderbolts at him and his shipmates with malevolent intent.

He secured the last cabinet and, on all fours, returned to his bunk, where he lay, longing for his room on Marlborough Street, longing to sleep for eight unbroken hours on a bed that did not rock, pound, and cant. He could hear the sea rushing past the hull with a fierce growl that made him acutely aware of how fragile the vessel was; all that stood between him and drowning were planks only an inch and a half thick, a few brass nails, a little tar and oakum. It occurred to him that the color of his and his shipmates' oilers—yellow—was appropriate; they were like chicks in a brittle egg that the sea could smash to bits any time it felt like. And yet, she held, she held, a tough little ship built by stern Yankees who knew a thing or two about heavy weather.

Before Nathaniel and Eliot could set the sea anchor—a long canvas cone with fifty fathoms of rode attached—they had to douse the staysail. In their rubber seaboots, walking the drenched decks was like walking on a skating rink that happened to be tilting violently side to side. Clutching at lifelines, at shrouds, at whatever they could grab to save themselves, they moved forward.

Everything went wrong at once. The halyard fouled. They were five minutes clearing it. Then a rogue sea, six feet higher than its brothers, thundered into *Double Eagle,* raised her up and dropped her down at a sickening, steep angle, and the sea following broke over her, burying her to the cabin tops. Nathaniel and Eliot disappeared momentarily under-water, arms locked around the foot of the foremast for dear life, truly, truly for dear life, the rushing flumes tugging at their arms and hands, trying to break their grips. The preventer stay parted, with a crack like a shotgun blast, and the fore boom swung to leeward, thudded at the end of its swing, swung back, and then forward again. The schooner heeled sharply; boom, gaff, and furled sail were thrust into the water and driven forward by the lunge of the boat. The boom split from the mast with a tremendous crash, the gaff broke an instant later, and both went overboard with the sail. Eliot tossed the sea anchor, but the vessel did not turn into the wind. From the helm, Will shouted, but Nathaniel and Eliot could not hear him. He waved and pointed, and they saw what the trouble was: The broken rig was still attached to the boat by the foresail sheet, which had ingeniously wrapped itself around a shroud. The shredded foresail was dragging through the water, pulling the bow to leeward and causing the ship to careen on her lee side. Drawing their sheath knives, the Braithwaites hacked and sawed at the fouled sheet. When it parted, boom and gaff—solid spars broken like straws—were carried away, and *Double Eagle* began to point up. Rolling into a gully, she angled up the face of a wave, swung through an arc, and finally set-tled down with her nose into the seas. She had taken a beating, but she had not been knocked down; now, recovering her wits, she squared off to face her adversary.

The wheel was made fast with the turk's head dead-centered. That done, the three joined Drew below, bolted the hatch, and took shelter in the cabin, huddling there like soldiers in a dugout during a siege.

The gale blew relentlessly, the sea scend pushing *Double Eagle* north by a little west. Hour after hour, she drifted, losing with each hour miles of the ground gained during her record run. How many miles it was difficult to tell. The boys sat or lay on the floorboards, while from outside came the ceaseless moan of high wind, and the thump of waves beating the decks. Inactivity was so opposed to Nathaniel's nature that he could barely stand the helpless waiting. He kept thinking there was some action that he ought to take; once, his restlessness drove him out into the wet howl to dump storm oil over the bow. Beyond that, there was nothing he could do, and doing nothing, he discovered, was an art unto itself.

After midnight, as the storm began to abate, Eliot performed the miracle of putting a kettle on for tea, and also managed to forage some salt cod and crackers from a storage locker. The boat climbed a sea, fell with a bang that shook her, stem to stern, her bell clanging outside like a shrill wind chime. Drew's plate skidded across the floor and struck a bulkhead, but remained right side up.

"Look at that!" said Eliot. "Aunt Phrony's looking out for you."

"Sure glad we made that detour to see her, she's doing such a fine job with this storm," Drew said, rising to retrieve his dinner. Another sea spared him the effort of volitional movement by tumbling him across the cabin. Sitting next to his plate, he decided it would be easier to finish eating right where he was. "Yeah, Aunt Phrony, she's doing all right by us, yes sirree."

"Maybe we brought her the wrong brand of chaw," Eliot suggested. "Could be she likes Redman instead of Copenhagen."

"Could be. So maybe now she'll drown us"—Drew, attempting to put his mouth and a handful of cod in the same place at the same time— "and then we can all have our own little gravestones right there with her kin."

"Shut up, Drew!"

"Easy, Nat," said Eliot, with a cautionary sidelong glance. Here, in such cramped quarters, with nothing to do but wait, and all of them exhausted and scared, it would be easy to get on one another's nerves.

At four in the morning, the worst was over, the storm's fury not appeased but spent. Will went above to take a look. A minute later, he thumped on the deck three times—their signal for all hands—and cried out, "Breakers to leeward!" The wind, down to fifteen knots, had veered due east, and the schooner was riding eight-foot seas toward a lee shore as yet invisible, for ragged clouds occulted the lowering moon. All ears were cocked for the sound of surf, but none was heard. Will assured them he had not been suffering from another sleepwalker's nightmare, for the simple reason that he, like they, had not slept a wink. Nathaniel broke out the lead and tossed it as far as he could to compensate for their drift. Fifteen fathoms. Another toss. Fifteen again. And then twelve, and on the fourth heave, ten. Now, all heard the breakers, a steady rush, as of a high wind through pine trees. The thing to do was to clap on the jib, raise the main, and luff up for sea room; but they were far too worn out, and dropped the hook instead, adding the kedge to be on the safe side.

"HALLO! Y'all livin', or y'all dead?"

The voice roused Eliot but not his shipmates. Looking at them, sprawled in their oilskins, he reckoned they were doing a pretty good imitation of corpses. After setting the anchors, they all four had sat down on deck for a breather, and there they had passed out.

"Y'all appear to be this side of the grave. How about your friends?"

The speaker, standing at the tiller of an oyster sloop hove alongside Double Eagle, looked a little like one of the risen dead himself. He wasn't just thin, he was cadaverous, with a worm of a neck, sunken chest, and knobby shoulders from which a white cotton shirt hung in loose folds. He had a fisherman's face, weather-seamed and burned to the color of cork, and though his voice belonged to a young or a middle-aged man, his hair was pure silver. Faded blue eyes goggled from behind spectacles whose thickness testified that he was almost as blind as he was scrawny.

Eliot gave Nathaniel, Drew, and Will each a poke in the ribs. They stirred, rubbed their faces, and cast confused gazes at the sloop and its skipper. Beyond, not two hundred yards away, a white beach, pierced here and there by inlets and river mouths, stretched north and south as far as they could see. The sun burned high in a flawless sky, and the air was like warm maple syrup but without the sweetness, reeking instead of the tidal flats spread all around, brown as coffee from mud churned up by the gale.

It came to them that they could not have been this close to land when they dropped the hook; the anchors must have dragged in the poor holding ground, and a flood tide carried Double Eagle inshore until the anchors grabbed again.

"Mornin'," said the oysterman, with a bobbing of his prominent Adam's apple. He squinted at the sun and added, "Make that afternoon."

They nodded, and he, giving a one-fingered salute, announced himself as Phineas Talmadge. He had spotted their vessel half an hour ago and thought he'd come on out for a look, schooners being a rare sight in these thin coastal waters.

"Mind telling us where we might be?" asked Will.

"Can't say where you might be, but I can say where you are, and that's off the mouth of St. Helene Sound, in the fine state of South Car'lina."

South Carolina! They must have been driven at least fifty miles north of Savannah.

"Now I see by your transom that y'all hail from Blue Hill. Where is that?"

"Maine," answered Nathaniel, and felt pride when he saw Talmadge's eyes bulge a little wider.

"Maine! I ain't sure how far that is, but I know it's got to be right far. Was your boat caught in yesterday's blow? She looks it. Whoo-ee! That blow was a honey."

"We were, Mr. Talmadge."

"Would like to hear about it, but we'd best not jaw too long. I'm here to tell y'all that if you don't pull your hook right quick and foller me into the channel, you're gone to *stay* in the fine state of South Car'lina till the Savior comes again. Tide's fixin' to turn, and when it does, it'll run outta here fifty mile an hour, and that fine-lookin' boat get herself stuck in a gumbo goes clear through to China. Gettin' her afloat will be harder'n hemmin' a hog, so foller me."

The boys, wondering what it meant to hem a hog, lost no time. Will and Drew hauled the kedge up by hand. Nathaniel and Eliot set the levers in the windlass drum and weighed the main anchor. With the jib out to port, the main to starboard, *Double Eagle* ran wing on wing behind the sloop down the channel—an ambitious name for a serpentine gutter that had nothing to mark its winding course except the flagged stakes planted on the bordering oyster bars. The tide did not fall as fast as Talmadge had claimed, but it moved right along, and by the time the two vessels passed through the mouth of St. Helene Sound, shoals and mud banks submerged ten minutes ago were glistening in the sunlight. Unwilling to entrust his vessel entirely to the piloting of a stranger, Nathaniel climbed the main ratlines to the top, the better to see the color of the water and so track the channel's meanderings. In all directions, rivers and estuaries spread like an immense vascular system around islands and peninsulas, through oak and pine woods and marshlands rippling in the breeze. As they approached a quaint settlement— unpainted shacks, some ashore, some on stilts at water's edge, their drabness relieved by a fleet of oyster boats lateen-rigged and rakishly sparred—he saw a few stunted, scrubby trees growing near the shore.

"Palms!" he called down. "Over there to port. Palms!"

Eliot and Drew ran up to stand beneath him and behold the sight. At the wheel, Will shrugged and concentrated on his steering, for he had seen the majestic royals of Bermuda, compared to which the Carolina palmettos were hardly more than shrubs. All the same, they were palm trees, the first the Braithwaites had ever seen—exotic, foreign, green emblems of how far they had come.

Double Eagle was anchored in deep water some hundred yards from the settlement (only someone given to hyperbole could have called it a town). Talmadge rounded up and brought his sloop alongside and invited the boys to supper. They said nothing, flummoxed by such impetuous hospitality; in Boston, you had to know someone practically five years before you got invited for a meal.

"Well?" asked Talmadge. "Y'all hungry, ain't you?"

"Sure. We'll be there," Nathaniel said. "Is there a boatyard around here? We lost a foresail, and a fore boom and gaff in that blow, and we're gonna need to replace them."

The oysterman thought a moment.

"There's Jeb Kincaid, what's got the sawmill and a carpenter works for him, Ray Sykes by name. Fixes up our boats when they need it. But we got no sailmakers here. Reckon y'all got to go to Beaufort for that."

"We're near Beaufort?"

"Twenty mile."

"Our mother was born in Beaufort."

"So y'all ain't a hundred-percent Yankee? Might stand you with folks around here, but still, you best have a pocket full o' money you go to Beaufort."

Nathaniel, not pleased to hear that, asked if Talmadge had any idea what Mr. Kincaid would charge.

"Don't know, but he's a right reasonable man. I'll need you gentlemen to come by early, say four, four-thirty."

And was there anything they could bring?

"Your own selves and a appetite." He paused, pushing his tongue into a cheek. "And if y'all got any magazines you're done with. Educated man is hard put to find readin' material in Snead's Landin'. Got to go all the way to Beaufort for a newspaper."

Will said that he had a bottle of Bermudian dark rum in his seabag and offered to bring it, along with some Coca-Cola.

"Sodee's fine. But y'all leave that rum behind. Three things ain't allowed here is niggers, strong drink, and cuss words, though we make exception, now and again, for cussin'."

He had asked them to come early to shuck the oysters they were to have for dinner. He said, apologetically, that he or his wife would have done the work, but his wife was sick with a fever and he had business to attend to that afternoon. Did they know how to shuck? They did not. Wasn't nothin' to it. What you do is take this here—he laid a heavy-bladed knife, hooked at the tip, on the fish-cleaning table at the end of his dock—work it between the lips of the oyster and cut the muscle in back with the hooked part; then you give the blade a twist or two and pry the shell open. A child could do it. In fact, children did do it, he informed them, in the oyster-packing plant in Beaufort, where they shucked hundreds of bushels a day for just pennies.

Nathaniel took one of the shellfish from the tub and gave it a try, succeeding only in cutting a finger. Talmadge then offered to demonstrate. With dextrous movements, he produced an oyster on the half shell in about two seconds flat. No sooner was he was done than a big ring-billed gull swooped down, snatched the meat, and flew off.

"Forgot to warn y'all about them. Gulls round here is mighty bold," he said, watching the bird pass over the chocolate waters of the Sound. "It's what comes from the abusin' of my gift, so the preacher told me. See you boys in a spell."

"That was a pretty strange thing to say," Eliot remarked, after Talmadge was gone.

Will shrugged and opined that Snead's Landing looked like a pretty strange place. "No niggers, strong drink, or cussing allowed—yes, shipmates, we are in the deep Baptist South, all right." Eliot said he had heard staid Bostonians express similar sentiments, only in more elegant language.

An hour and one more cut finger—Eliot's—later, the tub was full. Looking at the slimy mess, Nathaniel observed that the first human being to eat an oyster must have been very hungry or very brave. He and Will lugged the tub to the tiny cook shack out behind Talmadge's shanty, in a grove of long-leaved pine and moss-bearded oaks. A blond girl, tall and fat, opened the cookhouse door. She had large blue eyes that would have been pretty if they'd had any expression in them. Their blank stare fell immediately on Will and stayed on him, and they gave off a glint like cat's eyes in a darkened room when she stepped outside into a shaft of sunlight piercing the moss overhead. Without a word, she picked up the tub as easily as if it were a flower basket and dragged it over to the pump. Cranking the handle with one hefty arm, she bent over, displaying beneath her coarse, homespun dress the haunches of a mare, and stirred the oysters with the other arm as she washed them. Then she took the tub into the cook shack.

"His wife?"—Nathaniel, thinking aloud.

"He said his wife's sick and that girl is anything but sick," Will noted. "Besides, she can't be more than fourteen, fifteen. Must be his daughter. Did you see the way she looked at me? Gave me the creeps. Like being looked at by a stuffed head that happens to be alive."

14

AT SUPPER, Will presented their host with a three-month-old issue of *Scribner's* and Nathaniel donated a *Tip Top Weekly,* read and reread so many times it was almost falling apart. Talmadge thanked them with a gratitude almost pitiful. Pitiful too was the tenderness with which he smoothed the creased pages, the hunger with which he looked at the covers, as though he would sooner fill his famished mind with the words inside than his concave belly with the oyster stew cooked by the big, blond-haired girl.

He sat at one end of a pine-log table on his small front porch, facing the Sound, and she at the other. She did not speak and, large as she was, ate with sparing delicacy, while Talmadge, lean as he was, devoured two helpings of the stew along with cornbread and greens cooked in bacon fat. A smudge pot smoked to keep mosquitos and sandflies at bay. It wasn't too effective, and the meal was consumed to the sound of hands slapping forearms and foreheads. Talmadge begged their forgiveness for the outdoor dining. His ailing wife was recovering inside, and he did not think it proper to disturb her or to bring guests into a house where sickness dwelled. She'd been poorly for a week, suffering from a fever and headache brought on as a result of delivering a six-months baby, which had come out of her stone dead. He volunteered this, if not casually, then with such an absence of sorrow or bitterness that he might have been speaking about a stillborn pup or kitten.

"Come to Sunday, I asked the Reverend Dewey Jenkins—he's the preacher what ministers to us when the steamer's runnin' from Beaufort—if that dead child was another chastisement, and just when was the Lord gone to have done with me? Or was I to be like that Job feller in the Bible, gettin' one punishment after t'other for no reason? He thought on things a spell and told me that the dead child weren't a chastisement, no, sir. He told me, too, that Job didn't get punished for no reason. He was punished to teach him that the beginnin' of wisdom is fear of the Lord. And that's what the Lord was doin' with me. He was fixin' to end the chastisements and to get into the teachin' part, so's I could become a full-blowed Christian again. The Reverend told me I was in . . . Well, he used a word to mean I was in a time 'twixt and 'tween things. . . ."

"Transition?" Drew ventured, utterly at a loss as to what the man was talking about.

"That was it!" Talmadge stopped abruptly and looked at the girl. "Clara, reckon we could do with coffee and some of that pie of yours," he said, speaking very slowly, with exaggerated movements of his lips. Acknowledging him neither with word nor expression, the girl Clara picked up the dishes and went inside.

"Excuse me asking," Will said, "but is she your daughter?"

Talmadge shook his head. "Not by blood, but she was sent to me three year ago by the Lord, like a blood child would be. Her folks—they lived away back up in the marshes—died of the malaria, mama, papa, baby brother. I found her floatin' down a crick in a canoe when I was out huntin' ducks. Soon come to me that she didn't have no tongue in her head, I mean, she *got* one, it just don't work proper. Can't hear neither. She can understand, if you look right at her and talk real slow, like I just done, but she's deaf as a rock. Well, now, I had this here vision, kind of, after I come across her, floatin' midst the bulrushes like a girl Moses. The Lord had give her to me to raise as my own, and if I done a proper job with her, in time he'd been done with chastisin' me. Not that he was gone to stop all at once, no, sir, it would be like a convict, gittin' a little easier time of it for good behavior. Like that. So Clara—name I give her, 'cuz I never could find out what her real name was, her folks bein' dead and all—been with me ever since."

He pulled a pipe from his shirt pocket, and with head lowered as if in deep thought, filled the bowl from a cloth tobacco pouch. During the pause, Nathaniel, as bemused as his shipmates, asked how he knew Clara's family had died of malaria.

"She took me to 'em. Got in my skiff and rowed with her all the way up the crick, way back in there, and there they was, still livin', but sweatin' and shiverin' and ravin' like crazy folks. I know the malaria when I see it. Done what I could for 'em, took the girl back with me to here, got in my oyster boat, and sailed over to Beaufort to fetch a doctor. By the time I done that and by the time he got out to where they was, three days had passed and they was dead—mama, papa, and baby brother. We buried 'em there and it was then that it come to me, that I was to be father to this girl and that would start puttin' me to rights with the Lord."

Clara came out, bearing coffeepot, mugs, and a steaming pie plate on a pine board that did as serving tray. Eliot had been much affected by Talmadge's tale, his imagination supplying pictures to the words. A muddy creek, some tumbledown shack in some hookwormy swamp, a whole family lying dead. Yet, he could not comprehend it, so alien was it to his experiences. Once, when he had a bad cough, his mother summoned Dr. Matthews by phone, just like it said to do in the telephone company advertisements; he was at their door within an hour. Here, it would have taken three days. Such things shouldn't be, he thought, not in this new century; and yet Talmadge had spoken of them as if they were inevitable.

Nathaniel was thinking more pragmatic thoughts. Eager to repair *Double Eagle* and make up the lost miles as quickly as possible, he bluntly changed the subject and asked Talmadge if he had seen Mr. Kincaid that afternoon.

"Nope. But I hope to get around to it tomorrow," Talmadge answered, distantly. "Jeb's a busy feller. Owns the grocery store and the bait shop besides the sawmill. He's kinda the big man in Snead's Landin', which ain't sayin' much."

He struck a match to relight his pipe, then lit the kerosene lamp on the table. The sun had set, St. Helene Sound stretched away, a pool of pale black hemmed by the deeper black of the woods on the far shore. Crickets chirped, frogs chorused in the marshes beyond the town, and Clara had resumed her silent staring at Will. He could bear it no longer and, with a benign smile, asked, "Why . . . are . . . you . . . looking . . . at . . . me . . . like . . . that?"

At last, her broad impassive face, sallowed by the lantern, showed some animation. She swallowed hard, made a couple of unintelligible sounds, and turned to Talmadge with a look of appeal.

"Can't say for sure. . . . What did y'all say your name was, anyhow?"

"Will," said Will.

"Think maybe she's sweet on you. I ain't clear on exactly how old she is, but the curse come upon her last year, and she's gettin' twitchy in that way. Couple months past, she took to starin' at one of the boys in town, Billy Holcomb. Follered him everywhere like he had a leash on her. Drove him to distractedness."

Will puffed on a cigarette and nodded to say he understood, though it was plain to the Braithwaites, if not to Talmadge, that he did not relish being the new object of Clara's affections.

"Don't mind her, she's got no manners," Talmadge advised. Then, to the girl, emphasizing each carefully enunciated word with a wag of his pipe: "Now Clara, I don't want y'all starin' at this young man like you done Billy. Understood?"

She did not respond.

"Clara. Cla-ar-a?"

A quick movement, more a jerk than a nod. Her guardian told her to go inside and boil water to wash dishes, and she rose mechanically, a ponderous automaton. Talmadge slapped a mosquito, smearing blood on his wrist.

"Ought've knowed I'd have this problem when the time come, but I didn't think of it then. Not that I woulda done different. When the Lord tells you what he wants, ain't no choice but one." Moths swooped around the lantern, throwing bat-sized shadows on the porch wall. "Y'see, boys, about ten year ago, I got the gift of knowin' what was gone to happen before it did." It wasn't clear if he was beginning a new tale or continuing the previous one by going, in a roundabout way, back to its beginning. "Now, it wasn't like I seen pitchers in my head, or heard voices tellin' me what, it was just a kinda knowin'. Can't say it was Beelzabub give me this gift, but I shore did make the devil's work of it. Boys, I was what the Good Book calls a false prophet!"

Drew leaned back in his chair, folded his arms, and frowned.

"Don't expect y'all to believe me, but the truth of the matter was, I had the gift of second sight, except it wasn't a seein', like I told you, but a knowin'. Come to happen this way. I was out oysterin' on down the coast some. Blow come up and I put into this cove where nobody lived. Midst the blow, what d'y'all suppose lands on my boat but a young eagle? I figgered he figgered he had a better chance of ridin' out the blow on my boat than up in a tree somewheres. But after things got all nice and calm again, I'll be if that eagle didn't *stay* right on my boat. Brung him home and made a pet of him. Fed him fish and whatnot. That there eagle was on easy street and didn't he know it. He'd fly away for a spell, but come right on back. Well, one frosty day—it was in February—I was feedin' him shad I ketched up, and lookin' into his eyes and him into mine, and that bird done told me, in a way of speakin', where there was some new oyster beds ain't nobody ever dragged before. I just knowed it to be true, and sure enough, I come back with as many oysters as my boat could hold. Now, what do you boys think of that?"

"Uh . . . that's very interesting," said Nathaniel, reasoning it would be wise to humor him; they needed him to arrange things with Kincaid.

"It gits more interestin'," Talmadge resumed. "That eagle started into tellin' me what weather was comin'. Fair or foul, I'd know. Come the day when me and the eagle is lookin' each other in the eye, and this real bad feelin' come over me. There was gone to be a right bad blow, with loss of life. Warned one and all, but they didn't lissen, thinkin' me to be addled. That gale blew three whole days and three whole nights. Two boats and four men was lost. There ain't but sixty-odd men in this whole town, and to lose four wasn't no small thing, but folks lissened to me from then on. I become a weather prophet.

"But here's where the devil come in, boys. Figgered to get rich off my gift and started to charge folks for what the eagle had to say. Meantime, the eagle's startin' into tellin' me other things, like if a woman was with child, if it was to be boy or girl and what day it was to be borned. Charged for that, too. Soon enough, I become famous all up and down this coast, folks comin' from near and far, wantin' to know one thing or t'other. Well, there was times the eagle didn't have nothin' to say, so I'd make somethin' up. Some of them prophecies didn't come true, but a lot did—reckon it was luck—and the dimes and nickels and the quarters started to pile on up. Now I was a fortune-teller. The Reverend Dewey Jenkins heard tell what was goin' on, and was he hoppin' mad! Made me the subject of his sermon one Sunday. Points right at me in front of the en-tire congregation and says the Bible has got some things to say about sorcerers and what he called divinators, and wasn't none of them good. He read some scripture, don't recollect what now. . . ."

"Deuteronomy or Jeremiah," Drew interrupted. Listening to this nonsense insulted his intelligence. It was worse by far than all that baloney about Aunt Sophronia. "There's Jeremiah twenty-nine, verses eight and nine. 'Let not your prophets and your diviners, that be in the midst of you, deceive you. . . . For they prophesy falsely unto you in my name: I have not sent them.'"

Talmadge pushed his chair back and slapped the table.

"I'll be . . . Them's the words exactly."

"He reads a lot and he's got a photographic memory," said Eliot.

"Reckon he does, 'cuz them's the words exactly as the Reverend Dewey Jenkins spoke 'em. Done shamed me in front of the whole congregation, and after meetin', I asked him how come he done that. And he said he *meant* to shame me. Told me a true Christian puts hisself into the hands of Providence when it comes to knowin' the future. It's a sin to try to know the mind of God Almighty about what's to pass, and I was sinnin' twice over by chargin' money. If I persisted, I was gone to be chastised and good, he said to me, but Beelzabub had me in his clutches and I went on right with my divinatin'. Here's what stopped it.

"Some folks over to Beaufort heard about me and the eagle. Reckon they was put on to me by the reverend. These folks belonged to what's called the Human Sociation, and they sent out a whole delegation and said I got to let my eagle go. I said, 'Y'all see a cage? This here eagle is a free man and stays here of his own free will.' They wouldn't hear none of it, threw a sack over my eagle, and took him away. Stole him, but legal like. So that was the end of my divinatin', but the beginnin' of my troubles. My hair started to go white, and me not yet forty. Then my eyesight commenced to git worse and worse, till I was goin' to Beaufort once every three months or so to git new spectacles. Then, one day when I was out oysterin', more seagulls than I ever seed in one place at one time come along and snatched my whole ketch, shells and all. A oyster in the shell is a mighty big load for a seagull, but them gulls was heaven-sent and had the strength for it. That happened to me every time I went out. Purty soon, I didn't have no oysters to sell, and me and the missus started to go hungry, which is how I come to be the bag of bones I am today. Reverend told me the chastisements had begun. Didn't cut no ice with the Lord that I'd quit divinatin', 'cuz I hadn't quit of my own accord, only 'cuz the Human Sociation folks stole my eagle. I had not repented, y'see.

"It was terrible! Me and the missus goin' so hungry, folks took to bringin' us food. Oh, I repented then! Begged the Lord to show me a way to get back on His good side. Then He sent me Clara, and ever since then, He's done eased off considerable. But from time to time, He sends me a chastisement, like that gull you seen this afternoon with your own eyes, just to remind me that I ain't yet shed of my sins."

There was a long silence, filled with the sounds of crickets and frogs and the sough of wind through the trees and moss.

"So now you boys know my story," Talmadge said, as though they had begged to hear it. He knocked his pipe against the leg of his chair and, noticing that his listeners were stifling yawns, asked if they were ready to turn in.

They nodded as one, and the reformed false prophet picked up the lantern and led them down a path to the dock, then bid them good night.

"What did you make of all that?" asked Nathaniel, pulling the oars. The waters were so black in the hour before moonrise that he seemed to be rowing through the middle of the night air.

"What I make of it is that we ought to go to Beaufort first thing in the morning," Will said. "Bound to be a boatyard there where we can patch the old ship up for a decent price."

"Let's see what this Kincaid offers first."

"All right, Natters. But let's shove out of here soon as we can. This gunkhole is even weirder than I thought."

The next afternoon, as the tide was ebbing and great blue herons, posing still as artists' stuffed models, waited for the falling waters to expose schools of minnows to their quick, yellow eyes, a shabby little man poled his skiff across the flats to *Double Eagle*.

"Good day," he called, tossing a line to Nathaniel. He was short and wiry, with a gray stubble on his jaw and a nose set off by a wart big as a bee sting. "Here to see about this busted boat you got. Gimme a hand aboard. Think I'm as young as you?"

"You're Mr. Kincaid's carpenter?"

"Nope. I'm Kincaid."

Dressed in a patched shirt, greasy trousers held up by frayed braces, and a filthy straw hat, he looked more like an old swamp rat than the leading citizen of Snead's Landing. He spat tobacco juice over the side and said:

"Our local village idiot tells me you're from Maine and got caught in that blow day before yesterday."

"You're referring to Mr. Talmadge?"

"Who else? Tell you that yarn about him bein' a prophet?"

"Yes, sir . . ."

"Tells that one to every stranger who comes by, which one look at our town ought to tell y'all that that ain't exactly an everyday occurrence. Hope you don't think we're all like him. We ain't got a mayor, but if we did, I'd be it, and I wouldn't want folks to think we're a bunch of ignorant fools here."

Eager for the man's goodwill, Nathaniel assured him, truthfully, that they thought no such thing.

"Not that we ain't got our share of ignorant fools, the ones who was taken in by Phineas. Phineas, he's a little bit crazy and a whole lot lazy, and he's got an imagination. One day, his craziness got together with his laziness and the two of 'em had a talk with his imagination, and he figured out a way to make him some spendin' money without havin' to work for it. Only part of his story is true is the part about takin' in that poor gal. Phineas has got a heart, I'll say that for him, more heart than I got. So what is it you need done? Phineas wasn't too clear on that."

Nathaniel took him forward and showed him and made sure to let him know that Talmadge had promised that his charges would be reasonable.

"Compared to what they charge in Beaufort, sure," he said. "About your sails, there's a sailmaker over to Beaufort, name of Geslin. Frenchy, we call him. He's about as friendly as a cottonmouth, but he charges reasonable, too."

Kincaid studied the foremast with a canny, calculating look, then ran his hands along the main boom and gave a low whistle.

"This here's Sitka spruce. You boys millionaires or did you steal this here yacht?"

Taken aback, Nathaniel hesitated before answering that they were neither millionaires nor pirates. His mind turned this way and that for an explanation of how four teenage boys had come into possession of so fine a vessel. If Kincaid knew that it belonged to their father, he might feel free to demand every dollar they had.

"We're in the salvage business, and we've got our first job waiting for us down in Florida," he said, hoping his overly expressive face did not betray him. "We picked up this schooner a year ago, my brothers and me and our buddy. Went for a song, it was about ready for the break-up yard. We put every dime we had in her and all our labor, too, and got her shipshape."

"Son, when you're fibbin', it's best to keep it short," Kincaid said sternly, but with a twinkle of forgiveness. "This don't look like a salvage vessel to me, and even if it was, ain't nobody but a millionaire gonna fit her out with Alaskan Sitka masts and spars, when good old pine will do just as well and at half the cost. Now, why don't y'all tell me the truth, so's I know who and what I'm dealin' with here."

Eliot and Drew must have overheard the conversation below decks, for both their faces appeared in the hatchway to the forward cabin. Eliot took it upon himself to tell their story, and concluded with a statement of their financial condition: Of the thirty dollars their father had given them, a little over twenty-five remained, while their friend Will had about another twenty.

"Well, now, like the Good Book says, the truth shall set you free, but that don't mean everything comes for free," said Kincaid. He drew from his trousers pocket a length of twine, and with it and spans of his hand, began to take measurements—a method Drew found woefully imprecise and primitive. "Got me some Georgia pine sawlog over to the mill. Got cracks in it, but if you boys know anything about spar wood, you'll know the best kind got weather cracks in it and the worst is smooth, same as people. Do the whole job for twenty bucks, fifteen if you do the varnishin' yourselves."

"We can varnish," Nathaniel said. "You have yourself a deal, Mr. Kincaid."

"Take five up front," he replied, and then, folding the bill into his shirt pocket, advised that there was no way Frenchy Geslin, reasonable though he was, would cut new canvas for what funds they had left. They would have to find a way to beg, borrow, or steal the money, or work for it. The Beaufort oyster-packing plant was usually in need of new hands, though the work paid so little it could be weeks before the boys saved enough.

This was discouraging news, indeed. Nathaniel foresaw dreary weeks ahead, shucking oysters for pennies, and the end of all his hopes of seeing the Keys and finding the *Annisquam*. It was either that or make the rest of the voyage and the return without a foresail. Then, despair being parent to inspiration, he had one.

"Might be able to borrow. We've got family in Beaufort. Our great-aunt Judith," he said, more or less thinking out loud.

Eliot scoffed at the suggestion, which he thought typical of his quixotic older brother. They did not know if Great-Aunt Judith was still alive, and even if she was, he said, what were they going to do? Knock at her door and ask for a loan? They had never met her, did not even know her last name.

"Say, you boys sure don't *talk* like you got kin in Beaufort," Kincaid interrupted. "Talk as Yankee as blue-belly prisoners I heard talkin' durin' the war."

Drew, a little offended by the way the man had practically spit out the word *Yankee*—and by the implication that they were lying—said that their mother had been born and raised in Beaufort, and that her father had died fighting for the South in the Civil War.

"Oh he did, did he?" Kincaid's expression had darkened. "Died in the what, you say?"

"The Civil War, sir."

"I asked you, in the *what*?"

"The Civil War," he repeated, very puzzled. Not a minute ago, the old man had mentioned the war and now acted as if he'd never heard of it.

Bristling, the way Trajan bristled when a dog or strange cat came near, Kincaid laid hands on Drew's shoulders and breathed into his face (he wasn't more than three inches taller) the smells of bad teeth and stale tobacco.

"If you really had a granddaddy who fought for the South, you'd know that down here we call it the War Between the States, because that's what it was. Wasn't a damned thing civil about it. I'm bein' real civil right now, and the war wasn't that, son." The hands dropped, and Kincaid unbuttoned his shirt, revealing a scar that twisted from his sternum to his navel, like a long, pink worm. "Nothin' civil about this, is there? Seven Pines, May 28, 1862. I was with Longstreet, finest man ever to come outta South Carolina. The War Between the States, remember that. Y'all can go back to callin' it the Civil War when you're back in Maine, or wherever the hell it is y'all come from."

Drew gulped and said, "Yes, sir."

"So now that we're talkin' the same language, let's hear about this granddaddy."

His voice and body had relaxed, yet the man was so touchy they were afraid that anything they said would give offense.

"I sure hope you wasn't fibbin' to me about that. I truly do."

"He was killed at the Battle of Antietam Creek," Drew said.

"Sharpsburg. Down here, we prefer to call it Sharpsburg."

"Yes, sir. Sharpsburg. Fall of 1862."

"That's when it was. This granddaddy of yours have a name, or don't you know that, neither?"

"It was Lightbourne. Pardon Lightbourne."

Kincaid's head snapped back, but he recovered instantly and assumed again a look of flinty skepticism.

"Let's hear a little more."

"Our mother said he was a captain. That's what her aunt told her, our great-aunt Judith. She raised our mother after our grandmother died."

"Your maw got a picture of her daddy?"

Nathaniel answered that she had only one, a photograph showing a tall officer with very light hair and a mustache.

Murmuring, "Ain't this somethin'?" Kincaid removed his hat, uncovering a bald head ribboned in gray, and wiped the sweatband with a finger. "Boys, there was a Captain Pardon Lightbourne in the regiment of volunteers raised up in Beaufort County. Troopers called him 'Swede' because he was a tall man, hair like cornsilk and the mustache to match. I was in that regiment, a private when I got shot at Seven Pines."

"You knew our grandfather?" asked Nathaniel, feeling something move through him, a pleasurable chill.

"Can't say I knowed him, him bein' a cap'n, me a private, and us in different companies. But I knowed him to see him. Only time I talked to him, except to salute and say good mornin', was the time my cap'n sent me to him with a message. Recollect that real clear, it was before Longstreet's corps—our regiment was part of it—deployed to go up against Burnside at Seven Pines. Cap'n Lightbourne was settin' at the fire with his company sergeant and a lieutenant and they was jawin' about their families. The cap'n said he got a letter from his wife and that his son—reckon that would be your uncle—had spoke his first words, and that if he lived through the thing tomorrow, first thing he would do is ask for leave so he could get on home and hear his boy call him daddy. Yep, recollect that because them words, 'If I live through this thing,' was on everybody's mind, but nobody dared to speak 'em except the cap'n. Said it real calm and matter-of-fact-like. He was a brave man. And here's his grandsons, right here in Snead's Landing, all the way from Maine. How is it y'all got to be Yankees?"

Succinctly as he could, Nathaniel related that story, carefully editing out any reference to his father's service in the Union navy. He had been thrilled by Kincaid's brief reanimation of their grandfather, a man who had been little more than a name to him and his brothers, a figure in a cracked photograph without voice or personality. How wonderful to meet someone who had laid eyes upon the living man, had spoken to him and had heard him speak. The scene, suffused with the romance of the long ago, with the glamour of war, had composed itself in Nathaniel's mind: the fair-haired officer in rebel gray, seated at the watchfire with his officers on the night before battle. Only part of this captivating picture troubled him.

"Are you sure our grandfather was talking about a *son?*" he asked Kincaid. "That it was a son who'd spoken his first words?"

"Sure am. There's things I remember from the war like they was last week, some of 'em things I'd as soon not remember. That's a peculiar question. How come you asked it?"

An instinct told Nathaniel to keep the real reason to himself, but before he could formulate a plausible alternative, Drew blurted out:

"Our mother never told us she had a brother."

"That a fact?" Kincaid said, laying a finger against the wart on his nose. "Well, that's peculiar, too."

"Oh, Dad's side is the same way," Eliot tossed off lightheartedly. "We're a peculiar family all around."

"Ain't no business of mine. Maybe this great-aunty of yours can fill in the missin' parts. Said her name's Judith? Come to think of it, there's an old widow over to Beaufort name of Judith Wilcox. Her husband was Lucien Wilcox, what owned the biggest bank in Beaufort. Had some dealin's with him. Now, if that Judith is yours, y'all might be in luck. Banker's widow bound to have money to lend." Putting his hat back on, and giving it a smart crease, as if it were a beaver Stetson, Kincaid stood to leave. "But just in case she don't have it, or in case she ain't the right Judith, I'm goin' to do the job for y'all for the five in my pocket. Hell, I'll do it for that, no matter what."

Nathaniel thought of protesting for form's sake, decided against it, and thanked him.

"It ain't charity. It's because you're close kin to Cap'n Lightbourne. Makes up some for y'all bein' Yankees." He gave Drew's head a rub with his knuckles. "Just remember, it's the War Between the States."

15

ALL ALONG Bay Street and the Beaufort riverfront, the talk among merchants and fishermen was of the weather—hot enough to make the natives uncomfortable and the Braithwaites feel that they had landed in some Amazon port. Sweltering in their shore clothes, they proceeded through the business district, to which the adjective *bustling* could be applied only if your standard of comparison was a backwater like Snead's Landing. Half a dozen Negroes, speaking a sluggish dialect that sounded like English but wasn't quite, were stacking bales by a cotton warehouse with the movements of men afflicted by some minor paralysis. Two women came out of a shop and languidly strolled up Bay under parasols, while a team of panting horses slowly drew a freight wagon laden with furniture. Beaufort moved at a leisurely pace, and away from downtown, it wasn't moving at all on this broiling afternoon. Turning up Carteret, which wended between stationary parades of live oak past the frame or tabby mansions of town gentry, the boys didn't see a soul or a carriage. The same scene presented itself on Port Republic. All in all, the town had the look of one abandoned by plague or threat of invasion, and the deserted atmosphere heightened their feelings of uneasiness. At the corner, Nathaniel stopped and looked up the street with the bewildered air of a tourist in need of directions.

"Well, either we go through with this or we don't," said Eliot.

Not that he wanted to. With all his heart, he was opposed to the enterprise, first, on moral grounds—Nat's plan involved a certain amount of deception—and second, on practical grounds: they knew that Aunt Judith had been bitterly opposed to their mother's marriage; it followed that she would not open her heart, or her purse, to the offspring of that marriage. The only sensible thing would be to wire their father for the money; surely he had not meant his injunction to apply to emergencies;

surely he would want his precious damn yacht fixed up as quickly as possible. But Nat objected, without giving a reason. He didn't need to; Eliot knew what it was. Drew had taken Nat's side, not because he was proud but because he wanted to find out if they had a long-lost uncle and why Mother had never told them about him.

"I'm just taking a second to think things through before we go up there," Nat said now. "Remember, let me do the talking."

"Aye, aye, skipper."

They went up Port Republic, looking at the house numbers, and came to a scrolled iron fence behind which stood a white, two-story house with black shutters and verandas aloft and alow. Nathaniel opened the gate and led the way down a brick walk and up the stairs to a windowless front door. A mocha-skinned Negro woman, quite tall, with streaks of gray in her hair, answered his ring. She said something in the same peculiar dialect he had heard from the Negroes stacking bales. He didn't understand a word and asked if Mrs. Wilcox was in.

The woman uttered a phrase that sounded like "Shebeby-year," which he took to be an affirmative answer.

"Please give this to her." He took from his jacket pocket the note of introduction he had composed on the back of telephone company stationery.

They waited for a minute, for three, for five. . . .

"We know she has a telephone," muttered Eliot, mopping his face with a bandanna. "We should have called first."

"Better in person," Nathaniel said. "Makes it harder for her to tell us to get lost."

Another minute. Drew, squirming as though he had to go to the bathroom, wondered aloud if Judith Wilcox was not their relation after all.

Doubtful after what they had learned from the operator at the telephone company. Nathaniel had suggested going there to look up Mrs. Wilcox's address in the listings, reasoning that a banker's house would have a phone. He found an L. A. Wilcox at 414 Port Republic, and asked one of the operators if that would be Lucien Wilcox, who had owned the bank. She replied that it was, although Mr. Wilcox had died two years ago. His widow lived there now—poor woman, she'd outlived two husbands. Had she? Nathaniel asked, attempting to sound ingenuous. That wouldn't be Judith Wilcox, whose first husband died in the war of cholera, would it? Why, yes, it was, replied the operator; then, her face clouding, she asked the boys who they might be, and Nathaniel told her they were old friends of the family, and left immediately. He was proud of his detective work; hell, he'd told his brothers, he could get a job with the Pinkertons.

Some ten minutes had gone by when the maid returned. Opening the door, she said, "Pleaseya, coomin year." They entered a dim hall with a central staircase, and were brought to a sitting room whose walls were painted in stripes of sunlight falling through the louvers of shutters closed over closed windows, apparently to keep out the heat, though the opposite effect was achieved. The stifling air was made more so by a strong smell of cologne and medicine, the scents of boudoir and pharmacy combined. At the far end, an elderly woman, holding a cane in one hand and wearing a dark blue dress with lace sprouting from collar and cuffs, sat enthroned in an oval-backed chair.

"Thank you, Arthurlene," she said in a near whisper, then turned her small head to gaze directly at the boys. The shadows blurred her features, but a single slash of the barred light fell across her eyes—two steel-gray buttons fastened under gray brows bushy as a man's. "Would you gentlemen care for some lemonade? I would think lemonade would be in order on a day like this," she said; her accent reminded them of their mother's, adding a syllable to one-syllable words, two to three.

"Lemonade would be fine, ma'am," answered Nathaniel, and his manner of speech, compared to hers, sounded harsh, rushed, and somehow impolite.

"Three lemonades, if you please, Arthurlene," she said to the maid, and then, after looking at her great-nephews for another ten or fifteen seconds, murmured, "And so you are Elizabeth's boys."

"Yes, ma'am."

"Forgive me for making you wait in this ghastly heat. I wasn't prepared to receive callers."

"Oh, we didn't mind. . . ."

"You'll also have to forgive me for not standing up. I've an arthritis that afflicts me, heat or frost. Come closer so I can have a better look at you."

They crossed the floor and stood before her in a row, and she raised a lorgnette and studied each of their faces with a kind of detachment.

"And I had resigned myself to never setting eyes on you. How pleasant to be surprised at my age," she said. "I can certainly see Elizabeth in you"—motioning at Nathaniel—"but you, young man, you're the image of your father. I remember him clearly, and that strange quiet boy he had with him—why, yes, that's who you look like."

"That would be my half brother, Lockwood," Drew said, wishing someone would open a window.

"Was that his name? I guess I've forgotten. And yours? Your note said Nathaniel, Eliot, and Andrew, but which is which? Elizabeth sent me birth announcements—she was thoughtful enough to do me that one courtesy—but I cannot recall who came when."

After Nathaniel cleared that up for her, she gestured for them to sit down. He took the only other chair, his brothers a worn velvet settee, from which puffs of dust arose when they sat, the dust motes swirling in the slats of hot sunlight. Arthurlene returned with a pitcher of lemonade and three glasses. Thirst overcoming their manners, the boys drained theirs with greedy gulps.

"My, you must be parched!" said Aunt Judith. "But then, I don't suppose you are accustomed to such heat in Maine. Are you still living there? Oh, no, that's right. Boston. The last I heard from your mother, you had moved to Boston."

"Right after I was born," answered Nathaniel, "and after Dad's business got going. That's where Dad was from, maybe you remember?"

"I do," she said, and then plied them with questions about their mother and father and themselves, her manner neither hostile nor friendly but the way Mother's was with Lockwood: correct. When she was done, she begged their pardon for interrogating them so vigorously, but you see, boys, apart from the birth announcements, your mother has not seen fit to communicate with me—this with a venom that her mellifluous drawl not only failed to conceal but in fact emphasized.

"Really? We always thought it was the other way—" Drew started, but Nathaniel cut him off with a sharp look, and seeing a chance to flatter Aunt Judith, told her that their mother had always spoken highly of her, referring to her as "my dear aunt Judith."

"She always said that if we ever got to Beaufort, to be sure to call on you, and so here we are."

The old woman leaned a little forward, folding her hands in her lap, the veins in them prominent and blue.

"I'm surprised she would even know where to find me. I stopped writing to her, oh, it must be at least ten or eleven years ago. I was beginning to feel like someone putting notes in a bottle that are never picked up." She pursed her lips, from which vertical wrinkles sprouted. "Which brings me to ask, Whatever are you doing here all by yourselves? You are alone?"

"We're not with Mother and Father, if that's what you mean."

"It is. This is a terribly long way for three young boys to come on their own. Surely not just to visit me?"

The opening Nathaniel had been hoping for. He gave her an abridged account of their journey from its beginning, hewing strictly to the facts until he drew near the end, when he said that they had been making for Beaufort with the intention of visiting her when their vessel was caught in a gale, damaged, and driven into St. Helene Sound. They had sailed from there this morning to see about repairs.

"So we thought, Mrs. Wilcox"—fresh springs of sweat on his forehead, his will struggling to control his traitorous face—"that it would be best if we called on you now, before the repairs got under way. We're not going to have a whole lot of time, making sure they're done right, and then we've got to work at the oyster plant." He stopped to study her expression. "The boss told us they put in some awful long hours."

A puzzled frown came to Aunt Judith's bushy eyebrows. "Pardon me, but what do you mean, work at the oyster plant? Whatever would you be doing there?"

"Shucking oysters, ma'am."

"Oh, I know you would be shucking oysters, what else would one do at an oyster plant? It isn't work fit for gentlemen."

"I didn't explain, Mrs. Wilcox. We have to work there to pay for the repairs to our boat."

"I'm sorry, I know nothing of boats and their repairs. Is it expensive?"

"It can be. We blew out some canvas, I mean, we lost a sail in the storm, and we need a new one cut. We saw a sailmaker this morning, a man named Geslin. Frenchy Geslin, they call him. Do you know him?"

"I'm quite sure"—archly—"I do not know anyone called 'Frenchy.'"

"He gave us an estimate, and it's a lot more than we've got, so we decided to get jobs at the oyster plant. If the three of us work for about two weeks, we figure to have the money together."

She asked the amount, and Nathaniel told her, his emotions those of a poker player about to draw a hole card to fill a flush. Aunt Judith only cocked her head aside, asking if he and his brothers wanted more lemonade; if so, would he please pull that cord over there in the corner behind him. This he did.

"We do have a telegraph office here," said Aunt Judith, as Arthurlene materialized out of the shadows to take the tray. "Why don't you wire your father for the money?"

Eliot looked at Nathaniel, who said they could not do as she suggested.

"I can't explain why, because we don't know why. All he told us when we left was that the money he gave us—I didn't tell you, it was thirty dollars—was supposed to last us and he wouldn't send us any more."

The maid came back with fresh lemonade, filled three glasses, and when Aunt Judith said she would have some, a fourth.

"That is outrageous, Nathaniel," the old woman said. "Quite honestly, I find your situation outrageous. Do you mean to say that Elizabeth would not send the money, either?"

"Dad controls the purse strings, Mrs. Wilcox."

"Aunt Judith, please." She raised her glass with quaky hand. "Answer this for me, and answer on your oath. You boys aren't in any sort of trouble, are you? You haven't run away from home, have you?"

Finding it a relief to speak the truth, Nathaniel swore, his brothers seconding him.

Aunt Judith paused to gauge their honesty before saying what they desperately wanted to hear: Were she to lend them the money, would their father repay her? It seemed to her that any man with a thimbleful of honor would.

"I'm sure he would," Nathaniel answered, feeling not altogether honorable himself. "But you don't have to do that. I know we can earn—"

A palm, pallid and deeply fissured, was raised to stop his protest.

"I am fully aware I don't have to, young man. I don't have to do anything except breathe, eat, move my bowels, and die, which necessity is probably not very off. Kindly ring Arthurlene for me."

Spiritlike, she appeared again, and was instructed to bring stationery, pen, and ink. When this was done, Aunt Judith began to rise, shakily supporting herself on her cane. The Braithwaites practically tripped over one another in their rush to help their benefactress to her feet, but she waved them off and stood on her own, and they were surprised at how short she was—barely taller than Drew. Going to the table on which Arthurlene had placed paper and pen, she began to write, crumpled up her first attempt, and began again.

"Give this to that Frenchy person. I'm quite sure he knows who I am," she said, and handed Nathaniel a promissory note instructing Mr. Geslin to send all repair bills to her for payment.

From the three brothers, a chorus of thank-you's.

"Oh, you needn't thank me," she started. "On second thought, you can, perhaps. . . . There are some questions I should like answered. They have been preying on my mind for years. . . . Yes, that is how you can best thank me."

"Sure, if we can, Aunt Judith," Nathaniel said, and added, "There's something we're wondering about, too. About our grandfather?"

"Not now. It is time for my nap, and I never miss my nap. At dinner. Five-thirty sharp. I do mean sharp. Do not think me so Southern as to mean anytime between five-thirty and six-thirty."

"We'll be here. Would it be all right if we brought our shipmate? His name's Will Terhune, and . . ."

"I'm sorry, that won't be all right"—imperiously. "My questions are of a private nature. Five-thirty, boys."

They fairly ran down Port Republic to Carteret, down Carteret to Bay, Bay to the riverfront wharves, and then through the door of a brick building and up the stairs to a low-ceilinged loft where men in canvas aprons sat at long tables, stitching and cutting and pumping the treadles of heavy-duty sewing machines. The note was delivered to Frenchy Geslin, who had proved to be as irascible as Kincaid had described. Earlier, when Will and the Braithwaites had tried to negotiate a lower price for the new foresail, he had snarled at them, "I'm running a business, not a goddamned charity." Now he was as pleasant as could be, declaring Aunt Judith's pledge to be as good as cash in hand. He would start on the job that very day.

Down the stairs they flew, down the wharf to *Double Eagle,* and gave the news to Will, who was sunning himself on the cabin top.

"Splendid work, Natters. I never thought duplicity was one of your strong points."

The comment stirred Eliot's misgivings: They had buncoed a considerable sum out of an aging widow, a blood relative to boot.

"At least you kept it in the family," quipped Will.

"We didn't bunco her, and I'm dead sure that Dad will pay her back," Nathaniel said, and then reviewed their actions, concluding that they had not played Aunt Judith all that falsely. The story about the oyster plant was mostly true: They had inquired about employment there, hadn't they? (Though Nathaniel's motives in going had been to add verisimilitude to their tale.) And the foreman had turned them down, saying that he had all the hands he needed, hadn't he?

"Then we should have told her that," said Eliot, remembering that he'd been relieved by the foreman's rejection; when he'd seen the benches crowded with whey-faced women and children shucking amid steam and stink, he'd shuddered.

"Sure, but then we would have had to have come right out and begged her for the money, and Braithwaites don't beg," Nathaniel said. "The way we did it, we sort of nudged her into volunteering."

Really, he rationalized further, the only lies they'd told were to say that they'd been on their way to Beaufort to visit Aunt Judith and that their mother had spoken highly of her, and those untruths, because they made her feel good, fell on the white end of the spectrum.

"Oh, yeah? Wonder what your true-blue, two-cent magazine hero would say to that."

"Frank Merriwell doesn't exist," Nathaniel said.

Although it was two hours to sundown, an electric chandelier, augmented by a candelabra, burned in the dining room, for its windows also had been shuttered. Bathed, combed, the boys looked as presentable as they could at dinner, a Carolina low-country feast of rice and yams, fried chicken and baked ham and okra and fluffy rolls dusted with powdered sugar. Aunt Judith, changed out of her dark blue dress into a dark red one, presided at the head of the table but ate very little. Her digestion wasn't what it used to be, she complained.

The questions she had for them were not asked. Instead, she launched into a monologue about Marshlands, the rice plantation she and her first husband, one Caleb Maxey, had owned near Port Royal. Without bitterness but in the neutral voice of an historian, she spoke of its destruction by the Federal fleet that had blockaded Port Royal Sound in the fall of 1861, just before their mother was born, and of the Union occupation of Beaufort after the Confederate garrison on Hilton Head Island surrendered, the city becoming, for all practical purposes, a Northern outpost, what with bluecoats everywhere and their general, Stevens, headquartered on Bay Street, and sea-island slaves walking freely about among their former masters, emancipated by Yankee bayonets two years before Mr. Lincoln issued his famous proclamation. She told them about the Episcopal church turned into a military hospital, where she served as a volunteer, and oh, the suffering and horrors she had witnessed: doctors sawing off limbs on tombstones torn from the church graveyard to be used as operating tables, Southern blood and Yankee blood mingling to stain and blot the names of the long dead. Finally, she gave a sketch of their grandfather, her brother-in-law: his acumen in business (he'd started a successful cotton and indigo brokerage two years before the war), his handsome appearance, and his bravery. But she did not say a word about their grandmother, and they didn't ask, because she never gave them a chance.

Now, as Arthurlene cleared the dinner plates, Aunt Judith's narrative had rambled to the day when, in a letter signed by General Longstreet himself, news arrived of Pardon Lightbourne's death. The boys listened raptly but with divided hearts. It was hard, was in truth impossible, for them to reconcile their admiration for his courage with their repugnance, instilled by their father, for the cause he had died for. Nor could they reconcile their liking for their great-aunt and the knowledge that this small, frail, generous woman once had owned a hundred human beings. And there was one final, distressing contradiction: If their father and the father of their mother had met forty years ago, each would have done his level best to kill the other.

The maid came back from the kitchen and murmured something to her mistress, who asked the boys if they would like ice cream with their peach pie. The vote was unanimous, then Drew wanted to know what language Arthurlene was speaking, because he hadn't heard her utter a word that sounded like pie or ice cream. It was called Gullah, replied Aunt Judith, and it was spoken by the sea-island Negroes. Though she had little command of it herself, she and Arthurlene had been together so long that she could understand it.

"Your mother was fluent in it when she was a girl," she added, shaking her head when Arthurlene set a dessert plate in front of her. "The Gullah hymns and lullabies are quite beautiful, quite haunting. There was one Arthurlene sang to Elizabeth after her mother was taken by the consumption. Did she never sing it to you?"

They all three shook their heads.

"I suppose not," said their great-aunt after a few seconds' silence. "It's my feeling that your mother, after she left . . . Has she told you *any-thing* about her life here?"

"Yes, ma'am," Nathaniel said.

"And she has spoken fondly of me? Truthfully now, if you weren't earlier today."

"Sure. About how you taught her to be a lady and to speak French. . . ."

"French *phrases*, Nathaniel. Nothing of the grammar, which I frankly don't know myself. Phrases like *enchantez* and *au fond* and *comment allez-vous*, which do for a lady's speech what powder and paint do for her face."

"What do you mean by that?" asked Drew, with his characteristic bluntness.

"It is often necessary for a woman to present herself as more beautiful than nature made her, more refined than perhaps she really is. Women are illusionists. Theirs is the deceptiveness that is not necessarily fraudulence, because it makes the world a pleasanter place to live in. Arthurlene, I believe the sun's gone down. Kindly open the windows and allow the evening air to come in."

"We'll give her a hand," Nathaniel offered, not so much out of an earnest desire to be helpful as an eagerness to cool the steamy room as quickly as possible.

"You will do no such thing," said Aunt Judith as he pushed his chair back, he hearing in the imperative an echo of the former mistress of a plantation with one hundred slaves. "Arthurlene is in my employ, and has her duties. You are my kin, and have yours, which are"—more softly now—"to answer the questions I have for you, if you can, that is."

"We'll try," Nathaniel said. "Would you mind if we asked you one first?"

"I shall try as well."

"Do we have an uncle? Or did we?"

Aunt Judith looked down and tugged at her lace cuffs.

"Which side of your family are you speaking of?"

"Well, yours, of course. Mother's. Did she have an older brother?"

Her gray eyes rose from her sleeve to linger momentarily on Nathaniel's face before they shifted to Arthurlene, who, with her back to the room and both hands on a sash, half-turned to give Aunt Judith a startled look.

"Oh, dear. It's that warped window again. Nathaniel, it appears a man's strength is needed, after all."

He got up and gave the window a heave, expecting resistance; but there was none, and it flew up to slam against the top of the sill.

"Gracious! Elizabeth has a Great Sandow for a son," Aunt Judith flattered, when he sat down again.

Gracious! His mother's favorite expression.

"I'm not that strong," he said. "The window wasn't stuck."

"As to your question, did your mother ever mention having an older brother?"

"No, ma'am, but . . ."

"Well, that answers it, doesn't it? If she did, surely she would have said so. Wherever did you get this notion?"

He told her Kincaid's story, which she dismissed with a wave.

"That was quite a coincidence, your running into him, but I'm afraid that old man has mixed things up. Your grandfather would, of course, have been speaking about his daughter."

"That's what we figured, but if I've got everything straight, Mr. Kincaid overheard our grandfather talking before some battle that took place in the spring of 1862. So Mother would have been around six months old. Wouldn't that have been kind of early for her to be speaking her first words?"

From Aunt Judith, a brittle laugh.

"Elizabeth always was intelligent, but not that bright. Boys, if you wish to know anything about our side of the family, ask me or her, don't listen to some old cracker with a faulty memory." She removed the napkin from her lap and laid it on the table. "And now that I have cleared that up for you, perhaps you could tell me, if you know, why your mother has seen fit not to communicate with me all these years? Why every one of my letters has gone unanswered? Why she has deprived me of news about the closest thing I shall ever have to grandchildren? I can understand why she would have wanted to forget Beaufort. Life here was trying for her, it was for all of us. But I was like a mother to her, and this silence of hers, it's been cruel. It is a wound. It is a . . . like a . . . a repudiation of *me*. And I cannot understand the reasons for that and hope you can shed some light."

Nathaniel wanted to answer, her plea was so heartfelt, but he was too confused; the aunt's and the niece's versions of the breach between them contradicted each other.

"How am I supposed to take your silence, boys?" the old woman asked. "That you don't have an answer, or you do and are reluctant to give it to me? I am quite prepared for candidness."

Drew, unfortunately, took her at her word and said, "Maybe it's because you don't like our dad."

"Pardon me? Don't like your father? Why should I dislike your father, Andrew?"

"On account of he's a Yankee, and . . ."

"*What?* Young man, fifteen thousand federal troops occupied this city for four years, and while I can't say I was fond of them as a class, I did grow used to them and found some of them to be honorable men. Why, take a look at this city of ours. It wasn't destroyed, ravaged. I have to admit, they took rather good care of it, and there are people in the South who to this day would have my head for saying that. I considered your father a suitable match for Elizabeth. He had means, he was obviously ambitious, and I liked the way he treated that boy, that strange quiet boy. . . ."

"Lockwood."

"Yes, Lockwood. He was quite devoted to him, and he was certainly taken with Elizabeth. Head over heels in love. Wrote poems to her . . ."

"He did?"—Nathaniel, amazed.

"Yes. You didn't know that?"

He shook his head, feeling a pang of longing to have known his father then, before the poetry went out of him.

"There was only the problem of his age, and that was more your mother's problem than mine," Aunt Judith continued, in an agitated voice. "She came to me once and asked my advice on it, and I told her that an older man would be suitable, and probably better than a younger one. If there were any ill feelings between your father and me, I'm afraid to say they come from him. You see, I represented something to him, a Southern woman of a certain kind. Your father was a bit like my first husband—blind to shadings. Things were either one way or the other, and people, too. Never mind that I"—both hands gripping the edge of the table, real color seeping through the artificial one in her cheeks— "defied the laws of this state to educate as many of our Negroes as I could. Taught them to read and write. My own husband forbade me from conducting those lessons, I was causing talk, you know, but I defied him, too, because I was young and headstrong and considered such ordinances perfectly barbarous. If you wish to know the truth, I considered our peculiar institution perfectly barbarous, for which I knew, well before the war, we would suffer a Divine judgment. But that's neither here nor there. I never would have consented to the marriage if I hadn't thought that your father would make a decent husband. Oh, I wished he had thought better of me, but that wasn't important. The important thing was your mother's happiness."

"Aunt Judith, you said you consented to them getting married?" asked Eliot, in an innocent attempt to get at the truth.

"More than that, I encouraged it," she answered, and then Arthurlene made another of her sudden materializations. "Yes, by all means, I shall be retiring soon myself," the old woman answered to the maid's whispers. As Arthurlene left the room, Drew said:

"We always thought you were against them getting married. We were even afraid to come here. We thought you'd turn us away. . . ."

"Opposed to the marriage? Merely because your father was from the North?" A troubled look passed over Aunt Judith's face. "How ever did you get that idea?"

Blind to the effect his comment had had on her, Drew blundered on.

"Mother said so. That you were so against her marrying our dad that they had to run away."

Aunt Judith reacted as if she'd been slapped.

"They did not run off! Elizabeth could not have said any such thing!"

"Beg pardon, ma'am, but . . ."

Lacking legs long enough to reach under the table and kick him, Nathaniel told his youngest brother to watch his words, he was getting things all wrong.

"But you told me so yourself, Nat," Drew whined.

"No, I didn't!"

Aunt Judith rapped the table with the handle of her cane.

"Nathaniel, you are the eldest," she said, in a voice grown cold. "Now please tell me, did your mother say that I disliked your father and forced her into eloping?"

"No, ma'am."

"I shall take your word on that. Andrew, you should take care the things you say. Take care not to speak falsehoods, especially about your own mother."

"I'm not a liar," he mumbled.

She leaned toward him, cupping an ear.

"I said I'm not a liar, ma'am." The trembling lower lip, the injured expression. Before Nathaniel could stop him, he blurted out, "Nat told Eliot and me that he had a talk with Mother awhile back and that she said you made her run away to get married, because the only thing worse than marrying our dad would've been to marry a Negro."

Even for Drew, this was a stunningly obtuse thing to say, Nathaniel thought, as Aunt Judith looked at his youngest brother for a long time, or what in that hot oppressive quiet seemed like a long time; looked more in grief than in anger.

"Am I to be a policeman, interrogating you to find out . . . Oh, never mind. Elizabeth's silence answers the question. My, oh, my, what a wonderful impression you three must have of me." She folded her napkin and creased the fold and opened and folded and creased it again, and Nathaniel saw in her what he had seen so often in his mother—jaw muscles twitching as her will sought to subdue her emotions. "But that impression did not stop you from coming here to ask for money, did it?"

"No, ma'am! I mean, we didn't come here for . . ."

"Oh, please, Nathaniel. I'm very old, seventy-five this year, but I am not a fool. I do want you to know that I was so delighted to see you three, to see you at last, that I would have lent you five times as much if you had asked it."

"Aunt Judith, we didn't think anything bad of you, honest."

"Don't fret. I've no intention of withdrawing my promise. I have my honor, and I can look at the loan as my way of repaying you for explaining, even if you didn't mean to explain, why your mother has shut me out all these years. She was afraid that if . . . Better to cut herself off entirely . . ." This with a slashing motion. "Perhaps I would have done the same in her position, but I don't think I would have gone to the length of setting my children against the woman who raised me, and more—saved me. No, I don't think I would have done that."

"She didn't set us—" Nathaniel started, but the raised palm, pale and cracked, stopped him again.

"I am not a fool! I am also not the sort of woman your mother seems to have made me out to be. And your father, too, I suppose. The sort of woman who would have said that the only thing worse than marrying your father would have been to wed a Negro."

She sat still for a moment, hands flat on the table, then said, "I have a secret to tell, boys, come closer, for I must whisper it." One hand motioned to them, the other raised a finger to her lips. They leaned toward her, and she said in an undertone, "I believe that Negroes are human beings, no different than you or me. I always have. Hush, now. Don't ever repeat that to anyone around here. Things in some ways are worse now than they used to be. Did you hear what happened in Georgia only last year? Some crackers got hold of a Negro boy they believed had had relations with a white woman and they hanged him and then dismembered him and burned his body and then put the parts they cut off on display in a department store window. So hush, but come with me." Unhooking her cane from the arm of her chair, she slowly stood. "Come, I wish to correct your unfavorable impression of me."

They followed her, she hobbling on her arthritic ankles, her body trailing the scents of cologne and medicine, into a small room with no identifiable purpose except to house ancestral photographs and portraits. The largest were oil paintings of her two husbands: Astride a white horse, Caleb Maxey, the Southern cavalier, looked across to the opposite wall at Lucien Wilcox, the soberly garbed banker sitting at a desk. On the back wall, between two windows, hung a photograph of Pardon Lightbourne, identical, the boys observed, to the one in their mother's sitting room in Boston, except this print had been tinted by an artist to show the color of their grandfather's hair and eyes, the yellow epaulets and piping on his gray tunic and trousers, the silver in his sword scabbard, gleaming as if it had been forged from sunlight.

"He did cut quite the figure, did he not?" said Aunt Judith, noticing them admiring the picture. "That was posed just before he went off to fight with Longstreet at Seven Pines."

She passed over a carpet faded in patches and sat at a secretary, from which she withdrew a leather-bound album. While she turned its pages,

Nathaniel went to look more closely at his grandfather's photograph, and saw, just beneath it, a smaller one that showed him, in civilian clothes and without the mustache, standing beside a young woman seated with an infant in her lap. Her dark hair was parted in the middle and pulled back tightly over her ears, and the grim set to her mouth made her look like a matron of forty whom life had disappointed. The infant—Nathaniel's mother at a few months old—was swaddled in a frilly white gown.

"Is this our grandmother?" he asked, inadvertently stressing *this*. He was disappointed; she was nowhere near as attractive as he'd expected.

Her glance leaping from the album to him, Aunt Judith said, "What are you looking at?" in an accusatory tone.

"The woman in—"

"That is my sister, Henrietta. What about her?"

"Nothing. It's just that we've never seen a picture of our grandmother."

"No, I don't suppose you would have."

Puzzled by a few details in the photograph, he asked when it had been taken.

"Obviously, a little while after your mother was born," Aunt Judith replied, with a severe look and impatience in her voice; this was not the topic she wished to discuss.

"Mother had blond hair when she was a baby . . . ?"

"The powder flash, I'm sure," she said, without a change of expression, and placed a paperweight on the album to hold it open. "As you seem to have such an interest in photographs, please look at this."

They gathered behind her and looked at a light-skinned Negro wearing a starched collar and thick side whiskers of the kind in fashion twenty-five or thirty years ago.

"Hosea," she said. "Hosea Maxey. His parents had taken our name. My husband used to own them and, of course, him. He was a stable boy at Marshlands. He's now the principal of a colored high school in Virginia, and he and I correspond, now and then. I taught him to read and write at a time when, as I told you, it was illegal for Negroes in this state to learn to read and write. Hosea bears the scars of his knowledge, and I do mean that literally." As she spoke, her eyes did not lift from the picture, as if she were addressing it. "One day—this would have been in 1860—Mr. Foley, my husband's overseer, caught Hosea reading in the barn from a speller I had given him instead of grooming the horses. The offense was reported. Caleb confronted me. You'll recall, he'd forbidden me to teach our coloreds and that I had defied him. Caleb knew me well.

He knew that if he laid down the law again, it would only strengthen my resolve, so he had Hosea whipped and made me watch the proceedings. Owing to Hosea's young age, Mr. Foley went easy on him. A dozen strokes across the back. I won't forget that. Hosea on his knees, his wrists lashed to a wagon wheel, and the sound of the whip on his flesh and the blood and his cries." She shut the album softly and put it in a drawer and locked the drawer. "That was the end of my educational career. I could not bear ever to see such a sight again and know that I was responsible for it.

"After the war, Hosea attended school over to Mitchellville, on Hilton Head—that was a settlement for freedmen the Yankees had built during their occupation. He finished his secondary education and passed examinations to Howard University, up in Washington. He was in one of the first graduating classes. When he got his diploma, I heard from him. He wrote to thank me, to *thank me,* for all I had done for him. I cannot express how that moved me, because I thought that all I had done for him was to get his back laid open at the age of thirteen. Your age, isn't it, Andrew?"

"Yes, ma'am," said Drew, feeling ashamed of himself without knowing why.

"Hosea said that I had given him something that no one and no amount of whippings could take away," she resumed. "He told me that he'd had something in the nature of a revelation while the strokes were being laid on him. 'They can't unlearn me,' was what he had thought. 'They can whup me till I faint, but they can't unlearn me. Only way they can is to whup me till I'm dead.' Such, he said, had been my gift to him, and when the time came, he felt he owed it to me as much as to himself to make the most of it. I shall always treasure that letter. Would you boys care to see it, as proof positive that I am not the prejudiced witch who would have denied your mother her happiness? Who would have said what she claims I did?"

"We never thought that of you," Nathaniel reassured her, leaving unspoken the brutal truth that, busy with their own lives, he and his brothers had never thought anything about her, one way or the other.

"Considering what your mother told you about me, I don't see how you couldn't have."

He said nothing.

"Her welfare was always my first concern," Aunt Judith carried on, and Nathaniel was beginning to feel a double irritation: with Drew for the clumsy, stupid frankness that had hurt her feelings, and with her for being hurt to the degree she appeared to be. These Southerners, he thought, were oversensitive to slight.

"I did more than give her my consent, I gave her my blessings."

"Yes, ma'am. You told us that."

"It was plain that your father was the very best she could do."

He wasn't sure he liked the tone of that, but kept silent.

Eliot did not like the tone, either, and seeking Aunt Judith's meaning, asked if she was referring to all the men who had been disabled by the war. Their mother had mentioned how Beaufort was in those days: Confederate veterans with empty sleeves and trouser legs and barely a dollar in their pockets.

"Yes, that was true."

"But you didn't mean the boys closer to our mother's age?" Eliot inquired, cautiously. "The ones who'd been too young to fight in the war? I'll bet she could have had any one of them she wanted. She must have been awful good-looking—she still is."

"Yes, Eliot, but her looks . . . That wasn't the issue. . . ." She stopped herself, her lips, with their whiskerlike wrinkles, continuing to move silently. Suddenly, sharply gavelling the floor with her cane, she turned in her chair to look away at a point in space.

"I'm afraid I'll have to ask you to leave now. Please."

"Aunt Judith, did I say—"

"No, Eliot. Nothing you said. I don't wish to discuss Elizabeth any further, and I'm sure you would not want me to. Arthurlene has gone to bed, so you will have to show yourselves out."

As baffled as they could be, they stammered their goodbyes.

"I've one request to make of you," she said, just as they were leaving the room. "I don't blame you for Elizabeth's unkind—her ungrateful—comments, but please do not call on me again. Good night."

"WE SURE DID get the bum's rush, didn't we though," said Eliot as they started back to the wharves. "What do you reckon she meant, that we wouldn't want her to talk any more about Mother?"

"Why do you always think I can read people's minds?" Nathaniel asked, snappishly. Spurred by an agitation, he was covering ground in such long strides that Drew almost had to run to keep up with him. "And you, little man, if we ever end up at anybody's house for dinner again, *anybody's,* you're going to keep your mouth shut. Couldn't you tell that what you were saying was bothering her?"

"But she called me a liar," Drew complained as they passed under the streetlamps on Bay, the yellowish glow illuminating clouds of insects buzzing in the humid night.

"Not exactly," Nathaniel said. "I swear, sometimes you're like a tone-deaf man in a music hall."

In the main cabin, filled with the reek of cigarette smoke that fogged the gimbal lamp, Will lay on the settee, reading a newspaper. He asked how dinner had gone, and Nathaniel answered that the food was bully but he could not say the same for the conversation.

"Your great-aunt was not delightful company?"

"Never mind. What have you been up to?"

"Walked around, looked for diversion, found none. They roll up the sidewalks here *before* the sun goes down. So I thought I'd catch up on what's been going on in the world." He snapped the newspaper with a finger. "We are still fighting in the Philippines, and President McKinley still isn't sure if we should annex them or not, and Mr. Mark Twain has added his voice to the anti-imperialists'"—the pages rustling. "Closer to home, an automobile killed a man in Atlanta, and right here in beautiful Beaufort, the telephone company is looking for tall women to be hello girls because they have long enough arms to reach the switchboard. Anything else you care to know?"

"How long does it take to grow a mustache?"

"Is this the beginning of a joke, Natters?" Will asked, fanning himself with the newspaper. The hatch and portholes had to be kept shut against the mosquitos, and the cabin was stifling.

"No, Nat is going to try to look more grown-up," Eliot said.

"It's that picture of our grandfather with our grandmother and Mother. He doesn't have a mustache."

"So?"

"In the one above it, the one in his uniform, he does. But Aunt Judith said it was taken before that battle Kincaid talked about. Spring of 1862. In the other picture, Mother looks like she's about six months old, so it would have been taken about the same time."

"Maybe she was younger than six months?" Eliot offered. He sometimes found it difficult to follow the turns of his older brother's mind.

"Yeah, maybe. That's what I'm wondering. If our grandfather could have grown a big thick mustache like that in only a few weeks, say. Or if that picture was taken earlier than she said."

"It's Nat Pinkerton, star detective, on the case again. Are you saying that one of those guys isn't Granddad?"

"It's him in both, all right. I'm wondering if the baby isn't Mother."

And the wondering plagued him for most of the night. Was the infant their mother's older brother, and if it was, why had she never spoken of him? Why would Aunt Judith have lied to them? He turned and re-turned the questions in his mind, but could not find even the beginning of an answer before he fell asleep.

16

IN THE MORNING, after Frenchy Geslin told them it would be a few days before the new sail was finished, they returned to Snead's Landing by way of the Beaufort River and discovered that the carpenter had yet to put a saw to the pine sawlog. After some prodding, Sykes cut it to the desired lengths; prodded some more the next day, he began to mill and plane the spars to the desired roundness and smoothness, but with such slow movements that he appeared to be working against a resistance, like a submerged diver.

The muggy heat made the boys feel that they were indeed living undersea, and the sandflies were an added torment, the plague of insects aggravated by a plague of visitors—the townsfolk who found *Double Eagle* and her crew of young northerners an irresistible novelty. The gaunt worn women, the men wearing bib overalls or trousers held up with ropes in place of belts were a taciturn lot who boarded the schooner without asking permission, some to poke around her with the perfunctory inquisitiveness of detectives seeking evidence to support a conviction already decided upon, others to sit mutely on the afterdeck and watch the boys' every move with looks suspicious and curious at the same time. The greatest strain was not knowing what to say to the uninvited guests or what to do with them. Like Kincaid, the people had an air of touchy pride that might be offended with a wrong word or a wrong move, and that gave Snead's Landing the atmosphere of some foreign court, governed by social rules strangers were not permitted to know.

Will suffered under an additional burden: Every time he and the Braithwaites went ashore to check on Sykes's progress at the sawmill, poor Clara would appear and shadow Will, gazing with her usual trancelike expression. On their fifth day in Snead's Landing, after the carpenter promised to finish the spars tomorrow, Clara's manner changed. She approached Will, making gestures and guttural sounds whose meaning made no sense at first. Then, realizing she was asking him to kiss her or for permission to kiss him, he fled down the main street (the only street in fact, the others being but paths and dirt lanes between the shanties), the Braithwaites behind him, laughing at his distress (though even as he laughed, Eliot could not help but feel pity for the speechless girl).

Late that afternoon, they were called on by a man and a boy in a flat-bottom skiff, with a pile of dead birds between its thwarts and two shotguns propped in its bow. The boy, who was about fifteen, with slanted, slitty eyes and blond hair shorn to bristles, stood and held up three braces of marsh hens while his father, a broad-chested man with a hard, intransigent face, asked if they wanted the birds for supper. Nathaniel asked how much; the man replied by shaking his head, which was interpreted to mean that they were a gift. Nathaniel accepted and invited the hunters aboard for marsh-hen stew. They climbed on and, never uttering a word, plucked and gutted their kill with brutal efficiency. The birds stank of the marshes in which they had nested and of the crabs and fish on which they had fed. They stank raw, and they stank while Eliot cooked them in a big cast-iron skillet with onions and potatoes and garlic that, it was hoped, would disguise their taste.

In the middle of supper, which the man pronounced "right fine," *Double Eagle* had another visitor: Talmadge. He tied his skiff alongside the hunters', muttered hello to them, and, declining a helping of stew, told the boys that he'd heard from Kincaid that the work would be finished the following day, which meant they would be leaving soon, did it not?

"So I thought I'd show y'all a nice, safe, comfortable way down to Flor'da, where you don't got to worry about gettin' caught in another blow," he said. "It's a inland route. There's canals and channels what run clear through Georgia and across the Georgia sounds. Got charts aboard?"

Will brought them up and spread them in sequence on the cabin top, holding their curl down with his hands while Talmadge, squinting through his bottle-thick glasses, laid out a course from the mouth of the Savannah River to the mouth of the St. John's, just south of the Florida line. He had oystered, crabbed, fished, and duck-hunted all along that coast, he declared. There were some channels clearly marked, while with others it was navigatin' by guess and by God. Tides mighty tricky and mighty strong, but if they timed the ebbs and floods correctly, they could ride the currents southward even in a dead calm. The whole trip shouldn't take more than three, four days.

"Running on the outside, and with a fair wind, we could do it in two," Will said.

"Go right ahead!" Talmadge said, stiffening as though he'd been insulted. "It's a free country, ain't it? Y'all can go any way you please, but if you don't get that fair wind, it won't be my fault."

"I didn't mean any criticism, Mr. Talmadge," Will said. "The point is, this boat is too big to run in those canals. If we need to tack, we won't have room."

"With this here inland way, if it comes to a gale, you'll be safe, if it comes to no wind atall, you'll have tide to carry you where you're goin'. This here's a favor I'm doin', it's the benefit of my knowledge."

At that moment, Trajan bolted up the companion and onto the deck with a hen carcass in his jaws. Snake-quick, the boy's hand darted, snatched the cat by the tail, relieved Trajan of the carcass, and put it in his bloodstained game pouch.

"Them bones make a good soup," he said.

Drew picked up the distraught Trajan and stroked his head.

"I suppose they do," he said angrily. "But you didn't have to hurt my cat."

"Aw, I dint hurt him none." The boy's narrow eyes narrowed further. "I onest caught a catfish with a cat. Done snatched a kitten, fig-gerin' hit takes a cat to ketch one up. Stuck a big ole hook in that kitty and tossed hit in the river, and right enough, big ole catfish come up and swallered hit. Now that's what I call hurtin' a cat."

The man and the boy were beginning to make Nathaniel nervous. Thanking them for their generosity, he said he hoped they enjoyed their dinner and that he and his shipmates were pleased to have made their acquaintance, but now they had work to do and plans to make. After considering this diplomatic request to leave, the man said, "Let's go," and the two climbed into their skiff.

"That's Tom Holgrum and his son, Billy," Talmadge said, watching them row away, across a flat sound mirroring the sunset. "Y'know, the boy Clara was sweet on?" Pausing, he looked at Will amiably. "Which brings me to my main business in comin' out here. Clara tells me y'all kissed her today."

Will blinked.

"I ain't mad, son. That is, I ain't if you wasn't takin' advantage of her."

"I did not kiss her, sir."

"She says you did."

"Excuse me, but just how did she tell you?"

"We got our ways of communicatin'. Y'all sayin' that girl was fib-bin'? She ain't never fibbed to me before."

"No, I'm not saying that."

"So you did kiss her?"

"No!"

"Lemme get this straight"—rubbing his chin. "If she told me you kissed her, and you say she ain't fibbin', then in my book that says you kissed her."

The Braithwaites rushed as one to Will's defense, swearing that Will had not touched Clara in any way. He had in fact run from her when she made it plain that she wanted to be kissed. This confounded Talmadge, who said he had never in all his days heard of a normal young man run-ning from a girl eager to be kissed.

"Now, look here, Clara ain't just sweet on you, Will, like she was with Billy. Plumb in love is what she is. She knows you got to be leavin' right soon, and she is sick to heart about it."

Will expressed his regrets; sad departures, however, were part of the sailor's life.

"But what if she was to go with y'all down to Flor'da? She wouldn't be sad then."

The proposal was too shocking for any of them to respond.

"That's the reason I come here to show you the inland route. I'd want her to be safe if she did."

He had been thinking things over, and praying on them, too, he went on, and it had come to him in recent days that he could repay his debt to the Lord in full if he married Clara off to the right man. When he heard about the kiss, he was pretty sure Will was that man, and so was his wife—she was up and about again. He intended to speak about the matter with the Reverend Dewey Jenkins when he arrived to conduct Sunday meeting.

"That's but day after tomorrow, so I reckoned it would be proper to hear what you got to say before I go speakin' to the reverend."

Will, looking more stunned than when he'd been punched in New York, had nothing whatever to say.

"Now, I know this is springin' things on you suddenlike," said Tal-madge, sympathetically. "And I know Clara's got her liabilities. She can't talk, but if y'all look at that from the other side, you'll see that she won't never give her man any back sass, neither."

Eliot, who was standing back, leaning against the taffrail, realized that this scheming country boy had struck upon a way to rid himself of a responsibility that he no doubt had begun to tire of.

"Mr. Talmadge, there's something you should know," he said, stepping forward. He had had an inspiration. "Will's already married."

Talmadge flinched, then squinted skeptically at Will's hand.

"Don't see no weddin' band."

"He lost it during the storm," explained Eliot, pleased with his quick thinking.

"So where's his wife?"

"Boston."

"Thought you're from Maine. As I recollect, Boston ain't in Maine."

"We sailed the boat from Maine, but we're all from Boston."

Talmadge, not yet persuaded, pondered for a few moments.

"I can understand why you'd be a tad on the hesitatin' side," he said to Will, "and might want to fib to me about havin' you a wife. Could be you need a day or two to think and pray on this your own self."

Will, his powers of speech restored, said that he would not need to; he was well and truly wed. His own dear Susan awaited his return to Boston. Surely, Talmadge would not want Clara to be party to bigamy.

"Sure wouldn't." Bony hands to bony knees, he stood up and gave Will a censorious look. "But for a married feller to go kissin' a young girl, that ain't right. Maybe it's all right where y'all come from, but not down here."

"How many times do we have to tell you that I did not kiss her?"

"So she was fibbin'?"

"I'm afraid so," Will said.

"That ain't no small thing to fib about, in my book," said Talmadge, maneuvering into his skiff. "I'm gone to ask her again, and if she says the same, one of two things is gone to happen: You and me, Will, is gone to have us a man-to-man talk, or Clara's gone to get whupped, and good."

"Oh, please don't do that, Mr. Talmadge," Eliot pleaded. "She hasn't got all her wits and she probably didn't know it was a fib."

"You leave the upbringin' part to me, son," he said, pulling away. "Reckon we'll find out what's what soon enough."

As soon as he was out of earshot, they huddled in a quick conference and decided that they had to leave, if not at that very moment, then certainly before tomorrow. Nathaniel had an idea for retrieving the spars; whatever work remained they could do themselves in Beaufort.

They rowed ashore in darkness, made their way to the sawmill—it was at the edge of the settlement, in a grove of oak trees—and opened the shed door. Nathaniel lit the kerosene lantern they had brought along, and it revealed the boom and gaff, braced on sawhorses over piles of sawdust and shavings. Feeling like robbers (though they were only taking what belonged to them), their throats catching whenever a dog barked, they carried both pieces to the water, Will and Nathaniel the boom, the two younger boys taking the lighter gaff. The spars were lashed together, then to the stern of the tender, and towed back to *Double Eagle*.

Sails were raised, sheets made fast. Now came the most difficult part: picking their way down the narrow channel on a moonless night. With Nathaniel at the wheel, Eliot and Will stood in the bow, each holding a lantern to one side to illuminate shoal water. They called directions over their shoulders. "Port . . . Port a little more . . . Steady . . . Starboard now . . . Steady . . ." Two or three times came the sickening sound of the keel scraping bottom. Once, responding sluggishly to the helm, the schooner nosed into an oyster bar and became stuck. Poling with the tender's oars and the broken boathook did no good; they were too short to reach the hard bottom under the ooze. The spare anchor was taken out in the tender and dropped in deep water, and *Double Eagle* was kedged off. Her crew felt the joy, held in suspension, of escaped prisoners not yet certain of success.

An hour later, as the tide neared full flood, she had two full fathoms under her and was working against the current in the Beaufort River, which could be distinguished from the shoreline only by the occasional glimmer of reflected stars. The boys heard fish jumping but could not see them. Something big splashed near the woods on the starboard side; it sounded as if a log had been tossed into the river. Will and Eliot, keeping their places in the bow to light up channel buoys, swung their lanterns out to the right side, and saw what looked like a pair of burning coals bobbing on the surface two yards from the boat. In a moment, they recognized the eyes of an alligator, ten feet long and a yard across the back.

"First one I've ever seen outside a zoo," Eliot whispered, as if to hide his presence from the reptile.

"I hate it down here," Will moaned. "Gators and crazy fortune-telling hillbillies and enough mosquitos to suck the blood out of a million horses."

A little after midnight, the tide having turned to give them a push downriver, they caught the lights of Beaufort dead ahead.

All the next day they sanded and varnished the new spars: tedious, frustrating work because the moist heat caused the varnish to bubble in patches, and those had to be resanded and recoated several times over. Will was in a constant fret, half expecting a posse from Snead's Landing to come and drag him off to a shotgun wedding. Late in the day, as the no-seeums were boiling off the river to turn exposed flesh red with bites, he went into town with Drew to stock up on food; they had depleted their larder during the previous week and did not have stores enough to last them to Key West. Two of Geslin's employees, meanwhile, delivered the new foresail; though the spar varnish was still tacky, Nathaniel and Eliot decided not to wait to try it on for size. Peak, clew, and tack were lashed on, the foot laced to the new boom, the head to the gaff, the luff bent to the mast hoops, and the canvas was hauled up. It set without a flaw.

In the morning, well before church bells had begun to summon Beaufort's devout to Sunday services, *Double Eagle* set off once more in a light southerly air, glided into Port Royal Sound, then beat along the wild beaches of Hilton Head, crossed the mouth of the Savannah River, its waters muddying the sea's green, and passing Tybee Island at midafternoon, began its voyage down Georgia's broken coast.

They ran offshore, knowing it would be nearly impossible to navigate a forty-six-footer through the labyrinthine creeks and inlets of Talmadge's inland route. With what little wind they had blowing into their eyes, they got no further than St. Catherine's Island by nightfall. They sailed on, guiding on Arcturus and Spica and the low red beacon of Antares. A crescent moon rose, dolphins made fiery green wakes crossing the bow. An hour after dawn, Will took a morning sight, and fixed them off St. Simon's—they had logged only thirty miles in a full night's sailing. The barometer dipped, and soon, they were once again struggling in the face of a high wind and mounting seas, and when the wind began to turn to southeast, heading them inshore, the tide tables were consulted, so too the coast pilot. Falling off, they reached through St. Simon's Sound, the channel marked by leaning stakes with crude arrows nailed to them, and rode a rushing three-knot tide past salt meadows and rice marshes and offshore islands, wooded to their edges with pine and oak trees dipping moss-draped branches into the water like bearded old men bowing to drink. Night herons crouched amid the sedge, great blues and egrets raised stalklike necks above the marsh grasses, and nearing Jekyll Island, Drew spied their first pelicans, comical and clumsy-looking getting up to fly but thrillingly graceful once in the air.

An old-time riverboat passed them, its stern wheel thrashing, and its captain saluted *Double Eagle* with his steam whistle. They crossed St. Andrew's Sound and saw at the mouth of the Saltilla River crowds of sea-island Negroes wading the oyster bars, the sight reminding them of the clammers who worked the Gloucester beds. The tide turned, but the change did not follow the one predicted in the tables; now they were fighting a head current as well as a head wind, and making, at best, one knot over bottom. Further on, the tide turned again in their favor, and still further, in a wide, island-clogged channel between the mainland and Cumberland Island, it was on their nose once more. Talmadge was right—the tides were tricky, and an oysterman they met told them why: the rise and fall varied from sound to sound; a flood in one could be an ebb in another only a few miles down the coast, so that you could start down a creek connecting the two with a favorable current, and, in no time at all, run smack-dab into a foul, or what was worse, find yourself without enough water to wash dishes in. Forget your tables, he told them, you had to have local knowledge, and if you lacked that, the only thing for it was to sail when the tide served and drop your hook when it did not.

So drop the hook they did, hard by a small, nameless, unpeopled island cloaked in cypress and palmetto.

The wind kept the mosquitos off, allowing them to sleep with hatches and portholes open. The fog lifted in the morning and the wind died and the still water appeared in the red dawn like a river of lava. As Eliot was cooking breakfast, a shriek sent them all rushing outside, where they saw a great triangular raft of sawn logs bearing down on them, the tug behind it blowing its whistle, because *Double Eagle*'s stern, with the last turn of tide, had swung out into the channel. There was no time for anything except to haul on the anchor cable and pull the schooner out of the way, closer to the island. This was done, and just in time, the log boom swinging by so close they could have jumped onto it. Another shriek, the tug's captain leaning out the wheelhouse window to shake his fist and tell them what he thought of their intelligence and the legitimacy of their ancestry. With the crisis past, they settled down to breakfast. Drew filled a saucer with condensed milk to feed Trajan and, after calling him several times, announced, in a tremulous voice, that the cat was missing. Nathaniel said he must have been terrified by the tug's whistle and had hidden somewhere; but after they all four searched every possible sanctuary, even the bilges, the awful truth fell on them: Their mascot, who had sailed a thousand miles with them, weathering line squalls and fogs and a whole gale, had vanished without trace. He had probably leapt onto the log boom when the whistle blew the last time. Or he had jumped, in blind fear, into the water, to be swept off in the tideway. The thought of the little fellow, drowning alone, or riding that raft to an uncertain destination and fate, made them all desolate, Drew most of all.

"Nothing we can do," Nathaniel said, with as much sympathy as he was capable of. "The tide's serving, we've got to get a move on."

They had just begun to raise sail when Eliot caught a sound coming from the island, a faint wail, he said.

"It's him!" he cried. "He's on the island! He must've jumped off and swum to it! Trajan! Trajan!"

Though the distance wasn't great, Nathaniel didn't see how it was possible for the cat to swim it; from what he knew of felines, they could not swim at all.

"Yes, they can!" Drew said, and then called the cat's name. In a moment, they all heard the same strange, plaintive howl.

It took only a minute to lower the tender away, with Eliot and Drew aboard.

"Take this," Nathaniel said, handing down the L. C. Smith and a fistful of shells. "There's gators and Christ knows what else around here."

Two strokes of the oars were all that was needed to cross over. The tender was tied to a stump, and Eliot and Drew plunged into a cypress swamp, where a greenish light filtered through the trees to fall in circles on primeval ferns and tree trunks, bent like knees. The cat answered their calls with an anguished scream from off to the right, close to water's edge. They thrashed through the undergrowth, Eliot in the lead with the shotgun, and found Trajan half-drowned, his fur so matted that he looked as small and sleek as a baby muskrat, as he clung to a piece of sedge floating in a shallow pool. He must have leapt off the boat in his fright, latched onto the flotsam by sheer luck, and an eddy must have then swept it and him into the swamp. Drew splashed into the pool and picked him up; then he and Eliot rushed back to the tender, or rather, tried to rush through the muck and jumbles of stumps that bashed their legs, Trajan practically lifeless in Drew's arms. They saw the tender ten yards ahead when the cat, jumping as if shocked back into life by an electrical jolt, let out a screech and tried to escape, his claws raking Drew's shirt, drawing blood. An instant later, from out of the shadowy glades to their left, where the swamp rose to hard ground, a thing bolted straight for them; a thing big as a colt, with sable-black hair bristling and little red eyes in a huge head and tusks six inches long flashing in its jaws. Without thinking, Eliot swung the L. C. Smith and pulled the front trigger and the beast's front legs flew out sideways, its snout plowing into the mud; immediately it was up and charging again, making a sound like nothing Eliot or Drew had heard before, half bellow, half squeal. Something in Eliot's brain caused all movement to slow down. Though the animal was charging fast and wasn't more than fifteen or twenty feet away, he could see clearly where to place his next shot, and he himself seemed to be moving with great deliberation as he aimed for the hump behind its lowered head and pulled the second trigger. The crash of the shot, and the wild boar—for now he could name what it was—went down hard, legs thrashing and blood spurting from both wounds, the red shockingly bright against the black hide. Eliot reloaded and fired twice more, blowing off half the boar's head before it lay still.

When he and Drew got back to the boat, they were both so shaken they could barely gasp to Nathaniel and Will what had happened. Trajan was paralyzed by his ordeals.

"These goddamned backwaters are no place for schoonermen," Nathaniel declared, once the tender was triced up and secured again to the davit. "We're getting back out to sea, and it's Florida or bust today."

Excusing his brothers from further duties, he and Will took *Double Eagle* on the outside of Cumberland. Two miles or less ahead, they made out a town amid palmetto and pine on a spit of land; eastward, a river spilled into the sea through a breachway between the spit and the southern tip of Cumberland. To make sure they had read their charts right, they hailed a passing fisherman and asked what the river was called. "St. Mary's," he shouted, and they hauled on the wind and beat southward, down the Florida shore.

17

"THAT'S THE FIRST big animal I ever shot," Eliot said. "Never even shot a deer."

He and Drew were forward, trimming the foresail. A brown booby glided off *Double Eagle*'s starboard quarter, its wide wings spread to catch the wind deflected by the mainsail.

"That's well," called Nathaniel from the helm, and Eliot looped the sheet around the belaying pin.

"When I think about it, it scares the hell out of me," he said. "But I wasn't scared then, because I didn't have time to think. Reckon you know what I mean?"

Drew murmured that he did.

"I wonder why that boar charged us."

"For the same reason that guy wanted to knock Nat's block off," said Drew, and looked astern at the big brown bird hitching a ride. "I think that bird is like an albatross. Aren't they supposed to be bad luck?"

"Thought you didn't believe in stuff like that."

"I don't. I was just asking if they're supposed to be."

"Yeah, I think so," Eliot said as Drew sat against the mast and pulled his legs into his chest. "But I reckon we've had our ration of bad luck. Smooth sailing from here on in. Hell, we're as good as there."

"Take a look at the chart. Florida's more than three hundred miles long and Key West is another hundred past the end of it. That's like sailing from Boston to Chesapeake Bay."

And for four full days, measuring their progress by the lighthouses they passed—St. Augustine Light and Ponce de León and Cape Florida—they watched the Florida coast reel past the starboard rail. A coast drearier than the one expected: mile upon deserted mile of white sand fringing pine and palmetto barrens and swampy savannahs monotonous as midwestern prairies, the lush desolation relieved once by Daytona Beach, on whose strand they saw bathers and carriages and sun umbrellas, as if some little piece of Atlantic City had been floated twelve hundred miles south. *Double Eagle* bucked head winds all the way, yet it was the kind of sailing Drew liked: gentle breezes over benign seas, and with deep water lying close to shore, land was always visible by day, while in the unfailingly clear nights burned the signal lamps that he now knew by heart—the Summer Triangle, Libra's faint diamond, and Scorpius with Antares glowing near its head, its tail curved as if poised to sting The Archer, just beside it to the east.

The ice had melted in the icebox, and they had put into a shabby little town called Fort Pierce to buy fresh blocks, but by then their bacon had gone bad and the fresh vegetables bought in Beaufort had rotted. Low on cash, they decided not to buy groceries but to live off whatever the sea gave them. The rancid bacon was gobbed onto hooks and trolled with the rod and reel behind the log, the rod butt lashed to a taffrail post with a spare jackrope. The only fish hooked between Fort Pierce and Miami was a barracuda, to which they lost Little Israel when the fish chomped down on the small metal torpedo and its keen teeth sliced the log line in two.

Cape Florida Light on Key Biscayne marked the edge of the sea frontier. Beyond it lay the most treacherous waters on the southern Atlantic coast: another country where in earlier times pirate cannons thundered and Seminole raiders slipped out of the Everglades in long war canoes to torch island towns.

The boys were near Key Largo when they spotted clouds of birds over a lagoon—herons, egrets, pelicans, and white-crowned pigeons. Eliot, thinking the pigeons might be edible, persuaded Nathaniel to put in and let him have a try at bagging a few. *Double Eagle* slipped between the north end of Key Largo and Old Rhodes Key and into the lagoon—called Card Sound on the chart—and then cautiously felt her way down a channel marked with a few leaning stakes and decaying posts, the water on both sides brown and in spots barely deeper than mustard on bread. When the channel began to shoal up, the hook was dropped, the tender lowered away, and Nathaniel and Eliot rowed along the western side of Key Largo, past mangroves whose roots humped like gigantic spider legs and whose branches formed galleries over gloomy little creeks that had the look of harboring alligators. In a moment, they saw one, a baby some three feet long, basking on a log. Its mother, or father, appeared next, cruising out of a cove to cross the tender's bow. Nathaniel backed the oars, he and his brother held breathless, for the gator was longer than the boat by four or five feet, and when they noticed the pointed snout they realized it was not an alligator but a saltwater crocodile, one huge mass of armored sinew, with jaws that looked capable of swallowing either of them whole.

Pigeons cooed inside the mangrove fastness, from which there also came a kind of prehistoric croaking that sometimes swelled into a roar. It was being made by nothing more dangerous than a heron rookery, but it was unsettling, all the same. A flight of pigeons took wing off the bow, and Eliot raised the gun and swung, firing as he swung, and two birds dropped as if they had flown into an invisible wall. Nathaniel stroked to pick them up, but something else got to them first. It was hard to say what—a big fish, a gator, or a crocodile—because there was only a boil on the water before the dead birds vanished. Nathaniel said they might as well give it up, and so they did, rowing back down a wide crimson path made by the sun, a wound in the sky above the saw-grass plains of the Everglades. Long-necked cranes stood fixed in the reddened shallows while ibis and roseate spoonbills skimmed above them. Another crocodile, or maybe it was the very one they had seen earlier, waked alongside the channel in which *Double Eagle* lay at anchor, looking very lonesome. Nathaniel pulled hard for her, sweating in a heat unlike any he had known before, while Eliot swatted without effect at gnats and mosquitos, both boys feeling as though they had sailed out of their hemisphere and out of the new century, back to some primordial Eden innocent of the tread of man, ruled by reptiles and wild birds.

Double Eagle lost her wind after sunset, and she wallowed all night on a black sea plated by moonlight and filled with phosphoresence. She would have sat as still as an anchored ship if it weren't for the Gulf Stream's countercurrent, which nudged her along at a knot or two. A squall came down on her in the hour before dawn: a dense rain slanting before westerly gusts, blowing into her face and against the current, raising contrary seas that picked her up at the bow and slammed her down hard by the stern. Somehow or other, the port davit line sprung loose, the tender crashed stern first into the water. Hanging at a forty-five-degree angle, the tender's back end swamped, which made the steering heavy. Nathaniel standing to the helm, Will, Eliot, and Drew hauled on the davit line to trice up the tender, but the seawater in it made it as heavy as a boulder. The boat would have to be bailed out first. Drew, the lightest of the four, volunteered. One end of a lifeline was made fast to the taffrail, the other to his waist with a bowline. He grabbed a bucket and swung over the rail and stood for a moment, looking down at the dark waves, any one of which could sweep him away if the lifeline slipped. This wasn't like the brawl in New York; this wasn't reflex. He was conscious of what he was doing, and of the risk; but, to his happiness, he discovered that he could act at the same time that he was afraid. He dropped down and commenced to bail, but for every two buckets emptied, the lumpy seas tossed in one. We're not using our heads, he thought, and called to Will and Eliot to ease the starboard davit line. As they did, he crawled, or, rather, climbed, to the tender's bow and straddled it, his eighty-five pounds and the slackened rope lowering it, while raising the stern: only a foot, but enough to keep the seas from pouring in. With the tender now on a more even keel, he bailed her dry, and then Will and Eliot yanked on the lifeline, pulling him back on board. The tender was triced up, the ropes secured. Eliot whispered to Nathaniel, "If I ever hear you say he doesn't have a sailor's heart, I'll bean you with a belaying pin."

Saturn rose shortly before the sun and aligned itself with Jupiter. Nathaniel wasn't sure if that was a good or bad omen, or no omen at all; at any rate, the squall swept over the Florida Straits toward Cuba, the southeast breeze sprang up, and *Double Eagle* was away again on a reach. With the current on her stern, she clipped along swiftly enough to overtake a fruit-company steamer, lumbering toward the Gulf of Mexico and some distant banana republic. Following custom, the boys mastheaded a mop, and a ship's officer on the bridgewing jovially shook his fist to signal that he grasped the insult.

Flying fish launched themselves from out of the tide rips at the current's edge, and lines of sargassum miles long, and in places ten or twenty yards across, formed golden highways on the surface of the sea. A hook baited with bacon and a strip of white cloth to give it flash skipped in the wake. A Spanish mackerel struck, and then another, followed by a bonito. The mackerel were split on a cutting board and salted and stowed in the ice box for later consumption, the bonito chunked into bait. The red meat lured a big dolphin out from under a weedline. A flash of bright color in the rolling wake, and then the stout bamboo rod bowed, the 24-thread linen line hissing off the reel. The dolphin streaked away with astonishing speed and made several wild leaps, showing a butter-colored belly and flanks of iridescent green before it ran again. When Eliot pressed the leather thumb guard to apply drag, a sliver of smoke rose from the friction, and he could feel the heat in his fingers through the leather. With pressure on the line and the schooner towing it, the fish surrendered, its body tumbling in the wake as Eliot pumped it in—a big bull dolphin, flat-headed, twenty-five or thirty pounds. Nathaniel, swinging out over the gunwale, gaffed it on the first try and heaved the fish on deck, where it thrashed violently, spattering blood. Will clubbed it three times with a belaying pin and that scuppered it, and there was something tragic about the way its vibrant colors faded almost instantly. A quarter of an hour later, a thick fillet doused in lime juice was frying in lard and onions, and they all four ate it with fried ship's bread and agreed it was the sweetest fish they had ever tasted.

They sailed on, the compass almost unnecessary, for the reef line and the color change in the sea—a demarcation between the Gulf Stream's blue and the green of inshore waters as sharp as a bootstripe—guided them down the chain of islands, broken, twisted, suggesting the spine of a victim put to the rack. Dad had said that they were marked as "Los Martires"—"The Martyrs"—on the early Spanish charts. Lighthouses resembling drilling derricks towered above the reef, an immense necklace of rainbow-colored rock, and each one marked a station in the schooner's progress—Carysfort, Alligator, Sombrero: names Nathaniel had heard his father and Lockwood murmur in their reminiscences, and beholding them now with his own eyes, he felt like an immigrant's son returning to an ancestral homeland.

They came abeam of American Shoals Light, its red steel girders whitened with the guano of the seabirds roosting there. Offshore, a big four-master westered; inshore, the sails of small fishing smacks and trading boats made white triangles against the islands' somber green. American Shoals dropped astern, and now the bow sprit pointed dead ahead at another tower, rising taller and taller out of the sea, its framework silhouetted against a range of cumulus. Will checked the charts and said it was the Sand Key Light and weather station, and Nathaniel turned the wheel to bear off west by north, crossing the reef into Hawk Channel. Low cirrus spun like threads of red and purple silk around the cumulus, fringed with gold. A steamer ploughed southward, probably for Havana. A low island appeared some three or four miles off, a lighthouse at its western tip flashing white then green then white through the dusk. Will, standing at the rail, tapped a cigarette from his last pack of Duke's and said, "Well, Natters, despite ourselves, it looks like we made it."

18

FROM *Double Eagle's log of 21 July . . . Arrived Key West harbor 8:15 p.m. Found good holding ground in two fathoms outside ship's channel. Total time for voyage: 34 days, 8 hours. Total sailing days, 26. Distance covered, 1,644 n. miles. Average speed, 2.6 knots. Remarks: A mighty slow passage, due to layovers in New York and South Carolina, prevailing headwinds, and this vessel's inability to sail fast close to the wind.*

Reading what she has written so far, Sybil wonders if she's gotten the character of her great-uncle down right. There is a disparity between the Nathaniel who made that tidy, indeed anal, record of dry facts, and the restless romantic she has woven out of strands collected from Myles and Nathaniel's memorabilia (chiefly a scrapbook containing, among other things, Tennyson's *Ulysses,* which he had copied out by hand, clippings of his favorite Frank Merriwell stories, a photograph of Theodore Roosevelt in his Rough Rider costume, and an Andover essay, written in his freshman year, in which he confessed to his envy of his suntanned, sea-roving half brother). He and his crew had accomplished no small feat; he must have felt triumphant, but you would never know it from reading the logbook, Sybil remarks to me. Maybe he didn't have the vocabulary for his emotions; more likely, he intended to show the log to his father, and wrote it in a manner sure to win approval from that most unsentimental man.

She cannot find anything to say about what her grandfather and his brothers did during their first few days in Key West. She assumes they must have looked for Artemis Lowe, the Bahamian diver partially blinded while salvaging the *Annisquam,* or for someone who could tell them about the sunken ship; otherwise, those days are a blank. Her imagination is silent because the log is silent. For all its dull literalness, she seems to need it to open a window on to the past; needs to see Nathaniel's handwriting in the thin brown ink and to touch the mildew-spotted pages, as though his memories are embedded there, waiting for her to absorb them transdermally.

HIGH NOON and a white sun in an empyrean sky, cloudless overhead but with thunderheads walling the northern horizon, where the Gulf of Mexico seemed to end. Lightning sparked in the clouds' anvil tops, as though some smithy were hammering hot iron in the heavens, and the muted rumbling that would have made the boys apprehensive at sea cheered them now with its promise of deliverance from the heat. Simonton Street, its marl bed paved with crushed coral and seashells and a pellet-sized gravel called pea-rock, was whiter than the light it reflected back into their faces; faces that a week in the subtropics had seared to the color of nutmeg. Nathaniel's was the darkest of the three, and with his chocolate-brown eyes and wavy black hair, he had been mistaken for a Cuban just this morning by another Cuban, who had accosted him on the street, speaking in a rapid Spanish.

"Uh, no speakee hispanyoly," Nathaniel had replied, before Will stepped in and determined that the man was just off the Havana ferry-boat and was asking for directions to the Cortez cigar factory. He told him how to find it, the Cuban appearing a little confused to have gotten the response he did from Nathaniel while receiving an answer in his native tongue from blond, blue-eyed Will.

The Lower Keys Sponge and Fruit Company was at the foot of Simonton. Pyramids of sponges, giving off a pungent smell, had been set out to dry in the shade of a covered dock. A long, shoal-draft sloop was tied up to the dock, and a dozen more vessels like it, each with a kite tail of skiffs trailing from its stern, lay at anchor on the blinding harbor.

"How did the old man and Lockwood stand it here for nearly fifteen years?"

Eliot took off his cap and toweled his hair with a bandanna as they approached a board-and-batten shack at the foot of the dock. Key West looked like a Yankee town, with its wooden cottages and clapboard mansions graced by verandas and gingerbread, but it felt like a settlement in hell, its heat not a meterological condition but an affliction. The air never filled the lungs. Sometimes, desperate for relief, Eliot would dive off the schooner naked as a newborn, but the water did not refresh; it felt like the atmosphere, only in denser form. He had begun to yearn for home, to dream about it—the bracing slap of New England breezes, the cold green bays of Maine and Gloucester. But after what Nat had learned today, from a rum-reeking old Negro in the neighborhood called Africa Town, it looked like they were going to remain on this broiling rock for a while longer.

Nathaniel knocked at the shack's door, which was opened by a man with a long, narrow head and, incredibly, a bow tie cinched tight to a starched collar.

"Would you be Mr. Pinder?" asked Nathaniel.

"I'd be Mr. Carey"—motioning at an unpainted frame building across a lot where horse carts were parked, the nags' head drooping in the midday blaze. "Mr. Pinder's in the office."

"Thanks very much," Nathaniel said, turning.

"Won't get to see him for a spell. He's meetin' with some buyers right now. Maybe I can help you?"

"We heard you're hiring, and we're looking for work."

Hungry, all but literally hungry for work. Will was down to his last seven dollars, and the Braithwaites' treasury had shrunk to five.

"I'm the man you want to see," said Carey, gesturing to them to come inside, where a paddle fan twirled lazily overhead. He sat down at a rolltop desk and pulled a sheet of ruled paper from one of the slots. "Put down your names and where you're stayin'. You can write, I reckon?"

"Sure. But we're not staying ashore. On a boat."

"Then give her name and to where she's moored. That's in case you don't show up on time and I have to send someone to roust you out."

They gave the required information, and Carey told them the day began at eight and ended at six and that their pay would be five dollars a week for a six-day week. They were to proceed to the dock and see a man named Sweeting, who would show them what to do.

"You mean we're hired? Just like that?"

Carey, lowering an eyelid at Nathaniel: "What the hell do you expect, son? The U.S. Navy band to play a fanfare?"

"No, sir. Could I ask, do you know a man called Artemis Lowe? We've heard he's a sponge fisherman around here."

"Sure. Only nigger sponger on the island. Rest are Cubans, Greeks, or Conchs. He's up to Big Pine right now, due back today or tomorrow."

"So he really does still live here?"

"Has for years." Carey spun his swivel chair and made a show of reading some paperwork. "Stop askin' so many questions and get to work. You're on company time as of now."

After Sweeting, the balloon-bellied foreman, had told them what their jobs would be, he apprenticed them to a short, red-haired man called Popeye for the froglike bulge of his green eyes, and a muscular white Bahamian whom Sweeting addressed as "Doris," and who told the boys he had come to Key West five years ago from Great Abaco by walking across at low tide. Doris (no one explained how a man built like a wrestler had acquired such a nickname, nor why he stood it with such good humor) sat them on stools in front of tall straw barrels filled with sponges. "See these 'ere?" he said in his Bahama cockney, holding a sponge in either hand. "This 'ere nappy one is called a Sheepswool, and this 'ere yella one is called a Yella sponge. We want them sorted out from the rest, 'cause they're the best kind for bathin', washin' horses, cleanin' a wall. They're smooth, don't scratch."

He then taught them how to judge the quality of Sheepswools and Yellows by looking at the canals through which the sponges took their food; the smaller the holes, the better. Naturally, Drew the scientist wanted to know what sponges ate, and Doris replied that he wasn't sure, though he presented himself as an authority, lecturing that sponges were neither animal nor vegetable but "nuthin' more'n your common saltwater marine fossil," a point he said he would argue with any man, as though the nature of sponges were a matter hotly debated. Popeye tutored them in the arts of cleaning corals from the sponges' roots with paring knives, and in clipping off irregularities with sheep shears to give the sponges the pleasing round or oval shapes that drew buyers' eyes.

Thus, they spent their first day of labor: sorting Sheepswools and Yellows from trash sponges; cleaning and clipping. When they weren't doing that, they stuffed sponges that had completed their first drying period (to drain the blood out, that's what makes the stink, said Popeye) into traps resembling lobster traps and lowered them into the water to soak for a second time. Those that had been immersed for the required three to five days were hauled out and stacked to dry again, after which they would be ready for clipping. Eliot was grateful for the shade provided by the roof, though it had been put on to protect the sponges, which were ruined by direct sunlight, and not for the benefit of the employees. Drew pestered Doris and Popeye with questions about sponge habits and lifespans and what made Sheepswools and Yellows grow smooth while other types did not. Nathaniel (who considered the work pretty easy, compared with the granite quarries) sometimes looked out to the harbor, hoping to see a sponger's sloop coming in with a black man aboard.

At the end of the workday, the three tired brothers trudged past the Cortez cigar factory and the cigar-makers' cottages surrounding it, palms and Spanish lime and sapodilla trees motionless as plants in a greenhouse, royal poinciana ablaze. Going to the end of Porter's wharf, where the sidewheeler *City of Key West* was disembarking passengers, Eliot waved his cap to signal Will to come get them in the tender. As they waited, they watched big fish—tarpon, they'd learned—rolling in the harbor, thick bodies plated with scales the size and brightness of new-minted silver dollars. Westward, far across an expanse of bright tidal flats, a few out islands appeared as a flotilla of anchored ships. Miles and miles beyond them, hidden from the eyes in Nathaniel's head but visible to those in his imagination, lay the Dry Tortugas.

Back aboard *Double Eagle,* Will displayed the mess of fish he'd caught that afternoon—the locals called them "grunts," he said—and then had scaled, cleaned, and seasoned them, all ready to be fried and consumed with a heap of the grits purchased in Beaufort. His navigational skills unnecessary for the time being, Will had agreed to accept demotion to ship's cook if the Braithwaites found work ashore. The least the loafer could do, thought Eliot, still seething at Will's refusal to go job hunting with them. The snob said he was a Yale man and a yachtsman and would not stoop to menial labor unless faced with starvation—a remote threat, what with all the fish in these waters and most of the stores bought from Cudlip (that seemed a year ago) still in the lockers. He figured he could stretch his seven dollars another two weeks, by which time they would be homeward bound.

Actually, his account was down to six dollars and ninety-three cents; he'd gone ashore to buy cigarettes and the *Key West Gazette,* which he read aloud to the Braithwaites as they ate on deck, basking in the relative cool, while the sun fell toward the benediction of its setting. The Key West electric trolley service, inaugurated two years ago, was to be expanded. . . . A dispute between local spongers and a Greek crew down from Tarpon Springs had erupted into fisticuffs in a saloon. . . . And these items, telegraphed by the Associated Press: An Ohio preacher, speaking through a transmitter on his pulpit, had delivered a sermon to housebound members of his flock by telephone—"Long-distance salvation," Eliot cracked, his fork clicking on his tin plate. . . . The Chicago White Stockings had defeated the Milwaukee Brewers, three bags to one, in the year-old American League. . . . And General Funston, the celebrated captor of Aguinaldo in the Philippines, was due to return to the United States in the fall to lecture on his exploits. . . . The Anti-Imperialist League, claiming that Aguinaldo was a hero of Philippine independence, was urging people to boycott the general's speaking tour. . . .

"Those sissies. Sissies and traitors." Nathaniel spit a fish bone overboard. "Funston marched a hundred miles through the jungle right into Aguinaldo's camp and nabbed him, fair and square."

"Seem to recall it wasn't quite that way, Natters. He employed a *ruse de guerre*."

"What's that?"

"Funston tricked Aguinaldo."

"So what? Didn't the Greeks trick the Trojans?" Nathaniel's gaze stretched toward the out islands, now showing as black dashes against a purple sky. "Y'know, instead of going to college after I get out of Andover, maybe I ought to join the army or the marines and volunteer for the Philippines."

Eliot and Drew looked at him, and Eliot said, "This is the first time I've heard that one."

"That's because I thought of it only just now."

"The war will probably be over by then," Will said, running a comb through his hair. "Anyway, since you're still zealous to get yourself shot, why don't I bring up that L. C. Smith and you can do it to yourself. At least then you'll have been killed by someone you know."

That evening, they upped anchor, hoisted the jib, and brought *Double Eagle* further into the harbor, dropping her hook outside the clustered sloops of the sponge fleet. Now they had only a short row to get to work.

Eliot, the first to wake, was on deck, brushing his teeth with baking soda. It was the soft, gray hour seamen call morning nautical twilight. Toward the east, above trees and shingle roofs and the tall brick customs house, a pale glimmering told him to enjoy the moment; the furious sun would rise soon enough. With the ladle, he dipped the bucket of freshwater and rinsed his mouth and spit overboard, into a roil of bar jacks savaging a school of glass minnows. Unbuttoning his drawers, he began to pee, and tightened his groin muscles to squeeze off the flow when he jumped back from the rail, startled to see a tarpon of awesome size rise out of the depths, open a mouth as wide as a barrel, and with a lazy roll of its head, engulf two big jacks at once. Jesus, what a maw, could've gulped me down just as easy, he thought, finished pissing, and then heard a man's voice sing out somewhere in the distance, and several voices answer. Again, a call, a response: a quick and rhythmic chant, faintly drifting over the harbor. He could not make out the words, yet there was something vaguely familiar about the song. Looking south, toward the steam and sailing ships swinging on their anchors, he saw a white-hulled, scum-streaked boat glide out from behind a freighter some hundred yards away. She had the look of a yawl-rigged skipjack, with a pronounced sheer that gave her the appearance of a vessel overloaded by the stern. Three skiffs swam behind her all in a row, like ducklings following their mother. She came on slowly, driven more by the flood than by the wind, of which there was little.

The single, strong voice sang out again, and the others chorused:

> *Shallow, shallow in de mornin'* . . .
> *Shallow, shallow brown!*
> *Just before de day is dawnin'* . . .
> *Shallow, shallow brown!*

Five brown-skinned men standing or sitting around the deckhouse, keeping time with their hands, either by clapping or drumming on the deckhouse roof. A sixth, darker complected, wearing a wide straw hat and leaning into the tiller.

> *Thought I heard de Cop'in say* . . .
> *Shallow, shallow brown!*
> *Tamarra is our sailin' day* . . .
> *Shallow, shallow brown!*

Eliot went below, into the after stateroom, and shook Nathaniel's shoulder.

"Hey, Nat. Heave out."

Nathaniel, turning over, opened his eyes.

"What is it?" His voice thick with sleep.

"Come on deck."

In his drawers, slapping his face, he followed Eliot outside, where the day's new light colored the ratty sails of the yawl, now gone a little way past *Double Eagle*. She had pointed up and was slipping between the schooner and the sponge fleet toward the Simonton Street docks.

> *De blackbird sang and de crow went caw* . . .
> *Shallow, shallow brown!*
> *Let's set dis sail by half past four* . . .
> *Shallow, shallow brown!*

"Remember from when we were kids?" asked Eliot. "Lockwood used to sing that song when he was home, and one time I asked him where he'd learned it and he said it was from that old Bahamaian Negro who used to work for Dad. Well, there's six Negroes on that sponger, and one of 'em has got to be Lowe."

We're bound away for Nassau town . . .
Shallow, shallow brown!
So run aloft, den come on down . . .
Shallow, shallow brown!

His brown feet bare, wearing denim overalls shrunk two inches too short even for his short legs, Artemis Lowe slouched against the tiller of the *Euphrenia Mae* and tipped back his palm-thatch hat, lifting the shadow from his eyes, the left hazel, the right a sightless pearl, the whites of both red-rimmed. He was a strangely built man, no taller than five feet eight, and two-thirds of that was torso, the shirtless torso under the overall's bib like a stout barrel casking the lungs of the diver he had once been.

"Lord God Jehovah! I ain't seen Cop'in Cy in twenny year," he said, in a booming voice. "You're de Cop'in's boys, you say? You ain't joshin' me, are you?"

Standing on the dock, Nathaniel said, "No, sir. Why would we?" Beside him were Eliot and Drew; beside them, a crewman was taking wicker baskets full of sponges passed to him by two more men on the deck of Lowe's boat. Two others were inside the deckhouse, tossing the sponges from out of the hold.

"Well, some folks like to josh," said Lowe. "Make der lives interestin'." He turned his broad head, resting almost neckless on his shoulders, to look at *Double Eagle*. "And you come down all de way from Maine on dot boat? Lotta boat for a short trip, but not much for a trip like dot. Yeah, you ain't joshin'. You Cop'in Cy's blood, all right. Well, now, lemme shake your hands."

Stretching his squat legs with some effort, he stepped off and gave them each a handshake, his smile baring crooked teeth, the bottom tooth in the middle capped in gold.

"We'd been asking around town for you," Nathaniel told him. "Yesterday, we ran into a fella who said he knew you and that you were still around."

"And which fella dot?"

"Don't know his name. Tall, skinny . . ."

"White fella or black?"

"Black."

"Pretty drunk, too," Drew added, and then, with a reproving look: "And it was only nine in the morning."

"Tall, skinny nigger drunk at nine de mornin'? Dot be Desmond Knowles, and no other. Used to work with me till he get so deep into de rum dot he seein' sponges in *his* bed, but take him to de *sponges'* beds and he seein' everything but sponges." Lowe glared balefully at the crewman on the dock. "What you starin' at, Corey?"

"Wasn't starin', Papa. Was listenin'," said Corey, in the accents of the American South, rather than in Artemis's West Indian.

"Well, stop lissnin' and empty dem baskets, so's Sweeting can see what we got. He ain't gwan to buy what he can't see." Turning back to the Braithwaites: "Dis my youngest, Corey. Other two down de hold, and de two on deck be my nephews. Family business I got. We do the introducin' when dey done workin'. Goddom! Never thought I'd be meetin' Cop'in Cy's sons, de second batch. Knew de first, Lockwood. Wasn't but a boy when I last seen him, but a sailin' mon even den. First rate. Now how's he farin'? Must have him a wife and kids by now."

Shaking his head, Nathaniel answered that Lockwood was still single, and had himself tried to make a go of the sponge business in Tampa, but had gone broke.

"He did? Dot too bad. Wished he'd talked to me first. I'd of told him, Stay out de sponge business, 'less you be Greek." Artemis pulled off his hat, revealing a coffee-colored skull banded above his brows by a crease and above the ears by a ribbon of knotty hair dusted with white. "Goddom Greek foreign son-bitches, dey takin' it all!" he said, slapping the hat against his thigh. "Dey come to here from Tarpon Springs all de way and dey don't fish de sponges like we do, with a glass-bottom bucket and dese . . ." He reached into the boat and took up a long-handled hook with three prongs. "Nope. Dey dives for 'em in divin' suits, and dey go through a sponge bed like de locust in Egypt in de Bible times. And what dem foreign son-bitches don't take, dey kill, stompin' on de sponges with dem goddom heavy divin' boots. Yeah, I'm sorry Lockwood don't talk to me first. I'd of put him straight. I always liked dot boy. A sailorin' mon. First rate." He jammed the hat back on his head and glared again at his son Corey. "I see you lissnin' again instead of workin'."

"Who are these fellas, Papa?"

"Okay, we get to the introducin' part, then maybe you do what you supposed to be doin'." He rapped the gunwale of the *Euphrenia Mae* with the hook and called out to the two men in the hold, "George! Ethan! Come on out deah. Want you to meet somebody."

Bending double under the low deckhouse hatch, a young man of twenty or twenty-one emerged. Like Corey, he had his father's stocky build and broad, open face. He was followed by a wiry figure, with smooth skin only a shade or two darker than the sun-bleached butternut of his shirt. They stood leaning their backs into the main boom, around which the grimy sail was furled loosely.

"De first one out be George, my middle boy, and de second, what looks like a Sponnish mon—his mama be a Cuba nigger, with Sponnish blood in her—be Ethan, my oldest. Boys, you remember I told you about my old cop'in, Cy Braithwaite? De one take such good care of your papa after he goin' half blind, divin' dot packet?"

"'Course we remember," said Ethan. "Reckon you tell that story once a year, at least. Like a sermon in church, it is."

"Dot real funny. You work like you make jokes, maybe you get somewhere in life. Dese here t'ree, Nat, Eliot, Andrew, dey Cop'in Cy's boys, de second batch. And if you was lissnin' instead of workin', like Corey was, den you hear 'em tell me five minutes ago dot dey sail on down to here from Maine all de way. In dot fore-and-after yonder"—pointing—"two thousand mile, dom near. Dey got dere Papa's blood and dere brudder's, too. Sailorin' blood. First rate."

The two sets of sons nodded to each other, but no one moved to shake hands. Ethan pulled his thick neck into his shoulders and asked, "So how come it is you come so far?"

"Yeah, I forgot to ask dot myself," said Artemis. "What for you t'ree sailin' down to dis old rock, middle of no place?"

"It's about the *Annisquam*," Eliot said. He mopped his forehead with the back of his hand. Only seven-thirty and the heat was making itself felt already, the air damp, cloying.

"What about it?"

"We wanted to hear about it," said Nathaniel.

"Oh, he'll be happy to tell you," said Ethan, smirking, while George nodded solemnly. "Tell you about it till you sick of hearin' it."

"None of your sass!" Artemis looked up at Nathaniel, puzzlement creasing his leather-brown face. "I ain't never heard of nobody sailin' dom near two thousand mile to hear a story! Dot have to be one helluva story for someone to do dot, and de tale of de *Annisquam* is a good 'un, but it ain't dot good. Didn't your papa never tell you about it?"

"Not much, but there's more to it than just hearing about it." Nathaniel looked past Artemis's shoulder, toward a sponge sloop making sail, its wake putting folds in the slick water. "But if you could tell us about it, we'd sure appreciate it. When you've got the time."

Artemis turned and lowered his head, and seemed to be studying the fat snappers schooled around a piling fringed with green algae.

"Not today. Got to unload, clean up de boat, get some rest. Den tonight, I got to jolly up my Euphy. Been out five days dis trip. Now we gwan to be ashore tamarra, so it got to be den. You tell me where, what time."

"Tomorrow night, then? In our boat. We'll meet you here and take you out to her."

Artemis pointed to the gray smear beneath his left eyebrow. "Know what folks on dis eye-lond say about me and your papa after dis hoppen? Dot if you put us together, what you got is a mulatto what is blind in both or can see with both, dependin' on which eyes got put into that half-nigger's head. You boys got somethin' cookin', and I want to hear what it is."

19

ELIOT AND DREW were on the cabin top, drinking Coca-Cola, while Nathaniel, sitting against the taffrail, sipped rum from a tin cup with Artemis and Will. Far beyond the harbor's mouth, the slender, leaning coil of a waterspout dropped from a low cloud to briefly tether cloud to sea before it was drawn up again, like a rope on a winch. Artemis smacked his lips and said:

"Oh, dis Bermuda rum de finest kind, next to de rum of Haiti. Dere's folks who say Cuba rum de best, but uh-uh. It's too *white*." He let out a laugh, his big chest heaving under his overalls. "De good black rum of Bermuda or Haiti gimme any day."

"I thought Jehovah's Witnesses weren't allowed to drink," said Will; Artemis had mentioned earlier that he'd joined the sect some years ago.

"Where you hear dot? A Witness can drink, long as he don't make a fool of hisself like dot rummy, Desmond Knowles. Witness can smoke, too, but I don't have nuttin' to do with dem dom cigars and cigarettes." He looked up at a man-o'-war bird, a dark speck circling. A tarpon rolled off the port side, its back showing bronze in the slant of late sunlight. "Knew a fella come up with me on Harbour Island. Me and him divin' for conchs before we could walk. We got so we could stay down five minutes at five fathom, but when he got older, he start to smoke dem dom cigarettes like you do, Will, and he got so that he couldn't hold his breath long enough to fart. Dass what dem things gwan do to you, mon."

Will sucked in smoke and exhaled it through his nostrils.

"I can break wind with the best, and I can prove it."

"Don't do dot!" Artemis threw back his head and laughed again; a laugh that started in his knees and rose through him, gathering power.

He took another swig of rum, his good eye, deeply furrowed at the corner from years of squinting into harsh sunlight, wandering up and down the mainmast, over to the wheel and the binnacle in front of it. "Oh, dis one pretty little ship, it is. You can see Cop'in Cy's hand in it, yeah, you sure can." Rising to stand at the helm, work-thickened fingers grasping the spokes, his face expressing something like love. "How does she ride, boys? Your papa used to say of *Main Chance* dot she rode to make de seagulls weep for shame."

"Says the same about this one," Eliot told him. "She's got sand, too. She weathered a fifty-knot gale in the Carolinas when we were coming down."

"Would of figured your papa to make sure she got dot quality. *Main Chance* had it, too. Back in de wreckin' days, we used to storm ride in her. Storm-ridin', dass de riskiest thing a wrecker can do, dass when you stay *out* when every other cop'in with an ounce of sense is lookin' for some place to put *in*. You wait for some ship to hit de rocks and shoals. Dass about what we were doin' when de *Annisquam* run aground on de Tortugas reefs. Seventy mile from where we now sittin'." Motioning at the orange and scarlet horizon, above which filaments of cirrus had woven themselves into a crisscross pattern as symmetrical as the checks in a checkered shirt. "On dot day it was hot, too hot for de springtime, hot like it is today, and de glass fallin' some, but the thing your papa notice was de wind," he said, and sat down again between Will and Nathaniel. "Oh, dot mon could read de weather like he read de book de prophet Isaiah wrote.

"What de wind is supposed to do dot time of year is blow southeast, den south, den southwest, and go right round de clock and come north, givin' you a little norther for a day, maybe two, before it finish clockin' and come southeast again. But on dot day, tenth of March, 1879, de wind stopped after it go southwest. Stopped dead, den it commenced to blow, real, real light—not five knots—but stead-day out de west. A backin' wind, boys, and dot mean trouble. In dese waters here, when de wind backin' in de springtime, you most can count on a westerly gale comin' out de Gulf of Mexico, and dem springtime westerlies, hooo-hee, dey can blow like a hurricane.

"De *Annisquam* was a fast packet outta Boston, bound for Corpus Christi. She put in here for a couple days to unload some cargo and take on fresh water and dry stores, and she clear Key West harbor with de tide at five de mornin' of the tenth. Long about seven, your papa climb up de wrecker's lookout tower by Tifton's wharf to have him a look at de weather. He got his spyglass, and see de *Annisquam*'s sails away off—she didn't make too much westerin' in dem light airs—but he sees somethin' else way, way off to de west, and dass a black line way low in de sky. Dot wasn't no promise, wasn't no prophecy, dot was a goddom *guar-an-tee* dot a gale is comin', and dot gale and dot packet gwan to meet up somewheres near de Dry Tortugas. Ain't no guarantee dot de ship gwan to wreck up, but dere's a fair chance she will, 'cause dot wild water out dere, reefs and rocks and shoals dot ain't on no chart to dis day! Cop'in Cy got us all together, and we come runnin' with our Georgia bundles. Dot spare clothes and whatever food you can snatch up real quick. Dere was me and two other divers, Jim Wakefield and Bodden Cross—dey old Harbour Island boys like me, Bodden de one take up cigarette smokin'—and Hank Albury, de engineer who worked de salvage gear, and ten crew, sailors and lumpers together, your papa's first mate, a half-Sponnish fella name of Ben Moreno—he's dead now—and den your papa and Lockwood. Boys, we was one crack crew! When dot cry go out from de towers, 'Wreck ashore!' de *Main Chance* most times de first to speak de wreck and claim rights to be salvage master. So you can bet we had her under way in no time flat, and we sailed right into dot storm. . . ."

"But why—" Nathaniel started.

"Stead-day, mon. I'm comin' to dot part directly," said Artemis. "We did dot for de salvage, for de loot, but we did it too for de lives. Dere was one hundred one souls board de *Annisquam*, she a square rigger, got to carry a big crew, forty-four includin' her skipper, name of Robinson, and de rest was passengers. Folks used to say, de insurance folks most times, dot us wreckers was no better'n pirates, like Blackbeard hisself, but dere is many a soul walkin' dis sweet earth today what would of been sayin' 'Good day to you' to de fishes, if it wasn't for some wrecker savin' his no-account ass from de cruel ocean. Yeah, dere was some rascal wreckers, if it come to choosin' to lettin' dere own mama drown and gettin' to de loot, would of said goodbye to Mama, but Cop'in Cy wasn't dot kind."

No, he would not have been, thought Nathaniel, as Artemis paused to wet his lips with rum. Salvage and lives. Greed and duty—the coals that fueled the boiler of his father's ambition. The two didn't mix, in most cases, but he must have found in the wrecker's trade a calling that allowed them to be burned together.

"De money part now," Artemis resumed, while the first evening stars appeared. "We make it our business to know what a ship is carryin', if we can, and de rumor got started in town dot de *Annisquam* carryin' dese candle holders, no little ones like for a house, but great big ones long as a man is tall and gold clear through, seven of 'em, de tale went—it come from de ship's second mate, talkin' drunk de night before she left—and dey is bound for Vera Cruz, o'er to Mexico, for a church dere."

"Paschal candles, for Easter," Drew interrupted.

"Whatever dey called, dey big and gold and we all thinkin' what dot gwan to fetch at a salvage auction, if it come to dot. De Lord God Jehovah forgive me, but when we set out, I was prayin' for dot ship to hit de rocks, and I bet everybody else was, too, maybe even Cop'in Cy hisself, even if he wasn't dot kind. Say dere, Will, poss me dot rum gimme."

Will handed him the bottle, and he refreshed his cup.

"De gale was a sweetie pie, tell you dot. We run into it in Rebecca Passage, east of de Tortugas, and we got to ride it out. Wasn't long before I was prayin' to de Lord God Jehovah to save dis nigger's ass. Come to find out later dot when de storm poss o'er Key West, de navy people's gauges said de wind hit eighty mile an hour. Dere was a turtlin' schooner, hundred-and-twenty-footer, picked up clear outta de harbor and set down on Front Street. Small trees on de eye-lond got pulled out de ground like my Euphy pulls pins out her pin cushion, and dere was coconuts ripped from de palms and shot t'rough windas like dey was cannonballs, and out at sea, where we was, de seas looked to me high as de customs house yonder.

"It blew itself out in a hour, wind fall off to maybe twenty-five, and we go on our way, beatin' into dot west wind, with a lookout in de crow's nest, and it's about middle of de day and we got Fort Jefferson in sight when he calls out, 'Wreck ashore! Four points de starboard bow! Range, ten mile!' Cop'in Cy bears off and goes up Southeast Channel. Presently, we all see her, on de rocks way up on de reef at de north side of de Tortugas, way north of Hospital Key. Dere's seven eye-londs in de Tortugas, and Hospital one of de smallest. So dere she is, rocked head-on, and from de looks of her list, bilged, too. She was gettin' pounded by some rough seas, and Cop'in Cy is afraid she gwan to break up and wants to get to her before she does. Lot easier, salvagin' a ship dot still above water, and den dere's de salvage fee you get for savin' de ship and de' riggin, and den dere's de extra fee you get for goin' out in heavy weather and for showin' what de judges in de admiralty courts call enterprise. Even if we don't get dem gold candlesticks, we was lookin' at a pile of money. Albury, de engineer, gets his gear ready—de salvage anchors, de steam winch, and cables and pumps. De idea is, we gwan to patch her if she's bilged, den pump her dry, den pull her off stern first on de next high tide. We ain't a mile from dot ship when de lookout spots, away off to east'ard, two lifeboats, all full of folks, and dey pullin' hard, but de Lord Jehovah only knows where dey t'ink dey goin' out dere. Maybe for de lighthouse station on Loggerhead Key, maybe for de big fort on Garden Key, but dey rowin' de wrong way!"

Artemis took another sip and then went on, and they listened intently, the Braithwaites' chests swelling when they heard that their father had done the honorable thing. Ordering a change of tack, he picked up the survivors, who were wet and fearful and shivering in the wind. Among them was *Annisquam*'s first mate, and he told the crew of *Main Chance* that Captain Robinson's ship had been bearing northward through the blow on her lower main topsail, which was lost when the wind piped up unexpectedly to eighty knots or better. Crewmen were ordered aloft to clap on new canvas, and that had no sooner been done when the wind gusted some more and blew out the new sail, and then there was nothing for it but to run with the storm on bare poles. Robinson thought he was clear of the Tortugas Reefs, but he wasn't, and the ship cracked headfirst into the uppermost tip of a long reef shaped like a crescent moon. *Annisquam* drew twenty feet and she ran hard aground in two fathoms of water and was bilged. With her stern to seas most monstrous, Artemis said, she was rocking up and down with such violence that Robinson feared she would break in two and so ordered most of his crew and all the passengers to man the lifeboats and pull for Fort Jefferson while he remained aboard with the ship's carpenter and a handful of men.

"Now de lifeboats, in pullin' for Garden, got to quarter into ten-foot seas, even after dot gale let down. Dey gettin' nowhere except swamped, so dey come about and pull to east'ard with the seas, headin' for Middle or East Key, and ain't one of dem eye-londs a whole lot bigger den a backyard. De folks in de boats can't even see 'em. Dass when we picked 'em up. Den de mate give us de bad news. Dere was *t'ree* lifeboats lowered away. He don't know what hoppen to de third, but he reckoned it swamped and de folks was shark bait by now. Your papa, he can't go reckonin' like dot, got to find dem if he can, and it's close on to dusk when de lookout see a man signalin' from East Key with a white shirt. *Main Chance* can't get in dere. Lord God Jehovah, de water so shallow dere, man could lay down on his back and not get his nose wet. So we lower our longboat away and fetch dem souls, dey all huddled up and prayin'. Ain't nuttin' on East Key, no water, no trees, nuttin' but sand and coral, and de man who was signalin' us told us dey had give up hope. Dis one fella, he had him a gold watch on a gold chain and he t'rew into de sea, tellin' his friends, 'I got no more use for time, and nei-ther do you. God has abandoned us.' Dass what de signalin' fella tell us dot fella say."

Artemis spoke; Will and the Braithwaites listened and saw and heard as if they had been aboard *Main Chance* when she spoke the wreck after nightfall and dropped her hook a safe distance off the reef. The longboat was lowered and Cyrus was rowed to *Annisquam,* her stern lamp and masthead light aglow like stars. "What schooner is that?" Captain Robinson hailed through his horn. Cyrus called back, "Wrecker *Main Chance,* out of Key West!" and then offered his services and asked for permission to come aboard to see what needed to be done. But Captain Robinson replied that he wasn't letting some mooncussin' son of a bitch on board his vessel.

"You see, boys, de fast packets was crack ships and dere cop'ins was de cream of de crop. Downright embarrassin' for a cop'in like dot to run aground, and he figured to save de ship owners de salvage fee and his own reputation by refloatin' her hisself, soon as his carpenter had her patched and her pumps pumped her dry. Your papa give him de facts of de case. De tides dere didn't rise or fall more'n two, t'ree feet, so even at de flood, dere wasn't gwan to be enough water to refloat dot big ship. She was gwan to have to be *hauled* off, with de kedge anchors and winches. And best to get to it right away, 'cause dere was most likely a norther comin' behind de gale, and den de *Annisquam* gwan to be takin' seas on her beam and break her back, for sure. Cop'in Robinson a proud and a pigheaded cop'in and he says such words like he was on to de tricks of us scoundrels and to go to hell.

"Cop'in Cy row on back to *Main Chance,* and de idea now is we gwan to stand off de wreck till her skipper got some sense in his pighead. We got ninety-t'ree souls on board and dere ain't room for dot many on *Main Chance.* We got some of 'em on deck, some in de crew quarters, some even in de cargo holds, and dey all wet and shiverin'. With dot norther fixin' to come on down, it got chilly for dese parts. All wet and shiverin', and some of 'em was what dey call d'larious. Dere was one, a preacher from Texas, who kept talkin' about de Bible story about St. Paul gettin' saved from shipwreck. Over and over, his teeth chatterin', till it about to drive us out our heads. Den he shut up at last. He upped and died. Just like dot. Like he got shot. Dere's a few more look like dey fixin' to do de same thing directly, and Cop'in Cy was fearful dot he gwan to have him a ship full of dead people by de dawnin'. So back into de longboat he goes and he nails a copy of his wreckin' license to de side of *Annisquam.* Dot's what you do to let other wreckers know you spoke de wreck first. Den we weigh anchor and make sail and take dem folks to de navy hospital on Key West. Middle of de' night. Took us thirteen hours to make dot seventy mile, 'cause between de gale and de comin' norther, dere wasn't much wind."

But *Main Chance* rode the norther down the next day, making thirteen knots, and was at the wreck by afternoon. Her crew was surprised to see another wrecker, *Flying Storm,* skippered by a man named Sanford, anchored off *Annisquam,* from which Cyrus's license had mysteriously disappeared. The wreck was taking seas on the beam, as he had predicted, and Sanford's crew were throwing her top cargo overboard to lighten her up.

"Now dis Sanford fella, he a rascal wrecker, like de kind I told you about, a shady fella him, and he got nuttin' but rascals for crew. When your papa asks him—he's shoutin' t'rough de horn—where de hell his license gwan to, Sanford shouts back t'rough his horn dot he don't know what Cop'in Cy talkin' about. Your papa says he spoke de wreck de night before, but Sanford says *Annisquam*'s skipper told him dot de offer of salvage was turned down, so if—*if,* he says—Cop'in Cy claimed de wreck, he didn't have no right to. And now Cop'in Robinson changed his mind, Cop'in Sanford says, and de wreck is Sanford's to be master of. Fact is, he says, he got a contract from Cop'in Robinson agreein' to let *Flyin' Storm* save his ship.

"Now your papa notice, hell, we all did, dot dere is no salvage anchors set, no winches onboard *Annisquam.* Ain't no effort bein' made to get her off de rocks. Cop'in Cy got a feelin' dot what's goin' on is dot Cop'in Robinson and Cop'in Sanford made them a agreement. Work like dis. De ship run aground in a kind of little gully in de reef. Dis gully run east-west. To de north and south side of dot gully, de reef is even shallower—only a fathom. By lightnin' dot ship by t'rowin' off her top cargo, all dey gwan to do when de tide come up is drive her further up on de reef, and if de tide don't do it, dem seas smashin' into her beam will. Once she further up on de rocks, she'll break up for sure. Total loss. And dot, your papa figure, is de deal. Cop'in Sanford and Cop'in Robinson gawn to split Cop'in Sanford's share of de insurance claim for de vessel. Y'see, boys, when a wrecker is workin' a ship dot becomes a total loss, he got title to some of de insurance money. Dot kind of thing ain't done a lot, but it's done. Sanford must of figured your papa would take him to court for poachin' on his wreck and dot de court gwan to look with a kindly eye on Cop'in Cy and *Main Chance* for takin' so much risk and savin' all dem souls. So your papa is reckonin' dot Sanford told Robinson dot in exchange for de favor he doin' him, splittin' his share,

Cop'n Robinson gwan to testify in Sanford's favor if dey go to court. Not lie exactly but put some shadin' on de truth. He could say somethin' like dot he didn't trust Cop'in Cy or dot Cop'in Cy try to bully him into salvagin' and dass why he turn him down. It de right of a sea cop'in to turn a salvor away. Yeah, your papa knew all de tricks of de trade. He didn't never use 'em, but he knew 'em. De smart thing to do den was to sail back to Key West and your papa to see de judge, but none of us had no sleep in dom near two days and gwan t'rough a gale and saved ninety-t'ree souls from de cruel ocean, and your papa wasn't of a mind to do de smart thing. Say, Will, poss me more dot rum gimme."

Once more the bottle went from Will's to Artemis's hand, once more the splash of liquid on tin, and his audience, rapt, heard of how a small cannon aboard *Main Chance,* used for shooting lifelines and rescue harnesses to struck ships, was loaded with nails and bolts and aimed at *Flying Storm.* Leaving his first mate, Moreno, and the engineer on *Main Chance* with two men armed with Winchester repeaters, Cyrus sent Lockwood below, then boarded the longboat with his remaining crew and pulled to *Annisquam.*

"We got us Mausers, a couple breechloaders from de war, and your papa got his old Navy Colt in his hand and an owl-head pistol in his belt and a copy of *Marvin's Law and Salvage* in his pocket. Dot de wrecker's bible, wrote by Judge Marvin hisself. While we was rowin', Moreno calls over to Sanford on *Flyin' Storm* to sit tight on his ship with de men he got, and dot if he don't, mon, dere'll be a load of grapeshot tearin' into his riggin', and anybody try anything, dot mon gwan to get a Winchester bullet 'tween his sidelights.

"We pull up alongside de wreck, de lee side, next to *Flyin' Storm*'s longboat. Everybody up dere real busy tossin' off top cargo and ain't payin' attention to us. You should of seen your papa, he had a red beard den, look like old Barbarossa hisself, and dot gray eye of his, it look like a minié ball. I tell you, boys, if you don't know it already, dot when Cop'in Cy thought he was in de right, dere nuttin' could stop him, and when he thought he'd been cheated or someone broke de faith with him, he think nuttin' of shootin' dot fella. He de lass mon on dis sweet earth you want to double-cross or try stab de back. De grapplin' hooks go up, and your papa, he's de first one up and over. . . ."

Now the lilting West Indian voice carried the Braithwaites back through time so they did not need to imagine their father grabbing the first of *Flying Storm*'s men he could lay hands on, sticking the Colt in his mouth, and telling him to get off the ship with his mates. The boys did not need to imagine because they were no longer listeners, they were witnesses, hearing Cyrus warn the sailor that if he did not disembark immediately, his brains were the only part of him that would remain on *Annisquam* while his corpse went into the ocean and his soul straight to hell.

"Meantime, rest of us is comin' on up, oh, we like pirates den, and de mon your papa got, he looks at us, den into Cop'in Cy's minié ball eye and he knows dis ain't no play actin'. We send 'em all packin', back to *Flyin' Storm*. And bye and bye, she weighs and sails on back to Key West. Now dere's us twelve and Cop'in Robinson and his handful, facin' each other, and Robinson is mostways crazy, he's so mad. He yellin' dot your papa a buccaneer, dot he gwan to see Cop'in Cy hanged, but your papa, just cool as you please, go up to him with de *Marvin's Law* in one hand and de Colt de other, and read him chapter and verse. Dot he, Cop'in Cy dot is, got de right to board a struck vessel by force, if it be his judgment dot de vessel is in danger, a certain kinda danger, meanin' dot de danger about to come to pass. . . ."

"I think you mean 'imminent danger,' " Drew offered.

"Do believe dass de word. You a smart boy, Andrew."

"Don't tell him," said Eliot. "He already knows."

"Cop'in Cy say to Cop'in Robinson dot in his judgment *Annisquam* in dot kinda danger and in his judgment her cop'in not doin' all he can to save her, and in his judgment de wrecker Cop'in Robinson hired was showin' no skill in doin' things de proper way. No wreckin' anchors been set, no cables bent to de winches, nuttin' bein' done except t'rowin' off de top cargo, and dey wasn't even tryin' to save *it*. Just t'rowing' it in de water. So with or without Cop'in Robinson's permission, your papa said, he was gwan to save de ship before she broke up. And dass what we did, not save her, but try to.

"We set two big kedges astern her in deep water and we got cables fast to de winches, one a steam winch, the other an old-time kind you got to turn by hand. Dere is six of our men on dot one. De donkey engine to de steam winch was huffin', and our men is huffin' too, workin' like de devil, crankin' dot hand winch. Goin' round and round like oxes, dose men were. Dot big ship like she cemented to dem rocks, but she start to move at de last. Not much, but she's movin'. We got maybe ten, fifteen feet of her stern in deep water, and the other hundred ninety feet still on de rocks when dis big sea come in, driven by de norther, and lift the ship some and then set her down. Dere come dis most awfulest noise, a groanin' and a creakin'. Same time, more of her come off, and den her stern half floatin', and another sea come in and another, and she's bouncin' up and down and groanin' and creakin', and den we hear Cop'in Robinson shout out, 'She's gwan to break!' Now dass a big danger for us, boys. We got our men on dot ship. But your papa said to keep de winches turnin', and some more of her come off, but dass when we can see de ship is hogged mighty bad, dot her back is already good as broke and she gwan to break from de bottom up. She was bouncin' up and down like one dem things kids play on in de school playground, de seesaw."

A few minutes later, Cyrus realized that the game was up. He called to everyone onboard *Annisquam* to slip the cables and get themselves and the gear off, which they did, and none too soon. The ship broke; she twisted in half, her forward section remaining upright on the rocks, her stern half rolling over with a shriek of rending timbers, a terrible noise, as if the vessel were screaming in pain.

"We watch de stern roll and float for a while and den sink, and de forward parts flood and den dey roll in de surf and off de rocks and go down. Boys, we make our livin' off wrecked ships, but ain't no sailorin' mon can see a ship go down like dot without his heart bein' sick inside him.

"Wasn't deep dere, seven fathom, maybe eight, hell, we can *see* de top sides of de ship, not much more den ten feet under. But she down and dot de end of any idea of savin' her and her riggin.'

"We all get a rest den, 'cause we got to dive her de next day. Durin' de night, your papa ask Robinson where dem candleholders is stowed, but Robinson says dot far as he concerned, we all of us pirates and he ain't gwan to tell us what time it is. So me and Wakefield and Bodden Cross start de divin'. We got lowered on down in dese harnesslike things, weighted with ballast, and we got a rope to signal with and baskets and grapplin' hooks so de deck gang can haul de stuff up. Dass how we do it in dem times. No suits and hoses like dese goddom foreign Greek sponger son-bitches. Lemme tell you, boys, you need more'n' lungs for dot kinda work, you need de nerve to go down into de dark of a hold of sunk ship and feelin' around, never knowin' if you gwan to stick your hand in a shark's mouth. We brought up all kindsa stuff dot day—toothbrushes and coffee grinders and lamps and lanterns and bone knife handles and blastin' powder, but no gold candlesticks. We start again de next mornin', and a fine one it was, de norther blowed out, and de sea flat, but come de end of de day, me and Jimmy Wakefield, we feel dis burnin' in our eyes different den de burnin' come from saltwater. Bodden, he workin' a different part of de ship—de for'ard end—and said his eyes feelin' just fine. We go down de third day, and de fourth and dis time we come up with somethin'—de silks from China, and silver-ware, boxes of it, and de lamps from some expensive place in New York. Workin' like hell for four full days, and got a good bit of de cargo, but no candlesticks yet. Fifth day come, dot burnin' get worse, and after one dive me and Wakefield can't go down no more, de burnin' so bad now. Your papa wash out our eyes with de fresh water and de bakin' soda, but it don't do much good. Couple hours later, I'm havin' trouble seein', and so is Jimmy. Dass when dot goddom Robinson tell us dot *Annisquam* carryin' horse limmament. He call it 'Mexican mustang limmament,' and says we musta been down de hold where it was and dot de bottles musta broke when de ship did and all dot limmament mixin' with de seawater in de hold. Boys, me and Jimmy was scared! We up on deck in de light of day, and everything mostways look like it does down below. Your papa call off de whole operation. Bodden send up some kinda thing made of crystal, and dot was de last thing. Cop'in Cy sets sail for Key West, fast as he can drive dot ship, and me and Jimmy are brought to de navy hospital, but by den we can't see hardly at all. Jimmy was cryin', and I was fixin' to. While we in dere, de federal marshal arrested your papa on charges of grand larceny on de high seas, and dass what come of all dot."

"But there's more, isn't there?" asked Nathaniel, after a pause. He had lit an oil lamp and the soft glow gave a mahogany cast to Artemis's face, glistening in the tepid night air. The Milky Way arched overhead, a dusty white rainbow.

"Sure dere more, you care to hear it. I been talkin' one long time." He looked sidelong at Will, who passed the bottle yet again.

"You Jehovah Witnesses can sure hold your liquor, I'll say that."

"All de seawater in my belly, cuts de liquor some. Bye and bye, de sight return to my one eye but not de other, and it don't come back at all to poor Jimmy. Oh, he can see some light, some shapes, but if you was to put your hand in front his face and spread your fingers and ask him how many, he couldn't tell you. Your papa go to trial, a federal trial, held over to de Monroe County courthouse, dot big redbrick building over to Whitehead Street. We all dere, de whole crew of *Main Chance,* and some de crew from *Annisquam,* and Cop'in Robinson and Cop'in Sanford— he de one bring de charges when he sailed back to Key West. Dey testify against your papa, de crewmen from *Annisquam;* de rescued men, dey testify for him. Your papa got a lawyer who tell de judge dot Cop'in Cy had good reason to use force to board dot vessel, as her breakin' up proved, dot if Cop'in Robinson had lissened to him de first night, de whole ship and everything in her now be saved. Dis lawyer talk go on for t'ree, maybe four days, and you should of seen your papa, in his Sunday best, and not lookin' like no pirate and not like no guilty man neither, but just as sure of hisself as a preacher holdin' a royal flush. And his eye—he still got dot minié ball eye, and when Sanford and Robinson on de stand, dey can't hold de look of dot one eye with dere two.

"Dot judge lookin' kindly on Cop'in Cy for goin' out in a gale of wind and savin' one hundred souls from de cruel ocean. But he ain't so kindly about him boardin' a vessel with a gun in his hand and eleven men with guns in deres. He don't know what to do. Said your papa got to be rewarded and punished at one de same time. So dis what he do. He give your papa a choice. De reward for savin' souls be his captain's share of de salvage auction—ten t'ousand dollars! De punishment for usin' armed force when it wasn't called for would be dot his wrecker's license be suspended for five years. De other choice, he could keep his license, but forfeit his share de profits to Cop'in Sanford. Don't know how much your papa told you, but if you know him, den you know what he choose."

"He took the risks, he saved the people and the cargo, the salvage was his," said Nathaniel.

Artemis nodded gravely.

"De principle, not de loot. When de trial finished, your papa goes up to Cop'in Sanford and asks him what de hell hoppen to de copy of his license dot he nail to de ship. All he wants is a honest answer, but Sanford says he got no idea and dot your papa can go straight to hell. Cop'in Cy pop him hard 'tween the sidelights, and Sanford, he kinda stood dere a second before he start to fall, but he ain't fallin' fast enough to suit de cop'in, so he pop him again, and dot scuttled him. Right on de street in front of de Monroe County courthouse! Was de principle of de thing, you see. I tell you, boys, all of us on de eye-lond know dot your papa supposed to come from a right and proper family in Boston, and all I got to say is dot if a mon from de nice side de tracks can hit like dot, den I don't want nuttin' to do with one from de bad side of town." Artemis smiled at the recollection and said, "De principle and not de loot. He kept two t'ousand for hisself, for expenses for de ship and payin' off his lawyer, and turn over de rest to me and Jimmy Wakefield, fifty-fifty. He knew dere be no call for a one-eyed diver, and sure enough none for one got no eyes. He took care of us, and you know, with de four t'ousand I got I bought my house over to Petronia Street, free and clear, and de furniture in it, and I buy my sponge boat, free and clear. Ain't no bank, no mortgage mon can never take dem from me. Set me up for life, Cop'in Cy did."

"What about the other fella, Wakefield?" asked Eliot, and tossed his empty Coca-Cola bottle into the water.

Artemis, silent, craned his head to look above the main topmast.

"What dot star called? Dot real bright one just about straight up? Your papa used to steer by it in de summertime. Told me de name once . . ."

"Vega," Drew answered.

"Vega. Yeah." Lowering his gaze. "I could do somethin' with one eye, but Jimmy couldn't do nuttin'. De whole world for him like de dark ocean where he made his livin'. He mostways drank up all dot money and what he didn't drink he spent on de sportin' ladies. Dey only too hoppy to see him. Hey, mon, you got to *work* to drink up and fuck away four t'ousand dollars, but Jimmy done it in about t'ree year. When he was down to his last fifty dollars, he go into dis tap room over to Africa Town and buy de house all night, den with his last silver dollar, he tells dis fella dot he can have de dollar if he walks Jimmy to Tifton's wharf. And de fella did, and when dey get dere, Jimmy says 'thank you very much,' and takes de dollar out one pocket and gives it to de fella. Den he takes a pistol out de other pocket and puts it behind de ear and shoots hisself, and over he goes into de harbor on de ebbin' tide. Reckon it carried him out to de reef and maybe past it into de Gulf Stream, if de sharks didn't get to him first. And dere you have it, boys, de whole story about de *Annisquam,* and it all a true thing."

No one spoke, as often happens after a long tale; it was as if words themselves were tired from use. There was a quick spattering, like a sudden hard rain, across the water close by: a school of small fish in panicked flight from a big fish. Nathaniel looked at the constellation of anchor and masthead lights glittering over the harbor and said into the silence:

"And nobody ever recovered those gold candlesticks?"

"Nope, and nobody never will, 'cause dey ain't in her," Artemis replied.

They all four looked at him, expectantly.

"Dey never was, you see. Dot come out at de salvage auction. De auctioneer had him de cargo manifest, and wasn't nuttin' on it about no candleholders, no gold of any kind. De *Annisquam*'s second mate was talkin' drunk, and some fella hears him, but he's drunk, too, and he tells his buddy and adds a little spice to de tale to make it more interestin', and de buddy—you can count on him bein' into de rum and whiskey, too—he tells somebody else and puts in some seasonin' of his own, so by de mornin' of her sailin', it's all over town dot she carryin' seven solid-gold candleholders for a church in Vera Cruz, when, we all come to find out bye 'n' bye, she wasn't never bound to Vera Cruz in de first place. She was Tampico bound with dot horse limmament dot blinded Jimmy Wakefield and me."

Another long silence followed this revelation, Will and the Braith-waites exchanging glances, each trying to absorb the fact that they had sailed one thousand six hundred and forty-four miles in pursuit of a legend, a drunkard's ancient lie.

"Now how come you four lookin' all of a sudden like you lost your best buddy?" asked Artemis.

"We intended," Nathaniel began, and then, deciding that *intended* wasn't the word he wanted, said they had hoped to find the *Annisquam* and salvage her treasure themselves.

"Say, Will, any more dot Bermuda rum left?"

"Not much," said Will, and with what was now an almost reflexive movement, passed the bottle across his midriff into Artemis's hands.

"What the hell do you think you're doing!"—Will, looking stupified as Artemis poured the contents over the taffrail.

"Lookin' out for you, same as I would my own boys. You must of been drinkin' dis hooch all de way from Maine, 'cause it clear to me you thinkin' like rummies. You think dot divin' for salvage on a sunk ship is like divin' for conch or sand dollars? Now I know you first-rate sailorin' men, got to be, doin' what you did, but salvage divin' ain't no job for boys. Job for men, and men who know what de hell dey doin'. Oh, dom glad I told you dot story was dot and no more—a story. 'Cause if I didn't, den you been goin' out dere and get yourselfs drowned, and den when I get to heaven and see your papa dere, I got to explain why I didn't tell you the truth, and my one eye wouldn't hold on his."

Nathaniel felt suddenly diminished.

Eliot hopped off the cabin top and said in the tone of a prophet vindicated:

"Didn't I tell you, Nat? Way back in North Haven? That it was a job for professionals and you were nuts to think we could?" Then, to Artemis: "I told him. Before we even started out, I told him."

"You might have, boy, but I see you right here with him."

"Reckon that'll shut you up," said Nathaniel. He jumped to his feet and going below to the navigation station, rifled through the charts for the last one in the roll, the one bearing the legend: UNITED STATES—

EAST COAST. FLORIDA KEYS. MARQUESAS KEYS TO DRY TORTUGAS. *Soundings in Fathoms at Mean Low Water.*

He spread the chart on the cabin top, weighting it with the oil lamp.

"Would you show where she is, if you remember?"

"You think I was joshin' you, don't you? Uh-uh, ain't gwan to show you, 'cause den you go out dere to dive de wreck, lookin' for what ain't dere."

"I believe that, Mr. Lowe. All I want is to see on the chart where she went down. Honest."

Artemis threw him a skeptical look, frown lines stacking up beneath the deep crease made by his hat.

"Been twenny year. Don't know how good I remember." Bending over the chart, squinting in the lamp's weak light, a forefinger moving over water and islands. "Like I told you, she hit de west end of de reef on de north side. A fishermon buddy I got, he know her position down to de yard, but right here de best I can do." His finger pressed down, and where it pressed, near the upper tip of the blue crescent moon that marked the reef, Nathaniel penciled an X.

"Okay, now dot I show where she sort of is, you tell me what you fixin' to do, Nathaniel, and I don't want to hear no bullshit."

"I want to lay eyes on her, so when we get back, I can tell Dad that we did," Nathaniel answered, speaking from the heart. "You can see her from the surface, can't you? You said her side was only ten feet under."

"Maybe a little more den dot, and by now, she settle some into de mud and sand, but, yeah, you can see her, big dark thing layin' down there in two pieces, port side down. De water real clear out dot way. Hell, you can see de bottom, fifty foot down from a boat. And dass all you mean to do? Take a look so you can tell your papa you did?"

"That's all."

"Don't make sense to me, but you makin' it sound like it's real important to you."

"I'll single-hand this schooner out there if I have to," said Nathaniel, with a challenging glance at Will and his brothers.

"Know what I hear dis minute? Cop'in Cy hisself talkin'. Dot one determined mon." Artemis paused, rubbing the hatband's furrow. "But your papa wasn't pighead determined. Had common sense. When it look like dot ship gwan to break her back, he told de crew to slip dem cables to get de hell off. Lissen to me, now. I'm feelin' responsible for what you do. Got no idea why, but I do. You promise dis old eye-lond nigger dot you ain't gwan to dive on dot wreck."

"Promise. Honest."

"Don't know why dis is," Artemis said, with a grin. "But dere somethin' about the way you say dot word *honest* make me think the opposite. Dot dom wreck just plain old bad luck. De preacher shiverin' hisself to death. Me, Jimmy, your papa losin' his license . . ."

"But it brought you pretty good luck. Set you up."

"Dot partways Cop'in Cy's doin'. When you thinkin' of shovin' off?"

"We haven't talked about it, but I reckon Sunday, after we finish up the week working for Pinder." He looked again at Will, Eliot, and Andrew. "With your okay, shipmates."

"Thanks for consulting us, Natters. You're getting democratic in your old age. But all right. Sunday. How about it, my fellow peons?"

Eliot and Drew nodded.

"Now I'm figurin' it dis way. You boys can make de seventy mile to de Tortugas easy enough." He raised three fingers. "Calcalate ten, twelve hours dere, ten, twelve back, dot make one whole day." One finger dropped. "Calcalate a day for you to play around out dere lookin' at your wreck, dot make two whole days." The second finger folded. "Calcalate another day in case you get becalmed or some other things hoppen you didn't count on. Dot make t'ree." The third finger. "Sundee, Mondee, Tuesdee. You back here Tuesdee night, Wed-nez-dee mornin' de latest. You promise me dis, too. Dot you tell me when you leavin' and you let me know when you get back. Den, if you not back, I can report you overdue, dot de proper way seafarin' folks do things. I ain't to home, you leave word with my Euphy. Our house over to Petronia Street. You ask any nigger in Africa Town where it is, he'll tell you. You promise me dot?"

"We sure do, we'll do it," Eliot answered, before Nathaniel could utter a word; it had occurred to Eliot that this old West Indian, whom they barely knew, was showing more concern for their welfare than their father had.

"Okay," said Artemis. "Now, I gwan to do one thing for you, if I can find dot fishermon buddy. Ask him for a fix on de wreck, and den I get it to you before Sundee. Den you don't waste time, lookin' for her. Don't want to play around too long on de cruel ocean dis time of year. Hurricane time. Okay, Nathaniel. Mon de oars and take me ashore."

He swung over the rail and lowered himself into the tender and sat in the stern. Out came his blustery laugh. "Feel like de Phay-row isself, mon!"

"Think of how you'd feel if you were skipper of this schooner," said Nathaniel, fitting the oars into the locks.

"Oh, pretty fine. I sure do love a fine ship."

"Yeah, I get that idea." Nathaniel started to pull. "*Double Eagle* sails as pretty as she looks. If we get a beam wind Sunday, we'll fly to the Tortugas."

"Fore 'n' after on a beam reach, dere nuttin' sweeter on de sea."

"She can do ten knots, ten and then some. Coming down the Keys, we overtook a steamer. You would have loved that, Mr. Lowe."

"Suppose I would of." Artemis leaned back against the transom, his arms spread and a hand on each gunwale. "What you gettin' at?"

Nathaniel held the oars still.

"What if you guided us out to the wreck, after you talked to your buddy? Couldn't offer you any money, and, hell, you dumped the last of our rum overboard. But *Double Eagle* would be yours for three days. Whatever you'd say would go."

"Ha! Diss de first time I been made a cop'in by a boy. What is it, Nathaniel? You feel more sure of things with me dere? Got a livin' to make, sponges to fish, and I spend enough of my days on de water."

Nathaniel left it at that, and stroked across the dark harbor, in which the ships' lights in the distance, miniature moons, cast wavering white reflections.

20

SIX WEEKS AGO, Drew would have called crazy anyone who told him that the day would come when he would be happy to go to sea. He was certainly happy to be done with the Lower Keys Sponge and Fruit Company, and to have seen the last of Doris, who was an evil man. In the past week, Doris had not missed a chance to scold and humiliate him for sloppy workmanship. Drew never cleaned the roots thoroughly enough to please Doris, or he didn't clip the rough edges of the sponges quite right, or he mistook inferior breeds for the coveted Yellows and Sheepswools, requiring Doris to re-sort them, all the while cursing Drew for being the most useless little turd he'd ever known, a boy of such woeful abilities that he surely would never amount to anything (as if Doris were an example of how far a man could rise if he applied himself). He hated Doris but wanted to please him nonetheless, if for no other reason than to stop the criticisms, but pleasing the man was impossible. It wasn't that Drew could not get the hang of things; the work was so repetitive and tedious that he could not keep his mind on it for longer than half an hour before he lost himself in reveries of Boston and his mother, whom he missed at times with a physical ache, remembering long-ago winters when the sleighing season opened on Beacon Street and he snuggled beside her under a buffalo robe in the backseat of the family sleigh. Her warmth, the snug robe, and the horses blowing steam in the frosty air all combined in his memory to afflict him with longing, both for her and for the lively cold of a Boston January, which seemed, in Key West's swelter, as distant in time and space as a star.

Sometimes, he combatted his loneliness and the monotony of the work by solving mathematical problems in his head. He was in an advanced math class at Boston Latin, and had been privately tutored after hours in high-school algebra and quadratic equations. Clipping a sponge into the desired spherical or oblong shape, he would contemplate the mathematics of its curves—the elegant sweep of parabolas between vertical and horizontal axes. Or he would ponder the theory behind celestial navigation. Will did not have the faintest idea about the theory—why bother, when the *Nautical Almanac* and the Reduction Tables had worked all the problems for you? But, Drew had wondered, what would a navigator do if, by chance, he lost the *Almanac* and Tables? Will's edition of the *American Practical Navigator* contained an explanation of the astronomical triangle and complex trigonometric formulas that, if mastered, allowed you to calculate your position without reliance on the reference books. He studied it at night, but with all the arcane terms—cosine course, sine of the course angle, secant of the course angle—it was as impenetrable to him as to Will, the difference being that the impenetrability nagged him while it troubled Will not at all. It isn't necessary to reinvent the wheel, Will said; yet Drew wanted to.

Sort. Clean. Clip. Haul the traps up. Lower the traps down. Stack unfinished sponges in the drying shed. Stow the finished ones in the storage rooms, Drew musing upon the aspects of the theory that were within his grasp. The sextant reading measures the height of a star, let's say Vega, he would think. Ninety degrees minus the reading equals the distance between the observer's position and Vega's geographic position over the earth. But why? How? He made a mental picture of a diagram in Will's celestial navigation textbook: the globe and three lines. One line plunged vertically from the north pole to the imaginary center of the earth and represented the zenith angle, 90 degrees; the other two represented the observer's sextant angle and the angle of the star's geographic position. So, what's really being measured isn't the actual height of the star, he said to himself, but the internal angle of its GP with the zenith line, which should equal the difference between the observer's sextant angle and 90 degrees. If the sextant angle is 50 degrees, then Vega's internal angle is 40 degrees, and 40 degrees of arc over the earth's surface equals 2,400 nautical miles, because there are 60 nautical miles in each degree of arc. . . . Therefore, the observer's position is 2,400 miles from the point on the earth where Vega is directly overhead.

"Kid! Get your sweet dumb ass over here right now and look at this!" Rising from the stool, Drew walked warily to where Doris stood, in a dim, airless corner of the drying shed, near one of the storage rooms. (This happened yesterday afternoon.) He held out a Sheepswool sponge Drew had clipped. "This bloody thing looks worse'n it did when it come outta the goddamned ocean. What the 'ell are you thinkin' about?" Instead of apologizing and promising to do better, as he had on previous days, Drew replied, "Numbers, sir." Doris, squinting: "What d'yuh mean, numbers? What numbers? What's the matter with you? Are you crazy?" And Drew, affirming his sanity, said that he had been thinking about angles and the numbers of those angles, because numbers and angles and equations were as beautiful to him as poetry was to other people. To that declaration, Doris had no reply. He only stared down at Drew, who could not control the trembling in his lower lip. Doris stared for a long time and in a strange way, his expression hard and gentle at the same time: that big red ham of a face, and the hams for hands, one of which rose toward Drew's face, causing him to flinch. "Take it easy, kid, I ain't gonna smack you. Are you scared of me?" Drew thought it best to nod. "Well, you should be, 'cause I could hurt you if I wanted, but right now, I don't want to, because you're a nice-lookin' kid." Now the hand rested softly against Drew's cheek, its touch making him squirm, as if it were some clammy, slimy thing from the sea's bottom. "Too bad a nice-lookin' kid like you is so bloody fuckin' dumb and crazy. The craziest little bugger I ever met. Numbers! Nah, I ain't gonna hurt you. What I'm thinkin' I oughtta do is tell Sweeting to fire your sweet dumb ass for all the messin' up you're doin'. Want me to do that?" Drew, a fluttering in his throat, shook his head. "Bloody right you don't, 'cause around here, it's a full week's pay for a full week's work." Doris looked one side to the other, his hand falling from Drew's cheek to his collar, twisting it. "But you gotta be punished for messin' up like you have. Taught a lesson once for all. C'mere." He jerked Drew toward the door of the storage room, kicked it open with a knee, and dragged Drew inside, amid mounds of groomed sponges. "Takin' you to the woodshed, kid, and you ain't gonna make a peep, are you? Not one bloody little word." He whipped off his belt and wrapped part of it around his hand and told Drew to take his pants down. When Drew refused, he grabbed one of his braces, Drew spinning and bolting for the door to be pulled back by the elastic braces like a ball on a rubber band. He spun again, and one brace popped its buttons. "Wanta make it hard on yourself, do you, that's fine with me." Doris, breathing hard now, his lips wet, snatched the other brace, but Drew lunged away with such force that it, too, broke loose, leaving Doris holding the pair and Drew free to run, which he did, holding up his trousers with his hands, Doris shouting after him, "Hey, kid! I wasn't really goin' to! Was only trying to scare you! You keep your little mouth shut, or I'll . . ." But by then Drew had fled outside to the dock and out of earshot.

He did keep his mouth shut, though; out of fear, and out of something else, a kind of shame, although he could not explain to himself what he had done to feel ashamed about. When Popeye saw him snipping a length of trap warp for a makeshift belt and asked what he thought he was up to, destroying company property, he answered that his worn-out braces had broken and he couldn't think of any other way to keep his pants up. Popeye looked at him suspiciously, and then lifted his gaze and the suspicion with it toward the drying shed, where Doris stood with his arms folded across his chest. "Hey! That little bastard been messin' up!" he called out. "I was gonna teach him a lesson, that's all." Popeye nodded vaguely and turned back to Drew. "Keep that rope, kid," he said. "Best you stay away from him and work with me, from here on in."

When the day was done, he did not say anything to Will or his brothers. There was nothing to fear from Doris onboard the boat, but the peculiar shame, a feeling that he was dirty in a way that could not be cleansed with water and soap, remained with him. He had sensed that Doris meant to do something more than whip him, something he could not quite picture but that he knew would have been sinful; somehow or other, he must have made Doris want to do that sinful thing, and that was what made him ashamed. He retreated to his berth with the *Practical Navigator*, to study again the explanation of the navigational triangle, the trigonometric formulas. They still made no sense; but, he reflected, there were mysteries in men's hearts more impenetrable than any in mathematics, and in the world beyond the one from which he and his brothers had been exiled, as many perils as there were upon the sea. The latter, he thought, were to be preferred, for they could be explained.

"WEIGH UP dot anchor dere, and lively now!" Artemis laughed uproariously as Nathaniel cranked the port lever on the windlass and Eliot the starboard. "Oh, you gwan to be sorry you made me cop'in, 'cause I'm a mean 'un!"

The cable came in slowly, quivering with tension, shaking off droplets of water. Will flaked it into the chain locker, just aft the forepeak. The anchor's grip was broken, allowing Nathaniel and Eliot to crank faster. In a moment, the twenty-foot chain was rattling through the chocks. The anchor surfaced. Holding the chain, Nathaniel heaved and dipped it to clean the gray-white marl plastered to its flukes; then he and Eliot hauled the sixty pounds of iron aboard and made it fast.

Artemis, grinning broadly, his capped tooth like a small ingot set in his jaw, bumped the wheel to keep *Double Eagle* into the wind. The mainsail shuddered, and Drew hopped to the forepeak halyard, and with Will's help, raised the fore and foretop sails, then the jib and jibtop. Close-hauled, *Double Eagle* beat out of the harbor into a moderate southerly breeze in which the palm fronds ashore streamed like feathery green banners. The wind was opposed to the strong harbor ebb, making for a bumpy ride, but the stiff schooner's decks stayed dry. She slipped by the navy depot, a flag fluttering from its cupola; the customs house, high brick walls rising incongruously above weathered frame houses; the buildings of the naval station, white in the morning sun, and Government Wharf, beside which a frigate was moored, black cannon bristling in the embrasures of her armored casemates.

"Should of seen dis harbor durin' de war with de Sponnish, boys," said Artemis. "Hoo-hee! Battleships all over de place! De whole squadron, right here!"

Beyond Government Wharf loomed the massive battlements of Fort Taylor, joined to the island by a causeway. Artemis gestured, telling of the day he saw the U.S.S. *Maine* anchored off the fort, her stacks smoking as she got up steam for her fateful voyage to Havana. Nathaniel envied him for having witnessed that fragment of history, and watched the great red walls, topped by coastal guns, pass to starboard. The fort fell abaft the beam, and *Double Eagle,* beating still, entered open water. No longer channeled by the harbor, the tide lost its concentrated force, and the waves grew bigger but less choppy, heaving with wide troughs between them.

Dead ahead some seven miles, Sand Key Light craned above the horizon. Drew scaled the ratlines of the main shrouds for a better look, and made out the clapboard weather station, set beneath the light on a circle of sand not fifty yards across. Beyond, the Gulf Stream turned the ocean indigo. He was beginning to understand the magnetism that drew his father and Lockwood and Nathaniel to the sea. The sea, he thought, watching a solitary tern swoop to pluck some microscopic morsel from a wave, was like mathematics in the sense that it was pure and incorruptible. It was governed by its own laws, which men might learn but never master, nor bend nor twist to suit themselves. The sea's fogs had blinded him, his brothers, and Will; it had drenched and terrified them with line squall and gale; its dead calms had maddened them; but it never had intended to blind, discomfort, terrify, or madden anyone. It was in its nature to be foggy or clear, calm or stormy, and it did not care a whit for what effect its moods had on sailors and ships. He had heard his father speak of the ocean as if it had mind, heart, and will: It was cruel or kind, raging or serene, but in truth, it was none of those things. The sea simply *was,* in the same way that an equation or law of physics *was,* regardless of what men thought about it or wished it to be. And what about the land? The land he had missed so and yearned for when this voyage began? He thought about Mike Downey and crazy old Talmadge and orphaned Clara locked in her prison of silence; about Aunt Judith, embittered and alone, and about Doris and the obscene wetness glistening on his lips when he told Drew to take his pants down. The sea was a domain of purity; land, the province of violence, irrationality, suffering, loneliness, strange passions.

"Hey, dere! You aloft! Come on down and lissen to what your cop'in got to say!"

He left the perch reluctantly and joined Will and his brothers on the afterdeck.

"We're gwan to beat into dis another couple miles maybe, den bear off and reach due west, inside de reef," said Artemis, good eye fixed on some point in the distance. "Gwan to be passin' some eye-londs to north'ard, about two, t'ree mile off, den by-and-by, some more eye-londs, but further to de north. Dem de Marquesas Keys. Same time, to south'ard, gwan to see a small lighthouse, and dat be de light on Cosgrove Reef. When dot light pass abaft de port beam, we're gwan to bear off some more, west by quarter north. By-and-by, gwan to see a channel marker for de Rebecca Passage. Might have us some wild water in dere, dis wind pipe up. Gwan to leave dot marker to starboard, den we're gwan to see Fort Jefferson on Garden Key in de Dry Tortugas. Can't miss dat fort. It's big as a whole town! When it come into view, we're gwan to bear off again and run just about due north for Middle and East Keys. Dere's about five mile between dem and dey ain't no bigger'n gobs of spit, so keep your eye skinned for dem. We miss dem, boys, and de next stop gwan to be Texas, t'ousand miles away. You got all dot? Good. Next t'ing, I want a lookout aloft, keepin' an eye skinned for our marks and for coral heads. All kindsa coral heads in dese waters ain't on no mon's chart. Dass all, crew. Your cop'in done give his orders."

The islands were called Cottrell, Ballast, Man, Woman, Boca Grande, each with its ribbon of sand fronting a strip of sea oat, mangrove forests beyond, and the occasional coconut palm, bent by the prevailing winds, rising above the scrubby mangrove. Pelicans were bombarding schools of glass minnows and pilchards in a passage between two of the keys, the birds circling, then, with wings folded, swiftly diving to make successive splashes, like a salvo of bursting torpedos. But it was the water's color that held Nathaniel, taking the first watch aloft, in a hypnotic trance: a marbling of white jade and dark jade, emerald, aquamarine, chartreuse, turquoise. From the main crosstrees, he made out blind channels winding in coils of bottle green between the beige-tinted green of tidal flats. In some places, as the tide approached dead low, the flats lay high and dry, resembling meadows of mown wheat, and the white herons stalking them had the look of snowy scarecrows in motion. The deserted islands littered with sea wrack and driftwood, the wide, dazzling waters, the flocks of wild shore and seabirds—it all had a strange enchantment, a windswept lonesomeness, a beauty somehow threatening, the threat made manifest when he spotted long shadows finning just beneath the surface or the stationary shadow of a big coral head.

Will relieved him, and he went down to relieve Artemis at the helm, but Artemis was having too good a time and stayed by the wheel.

"She's headstrong, wants to go to wind'ard, and you got to rein her in, like a horse ain't yet broke, she is."

"She'll never be broke, and you wouldn't want her to be," Nathaniel said. "So you're glad you decided to come along after all?"

Artemis whistled a bar or two from that Caribbean chantey, "Shallow Brown."

"How glad gwan to depend on how good Ethan and George do with de spongin'. Oughtta do good, been teachin' dem since dey was kids. Reckon I'm gladder now den I'd be, you'd gwan out to dot wreck without me supervisin' and do somethin' dumb and drown yourselfs. Den I gotta answer to Cop'in Cy, in dis life or de one to come, Lord God Jehovah willin' I get dere." He squeezed the spokes, looked at the compass card, holding steady on the black W. "Now my Euphy, she think I gwan some in my head. Man who spends five days of seven on de water, goin' on de water for a holiday! Dot's like de postman takin' a walk, my Euphy says. But Euphy don't know what's it like. Sometimes I hate de sea, boys, but I can't stay away from her. Dot's what Euphy don't understand. Ain't sure I do. But it one fine thing, steerin' a boat like dis with a crew know what dey doin'."

Nathaniel nodded to the compliment. From above, Will shouted that he could see an island in the distance, about three points off the starboard bow. Artemis crouched, and leaning to his right to look under the main boom, said those were the Marquesas Keys.

"Hoo-hee! Just about to dem already! My spongin' boat, it'd take most de day to make de Marquesas. Got your beam wind, Nathaniel, and this schooner is crackin'! How fast you reckon?"

"If we still had our log, I could tell you, but we lost it to a barracuda. How far are those keys from Key West?"

"Dunno 'sactly. Eighteen, maybe twenny mile."

Nathaniel, glancing at his pocket watch, struggled with some basic arithmetic, and declared that if the Marquesas were twenty miles away, *Double Eagle* was making over eight knots.

"Doesn't feel like eight to me," said Eliot, feeling contrary. It was the way Nat had announced their speed—like he was speaking holy writ—that annoyed. "For one thing, the Marquesas aren't off our beam yet—they're still ahead of us. And for another, maybe they're eighteen instead of twenty miles. Yeah, bet you a quarter of my hard-earned pay that it's seven knots, tops."

"Go ahead. How are you going to prove it?"

"When those islands are directly abeam, check your watch then. You'll see. Seven."

"I can tell you right now," Drew said, then went below, and came back up with an empty box of kitchen matches. "Okay, Nat, you give me the time," he said, moving forward. Kneeling down, he flung the box slightly forward of the lee bow, hollering "Mark!" the moment it hit the water.

"Four seconds!" Nathaniel called, as the box bobbed past the stern, to be swamped by the wake.

Drew returned aft and sat on the cabin top, eyes closed and head bowed and lips moving, as one in silent, fervent prayer.

"Eliot wins," he announced about a minute later. "I figure six point nine knots on the nose, but give or take a tenth."

"You couldn't have done all that figuring in your head," Nathaniel said.

Drew blinked and, in the voice neither boy's nor man's, affirmed that he had. Just calculate what part of a mile forty-six feet was, and what part of an hour four seconds made, and divide the distance by the time. It was easy.

Now, Nathaniel went below, where he remained for some ten minutes, scrawling fractions on a piece of paper. He came up the companion triumphantly and waved the paper in Drew's and Eliot's faces.

"So sorry, little man. The family genius is wrong for a change. It's eight knots. Eliot, I'll take that quarter."

"Could I see that?"—Drew, extending a hand.

Nathaniel gave him the calculations, which needed only one look to bring a smug smile to his brother's face.

"Slipped up, Nat. You used fifty-two hundred and eighty feet, a statute mile instead of a nautical mile, six thousand eighty. We're doing eight land miles an hour, and that works out to six point nine knots."

"You can pay me when we get back," said Eliot as Nathaniel, upset with God for making his youngest brother such a little smartypants, crumpled the paper and pitched it over the rail.

Falling off past Cosgrove Light, *Double Eagle* bruised the water as though she were getting even for all the knocks the sea had given her. In the fifty miles between the Marquesas Keys and the Dry Tortugas, no land could be seen, and cumulonimbus towered on the horizon in all directions, so that the schooner seemed to be crossing an immense, round, cobalt-green plateau ringed by snow-covered mountains. High overhead, frigate birds soared on the thermals. A leopard ray six feet long and six wide breached within yards of the weather rail, rocketing into the air with its broad, white-spotted wings spread, and Artemis told of the day when one of the creatures leapt into his sponge skiff, thrashing with such power that it splintered a thwart, broke his partner's ankle, and sent Artemis diving overboard. "Would of smashed dot little skiff to bits, it didn't jump back into de sea where it belong, and when it did, you dom well sure I jump right back in de boat, where I belong." He whipped off his hat and waved it with an expansive gesture. "Oh, dese Keys waters, dere wild country, boys, wild as de Wild West, only dey wet!"

At five o'clock, with the lowering sun slanting into their eyes, they raised the high brick walls of Fort Jefferson on Garden Key. Eliot, who now was standing the lookout trick, thought it one of the oddest sights he'd seen: Backlit by the sun, the fort looked like some magical castle afloat in the middle of the ocean. Sheets were slacked, booms swung out, and *Double Eagle*'s wake described a rounded L, as she hooked northward and ran up Southeast Channel for East Key.

It was three or four acres of limestone, sand, and bleached coral, utterly lifeless except for a few mangrove shrubs and a few cormorants and gulls, roosting on its windward side, beaks into the wind. An anchorage was found in a tongue of deep water between two reefs that didn't have more than six feet of water over them. The pale brown dorsal of a big hammerhead cut a wake across this channel and passed within a yard of the schooner's stern with slow sweeps of its sickle tail, its head turning side to side a couple of feet beneath the surface. The head was a thing of nightmares—eyes set into the tips of bony protrusions extending from its nose—and Eliot fetched the shotgun from below and took aim at the shark. Artemis shoved the barrels aside.

"He out of range now and de only thing you gwan to do with dot is make him mad, and we don't want him mad."

Eliot laid the gun down. Looking at the shark's dorsal, at the barren key, and at the Gulf of Mexico, reaching away into infinity, he felt that he'd arrived at the farthest outpost of the known world.

"This is where the people in the third lifeboat got stranded?" he asked.

Artemis nodded as he rigged a handline to catch their supper.

"Well, I can sure see why they'd given up hope." An uneasiness stole into him.

"Yeah. Nuttin' out dis way but a whole lotta nuttin'. Just a rock in de cruel ocean."

The handline rig consisted of sash cord wrapped around a grooved wooden reel, roughly twice the diameter of a wagon-wheel hub. An egg-shaped lead sinker was tied to the line about a yard above the hook, which Artemis baited with chunks of salt mackerel. He stood up, gave the line a twirl, and cast it out, leaving about ten feet of slack on deck.

Sunset, moonrise, Artemis sitting at the rail, humming to himself, the line held delicately between his fingers. "Uh-huh. Somethin' takin' it," he murmured. "Gwan to let him swalla it." The slack paid out between his hands, and when it came taut, he jerked the line hard, setting the hook. Standing again, he played the fish for a while, the line softly hissing as it zigzagged through the water; then, with deft turns of his hands and wrists, Artemis spooled it back onto the reel, and brought up a fat, oval-shaped fish, its tail fluttering on the surface. Putting a wrap around both hands, he heaved the catch on deck, where it thrashed, gills pumping, flanks showing reddish orange in the twilight. "Mutton snapper, and fifteen pounds of him," Artemis said, breathing hard from the struggle. "Hoo-hee! Gwan to have us some fine eatin' tonight, boys."

As smoke drifted leeward from the Charley Noble, Artemis and *Double Eagle*'s crew ate on deck, under constellations turning like the jewels in a majesterial clock, the Dipper in the middle of the northwestern sky, pointers aimed at Polaris in one direction, at Leo in the other, and low in the southern heavens, glimmering above Cuba across the Florida Straits, four stars arranged in an elegant crucifix.

"Didn't know you could see it this far north," Nathaniel said, pointing.

"Up to twenty-five degrees north latitude, and we're at about twenty-four and a half," said Will.

Nahaniel was thrilled. Now he could say he had been somewhere and seen a rare sight, and making a great imaginative vault deep into the new century, he heard his aged self telling his grandchildren of how at the age of sixteen he had captained a schooner from Maine to the latitudes of the Southern Cross.

Artemis filled a tin cup with coffee and began to reminisce about his childhood on Harbour Island, from which Bahamian wreckers had set out for the Florida reefs in his father's and grandfather's day, back when Florida was still ruled by the kings and queens of Spain. He remembered white wreckers like old man Albury, who had filled the streets of Dunmore Town with goods salvaged from Spanish ships grounded on their way to Havana, and Negro wreckers from the Black Fleet, which Artemis joined at fourteen as a diver, and the wandering among the Bahama out islands whetted his longing to see the world. He signed on as an able-bodied seaman with the British merchant fleet.

"Sailed all over for t'ree year, seen London town when I was twenny," he said. "It was de trip back from London dot lond me in Key West. I was on de worstest ship I ever had de misfortune to sail on. De *Sophia,* leaky old square-rigger full of rats, and de biscuit mealy and de pork gone bad and de cop'in, name of McIntyre, worser den de food. Dis is eighteen and sevenny t'ree, but dot skipper actin' like it still de days of dot Bligh fella. We off-load in Santiago and take on sugar for British Honduras, but dot ship leakin' so bad, de sugar ruint and she got to put in to get caulked up. Key West de closest, and when we got dere, Artemis walked off dot hell boat and didn't look back! Yeah, I jumped ship. My old 'Br'iland mate, Jimmy Wakefield, was in Key West by den, and he hid me out in Africa Town in case dot McIntyre son-bitch come lookin' for me.

"Now in dem days after de war, all kindsa Africa slaves rescued from de slavin' ships by de Yankee navy was livin' in Africa Town, and sometimes you hear drums. Drums!" Artemis bobbed his head to affirm the truth of what he was saying. "Dem Africa niggers wasn't yet Christianed. Practicin' dis voodoo from Africa, *obeah,* and sometimes I was hearin' dot drummin' and wonderin' what I got myself into. But Jimmy was already workin' for your papa and put in a good word for me and de next thing I know, I'm on de crew of *Main Chance.* So dom good, if I do say so myself, boys, Cop'in Cy make me chief diver in one year. I was with him six year, up to de day dis *Annisquam* we gwan to look for tamarra wrecked up and took my eye."

REDNESS in the east, a point of white light in the west, the sun rising as the moon set. On mainsail and jib, *Double Eagle* ranged northward, following the curve of the crescent-shaped barrier reef. A Portuguese man-of-war drifted along, its translucent purple sail lit up in the sunrise. Balanced on the ratlines, one arm crooked around the main crosstree, the other arm around a shroud, his jersey billowing in the wind, Nathaniel scanned the morning sea for the buoy with which Artemis's fisherman friend had marked the wreck.

"Seen anything yet, lookout?" Artemis called up from the helm.

"I'll sing out when I do," Nathaniel said. Leaning into the ratlines, he took his right hand off the shroud and made a visor over his eyes. Barefoot, his unshorn hair streaming back, a sheath knife hanging from the belt of duck trousers rolled up to the knee, he resembled a sailor of bygone times. Looking astern, he could make out Hospital Key, another lump of barren rock covered with low mangrove, and Fort Jefferson some two miles beyond it. Looking below, through seas almost as clear as the air, he watched coral heads passing darkly under the keel. A lone frigate bird circled dead ahead on black wings shaped like boomerangs. That was all he saw—coral rocks and a solitary bird and broken ribbons of surf driven up on the reefs by the south wind. He was beginning to doubt himself. All this effort merely to look at a sunken ship? And yet, because that was what he had set out to do, he would think less of himself if he gave up now. *Don't quit,* his father had told him before his first boxing match two years ago. *You can win, you can lose, Nat, but no son of mine quits.*

He caught something dead ahead, a flicker of red, bobbing on the waves near the westernmost end of the reef. He squinted into the sea glare.

"There it is!" he shouted.

"What is it? Whachya see?"

"The buoy, Artemis! Dead ahead about half a mile!"

Artemis ran the schooner on, rounded up, and dropped the hook a respectful distance from the marker, to make sure the anchor did not foul in the wreck. The tender was lowered. Nathaniel got into the small boat. Eliot and Drew climbed in after him, Eliot manning the oars. The sea was flattening as the wind died off. To Nathaniel's mind, the growing calm seemed deliberate; nature was arranging her elements to make things easier for him.

"Believe I'll stay here," Will said, leaning over the rail. "Let me know if you see any mermaids with robust mammaries."

"Any mermaids down dere, you see dem better with dis." Artemis passed down an oaken, glass-bottomed bucket he used for sponging.

The buoy was a steel drum thickly coated with red bottom paint against rust. Eliot reached under it with an oar and scooped up the mooring line, to which Drew tied the painter. A hawksbill, its shell a yard wide, hovered on the surface nearby, then leisurely submerged. Nathaniel dropped the bucket over the side and lowered his face into the open end, and was stunned by his first unfiltered view of the undersea world, a world of brilliant colors and bizarre shapes: corals like forests of stag horns painted ochre; corals with whorled grooves and ridges, resembling gigantic human brains; corals that leapt like tongues of flame; purple sea fans waving in the current. Brightly hued fish swam by in flotillas, at times blotting out his view of the sea bottom: speckled fish and striped fish, fish scaled as parrots were feathered, in reds, greens, and yellows. He passed the bucket to Drew, who was also wonder-struck—it looked like an immense, fantastic aquarium down there. He tried to identify one of the species of fish, but there were too many, darting too quickly through his field of vision. Then it was Eliot's turn. He was watching a school of light-blue chubs when something lunged out of a little cave in the coral wall: a hideous, green, eel-like thing as thick as a man's arm and twice as long. It sucked one of the chubs into its maw and shot back into its lair, all in less than a second. Raising his head, he reported what he'd seen.

"Life's sure cheap down there," he commented. "Where the hell is the wreck? I didn't see anything that looked like a wreck."

"That way," Nathaniel said. "The float got carried by the tide."

Drew untied the painter and Eliot began to row again while Nathaniel looked through the bucket. The mooring cable, furred with seaweed, curved away from the slope of the reef and ended some twenty yards uptide, shackled to a mooring stone eight or ten fathoms below. Just beyond the stone, the stern half of the ship loomed, her broken barn door of rudder, her rails and rigging encrusted in barnacles, her hull covered with a gray-brown silt, her splintered mizzenmast leaning out and away from her worm-eaten quarterdeck. She lay as Artemis had described, on her port side. The forward end—what had been her middle when she was whole—was sunk several feet into the bottom, and her keel was gouged and scarred from the rocks that had ended her life. Fish swam into and out of her gaping scuttles and hatchways, nibbling at the organisms that were patiently, inexorably devouring her. Eliot pulled slowly along the length of the ship, Nathaniel directing him: port, starboard, steady now. Past the front part of the stern section lay a swath of wreckage—beams and knees and ribs and cargo boxes showing in outline from beneath the white bottom sand, like pieces of furniture covered by bed linen. Beyond that, her forward section lay upside down. Bowsprit and boom had been carried away, or consumed by worms, or were buried in the sand, which wasn't sand but the bones of dead coral milled into powder by the ceaseless motions of the sea.

"Row on back, Eliot, then you two can have a look."

Once more, the wreckage passed beneath, unfolding like a diorama.

"Hold it right here," said Nathaniel when the tender was once again over *Annisquam*'s stern. He gave the bucket to Eliot, then stripped off his jersey.

"Hey, what're you doing, Nat?"

"Top parts of her ain't twenty feet under"—wriggling out of his trousers—"and I'm gonna get a piece of her and bring it back to Dad."

"Artemis told us not to dive her!"—Drew, motioning at *Double Eagle,* lying to a hundred yards away.

"He's the skipper only because I said he could be."

Nathaniel grabbed the tender's mushroom anchor to hasten his descent. Standing, he took several deep breaths, then jumped in, cradling the anchor in both arms against his stomach. The ten pounds of lead carried him down in two seconds. His feet touched the silted hull, its decayed planks, mushy as sedge, threatening to collapse under his weight. The pressure at over three fathoms sent a sharp pain shooting through his eardrums. Holding the anchor with his right hand, he pinched his nostrils between two fingers of his left and blew out. His ears cleared with a pop, the pain subsided. He could hold his breath for two minutes in shallow water and so gave himself half that at this depth. Reckoning that he had already used up fifteen seconds of his allotted minute, he looked around for a suitable souvenir; but without the aid of the bucket's glass bottom, everything was blurred, the wreck an indistinct, brownish mass in the beveled shafts of sunlight, the schools of fish smears of dimmed color. Still, he was able to recognize the ship's taffrail, parts of which had been broken off so that it resembled a grinning mouth with gapped teeth. He dropped the anchor, clutched one of the stanchions in both hands, and, with his legs buoyed upward by the sea, pulled as hard as he could. Six feet of rail came away in a piece. He kicked hard to drag it to the surface, but it was too heavy and pulled him down instead. He let go, snatched the anchor line, and watched the rail float toward the bottom, another thirty feet below. When it struck, there was a silent explosion of sand and marl as a big leopard ray, startled by the disturbance, burst out of its hiding place and swam off with powerful sweeps of its wings. Their motion blew away the billows of mud, revealing a flash of gold in the cavity the ray's body had made in the bottom. Nathaniel's first thought was that the legend of the ship's treasure was not a legend after all; then he realized that he was looking at a fragment of gold-leafed lettering. He could not read the letters, and he didn't have the air to dive down for a closer look. Close to blacking out, he quickly surfaced in a trail of bubbles, swam back to the tender, and clung to the gunwale, gasping.

"Goddamnit, Nat!" said Eliot. "Were you planning to spend the whole morning down there?"

He regained his breath and pulled himself aboard.

"What're you so nervous about? Damn, Eliot, you're getting to be a grandmother in your old age."

Eliot said nothing, unwilling to admit to the uneasiness these waters induced in him; these dazzling waters in whose depths hammerhead sharks swam and big green eels lunged out of coral caves.

Nathaniel took the bucket and, lowering his face, confirmed what he had glimpsed on the dive. Glimmering below, their gold leaf partially flaked off, were the letters A N N I, carved into half of a scrolled board two or three feet wide. The other half was buried.

"Her escutcheon's down there," he said. "The fastenings must have rusted through and it fell off, and now it's lying down there, just waiting to be picked up. That's what we're going to do, that's what we'll bring back to the old man."

"*What?* It probably weighs a ton."

"No, it doesn't. Heave up the anchor. I've got an idea."

"Don't doubt you do. You've always got an idea. You're a regular factory of ideas, most of 'em crazy."

Yet Eliot heaved the anchor, knowing he would go along with whatever idea Nat had, because what was often true in the world of men was always true in the world of boys: The strongest prevailed.

"Don't come no closer!" Artemis called to them. Bareheaded, with a cast net slung in his arms, he was perched on the stern alongside Will, who was tossing scraps of food behind the schooner. "Dere a fine school of yellatail come up, and if Will can chum 'em in closer, I'm gwan to catch us some for lunch."

Eliot backed the oars, holding the tender in place. The wind had died off completely, and the schooner and the chunks of chum appeared to be floating upon a vast plate of molten green glass. Squinting into the limpid water, the net draped over his left arm while his right hand held it partially open, Artemis was a study in concentration. So he stood for a full minute; then he torqued his body to one side and, flinging his left arm out, launched the net, which spread against the clear sky a white, gossamer circle ten feet in diameter. It swooped down on the water, the lead sinkers sewn into its edge making a light splash. Artemis crouched and struck the net by giving its cord a vigorous yank. "Hoo-hee!" the Braithwaites heard him yell as he hauled the net up, hand over hand. "Hoo-hee! Mess o' yellatail. You boys can come ahead now."

As they climbed aboard, leaving the tender to trail astern by its painter, the fish were flopping inside the net, ten of them, each about the size of a small bass, with powder-blue bodies set off by yellow lateral lines and butter-colored fins. Drew thought them almost too beautiful to eat. When the last one ended its death throes, Artemis opened the net, spilling them on the deck. The smell of them drove Trajan into a frenzy; he shot up the companionway in a blur of orange and made off with the smallest of the fish. Will got down on his hands and knees and scooped the rest into a bucket, muttering something about the sorry state to which he, a Yale man and yachtsman, had fallen.

Hands on his hips, Artemis surveyed his catch with satisfaction. "Yeah, de yellatail snapper, next to de mutton, be de finest eatin' dis ocean can give a mon," he said, then returned his hat to his head and fastened his sighted eye on Nathaniel. "So did you get a look at her? See what you come to see?"

"Yeah, we did, and—"

"You must of seen a whole lot," Artemis said, before Nathaniel could finish. "I watched you. I de cop'in for dis trip, and de cop'in's word is law, and you broke it. Olden times, I'd take de cat out de bag and tell de bosun to give you a few crost de back."

He flashed his teeth to show that he wasn't being entirely serious. Still, Nathaniel thought, there was nothing like taking command of a few planks of floating wood to bring out the despot in a man.

"Her scut is down there. Broke loose. I want to bring it up and take it back with us. It would mean a lot to Dad."

"And what your papa gwan to do with it? Hang it on a wall? Dot dom thing twelve foot long if it's a inch."

Nathaniel hadn't thought of it before, but mounting it on a wall struck him as a fine idea. He saw it already, spread over the fireplace in

Mingulay's dining room, the gold letters restored to their original brilliance, and the name *Annisquam* gleaming on through the years, his grandchildren looking at it and telling their children how the escutcheon had come to hang there.

"How you proposin' to get dot big hunk of wood from down dere to up here?" asked Artemis. "Haulin' it up by hand would be some tough work, mon. You got no winches aboard, except dot anchor windlass."

"That's what I'm proposing. We move the boat close as we can, so the scut comes up as close to straight up as we can make it. We anchor with the kedge, unshackle the main anchor from the chain, drop the chain down. One or two of us dive and lash it to the board. Then we crank it up. It shouldn't take long at all."

Artemis lowered and shook his head, the crown of his straw hat brushing past Nathaniel's nose.

"You don't think that would work?"

"Oh, I reckon it could. Piece of wood, dot ain't nuttin'. My day, we salvaged ship's anchors, two ton of iron. No, I just thinkin' dot you somethin'. Dot hunk of rotted wood, maybe it mean somethin' to your papa, maybe not, but it sure mean somethin' to you, don't it?"

"So what if it does?"

"So nuttin' whatever." Raising his clasped hands overhead, Artemis stretched his arms and cracked his knuckles. "Now, if we do dot, you gimme your word dot will satisfy you? Den you be hoppy? Den you ain't gwan to get some other notion in dot young head of yours?"

"Oh, he'll get another notion, sure enough," said Eliot, who, seated beside the wheel, was attempting to pick up a cup with his limber big toe. "Next thing, he'll want to salvage the whole damn ship and fix her up and sail her home. You watch, Artemis. Nat's whole purpose in life is to get crazy notions."

He succeeded in curling his toe around the handle. Bending his knee and leaning far forward at the same time, he lifted his foot and brought the raised cup to his lowered lips.

"Now dere's a trick I ain't seen. You got de monkey in you, Eliot." Artemis looked down at the bucket of fish, stiffened in death. "Let's get dese split and cooked up before dey go bad. Den we fetch up Nathaniel's hunk of wood. I gwan to help you with dot as a favor to Cop'in Cy for settin' me up in life, and you be sure to tell him dot when you get home. Soon as we get it aboard, we make sail for Key West."

"It's only Monday," Nathaniel said. "We've got till Wednesday morning."

"I don't like dis calm and I don't like de looks of dot sun."

"What's wrong with it?" Drew asked.

"Dot ring around it, dass what."

Shielding his eyes with the palm of his hand, Drew observed a hazy, shimmering corona and remarked that it was caused by water vapor or ice crystals in the upper atmosphere.

"Now just what is dot supposed to mean?"

"Nothing. Only that the vapor or the ice is bending the light rays. Kind of like a rainbow."

"Dot real interestin'. Now, I tell you what it means. Dere is dirty weather knockin' around somewhere, two, t'ree days away. Dis time of year, could be a hurricane. Cop'in Johnny Sawyer, my first skipper in de Black Fleet, taught me dot, and now Artemis is teachin' you. Get to splittin' dem yellatail, boy. De cop'in is hungry."

STANDING AT the rail with the L. C. Smith jammed butt-first against his thigh, Eliot tried to adopt the agate glare of a man engaged in serious business. The pretense didn't quite come off. He might have fooled a stranger who chanced to sail by, but he could not fool himself. Undeniably, guarding Artemis and his brother against shark attack *was* serious business, but it was serious business employed in service of a stunt, like manning a rescue boat for that crazy woman he'd read about in the newspapers, the one who went over Niagara Falls in a barrel. Recovering the escutcheon was not as risky as that, but it was as pointless. The shotgun was loaded with slugs, of the sort used to shoot deer. Eliot had found a couple in the box of mixed shells his father had put on board. Unlike birdshot, a well-placed slug would do a lot more to a shark then make him mad; if it didn't kill him outright, it sure as hell would kill his appetite.

Artemis and Nat were over the wreck in the tender, about ten yards from where Eliot stood on Double Eagle. The chain was in the small boat, and thirty-odd feet of cable hung over the space between the two vessels. The rest of the cable, all fifty fathoms of it, lay in stacked coils on the schooner's foredeck, alongside the windlass. Nat was looking through the glass-bottom bucket while Artemis, at the oars, turned the tender around and around, in ever tighter circles. The two were having trouble spotting the object of their quest. Finally, Eliot heard his brother cry out, "There it is! We're over it now!" Artemis rowed a short distance uptide, Nat cast the tender's anchor. As the line paid out, the boat drifted back to the original spot. He snubbed the line to the tender's bow cleat, then he and Artemis heaved the chain overboard. The thirty feet of horizontal cable went suddenly vertical, pulling several of the coils on the schooner's foredeck into the green depths. When the chain hit bottom, Will, standing by the windlass, hitched the cable to the windlass.

Everyone was behaving with admirable professionalism, Eliot thought. But it was just a stunt. He wondered how Nat managed to get people to do what he wanted, even against their better judgment. It wasn't his strength or the quickness in his fists; he didn't bully, he had some other quality that made you *want* to follow him into places or situations you would otherwise avoid. Eliot did not know what to call that quality; he did know that he didn't have it.

"You t'ree fellas, we gwan to go down, presently," Artemis called. "One of you keep an eye on de port side, other 'un on starboard. Eliot, you be ready with de shotgun. Cop'in hommerhead show up, you let him have it 'tween de sidelights."

"Aye, aye!" Eliot tossed a jaunty salute.

Serious business.

Turning to Nathaniel, Artemis picked up one of the four ballast blocks they had pilfered from *Double Eagle*'s bilges. A cord was lashed around it, end to end, and the two ends of cord, he said, were to be cinched around the waist with a running bowline; the weight was to be carried against the small of the back.

"Den you ease into de water. Don't jump, ease on in," he instructed. "You hold on to de boat and blow out five, six times, blow all de dead air out your lungs. Den you take in deep breaths, but only let a little bit out each time, till you feel dizzy. Dass when you go down. When you get to de bottom, you maybe start to floatin' up again. Dot hoppen, you let out little bit of air, and dot will help you sink. Free divin', mon. Dass how we doin' it in olden times. Understand?"

Nathaniel swallowed and said he did.

"Now I 'spect dot even at my age I can stay down longer'n you. So I do all de work, you gimme a hand if I signal you. You get to feelin' you got to go back up, you drop de weight and up you go, but slow. Hear me? Slow."

"Hear you."

"We got us four pieces of ballast. Dot mean two dives. We don't get de job done in two, we quit. Understand me still?"

He nodded.

"You one stubborn boy, got de pig's head sometimes, so I makin' it clear. Two dives and no more." He made a V with his fore and middle fingers, then took the bucket and, sweeping it back and forth through the water, surveyed the wreck. "Yeah, dere she is. Dot bad-luck ship.

Ain't seen her since de year Ethan was born. Oh, my Euphy, she for sure think I'm crazy in de head if she see me doin' dis and no money in it."

"It ain't the loot," Nathaniel said.

Artemis looked at him.

"No, it ain't."

"Maybe this means something to you, too."

"Maybe so." He stood, unbuttoned his overall's straps, and stripped off his shirt. "Yeah, Nathaniel, dot just may be so."

The ballast blocks made the descent feel more like a controlled fall through empty space. Headfirst, they plummeted. The bottom—ribbed sand dappled by a dim shimmer, coral heads resembling undersea rock gardens—seemed to lunge up toward them. The foggy vision of his naked eye distorted Nathaniel's depth perception, and he almost crash-landed, thinking the bottom farther than it was. By the time he righted himself, got his bearings, and blew through his pinched nostrils to ease the pain that spiked through his ears, Artemis already had the anchor chain in hand. The cable sliced upward at an angle toward the schooner, the coppery red of its bottom visible even from almost fifty feet down. Overhead, the tender made a dark, oval smudge on the silvery roof of the sea; a few yards to the left, *Annisquam*'s stern rose thirty feet, an umbered wall, its vacant scuttles offering glimpses of the darkness within. Artemis, down on both knees, passed the chain under the escutcheon, then signaled Nathaniel to take the bitter end. This he did, then the two of them pulled seven or eight feet through. They had been down about a minute, and Nathaniel's brain sent the first signal that it was starving for oxygen. Artemis picked up the chain, and walking with a queer, ponderous gait, knelt again and passed it through a second time, pulling it snug. The procedure was repeated once more. Now, with two tight wraps around the board, Artemis took the snap-shackle at the bitter end to clip it to the standing part of the chain and make a triangle, with the scut as the base, the short end of the chain as one side, the standing chain as the other. He signaled for help, but Nathaniel could stand no more. Pointing up with one hand to let Artemis know that he was surfacing, he tugged the running bowline with the other to drop the ballast block. For some reason, the knot would not loosen. Kicking hard to rise against the weight, he banged his right leg against a sharp coral head. Panic seized him. Reaching for his sheath knife to cut the cord around his waist, he remembered that he'd left the knife on his belt in the tender; and that was the last coherent thought he had until he was on top, thrashing like a madman, gulping for breath with such desperation that he swallowed as much seawater as air. Artemis grabbed his hair and, paddling with his free arm, dragged him the few yards to the tender. Nathaniel clutched the gunwale, but didn't have the strength to pull himself in; he could only hang there, gagging. Artemis clung beside him.

"What de hell hoppen, mon?"

He shook his head to say that he couldn't yet answer.

"See you kickin' down dere, cut de weight off with my knife, and shoot you right up. No time to go up slow. What hoppen to you?"

"Knot . . . wouldn't . . . Got tighter . . . Thanks, thanks . . ."

"Where your knife?"

He slapped the side of the boat.

"Oh, mon. Dot my fault. Should of made sure you had it with you."

Nathaniel hung on for another half a minute, drawing in breaths.

"The job? Finished?" he asked, recovering.

"Too busy savin' you from drownin'. All dass left is to shackle de chain. Take me a jiffy, but you stayin' up here. You ain't goin' below again."

He didn't argue but hoisted himself into the tender. There was a stinging sensation on the inside of his right leg, just above the ankle, and he noticed a bleeding abrasion, as though his flesh had been scraped by a grindstone. Coral is beautiful to look at, but nothing you want to touch, he thought.

"Gimme a hand gimme," said Artemis, his elbows propped on the gunwale.

Kneeling down, he reached under the other man's arms and helped him in, Artemis rolling into the boat belly first. He sat on the aft thwart to rest, knees spread, his cotton drawers wetted to transparency so that the color of his skin showed through.

"Gettin' too old for dis bizness, dot for sure."

"Maybe we should forget it?" Nathaniel said.

"Uh-uh. Gone dis far"—looping another piece of ballast around his stout waist—"go de whole way. Take a jiffy." He glanced up at a frigate bird wheeling low overhead on motionless wings. A male, with a throat like the bulb of a crimson flower. "Yeah, dis mean somethin' to me. Break de spell of dot goddom bad-luck ship. She take my eye from me, now I'm gwan to take her name from her."

"You can keep it. It's yours," Nathaniel said, in a burst of gratitude.

"Nah. Got nowhere to put it. Just want to say I done it."

Nathaniel shuddered.

"What de matter? You cold?"

"What happened down there. It felt like . . . I don't know. . . . Like there was a steel cable around my lungs, and it gives me chills to think about it."

"Den don't think about it." Artemis snorted. "Dere's folks who say dot drownin' be a peaceable way to go, but I come close to it couple of times, like you was a little bit ago, and I know it ain't so. Okay, I rested up now."

He cleared his lungs, took three deep breaths, and slipped into the water. Nathaniel watched his descent through the glass, and he looked graceful as a dolphin, kicking with short, economical strokes, his arms held tight to his sides. The water was so transparent that he did not seem to be submerged but to be diving through a lambent aquamarine light. He reached bottom in a few seconds, his figure diminished by the looming wreck. Taking the end of the chain, he bobbed up several feet and, with quick, expert movements, shackled it to the standing chain. He gave the joint a tug to make sure the shackle was secure, then slipped out of his weight belt and ascended as gracefully as he'd descended, his back arched, bubbles trailing from his mouth. Surfacing with a loud expulsion of breath, he grabbed the gunwale and called over to Will and Drew to start winching.

"Nathaniel, you watch t'rough de glass, make sure dot dom thing comin' up okay. Chain start to slip, lemme know."

As Will and Drew cranked the windlass, the chain and anchor cable came taut and the long board lifted off the bottom in a cloud of stirred marl. It rose gradually at a shallow slant, fifteen feet . . . twenty . . . thirty. . . . The escutcheon canted slightly in its harness, and now Nathaniel could make out the scrolled ivy at each end, and the whole name, ANNISQUAM, carved from end to end, the chips of gold leaf flickering in the undersea light. It came to the surface, and with a few more turns of the windlass, one end was hoisted out of the water and the board lay angled against the side of Double Eagle's bow, like a gangplank. Eliot put the shotgun down and went forward to help Will and Drew haul it on deck.

"Got it done, mon," Artemis said to Nathaniel. "Give dis old man another hand."

Again he kneeled and slipped his hands under Artemis's arms and started to lift just as a huge, phantom shape shot up from the depths. There was a flash of bronze and creamy white beneath Artemis's dangling legs, and Nathaniel felt a powerful, resistless tug as Artemis was torn from his grasp, eyes bulging, mouth opened to scream, but he never made a sound, dragged under in the time it would take to snap a photograph. He appeared briefly a few feet below, arms flailing, his mouth still open and the gold tooth giving off a dull gleam, before he vanished in a dense billow of what looked like dark green ink. Nathaniel caught a fleeting glimpse of an enormous brown tail, scything swiftly downward through the billows. The whole thing happened in two or three seconds. Too stunned to speak or move, his brain utterly unable to interpret what his eyes had seen, Nathaniel remained on his knees, staring at the inky cloud spreading across the calm sea. In a few moments, the water was clear again, and he could see the sand and coral heads eight fathoms below and nothing more. It was as though Artemis Lowe had dissolved in an instant; it was as though he had never been.

Busy with their task, the other three boys had not seen a thing. Eliot was taking the shackle off the chain when he heard Nat scream, "Shoot! Eliot! For Christ's sake, shoot! SHOOT!"

He ran aft for the shotgun; but when he looked around, he could not see anything, yet Nat cried out again for him to shoot.

"At what?" he hollered.

"SHARK! SHARK!"

"Where? Where away?"

"SHOOT IT! SHARK! IT'S GOT ARTEMIS! SHOOT, FOR GOD'S SAKE!"

At the word *shark*, Will and Drew ran back to join Eliot.

"What's he mean, a shark's got Artemis?" Drew asked. "Wasn't fifteen seconds ago, I saw him hanging on to the tender."

Eliot narrowed his eyes against the glare.

"He ain't *in* it, Drew."

They all three went silent, and the dread that fell on them equally was almost visible, almost tangible. Their glances swept the sea, but that's all there was: sea and sky, reef and bird.

"GODDAMN YOU, ELIOT! I'LL SHOOT THE THING IF YOU WON'T!"

They watched Nathaniel seize the oars and begin to row; to row furiously but move not a foot.

"Natters! You forgot to haul the anchor!" Will called, with forced calm.

Paying no attention, Nathaniel continued to pull, with a futility that would have been farcical under different circumstances. All three shouted to him to pull up the anchor, but he was as one gone deaf.

"Your brother's out of his head," said Will. "Jesus Christ, what could he have seen to do this to him?"

"Artemis get eaten, what the hell do you think?" Eliot said.

Will quickly stripped off his jersey and trousers.

"Don't, there's a . . ." Drew began.

"Let's hope its appetite is appeased for the moment."

Will stepped to the rail, took a careful look around, and launched out in a long, shallow dive that carried him almost halfway to the tender. The two younger brothers watched with stilled hearts, Eliot shouldering the L. C. Smith, determined to fire at the first suspicious shadow he spied gliding under these lovely, limpid, terrible seas. Will was to the boat in two strong strokes. He appeared to leap over its transom, as though springing from solid ground, and eased past Nat, who seemed oblivious to his presence. In a moment, the anchor was weighed, and that was when Nat perversely chose to stop rowing. He slumped in his seat, his head falling to his knees, his shoulders heaving. Will pulled him off the thwart and took the oars.

At first, Nat would not get out of the tender. He sat, sobbing quietly to himself, but Will at last cajoled him to come aboard and tell them what happened. He flopped down on the afterdeck, legs spread, hands lying limply between them.

"Goddammit, why didn't you shoot, Eliot?" was all he said.

"There was nothing to shoot at. We never saw a thing."

The tears streaking his older brother's face shocked Eliot. He could not remember seeing him cry, even when he was little. Their father had taught them that tears did not become a boy, but Nat was the only one to take the lesson to heart.

"Because you weren't looking," he said, choking. "If you'd been looking, you would've seen it and shot it before it . . . Aw, Christ . . ."

"Nat, all I did was go forward for a second to help out," said Eliot, feeling a sudden stab of guilt. "No shark could've come in that quick."

"This one did. It sure as hell did."

Some quick-acting alchemy transformed Nat's grief and shock into rage, and he snatched the shotgun from Eliot's hands, took aim at the spot where the tender had been anchored, and fired both barrels, the slugs geysering.

"Like that! That's all you had to do, and then he'd still be here!"

"You're saying it was my fault?" Eliot cried out. "You son of a—"

Will took hold of Eliot's arm and with a shake of his head told him to keep still.

"Want something to drink, Natters?"—soothingly. "Wish I had another bottle of that rum. How about a cup of coffee?"

Nat motioned that he did not want anything.

"All right, then. What went on? Last thing we saw of Artemis, he was about to get into the tender. What happened? We need to know because we're going to have to tell his wife. What did he call her? Euphy? Euphrenia, I guess. We're honor-bound to tell her. You realize that, don't you?"

"Nat's the one for that job," said Eliot. "This whole cockeyed thing was his idea, so he can be the one who knocks at her door and tells her that her husband got killed salvaging a hunk of rotten, wormy, worthless wood. I'll bet that'll sit real well with her."

Nathaniel's expression turned murderous, and Will told Eliot to shut up.

"It's all our faults, so we're all going to knock at the door," he said. "All right, Natters."

"I told him to forget it. Just before he went down for the second dive, I said that maybe we ought to forget about it, but he went anyway." Nathaniel realized that he sounded like a man accused of a crime, spouting alibis and excuses. "He wanted to for his own reasons. Said he wanted to break the spell of that bad-luck ship."

"That isn't what we need to know," Will said.

He told them then, and the telling took several times as long as the event.

"Happened so fast, I never got a good look at the shark," he added. He found that he could not hold Will's gaze, and looked up at the same frigate bird that had been circling over the tender: the male with the scarlet throat. "I don't know where it came from, because there wasn't a sign of a shark on the first dive. Maybe it was this"—pointing at the wound in his calf. "I cut myself on a coral head, and I guess the blood, I guess that drew it in from somewhere, and it was down there, waiting. . . ."

No one said anything. He could not bear the silence, which somehow seemed like the silence of a jury listening to damning testimony. His throat tightened, and he pleaded.

"I didn't do it on purpose, for Christ's sake. And it wasn't carelessness. I'd run out of air, and I was kicking up to the top, and I never saw the coral. . . ."

Will, squatting down in front of him, laid both hands on his shoulders.

"No one's accusing you of anything. That's not the point."

"Damn right, it ain't. What the point is . . ." Eliot broke off, went forward, and unshackled the chain. Bending low, he gave the escutcheon a heave, then another, and shoved it over the side. Scored with the holes and channels seaworms had bored into it, it floated for a while faceup: ANNISQUAM. "There's the point right there!" Eliot shouted from the bow. He waited for his older brother to do something, to run at him and throw a punch, to dive in to retrieve his prize, but Nat did not move, and the board sank gradually back to where it had lain for twenty-one years.

After that, none of them spoke. They stayed apart from one another, their shipmates' bond broken for the moment, Eliot sitting on the bow, Drew atop the main cabin, Will standing by the taffrail, Nathaniel lying below on the bunk in his father's stateroom. He was still in shock, and though his gaze was fixed on the painting of *Main Chance*, he did not really see it. His stare was as blank as his mind, and his heart was empty also, a vacuum of numbness except when an image of Artemis's face, jaws agape and white eyes bulging under the sea just before they were enveloped by the inky green billows, swam to the surface of his memory; then the numbness inside him was overcome by a dry nausea. He had never seen death before, even in its most benign guises—the aged aunt who sighs her last and expires in bed. Death had been a word to him, an abstraction, signifying no more than "forty below" would to a South Sea islander.

A word was all it had been to Will, Drew, and Eliot, who, seated on the foredeck with his knees drawn up and hands clasped around his legs, recalled the chub he had seen, swallowed up in a twinkling by a moray eel, and the rest of the school swimming on, as if nothing had happened. It seemed impossible that a human being, a man whom he had seen only minutes before, quick with life, could have met with a similar fate. Dragged under, torn to pieces, eaten, and all in seconds. He trembled, and wondered if he would have seen the shark if he had kept his look-out, and then if he could have shot it before it got Artemis. From what Nathaniel had told them, he didn't think so. He might have shot Artemis instead. The schooner began to swing on her rode. The tide was turning. In six more hours, it would turn and then turn again, ebb, flood, ebb, flood. The frigates still soared on the thermals. The heavens were no less blue than they'd been before Artemis's death; the haloed sun shone no less brightly. This continuing on of things outraged him. He felt like loading the shotgun and blasting the sun's indifferent eye. He wanted to wound the sea and force all nature to acknowledge that a good man had died for no good reason.

Those were not Drew's thoughts and emotions as he sat with an arm resting on the warm metal of the Charley Noble. The sea doesn't care a whit for what happens to those who sail upon her, he reminded himself. Or for those who dive into her depths. Yet, of them all, he, the youngest, was the least able to grasp that Artemis was gone forever. He found himself turning around, every now and then, with the expectation of seeing Artemis beside him. When he spotted a mossy lobster pot drifting on the tide in the distance, he thought for a moment that it was Artemis's head, bobbing to the surface. He squinted at the far-off object, half hoping to see the strong brown arms stroking toward the boat, and then Artemis climbing up the Jacob's ladder to laugh that wonderful laugh of his and tell them that he had gone for a long, refreshing swim.

And so the long day waned. They did not shape a course for Key West, or cook dinner, or check the barometer, which had fallen. They did not do anything, bound to inaction by a profound, paralyzing gloom that had become a fifth member of their crew. It stood by the helm, inhabited the cabin and the bunks below; it crouched in the bilges and hung from the crosstrees and shrouds aloft. And so the long day waned, and the sun bloodied the escarpment of cloud that had just begun to rear above the western horizon. Each boy recalled the hoary adage "Red sky at night, sailor's delight," and naturally it struck them now with a cruel mockery. Had Artemis been able to speak to them from the world of souls, he would have told them not to concern themselves with such thoughts; he would have told them to snap out of their funk and set sail for safe harbor, because in tropic latitudes during hurricane season, a deep crimson sunset was anything but a sailor's delight.

Part Three

IN ANOTHER COUNTRY

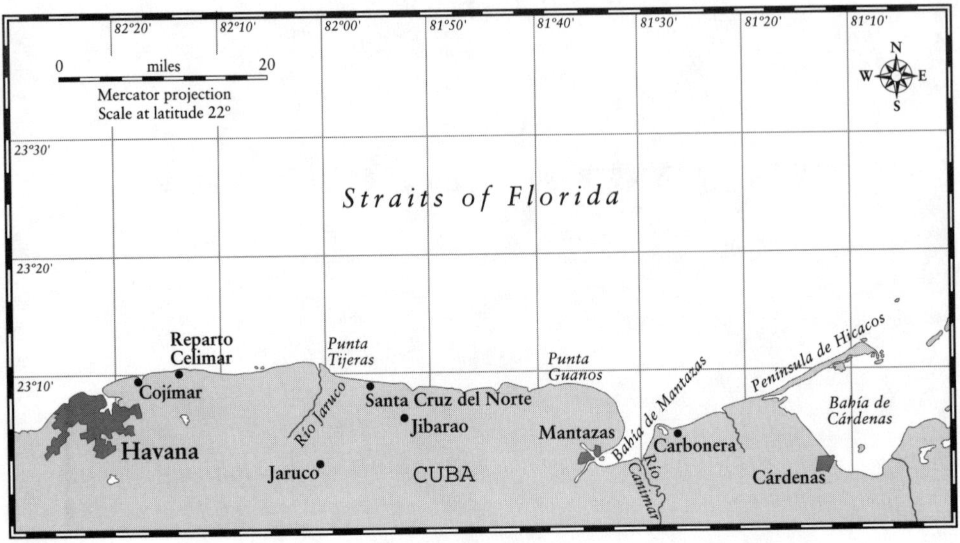
82°20'
82°10'
82°00'
81°50'
81°40'
81°30'
81°20'
81°10'
0
miles
20
Mercator projection
Scale at latitude 22°
N
W
E
S
23°30'
Straits of Florida
23°20'
23°10'
Reparto Celimar
Punta Tijeras
Punta Guanos
Peninsula de Hicacos
Bahía de Mantazas
Cojímar
Santa Cruz del Norte
Río Jaruco
Jibarao
Bahía de Cárdenas
Mantazas
Carbonera
Havana
Jaruco
CUBA
Río Canimar
Cárdenas

21

STRANGE DREAMS are dreamed at sea, for the sea is home to spirits all
its own, the immaterial correlatives of its fishes, whales, and squids, and
these spirits enter the minds of sleeping voyagers. As water roared in
through the shattered skylight and portholes and stoved hatches, Will
leapt from his bunk, ran through the main cabin and up the companionway, and scaled the mainmast shrouds to its top. Like thousands of ship-
wrecked sailors before him, he was trying to buy a few more minutes of
life before the vessel sank. When he woke up, he was so startled to find
himself aloft, in the middle of the night, that he almost fell. He didn't
know the hour—his pocket watch was in his trousers below—but by
observing the Pleiades in the bottom quarter of the eastern heavens and
the Dipper lying low on the northern horizon and almost parallel to it,
he estimated that it was between one and two in the morning. The telltales on the shrouds fluttered in one direction, dropped, and fluttered in
the opposite direction, then dropped and fluttered again in a third direction: Fingers of wind were swinging the compass, picking up the telltales
and letting them fall, like an idle girl toying with the ribbons in her hair.

He climbed down and noticed that he could not see Sagittarius,
which should have been visible as it dipped below the ecliptic in the
southwest; nor could he see Rasalhague, the bright star of the constellation Ophirechus in the west. It and Sagittarius were blotted out by a
solid-looking bluff blacker than the black sky. Turning his hand on its
side, he extended it an arm's length to measure the height of the clouds.
At sunset, they had been merely a ruffle on the western horizon. He
could have covered it with two fingers; now he needed three hands'
breadth. The sea was rising and falling very gently; there were none of
the long, glassy swells that portended a cyclone. This did not reassure

him, however; the schooner was anchored in the big basin ringed by the Tortugas reefs, and the one west of her—Loggerhead Reef, it was called—was probably flattening the swells, if any were out there, rolling across the Gulf of Mexico.

He went to his berth and looked at his watch. His guess at the time had been on the money: It was one forty-five. Going into the main cabin, he lit the gimbal lamp, peered at the barometer, and lost no time rousing the Braithwaites.

"Something's coming and we'd better figure out what we're going to do," he said, as they gathered around him at the chart table, yawning, rubbing their eyes. "It was a thousand twenty millibars yesterday morning"—motioning at the barometer. "It's a thousand six now and falling, and there's a wall of clouds to the west, headed our way."

"That ring around the sun yesterday," Drew murmured. "Dirty weather, Artemis said."

The mere mention of the name cast a pall. They stood looking silently at one another, or at the floor, where Artemis's Georgia bundle—a piece of sailcloth tied around an oilskin jacket and a spare shirt—lay with his cast net furled atop it. Nathaniel's face was a desert of emotion. He looked exhausted, and he was: exhausted on the inside. All he could think about was how the shark had ripped Artemis from his arms as effortlessly as he could snatch a rattle from a baby's hands. If he had been more alert, if he had seen the shark sooner and reacted more quickly . . . But he could not have. No one could have. . . .

"Dirty weather it's going to be," Will was saying, as he spread charts on the chart table. "The question is, what kind of dirty weather and how much of it is there going to be and what we ought to do. Stay put and see what comes? Get the hell out of here, and if we do, where to?"

With Artemis guiding them, Will had had no need to make a careful study of the Dry Tortugas' geography. Now, lighting a cigarette, he examined it with a scholar's attentiveness. The oblong basin of deep water, some eight or nine miles long by four wide, was blockaded to the northeast, east, and southeast by the crescent reef called Pulaski Shoal, to the south by the reefs surrounding Bush and Garden Keys, and to the west by Loggerhead Reef and Brilliant Shoal. Three channels, called Northwest, Southwest, and Southeast, allowed passage through the barriers, but the channel bottoms were an obstacle course of patch reefs, banks, coral pinnacles, and sea mounds. Some lay deep enough to allow the schooner to pass over safely, but in other places, the sea floor jumped abruptly from sixty feet to six or less. There were only a few markers, and none were lighted. The only beacon was the lighthouse on Loggerhead Key. Clearly, said Will, to try to sail out of this maze in darkness could be disastrous.

He gazed at the chart again and traced a line with his finger.

"We're just about in Northwest Channel right now, and the patch reefs in it look like the deepest. See here—the shallowest is two and half fathoms, more than enough. We could sail due north from this anchorage for about two miles, then head east along the north side of Pulaski. Four miles and we're clear of it. Then we bear south southeast through the Rebecca Passage and back into the same channel we followed coming out here. Then east by north to Key West."

Eliot and Drew frowned.

"Yeah," said Will. "Yeah. If whatever's brewing out there catches us between here and Key West—nowhere to hide."

Yet the second alternative—sitting tight—wasn't very attractive, either. Loggerhead Reef, less than a mile wide, would not provide much of a lee.

"But maybe it isn't a hurricane," said Eliot, with hope in his voice. "Maybe it's just a line squall."

"Maybe," said Will, turning to the chapter on tropical cyclones in the *Practical Navigator*. Reading aloud, he informed his shipmates that hurricanes spawned in the Gulf of Mexico generally occurred early in the season and generally tracked northeast or northwest. This was August, the middle of the season, and the cloud bank was traveling due east. "So maybe that's all it is, a line of thunderstorms," Will added. "But a damned big one. What do you think, Natters?"

"I don't know," Nathaniel replied, with a listless shrug and in a listless voice. "You're the expert."

"I meant, what do you think we should do? You're the skipper."

"There any kind of safe harbor around here?"

"There's Tortugas harbor, only five miles southwest of where we're sitting"—pointing at the chart with the dividers—"but I can't say how safe it'll be. It's on the west side of Garden Key, so it would be open to whatever's coming from the west. But if we could tuck in there, set both anchors with plenty of scope, we could take the tender ashore and hide out in the fort if things looked like they were going to get real nasty."

"What happens to *Double Eagle* if she gets blown onto those reefs? She'd be busted to bits."

"In that case, I'd much rather be in the fort. Only problem is, the harbor entrance is corked by this big rocky shoal here, and the channels on either side don't look fifty yards across, probably less. If I knew these waters, I'd chance it, but I don't. It's nothing I want to try in the middle of the night. We ought to wait till we've got some daylight, but it might be too late by then."

Again Nathaniel shrugged. Eliot and Drew had never seen him like this—not merely subdued but indifferent. They and Will waited for him to speak, but he remained still for half a minute, his palms flat on the table, his gaze on the chart but far away at the same time, vacant and somber.

"Natters, we haven't got a month of Sundays. What happened . . . We can't dwell on that now. . . ."

"No, you can't, because you don't have to," he said, turning aside a little, as though addressing the bulkhead upon which the barometer and chronometer shone in their brass housings. "You didn't see him, the way his eyes almost popped out of his head and his mouth opened like he was going to scream, but he never got the chance even to do that. And then that big tail, going back and forth and down and down, through the clouds of his blood. Uh-uh. You didn't see that, but I reckon I will, if I live to be a hundred."

There was nothing to say to this. Will lit a second cigarette off the butt of the first, let the smoke drift out of his mouth, and inhaled it through his nostrils.

"All right, then here's what we'll do," he said. "Lash down and batten down. Sea anchor at hand. Test the pumps to make sure they're drawing. That should take an hour at the longest. Then we start toward the fort with a triple-reefed main and foresail and stays'l. We'll need the stays'l for balance." He spoke with authority, the cigarette jigging between his fleshy lips. "If our timing is right, we'll be near the harbor toward daybreak. Then we'll have enough light to sneak in through those tight channels."

"A plan," said Eliot. "The best thing about a plan is to have one."

And it was a good plan (Sybil comments, aside). Men who had earned their salt would have approved it for its caution and sagacity, qualities seldom found in twenty-year-olds, even those with Yale educations. Will figured they would be sitting snugly behind Fort Jefferson's eight-foot-thick walls by the time the outer winds struck. That was the one flaw in his plan, a forgivable one, since in those days before marine radio or even wireless telegraphy, before aerial reconnaissance and satellite telemetry, there was no way for him or anyone to know that the hurricane, coiled as tightly as a serpent prepared to strike, was flying eastward at the speed of the fastest liner then on the ocean—much faster than Will had counted on.

The younger boys checked and secured things below—locker doors, portholes, steering cables. Above decks, Nathaniel and Will inspected shrouds, stays and the anchor cable, bolted hatches to the skylight. The cloud wall had risen, resembling an anthracite cliff emerging from the sea. Will, feeling the first touch of west wind on his face, worked with urgency, but Nathaniel moved about sluggishly. None of Will's pleas to "hurry up, give a hand here, get the lead out" had the least effect on him. They were like the consoling platitudes offered to someone suffering from an inconsolable loss.

The wind accelerated to twenty knots and the black seas rose and breakers charged in serried ranks over Loggerhead Reef. Drew went above, filled two buckets with seawater, then returned below, opened a hatch in the floorboards, and emptied one bucket into the bilges. Eliot, bowing over the midships pump, pushed and pulled the plunger. The water went out with a sucking noise. They went to the forward pump with the second bucket and repeated the procedure. Both pumps were drawing well.

Four o'clock. Will said he'd never seen a barometer fall so fast, and they all knew, as they got into their oilers, that they were in for it. Will took the helm, Nathaniel beside him in case the wheel needed two pairs of hands. Eliot and Drew winched up the anchor, then stood ready to tend the sheets, hunching their shoulders against a wind already keening at gale force. The eastern sky had taken on a gray luster, like the inside of an oyster shell. To the west towered a mountain range in motion, wild, menacing, with smoky plumes flying off its ragged crest. The storm was barreling toward them, and the most rational meterologist, had he seen it as the boys did, from the deck of a forty-six-foot schooner, would have forgotten everything he'd learned from books about heavy weather and felt himself one with the Carib Indians, the first men who had quaked before that wrath and given it a name—*huru-can,* demon wind.

Double Eagle tore southwestward under morning stars winking out one by one, her deck slanted thirty degrees. To her weather side, waves broke over the patch reefs in the Northwest Channel—the wide breach between Loggerhead Reef and Pulaski Shoal—reformed their ranks, and advanced to batter the schooner abeam. She rolled and banged in the crowded, eight-foot seas.

"At this rate, we'll be in the harbor in less than half an hour," said Will, standing, as they all were, at a thirty-degree angle. "It'll be easier once we're in the lee of Loggerhead. That reef will take some of the starch out of these waves."

Only minutes later, the storm forced Will to go back on his promises. Though it seemed to the boys' minds to do so with evil purpose, though it seemed a conscious being, it had no more concern for the promises, the plans, the paltry hopes and dreams of those four adolescents than its ancestor storms had had for the grand schemes of empire and the lust for riches dwelling in the minds and hearts of Spaniards homeward bound from the New World in galleons ballasted with bars of looted silver, their sea chests filled with emeralds and gold plundered from mines where Aztec and Inca labored under the Spanish whip, and all—ships, chests, coins, jewels—driven onto the reefs, smashed, and sunk, the Sevillean and Valencian lords and ladies crying out futile *Aves* as the waters closed around them and the great wind tore the prayers from their lips and shredded the words before they reached the ear of heaven; no more concern than one of this storm's big sisters had shown for the souls of Galveston only the summer before, September 8, 1900, when it roared into that city and in a few hours left it looking as if it had undergone a monthlong naval bombardment, the corpses of six thousand of its citizens bloating amid the ruins of their civic pride. Six thousand lives or four, Spanish galleon or Yankee schooner, conquistador or ordinary American boy—it was all the same to *huru-can*, a true egalitarian in its administration of destruction.

Double Eagle had crossed a mile of Northwest Channel and was within half a mile of the lee when the first of the storm's flailing bands struck her. The sky vanished, and in the roiling murk, Loggerhead beacon was extinguished like a fragile illusion in the face of an implacable reality. The rain did not fall but swept across the fractured sea horizontally, goaded by a wind that did not rise but leapt almost instantaneously from thirty-five to fifty-five knots. The ship went over on her beam ends, and was driven headlong, white water slashing past the cabin portholes. Nathaniel, Eliot, and Drew tumbled to the lee side, grabbed stanchions and lifelines to save themselves, and lay in a heap with a torrent rushing over their prone bodies; it was as if they had fallen into a salty mountain rapids. Will, with his legs clamped around the wheelbox, had managed to keep his footing and his grip on the spokes. He was shouting, but the three brothers could not hear him over the wind and the vibrato of shrouds and stays strung to the limit of tolerance. Getting to their hands and knees, they crawled up toward him, an effort as difficult as crawling up a steeply pitched roof in a rainstorm.

"Fall off!" Will cried as Nathaniel embraced the wheelbox and Eliot and Drew clung to the weather rail.

Yes. Yes. They understood. The rigging could not withstand the strain much longer; either the shroud would part or the sails would blow out, and if neither happened, the vessel would be knocked down and very likely founder. She had to be turned off the wind.

On their bellies, the Braithwaites slithered along the weather deck between the rail and the main cabin, its two-foot height all that prevented them from sliding back to the drowned lee side.

"You two! Main!" Nathaniel yelled. "I . . . for'ard!"

He returned to all fours, tensed like a runner in the starting block, and scampered across the ten feet of open space amidships, between the main and forward cabins. He started to slip, hooked an arm around a shroud, then continued to the safety of the forward cabin bulkhead. Crawling to the foremast, he kneeled against it, groped amid the pins in the pinrack, and took the turns off the staysail sheet. He did not have to look up to see the sail; he looked out, for the masts now were canted almost to forty degrees, the crosstrees dipped to within a few feet of the lunging wavetops, and the staysail was skimming the seas like a bird. The water over the lee deck hissed only inches away.

"Ease sheets, then down peak!" he howled over the cabin top to Eliot and Drew, who were at the main, Drew sitting with both legs wrapped around the mast, Eliot seated behind, his legs around Drew's waist. Their arms were held high, their hands gripping the main sheet. "Ease sheets, then down peak, all together now!" Nathaniel repeated. They were only fifteen or sixteen feet behind him, but he wasn't sure they'd heard, so he gave the command again, his voice breaking.

They paid out the sheets, watched the booms swing to leeward, and then made fast. The ship swung off to a reach, but did not begin to right herself; she continued to race on her side. She had too much sail on her.

"Down peak now!" Nathaniel screamed to his brothers and dashed aft to give them a hand. "She needs our help! Down peak! Down peak!"

He stood, and fell belly first against the mainmast. From above, he would have looked like a man crawling along an inclined log. He loosened the halyard, let the rope burn through his palms, and grabbed the luff of the sail, pulling it down. The unloveliest dousing he had ever seen. Eliot and Drew, clambering to the cabin top, stood doubled over the boom, like square-rig sailors on the yards aloft, and snatched handfuls of canvas, snapping so violently that it almost jerked them off their feet. Gradually, they stuffed it between boom and gaff and used the main sheet to tie it down.

"Right yourself!" Nathaniel bellowed. "Goddammit, come right!" Turning to see what Will was doing at the helm, he was pelted in the side of the face by what felt like gravel blasted from a cannon: rain, driving at

sixty miles an hour. A high wave, every foot of twelve and the color of
gun metal, charged *Double Eagle.* Her stern lifted to it as the schooner
laid off another point. Too much. For several seconds, she rode the face
of the wave at an angle to the trough, her stern high, bow low; then a
breaker caught her mercilessly and rolled her past forty degrees. The
bowsprit knifed into the back of a sea, the tips of the booms sliced
through spray and froth, and four hearts banged against the back of
four sets of teeth, as the boys waited for the booms or the bowsprit to
crack, or the ship to broach to. Then Nathaniel felt the ship lurch. Or
had he imagined it? Confounded hope with fact? No. He was standing
straighter now. In a moment, the lee deck reappeared, water streaming
off it, and then the rail burst to the surface.

"She's doing it! Oh, she is!" he shouted exultantly.

Looking amidships, he saw Eliot's and Drew's mouths open—dark
cavities beneath the hollows of their eyes—and heard their cries flying
away on the wind. "She's coming right! She rights herself!"

Forward, the staysail held.

They pounded Will's back and punched his shoulder and yelled glee-
fully that she was an Essex-built schooner, tough, buoyant, and brave,
and nothing could knock her down.

"Don't go passing out any medals yet, this is just the beginning,"
Will warned, and carefully brought *Double Eagle*'s nose to windward,
steering her back on course. All the rigging hummed, and he looked anx-
iously at the staysail, deeply concave. "Can't see the fort, can't see the
lighthouse, can't say exactly where we are. We'll never be able to negotiate that harbor channel in this mess. Any ideas?"

No one spoke, in part because the ferocity of the hurricane induced
silence, in part because they weren't sure what was the best strategy.
Each had its advantages, each its dreadful liabilities. They could drop
both hooks immediately and try to ride things out, but they were in the
middle of the basin, almost as exposed as they would be in the open sea,
and in ten fathoms of water, with high waves pushing the boat, the
anchors might drag or the cables break; then they would scend to leeward, and to leeward lay the middle of the big crescent reef. They could
lash the wheel and heave to under a shortened foresail, but in a seaway
such as this, the rudder would be subjected to unnatural stresses; they
could lose it, or the foresail sheet could chafe and part, and then the vessel would go scudding off toward the rocks.

"Well, if nobody else has got one, I do!" Nathaniel spoke through
gritted teeth. He was beginning to feel in command again, of himself and
the ship. "Change course. Head more west of south, toward Loggerhead

Key. . . . Get as close into the lee of the island as ever we can. . . . Anchor up and ride it out there."

Will objected: The altered course would bring the ship closer to the wind; the strain on the rigging would be tremendous. And when the back side of the hurricane blew in, the wind would reverse course, forcing them to up anchor and get *away* from Loggerhead.

"Ain't time for debates!" Nathaniel interrupted. "Drew, Eliot, lay for'ard and sheet in the stays'l! Stay there! Tie yourselves to the foremast if you have to! Lots of shoals between us and Loggerhead! Need lookouts!"

They staggered toward the foredeck, with the ponderous steps of men pushing a block of stone. They took the turns off the staysail sheet, hauled together, made fast. As they lashed themselves to the mast with the foresail sheet, the ship crept up, until the wind was just forward of the beam. It slashed their faces, and they thought the driving rain would put their eyes out.

"Lookouts!" Eliot hollered. "Goddammed joke! Can't see a thing!"

At the wheel, Will said he could not hold her on course by himself. Nathaniel wedged in beside him and seized two spokes. Immediately, he felt the pressure on the rudder and the strain on his forearms, and was amazed that Will had held her alone for this long.

Ahead, slate-colored waves surged and broke, flinging back glints of the eerie, yellow light that pierced the clouds, racing overhead like shredded rags. The rigging sang—a single note, high and piercing—and the wind changed tone, from a shriek to a deep, operatic moan.

A hail of rain and sea froth scourged Drew's face. He bowed his head. Sinners in the hands of an angry God, he thought. Mr. Hayworth, his Sunday school teacher, reading from Jonathan Edwards's famous sermon. But neither Mr. Hayworth nor Jonathan Edwards himself had the slightest idea of what it was like to be a sinner in the hands of an angry God. *This* is what it's like, thought Andrew Braithwaite, and yet, he felt a strange exultation, inseparable from terror. I am a sinner in the hands of an angry God. . . . But he must not think of the storm that way. It was a hurricane, not a punishment. It was a natural phenomenon, without mercy or cruelty, without a heart or mind: a cyclonic weather system caused by the Coriolis force—the effect of the earth's rotation on air currents over warm ocean waters. So said the *Practical Navigator*. That's all this is, Drew muttered to himself. Weather.

The staysail sheet parted. The top half of the line flew out straight as a stick, and the sail, jerked to a horizontal, flapped two or three times before it became a mass of tatters, some of which soared off while the rest whipped themselves around the stay. Without canvas to control her, the schooner swung and rolled broadside into a ravine alive with foamy spindrift. Will and Nathaniel brought the helm hard over, fighting to bring her head round on the rudder alone, but she was a plaything of the storm now and would not answer.

"The anchor!" Eliot yelled into Drew's ear, and loosened their bonds. Dropping, they belly-crawled to the chain locker and pried the hatch cover open. A vicious gust caught it and slammed it down on Eliot's fingers. He screamed. Drew wedged his hands under the cover and yanked it open again. Another gust tore it from its hinges; the screws pinged off like bullets, the cover careened over the lee rail. Rolling to the starboard rail, to which the main anchor was attached, Drew undid the lashings and let the hook fall. The chain banged through the starboard bow chock, and the cable uncoiled from the locker without a foul. Thank God for that, Eliot thought. No, thank Will for doing such a nice job of flaking it. Lying flat, cradling the throbbing fingers of his left hand in his right, he watched the cable pay out across the deck and through the chock. He knew the anchor had found bottom, although he didn't know how he knew; he hadn't seen the line go slack, even for a moment. When about a hundred and fifty feet of scope had gone out, Drew snubbed off on the samson post. The one-inch manila line came taut, creaked and quivered from the tension on it. The bow swinging back into the wind, the two boys rose to run aft for the kedge, were nearly blown off their feet, and so, once again, crawled like dogs.

"Quick work!" Nat said.

"Kedge . . . Help Drew set . . ." gasped Eliot. "My hand, think it's broke. . . ."

The kedge, with its twenty-five fathoms of cable, was dragged forward, foot by bouncing foot, and dropped over the port side. Nathaniel threw a turn around the samson post and, sitting with his feet braced against the bow rail and the line in his hands, let out scope.

"Okay! That's all of it!" he yelled.

The boys lay still, exhausted, clutching the samson post. Nathaniel's lips twitched, and he muttered that the old man would be proud if he could see what they had accomplished, a comment that inspired an outburst of uncharacteristically foul language from Drew.

"Fuck the old man!" he screamed. "If it wasn't for that son of a bitch, we wouldn't be in this goddamned mess!"

Irrefutable truths require no reply, and Nathaniel made none.

A moment before he and Drew ducked into the forward cabin, they had a chance to catch their breath. The wind fell instantly to a benevo-

lent forty knots and a break appeared in the clouds. They saw a teasingly
serene strip of blue and, about half a mile to the northwest, Loggerhead
Light, tall and white, its green Fresnel lens casting across an anarchic sea
a radiant beam of hope and salvation; a salvation out of reach, a hope
they dared not allow themselves to feel, as they dared not allow themselves to be seduced by the thin, fleeting patch of blue. Westward,
another dark gray precipice reached to heaven, promising more, and
greater, wind.

Below, the main cabin looked as if it had been ransacked by a team
of burglars in a hurry: strewn dunnage, broken bottles flung from the
medicine chest, charts, books, tin plates, and pots and pans, which clattered with every roll and thud.

Will, on his knees, was at the midships pump, pushing, pulling.

"Taken on water," he said, unnecessarily.

"Not surprising, considering how much of it there is out there," said
Eliot, sitting on the cabin sole beside the chart table. A rag was bound
around his left hand and a terror-stricken Trajan lay in his lap.

Nathaniel and Drew stumbled through the short, narrow passageway between the forward and main cabins. The ship rose, came down
with a bang, and they toppled, Drew into the companionway, Nathaniel
on top of Will.

"Sorry," he grumbled, and wedged himself into the corner of the
L-shaped settee that bracketed the dining table.

"Quite all right." Will closed the hatch over the bilge pump.
"Reckon I'll fall on you before this is over."

"Maybe it'll be over soon," Drew said, sucumbing to hope. "The
wind fell off a minute ago."

"It piped right back up, though, didn't it. That was just a hole. There
are holes in a hurricane wind, just like in an ordinary wind. Nope, shipmates, it'll get worse before it gets better. The eye wall hasn't hit us yet."

They looked at Will. He was tired, his head thrown back slightly, his
eyes half closed.

"What's an eye wall?" Eliot asked.

"The winds around the eye, the middle of a hurricane. They're the
strongest."

"You mean . . ."

"Right. Ain't seen nothing yet. Figure we're in for a hundred knots
and then some. The really horrible news is that I'm down to my last
three cigarettes."

"And then what?"

"Without a smoke, Eliot, I shall become unpleasant company. Far as the storm goes, the eye will pass over us after the eye wall, assuming we're not on the bottom by then, and it'll get real calm for a while. How long depends on how big the eye is. I'll bet my last pair of dry socks that this one won't be very big, twenty miles across at most. The stronger the storm, the smaller the eye. Then, oh, maybe half an hour later, we'll get hit by the back side. As a rule, the back side of a hurricane isn't as nasty as the front."

"Learn all this from that book of yours?" Eliot grimaced as the floor slammed under him and pain darted through his injured hand.

"My skipper in the Bermuda race gave us a primer on these daisies, just in case we ran into one during the race." He lighted one of the remaining cigarettes, rationing himself to two deep drags before he snubbed it out and returned it to the pack. "We'll be busy lads when we're in the eye. That's when we'll haul up both anchors, if we can, or cut the cables if we can't, then make sail and claw away from Loggerhead, to be ready for the winds from the back side."

"Loggerhead's about half a mile off," Drew interjected. "We saw the lighthouse, Nat and me, a couple of minutes ago."

"Proves my point," Will said. "Half a mile is too narrow a margin."

"All this will be just bullshit if we lose the anchors altogether," Nathaniel said, wearily. He was beginning to find the strategizing tiresome, and possibly pointless, as well. It allowed you to think that you had some control over what was going to happen to you, when you probably had none whatever. "And we might lose 'em, y'know," he added. "The cables could chafe right through in the chocks, or if there's enough strain on 'em, they could part, just like the staysail sheet did."

"So, *Capitano Furioso* Junior, what do we do then?" asked Eliot.

Nathaniel said nothing. Die, he thought, overcome by a fatalism foreign to his nature. Reckon we'll die.

Will, on all fours, his head bobbing with the motions of the boat, rummaged among the charts papering the floor.

"We're in Southwest Channel. Okay, if we lose the anchors now, on the front side, we'll get blown away from Loggerhead onto the Garden Key reef. If we lose 'em on the back side, we'll get blown into Loggerhead. What do we do to prevent that? Okay . . . Only thing I can think of . . . set the foresail, triple reefed, and . . . and . . . Well, if we're exceptionally fortunate, and lose the anchors just before the eye passes over us, we could sail through the eye into Tortugas harbor, abandon ship, and get ourselves into the fort before the back side hits. We'd have half an hour to do all that. Otherwise, we try to sail down channel till we're clear of the rocks and in the open sea. It's only about two miles. Pray the canvas holds long enough till we're clear. Once we are, we run with the wind. And if the sail blows out, we run under bare poles."

Run with it under bare poles—the last resort in heavy weather. Run with it under bare poles in the open sea. They were all silent as the words sank in.

"But listen," Will continued, on a second thought. "We can't run with the wind dead astern. That's what our skipper told us in Bermuda. You could pitch pole that way, but there's this, too. He said the idea is to run away from the eye, and if you're already in it, to run out of it. And he said you do that by keeping the wind on your stern quarter and your bow angled away from the eye. That way, the winds propel you out toward the edges of the storm. They're spinning counterclockwise, see, and eventually they'll spin you out to the edges. The only thing I don't remember"—this with a caustic laugh—"is *which* stern quarter: port or starboard."

There was an interval of silence, then Drew traced with his finger an imaginary diagram on the floor.

"Starboard," he said. "If the wind's backing the clock and the bow's angled away from the middle, it would have to be starboard."

Will paused, thinking.

"Yeah. Right. That's what he did say. Starboard quarter. Better reef the foresail now, while we can. Might not be able to when the eye wall hits. Reef it, rig a couple of lines as extra preventer stays so the fore boom doesn't swing an inch unless—until—we want it to."

Nathaniel stood, and was flung backward onto the settee. A cooking pot rolled one way across the floor, then the other way.

"Will and I will make ready above. Drew, Eliot, stay below. You can't do much with that hand, anyway, Eliot. But you can help Drew break out the life jackets and the mooring lines." The fatalism that had seized Nathaniel only moments ago was gone. It was weird how his emotional winds were swinging like the storm's. "Make four safety lines out of the mooring lines, long as you can, good, stout running bowline in each. I want everybody in a life jacket and with safety line and a sheath knife belted on the outside, the *outside,* of his oilers. Got that? Turn to."

"Ah, Nat, it's great to have you back, giving orders," Eliot said, and then put Trajan down.

The cat bolted into the illusory safety of a locker in the galley aft. Will and Nathaniel lurched up the companionway and went out.

"Life jackets. How do you like that?" said Eliot, sarcastically, even as he fumbled for the jackets in the foul-weather gear locker. "Know what a life jacket will do in this? Keep you alive just long enough to shit your drawers before you drown."

"Shut up," said Drew, cutting a mooring line into ten-foot lengths with his knife.

"And those. Sheath knives. On the outside, he said, so they'll be handy. Yeah, if we get blown onto the rocks, we can stab each other to death and put ourselves out of our misery."

"Shut up!"

After Will and Nathaniel returned, drenched anew, faces pale, they reported seeing two distressing sights. The first was the chafing in the anchor cables; the second, far off to windward, was what appeared to be a rolling pall of coal dust thousands of feet high and stretched from horizon to horizon: the eye wall, the black core of the hurricane. All four hunkered down with the tense resignation of townsfolk beseiged by a barbarian army.

22

A QUARTER of an hour passed. Then they heard a terrible, onrushing rumble. In seconds, as the central winds roared over the ship, shaking her till her crew thought she would come apart, the rumbling changed pitch and character, ranging from a demonic howl to a bellow to a prolonged bass groan, deafening and demented, as if a lunatic were pounding the keys of a cathedral organ. They all remembered the words of the old trader, Cudlip. None of them knew what the lamentations of the damned were supposed to sound like, but they could not possibly rival what the boys heard now, or, rather, felt. They felt it, as Cudlip told them they would, first in their groins, then all through their bodies and in their bones. *Double Eagle* reared to monstrous breakers, reared and bucked against the cables tethering her. Hatch covers lifted off their battens and slammed down, the masts trembled, booms thudded, cordage rattled; a great sea hammered the cabin tops and saltwater surged through the Charley Noble into the stove, transforming it into a washtub. All the while, the awful noise never abated. It was, each of them thought in his own words, the cry of that power in the universe which hated integrity and sought disintegration, which despised order, peace, and contentment and sought their opposites. It was the voice of chaos. Drew clamped his hands over his ears and recited his incantations silently . . . coriolis force . . . cold air in the upper atmosphere, low pressure on the surface . . . weather, only weather . . . but they did no good. He could not help himself. Convinced his life was going to end among these forlorn reefs, he began to cry, curled up, and fell across Nathaniel's lap.

"C'mon, Drew." Nathaniel felt awkward, as he always did in situations that required compassion. "C'mon, we'll get through it, you'll see."

"Why don't you sing?" Will said to Eliot, who gave him a stupefied look. "You're the one with the voice. Lead us in a tune. Let's see if we can sing louder than the wind can blow."

And he led them in the "Mingulay Boat Song" and in other old chanteys his father had taught on summer cruises, or that he had heard Lockwood sing in the house on Marlborough Street: "Heave Away Me Johnnies" and "Cape Cod Girls" and "The Leaving of Liverpool." They hurled their voices defiantly into the mad imprecations of the storm; but in the end, they were like a quartet trying to make itself heard amid the roars in a football stadium. In the middle of a verse, the ship gave a quick lurch to starboard, then swung back and held. They grew silent, all but certain that they had lost an anchor. In a crouch, Nathaniel stumbled to the fo'cs'l and fetched the sea anchor and two kegs of storm oil, with lanyards attached to the handles.

"Think we'll be going above before too long," he said to Will, in a doleful tone, and slumped to the floor.

It wasn't too long at all—about five minutes. A gust screamed through—Will thought it reached 120 knots—and was followed thirty seconds later by another just as violent. *Double Eagle* lifted and shook her head, and as the wind settled back to a steady 100 knots, the second anchor cable gave way and the schooner shot sternward then fell off broadside to the seas. Will grabbed the storm oil, bolted up the companionway, and forced the hatch open, Nathaniel following with the sea anchor. Outside, they could not stand or even get to their hands and knees; raging over them at nearly twice the speed of an express train, the wind pinned them flat to the afterdeck. It eased somewhat a moment later, and seizing their chance, they sprang to their feet. Sea, sky, and cloud were mingled into a single element, a maelstrom of thundering air and exploding spray, of whirling vapor, rain, and wash as blinding as fog. With the boat heeling to the storm and yawing in the eddies atop the waves, the boys were disoriented, unable to tell which direction was which. They seemed about to lose their sense of up and down. Bowing his head, Nathaniel peered at the compass card, and saw that the schooner was heading, or, rather, drifting, a little south of east. To get through the channel and clear of the reefs, she had to go west of south. The ship jumped, the top of the brass binnacle gave him a hard rap on the nose, and he felt blood start.

"Hoist . . . Foresail!" he cried.

Reduced by the wind to a reptilian mode of locomotion, they crawled forward on elbows and bellies. They lashed their safety lines to the foremast, struggled to their knees, and hauled on the halyard with all their strength. The gaff began to rise, but as the foresail filled, the forces on it made hoisting it as difficult as hoisting a barrel of lead up from the bottom of a well. The boys pulled, howled, pulled. They had to get the ship to sail; she would be crushed on the rocks in minutes if they did not. They howled and pulled some more and thought their straining muscles would burst through their skin. The gaff rose another foot, and then a foot more, and the reefed sail, struck by a hammer blow of wind, formed a deep, horizontal trough. It was up! Sheets and preventers were eased for sailing off the wind. Will and Nathaniel slithered back to the helm, tied their safety lines to the wheelbox, seized the spokes, and, bending their knees to put their weight into the effort, turned the wheel to bring the ship on course. She had a large rudder, but a barn door seemed too small for such a seaway. She would not answer and continued to drift on her side, lifeless as a log, indifferent to her fate. Nathaniel glanced eastward, to see how close they were to the reef, but everything ten yards beyond the rail was an impenetrable murk. Then *Double Eagle* stirred, making a final effort to save herself. She began to sail. Soaring sideways up the faces of seas, sliding down, she wasn't sailing well; yet she was sailing, against all odds. Nathaniel, gripping the wheelbox with his knees, his fingers feeling as if they were frozen to the spokes, his forearms aching, held his gaze dead ahead, trying to see through the white merge of sea and sky, the blown spray that stung like a knotted whip. As the schooner passed out of the lee of Loggerhead Reef, the waves soared to sickening heights. He dared not look at them, afraid the sight would unnerve him entirely.

"Bear off . . . Now . . . Slow . . ."

Will's yell was reduced to a barely audible whisper.

By quarter turns, they nudged her away from the wind, until she was poised between a broad reach and a dead run. Nathaniel was about to go forward to douse the foresail, but a sudden gust did the work for him. The sail exploded in a shower of canvas shards. The brand-new sail sewn by Frenchy Geslin and paid for by Aunt Judith. Letting the helm go, Will pulled the stopper on a keg of storm oil and dropped it off the weather quarter to do what little it could to smooth the waters. The sea anchor, which had been rolling across the afterdeck when it wasn't flying like a tethered balloon, was tossed off the port quarter. The wind picked it up and flung it forward. It struck the water as the schooner surfed down a wave, and the coiled cable flew off the deck and came tight. The anchor, theoretically anyway, would help the ship maintain her track and slow her wild journeys down the seas.

Will stood again to his side of the wheel, the port side, but kept looking astern, to watch for rogue waves. Nathaniel did the same on his side, and felt his heart shrink as he looked directly into the steep face of an oncoming wave, shattering into white at its top. *Double Eagle* climbed, her after sections first. Instead of making headway, she seemed to be going backward. The crest frothed around her, the wave pushed on with relentless drive, and the bow rushed into a trough so broad that for a moment the schooner appeared to be sailing in a narrow lake between two high ridges. Then she scaled the next sea and plunged again. Thus, she ran into the Florida Straits to live or die amid the wandering peaks of a vast and roaring gloom.

Nathaniel wished he could take one hand off the wheel to wipe his bleeding nose. He wished he had some idea of when the storm would pass. The schooner's topmasts were bent like wands; the masts trembled, threatening to break the shrouds. How much of this punishment could she take? How much could *he* take? He knew it was axiomatic among sailors that a small vessel, if she were made right and had sand, stood a better chance of surviving severe seas than a big ship; she floated on the waves instead of driving through them. There was in the small craft a certain necessary submissiveness that was not surrender. Yet, the sturdiest, bravest vessel had her foundering point—the moment when her strength was sapped, the last coin in her treasury of courage was spent, and she quit; or, still having some left, she met the sea, the wind, to which her strength and valor were not equal, and she was defeated. And what about a man? Did each man have his own foundering point? he asked himself. Do I have one, and where is it, and what will find it out? He awaited the climax of the storm with anticipation and dread, in equal measure.

The eye passed over them, creating the illusion that they had passed into an oasis of calm. The wind tumbled to a breeze, the waves shrank, the noise abated, and a circle of blue showed overhead, though the horizon all around was walled by gray. Eliot and Drew came on deck, hoping the tranquillity was deliverance, even when they knew it was only a respite. Worn-out and bruised, Nathaniel wiped his bloody nose with his sleeve and slumped over the wheel. Will sat down and looked with bewilderment at the sky.

"I don't get it. When we lost our anchors and bore off to south'ard, we should have been sailing away from the eye, but we've been sucked into it," he said, and then, thinking aloud, tried to account for the turn of events. Had they sailed the wrong course? Had the hurricane stalled or changed direction? He muttered things about navigable quadrants and steering currents and speculated as to what would be the best course of action, when the back side struck.

"Doesn't make sense," he said. "The storm must've changed direction. It's heading south, but hurricanes almost never go *south*. The only way that could happen is if the steering currents collapse, and then the storm just kind of goes wherever it feels like."

Nathaniel slammed him hard in the shoulder with the heel of his hand.

"Shut up! Stow it!" he said, in a voice verging on the hysterical. "That's all a lot of crap, and I'm sick of listening to it! If this storm wants to kill us, it will, and there's nothing we can do about it." He turned savagely on his younger brothers. "You two, get us something to eat, instead of standing there like idiots!"

Below, picking up tins of corned beef from the floor, Drew murmured that Nat was acting strange.

"No, he ain't," said Eliot. "He's pretty much acting like Nat."

"It's different this time," Drew said, although he could not articulate in what way.

His own crisis had passed. He wasn't going to cry again, no matter what happened, but not because crying was unmanly. He'd broken into tears earlier because he'd forgotten, in the fright of the moment, that the hurricane had no intention of ending his short life. His life did not make any difference to the hurricane, so it was foolish to take the storm personally. The trouble with Nat was that he took almost everything personally. He couldn't get into his head that his life also was not the hurricane's concern. None of their lives were. Drew did not agree that there was nothing to be done. Their lives did not depend on the storm's whims, but on the actions they took in the storm. It was up to them and maybe to luck, as well.

He split the cans with a hatchet (the opener had vanished amid the wreckage in the cabin) and dumped the contents into two tin platters. On deck, they all shoveled the food into their mouths with their fingers. Very shortly, they heard the rumbling again.

It swelled in seconds to a thunderous vibration, like a hundred locomotives speeding through a tunnel. The seas built up and tightened. All ran as high as the foremast—about thirty feet, but every now and then, one lifted another ten feet, nearly to the height of the mainmast. The schooner skated down the faces exceptionally fast; too fast for safety. Will noticed, by the way the cable was swinging wildly astern, that the sea anchor was gone. Either it had broken off entirely, or its canvas had been shredded, leaving nothing but a bent metal frame and fifty fathoms of line to restrain the ship.

"Brace!" Will cried.

A hundred yards off, a sea mounted to an astonishing altitude, perhaps fifty feet. As it approached, Nathaniel could hear the crash of its breaking crest. He wanted to run, as from a charging lion, but of course there was nowhere to run to. The sea chased the ship down with implacable malice—so it seemed to him—and lofted her toward the invisible sky. Nathaniel stood paralyzed with awe, for here was an almost sheer wall of blue-black water, streaked with foam and spume and spindrift. The schooner reached the summit, where, with white water churning all around her, she seemed to be riding through surf or a tide rip. It took all his strength, and all of Will's, to hold the helm steady against the eddies, currents, and countercurrents crisscrossing the crest. *Double Eagle* was poised briefly there, offering the boys a dispiriting gull's-eye view of a seascape that might have been painted by a madman: a heaving, tossing wilderness that had no end. The ship rocketed down the wave, yawing in the confused water, and buried her nose. For an instant, she seemed intent on plunging straight for the bottom, but she rose valiantly, her head breaching. An immense volume of sea flushed backward, drowning the cabin tops and sweeping Will and Nathaniel off their feet. As they fought to rise and the water tumbled through and over the taffrail, the helmless ship slewed to windward, rolled, and went over, her masts pointing straight down at the nearest land, five hundred fathoms below, her keel slicing through the air.

Inside, as the hull turned turtle with a tremendous thud, Eliot and Drew were flung against the side of the cabin, tumbled with Trajan, tin cans, charts, instruments, and a hundred other things from the floor to the ceiling, which became the floor. The cat screeched and ran in circles. Drew crashed into the skylight, shattering the glass and cutting himself. If the storm hatches had not been battened down, he would have fallen through into the sea. The hatches were designed to shield the skylight from breaking waves, not for submersion, and saltwater was forcing its way through the spaces between the storm hatches and the skylight frame, creating a pond in the middle of the boat. More seeped through cracks between the main cabin hatch and the bulkhead. The battened hatch, if it did not hold, would be an open door to the ocean. And still more water was bubbling through the stove, which hung above them by its floor bolts, the stovepipe forming a hole in the new bottom.

Nathaniel and Will, tethered to the boat by their safety lines, were being trolled like baits, skipping the surface one moment, sucked under

the next by the schooner's motion and by the power of the seas. Their
life jackets had been rendered useless. Nathaniel was dimly aware that
the tender had been torn away and that the falls were bouncing along
near his head. He didn't care. When he was pulled beneath the tumultuous surface, he welcomed the quiet. He imagined he saw things: brilliant tropical fishes, glowing squids, phosphorescent porpoises, lights
twinkling as stars in some submarine heaven. Signs and wonders. There
was no thought in his mind that he was drowning; there was no thought
of anything. A warm ether coursed through his veins, creating a blissful
drowsiness. The struggle against the storm was over. The noise, the fear,
the strain on his hands, arms, and back—it was all over. . . .

Less than half a minute after capsizing *Double Eagle,* the unbiased
ocean righted her. Eliot and Drew fell through space again, landing on
the floorboards with the same items that had fallen with them the first
time. The water in the V-shaped skylight showered down, the stove door
banged open, and the gallons in the belly poured out, flooding the main
cabin. Eliot, quickly yanking a floor hatch open with his good hand, got
it to drain into the bilges. Drew leapt to the pump.

Nathaniel and Will were catapulted back into the boat—morsels,
they were, spit out by the sea. Spit violently, too. Nathaniel cracked his
skull on the taffrail, Will howled with pain when his ribs struck the
wheel. They had been returned to the world of struggle, of effort, of terror, of strife. Nathaniel was amazed that they had not lost their masts
and rigging and yet he almost resented their deliverance. He felt that the
storm was toying with them. At some point, five minutes from now, or
an hour, or two hours, it would tire of the game, and that's when the end
would come.

Drenched, chilled by the wind, he shivered uncontrollably. In a few
minutes, a dreamy lassitude came over him again. All he wanted was
rest, to fall down and go to sleep. Once more *Double Eagle* scaled a
gigantic wave, once more he and Will surveyed the crazed painter's
panorama. A moment before the plunge, they glimpsed a dark cloud
stretched all across the windward horizon. Was it the eye wall again?
Were they merely spinning aimlessly around the eye, condemned to be
drawn into it again and again, until the storm blew out or the schooner
foundered? As the ship rose on the next wave, they saw that the cloud
had reared higher; it was drawing toward them rather than they toward
it: an immense, oncoming shadow, with white curling from its top.
"Ah," Nathaniel said to himself. "Ah." The boat skidded into another
trough, and his spirit fell with her. Until this day, the sea had been as
kind and generous toward him as life in general. It had never shown him

what it was capable of when roused to the fullness of its passion, had never visited upon him that wrath which cannot be appeased or placated but only endured. Now it was making up for that deficiency in his education by presenting him with the greatest sea he had ever beheld, a sea the likes of which an ocean liner might not encounter in her lifetime; and he knew he could not endure it. Nor could *Double Eagle*. She was too small and fragile to survive the monster charging her with a momentum as unstoppable as the rush of time itself and with a vindicative purpose that nothing could turn aside. She would not live, and so, neither would he, his brothers, and Will.

The idea of watching the end come was intolerable. He would sooner stare into the jaws of an enraged grizzly bear. Letting go the helm, he loosened the bowline around his waist, slipped out of his safety line, and gave Will a pat on the shoulder before he pulled the hatch open and tumbled below. His confidence that the world was arranged for his benefit had collapsed entirely, and with the loss of that faith, he had lost faith in himself and the conviction that there was nothing he could not do. It had been shouldered aside by a feeling that he was a puny thing, incapable of any meaningful action.

"It's all up," he said to Eliot and Drew, then flopped on the wet cabin sole. His voice was level, his face wore a calm expression that was something of a mask; he wasn't calm inside so much as filled with the resigned despair that is, in battles on land and in storms at sea, sometimes mistaken for stoic courage. "Not a cloud . . . It's a sea. It's all up," he repeated, and closed his eyes.

His two younger brothers stared at him. A gust blasted into the cabin, rearranging the debris: Nathaniel hadn't bothered to shut the hatch.

"What about Will? Where's Will?"—Drew, fighting panic.

Nat didn't stir, except to make some indeterminate movement with his hand.

"Did you leave Will to steer by himself? What . . ."

Sensing that some crisis was only minutes and perhaps seconds away, Drew broke off and hopped on deck, dogging the hatch behind him. Will did not appear to be aware of his presence as he lashed his safety line to the wheelbox. Will was transfixed by the lifting plane of water a hundred yards astern, many times more massive than a building, its tumbling cap ranging beyond the maintop, which stood higher than the schooner was long. The sea was so huge that there were seas upon it—smaller waves quartering its face, leaping mounds three and four feet in height—and its upper slope was inverted, appearing in the glimmer of gale light as a watery cavern. It was majestic. Drew was held breathless, too mesmerized to be scared, as the wave reared above him. If there had been sunlight, it would have cast a shadow over the schooner, stem to stern.

The sea reached her in seconds. She ascended swiftly, voyaging almost vertically, fighting to keep herself upright on the face. Just before she reached the summit, she was canted so steeply that Will and Drew would have fallen to the bow if it had not been for their safety lines. Then, suddenly, she was level. The top of the wave, exposed entirely to the wind, had been blown almost flat. It looked as wide and wild as the salmon rivers in Maine, an asylum of hurling froth. Drew tried to follow Will's movements as he deftly nudged the helm to one side or the other to hold course. They could feel the rudder vibrating through the wheel. The whole hull was vibrating. At that moment, a part of the crest made a freakish leap and became peaked. The body of the wave trembled, as the earth trembles in a quake, and the peak collapsed over the ship in a thunderous Niagara. The impact almost hove her under, and she thrilled in every timber. Will and Drew were knocked breathless and driven backward, the force causing the safety lines to burn into their flesh through their oilskin jackets. As the great sea passed under them, rolling away into infinity, a howl of wind tore through the rigging, weakened by the capsizing. There was a loud crack and then another, and then a terrific bang. The foremast had been carried away. When it fell, the triatic stay between it and the main toppled the maintop and part of the mainmast, which stove in the storm hatches over the forward cabin skylight. Now, the two-masted schooner had been reduced to a half-masted schooner, twenty feet of broken mainmast standing like the stump of a lightning-struck tree above a deck littered with a wreckage of shrouds and rope. The foremast was dragging along to starboard, held by the shrouds and stays. It was the Carolina gale all over again. The whole rig was dragging—the mast, the new boom and gaff crafted by Ray Sykes in Snead's Landing. The spars battered the hull, threatening to hole the ship.

"Get rid of it!" Will bellowed.

Drew flew below to summon Eliot and Nathaniel, but only Eliot responded. Armed with a hacksaw and a hatchet, Drew and he worked their way through the web of fallen lines to the foredeck. The wind began to moderate somewhat—over the past several hours they had become as attuned as anemometers to its rhythms—and the seas appeared to be falling to thirty feet or less, a mere chop compared to the monster that had joined forces with the wind to dismast the ship. Safety lines bent to the windlass, the two boys chopped and sawed the god-awful mess of cordage for twenty minutes, Drew vomiting because the ship, with her masts gone, no longer rolled but rocked side to side with the twitchy motion of a toy boat. Finally, the rig floated away on the scend of the sea, either to sink and add its little bit to all the other wreck-age lying on the bottom, or to drift onto an unknown shore, where it might or might not be picked up by a beachcomber, who might or might not ponder what fate had befallen the vessel it had belonged to.

23

THE LATE AFTERNOON sun illuminated a green-hulled schooner grounded in a vast, muddy bay, her decks looking as if she had been used as a practice target for small-caliber guns. She was heeled far over on her port side far enough to show a rudder cracked in two and the upper portion of a damaged keel. Islands speckled the bay like green patches sewn onto clay-brown cloth, the archipelago reaching eastward as far as eye could see. To the south, girt by a narrow beach, low mangrove jungles steamed in the brilliant heat.

Eliot, Will, and Drew, sitting on the high side of the afterdeck, under a jury-rigged dodger, delighted in the calm as survivors of a blizzard delight in a roaring fire. But they had been delivered from the storm into a new predicament: They were stranded in some tropical middle of nowhere, with food and water to last them a week at the longest. The hurricane had cast them here, somewhere off the north coast of Cuba, in a final tantrum of wind. Rollers had swept *Double Eagle* over a broken reef that materialized out of nothing. In what had seemed like seconds—certainly it hadn't taken more than a few minutes—she was tossed from the abyss of the Florida Straits into water that wasn't ten feet deep. Drew remembered, with a shudder, the huge shadows that had suddenly appeared through the surge and Will hollering, "Rocks! Those are rocks!" just before the ship struck the first time, with a thud that shivered her throughout. The tension went out of the wheel instantly, and they knew they'd lost their rudder. A breaker lifted the schooner and flung her forward, and she struck again, this time with a shriek of rending planks and timbers. In moments, her bilges filling, she began to settle. Holed beneath the waterline, rudderless, mastless, she was without defenses. Drew and Will, their hands still on the useless helm, were all but certain that she would swing broadside to the surf, broach to, and sink; but she continued to run with the wind, defiantly, miraculously, until she ploughed into a sand shoal that stopped her wild career as suddenly as a stone wall. The wind slid rapidly down the scale, from gale force to strong breeze to gentle breeze, ragged windows of blue opened in the clouds. The high storm tide rushed out, the water falling from six to three feet. It was three o'clock in the afternoon, and Will, slumped on the deck, cradling his left side in both hands, said that by his reckoning, they had been driven one hundred miles across the Straits in about nine hours. That did not amaze Drew as much as the time of the day. The storm has lasted a little under twelve hours, but with its unearthly roar still echoing in his ears, it had seemed like a week. He sensed even then that those twelve hours had separated him from his childhood forever.

When he and Will went below to inspect the damage, they found Nat lying in the after stateroom, uninjured but looking as if he'd been clubbed. Eliot was in the main cabin, which was flooded on the port side. He too appeared dazed as he waded knee-deep in the muddy water, sifting through a thousand floating articles. "Aw, damn!" he said, dipping down and coming up with Trajan's corpse. Realizing it was no time for sentimentality, Drew took the small body by the scruff and went outside and tossed it overboard. "You were a good old cat," he murmured, then returned below to help Will and Eliot salvage whatever could be.

Their principal concern was for food and water. The copper tank forward was empty; the fallen mainmast had speared through the floorboards, severing a hose pipe, and all fifty gallons had drained into the bilges. The tank aft was half full. Thinking they would be in the Tortugas for the three days at the longest, the boys had neglected to top it off before leaving Key West. A box of canned goods and a few loose tins of salt pork and beef were retrieved from the drowned galley. Everything else—sugar and salt, coffee, tea, beans, rice, onions—had been rendered unfit and was cast into the sea.

Drew had felt a need, an obsession, really, to impose order on the chaos of wreckage and went into a frenzied cleanup campaign, jettisoning whatever had been destroyed or was not of immediate practical use, like Eliot's water-logged guitar. A whole chanderly of items that had once seemed indispensible either went to the bottom, or drifted off on the tide. He spared the logbook, which had survived the storm; he wanted to keep it as a memento. The mirrors on Will's sextant had been shattered, but the Plath, protected by its sturdy teakwood case, was still in working order. The *Almanac* and the Reduction Tables were drenched clear through, and he set them on deck to dry. The chart of Cuba was also soaked, almost to a pulpy transparency, but he carefully spread it out on the cabin top and weighted its corners and hoped the sun would restore it. When all that was done, he helped Will and Eliot drag the jib out of the sail locker and rig it as a dodger against that same ferocious sun.

Now, clustered in its shade, they surveyed the surrounding waters for a sign of human life. About a mile away, between them and the mainland, white birds lofted from a small island in such numbers as to resemble smoke. Closer to the stricken schooner, flamingos waded a sandy flat on long, twiglike legs. That was all they saw—birds, thousands of birds, and deserted keys and a coast as wild, they imagined, as when it was first charted by Spanish navigators four hundred years ago.

"First things first," Will said, wincing, again pressing his hands to his injured side. "Got to figure out exactly where we are, if we can. Best do it before we lose the sun. Damn, I must've busted half my ribs."

Drew did not want to think about that, or about Eliot's broken hand, or about the weird funk that kept Nathaniel below in a state of speechless immobility. The physical and mental infirmities of his shipmates suggested that he was in charge, and he did not feel that he was ready to be in charge. Fetching the Plath and the reference books, he took a sight on the lowering sun. The calculations proved more tedious than usual, for the books' pages were plastered together and had to be carefully pried apart, and then the columns of figures were smeared and nearly illegible. Nor was there a dry piece of paper to write on, so he and Will did the arithmetic on the deck planks.

While they were at it, Eliot watched the sun drop and hover over the western end of the bay. Just before it vanished, the last red sliver turned bright green, gleaming like an enormous emerald.

"I just saw it!" he cried. "First time ever! The green flash!"

Drew and Will, busy with their numbers, said nothing.

"Hey! I just saw the green flash!" Eliot repeated. "Like Dad told us about! It's supposed to bring good luck!"

"It's caused by refraction through the lower atmosphere. Doesn't have anything to do with luck," Drew said, with the wearied patience of a missionary instructing a particularly benighted savage.

As the light faded, he and Will determined their azimuth and HO, and, going to the chart on the cabin top, laid the parallel rule on the Compass Rose.

"We're somewhere on this line, then," he said. "Somewhere in here. Bahía de Cárdenas. What's that mean, Will?"

"Cárdenas Bay," replied Will, adding, with what struck Drew as an absurdly finnicky attention to linguistic niceties, that "bahía" was pronounced *buy-uh* not *bah-high-ah*. Leaning over the chart, the movement bringing a grimace to his lips, Will pointed with the pencil. "Looking at the shoreline, I'd put us right about here, on this sand shoal, just north of this little island, and maybe five miles from this headland. Punta de Piedras, it looks like." He spread his thumb and forefinger and measured off ten miles on the longitude scale, then fixed his thumb on the schooner's estimated position, his finger on a point at the head of the bay, half an inch from a place marked CÁRDENAS.

"There's civilization, a town, maybe a city. Twelve miles, give or take, southwest of where we are. Straight line distance over water. Soundings show an average depth of a fathom and a half. Too bad. A little shallower and we could wade it. Wish to hell we hadn't lost the tender."

Drew squinted at the chart, then lifted his gaze to the coastline immediately to the south. It was shaped like a crooked thumb and formed the eastern shore of the bay.

"Look here, Will, we're just about two miles off the mainland and the soundings show nothing but shallows between us and it. Half a fathom only. We could wade from here, follow the coast right along the bay to that town."

"That looks like a twenty-five-mile walk, and I'm in no shape for a hike like that."

"I say we stay put," Eliot interjected. "We ration the food and water and wait for a fisherman or a boat to spot us. There's bound to be a boat coming out of that town, sooner or later."

"But what if all the boats there are in the same shape this one is?" asked Drew, more or less rhetorically. "I'll give it a try. I'm the shortest. If I can wade it, then everybody can."

Without waiting to hear opinions, he slipped off the port side, and found himself up to his chin as he sank past his knees in the boggy bottom. Wading two miles through such a gumbo would take forever, he thought. He grabbed the rail and hauled himself back on board, the muck caking his trousers and giving off a sulphurous stench.

"Reckon that takes care of that bright idea," Eliot muttered. "Water's shallow, the mud ain't."

They all four slept on deck, for it was suffocating below and stank of stagnant bilgewater and mildew. Their limbs twitched, and sometimes one of them would cry out to reef, haul, or make fast as the hurricane returned, howling in their dreams. Nathaniel bolted upright in the middle of the night, startled into consciousness by a nightmare in which the great wave reared again, its dark body hurtling toward him with the single-minded, appalling purpose of tearing the breath from his body. He saw it still, as he sat fully awake beneath the cold and lofty stars, and it pronounced a terrible judgment. He had turned his back on Will, abandoning him to steer and confront the monster sea alone. He had failed Will and his brothers, as he had earlier failed Artemis; worst of all, he had failed himself and his own best image of himself. He had proved wanting in the first grave crisis of his life: the exalted test for which he had so diligently prepared with his boxing and football and mail-order dumbbells. In that towering mass of angry water, he had encountered a power to which his spirit was not equal. If his shipmates had cowered before it as well, he might now think better of himself; but they had found the resources to look the beast in the eye, while he had searched his own heart and found only an emptiness, a hollow, a shameful lack. He could not face his father now. He wasn't sure he could face his own reflection in a mirror without spitting at it. To go on living with so much self-loathing would be impossible, and a thought of suicide, chilling in its attractiveness, flitted through his mind, but was checked by the hope that life, in its infinite justice and mercy, would someday offer another challenge to his courage, one that he would meet and overcome and prove himself to be the man he thought he was. And if life did not present it to him, then he would be required to seek it.

And so passed three interminable days and nights. When they weren't sleeping, they sat and sweltered and scanned the bay for a boat, never seeing anything more than blinding water, wild birds, and the mangrove-tangled shore, brooding under a sun that offered no consolation. They grew silent and sullen and instinctively tended to stay out of one another's way. *Double Eagle,* what was left of her, had become as much a prison as a refuge. The water was rationed ever so carefully, doled out dipperful by dipperful, but they were privileged American boys, as unaccustomed to deprivation as they were to the alien heat, and each of them sneaked an extra ladle or two when the others weren't looking. By the morning of the fourth day after the storm, the tank was down by a third.

When Drew woke up, the tide was on the ebb. There was dry land all around the small key to the south: a broad ring of sand exposed by the falling water. It beckoned like a mirage on a desert. Though he had lost his fear of the sea, he longed as much as ever to feel firm earth beneath his feet once again. In a little while, he would *need* to feel firm earth beneath his feet. They all would, he thought, for the remaining water would not last much longer. He had learned one big thing on the voyage: that the first necessity in life was to face necessity with a clear eye and a cold head. You ignored what you wished were so, looked only at what *was* so, and then acted—ruthlessly, if ruthlessness was demanded by the situation. He realized that the older boys were going to wait for a boat to appear until the last morsel of food turned to shit in their bowels and the last drop of water was pissed over the side. Sure, a fishing boat might turn up to rescue them; then again, it might not. The one certainty—if he and Will had plotted their position correctly—was that the town of Cárdenas lay some twenty-five miles away by land. To Drew, there was no choice but to try and ford their way to the mainland while they had food and water to sustain them on the march.

He announced this conclusion, eased over the side, and again sank past his knees in the muck that occupied some nether state between liquid and solid. Walking in it was like walking in wet cement, but he forced himself to go forward. Ten minutes later, he was parched and pouring sweat and had covered less than a hundred yards. At this rate, he calculated, the two-mile journey would take about eight hours, assuming the mud did not get any deeper. He jerked his left leg out, planted it, jerked out the right and planted it. Again and again. A thrill of relief passed through him when, taking one more step, he suddenly stood in a foot of water, on a bottom almost as firm as pavement. He reached down and scooped a handful of what looked like crushed limestone. Pressing on, to make sure the hard bottom was not temporary, he trudged another hundred yards in less than half the time it had taken to cover the first. Turning, he slogged part way back to the schooner, cupped his hands around his mouth, and yelled, "We can do it!" Will signaled with his arms that he had been heard. A quarter of an hour passed, during which he saw Will and his brothers busying themselves with some task—what, he could not tell. When they finally joined him, he saw that they had rigged a harness for a water cask out of rope. Two lengths were bound tightly to the top and bottom, and two more had been tied perpendicular to those to make shoulder straps. Nathaniel was carrying the cask, while Eliot had the shotgun over his shoulder, with a Georgia bundle, composed of sailcloth wrapped around a few tins of food and the logbook, slung from the barrel. The log had been Will's idea: He thought they might need it to document their story to the Cuban authorities in Cárdenas. If they were lucky—very, very lucky—they would run into U.S. soldiers, for the island was still occupied by the American army.

They trekked to the key, reaching it in two hours, and rested and drank and looked with awe at the destruction wrought by the storm. The mangroves were flattened, as if trod upon by an angry giant. In the distance, the hulk of *Double Eagle* was silhouetted against a bleached sky. They had sailed and loved her; she had been faithful to them, delivering them from what Artemis called the cruel ocean, and the sight of her now brought to each boy an ache of loss and regret, such as might be felt by a refugee, stealing a last look at a home destroyed by war or natural disaster. None felt that grief as strongly as Nathaniel, and it was compounded by guilt; he had failed her, too, his ship, and to abandon her now, on a foreign shore, struck him as the ultimate betrayal. He stood staring at her with a tightness in his chest until Will touched his shoulder and said, "C'mon, Natters. Let's go."

They went on, fording a broad stretch of deeper water between the key and the mainland. Drew was up to his chest in a few places, and once, stepping into a white sand hole, over his head. Pale brown sharks no more than a foot long finned lazily over meadows of turtle grass; small stingrays glided by, trailing whiplike tails from their black, pieplate bodies.

Drew offered to spell Nathaniel, but he refused, vowing to carry the barrel all the way to Cárdenas. It was the beginning of a self-imposed penance. If life was to offer him a chance to redeem himself, he reasoned, then he had to prove himself worthy of it, purifying himself through suffering and sacrifice. He welcomed the chafe and burn of the hemp straps, the strain that twenty pounds of water and wood put on his back. He exulted in the heat, his thirst, and in the pinch of the limestone gravel on his bare soles. As far as he was concerned, he could not suffer enough.

Five hours after starting out, they set foot on a beach no wider than a sidewalk and littered with storm wrack: coconuts, broken lobster traps, coils of pot warp, driftwood, a tree trunk borne from some distant place. Behind the beach lay more flattened mangroves and fallen casaurinas, jumbled like the slash at a logging site. A few palms remained upright, leaning at crazy angles, some with all but one or two fronds stripped off. The boys rested and drank again and ate cold salt pork out of a tin with their fingers before setting off, single file. Sometimes the beach constricted to the width of a footpath; frequently, it gave out altogether, forcing them to struggle over the mazed hoops of mangrove roots or to wade the waist-deep channels, dredged along the shore by tidal currents. They swam the mouth of a small river, Nathaniel pushing the scuttlebutt out ahead of him, Will gasping from pain, Drew taking the shotgun and the tramp's bundle from Eliot, who needed his good hand to paddle with. They reached the head of the bay at nightfall, flopped down on the sand, and closed their eyes, but the mosquitos, swarming out of the mangrove swamps, would not allow them to sleep, so they went on, their way lit by a quarter moon. Finally, around midnight, exhaustion overcame them and they slept.

They were off again with the dawn, trying to make as much distance as possible in the relative cool. Weeks on a small ship had softened their legs. Their muscles were stiff and refused to move quickly. Will, noting that the shoreline now headed due west, said that if he had read the chart correctly, Cárdenas could not be more than ten miles off. Two hours, and perhaps that many miles later, they drank the last of their water, and Nathaniel dropped the scuttlebutt, that portion of his penance done. Still seeing no sign of civilization, not a boat, farm, or village, they sat down and indulged in dreadful speculations. Maybe they had plotted their position incorrectly and were not on Cárdenas Bay, but on some other utterly deserted stretch of the Cuban coast. They dropped off to sleep, clubbed into unconsciousness by weariness and the heat. Their dreams now were of clear northern streams and sweet springs bubbling in shady New England glades.

Will did not think he was dreaming when he was awakened by a sharp nudge in the ribs; he thought he was hallucinating. Three people stood over him, their figures backlit by an afternoon sun. Sitting up, he shielded his eyes with his palm and saw a dark-complected boy of fourteen or fifteen wearing a straw hat and ragged cotton trousers, belted with a rope from which a sheathed machete hung. Beside him, an old Negro woman, her face a riverine map of wrinkles, stood holding a bundle of leaves, and beside her was a tall woman of twenty or so, with fawn-colored skin. A blue kerchief was wound turbanlike around her black hair, and her eyes, as black as her hair, were large and oval and tilted slightly at the corners, like the eyes of a woman on an Egyptian frieze. A gold pendant hung between her breasts—generous breasts that nevertheless seemed disportionately small for her wide hips. That flaw heightened rather than detracted from her beauty; she was the most striking female he had ever seen. Behind the trio, a gaff-rigged skiff, sixteen or eighteen feet long, with a bright blue hull and red gunwales, was drawn up on the beach, its painter tied to a mangrove root.

"Quién es?" the boy asked.

"Yo?"

"Sí. Usted." The boy grinned, as if to say, Who do you think?

"Me llamo Willard Terhune."

"Usted no es cubano, verdad? De dónde es Usted?"

"Soy norteamericano."

The boy, who looked like a tough little character, older than his years, cocked his chin at the Braithwaites, lying propped on their elbows, blinking against the light.

"Ustedes también son yanquis?"

"Mis amigos no hablamos español," Will informed him. "Somos yanquis. Todos." Pausing, he noticed the boy's hand resting on the handle of the machete and the alertness in his dark eyes, which moved quickly across their faces and then rested on the shotgun braced across Eliot's lap. Realizing that the four of them must look like desperados, Will added, to reassure him, "Somos marineros. La barca de nosotros . . ." He hesitated, forgetting, if he ever knew, how to say "was wrecked" in Spanish. "La barca de nosotros," he began again, and made motions to indicate a sinking ship. "Comprende?"

The boy nodded and asked if their boat had sunk in the storm, and Will affirmed that it had. The boy replied that it had been one bad storm, and a very unusual one as well, coming from the north and west instead of from the south and east, the direction from which hurricanes usually came this time of year.

The old woman, speaking in a rapid dialect of the classical Spanish Will had learned in school, said something that he translated as "Olokun does as he wishes."

"Sí, Madrina," the boy replied, his tone respectful. "Veramente."

He told Will that the bohío in which his family lived had lost its roof to the wind, which had also taken down one of their Spanish lime trees, and that the heavy rains had washed away part of their garden, and that the noise of rain and wind had made one of their pigs muy loco, causing it to flee into the countryside, from which it had not returned. His family had known the hurricane was coming, he said, for his madrina was a santera of high repute who spoke to the orishas of Olokun and Shango and could divine their future intentions. On her instructions, his family had slaughtered a rooster and fed it to Olokun with a little rum, in the hopes that the Lord of the Sea would turn the storm aside, but that was not to be. As his madrina had said, Olokun did as he wished.

"Pero, quién sabe? If we had not sacrificed, perhaps the hurricane would have swept us away with our plantanos. Perhaps it would have made us all crazy, like our pig."

"Sí. Que es posible," said Will, who wished to be agreeable, although he hadn't the vaguest idea what the boy was talking about. Olokun, Shango, orisha—what did all that mean?

"Sus amigos—cómo se llaman?"

"Nathaniel, Eliot, Andrew," Will answered, pointing to each and pronouncing their names slowly. He watched the boy silently mouth the foreign names and then asked his. The boy replied that it was Francisco Casamayor and that the old woman, his aunt as well as his madrina, or godmother, was called Rosaria Balbontín. The young woman was his older sister, Elvira.

Rising to shake hands with the three, Will sucked in a breath as a dull pain shot through his ribs. He was surprised to notice that Elvira was as tall as he in her bare feet. She wore a loose white shift translucent from sweat—apparently she and Francisco and Rosaria had been cutting plants in the forest, for what reason he did not know—and her nipples, her navel, and the fork of her thighs showed through the damp cloth. She neither smiled nor frowned as Will took her hand, but her face was not expressionless; rather, it wore an expression he could not read: an opacity that intrigued. There was something ancient in that look of hers, something profound and penetrating, as though she could see past the surface of an object or a person and know its essence in a glance.

"You have been injured?" asked Rosaria, noticing him flinch when he withdrew his hand from Elvira's.

"Sí . . ." Will did not know the Spanish for *ribs* and so gestured at his side and said, "Huesos . . . aquí . . . Mi amigo también"—gesturing at Eliot—"en el mano."

Stepping forward, Rosaria pressed Will's side up and down with her fingers and frowned thoughtfully, asking him where it hurt and where it did not, and then, motioning to Eliot to stand, took his hand and kneaded the knuckles with her thumb. When she concluded the examination, she said she had herbs for curing broken bones at her house; if Will and Eliot accompanied her there, she would heal them—with the herbs and the proper rites to someone or something called Babaluaye.

"Eres una médica?" asked Will, incredulous.

"Soy curandera," she replied firmly.

"Mind letting us in on what this is all about?" asked Eliot. "Who are these people?"

"The kid's name is Francisco, the six-foot beauty is his sister, Elvira, and the old lady's name is Rosaria. I think she's some kind of healer, you know, like a witch doctor. She said that she's got some sort of potion that's going to cure my busted ribs and your busted hand."

Eliot scowled and said, "I ain't drinking some potion brewed by an old lady who doesn't even speak English."

"We're in Cuba," Will reminded him. "They speak Spanish in Cuba." Then to Rosaria: "Dónde está la casa de Usted, señora?"

"Cárdenas," she answered, and, turning around partway, pointed to the west.

Will told her that Cárdenas was their destination, for they now had no food or water; they hoped to find someone to help them return to their homes. The woman said something so quickly that Will could not quite make it out.

"Habla Usted más despacio, por favor," he said.

"I said to you that you have found help already. Olodumare, the father of destinies, has guided you to us, us to you. We have food, water, herbs for your injuries. Perhaps we will find someone to help you with your return. You will come with us."

She made it sound more like a command than an invitation.

"Madrina, con permiso," said Francisco, stepping in. He looked at Will, then at Eliot, and gestured at the shotgun. "Give that to me."

"You wish it as payment? We have a little money. . . ."

Francisco shook his head, giving Will a cool, flat stare. "I don't want the gun in your possession while we take you."

Will passed on the offer and the terms to the Braithwaites. Eliot hunched his shoulders and refused to hand over the L. C. Smith.

"You don't get it," said Will. "The kid doesn't trust us yet, and frankly, if I was in his shoes, I wouldn't either. We look like some pretty rough hombres. Give him the goddamned gun, unless you want to walk the rest of the way."

Eliot crotched the barrels in his elbow, opened the rusty breech with his good hand, shook out the shells, and passed the weapon to Francisco.

"We will ride in the stern, you four in the bow, where I can see you. That will be agreeable?"

"We have walked for almost two days," said Will. "Anything you ask will be agreeable."

Francisco, grinning at Will's remark, set the patched sail to the southeasterly breeze, tugged the pendant to the centerboard, dropping it, and ran offshore for a quarter of a mile, where he sheeted in and came up, the little skiff reaching westward, her freeboard reduced to inches by the weight of her seven passengers. The boat was making two knots at best, it needed a good hosing down, and the heat was crushing, but the four boys were joyful to be off their feet and grateful for the water jug that Rosaria handed them.

"De dónde en Estados Unidos son ustedes?" asked Francisco, leaning into the transom, the tiller under his arm.

"Tu sabe Boston?"

The boy shook his head.

"Somos de Boston. Está un ciudad en el norte. Tu sabe Cayo Hueso?"

"I have heard of it. It's across the Straits."

"Sí. We had sailed from Cayo Hueso when we were struck by the hurricane."

"José Marti went to Cayo Hueso for money and guns to fight the Spanish. He was our great poet, our great patriot."

"Cuba Libre!" said Will, toasting with the water jug.

"Cuba Libre!" Francisco echoed.

"Looks like our luck's changed," Will said to Nathaniel, who did not reply. "That girl is really something to look at, isn't she?"

Nathaniel, who was squeezed against the port gunwale, remained silent.

"Something wrong, Natters?"

"I'm sorry," he said. "Leaving you on deck like I did. I went yellow on you. No other way to say it."

"Is *that* what's been bothering you the last few days?" Drew interjected.

"Wasn't talking to you."

"I'm sitting a foot away from you. It's a little hard not to hear you."

Will laid a hand on Nathaniel's shoulder in the manner of an older brother. "I don't hold that against you. None of us do. You shouldn't hold it against yourself."

Nathaniel did not say anything but mulled his friend's advice, even though he knew he could never follow it. His mind leapt from thought to thought, but there was a direction to its apparent randomness: It led him back two years, to the last day of the Black Island quarry strike. The quarrymen, in retaliation for Cyrus's importation of scab workers from Boston, had armed themselves with clubs and stones and marched on the company wharf, where a drogher was being loaded with paving blocks cut by the scabs. The mob dragged the teamsters off the wagons parked alongside the ship, cut the traces to the horses, overturned the wagons, tossed the blocks into the water, and stoned the handful of company men—six engineers and blacksmiths—who tried to stop them. Cyrus, who was in the office with his manager, the big Swede named Pedersen, ran outside and told the strikers to return to their homes, promising he would discuss their grievances with their leaders when order was restored. One of those leaders, a tall Finn, said the time for talking was over. Brandishing three-foot cudgels, throwing stones, the men advanced on Cyrus and Pedersen, forcing them to retreat closer and closer toward the end of the wharf. When his heels bumped against the railroad tie used as an edge timber, Nathaniel's father pointed at the tall Finn and asked if he could swim. The man, taken aback by the question, shook his head.

"Neither can I," Cyrus said. "And if I go in, you're going with me. We'll drown together. I'm willing to drown for what I stand for—how about you? Are you willing to drown for time and a half?"

The strikers' advance stopped instantly; so did the shouting and shoving. The clubs were lowered, along with the fists that held the stones.

"Come ahead," Cyrus challenged the Finn. "C'mon ahead, and so help me God, you're going into that cold water and down to the bottom with me." Still, no one moved. "If that's as far as you're going, then turn around and go back to your homes, cool off, and we'll talk things over in the morning, like reasonable men."

And they did exactly that. Although the men stayed out of the quarries for another two weeks, the strike, for all practical purposes, was broken at that moment. If Nathaniel's sympathies were for the quarrymen—even then, a year before he'd gone to work alongside them, he had thought they were in the right—he could not help but admire his father. It must have taken a tremendous amount of raw guts and moral authority to stand unarmed, with the ocean to his back, and face down one hundred and twenty angry, club-wielding men. Such was Nathaniel's legacy, along with those bequeathed by the grandfather who had risked jail to help fugitive slaves to freedom, by the great-uncle who had remained on the quarterdeck of his clipper ship for an entire day and an entire night till she was safely through the typhoon. How, with a heritage like that, could he not hold his own cowardice against himself?

The skiff sailed into a harbor as fetid as any swamp, its waters coated with a green scum that glowed with an unnatural radiance under the sun. A wooden quay and wharves, battered by the storm, ringed the shore. Low stone buildings with red-tile roofs and pastel walls stood behind the quay, and the cupola of a Romanesque cathedral raised a crucifix against the southern sky.

"Cárdenas," Francisco said to Will. "We live just outside the town, to the west."

A short time later, he hauled on the breeze and beat toward a slender, rocky beach, upon which a dozen wrecked fishing boats, painted in festive colors that made them look all the more desolate, lay on their sides or bottoms up amid mounds of baking seaweed that stank worse than fertilizer. Beyond were rows of wooden shacks, many without roofs. Those closest to the bay had been reduced to piles of planks and rafters and posts. With a jerk of the pendant, Francisco raised the centerboard and nosed the skiff into the beach. Everyone climbed out into mud-brown water, warm as bathwater. Will watched entranced as Elvira hiked her skirt to wade ashore, revealing long, bronze calves and a few inches of her ample thighs. The sight shocked the Braithwaites, who had never in their lives seen more of naked female limb than an exposed ankle. Nathaniel, as he helped Francisco pull the boat out of the water, thought of Constance—his beautiful, modest Constance, who would have sooner ruined her skirts than to brazenly raise them in full view of young men.

Francisco led them inland for perhaps half a mile, down a winding dirt road between shanties walled with uneven planks gapped by mortarless chinks. Each had a little garden and chicken coop and hog pen. Bare-chested men—some black, some brown, some white, some a fusion of all three races—were up on crude ladders, re-roofing the hovels with palm thatch, bundles of which lay in ox and donkey carts drawn up everywhere. Here and there, women were grinding coffee beans in tall wooden mortars. The savor of the crushed beans mingled with the stench of excrement and the fragrance of flowers and herbal gardens to play havoc with the boys' nostrils, delighting them one moment, offending them the next. The men and women often stopped whatever they were doing to gawk at the four strangers trudging behind Francisco, who, with the shotgun in one hand, looked as though he were leading prisoners to jail.

They came at last to a bohío that looked no different from the others, its raked dirt yard shaded by coconut palm and a spreading royal poinciana ablaze with scarlet blossoms. In the back was a plot, bigger than a garden but smaller than a farm field, planted with a crop of some kind, and beyond it, the land rose toward what looked like a high desert plateau, bristling with agave and cactus.

It was dark and musty inside. Solid wooden shutters, like ship's hatches, were battened over the glassless windows. Francisco threw them open and dropped the muslin bedsheets furled over the openings, permitting a hazy light to fall on three beds, arranged in a U along the partition walls of a room twelve feet square; a room only sailors would have found commodious. There was a washstand bearing an earthenware pitcher and bowl, and a thin draw curtain over the doorway, which led into a second room that combined kitchen, dining room, and parlor. A picture of an anguished Christ, baring a heart wrapped in thorns, hung over the washstand. Otherwise, the walls were as bare as those in a monk's or a captive's cell.

"I am afraid one of you will have to take the floor," Francisco said, looking apologetically at Will, while motioning at the three beds. "This was my father's house before he was killed. He died, you know, at Santiago, fighting with the guerrillas alongside the yanqui army. No one has lived here since then, but my sister keeps it clean—in case our father's spirit comes back to spend a night in the old place." He propped the shotgun aganist one of the corner posts. "I return the gun to you. You four look like cimarrones, but I am satisfied that you're not. I go now to find my uncle, Enrique. He knows a lot about what to do, and I think he can help you return to North America. Buenas tardes."

"Más tarde," Will said, with a wave, and then informed his shipmates that they were to wait for Uncle Enrique, who might aid them in getting home. He flopped on one of the beds. After four nights sleeping on deck and one on the beach, the straw mattress felt like down. Drew went out to have a look at the other room, Eliot took a bed, and Nathaniel lay on the floor, because he thought he deserved it.

24

"HEY, WILL, what does 'San Pedro' mean in English?" asked Drew, poking his head through the draw curtain.

"You can't figure it out? Saint Peter."

"So, these folks here, these Spaniards, they're Christians, is that right?"

"They're Cubans. They're no more Spaniards than we're Englishmen. And yeah, they're Christians. Roman Catholics."

"Our old man doesn't think Catholics are exactly Christians," said Eliot, curling his big toe. "But, I wonder if they're going to do the Christian thing and feed us. I'm hungry enough to eat the tail off a wooden horse."

"C'mon out here and look at something," Drew said to Will.

In the other room, he opened the doors to a shelved cabinet. On the top shelf was the wooden figure of San Pietro, standing on a base carved to resemble a rock. The shelves below it were occupied by a rag doll, its hair crudely dyed with paint or shoe polish, a peculiar little statue with seashells for eyes, a garishly painted bowl containing a few stones, and miniature models of weapons and tools—a pair of tongs, a hammer, a sword about two inches long.

"This doesn't look Christian to me," Drew said, in a tone of disgust.

"Kind of pagan," Will said.

The door flew open, a sultry breeze blew through the room, raising dust from the hard-packed dirt floor.

"Ohe! Qué carajo hacen?"

The loud voice was as startling as a thunderclap. Standing in the doorway was a man of about five feet six, with walnut-brown skin stretched over a bony frame as tautly as hide over a drum. His dark hair, cropped short and tipped with silver, had retreated to the middle of his skull, and he wore a drooping mustache that gave his mouth the grim set of someone resolved to do an unpleasant duty. A faded red shirt hung outside a pair of khaki trousers that must have been cut for a fat midget, for they were too baggy for the man's scrawny legs and at the same time too short, the cuffs three inches above his feet, which were shod in rope and leather sandals.

He spoke again, in the same rapid-fire dialect as Rosaria.

"Cómo se dice?" Will asked. "Más despacio, por favor."

"That was the canastillero of my brother-in-law," the man shouted, but more slowly. "It's not for you to look at."

Will closed the doors and apologized, telling the man that they did not know what a canastillero was. "Please excuse our ignorance."

"Sure I will. You're yanquis—what the hell do you know? But watch out, sticking your nose where it doesn't belong." He stepped into the room, swaggering like the pugnacious little cocks that crowed and strutted in the yard. "So you're the one who speaks Spanish, eh? How are you called?"

"Will Terhune."

"Me llamo Tío Enrique. Enrique Balbontín, esposo de Rosaria." He thrust out a gnarled brown hand. "Soy el jefe aquí también. I'm the one who makes things happen. My nephew told me that you met with misfortune at sea and that you wish to return to the United States. Where to? I've heard of Texas. I've heard of California and New York. They're far away. If that's where you're going, I cannot be of help."

"Cayo Hueso."

"Cayo Hueso? No habrá problema." Pausing, Tío Enrique sat at the small, square dining table and, rubbing his bald pate, looked at the floor. His booming voice, so far out of proportion to his size that Will almost believed it was a ventriloquist's trick, had brought Nathaniel and Eliot out of the bedroom. "It would not be a problem," he continued, "except most of the boats around were damaged in the hurricane, and the ones that weren't are too small to take the four of you across to Florida." He raised his bloodshot eyes. "The best thing for you would be to go to Havana. I know you would find passage to Florida in Havana. All the world comes to Havana. Also, there are a good many yanquis there who could be of assistance to you."

"And how, Señor Balbontín, do we get to Havana from here? Is there a coach?"

He laughed sharply.

"You could call it a coach. It's more like a donkey cart and the road is very bad now, with the summer rains. Going by sea would be much faster. Havana is two or three days away by sea."

"But if all the boats . . ." Will started to say.

"Listen. I know a fisherman. His boat is in good condition. Maybe he'll take you when he's in between fishing trips. Got any money?"

"Repita Usted, por favor, y más despacio," said Will. He'd understood, but he wanted to stall before answering. The Braithwaites still had their pay from the sponge factory in Key West—fifteen dollars—and he had another three.

"Cuántos dólares tiene Usted?" said Tío Enrique, very slowly.

Will reached into his pocket and opened his palm, displaying three silver dollars. Tío Enrique took one between his thumb and forefinger and, holding it up to the fading light pouring through the open doorway, squinted appraisingly.

"This one's mine for taking the time to help you." Flashing tobacco-stained teeth in a cockeyed grin, he pocketed the coin. "This fisherman, he'll take you for the other two dollars. That will leave you with no money in Havana. Unless you have more, hidden away maybe?"

"No, Señor Balbontín. Está es todos."

Tío Enrique pulled a thin, twisted brown cheroot from his shirt pocket and lit it. Will looked hungrily at the glowing tip, the smoke.

"Quiere un cigarro?"

"Very much," said Will, trying, without success, not to sound too desperate.

The cheroot was the tobacco equivalent of moonshine whiskey, and Will gagged when he drew the smoke into his lungs.

"Ohe! You do not inhale these like they are cigarettes," Tío Enrique said, laughing.

"Can I get cigarettes around here? American cigarettes? Duke's?"

"I will see. But that will cost you something. Here, take these to last you. My favor to our yanqui guests."

He gave Will half a dozen cheroots, then planted his hands on his knees and stood up.

"All right. Who are the two injured ones? Rosaria has something for you. You will be good as new in no time. She knows her stuff."

Will asked for a moment to explain what was happening to his friends. When he was done, he and Eliot followed Tío Enrique outside into the gathering twilight, the sky a velvety purple in the west, candle- or lamplight slivering through the cracks in the shutters of the bohíos, palm fronds rattling in the breeze.

"I ain't drinking any hag's potion," Eliot grumbled as they entered a hut.

The middle of its earthen floor was taken up by a wooden bathtub. A large iron pot simmered on a hearth in one corner, its steam filling the cramped room with a dense, pleasant odor. Bundles of herbs hanging from the rafters added their fragrance, and candles guttered on an altar, which was dominated by a three-foot plaster statue of Jesus wearing a scarlet cape, his exposed heart dripping blood from the thorns twined around it. Beside the statue was a bohío the size of a dollhouse, complete with a straw roof decorated with seashells, a tiny window, and a door against which a pair of miniature crutches leaned. None of this, exotic as it was, drew Will's attention as much as Elvira. In a fresh white gown that reached to her bare ankles, her wrists adorned with bracelets of black and pale blue beads, her throat with the gold pendant, she sifted dried herbs into the pot, hearth coals and candlelight burnishing her skin so that she looked like a living icon cast in bronze and gold. She turned around when the two boys entered, and her eyes lingered on Will before they shifted to Enrique, the sight of whom appeared to frighten her. She quickly averted her gaze and went back to her sifting and stirring. After he left, Rosaria, sitting on a footstool in front of the altar, beckoned her patients to come forward.

They sat on a reed mat in front of her. Eliot, feeling a mild terror, flinched when the old woman, her seamed brown face like the masks Lockwood had brought from Africa, took his hand in hers and began to rub the back of it with the broad, bright green leaves of a plant. Next— and this almost made him yelp—she produced a headless pigeon from a basket beside her and dripped blood from its severed neck onto his hand, chanting as she did in a high, quavering voice and in a language neither he nor Will had heard before. Elvira accompanied her, the chant like a litany, with one word—"Babaluaye"—repeated several times. Rosaria interrupted once and, reverting to Spanish, said something to the younger woman, who repeated the chant. Although Eliot could understand none of it, he divined that Elvira was a pupil, engaged in some sort of recitation exercise. My God, he thought, he and Will were guinea pigs in a school for witch doctors! Nevertheless, he submitted to Rosaria's ministrations, mostly because he was afraid he would insult her if he did not, partly because the treatment was having an effect. A soothing warmth penetrated his skin, like the camphor rubs his mother gave when he had a cough.

Rosaria nodded to Elvira, who dipped a strip of cotton cloth into the pot with a pair of wooden tongs, then passed it to Rosaria. The old woman lay a sprig of herbs across Eliot's knuckles and bound it with the damp cloth, which sent waves of heat into his fractured joints. She spoke to Will.

"She says you're to keep that on tonight and come back to her for a fresh one tomorrow," Will translated.

"Okay, but I ain't drinking any potions, Will."

Rosaria gestured to Will to take his jersey off and told him to raise his arms above his head. He was surprised that it embarrassed him to bare his torso in front of Elvira; he'd never suffered such shyness in the whorehouses in New Haven and New York. She knelt beside him and began to massage his cracked ribs with a bundle of pungent leaves. Her strong hands moved over his side as softly as a mother washing an infant, and the chant she sang, following Rosaria's lead, was hypnotic in its drumlike cadences.

She fell silent, rose, and dipped more cotton strips in the herbal brew and held them, steaming and dripping, over the pot before returning to the mat to kneel and bind them around Will's chest. He caught the scents of aloe and sage, and Elvira's cheek came within an inch of brushing his and warmed the air between their faces. The sensation suggested a touch, and the suggestion was more arousing than a touch itself would have been.

"Well, that takes care of you for today," said Rosaria. Few words could have been more disappointing to Will. He felt ready to be wrapped up like a mummy, so long as it was Elvira doing the wrapping. "Tomorrow, you'll take an herbal bath in this tub you see here. I will speak with Babaluaye and we'll see if the power of his herbs works on those who don't believe in them."

"Rosaria, qué es Babaluaye?" asked Will.

"Es orisha—una anima. Entiende Usted?"

"No."

"The spirit of sickness and healing. The same as San Lazaro." She twitched her small, round head at the miniature house. "His ashe is in there. Entiende?"

"No. Ashe. Orisha. These are words I've never heard. Nor the words that you and Elvira were singing."

"Lucumi." Leaning forward on the stool, knees spread beneath her dress and her hands folded in the furrowed cloth between them, she cast a slightly mischievous look at Will and Eliot. "The language of the old people, the ones the Spanish brought here in chains from Africa. It's their words. It's their religion."

"I thought you people were Catholics," said Will, with a puzzled frown.

"Somos Católicos, seguramente. Pero, somos orisha también. Hijos de santos."

"Disculpe. No entiendo."

"We follow the way of the saints. It's a more beautiful religion than the Catholic. But it's too complicated to explain." She motioned him to come closer. He cocked his head toward her, and she whispered, "What did my husband say to you?"

Will related the conversation. The old woman snorted and tilted her chin haughtily.

"It's like him to ask money for doing nothing. Let me tell you what he'll do next. He'll tell you that he has not been able to find his fisherman and ask for another dollar to go find another fisherman. Don't give it to him. Take my advice and now listen to me. I've got a cousin here, Luis Figueroa. He trades in coconuts up and down the coast between here and Havana. He's got a big boat. I'll talk to him and see if he can take you, and I won't ask a peso of you. Neither will he. I am santera, I've made Olokun and seek Olokun's blessings for each of Luis's voyages, so he'll do it for free if I tell him to." She lowered her lips to Will's ear. "But I will ask you to do something for me in return," she whispered, so softly only he could hear. "I think it will be something you will want to do, but before I tell you what it is, I must speak first to Luis. All right?"

Will hesitated, uncertain about what he would be committing himself to—and his shipmates as well.

"Believe me, you will not find it an unpleasant task," she said, sensing his reluctance. She drew back and sat up straight. "I have been waiting a long time for someone like you to come. I have been expecting you, I think. I want to say that finding you on the beach today was luck, but there is no such thing as luck. Nothing happens by accident. Do you believe that?"

Will shook his head, his recent experiences having convinced him that life, whether on land or sea, was a chain of accidents ruled by blind chance.

"Well, you will," Rosaria forecast. "Oludomare guided you here for a reason. Think about how you came to be here and of all the little things and big things that could have prevented you from coming here. Think about that and you will see what I mean. It was destiny. What have you boys had to eat?"

"Nada," replied Will. "Tenemos mucho hambre."

"Vayan al bohío, Usted y su amigo. I will see that you get something. Yellow rice, black beans, plantanos. Maybe some sofrito."

Elvira, standing by the hearth, turned to her aunt and godmother.

"I would like to cook for them, with your permission, Madrina," she said, in a voice that tore at Will's heart. They were the first words he had heard from her since meeting her hours ago, in the fire of afternoon.

"Not alone, you won't. It would not be proper," Rosaria admonished. She looked at her niece and then at Will. "I will come. I am tired and it is late, but I will come and help you feed these boys who came to us from the sea."

AFTER DINNER, when the two women had left, Will paced around the small room, as agitated as the Braithwaites had ever seen him.

"That was a bully feed," Eliot remarked, balling a fist over his mouth to stifle a belch.

"What?" Will muttered, distracted. He fumbled in his pocket for one of the cheroots Tío Enrique had given him but came up empty, so he went into the bedroom and took a butt from the tin plate he used as an ashtray and lit it. Once again, he paced, opened the door and looked outside, and paced some more.

"Jiminy, Will, aren't you tired?" said Eliot. "It makes me tired looking at you, walking back and forth like that."

"Then why don't you turn in, sailor boy?" Will snapped.

"What's eating you?"

"Not a damn thing, Eliot. Why don't you pipe down and turn in."

"Maybe we all should," Nathaniel said. He looked at Will. "Hey, it's not that girl, is it?"

"What about her?"

"She's colored, for one thing."

Will turned sharply and crushed the cheroot on the earthen floor.

"Not completely. Maybe not even half, I'd say."

"Half is enough," said Nathaniel. "You can't be falling for a colored girl."

"Who the hell said anything about falling for anybody? Anyhow, what if I was? I'd think that after everything you've seen on this trip, you'd be a little more broad-minded about some things."

"Well, she is pretty good-looking, I'll say that." Nathaniel commented, withholding his true feelings. When he thought about the shameless way Elvira had hiked her skirts, she seemed to him to be like the Cuban air—excessively humid and unwholesome.

"It's not the architecture, although that's pretty splendid," said Will, fingering his hair. "Not the eyes either, although they're pretty splendid, too. Something else. Never seen anything like her."

"Me neither," Nathaniel said. "But I'm not falling for her."

WHEN THE SHUTTERS were closed that night, the bohío felt like the inside of a safe on a hot day, and the boys slept fitfully, sweating through the coarse bedsheets. When Drew flung the shutters open, mosquitos came in by the squadron and kept everyone from sleeping at all. Hadn't these people heard of window screens? Drew complained, closing the shutters again. A few strips of cheesecloth would have been sufficient to allow the cool night air in and keep the bugs out. The house had other inconveniences—among them, no privy—and the boys peed and defecated in the bushes behind the yard, a lair of snakes and scorpions. Drew expected hardships at sea, but he found such backwardness ashore inexcusable, and as one day wore into two, two into three, he found himself disliking Cuba and Cubans. He hated the dirt and dust and the intemperate heat that built until late afternoon, when black clouds marshaled in the southeast and rain fell as if an immense water balloon had burst in the heavens. He hated, most of all, being among strangers whose language he could not understand and whose lives were a mystery. Will had passed on what he'd learned from that strange old lady, Rosaria—that the religion here was a little bit Catholic and a whole lot heathen mumbo jumbo. It came from Africa, Will had said at supper, and that tall colored girl he was sweet on told them that the rag doll in the cabinet—the thing that was called a canastillero—commemorated her dead father. Not a photograph or a portrait, but a doll! What kind of superstitious nonsense was that? Drew wondered, his empirical mind offended. By the end of the third day in Cárdenas, he was desperate to escape, his longing for home and all its familiar comforts subverting the reign of logic in his thoughts. He lay sweating in his bed, listening to Will's bed creaking as he committed a sin—thinking about Elvira, no doubt—and schemed to hijack a boat. He laid plots to steal an oxcart and drive it to Havana himself.

There used to be, and perhaps still is (writes Sybil in another of her marginal comments), a type of patrician Anglo-Saxon who felt at odds with what he was. He fancied himself possessed of a dusky, sensual, and passionate soul imprisoned within pallid skin, of a heart Latinate and tropical, beating in opposition to the hymnal rhythms of the stern Protestant virtues. He was drawn to the sun, dark-skinned women, and exotic landscapes, where he imagined his true nature, liberated at last, would blossom in all its brilliant hues. Willard Terhune was of that romantic type.

His thoughts were also taking an illogical turn, but led in the opposite direction from Drew's. He felt curiously at home in Cuba, repatriated rather than expatriated from the somber cold of New England skies. The island's venereal soil and seductive climate, its aura of magic and mystery, were incarnate in Elvira. She was earth and sea, fire and air; she was moist with a fecundity beside which the girls he'd known in Boston seemed made of sand, corseted in the whalebone of barren proprieties. He'd begun to court the idea of staying in Cuba with Elvira as his wife and was seized by images of them living together in a bohío all their own, or in one of the pastel brick-and-plaster cottages in the center of town. They would eat arroz amarillo and frijoles negras and pollo arrosto in the shade of a porch or inner patio, and in the drowse of siesta, retire to the bedroom and make love till nightfall, while humid sea breezes blew through shuttered windows. They would get drunk on love. He felt drunk thinking about it. Savory creole dishes, the perfume of herbs, shuttered rooms, sultry air, bright sun, pagan spirits, Elvira's black eyes and lush brown flesh—it all blended in his mind into an intoxicating brew.

For three days, he walked to Rosaria's bohío for his herbal bath not because those immersions were doing any good beyond effecting a temporary respite from pain, but because it offered his only chance to be near Elvira. Her movements, as she changed his wraps, were a flowing of skin and muscle, and when she stood and the light, piercing the chinks in the walls, passed through her shift, the silhouette of her body was so erotic that he lost his breath. He yearned for her lips, her breasts, and to plunge so deeply into her that he would lose himself; but she was hardly ever out from under Rosaria's gaze. Evidently, there were proprieties in Cuba as stringent as those in Boston, but where the latter suppressed desire, the other inflamed it. It was exquisite torture to be close to her and not be able to touch her.

He practiced his Spanish, telling the two women about himself, describing Boston, relating his adventures and misadventures at sea, holding them spellbound with the story about the hurricane. By the third day, Elvira felt free enough to speak about herself and told him, there before the shrine to Babaluaye, amid the scents of sarsparilla, aloe, and sage, kneeling on the reed mat beside a headless dove whose blood had sanctified the herbs, that she was striving to be an iyawo of Babaluaye, a bride of the orisha; that is, she was in her novitiate as a priestess of santeria. Her mother, Mercedes, had died when she was thirteen; died of a broken heart because her father had given himself to another woman, that adulteress having been the insurrection against the Spanish. Her father, Tomas Casamayor, had been criollo, tall and fair, as fair as you, Will (it thrilled him to hear her speak his name), and her mother had been black and had died from longing for Tomas, ever absent in his devotions to the insurrection and José Marti. After a Spanish bullet found her father at Santiago and her mother died, Elvira was so grief stricken that she could not eat and would have starved herself to death if Rosaria had not healed her sorrow with her special cures. That was when Elvira became interested in the religion, but it had only been in the past year that she'd begun to study it seriously, learning the herbs by sight and name and use, along with the ancient chants that had crossed the seas on the slaving ships. She hoped soon to make her asienta, the ceremony of initiation, when the orisha of Babaluaye would be seated on her head.

Will was enchanted, thoroughly captivated, and so touched by the tale of her orphaning that he very nearly cried out, Marry me! Be my wife! I will take care of you forever!

On the next day in Rosaria's bohío—Eliot had taken to calling it the "witch doctor's clinic"—Elvira again stroked his ribs, boiled the herbs, and sang her songs of Africa, and Rosaria rectified each small mistake. The two women, as usual, turned their backs when Will stripped to get into the tub. While he soaked, Elvira spoke about a ceremony called quinces. Her father had died when she was fifteen, so she'd had no one to hold a quinces for her. There was only Tío Enrique, who had become her guardian, but he did not want to give her a quinces because it cost a lot of money. In time, however, Rosaria persuaded her husband to part with a few pesos and throw a party in honor of Elvira's womanhood. Rosaria had sewn her a new dress, people from all over town showed up, except the rich, of course, and there was music and dancing and feasting—plantanos and wine and porco arrosto marinated in the juice of the sour orange. And what was a quinces? Will wanted to know. From her description, he gathered that it was a kind of cotillion for Cuban girls who had reached the age of fifteen—hence its name—and its purpose was to declare that the girl was now eligible for marriage.

You must have had a thousand offers, said Will, leaping at the chance to flatter. She cast her eyes on the floor and shook her head. Then was it ten times a thousand? he asked, smiling to her back. She shook her head again. More still? A hundred times a thousand? A thousand thousand? Did all the young men in Cuba come to your door?

"Silencio, Will!" she burst out, daring in her anger to look at him. "Stop ridiculing me!"

Her expression was at once injured and furious, and the display of temper flummoxed him. "Lo siento, lo siento mucho," he said, assuring her that, far from ridicule, he had intended only to compliment her beauty.

"The truth is I did not receive one proposal," she said, with a ferocity that made him start. "Because of my uncle! He charges for everything, and he had his price for what my quinces cost him!"

Rosaria hissed, and her niece turned around and bowed her head, muttering that she was sorry, she had forgotten herself.

"My husband is very . . ." the old woman began, then paused, searching for the right word. "Protective. He is very protective of Elvira, and most of the young men in this neighborhood are afraid of him, even though he is a shrimp, let's face it. He is el jefe in this neighborhood. He sells lottery tickets and he blesses them, for the luck, comprende Usted? He runs the cockfights and he blesses the roosters, also for the luck, and if the rooster wins, he takes half the winnings."

"But why does that make the young men afraid?"

"My husband is what we call a father of the mystery, a high priest of the religion, a babalawo, but he . . ." Rosaria looked right and left, as if to make sure no one was eavesdropping. "The saints pardon me for saying this to a stranger, to a yanqui. He uses his powers sometimes for evil purposes. He has cursed people. He has caused, with his powers, sickness and death to those he calls his enemies. So the young men around here, knowing of his passion to protect Elvira, have been afraid to ask him for her hand."

Will had been clinging to the edge of an emotional cliff for four days. Now he let go.

"What if I were to ask him?" he said, amazed at himself for speaking so calmly, for feeling no nervousness or uncertainty. He'd never been so sure of anything in his life. "If it's agreeable to Elvira, I will ask him. I'm not afraid of him. I do not believe in curses or in any kind of black magic."

There was a prolonged silence, Rosaria and Elvira sitting as still as figures in a portrait, their backs to him.

"There are people who are not afraid of poisonous snakes, but that does not mean the snakes will not bite if they are stepped on," the old woman said finally.

"I'm not afraid of him," Will repeated, and his firmness and sincerity were not manufactured, not after all he had been through in the past two months. "I will ask him if Elvira wishes it. I am in love with her."

"That requires no saying. It has been obvious that you were stricken the moment you saw her. And she feels the same. Que es verdad, no, Elvira?"

He saw the slight shy movement of her head under the pale blue kerchief, and now his heart tumbled joyfully.

"Get out of the tub and dress," Rosaria commanded. "This is a time for you to have a cool head, even if the rest of you is not."

After he had dressed, the two women turned to him. Elvira smiled—the first smile he'd seen on her lips. Rosaria went to her canastillero and took a bundle of herbs, which she dipped into a pan of water on the cold hearth; then she soaked a cloth in the preparation.

"Kneel down," she said, beckoning Will to come forward.

He did, moving like a man under a spell, and the old santera began to wash his head with the cloth.

"You have very thick hair. I think it keeps your head too warm and causes confused thoughts. I'm purifying your head with omiera, because it must be kept cool and clear. I'm not sure it will work, I am not sure it is proper, because you are not a child of the spirits, but I am doing it anyway because it is necessary." After the bath, she filled a large seashell with clear water from a bucket and rinsed his head, singing in her high-pitched voice a long chant in the language called Lucumi. Will felt a little foolish, kneeling before this inscrutable woman, listening to her unintelligible prayers. If the Braithwaites walked in, they would think he'd lost his mind, and, he reflected, they probably would be right.

"I have just sung the rogación de la cabeza. I have prayed over your head to Oshun. She is a beautiful orisha, the spirit of cool, fresh waters and clear thinking. Maybe it will work on you." She took her footstool, occupying it as if it were a throne. "All right, sit down. Escúchame. Whether you fear or do not fear my husband makes no difference. You may ask him for permission to marry Elvira, but he will not give it. Never. And because he stands for her father, there is no priest here in Cárdenas who would perform the ceremony."

"You are saying it's hopeless."

"Escúchame, Will. I saw my cousin yesterday. He agrees to take you and your friends to Havana without charge as soon as he has enough coconuts to sell in the market. He thinks he will be ready to sail in two days' time. When he is, he will tell me and then I will tell you. Now for the thing you must do in return, the pleasant duty. You will take Elvira to Havana with you."

Will did not say anything. Elvira had contrived an expression as impenetrable as the shutters on the window, but her composure, her lack of surprise, told him that she and her madrina must have hatched the scheme in concert. His mind shot back to Talmadge and Clara. There was a weird symmetry between what that addled man had asked him to do and what this woman was asking, the difference being that Will was now more than ready to agree.

"But how can you allow her . . ." he began. "If we aren't man and wife . . ."

"You are going to watch over her as if you were her husband, but you will not be permitted to take a husband's privileges. Comprende? I think you can be trusted to behave honorably, and"—with a twinkle— "my cousin's boat has nowhere to be private, and so there will be no temptation to behave dishonorably. For you or her."

Elvira's mask broke, her cheeks flushed, and Will felt a fever in his.

"I will have to speak to my friends first," he said. "I have to ask if they agree to this arrangement."

"Por qué?"—sharply.

"Porque ellos son mis amigos. En inglés, 'shipmates.' Amigos de la barca. Entiende?"

She nodded gravely and said, "Escúchame. It has been necessary for some time for my niece and goddaughter to leave here, but that has not been possible because of my husband. I could not very well send her away alone, a single girl of eighteen, without a man's protection. And there is no man here willing to be her protector because their fear of my husband's revenge is stronger than their desire for her. Do you know what I am telling you? Lo siento, I must speak brutally. Your friends have no choice in this matter. If Elvira cannot sail with you, then I will tell my cousin that he sails without any of you."

"Entiendo," said Will. "May I ask why it is necessary for her to leave?"

In an exchange of glances, some encrypted message passed between the two women.

"Because it's necessary for her to make her asienta, which is not possible here for reasons that are complicated," Rosaria answered. "I know of a woman in Havana, a woman of quality, one of the gente de color, who is also a great santera, a sister of Oshun and Babaluaye. One of the sisters here is composing a letter of introduction to her for Elvira. I myself cannot write. This woman in Havana will be Elvira's new madrina and Elvira will continue under her." The old woman paused. "I am going to say in this letter that if you and Elvira wish to marry, you will have my blessings. The new madrina and her husband will then act as Elvira's family. They will arrange for a priest. . . ."

"Un padre Católico?"

"Por supuesto."

"No soy Católico."

"Do not worry. Sometimes priests can be persuaded to look the other way if there is something in it for them. Now listen to me very carefully. When Elvira makes her asienta, the orisha descends and mounts her. She becomes his bride for one year. Understand? The act of love will be forbidden between Elvira and a man, even if he is her husband, for one year. Do you think you love her enough to do that, Will?"

He did not answer. He had not expected anything like this.

"Yes, we will see how much love you have," Rosaria stated with a tight, wry smile. "Better think it over with a cold head."

"I think I could. . . . Yes, I could. . . ."

"We will see. Now, go and talk to your amigos de la barca, but I advise you to tell them what I told Luis. As little as necessary."

Will looked at her.

"He doesn't know that Elvira is going without my husband's knowledge or approval."

"But should he not know? What if he sees Tío Enrique and says that he is taking Elvira, then . . . ?"

"Leave that to me. I leave your friends to you."

He told them, in fact, next to nothing, saying only that Elvira was sailing to Havana with her godmother's cousin and that they would be joining her as fellow passengers. Put that way, the arrangement met with the Braithwaites' approval. They were all three so impatient to get out of Cárdenas, they probably would have agreed to anything.

Later, the two women appeared to cook la comida, as they had every evening. The bohío was again redolent with the aromas of green pepper and onion and garlic sautéing in an iron skillet, and the boys gorged on plantains and rice and a spicy shredded beef called ropa vieja. While strong coffee brewed in a small octagonal pot, Rosaria told Will that Luis Figueroa planned to sail earlier than expected, with tomorrow evening's tide.

"Here is what will happen," she continued. "Tomorrow afternoon, I am going to tell my husband that Elvira and I are going to gather herbs.

We will be waiting at a place on the beach beyond town. Luis knows about it. You will go to the harbor later on and board his boat and he will sail to where Elvira and I are waiting, and then she will join you, and then I, for the first time in many years, since her mother died, I will walk home without Elvira."

"And that makes you sad?"

"Both sad and happy," she replied. "Luis said the tide is at five o'clock. He asks that you be at his boat before then. It is called *La Esperanza.*"

They drank the bitter coffee from demitasses, the two women joining them, and when the pot was drained, Rosaria went outside to relieve herself. Elvira sprang from her chair and began to clear the table, carrying the cups and saucers to the washtub. One cup dropped and broke against the dirt floor, which was trod to the hardness of stone. Will went to help her clean it up, but she waved him away, stooped, and with one hand, swept the fragments into the other.

"You seem nervous," he said, stooping beside her.

"Of course I am. You would be, too, if you were in my position."

"There's nothing to be afraid of."

"Yes, there is."

"This morning, when Rosaria asked if it was true you loved me, you moved your head to say yes. Can you say that now with your lips? I want to hear it. I want to hear you say, Will, sangre de mi corazón, me encantas, te quiero, te amo."

"Please, this is not a love song we are living. This is not an adventure. Be serious."

"I am."

"One hour from now I must go to the woman's house to pick up the letter," she whispered, with an agitated glance at the door. "Please go to the bohío where you take your baths. I have something to tell you. Now, go sit with your friends and don't speak to me."

Slipping in the mud of the afternoon's rain, Will walked to the bohío with the feeling that he was no longer in possession of himself, nor in command of events. The sensation reminded him of the moment when *Double Eagle* lost her rudder, and he and Drew found themselves piloting a piece of driftwood, helpless in the waves and currents. There was one big difference, though: The powerlessness he felt now thrilled as it frightened, and to the romance of that delightful terror, the glamour of intrigue had been added. Tomorrow's departure would have the elements of an elopement, or an abduction, although he could not say for sure who was being abducted, Elvira or him. If he married her, he would be turning his back on his family, his friends, and the whole world he had known. Banned in Boston, he thought, with silent laughter. Yes, Elvira Terhune would be banned in Boston, and probably in New York and Chicago and Philadelphia as well, certainly in any city in the South, with the possible exception of New Orleans. Maybe they could live there one day; if not, then he would have no choice but to remain in Havana. He had a dim awareness that closing off his avenues of retreat had something to do with his desire for her, that her magnetism was seated as much in her taboo as in her beauty. If Willard Terhune had been older and more experienced, he might have summoned this foggy perception into the full light of his consciousness and questioned the authenticity and purity of his passion. He might have seen that what he sought from this alluring and exotic bird was not her heart but her wings, to bear him aloft in flight from the ordinary. He might have paused to ask himself what it would be like to live with her day after day, in a self-imposed exile, and what would happen to his passion once the extraordinary became ordinary, the exotic familiar, and all the abrasive cares and vexations of wedded life, which are as universal as love itself, began to wear on his idyll.

The bohío's door was closed. It was very dark inside, except for a leaning pillar of moonlight that fell through a vent between the roof and one of the peaked side walls. He heard Elvira ask, in a tense whisper, if it was he. He answered that it was, and with a low laugh, said he could not see her.

"Shhhhh!" she scolded. "Ven aquí, Will."

He walked toward her voice and, his vision adjusting, saw her white shift in the darkness. Legs tucked beneath her, she was sitting on the reed mat in front of the altar shared by Christ and the orisha Babaluaye. He sat beside her, leaving a discreet distance between them but close enough to smell her: a female musk mingled with a scent like his when he came out of the herbal baths.

"Do your friends know you're with me?"

"I told them I was taking a walk, but I am not sure they believed me. What about Rosaria and your uncle?"

"They think I am with Lydia, the woman who is writing the letter, but I cannot be delayed too long."

"Then what is it you have to tell me?"

"Three things," said Elvira Casamayor, and then fell silent. His eyes were accustomed to the blackness now and he could see her more clearly, sitting back on her heels, her hands cupping her knees, her gaze not on him but on the slant of moonlight. "No soy virgen," she began, matter-of-factly. "I wish you to know that. I don't know if that's important in North America. It is here."

"Está no importante para me," he declared, not sure if he had said it correctly. "No soy virgen también," he added, attempting a light-hearted tone.

"Of course you're not. You're a man. Don't make jokes. I have heard it said about you yanquis that you are always making jokes. I think that is so because you yanquis are rich and do not see that most things end badly."

"Things can end badly, even for the rich," he said. "And the second thing?"

"What you wish me to tell you, but not because you wish it, not to please you. Pero porque es verdad. Te quiero, te amo."

"It pleases me even if that's not why you said it. I have never felt so pleased. And I am not making a joke. Tell me the third thing."

"What my madrina told you is true. When I make asienta, I am mounted by the orisha. He enters me. Not my body but my spirit. He becomes my husband, and I must be faithful to him for one year. And I will be. It is very important to me to become a santera. To be a santera is to have respect, honor."

"Sí. Entiendo."

"You say you do, but you don't. You understand only the words. Listen. I do not know how long it will be before I become asientada, but I do not think very long. If you and I are married, that will be a torment, no?"

He nodded, and yet—maybe he *was* losing his mind—the torment appealed to him. To be sanctioned to love her and prohibited from it at the same time cast a powerful spell over him—the aphrodisiac of piety and devotion and an abstinence constantly at war with desire.

"Now listen some more. Lydia is a sister of Oshun. When I was with her, I confessed what was in my heart and asked her to seek the orisha's counsel. She came here with me a little while ago and threw the oleinus and said the mayuba, the prayer, and . . . Will, strike a match, look at the mat beside me, and tell me what you see."

He lit a match, its flare illuminating her face, glistening with sweat, and the pieces of a quartered coconut, all lying with the pulp side up.

"No entiendo," he said, waving his hand to extinguish the match.

"The oleinus landed with the white side up. Alafia. That means yes in the old language. Oshun will bless us. Sangre de mi corazón. Sangre de mi sangre. Sangre de Usted, mi sangre. Uno," Elvira said. While her expression was indistinct, he somehow sensed that it was the same one he had seen on her face the first day—intense, sagacious, leaving him with no refuge for his secrets even while it guarded all of hers. "Oshun consents that we can make each other man and wife without the priest," she went on, in a tremulous whisper. "We do not need the priest now. The priest can come later."

He felt like he was drowning. She straightened to her knees and, raising her arms overhead, pulled off her shift.

"Oh, my Christ," he murmured in English. She wore only the bead necklace from which the small gold amulet hung between her breasts. He cupped them, tentatively at first, then took her nipples into his mouth. She drew in a breath, sharply, quickly, through clenched teeth and, taking his chin in her hand, lifted his face and kissed him while she unbuttoned his shirt without looking at it. No, she was no virgin.

He kicked off his shoes, fumbled with his belt, tore off his trousers, and they fell on the mat together, lying on their sides, her legs crossed over his, his arms around the small of her back, their tongues flicking inside each other's mouths. She took the core of him in one hand; it was as if he had no flesh there, every nerve and vessel laid bare, and he softly pushed her away, fearful that he would burst instantly. He caressed her buttocks, the smooth mound of her belly, and touched the damp, fervid bristle between her thighs, piercing her with his finger.

Suddenly, she stiffened, clutched his wrists, pulled him out of her.

"What's the matter?" he asked, choking. "Should I stop?"

"Lo siento. It's difficult for me."

"Should I stop?"

"No. Por todos los santos, no."

He thought of the little moves and tricks he had learned in brothels, but those seemed out of place now, the techniques of love without its substance. Abandoning himself to instinct, he touched and fondled and kissed her, and then, prying her thighs apart with his face, licked the lips of her sex, breathing in the odor of seabottom, fetid and fragrant, salty and sweet. She stiffened again.

"Should I stop?"

"No."

He kissed her all the way up to her neck, biting the necklace beads. She moved under him, thrusting her hips, and pressing her lips to his ear, cautioned him not to make a sound.

"Now you must mount me before the orisha. You will be my first husband, he the second. Now," Elvira said, and turned over onto her belly. Lying with her face on the mat, her hands clasped over the back of her neck, she heaved up on her knees to present her bottom. He kneeled behind her—it seemed fitting to kneel, for this that they were doing seemed sacred—and he gloried in the graceful arch of her back joined to her broad buttocks, shaped like a heart, spread in invitation. He entered her gently, but her body tightened once again, and he held himself for a moment, until she, reaching behind with one hand, shoved him into herself greedily. She was scalding inside—a shaft lined with hot, wet satin. He thrust once and again, burying himself, while his arms enfolded her waist. She hissed, pulled away from him, shoved back, her buttocks writhing against his groin, both of them drenched in a warm, thick dew. Now his hands fell to the floor below her ribs, and they moved for several seconds like stallion and mare, Elvira biting down on the mat to stifle her cries, Will moaning, his jaw clenched as, with exquisite agony, in wild spasms, he filled her with his seed.

They lay for longer than wisdom dictated, bathed in each other's sweat, gasping softly, neither speaking, beneath the little house in which the ashe of the spirits dwelled, beneath the statue of Christ gazing toward the ceiling with his plaster eyes, his plaster heart dripping plaster blood. Then Elvira rolled over onto her side and embraced and kissed Will.

"Otro vez?" he asked, with pleading in his voice.

"No. It is late. When we get to Havana, then as many times as you wish, but not now, no, not now. . . ."

She began to cry, softly.

"What is it?" he asked.

"Tío Enrique will be expecting me by this time, and I'm afraid of him, like everyone else," she said. Abruptly, she got up and pulled her shift over her head, patted her hair, smoothed the dress. "I am afraid for myself and for Rosaria." Elvira had fought back her tears, and her voice had grown cold and distant. "Tomorrow, when she returns home, she is going to tell Tío that I ran away with you, which will be true. I don't know how she will explain how she allowed it to happen. I am afraid that he will suspect she had a hand in it and will do something bad to her." Elvira paused. "Unless she does something bad to him first. She knows some of the things he knows. Maybe she will poison him. I think she should. I hate him."

Hearing this spoken with such venom, after the warmth of love, was a little shocking to Will.

"You hate him that much? Why?"

She shook her head.

"Por qué? Por qué?"

"This"—touching the amulet—"was given to me by Rosaria to protect against evil, but Tío Enrique's evil is stronger than it. . . ." The icy composure that had fallen on her so swiftly now shattered, and she started to cry again, not as before but in a hoarse clutching of breath.

He stood and held her close, and despite her height, she felt very small.

"What is it? What is wrong, Elvira?"

She uttered a few disconnected words—Should have . . . A fourth thing . . . Lo siento, should have . . .

"What?" he pleaded. "What fourth thing? Should have what?"

She repeated that it was late and told him to go back to his friends, but he sensed that she had said this only for the form of it.

"Not until you tell me what's the matter," he said.

She broke from his arms, dried her eyes with the backs of her hands, and turned away.

"Do you think I found pleasure in what we just did?" Elvira asked, in a voice grown cold again. It appeared that her emotional climate was subject to sudden and dramatic changes.

"If you didn't, then you will become rich as an actress."

"Not an actress. Puta. I pretended, como una puta, because maybe that is what I am. The act of love is painful for me. Sometimes it disgusts me, but I pretended to find pleasure, because I know how to pretend. I pretended but not to deceive you, oh, no, my Will, mi corazón, not you, because I do love you. To deceive myself."

Elvira spun around to face him, and what she said next was spoken in a Spanish so highly nuanced that its meaning escaped him entirely.

"You are used, as was young Rosaria?" he said, repeating the phrase as he'd heard it. "That makes no sense."

"Escúchame. I am used *as* Rosaria was when she was young. That is what I said." As Will took a moment to translate these words into English, she added in an undertone, in a whisper's whisper, "By him. By Tío Enrique."

There was a lag of several seconds between her utterance and his comprehension, and then Willard Terhune's façade of worldliness crumbled, as false things do when put to the test. He had heard of such things, in the brothels, in conversations within the protective walls of Yale dormitories, but they occupied the same place in his mind as tales of gruesome murders, as newspaper reports about conditions in the slums or wars in distant countries. He could not fully grasp the abomination just described, though its victim stood before him, breathing into his face.

"That was the price for my quinces," Elvira carried on, in a voice so subdued Will had to move closer to hear. "It happened that very night. The party was held in the cabildo Tío Enrique belongs to in Cárdenas. When it was over, he asked me to stay, because he said he had a special present for me, a dress prettier than the one Rosaria had made for me. He took me into a room in the back and told me to take off Rosaria's dress, and then he went out. I tell you, I was scared, I knew something was not right, but I did not know what until Tío Enrique returned, with no clothes on. He locked the door and told me not to make a sound and said he had had his eye on me since I was thirteen. And then he said to me, 'But now you are fifteen, you are old enough to bleed, you are old enough to cut.' I fought him, believe me, I did. Even then, I was tall and strong. But Tío is strong for a small man. He did, you know, pelote, for money when he was a young man. He knew how to hit, and he hit me, and then he took me like a wild beast, as I had you take me tonight, because I thought that if a man I loved could have me like that but with love, with sweetness, with tenderness, then perhaps . . . But it felt the same as with him. Lo siento, it did. Not because of you, O my Will. Because of him. For three years now, he has me whenever it comes upon him. He's ruined me. So you see, he is not protective of me, as my madrina lied to you. He is jealous. So you see, if I made my asienta here, it would be impossible for me to keep my vows."

Will did not say anything, because there was nothing to say.

"I have never given him my consent," she said into that stony silence. "Not once. Believe me, Will. You must believe me."

He did and he did not. He believed her with his mind, but in the depths of his heart lurked a small suspicion that she must have, at one time or another.

"And Rosaria?" he asked.

"For a long time, she pretended not to know, but it is a very great effort, pretending all the time. Now this chance has come. To send me to Havana. She is sending me for my sake, but for hers, too."

She kissed him chastely on the forehead and asked, with a plaintiveness that broke his heart, if she would still see him tomorrow. Of course, he answered. Certamente.

"We must leave the way we came," she said. "I will wait here a moment."

Will went out with his thoughts and feelings in a riot. As he opened the gate to the yard, a fleeting shadow appeared in his peripheral vision and he heard someone or something rustling the bushes behind the bohío. He walked toward the sound, fearful that he and Elvira had been spied on. A snuffling noise came from a tangle of shrubs beneath a poinciana, and in a moment, a pig waddled out of the pool of blackness created by the spreading tree.

He threw a rock at the animal, only to vent his emotions on something, and walked on down the lane, its beige dust blanched by the half-moon. He tried to quell the melee in his mind, with little success. Thinking about what Tío Enrique had done, Will, who had always sought to avoid violence, considered taking the shotgun and blowing the bastard's head off. An instant later, his rage turned on Elvira, for waiting until after they had made love to reveal her secret—a timing he felt sure had been calculated. Images of her in her uncle's embrace swooped past his mind's eye, like the bats and night birds swooping past the eyes in his head, images that heightened his fury, excited both pity and revulsion, and perversely aroused him, so that he was almost as appalled with himself as he was with the man who had raped his own kin. He could not rid himself of the suspicion that Elvira, sometime after the first rape, had become a willing participant—a suspicion he knew to be cruel and unjust yet one that possessed an existence beyond the governance of his reason. He was angered as well by Rosaria's duplicity. He could not blame her for using him to further her plan to end her own humiliation and to spare her niece further degradation, but that understanding did not prevent him from feeling used. Now that he knew the truth, he had every right to back out, but he knew he wasn't going to. The truth made it all the more imperative for him to play his part in Elvira's salvation. It just might be the first truly brave and honorable thing he had done in his life.

When he came to the shack where he was staying with the Braithwaites, he had achieved some measure of that coolheadedness the old woman said he would need. In most cases, love and duty were in conflict, but in this one they were allies. He would do what love demanded, and he would conceal his knowledge from his shipmates, certain of what their reaction would be if he did not. So he guessed he was not without a capacity for duplicity himself and felt a little like a traitor as he entered the bedroom, where Eliot and Drew were asleep while Nat lay awake on the floor.

"That was sure a long walk, Will," he said quietly.

"A lot longer than you can imagine," Will muttered, and lay down on his bed, wishing he were at sea with his sextant, amid the certitudes of angles and degrees of arc and the fixed and steadfast stars. All night, the palm fronds scraped in the wind.

25

La Esperanza was a strongly built boat of some thirty-two feet, single-masted, and so beamy that she was almost round—a true tub. She had a cramped cuddy forward, where her skipper slept, a long tiller pinned through the head of a massive rudder, and a cargo hatch amidships, immediately abaft the mast. Into this opening, roughly the size of a storm cellar's door, Will and the Braithwaites dumped coconuts from high-sided handcarts. Luis Figueroa wasn't charging them for their passage, but he was making them work for it. He lay below, distributing his cargo evenly in the hold.

"Más rapido!" he commanded, poking his head out of the hatch. He was a tall, brown-skinned man with a flat nose and brows that perpetually scowled, as if he were plagued by some persistent worry. "The tide makes in half an hour."

Will translated for his shipmates, then they pushed their empty carts down the sagging, guano-spattered wharf to the quay, where the coconuts were stacked in pyramids. Twenty minutes later, while Nat and Eliot were helping Luis make ready to cast off, Will and Drew filled a cart with the last load. The labor caused Will's ribs to throb again, and he grimaced each time he stooped to toss a coconut into the cart.

"Y'know, this whole operation would've gone a heck of a lot faster with a derrick and a cargo net," said Drew.

"Well, why don't you bring that up to Luis? I'm sure he'll be impressed with your engineering genius."

"What's gotten into you?"—Drew, frowning. "You've been mean as a snake all day. You sound like Nat when he's in a bad mood."

"Hurting again," said Will, pointing to his side. "And the heat," he added, indicating the dried sweat that made white rings on his dark jersey. "Sorry."

"Nat says you're all flummoxed by that colored girl."

"Her name's Elvira."

Drew dumped the last armload into the cart.

"You're not really sweet on her, are you, Will?"

"No, I'm in love with her."

Drew blinked.

"How could you be? We haven't been here a week. You must be crazy."

"That's possible. How about you push this thing back to the boat. My side aches like hell."

Drew got behind the cart and wheeled it along the wharf, Will following.

"Ohe! Yanqui!"

Turning, he saw Francisco calling from the quay behind him. Misbehaving locks of his curly hair tumbled across his forehead and an unlit cigarette dangled from a corner of his mouth, so that he looked one part urchin and one part waterfront ruffian.

"I came down here to say goodbye, tú sabes? I heard you're leaving for Havana today," he said, starting toward Will.

"And how did you know that?" asked Will, walking to meet him.

Francisco stuck the cigarette behind his ear and shrugged casually, but there was something in his manner that suggested nervousness or fear. Will noticed a welt under his right eye, and he was sweating heavily and breathing hard, though that might have resulted from running all the way to the harbor.

"How stands everything, Francisco?" Will asked, probing circumspectly. "Sta bien?"

"Bien. Except we have not seen my sister all day. My uncle is looking for her right now. Know where she is?"

His heart flipping, Will affected a look of indifference and shook his head.

"Oh, sure, how would you know?" Francisco half turned to glance briefly at one of the large carriages called volantes as it rattled down the quayside street, through the long afternoon shadows cast by the trees and buildings lining the waterfront. "But listen, Tío Enrique, he felt bad that he did not find you a boat for your dollar," he said. "So he bought you a present with it for your voyage, tu sabe? And he sent me down here and said to make sure I gave it to you before you left." Francisco pulled a package of Duke's from his shirt pocket and, with a tight smile, handed it to Will. "They were difficult to find, but Tío found them. I stole one," the boy confessed, gesturing at his ear. "Lo siento, I could not resist. They are rare."

"Keep it," Will said, and then, feeling he could not accept anything from a man like Tío Enrique, stuffed the package back into Francisco's pocket. "Keep them all. I've quit smoking."

The boy tucked in his chin and glanced down at the cigarettes, befuddled. He removed the package and again pressed it on Will.

"Por favor . . . Tío, he will be . . . If I take the gift he meant for you . . . He'll be angry with me."

"Oh, all right," Will said in English. He pocketed the Duke's and held out his hand. "Gracias. Hasta luego, Francisco."

"Hasta luego. . . . Oh . . . y tome está también," the boy said, reaching into his back pocket with his left hand while his right clasped Will's.

Will heard a distinct, metallic click and felt a sharp pricking in his belly, but did not see Francisco's hand move because it moved too fast to see, fast as a snake striking, a split-second thrust and withdrawal. "Esto es de mi tío y mi, por singarla, cabrón," he spat, and then bolted to the quay and vanished behind the stalls of a fish market, all in no more than five seconds.

Staring stupidly at the stalls and the blue and yellow buildings across the street, Will would not have known that anything had happened to him if it weren't for the blot spreading over his shirt and the warm, sticky flow of blood down his trousers. The blade had been so thin and keen and pulled out so deftly that he barely felt it pierce him just above his belt buckle. There had been only that pricking, like a wasp's sting. A peculiar, detached calm flowed over him, and he unbuttoned his shirt and wiped the blood from his abdomen with his bandanna, revealing a puncture no larger than his navel running alongside it a fraction of an inch away. The smallness of the wound led him to believe, or hope, that he had not been injured too seriously. Thinking of Francisco's parting words, he suspected that a lower part of his anatomy had been the target, but the boy, in his fear, had struck too high.

Will staunched the bleeding with the bandanna, buttoned his shirt, and hitched his trousers up an inch, tightening his belt over the bulge made by the bandanna. Walking toward the boat, he felt the first waves of pain and forced himself to climb the gangplank with as normal a stride as he could manage. He made a credible show of helping Luis pull it aboard and of giving Drew a hand, casting off the stern line while Nat and Eliot handled the bowline. The cumbersome craft, under a huge triangular mainsail, eased away from the wharf.

"Yahoo!" said Eliot. "We're bound for being homeward bound."

Will faked a smile. It was essential to hide his injury from his shipmates, who, bless them, would insist that Luis return to shore and fetch a doctor. Then would come the complicated business of explaining who had stabbed him. . . . Police would be summoned. . . . Luis would be held back from sailing, he and the Braithwaites questioned about what they had seen, giving Tío Enrique plenty of time to find Elvira. A lucky thing Will had worn his navy-blue jersey and denim trousers today; the bloodstains were almost indistinguishable from sweat stains. It was also lucky, if he had to be stabbed, that he'd been stabbed with a stiletto instead of, say, a kitchen knife; the puncture wasn't a great deal larger than an ice pick would have made, and his bandanna would stem the bleeding for a while, for long enough, he hoped, to get Elvira aboard and make course for Havana. But the natural reactions of his body threatened to undo the camouflage of his clothing; as the boat, trailing a small tender, lumbered across Cárdenas's filthy harbor, Drew remarked to Will that he looked unnaturally pale. Was he all right?

"Ribs," he said. "Loading the boat . . . I'm going to lie down in the cuddy for a bit. I'll be okay in a jiffy."

He looked to Luis, clutching the tree trunk of a tiller, and asked permission to use his bunk. The big trader nodded, and Will went forward, gritting his teeth as a honed needle jabbed his guts, through and through.

The windowless cuddy had the distressing size and feel of a burial vault. Will stretched out in the hot enclosure on a moldy straw-tick mattress. He would be better off prone—blood less likely to run out of the wound. A cockroach darted across the floor, paused to test the air with its feelers, and then slipped into a crack in a vanishing that was the next thing to a dematerialization. Another scampered across Will's leg. He whisked it off, listened to the welcome sound of water moving under a keel, and felt the old, familiar motions of a vessel under way. Then he arched his back against another jab, sharper and more sustained. Son of a bitch. Must think about something else, he said to himself, something that requires concentration. Will Terhune, his hands folded tightly over the bandanna under his shirt, tried to assemble a plausible narrative explaining how Francisco and Tío Enrique had found out and when. How much did they find out? he asked himself. Only that I slept with Elvira, or do they also know that we're smuggling her to Havana? If Tío Enrique knows that, then Rosaria had better come with us, because things will go very badly for her. She was right. Must think with a cold head. Not that it made any difference now, but tracing a hypothetical chain of conscious action linked to random accident helped Will detach his mind from his body's suffering.

There is no such thing as luck, Rosaria claimed. Well, sorry, old woman, there is, thought Will, and what happened to me was bad luck. If Francisco had arrived at the harbor five or ten minutes later, I would have been gone; if Nat had been loading the last cart with Drew instead of me, Francisco would have had to board the boat to get near me, and I doubt he would have had the nerve.

He began to feel a drowsiness induced as much by the heat inside the cuddy as by loss of blood. Maybe it would be better to lie down on deck in the open air. No. Too much risk that his condition would be discovered, and the boat had not yet cleared the harbor. Will touched the bandanna gently. It was wet but not soaked clear through. He wasn't bleeding too badly, at least on the outside. But how long could he last without medical attention? A two-day sail to Havana, possibly three. He could endure that long, surely he could; he was twenty years old and in otherwise strong condition. There had to be plenty of doctors in Havana, maybe even an American army doctor, skilled in treating battle wounds. Sure. A U.S. army surgeon would sew him up, and when he was well enough, he would marry Elvira and they would eat lunch on an inner patio and then make love in a shuttered room.

"Say, Will, how are you feeling?"

It was Nat, squatting down in the low hatchway to the cuddy.

"All right."

"Drew said it was your ribs again."

"Yeah. Not bad. Need a little sleep. Didn't get much last night," Will said, and that was true as far as it went.

"Sure you're okay to make the trip?"

"Yeah. Let me get some sleep, Natters."

And trusting that he had done a good job of mimicking a man suffering nothing more than a cracked rib or two, Will Terhune shut his eyes.

Voices awakened him less than an hour later; Luis's voice and the voice he longed to hear more than any other. Dónde está el otro señor? he heard Elvira ask, and Luis grumble in reply that el otro was asleep in the cabin; he had injured himself loading cargo because, no doubt, he was a soft one, unaccustomed to man's work.

Gathering his strength, Will pushed himself up, bumping his head against the ceiling. In a moment, Elvira came through the hatch and crouched beside him in the narrow space between the bunk and the opposite wall. Her white shift hung in folds; the loose neckline fell away, exposing her breasts and allowing her scent to flood over him. Uttering his name and not a word more, she clasped the back of his head and kissed him fervently on the cheeks, the chin, the nose, eyebrows, lips.

This was indiscreet of her; Luis did not know that they were lovers. Elvira's tongue sought his and savored the taste of him. "If there was room in here, I would throw myself on top of you right now!" she whispered.

"Do not. Please, do not," Will said.

She kissed him again. Mistaking his lack of ardor, she drew back and looked at him questioningly. He forced a smile and assured her that his feelings had not changed because of what she had told him; no, it was because his side was hurting again that his kisses were not equal to hers.

"Luis said that—" she began.

"Never mind Luis right now," Will interrupted. "You are here. You are safe."

"I had expected you to come for me in the little boat," she said. "I had hoped it would be you, mi corazón. That would have been very romantic."

"I would have, except for—" He could not finish: Another bolt of pain branched from his abdomen down into his groin, up into his chest.

"Does it hurt that much?" she asked.

As she reached across him to touch his side, her bare arm rested on his stomach. He flinched and she, feeling the wetness on her arm, slipped a finger between his shirt buttons and then put the finger to her tongue. Her dark brows pursing, she opened his shirt and removed the bandanna and looked with alarm at the wound, the dried blood smearing his belly.

"Madre de Cristo!" she hissed. "It looks like—What happened?"

He did not answer. She raised her eyes to his face; those black eyes so full of comprehension that it seemed almost unnecessary to explain what had happened, and why.

"Will, this did not happen loading the boat."

"What we did last night," he started, but the pain was now like hot coals in his guts. He took a breath. "A beautiful thing . . . but . . . not intelligent . . . Francisco saw . . . I think maybe he was sent looking for you because you were late . . . and this afternoon . . . at the wharf . . . Francisco . . . knife . . . ."

"What? What did you say?"

"Francisco stabbed me."

"Francisco?" she cried. "He did this? Francisco? Mi hermano? Imposible!"

Will repeated, "Francisco," thinking that in a way his wound had been self-inflicted.

Elvira, silent, stared at the puncture again before covering it with the bandanna and refastening the buttons.

"No mi hermano," she murmured. "Mi tío. Francisco held the knife, but that cabrón, that shit eater who calls himself my mother's brother, that pig who would have stuck his curo into his own mother's cunt, he put my brother up to it. Oh, I know it was him. . . ."

"Calm yourself," said Will, as impressed with her rage as with her profane vocabulary. "I think you're right, but Francisco could not have told him last night. . . . He—Tío—he would have beaten you then and come after me. No, I think Francisco did not know what to do at first. But then, today sometime, maybe after you and Rosaria left . . . maybe then he told Tío. . . . And then Tío hit him for not talking sooner. . . . Tío must have said to him if he was to be a man, then he must avenge your honor. . . ."

"My honor!" She practically shrieked with laughter.

"Say nothing. . . . My friends . . . make Luis go back to Cárdenas . . . doctor . . . cannot go back there . . . Tío . . . looking for you . . . must pretend some more, Elvira, until we're far away . . . only my side, say that . . . Comprende?"

"Sí, sí. Comprendo. I have some herbs in my bag. They will help until we get to Havana. Ah, Will, my Will . . ." She took his face in her hands and kissed him once more. "I will take care of you, but dica mi, why is it that good things must always end badly?"

"This . . . not ended yet. Let us see how it ends."

She prepared some kind of poultice, a sack of ground herbs that she laid over the wound. It would draw out the poisons, she said, and then, reaching into the straw bag that contained the letter and all she owned, took her one spare dress and tore it into strips for bandages. She tied one over the poultice and around his stomach, singing a Lucumi chant, which drew the Braithwaites to the cuddy.

"Will? Will?" asked Nat, outside. "What the hell's going on in there?"

It was dusk now, and the cuddy was so small that Elvira, with her back to the hatchway, blocked all view of its interior.

Will put on as ordinary a voice as possible.

"Under excellent care, Natters."

"What's all that weird singing?"

"Eliot . . . Ask him. . . ."

"It's witch-doctor stuff," he heard Eliot tell his older brother. "But I guess it works. My hand's better, anyhow."

Will suspected that that was due to the natural process of healing and not to the influence of African spirits. If those orishas had curative powers, they were probably reserved for people who believed in them, not for Eliot Braithwaithe, a white Congregationalist from Boston, or for Will Terhune, a white Episcopalian from Boston.

Elvira finished, laid a damp cloth over his forehead, and withdrew, kissing him lightly on the mouth.

"I will pray for you," she said in an undertone, and, as if to make sure she had all the bases covered, made the sign of the cross.

Alone in the blackness, Will called upon his own God to lend a hand, reciting the Lord's Prayer silently. He'd almost forgotten the words, and he feared the Deity was a bit upset with him for not having kept holy the Sabbath Day for several years, for failing to honor his father and mother, and most of all, for repeated fornications. Yet, a merciful God surely would forgive him those and other trespasses and not allow him to die. The thought of death had not occurred to him until now; it had come with nightfall, it was in the cuddy with him, but he could not imagine or accept that the treasury of his future, which had seemed inexhaustible when this day began, was now drawn down to a few hours or less. Drawn down, moreover, by an addled Cuban kid avenging his sister's loss of a chastity she had not possessed in the first place. It could not be, it must not be, that Will would lose his life for that, for an illusion, while the man who had stolen Elvira's honor in the most brutal way possible went on living. That was too unjust to contemplate; worse than unjust, it was ridiculous.

As these reflections tumbled through Will's head, the pain in his middle parts climbed up and up the scale. It reminded him of the hurricane; just when he was sure it could get no worse, it got worse. Finally, he felt as if someone were tearing his entrails out, and he clenched his teeth until he thought he would grind them to powder. Then he opened his jaws wide and screamed.

There came the sound of footfalls on deck, and of voices. Nat's voice, Eliot's, Drew's, Elvira's . . . "Will, what is it?" . . . "Let's see what's wrong." . . . "Get him out of that sweatbox." . . . "Fresh air." . . .

Someone took him by the ankles, someone else crawled inside and lifted him off the bunk. He was dragged outside under the mainsail, and he screamed again from the rough handling.

"Will, what happened? Was it a nightmare? Say something."

It was Nat. His eyes shut from pain, Will said, "Cold," for he was, suddenly.

"Cold?" asked Nat. "It's hot as blazes tonight."

Opening his eyes, he saw Elvira, kneeling over him.

"Frío," he said to her. "Soy frío."

She got up. He heard her muttering to Luis. Soon, she returned and laid something over him, something heavy and stiff—a sailcloth. Looking past her face, toward the zenith of the sky, he noticed a bright star. Which one was it?

"Will, c'mon. Tell us what it is?"

Nat again, kneeling beside Elvira.

"Hurt," Will said.

"Where?" asked Nat, sounding panicky. "What does?"

Will laid a hand over his stomach and tugged at the sailcloth, but he didn't have the strength to remove it. Better tell them now, while I can, he thought.

"Francisco," he said. "Francisco . . . stabbed . . ."

"*What?*"

Someone pulled the sailcloth off, Elvira maybe. . . . It was hard to see in the dark. He felt her fingers, fumbling with his shirt, and then heard Nat exclaim, "Oh, Jesus Christ!"

"Okay. Better now," Will murmured, as the waves of pain subsided, at least for the moment. But he felt very tired now, and colder. He shivered.

Luis lashed the tiller to keep the ship on course while he lit a lantern, which he now held over Will.

"Jesus Christ!" Nathaniel cried out again as he looked at the makeshift dressing, the pale skin around it smeared with blood, shockingly red in the light. He removed the dressing, puzzled by the bundle of leaves it contained, and was transfixed by the small perforation from which blood seeped with slow but relentless pressure.

"Francisco? Is that what he said?" he inquired of no one in particular. "That Francisco stabbed him? Is that what he said? *Stabbed* him?"

"I saw him talking to Francisco just before we shoved off," said Drew, in a tremulous voice. "But I didn't see . . . They weren't arguing or anything. . . ."

"Why would Francisco stab him?"

"I don't know." The sight of the wound brought on an incipient panic, and Drew fought to contain it. "Nat, we've got to boil water. That's got to be disinfected."

Nathaniel turned to Luis.

"Water?" he asked. "Ah, I mean agua. Agua?" He had learned a few Spanish words during the stay in Cárdenas. "Agua? You have?"

"Sí. Tengo," Luis replied, and setting the lantern down, moved away to fetch one of the clay jugs stowed in a box in the stern. "Agua," he said, uncorking the jug, handing it to Nathaniel.

"No. Hot. Must be hot. Boiling. Understand? Jesus, what's the Spanish word for hot?"

Luis's natural scowl deepened.

"No comprendo. No hablo inglés," he said.

"This water must be hot. Boiling. Stove? Galley? You have a galley stove on board?" Nathaniel lowered his face to Will's. "What's the Spanish word for 'hot'? Will? Will?"

Will opened his mouth and started, "Cal . . . cal . . . cali . . ." but he could not get the rest of the word out.

"C'mon, Will, what is it?"

"Leave him be," said Eliot. "Don't try to talk, Will. Take it easy."

"Then what is it?" pleaded Nathaniel. "The Spanish word for 'hot'?"

"How the hell do I know?" Eliot said, regretting every bad thought and feeling he had ever had about Will, wishing he could make it up to him now.

Nathaniel employed every gesture he could think of to mime the act of boiling water, but Luis kept shaking his head and mumbling that he did not speak English. Nathaniel gave it up, poured the cold water over the wound, and wiped the blood with the strip of cloth that had bound the dressing. He tried to think of something else to do, but nothing came to him, not a single idea, so that, when Elvira brushed his hand aside and replaced the bundle of leaves, he drew back and left things to her.

Down on her knees, lowering her head, she slapped her thighs, beating out a quick, irregular rhythm, and began to chant again, in a voice deeper than her speaking voice, the words issuing from her lips sounding like a language out of some distant time:

> *Ibarago moyuba*
> *Ibarago moyuba*
> *Ibarago moyuba Elegba Eshulana . . .*

She looked beautiful and magical, the hollows and angles of her face brought into bold relief by the lantern light. Nathaniel was momentarily arrested by the depth of her possession. Her head and shoulders swaying in time to her drumming, the beads around her neck swinging with her movements, she seemed no longer aware of anything or anyone around her.

Will heard her voice, coming from what seemed very far away. He felt a surge of strength and opened his eyes wide, but he did not see her. He saw instead the star in the heart of the heavens. Vega. Vega in Lyra.

He also made out the constellations of Cygnus and Cepheus, nearly straight overhead, Cygnus, with the beacon of Deneb in its middle, a little ways astern of Lyra. Astern was east. We're sailing almost due west, he thought, we've cleared out of Bahía de Cárdenas and are westering toward Havana, following the edge of the Gulf Stream. It's about ten o'clock. The stars told him the course and time: the fixed and steadfast stars, all in their appointed places.

Ago, ago
Ago, ago . . .

The eerie incantation got on Nathaniel's nerves, and he told Elvira to stop. She kept on. He seized her arm and said, "Stop it! I can't think," but she did not break her swaying.

Ago ile ago . . .

"Stop all that! It's not doing him any good!"

"Señor, por favor, no." Luis, standing behind Nathaniel, laid a hand on his shoulder and told him with gestures to let Elvira go.

"Su amigo . . . Lo siento . . ." he murmured.

"What? What are you saying? Eliot, what's he saying?"

"Damnit, Nat, I don't know. . . ."

"Su amigo," Luis repeated, and jerked his chin at Will, whose eyes were slitted open and still. His chest had ceased to rise and fall, his head had rolled to one side and the tip of his tongue stuck out of a corner of his mouth. Nathaniel put an ear to Will's heart and, hearing the worst, the loudest silence in the world, shook him by the collar and said, "Aw, come on, Will, come on," as if his friend were running a race and needed to show only a little extra effort to win.

Luis closed the eyes with a brush of his hand and pulled the sailcloth over the corpse's face, and then he and Elvira and the three boys confronted the great conundrum of death in their own ways: Luis crossed himself, the Braithwaites looked at their covered shipmate in silence and disbelief, and Elvira let out a shriek that flew a little distance over the dark waters of the Gulf Stream, rolling on into oblivion.

26

"VERY WELL, thank you, gentlemen. Quite a story." Mr. Carrington, the American consul, a tall and ponderous man wearing a cream-colored linen suit, looked at his notes. "We'll have to go through it again, with my secretary present to record it. Hope you don't mind."

"All of it, sir? From the start?" asked Nathaniel, seated with his brothers in front of Carrington's desk, an impressive expanse of dark wood bearing a brass lamp, pens in holders, and papers tidily filed in labeled trays.

"No. We'd be here until tomorrow," he said, running a finger under his starched collar, yellowed at the edges with dried sweat. An American flag, uncased behind him, and photographs of President McKinley and Vice President Roosevelt lent a patriotic flair to his otherwise stark office. "Only the incident involving your friend. Mr. Terhune, is it? That's our concern here. A U.S. citizen murdered—I should say, who appears to have been murdered—by a citizen of Cuba."

Rising, the consul opened a set of double doors and called quietly into an adjoining room, "Joseph, would you come in, please?"

Joseph appeared, garbed in a striped shirt with sleeve garters, and asked his boss if it was all right to leave his jacket off, for it sure was a scorcher today.

With a wave of his pen, Mr. Carrington gave his approval, observing that just about every day in Havana was a scorcher. The secretary sat down alongside the desk, under high casement windows facing the street, the windows open to admit the breezes, the louvered shutters closed to break the direct afternoon sunlight. Joseph opened a stenographer's pad on his crossed legs, adjusted his steel-rimmed eyeglasses, and waited, pencil poised.

"This will be to the Department of State," Mr. Carrington began. "Dated today, August fourteenth. Subject—Alleged homicide of a United States citizen in Cárdenas, Cuba, by a citizen of Cuba. . . ."

Joseph scribbled in shorthand and looked up, all ears for the rest of the tale.

"Dear Sir," Carrington continued, "I have the honor to inform the department that I conducted an interview today with three United States citizens, who presented themselves to me to report that their companion, also a U.S. citizen, was the victim of a knife attack in the port of Cárdenas, Republic of Cuba, on or about the tenth ultimate. The victim, Mr. Willard Terhune"—the consul again glanced at his notes—"age twenty years, a resident of Boston, Massachusetts, died as a result of his wounds approximately five hours after the alleged assault occurred. His death took place, according to the information supplied to me, on a Cuban vessel, *La Esperanza,* while it was in Cuban coastal waters, bound for Havana from Cárdenas. Those reporting this incident knew the alleged assailant, Francisco Casamayor, and they believe that he was about fifteen years old. . . . All correct so far?" asked Carrington, looking at Nathaniel.

"Yes, sir."

Carrington then resumed dictating. "I was informed of this incident by three brothers, Nathaniel Braithwaite, sixteen, Eliot Braithwaite, fifteen, and Andrew Braithwaite, thirteen. They gave their residence in the United States as 239 Marlborough Street, Boston, where they live with their parents, Mr. and Mrs. Cyrus Braithwaite. Henceforth, for the sake of convenience, they shall be referred to as 'the informants.' I wish to apprise the department of the following before going on. First, the informants and Mr. Terhune comprised the crew of a schooner, the *Double Eagle,* which is the property of the informants' father. Nathaniel Braithwaite was the captain and Mr. Terhune the navigator on a voyage from Maine to the Florida Keys, where their vessel was caught in the hurricane of the fifth ultimate and driven into the Bay of Cárdenas, where it ran aground and eventually had to be abandoned. Second, because the informants arrived in Cuba as a result of shipwreck, they were unable to supply to me passports or other documents identifying them as U.S. citizens; however, after speaking to them at length, I am satisfied that they are. Third, after sojourning in Cárdenas for several days, the informants and Mr. Terhune accepted an offer to sail to Havana aboard the aforesaid *La Esperanza,* their intention being to secure passage from Havana back to the United States. Fourth, although one of the informants,

Andrew Braithwaite, saw Mr. Terhune engaged in conversation with the aforesaid Francisco just prior to *La Esperanza*'s departure from Cárdenas, none of them witnessed the alleged assault on Mr. Terhune. Their claim that Francisco attacked him with a knife is based upon a puncture wound they observed in his lower abdomen, and on a statement they said Mr. Terhune made to them immediately prior to his death, to wit: 'Francisco stabbed me.'" Carrington paused to mop his brow with a handkerchief. "Do you have all that, Joseph? Am I going too fast?"

"No, Mr. Carrington," Joseph said.

"Still all correct?" asked the consul, turning again to Nathaniel.

"Yes, sir. But . . ." Nathaniel hesitated.

"But what, young man?"

"Well, it doesn't sound so good, the way you put it. I mean, that we didn't see him stab our shipmate."

"I am not an attorney," said Carrington, "but I would say that as evidence for a homicide case, it sounds absolutely terrible. However, you've come with this information, and I am required to report it. With your permission, I shall continue."

When he finished, some twenty minutes later, Joseph closed his notebook and asked if that would be all.

"Not yet." The consul leaned back in his swivel chair and ruminated for a few moments, brown mustache twitching, hands folded over his substantial waist—the waistline of a plutocrat rather than a diplomat, Eliot thought. "Would any of you boys care to speculate on what this Francisco's motives were?" he asked. "Andrew, you were the one who saw them talking, but you said they weren't arguing."

"I couldn't understand what they were saying, but it didn't sound like an argument, no, sir," Drew replied. He did not like the look of chilly skepticism on Carrington's face.

"Nathaniel? Eliot? Can you think of any reason why this boy, in the course of what to all appearances was a friendly conversation, or at least not a hostile one, should suddenly stab your friend?"

They shook their heads.

"And then we have your fellow passenger, Francisco's older sister. Perhaps she could shed some light, but you say that she disembarked as soon as *La Esperanza* docked and that was the last you saw of her?"

Nathaniel, recalling Elvira's departure—she had vanished into the crowds around Havana's inner harbor—confirmed that that had been the case.

"So that leaves us with the master of *La Esperanza*, but you say he sailed back to Cárdenas today. Thus, we have no one to corroborate your story. Nor do we have a body. Jurisprudence here may not have the fine points of our Anglo-Saxon variety, but it does have writ of habeas corpus."

"What's that, sir?" asked Eliot, thinking, He doesn't believe a word we've said.

"It means that if you're going to allege a murder, you had better have a body to prove that a murder was committed. But you say Mr. Terhune was buried at sea." Pausing, Carrington daubed his forehead once again with his handkerchief. "On that topic, perhaps you could go over the details of the burial again. Mr. Terhune's family will doubtless have questions, and it is best that we have as much information as possible. Joseph, be sure you get this down."

Nathaniel found the second telling no less painful than the first. The morning after Will's death had come with barely a wind, so that Luis had to tack his ship inside the reef to avoid being pushed backward by the Gulf Stream. *La Esperanza* wallowed some two miles off an inhospitable shore marked by tall cliffs and made headway only because of a sluggish, west-setting current.

Will's body lay under the sailcloth, in the broiling sun. Around midmorning, Luis, with extravagant gestures, communicated the urgency of disposing of it, but Nathaniel was determined to bring the remains home for Christian burial. He had no clear idea of how this was to be effected, but he was resolved to do it, and to allay any doubts the others might have about his resolve, he seized the L. C. Smith and stood vigil over the corpse for some three hours. By then, there was nowhere aboard the small vessel to escape the stench. So dense it seemed almost visible, burning the nostrils and causing everyone's eyes to water, weaving itself into the threads of their clothes; it was an odor the Braithwaites had never experienced before, unlike Luis, who had made its acquaintance fighting in the insurrection against the Spanish. Handing the tiller off to Eliot, he angrily stripped the sailcloth from Will's body and said to Nathaniel, "Mira!" Will's chest and abdomen had swelled, straining the buttons of his shirt; his bloated face was dark yellow blotched with pale green.

But even that appalling sight did not quite dissuade Nathaniel. It was Drew who finally convinced him that his notion was pointless, because that wasn't Will, it was a mass of decomposing flesh and chemicals breaking down. Whatever had made Will Will was gone—to heaven, to hell, or into thin air, but gone. Nathaniel gave in but insisted that the mass of decomposing flesh was not to be unceremoniously tossed overboard; it would be given a proper sailor's interment in the deep. He signed to Luis that a weight was needed. Luis dropped into the cargo hold, and came out with a ballast stone. Masking nose and mouth with a bandanna, Nathaniel covered the body again, lashed the sailcloth tightly with the bowline, and tied the stone to the line. Luis then took the shrouded corpse by the ankles, Nathaniel its shoulders, and the two lifted it to the gunwale.

A proper seaman's burial required prayer and hymn, so Nathaniel petitioned God to allow the soul of Willard Terhune into the kingdom of heaven, then told Eliot to lead them in the "Navy Hymn." Eliot demurred, saying that he thought that was overdoing things a bit; after all, Will had not been a bluejacket.

"But he was our shipmate, so you sing," Nathaniel commanded.

Eliot cleared his throat and began,

> *Eternal Father, strong to save,*
> *Whose arm has bound the restless wave . . .*

As he sang, Elvira chanted in praise to the orisha of the ocean depths, the spirit that had kept her ancestors alive on their voyages enchained to the New World, and she called upon it now to safeguard Will on his journey:

> *Olokun, Olokun,*
> *Baba Baba Olokun . . .*

So they continued, singing against each other to Christian deity and African spirit:

> *Who bade the mighty ocean deep . . .*
> *Olokun, Olokun . . .*
> *Its own appointed limits keep . . .*
> *Baba Baba Olokun . . .*
> *O hear us when we cry to Thee . . .*
> *Olokun, Olokun . . .*
> *Baba Baba Olokun . . .*
> *For those in peril on the sea . . .*
> *Moyuba Baba Olokun.*

Nathaniel and Luis rolled the body overboard and watched it float briefly before the stone pulled it down.

Luis crossed himself again, and then, pulling out the linings of his pockets, pointing at the sails, the ropes, the water into which Will had sunk, made it known that he was a poor man and that it would be fitting to compensate him for the sailcloth and the bowline. Nathaniel gave him the shotgun, figuring he could pawn it for a fair price.

"The consul turned to his secretary. "Did you get the gist of all that?"

"I did," Joseph answered. "May I add, Mr. Carrington, that, judging from the description of the coastline—the cliffs—the victim was buried at sea at a point west of Veradaro, in the vicinity of the mouth of the Rio Camarico. His family might like to know the location."

"Thanks, Joseph. Joseph was raised in Cuba. Parents Protestant missionaries," Carrington informed the Braithwaites. "Pretty thankless task in a country full of papists, when they aren't beating voodoo drums. That will be all, Joseph, unless you boys have something to add?"

They said they did not and Joseph left, flicking a finger across his brow and remarking again that it sure was a scorcher.

Carrington opened a drawer and produced a squat cigar, which he clipped at the end with a device that looked like a miniature brass guillotine.

"There isn't much done right in this country," he said, striking a long match, "but these Cubans sure know how to make a see-gar." He exhaled slowly a plume of smoke that twirled lazily in the ribbed light. "Now I'm going to tell you boys about the birds and the bees. Without a single witness and without a body, I am afraid that nothing can be done."

"Nothing?" asked Eliot, with an indignation all three shared. "What do you mean, Mr. Carrington, *nothing* can be done? We're witnesses, sort of. Don't you believe us?"

"Frankly, I do. But that is not the point." The consul set the cigar in an ashtray and clasped his hands on the desk. "Even if this Francisco could be found and charged on the existing evidence, of which there is next to none, the case would be tried in a Cuban court, and I'm sure no Cuban judge and jury would believe one word of what you say. I would imagine that Francisco's attorney would plant an idea in the judge's and jury's minds that Mr. Terhune died in, ah, let's say different circumstances—circumstances that you three tried to hide with a fabricated story about a knifing. Is my drift clear, gentlemen?"

"I think so, Mr. Carrington," replied Nathaniel, his indignation cooling rapidly. "We could get into trouble?"

"And maybe a heap of it, so my very strong advice to you is not to pursue this matter any further. I'm as far as you can go, in any case. You're in another country, boys."

A pall of resignation settled over them. Recalling Carrington's summary of their story, it sounded unbelievable, even to them.

"The problem we now have is getting you three back home," the consul said. "You say you're almost broke?"

They were. They had bought dinner last night, after arriving in Havana, and breakfast and lunch this morning. To that was added the expense of the two telegrams they had sent yesterday (a pair of American sailors had shown them where the cable office was in the maze of the city's narrow streets): one to their father begging for money for passage home, the other to Euphrenia Lowe (Nathaniel knowing that the wire did not release him from the obligation to tell her face-to-face).

"And as of this morning, you had not received a reply from your father?" asked Carrington.

"Not this afternoon, either," Nathaniel answered, with some embarrassment. "Maybe he's on a business trip or something."

"And you have nowhere to stay while you're waiting for a reply?"

"Luis let us sleep on the boat last night, after we unloaded his coconuts for him. But he's gone now, like we said, sir."

"Then take this, Nathaniel." Carrington pulled a billfold out of his inside coat pocket and passed seven dollars in one dollar bills across the desk. "The Yankee buck goes a long way in this country. Five should buy a meal for the three of you and a night in an inexpensive hotel. I'll give you the name of one close by. It has baths and a barbershop next door, and that's where I strongly recommend you spend the other two dollars. A thank-you would not be out of order," the consul added, when the Braithwaites failed to offer one.

"Guess we forgot our manners," Nathaniel apologized. "Thanks. If we don't get an answer from our dad by tomorrow, what should we do then?"

"I am eager for you to be on your way and out of my hair. You three have a halo of disaster about you, and I do not intend to pay you a per diem for an extended stay in the tropics." Carrington lifted his eyebrows comically to show that he intended no malice. "It's possible the cable did not reach your father, considering that commercial traffic is relayed from here to Key West and then routed on up the coast. Tell you what. I will send a wire to your father through official channels, at legation expense." He took a pen from the holder and dipped the inkwell. "What's the message?"

"Same as the first, I guess," said Nathaniel. "'*Double Eagle* wrecked storm Cuba Stop. Stranded Havana Stop. Urgent you wire money passage home Stop. Nat Eliot Drew Stop End.'"

"Anything more? The government's paying," Carrington offered.

They thought for a moment, and then Drew recalled words Nathaniel had spoken in what seemed a long time ago.

"Could you add this before our names?" he asked the consul. "'We have looked to the quarry and the pit. Stop. Found *Annisquam* Stop.'"

"And he'll know what that means?" asked Carrington, writing.

"He should," Drew answered.

"All right. Check with Joseph in the morning to see if there's a reply. None then, check in the afternoon, about one o'clock. The hotel is the Cojimar. Joseph will show you how to get there." A long, luxurious drag on the cigar. "If you boys were a shade older, I'd offer you one of these."

THE HOTEL COJIMAR—aquamarine walls blotted with mildew—was in one of the plazas that made oases of light in Havana's labyrinth of narrow, shadowed arteries. The boys ate chicken and rice in a cheap bodega and slept all together in a tiny room where small lizards clung to the walls and a single window overlooked an enclosed courtyard into which clay gutters spilled the evening's rain. In the morning, they went to a coffee shop and drank café con leche, thickly sugared to kill their appetites, and then walked to the legation, where Joseph told them that no reply to their cable had been received, and so they wandered about, killing time, fighting anxiety and the melancholy that descended when they thought of how Will would have delighted in the city—the sensuous women, some in fancy dresses, some in the peasant shifts that Elvira and Rosaria wore, the pastel buildings with scrolled iron balconies and bars on the windows, which reminded Eliot of a menagerie and made Nathaniel think of the cities described in *Don Quixote*. Carriages driven by booted Negroes, whipping the horses unmercifully, clattered down the stone streets, and mules, so laden with fodder that all that could be seen of them were tiny hooves, stepped daintily along. At noon, they came upon a donkey carrying panniers of oranges, and they asked the driver if they could buy some, but he could not understand them nor they him, until Nathaniel showed him a quarter, and money being a universal language, the man sold them three oranges, which did for lunch.

Returning to the legation at one, they were told that a reply still had not come in and to try again in a couple of hours, when all the cable traffic had been sorted and filed. Speculating on the reasons for their father's silence, but coming to no satisfactory conclusion and suspecting they might have to find their own way home, they went to the harbor to check on the possibilities of hiring on board an American ship bound for Boston or someplace near. Across the harbor rose Moro Castle, its ramparts running along a rocky hill and dipping into ravines, blending so smoothly into the rock that the walls did not appear to have been built upon it but hewn from it. There were many ships, steam and sail, flying the ensigns of many nations, all discharging waste into the harbor, which, with its modest tides, stank like a landlocked bog. Eliot spotted a Standard Fruit Company steamer, but the second mate told them she had a full crew. He directed them to a down-easter, the sight of which made them almost cry with homesickness. The ship needed hands, but she was bound for Caracas, and the wrecking sloop moored nearby, out of Key West, had only one berth open; besides, she was headed for a salvage job in the Bahamas.

They headed back in the worst heat of the day, the streets nearly empty, as the Havaneros took their siesta. It was so hot that, halfway to the legation, the boys sneaked into the interior courtyard of some grandee's mansion and dunked their heads into a fountain. Cooled off, they made a third climb up the stairs to the office where Joseph labored with several other functionaries.

"I believe this is what you've been waiting for," he said, handed a yellow envelope bearing the stamp OVERSEAS CABLE to Nathaniel, and looking at his wet hair, said, "One heck of a scorcher today, isn't it?"

Nathaniel tore the envelope open, read the message once, and again, and a third time, and felt something close around his heart like a fist.

"What's it say?" asked Eliot, alarmed by his brother's expression.

Nathaniel passed it to him and Drew, and they looked at him, frowning, and he said to Drew, "You're the one with the Kodak memory. Got any idea what he means?"

Drew thought for a long while. If his mind were clear, perhaps he could summon up a chapter and verse that would solve the riddle, but every channel in his brain was clouded by a bitter anger. There is something seriously wrong with the man, he thought. Maybe he's crazy. Maybe he's been crazy all along but we couldn't see it. And if he isn't crazy, then he ought to be horsewhipped.

"He means he's not sending us a penny," he said to his brothers.

"We can figure that much out, and that isn't enough," Nathaniel remarked, and went to Joseph's desk.

Joseph was typewriting a letter by hunt and peck, and he raised one hand to tell Nathaniel to wait.

"I must say I prefer a pen and foolscap to these machines," he muttered to himself, and then gave Nathaniel his attention.

"Could we see Mr. Carrington again?" asked Nathaniel. "There's a problem."

"He's engaged presently," said the secretery. "But I'll tell him you're here."

"Thanks. Do you happen to have a Bible around here we could borrow?"

The missionary's son produced one from his drawer, bound in soft, black leather and so frequently consulted that its binding was coming apart.

They waited on a bench in the corridor outside, under an electric fan that listlessly paddled the air, Drew reading the first epistle as quickly as he could, salutation to benediction, waiting as he read for a line or a verse to leap from the page and say to him, "Here it is, the key to break the code." He was into the second epistle when he closed the book and slammed it on the bench.

"This is just what the bastard wants us to do," he said. "Drive ourselves nuts trying to figure it out. I'm sick of him playing the tune and us dancing to it."

At four, Joseph appeared and said Mr. Carrington could see them now, but briefly—he had an appointment in a quarter of an hour.

The consul, his collar open and necktie pulled down, pondered the telegram for a full minute, scowling.

"Boys, don't know what to tell you. This sure beats me," he grumbled, and the three brothers felt ashamed, ashamed to be their father's sons, ashamed of what Carrington must think of a man who would abandon his children in a foreign land, and ashamed because they were now reduced to begging. Beg they did, telling Carrington of their earlier efforts to find a berth on a ship, more or less to assure him that they did not want to be charity cases.

He blew out his cheeks, then drew a form from one of his desk drawers and signed it, with an impatient movement.

"Present this to Joseph," he said, in an exasperated tone. "It authorizes him to draw from an emergency fund we keep for American citizens who get stranded without any means to get back to the U.S. There'll be enough to buy you tickets on the Havana to Key West ferry and for reasonable travel expenses from there to most places on the East Coast. There's a ferry leaves at midnight tonight, gets in at eight in the morning. All right?"

"That would be grand, sir. We can't thank you enough."

"Thank your government." Carrington picked up the telegram. "Want this or shall I throw it away?"

Nathaniel hesitated for a moment before taking it, his heart, within the fist's clasp, crushed down to the size, and the hardness, of a walnut.

"Sure does beat me," Carrington repeated. "And you have no idea what your father means by it?"

Nathaniel scanned the words, LOOK NOT TO ISAIAH BUT TO CORINTHIANS FOR PASSAGE HOME. STOP. C.R.B., as if, on fourth reading, they might yield some glimmer of sense. Didn't even sign *Father,* he thought. Just his initials.

"No, sir, we don't," he stated to Carrington. "But we sure mean to find out."

Epilogue

HIS FATHER'S WIFE

SYBIL DOESN'T KNOW if they did. She doesn't know, for that matter, if she herself has the answer, although she has a few ideas. She has been trying to explain to herself why her grandfather and his brothers never told the tale of *Double Eagle*'s voyage and left no record of it except for the logbook that lay in a trunk in Mingulay's storage room, unread for over ninety years until she discovered it, with Cyrus's cryptic telegram folded into quarters between the last page and the back cover. The reason for the boys' silence may have been simple—the deaths of Artemis and Will had made the entire experience too painful to recount, affecting them with the muteness that overcomes war veterans. She doesn't think the analogy is strained. The voyage taught the lessons young men learn in battle: that the world is indifferent to our fates; that life is fragile and our grip on it tenuous; that when the great crisis comes, though we may face it bravely and act well, we are nevertheless not as brave or as good as we might have hoped. And so, Nathaniel, Eliot, and Andrew returned home stripped of that illusion of invincibility which is the chief glory and liability of youth, which is youth itself.

There is something satisfying about this explanation, and it is probably true, as far as it goes. But it doesn't go far enough. Wouldn't their sorrow and guilt have softened over time, releasing them to speak? What's more, Cyrus and Elizabeth never breathed a word to anyone, either. The story would have been lost but for Gertrude Williams and her daughters, who, after learning of Will's fate, had made it part of their family lore. The absence of testimony from the Braithwaites leads Sybil to suspect some kind of conspiracy; she knows her family and its propensity for suppressing the darker chapters of its history.

The power of stereotype should not be underestimated. Its distorting prism can affect the way we see ourselves; sometimes, we strive to imitate the images others have of us and thus turn a picture essentially false into one that is true—a case, more or less, of life imitating art. That goes for families as well as for individuals. If old Southern families (like Sybil's mother's, the McDaniels) are supposed to be dysfunctional by nature—asylums without walls, swamps of forbidden desires and passions populated by drunks, drug addicts, beautiful but self-destructive females who depend on the kindness of strangers, murderers, suicides, and idiot cousins—old Yankee families like her father's are expected to be ruthlessly functional, composed of virtuous pragmatists immunized to the more destructive promptings of the libido and the id. The House of the Seven Gables (according to this view) has become a museum of extinct curiosities, the descendants of its inhabitants having moved out to the suburbs to shuck off their black lunacies for nothing worse than quaint eccentricities or madnesses temperate enough to be cured with a martini or a few Valium.

But Sybil knows that the real difference between the Braithwaites and the McDaniels is her father's family's greater talent for concealing their Gothic pathologies. Its good name is its most precious asset, the glue that has held it together while the Great American Cyclotron has smashed the extended familes of Sybil's grandfather's day into the nuclear familes of her father's day, and those into the single-parent leptons and no-parent quarks of her own day. Not that Braithwaites haven't been touched by divorce or any of the other centrifugal forces that knock families to pieces; but divorces and the like seem to have had no lasting effect on their coherence, on the unity signified by the Wheel Chart, a copy of which hangs in Sybil's bedroom here on her Arizona ranch, a good long way from her roots in salt marsh, granite coast, everlasting sea. The Wheel Chart is the Braithwaite family tree—not the diagrammatic type usually found in genealogies but a series of concentric circles. In the center are the names of the clan's progenitors, Joshua Caleb Braithwaite (1647–1711) and Sarah Siddons Braithwaite (1653–1722). Around them is a slightly larger ring, with the names of their children and their spouses, and then a still larger ring of grandchildren, and so on, generation after generation radiating outward through time to the present. The impression is not so much of a wheel as of a solar system, ordered and impregnable.

Sybil's name is in the second-to-last orbit, the twelfth. With one glance, she can find her position within her family's history, her coordinates, so to speak. Any other Braithwaite can do the same, and that gives them, in a time of deracination, an abiding sense of place. Most of Joshua's and Sarah's descendants still live close to the flinty, unyielding soil from which those first two settlers wrested their bread and in which their dust lies today (in the cemetery in Dedham, Massachusetts). For the most part, the Braithwaites did not scatter themselves across the American wilderness, as if they feared that they would lose themselves in the raw vast vacancy of the continent, would forget who they were and from whom they had sprung if they lost sight of one another and the tombstones of Joshua and Sarah and of all the Seths and Hannahs and Enochs and Abigails who followed. Yet, there is a Braithwaite diaspora (which Sybil joined when she moved west in 1992). Small branches of the family—twigs, really—dwell in Ohio, Washington, and California; a few retired Braithwaites inhabit the golf-club communities of the Sun Belt; two expatriate Braithwaites live overseas. But every year, at different times during the summer, different branches convene at Mingulay, just as Cyrus had envisioned when he built the place in the late 1880s. They come together to play tennis and bridge and billiards, to sail and swim and fish and hike in the woods, or to sit reading on the verandas when Maine fogs descend; but the true purpose of these assemblies is to reaffirm their bond of blood. The bond is almost palpable when large numbers of them gather. A visitor sipping cocktails with them at the appropriate hour is likely to feel, amid the polite conversation made by people in blue blazers and Lands' End dresses, that he is observing the tribal rite of some white, Protestant Yanomami, preserved in the isolation of their metaphorical Amazon.

In the courtyard of her ranch house on this winter's day in 1998, Sybil and I reminisce about the Fourth of July, 1974, when we, roommates recently graduated from Mount Holyoke, stood on Mingulay's lawn with a mob of Braithwaites, from septuagenarians to toddlers, to watch fireworks burst over Blue Hill Bay. We remember how the thunderous finale that made noon of night seemed to shine on the firm clean patrician faces of her relatives, like a light of grace. Yes, they had it even at that late date in their history: that air of belonging to an America that belonged to them.

When Sybil's father died sixteen years later, some of the same people assembled to lay him to rest in Mount Auburn cemetery, but there was something different about them, beyond the obvious changes time had brought about, something less confident, less commanding; their movements as they gathered around the small marble slab, simply inscribed WADE EDWARD BRAITHWAITE: FEB. 19, 1920—JUNE 30, 1990, suggested a people no longer as sure of their footing as they once were. The service was brief and plain, there amid the mansions of Wade's ancestors, under groves of maple and copper beech whose long shadows lay like fallen pillars over headstones bearing ancient names of the Republic—Thayer, Greenleaf, Bryant, Peabody. Sybil and her brother, Jason, spoke a few words about their father, then a craggy Congregational minister delivered a eulogy in a Brahmin accent that struck my ear like a scratchy recording made sixty years ago.

The memory of that scene reminds her of something Cousinuncle Myles told her that somber November afternoon in his somber Gloucester house with its scent of roses slightly past their prime: that families like theirs had not suffered a dramatic fall from grace, but rather a slow withdrawal of its light. No, that was not quite how he put it, she recalls. We've slipped into irrelevancy, that is what he said, but it means the same thing.

She recalls another of his observations as she sits and ponders whether Nathaniel, Eliot, and Andrew ever discovered the meaning of their father's message.

Myles had been in the middle of an anecdote about how his grandfather's granite business had won its first big contract, the profits of which helped to build Mingulay, when he lost his train of thought, and began to reminisce about past summers at the capital of the Braithwaite family-nation. The reminiscence led him to a recollection of his daughter, Allyson, the "blueblood bomb-thrower," as the newspapers referred to her after she had been arrested in 1970, with several other members of a Weather Underground cell making pipe bombs in a New York basement.

Myles had fallen silent for several moments, and then made the observation that sent Sybil off on the quest that has taken her six years.

"Our lives are a kind of inherited disease, Cousinniece. We Braithwaites have been condemned to commit the sins of our fathers over and over," he'd said, and when Sybil had asked what he'd meant by that, Myles replied, "Parents who destroy their children, unless the kids get to them first, that's us."

"Myles!" Sybil had said, confused and haunted by his choice of verb: not "hurt," not "abuse," but *destroy*. "That's an awful thing to say. A little while ago you told me you hoped that I wouldn't end up hating our family like Allyson does. How could you have said that, then tell me what you just did?"

"I learned as a clergyman, and it wasn't an easy lesson, how to hate the sin but love the sinner."

Sybil heard the ticks of the hall clock in the quiet house.

"Like my father? My father and Hilary?" she had asked.

Hilary, golden Hilary, sporty and daring, who in her sophomore year at Mount Holyoke broke any number of taboos and precedents by crewing on a Gloucester swordfishing boat for a day to write an article for her journalism class. The skipper and mate gave her a chance to harpoon a swordfish—a challenge they were sure she wouldn't accept. They were dumbfounded when the child of privilege walked out onto the bow pulpit with a harpoon, and with an aim as true as if she'd been schooled by her whaling forefathers, ironed a three-hundred-pounder basking on the surface. As the great fish thrashed and the barrel at the end of the rope dipped and rose like a bobber, she further astonished captain and mate by quoting Melville, something to the effect that a harpooner casts his lance not out of toil but out of relaxation.

Hilary, Sybil's sistermother because Catherine, the Garden District deb, queen of the classiest krewe in the 1941 Mardi Gras, was appalled by children younger than six or seven. Their stink and shrieks and incessant demands, their irrationality. Hilary was the one who daubed iodine on the knees Sybil was forever skinning as she scrambled in summer tide pools to net crabs and shellfish and minnows. She comforted Sybil when she came home from school crying because the teacher scolded her for not participating in class. Come on, dry your eyes, Fudge. You're a little bit of snail, and she was only trying to get you to come out of your shell. Her voice was husky (a little like Lauren Bacall's, their mother used to say) and her hands were strong from all the sailing and rowing she did; oh, sistermother was quite a woman, and her death had left Sybil feeling more orphaned than if Catherine had died.

The summer of 1963, the summer before things started to go wrong—and not just in Sybil's family. Wade was sailing his Concordia yawl, *Double Eagle III,* in a class race at Newport. He was helmsman and captain; the editor of one of his magazines was navigator; his son, Jason, seventeen that year, was being trained to handle the main and mizzen sheets like a crack crewman; and Hilary was foredeck man— the toughest job, the one that required a fine sense of balance and timing. There was nothing particularly critical or prestigious about the race, but Wade, former Dartmouth boxer and hockey player, marine fighter pilot in World War II, intended to win it, wanted to, needed to. He had inherited, like his uncle Nathaniel, a competiveness almost pathological.

Double Eagle III was in the lead, though not by much. She was being challenged by another yawl, only a half-boat length behind, as the two vessels bore off on the downwind leg. Wade knew he would seal the victory if he could keep his opponent outside him at the downwind mark, then hook around it in the nautical equivalent of a hairpin turn.

He fell off ever so cautiously to a dead run, his navigator warning him that the wind was fluky and that he was running the risk of an accidental jibe. "I know that!" Wade snapped, and the man kept quiet, for Wade was not only his skipper but his employer. *Double Eagle III* cracked toward the buoy, her green and white spinnaker ballooned out in front, Wade, alert for any shift in the wind, warning Jason to stand by the sheets and Hilary to be ready to douse the spinnaker. "Prepare to jibe!" he said, and as Hilary rose and scampered forward, the wind veered suddenly, with more force than Wade, or anyone, could have expected. The boat jibed a split second early, the heavy boom slammed over, struck Hilary in the back of the head with the power of a bat swung by a cleanup hitter, and knocked her overboard. She floated facedown in her life jacket, until Wade and his crew, acting with a competence and calm everyone later agreed was remarkable, doused the spinnaker, brought *Double Eagle III* around, and pulled Hilary out of the water. All attempts at resuscitation failed. The autopsy determined that the blow to her head had killed her almost instantly.

"I could be speaking about that," Myles had replied. "It's merely another way of urging Christian forgiveness."

"I've tried to, but it's hard. It's hard even now, with him gone two years. And what's just as hard to forgive is the way everyone just automatically covered it up and pretended he had nothing to do with it. But he did. It was his pride that killed her, as much as that freaky gust of wind."

"Yes. Yes," Myles had mumbled, and then, in the stentorian voice of homily and scripture: "There is nothing more corrupting of a family's integrity than keeping secrets. And I don't mean integrity in the sense of reputation. The family that conceals certain truths about itself, or denies those truths, or in some other way falsifies its history, is going to suffer consequences, but those won't necessarily fall on the creators and bearers of the falsehoods, nor even on those who belong to the same generation as the creators, the bearers. They could just as easily fall on a future generation, at some unforeseen, unexpected hour, without making any fine distinctions. . . ."

"I'm not following. Do you mean that Hilary, what happened to her, that it was because of something someone did a long time ago?" Sybil had asked.

"I consider myself an enlightened man, Cousinniece. I am aware that, as often as not, things just happen for no reason beyond the mechanics of their happening. A man slips on the ice and falls off a cliff. Why? Ultimately, because of the laws of friction and gravity. Intermediately, because he was wearing the wrong shoes for conditions, or put his foot in the wrong place, or was stupid enough to be walking on ice near a cliff in the first place. I know that! And if what happened to Hilary had been an isolated thing, if you and your family hadn't lost her and I hadn't lost Allyson in a different way, and . . ."

"Everything that happened afterward," she had finished for him. "The string of disasters. More than our fair share. We're back to that Original Sin idea, and that family history you're putting together. . . ."

"*You* are doing that now," he reminded her. "It's your baby. Do whatever you want with it, including nothing. As for myself, maybe I had hoped that bringing certain things out into the sunlight—and sunlight's the best disinfectant—would be an expiation in and of itself."

And so she had assumed from him the roles of family historian and etiologist, seeking to trace cause and effect, searching amid the sins of the fathers for the one great sin that might explain to her satisfaction why her sister had to die, senselessly, at the age of twenty. This has not been her sole occupation for the past six years. She breeds and trains reining horses on San Gabriel ranch: 160 acres of grass meadow and oak and juniper uplands more than twenty miles by dirt road from Nogales, on the Mexican border. The ranch keeps her busy all day, but there is nothing to do at night in such an isolated and lonely place, and rather than drink or sit up watching her satellite TV, she pores through the trove of stuff she got from Myles, from the trunks and boxes at Mingulay, from the Williams family, and from a Boston genealogist, a man named Buckmayer.

Sybil began with the fragmentary tale her mother told her. Willy-nilly, she found herself re-creating the voyage, inventing things, not out of whole cloth but out of the threads in the logbook. I don't believe that she has the power to see into her family's past, as she claims she does; but I'm not going to make fun of her or deny that it's at least theoretically possible to possess a kind of extraordinary genetic memory that can be summoned up from time to time. At any rate, she has tried to resurrect that summer in Nathaniel's, Eliot's, and her grandfather's early lives as it probably was lived. She says I should consider her story an exhibit in the natural history of her family. She has taken shards of authentic bone, fossil ribs and partial mandibles and broken joints of fact, and fused them back together with fabrications to create a whole thing. That is what she has been after all this time—the creation of a whole thing, with what art she commands, and there is truth in art.

But now she has come to the riddle of Cyrus's message, and she doesn't want to leave its interpretation to the imagination, for within those words, "Look not to Isaiah but to Corinthians," may lie the hidden sin whose legacy has been passed down to her generation. Keys to its meaning now lie all around her on a table in the courtyard—fragments of letters and diaries; a few yellowed newspaper clippings covered in protective plastic; copies of a transaction between Caleb Maxey, Aunt Judith's first husband, and Sybil's maternal great-great-grandfather, Pardon Lightbourne; the log Cyrus kept when he was master of *Main Chance;* a letter to him from a lawyer advising him not to file for divorce; two letters to Gertrude Williams from Elizabeth Braithwaite; and more than a dozen other items, some seemingly irrelevant, like a century-old advertisement for Lydia Pinkham's tonic. Those are the written documents. There is also an oral record of sorts, stored in Sybil's memory: the stories Myles told her about Cyrus, the man "hard as a white oak plank."

This is what she knows happened after the three boys left the U.S. Legation in Havana:

Nathaniel, Eliot, and Andrew took the night ferry to Key West, arriving early in the morning, and immediately (before their nerve failed them) went to Euphrenia Lowe's house on Petronia Street to tell her that her husband had died. They'd decided, in the interests of sparing her feelings, not to tell her how but to say that he had been lost during the hurricane. Mrs. Lowe, sitting on the steps of her front porch, murmured, "I always knew something like this was goin' to happen." The boys attempted to give what solace they could, but the eldest son, Ethan, told them that the best thing for them would be to leave immediately, before he took a whip to all three of them.

By the next morning, they were on a Mallory Line steamer bound for New York City, where they intended to entrain for Boston. They had bathed and gotten their hair cut in Havana; in Key West, they brought their clothes to a laundry, hoping to present a civilized appearance for the voyage home. But, in Sybil's imagining, they must have presented a different sight to the passengers: bodies winnowed to muscle and bone, hands chafed and callused, faces that had been tanned, burned through the tan, then tanned through the burn: three boys who did not have the look of boys in their eyes.

The trip that had taken *Double Eagle* a month was made in four days. For all their distress about their father and the knowledge that they had another door to knock on when they got to Boston, it must have been a joy for them to loll about the ship, without having to reef, haul, make fast, or steer, a joy to ride aboard a vessel ploughing a straight line across placid seas, and never a worry about the wind, a joy to eat three hot meals a day instead of wolfing cold hash out of a tin.

Sybil imagines that Nathaniel must have steeled himself, during the voyage home, for a confrontation with Cyrus. He would have rehearsed the words he intended to speak, imagined those his father would say and the replies he would make. He would have pictured himself, standing firmly and as a man, demanding answers and getting them.

On August 20, 1901, the last entry was made in the logbook-cum-diary, and Sybil would have known it had been written by Nathaniel even if she didn't recognize his handwriting: "Arrived New York City 1:45 p.m. Cloudy, muggy day—almost feels like Havana. Wired home to say we're arriving by train this evening."

And then she loses sight of them. Without the medium of the logbook, her vision of the past is obscured, the voices of her forebears as young men are stilled, their youthful faces vanish, and so she can barely imagine the way it was when they appeared at the Marlborough Street town house. She sees, vaguely, her great-grandmother, sitting in a chair with the martial brace to her shoulders and back. Elizabeth embraces her boys, kisses them, perhaps she cries, but she soon becomes the iron maiden again, restraining the joy of seeing her children alive and safe, for there are things she must tell them, difficult things, and she cannot allow her emotions to get the better of her. And Sybil hears her, oh so faintly, breaking the news that their half brother had been run over and killed by an elevated train in New York City, only the day before they had arrived there and talked to Mrs. Gleason, the boardinghouse owner. Lockwood had been drinking and had fallen off a platform somewhere in lower Manhattan, she whispers. And then comes the hardest news: Their father has left on an extended business trip. . . . *But that, boys, is not the entire truth. Your father and I, though we remain married, have decided to live apart from now on. . . . And, no, please, please, do not ask me why now, perhaps I will tell you when you're older, but please not now. . . . You will be seeing very little of your father from now on, perhaps you will not see him at all. . . .*

How did the three brothers react to those twin shocks? Sybil wonders. She supposes Nathaniel felt cheated—now he would be denied catharsis, now he would not learn the meaning of the riddle in the telegram, now the drama that had been taking place on one stage while he and his brothers acted out theirs on another would forever remain a mystery. Did he demand from his mother the answers he sought from his father? Did he and Eliot and Drew insist that she tell them why

Lockwood had been drinking so heavily that he fell off the train plat-form? Why their parents, who had seemed in love when the summer began, were now to live separate lives? They must have, but not with the insistence of modern adolescents. This was the late-Victorian era, after all, and the boys must have understood implicitly that something had happened which they were not to know, but there would have been another reason for their docility. They sensed, perhaps through their mother's gestures, her expressions, her tone of voice, that it was some-thing they would not want to know.

How, I ask Sybil, did she learn about Lockwood's accidental death and discover that her great-grandparents had begun to live apart that summer? Myles told her, she answers, Myles having learned those facts from his father when Eliot was late in life. No, Myles did not know the reasons for his grandparents' unusual arrangement. All he knew was that Cyrus had considered divorcing Elizabeth, had decided against it, and then took up residence at his club in Boston; when he wasn't there, he stayed in Gloucester to oversee his quarry operations on Cape Ann. He never spent another summer at Mingulay and had no contact with his family for the rest of his life, which ended in 1908.

"When Myles told me that his grandfather had thought about a divorce, I wondered if that was the reason he sent the boys away. You know, to spare them the scandal, or just to have them out of the way. He wanted to clear the decks, but he could have packed them off to a camp or to a relative, if clearing the decks was all he intended."

Far overhead, in a square of unblemished blue formed by the roof-less courtyard, a hawk wheels, probably a red-tail, but I'm not sure. The winter sun has advanced across the courtyard, the morning's shadows retreated to one small corner on the north side.

"He intended something else?" I ask. "The character-building idea?"

Sybil takes off her glasses. I notice that she hasn't lost a nervous habit I remember from our childhoods: She rubs the middle knuckle of her thumb against her teeth.

"I imagine a kid like Nathaniel would have thought that was his father's intention," she answers. "But remember, I wrote that his love, his respect, were the last things they could expect from him? I don't think character building was what Cyrus had in mind. Whatever it was, I don't think he was completely in his right mind when he did it."

She compares him to a severely depressed person who, gripped by despair, gets in a car, drives at reckless speed, and then jerks the wheel and crashes into a wall or a tree, not with full, cold-headed, cold-blooded intent to kill himself, but with a blind, unconscious compulsion—Cyrus, she says, might have been in a state of mind like that when he threw the boys on the mercy of the sea.

I back my chair against the wall, under the glazed tiles of a mosaic of the Virgin of Guadalupe, its colors vivid in the vivid light. Sybil isn't quite herself. Less contained than usual.

"If that's the case you're making, you'd have to show him to be a reckless man, and you haven't," I say. "Just the opposite. Methodical, thorough. Inspecting the ship to make sure everything worked all right, to make sure the boys had a good sextant, charts, food, everything they needed to survive."

Some of that, she answers, would have been habitual for an old sea captain, but, she adds, a man's actions can appear orderly and rational while the impulse driving them is disorderly and mad. She urges me to look at things from this angle: The food, the instruments, the charts of unfamiliar shores and waters, and giving Nathaniel command of the vessel—that above all—was as irresponsible as putting a whiskey bottle in front of an alcoholic.

I shake my head. She leans forward in her chair as an eddy of dry wind drifts into the courtyard and rustles the papers on the table.

"How could he *not* have known that Nathaniel was a restless kid, a kid with an adventurous temperament, a kid with a habit of taking chances, and sometimes stupid chances?"

"Ah," I say. "All that stuff was a way of encouraging Nathaniel, even tempting him? Cyrus could not have known that he would decide to sail to Florida, but he must've known that Nathaniel would take some sort of risk, eventually?"

Not known it in the sense we know things for certain, she expounds. Hoped it maybe. Wanted it maybe, way down in some rank and secret cellar of his heart or mind, the place where bugs and lizards crawl. Hoped it, wanted it, but could not consciously admit to the hope, the desire, because it was too malignant . . .

"Wait a second," I interrupt, she sitting tensely before me, knees clamped, hands folded in her lap. "Are you suggesting that the thing he wanted, that he hoped would happen—Are you saying that he was trying to *do away with* his own sons?"

"He hoped the sea would do it for him. At the very least, he didn't give a damn what happened to them. Maybe. Yes."

"Could you tell me what 'Maybe, yes' means?"

"Not 'Maybe comma yes,' but 'Maybe period. Yes period.' Yes, that's what I suspect, but only suspect, because I could never prove it."

"But Sybil, you said that he said they were to come back in September, so if what he was trying to do was . . ."

"I think that instruction was part of his derangement," she interjects. "It was to assuage his own conscience. He said it to pretend to one part of his mind, call it the upper part, that he wasn't trying to do what the lower part wanted. Or maybe he said it because he knew that if he told the boys what he really meant—*Don't ever come back*—they would have panicked, made a scene, caused a lot of fuss he wasn't prepared to deal with. Anyway, I don't think that he, knowing what he did about the sea, expected them to last the summer."

Her composure has returned, which is odd, considering what she's telling me.

"Maybe you've been affected by what Myles told you?" I suggest. "What was it? Parents who destroy their children?"

"Unless the kids get to them first," she says, finishing up that cheery observation. "Yeah, I've wondered if that colored my thinking. It's just that I can't explain why he did what he did—not only banishing them, whatever you want to call it, but denying them. Sending that cruel telegram. Stranding them, after all they'd been through. I've tried to put myself in their shoes. What would I make of such a denial? Would I start to wonder if my survival was a disappointment?"

"Now that you've turned this into a kind of crime story, you need three things, y'know. Evidence and a motive and witnesses. Live witnesses, I mean witnesses who were alive then. Otherwise . . ."

One hand is raised, like the hand of the Virgin in the mosaic at my back.

"That's one of the reasons I've tried to make these people come alive for you, and for myself, too," she comments, and picks up her manuscript again. I notice that her handwriting resembles Nathaniel's. A bit more decorative and feminine, but the letters have the same sharp forward slant, as if they are about to fall over.

Then, in a tone oh so lawyerly, she tells me that there are threads of evidence that can lead to establishing a probable motive. There also are three witnesses, and the first one she calls is Lockwood.

Lockwood's Testimony

Begins with his birth . . .

Swinging her boots off the table to the tiled floor, spurs jinglejangle-jingling, Sybil draws her chair up to the table and flips through an album with a black cover and stiff black pages upon which captions are written in white ink under antique photos. Sepia images of people, boats, houses, seascapes, and landscapes flicker past until she comes to a photograph of a man with a wide head, what appears to be sandy brown hair and beard, and a stare whose bright, fixed intensity is doubtlessly an effect of a box camera's powder flash, but suggests fever or madness. He is wearing a suit, a high starched collar that looks a little too small for his athletic neck. The caption reads: "L. R. Braithwaite, 1899."

"And this," she says, turning more pages, "is a photo of the portrait that used to be in Myles's house. Cyrus at about the same age."

It is as she's described: Lockwood could be the younger Cyrus re-incarnated. The only noticeable differences are in the breadth of Lock-wood's head and the shade of his eyes: darker than his father's.

"Lockwood's exact age is one of the thousand little facts I couldn't nail down. No birth certificate that I know of, no records of any kind of when or where he was born, and he's not in there."

Motioning at a green, cloth-bound book on the patio table, *A Braithwaite Genealogy*, she comments that in a family like hers, keeping the kinds of records it does, there could be only one reason for the omis-sion of Lockwood's name.

"That's not a guess," she adds. "Myles told me, while we were hav-ing dinner. His father told him, and Eliot and my grandfather found out from Elizabeth. That's the chain of information. My great-grandmother let Eliot and Andrew in on Lockwood's secret when she was pretty old—lived to be eighty-six—and they were a long way from kids themselves. Up until then, they didn't have a clue, I guess. What Myles didn't know was Lockwood's mother's name, because Cyrus had never spoken it to his sons. I dug that out on my own."

She thumbs through the album again, her chin raised at an angle that allows me to picture the haughty tilt of her great-grandmother's that morning when the carriage rattled down the drive, taking her to the train station to see her doctor in Boston. Now, her head inclined toward mine, Sybil presses down on a page with an earlier photograph of Lock-wood, taken before he grew the beard. She carefully removes the photo from its corner slots and turns it over. Pasted to the back, the paper darkened to a buckskin color, is a notice from the church records of a New York City parish, St. Agnes. "A Mass was said today for the repose of the soul of Maureen Keough, beloved daughter of Thomas and Margaret Keough, members of this parish. Died October 20, 1865, age 19. May her sins be forgiven and the Perpetual Light of Heaven shine upon her."

Sybil, drawing away—"I have no idea who pasted it to Lockwood's picture. But I can't imagine why it would be there if Maureen Keough wasn't his mother. So, if she did die in childbirth, then October 20, 1865, must have been when he was born."

"But how could Cyrus have been the father?" I ask. "He was off with the navy."

"He was medically discharged after Mobile Bay, September of 1864," she explains. "He returned to Boston for a while, then went to New York. His older brother, Alexander, helped him get a job there, sometime, I figure, in the late fall, the early winter of 1864. Their father, my great-great-grandfather, Theophilus"—she raises a berry-brown hand as if swearing an oath —"that was his name, Theophilus. A Boston physician. Doctor to the Brahmins, and I guess a Brahmin himself."

"The abolitionist?"

She nods, then offers a portrait of the man put together from things she had been told by Myles, from bits of information gathered here and there: A true son of nineteenth-century Boston's upper levels; a man with an ascetic physique and turn of mind; a devout Congregationalist, stiff, crabbed, taciturn, his heart so full of rectitude that there was little room in it for much else—not so much as a cupboard wherein he might accommodate an understanding of moral failings, much less tolerance for them. But if you were going to aid fugitive slaves in the 1850s, that's how you had to be.

"In that sense, Cyrus was a chip off the old block," she says.

There was no finer example of her great-grandfather's virtue, she continues (assuring me she is not digressing), than his refusal to have another man serve in his place when he was called up by the Conscription Act of 1863—the infamous Conscription Act that had set off draft riots in New York City. She found documented proof of this old family legend. Among Cyrus's logbooks, among his granite company's account books, among the photos, scrapbooks, birth and baptismal records, and newspaper clippings—the odds and ends of a life, all that was left of an entire life, her great-grandfather's life—she had uncovered a bundle of correspondence bound with a dry-rotted ribbon; among those letters were two that Alexander had sent to Cyrus at Harvard (he was studying to be a doctor to please Theophilus, not because he wanted to be one). Twelve years older, a compact, dark-haired, bewhiskered man, Alexander was working as a junior partner in his maternal uncles' shipping business in New York City when he heard that his younger brother had been conscripted. Alexander had witnessed the riots, and he wrote in his first letter that he had found a German immigrant willing to serve as

Cyrus's substitute for the standard fee of three hundred dollars. That was customary for privileged young men in the Civil War. Cyrus's reply has been lost, but he must have answered that he would do nothing of the sort, must have said something to this effect: How could he, son of a man who had risked so much and done so much to liberate the Negro, *pay* someone else to fight in his stead in the war whose purpose was to wipe from the land the sin, the taint of slavery? In the next letter, Alexander told him he was being a fool, that not one of his, Alexander's, classmates from Yale had volunteered, and even the Irish rabble had rebelled against the Conscription Act, practically burned half of New York down in the riots. Why should Cyrus allow himself to be dragged into uniform when those ruffians weren't willing? He might think his life was his to do with as he chose, but it wasn't; he should think of their mother and how she would feel, were he to die for no good reason other than stubborn pride and too fine an observance of principles. Perhaps he had learned their father's lessons too well; he should reconsider. Sybil assumes he did, that mindful of his family's concerns, wishing to do the right thing, but not to worry his mother unnecessarily, he volunteered for the navy rather than be drafted into the army. Already an expert sailor, he would have felt more at home aboard ship than in a regiment; moreover, the navy wasn't involved in heavy fighting—mostly enforcing the blockade against the Secessionists and bombarding forts from a comfortable distance—and if he was fated to die, at least it would not be in some malarial rebel swamp but in the bosom of the great sweet mother of the sea.

And, of course, he almost did die in the great sweet mother's bosom, and he only nineteen at the time. Afterward, he appeared to suffer emotional problems, and those led him into a spell of less than virtuous conduct after he returned home. Sybil explains that she formed this analysis after reading the diary of her great-great-grandmother, Ada Wallace Braithwaite. Reaching over to the table, she takes up a sheaf of photocopies held together by a binder clip and marked with Post-it notes: a copy she has made of the diary. In it, Ada described her son's "seizures of black melancholy," which alternated with episodes of belligerence and heavy drinking. It was as if the war had erased his upbringing and conjured up the "mad wild" blood in him, the blood of those mutinous, pugnacious Scots from whom she herself was descended and whose heritage she had struggled to eradicate by teaching her son good manners and poetry and to say his prayers morning and night. In a later entry, Ada recorded that her husband decided a good dose of hard work would exorcise Cyrus's devils and prevailed upon his elder son and his brothers-in-law, Douglas and Tyler Wallace, to give Cyrus a job, the tougher the better. If he proved a sober, able hand, then perhaps they could give him a more responsible position in the office. The company was called, simply and unimaginatively, Wallace Brothers Shipping, and as best as Sybil can determine, it was located in lower Manhattan, on the Hudson River, not far from Hell's Kitchen, the old Irish immigrant neighborhood.

"They put him on the loading dock, he was a stevedore, and then he somehow or other must have gotten involved with Maureen Keough. What kind of a woman was she? A good girl who lost her heart to a handsome war hero? Maybe something a little shadier, like a barmaid in a waterfront dive? Can't say, but I'll guess that my great-grandfather would have been attracted to a girl who wasn't from his own class. Not because of the wild Scot in him, or because getting involved with a woman like that was a way of rebelling against what he'd come from. No, she brought him back to life."

"And you can say that for a fact, or . . . ?"

"Both," she replies. "Or maybe neither, not fact, not imagination, something else."

She means one of her visions of the past. Thus, she saw Maureen Keough and her great-grandfather one night late in 1864 or in early 1865, eating dinner in a cheap café on the riverfront. Maureen, as drawn by Sybil, is a not particularly pretty young woman, plump, even by the generous standards of that day, brown-haired, coarse-featured, but full of ruddy good humor, a certain raw appetite. The women who would meet with his family's approval, bound by rigid social rules, cannot give Cyrus what Maureen does. For reasons beyond his understanding, she banishes his spells of black melancholy; he forgets that terrible day aboard the *Brooklyn* after its sprint across the rebel minefield and past the guns of Fort Morgan, the deck a chaos of broken rigging, shattered spars, torn bodies tangled up in torn splinter nets like seined mackerel savaged by sharks, and Cyrus, too terrified even to realize he is terrified, trying to will sight back into his darkened eye, stumbling with a shipmate's help below decks to sick bay, and for a moment, wishing himself altogether blind when he sees that butcher's bin where surgeons labor in leather aprons black with blood, yes, the veil of Maureen's laughter makes all that fade away. . . .

"Maureen probably was the kind of girl who never had any luck, because she must have gotten pregnant right away," Sybil continues. "There was no way for an Irish Catholic in those days to marry outside her faith, and it's for sure Cyrus couldn't bring her home to Boston.

Even if she'd had all the breeding and manners in the world, Theophilus would not have given his blessing. He'd made his wife renounce Presbyterianism before he would marry her, because Congregationalists thought Presbyterians were the next thing to the devil himself, and Roman Catholics *were* the devil himself. So, if they did get married, it would have been in secret, in some civil ceremony, but I don't think they got married at all. The obituary lists her as Maureen Keough. And then there's this. . . ."

She lays the diary in her lap as she draws knees and heels together—a posture that would make her look like the prim, earnest schoolgirl I remember, if the tabloid glare of the desert light didn't expose the gull's tracks at the corners of her eyes, the whisker-thin wrinkles in her cheeks, other signs of too much sun and weather and her forty-four years.

Putting on her glasses, she reads aloud:

"November 12th, 1865. I have not written for the past three days because of dreadful news arriving in last week's mail from Cyrus. His conduct has been worse than scandalous and has become a source of the deepest anguish for us. While my dear Theo and I have tried to persuade ourselves that our son, whose soul had been so much troubled since his return from the late war, was the victim of temptation, we fear that, in truth, he was the source of it. Now, we must contend with the inevitable consequence of his sin, as he must as well. Of course, my heart goes out to the unfortunate, and to her family, and most of all, to the poor innocent. Of course, we will strive to grant our Cyrus Christian forgiveness, but as to the other thing he has asked of us—Oh! My heart is divided, for in part it is inclined to grant his request, to find some way to accommodate him. Sometimes I cannot bear the thought that I will never see, never know him. Indeed, Theo and I have actually quarreled over this matter. But he is a man with more moral fortitude than I. He said certain material provisions could be made, but as to the other, he will have none of it, will not even hear of it, and as Cyrus and I are bound to obey his wishes, I fear that is the end of it."

Sybil looks at me, her eyes sad but composed, as if she harbors a grief to which she was long ago resigned.

"Even when she's writing in her diary, talking to herself, Ada can't say a thing directly," she comments. "And that particular entry is candid, compared to some of the others. You should see them. You almost need a decoder to figure them out."

"All right. The 'him' she's afraid she'll never see is her grandson, Lockwood," I say. "But the request that the old man, that Theophilus wouldn't grant—I need the decoder there."

"After Maureen died, Cyrus must have written to his father and mother, confessed everything, asked for forgiveness and for them to help him raise Lockwood. Accept him as their grandson. No one in Boston had to know the boy was a bastard, his mother an Irish girl from the slums, but, of course, Theophilus would have considered that adding sin to sin, lying to fornication. No dice, that must have been what he wrote back to Cyrus, in so many words. He must have told my great-grandfather to place Lockwood in an orphanage, maybe promise to set something aside for the kid, but if Cyrus persisted in the notion of keeping the child, he would be cut off. Financially and otherwise. I couldn't find the letter. I assume Cyrus destroyed it. He didn't want any evidence lying around that Lockwood was illegitimate."

And that, she carries on, must have been the end of things between Cyrus and his parents. They cut him off, he cut himself off from them. In those days, with those kinds of people, there was no going back, once you made a choice. And Cyrus made his. He was going to be loyal to his child. He raised Lockwood himself.

"A single father in the 1860s!" Sybil looks over my shoulder, at the mosaic of the Virgin, and shakes her head in wonder. "How he did that in those days is something I have a hard time imagining, but it's the kind of thing that makes me wish I could love his memory, think the best of him. He took Lockwood with him to Florida when he took up the wrecking trade."

Wrecking and salvaging was a way to riches for someone who knew the sea and how to handle a ship, and Cyrus, cured by his new responsibilities of his melancholy, belligerence, and hard drinking, wanted to get rich as quickly as he could. He wanted to, because he couldn't expect a dime from dear Theo, and for another reason that she will go into later.

He turned up in Key West in late 1866, stepped off a packet with his infant son, and hired a Negro wet nurse named Clotil or Clothil or Cloteal—Sybil isn't sure of the spelling. He had been stationed in Key West during his first few weeks in the navy, aboard a frigate that captured slavers on the high seas and freed their human cargo. He would have learned that reefs and hurricanes made the Florida Straits the most fertile wrecking grounds in the country. And there would have been this to draw him there as well: the remoteness of the place as it was then, a lonely little island on the sea frontier, far from his family. A place of exile. He must have caught on to the trade quickly, because by 1870, he was owner and master of *Main Chance*.

"From what I could piece together, when Lockwood wasn't sailing with him, he was watched over by Clotil or Clothil or Cloteal, and sometimes by Ursuline nuns. They educated him—can you imagine what Theophilus would have thought of that? *Nuns?* I've read through the *Main Chance*'s logs, and you'll see references to the wind, the weather, what was salvaged from some wreck or other, and then, 'Lockwood didn't do well on his spelling lesson, but arithmetic satisfactory.' You've got to read between the lines, but you can tell that he really loved the kid. That's a key to what happened. He really loved him."

"Which Lockwood didn't return? You suggested that somewhere in the story, earlier on."

She nods. I mull things over for a moment, and maybe I'm getting into the spirit of the thing, acquiring my own insight into past lives, because I have an illumination, quick and bright, revealing an aspect of Lockwood's interior as a landscape is revealed in a flash of lightning.

"Because he felt guilty that his life had been bought at the price of his mother's?" I say, or ask, or both say and ask. "But you can't go around, day after day, feeling guilty about your own existence, so he shifted it, the blame, I'm saying, to Cyrus?"

"I'd say so, yes," Sybil replies.

"Because somewhere along the line, he found out he was a bastard, and maybe—it would be irrational for him to think this, but it would be understandable—he wondered if his mother would have lived if Cyrus had married her. That her death in a way was a kind of punishment, a retribution for living in sin."

"I'd say so, yes."

The album again, her hands again turning pages, Sybil's hands that I remember as smooth, youthful, now cracked and fissured beyond their years by this arid climate she's chosen to live in. The page-turning stops at an oval portrait of a woman with close-set eyes whose irises are the same midnight hue as their pupils.

"She told him. Elizabeth."

Lace covers the shoulders and bodice of Elizabeth's dress, and what looks like a giant butterfly with billowy wings and a jeweled body clings to the center of its modest decolletage. She is looking slightly away from the camera, and I remark that strong resemblances must run in Sybil's family, because the dead woman's likeness to the living one is such that the two could be sisters instead of ancestor and descendant. There are some notable differences: Sybil's eyes are golden; her hair is brown, long, and loose, while her great-grandmother's is wound into a turban of rich black whorls—she looks as if she could be South American or Italian. But both women have the same nose (its prominence creating that strong beauty people call handsome in a female), the same mouth, upper lip thin and bowed, the lower thick and lubricious, and the same high, broad forehead and hollow cheekbones. Yet, it isn't a similarity in the architecture of their features that makes them appear like siblings; it's a kinship of expression. Sybil has an old face—old in the sense of archaic—its look of somber serenity belonging to a time (unlike our own) that had lost neither its sense of the tragic nor the certitudes of faith: an age when both the awareness of death and the hope of salvation were writ on every face.

"Myles mentioned it to me," she says. "When Elizabeth told Eliot and Andrew that Lockwood had been illegitimate—don't know how she found out herself, maybe Cyrus 'fessed up when his guard was down—she also admitted that she had told Lockwood the truth, years and years before. No information on exactly when, or why she did."

"I suppose someone had to," I say. "She must have figured that Lockwood would have found out eventually and it was better he heard it from her, if Cyrus wasn't going to let him know. You can't keep a secret like that forever."

"That might have been her reason. . . ."

Sybil stops herself abruptly, leaving something unsaid, and sits silently in that schoolgirl pose.

"But Lockwood," I say. "His testimony."

"It's brief," Sybil responds. "He didn't fall off an elevated platform, he threw himself off, into the path of a train."

She hands me a copy of a *New York Times* article, dated Thursday, June 22, 1901. It begins with the multidecked headlines of the day.

SUICIDE IS IDENTIFIED!
MAN WHO LEAPT FROM TRAIN PLATFORM
SON OF PROMINENT BOSTON BUSINESSMAN!
LANDLADY DESCRIBES VICTIM AS "TROUBLED."
DID NOT LEAVE NOTE.

The story goes on to say that police had identified the man who had jumped from the Third Street elevated platform Monday night as Lockwood Robert Braithwaite, son of, et cetera, et cetera.

I read on down the column of small type. . . .

His supervisor at his place of employment, the marine insurance firm of Merrill, Chapman and Scott, stated that when Mr. Braithwaite, a valued and faithful employee, had failed to report to his office by Wednesday, a member of the firm recalled reading about the suicide in the newspaper and that the initials "L.B." had been found sewn into the victim's coat. A representative of the firm was then dispatched to the morgue, where, et cetera, et cetera. . . .

A search was made of Mr. Braithwaite's rooms at Gleason's Boarding House, James Slip. . . . Detectives found scraps of what appeared to be a letter, burned in the fireplace, but a suicide note was not discovered. . . . Mrs. Thomas Gleason, proprietress, informed the police that Mr. Braithwaite had been in an agitated and distracted state the last time she saw him, which was Monday morning. "He appeared to be most troubled," Mrs. Gleason said, but did not wish to speculate on what his motives may have been. However, the *Times* learned that Mr. Braithwaite's wages were being garnisheed to pay off debts incurred in a business failure in Florida. . . .

"Pretty straightforward, Sybil. His creditors were after him, he asked his father to help him out again, he was turned down, he had nowhere to go."

"Maybe. Maybe that's what it was," she says, in an undertone. "As near as I could figure, Lockwood probably went to him at Mingulay, sometime in early June. Remember that? From the first chapter?"

I nod.

"I did not make that part up. The reason I know is from a letter that Eliot wrote to Andrew in the 1930s, when Eliot was working for FDR in Washington. It was in one of my grandfather's scrapbooks. Both of them knew by that time that the story their mother had told them about Lockwood's death wasn't completely true. Anyway, it was a chatty, personal sort of letter—it's in this pile somewhere—and in it, Eliot makes a reference to the voyage and to the argument between Lockwood and their father that took place before it. That's how I figured out about when the argument happened."

"All right, Lockwood goes to him in early June, asks for help, doesn't get it, and then kills himself."

"Two or maybe three weeks later. I wonder why it took that long. . . . Oh, I know, he may have brooded over it, but . . . Well, maybe I should just go on, take this step by step," she says, and then picks up a file folder filled with papers.

Elizabeth's Testimony

Begins with a photocopy of the transaction between Caleb Maxey and Pardon Lightbourne, dated Oct. 20, 1858.

But the story really begins earlier, with an entry from the diary of Carleton Maxey, Caleb's father and the founder of the rice and indigo plantation called The Marshes:

June 19, 1843—Rose at five-thirty, said my prayers, read from Amos ... Learned from O'Brien that Samuel, the mulatto acquired from JPT last year, has run off ... Reported Samuel missing, with description.

Which continues:

September 12, 1843—Rose at six a.m., said my prayers, read from Psalms ... O'Brien reported that Samuel discovered by patrols living with Creeks about seventy-five miles from here ...

And with this:

September 17, 1843—Rose at five-thirty a.m. Prayers. Continue with the Psalms ... Samuel returned, with half-Creek, half-nigger wife, name unknown. The woman is with child ... Had Samuel whipped, twenty-five strokes, and warned that if he attempts again, will amputate a foot ...

And with this:

Jan. 21, 1844—Rose at six-thirty. Said my prayers, read from Matthew. The day spent with accounts ... Entered into inventory one female, named Julietta, born recently to the half-Creek, half-nigger woman. Samuel is the father.

And finally, the 1858 bill of sale, written with a Victorian flourish, in the thick black letters made by the nib of a quill pen:

Sold to Pardon Lightbourne, of Federal Street, Beaufort, for the sum of fifty dollars, one female Negro, Julietta, age thirteen.

Height: 5 feet 4 four inches; 125 pounds; light mulatto complex-
ion. I attest that she is my property, that there are no prior
claims upon her by other persons, and that her health and condi-
tion are sound. Caleb Maxey.

She goes from that to excerpts from Pardon Lightbourne's Civil War
diary, obtained by Buckmayer, the genealogist, from the Beaufort His-
torical Society.

Sybil mentions that when she read through it the first time, following her great-great-grandfather from his departure with his South Carolina regiment in May 1861 to the day before his death at Antietam the
following year, she was struck by the absence of a single word about a
baby daughter (Elizabeth was born in late November 1861, shortly after
Union forces occupied Beaufort). The only child Pardon spoke of was
his three-year-old son, Henry.

Sybil read the diary again, more slowly, and that was when she
noticed what she had missed the first time around.

She removes a printout from the folder and hands it to me.

Dec. 17—I received today from Henrietta a most painful com-
munication that causes me the deepest shame. . . .

Dec. 20—Rain continues. Feel an ague coming on. Wrote to
Henrietta today. Confessed all & begged & begged for forgive-
ness but said I would understand if it was not forthcoming. This
unburdening has brought some relief. I could not face Christmas
with so much on my conscience. . . .

Feb. 3 (1862)—Bitterly cold today, but a letter at last from Hen-
rietta. There is a good deal of news from home. Foremost, I am
forgiven! The relief this brings me cannot be described. I have
been in torment these past weeks, and have almost wished for a
Yankee ball or bayonet to find me. . . . Federals are building a
town for freed Negroes on Hilton Head, and the girl ran off to
live there with a buck Negro who wanted nothing to do with her
infant. She abandoned it. H. is quite happy to be rid of her and,
not desirous of caring for the issue of a husband's sin, accepted
an offer from Judith to take the child in until a Negro family is
found for her, if one can be. Negroes may find her too fair and
fear they will be accused of abducting a white child. I will write
that the arrangement with Judith is appropriate, considering my
sister-in-law's opinions. . . .

The excerpts end there, and Sybil and I are silent while I, so to speak, metabolize the astonishing fact implied in Pardon Lightbourne's oh so guarded confession.

"When did you find this out?"

"A couple of years ago."

"Did you tell your brother?"

A curt nod.

"So that makes you . . ."

"Depends on how much of a mulatto Elizabeth's grandfather was. . . ."

"Samuel?"

"Samuel. And how much black there was in his Creek wife. But I think it's safe to say that Jason and I are one two-hundred-and-fifty-sixth. I remember hearing a story from my grandfather that his mother had Indian blood. He never said anything about her other blood, because I don't think he knew. I'm sure Cyrus didn't, either. The only ones who knew were Elizabeth and Aunt Judith."

They would have covenanted between them to keep the truth from Cyrus. When he left Florida to begin a whole new life for himself in Maine, he turned *Main Chance* into a cargo ship to make the trip pay for itself—thirteen years in the tropics had not diluted his Yankee enterprise. He sailed into Port Royal on a winter's day in 1879 to sell off a load of pineapples, take on cotton for Boston, and look for a couple of crewmen, because he was short-handed. A torn peacoat and a hankering for a decent meal brought him into Beaufort, a few miles from the port, and when he brought the coat into a tailor shop on Bay Street, he fell instantly in love with the eighteen-year-old seamstress with ebony hair and onyx eyes, who told him she would have it repaired by the next day. He took one look at her and said he wished he had a trunk full of clothes that needed sewing. Elizabeth had been well schooled by Aunt Judith and made no reply, turning aside with a coquettish glance that encouraged by failing to discourage. And so the courtship began, the courtship that was so ardent and swift as to be almost an abduction. It was one of those times in life when chance colludes with design. He had determined to marry and wanted more children, and this girl, who was young and healthy and extraordinary looking, struck him as a gift to be seized without pause or reservation, and he, a stranger bound for the distant North, a man of some means and ambition, must have struck the women in the same way, and they covenanted to deceive him. They could not afford to do otherwise; Cyrus was Elizabeth's only chance, for this was Beaufort,

South Carolina, during Reconstruction, a city of five thousand souls, at most, and far too many people in town knew the secret of her birth, much as Aunt Judith and she tried to conceal it. For all her beauty, for all the charms and manners and French phrases and domestic skills Aunt Judith had taught her, there wasn't a white man in the county who would have considered marrying her, or a black man who would have dared to take to wife a woman who looked and was, for all practical purposes, white.

Cyrus was a gift, not to be lost through pointless candor. There were the liabilities of his age and his son—Elizabeth would become an instantaneous mother—but Aunt Judith probably argued that these were not of sufficient weight to affect his assets. Better an older man who knew what he was about than an untested youth; as for the son, he was so close to Elizabeth's age that he would be more of a younger brother than a stepson.

In less than two weeks, Elizabeth was the captain's wife, the ceremony performed by another captain whose ship was docked alongside *Main Chance*. The next morning, she left for the iron skies and waters of the Maine coast with a small trunk, her copy of *The Manners, Culture, and Dress of the Best American Society,* and her secret. Two secrets, actually, one of which was being kept from Aunt Judith: Elizabeth intended to reinvent herself. That necessitated severing herself entirely from her former world and life, which had the additional benefit of insuring that her husband would never find out her true parentage.

Cyrus had his plans, as well, and he must have told his bride about them during the long voyage to Maine. Losing his wrecker's license had been a disguised blessing. It was time to get out of the business anyway. He had fought storms and ship owners and underwriters for thirteen years, and he had too little to show for it. Yes, he'd become modestly rich, but modest wasn't rich enough. Now he was thirty-five, and he craved more. In Key West, he'd met a down-east skipper transporting paving blocks to Havana. The man told him about fortunes being made quarrying New England granite: Cities had to have it for their streets; bridge builders needed it; it was used for facing, monuments, fountains. Cyrus made inquiries by mail, obtained by various means statements of profit and loss from several quarrying companies, looked into labor and equipment costs, and when one of his correspondents sent him a newspaper advertisement for the sale of a quarry on Hurricane Island, "complete with shops, sheds, wharf, derricks and forty acres of land," he wired the owner and bought the operation sight unseen, and without knowing the difference between feldspar and hornblende, a scotia hammer and a plug drill. That didn't bother him. He'd landed in Key West not knowing the first thing about wrecking.

He presented all of this to his Elizabeth (when she wasn't too seasick to listen to it), and his vision of what the profits would buy: a house in Boston, a country house on the coast of Maine. By force of will, by unremitting toil and enterprise, he intended to reclaim that place in Boston society he had lost when he defied his father's wishes and kept custody of Lockwood. (It might have been then that he confessed to Elizabeth Lockwood's illegitimate birth, Sybil adds parenthetically.) He also wanted more children, before he got too much older. He knew the exact number—five, and he hoped for three sons. That was where Elizabeth came in; her womb to be the servant of his ambitions.

There is no record in letter or diary of how she fared during the four years she lived in Maine, nor had any stories been passed down to Myles. All he had heard was that they were difficult years. They must have been. Cyrus rented a house in Vinalhaven, across a strait from Hurricane Island. Sybil imagines what it must have been like for the young woman, who had never felt anything much below forty degrees Fahrenheit, to endure a Maine winter; a spring that was not a spring, at least not one as she understood the term; a cool summer, the mornings obscured by fog; a brief autumn; and then another winter, with its short days and frigid palls of seasmoke. Cyrus would have been gone much of the time, spending long days at the quarry, learning the business from his manager, the Swede named Pedersen. Lockwood, when he wasn't in school, was her only company, and, she must have judged, was likely to remain so; for inhospitable down-easters would have come along with the inhospitable climate. The woman from a region that loved words and talk and bombast listened to the monsyllabic "nups" and "ayups" of stern Calvinists who ate milk and crackers on Sundays, because it was sinful to fill your belly on the Sabbath, and who declined to accept as friend anyone who had not lived among them for at least a decade. To their flinty minds, Elizabeth, with her olive complexion and strange, lilting drawl, would not have seemed exotic but suspiciously foreign.

And at night, Cyrus, home from the pits, would have ploughed and harrowed and seeded her in the same rough, single-minded way he did everything else, but her menses came month after month with depressing regularity.

"I found these with my great-grandmother's things. Take a look at the articles," says Sybil, producing several antique issues of the *American Gynecological Review,* the *Boston Medical and Surgical Journal,*

Harper's Weekly, Century Magazine, American Magazine, and an 1883 copy of the *Practical Home Physician.*

They form a chronicle of a young woman suffering from the great fear of the Victorian wife, the fear of the empty cradle, which she must have felt more acutely than most: a terror of barrenness that was conspiring with a chilly climate, chilly neighbors, and isolation to disorder her nerves, and maybe her mind, as well. "The Treatment of Neurasthenia" . . . "Does Excessive Education Make Women Barren?" . . . "Remedies for Uterine Catarrh" . . . "Causes and Treatments of Female Infertility" . . . "Neurasthenia and Its Relation to the Diseases of Women" . . . And stuffed inside the journals were several ads for bromides and electuaries and other snake-oil remedies like Worden's Restorative Nervous Elixir—"guaranteed to remove the causes of female sterility" . . . Lydia Pinkham's Tonic—"A baby in every bottle!" . . . Dr. Pierce's Golden Medical Discovery . . .

"I don't know how she got hold of all those periodicals, living out there in the middle of Penobscot Bay, but she did," Sybil remarks, and then lifts from between the covers of the *Practical Home Physician* a page torn out of the *Boston Medical and Surgical Journal,* dated fall 1883. The article, by a gynecologist named Bigelow, describes how he treated a young woman who had come to him seeking an operation to cure her infertility. The beginning of one paragraph is underlined: "This patient verged on hysteria, stating to me that she had been married for seven years without a pregnancy, and that she was now desperate, fearing that her husband would desert her if she did not give birth. . . ."

"My great-grandmother must have identified with that woman, whoever she was."

But, my friend goes on, Elizabeth's thinking began to change. Sybil doesn't know what brought the change about. An article in one of the magazines? A word from her family doctor? At any rate, although Cyrus had a son to warrant his manhood, something caused her to question if it was the seed and not the ground that was barren in their marriage. She began to clip stories about the causes of male sterility, one of which, gonorrhea, must have caused her some worry. Her husband could not have remained celibate during his seafaring years. Had he contracted the disease from some waterfront prostitute? But it is doubtful that she suggested anything of the sort to Cyrus, no good Victorian wife would have; so she probably went on guzzling her Lydia Pinkham's tonic and Dr. Pierce's Golden Medical Discovery while her terror of desertion mounted, and her neurasthenia with it.

A terror that might have been aggravated by the concoctions she was drinking—those fradulent brews of opium, laudanum, and cocaine—but not caused by it. No great powers of imagination are needed to picture the disappointed and recriminatory looks that Cyrus had started to give her, to hear the silences that were not silences, and to feel him, as Elizabeth must have, slowly drawing away.

At that time—late 1883—he moved his family from Vinalhaven to Hurricane Island, where he had established a new quarry, the Norawhega, whose granite was being shipped to face the Museum of Fine Arts in Boston, the New York Customs House, the U.S. Naval Academy. A gold mine for Cyrus, which was why he named it after the legendary jeweled city that, early Dutch explorers had been told (by some Indians with a sense of humor), lay somewhere in the forests around Penobscot Bay. He had learned the business quickly and had built a company town on Hurricane, with stores, a boardinghouse, a school, a church, and a dance hall, and he was the unelected mayor, ruling it as he had his ship, his iron reign eventually earning him the title (seldom uttered in a complimentary tone) "Emperor of the Isles," to which the Italian stonemasons later added their *Capitano Furioso*.

So now, Elizabeth and Lockwood found themselves living in greater isolation, Hurricane Island being a fraction of the size of Vinalhaven. Their house wasn't large, and it had only its location atop a hill overlooking the new town to distinguish it from the clapboard cottages of the quarrymen. They were a friendlier lot than the down-easters of Vinalhaven, but they spoke Finnish, Swedish, and Italian, leaving the Emperor, his Empress, and his heir apparent with no one to speak to but themselves. That suited Cyrus, who was still the sea captain at heart, alone on his figurative quarterdeck. But it had to have been boring and lonely for Elizabeth and her stepson, and when Cyrus was gone (continually prospecting, from Maine down to Cape Ann, for new quarries to buy or for new ledges of untapped granite), they were stranded in an unnatural solitude, with only the occasional town dance or party to relieve it.

In the spring of the following year, Cyrus left on a trip that was supposed to have taken a couple of weeks, but lasted six. He had sailed away aboard one of the droghers that regularly shipped his granite, *Caitlin Adams*. She was carrying two great pedestal stones for a monument in New York City, but was caught in a gale for six days and driven over a thousand miles into the open Atlantic, before she was able to resume her original course. When Cyrus finally got back to Hurricane Island, says Sybil, Elizabeth must have been joyful for two reasons: Her husband had not been lost at sea, and she was pregnant. A perfect time, the land greening and she with it, the light after the long winter, the world awakening. The first of the coveted sons was born March 3, 1885. . . .

"That would have been about a month late. Just right. A month wasn't enough to raise eyebrows."

"How do you mean, late?" I ask.

"I've got a newspaper story about the trip. Cyrus gave the Camden newspaper an interview about the trip and how harrowing it was. Anyway, the ship set sail on May 5—this is 1884—and finally docked in New York on June 11; Cyrus got back to Maine around the 17th or 18th. So, let's say that my great-grandparents made love just before he left, the nights of May 3 or 4. Counting nine months exactly, that gives a due date for Nathaniel of February 4, 1885. Okay, it's never exact, give or take a week to ten days, on either side. If Nat was a week late, he would have been born February 11, or thereabouts. But for her to deliver him on the 3rd of March means she had to get pregnant on the 3rd of June, if he was right on time, on the 10th of June, if he was a week early, and around May 27 or so, if he was a week late."

I have a hard time following this without a calendar; so I give her arithmetic the benefit of the doubt.

"All right. But do you know that she knew she was pregnant when Cyrus got home?"

"Not know it as in I-swear-on-the-Bible know it. But that's what I'd heard from Myles—my great-grandfather was thought lost at sea in the spring of 1884, delivering this granite, and found out that he was going to be a father again right after he got back."

"That'll have to do, I guess. Still, you're cutting things close. It could have been him."

"But have I made a good case for her desperation?" Sybil asks earnestly. "Her history, her situation? A woman with very limited choices? With him, she could have everything, without him, well . . . And to keep him, she had to deliver a baby. A desperate woman is likely to do desperate things. . . ."

Now, she reaches for another exhibit in her pile of evidence, a Bible, which she opens.

"You know, I would believe Cyrus had been the father, except for this. When I read the telegram, the first thing I did was go to St. Paul's letters to the Corinthians. Still couldn't figure out what the man was talking about. That was a couple of years ago, before I had a chance to look at all this stuff"—gesturing at the table. "But after I did, this verse lit up like it was written in neon."

She gives me the Bible, opened to First Corinthians, chapter five, verse one. It's the New Revised Standard Edition, so the language is clearer, if less majestic and ominous, than in the old King James. I read the passage, take a moment, and I read again, to make sure I understand the implications.

> *For it is actually reported that there is sexual immorality among you, and of a kind that is not found even among pagans; for a man is living with his father's wife.*

"Oh, my God, Sybil."

She looks over her shoulder through the courtyard gate, its carved leaves, blackened as if by fire, opened under an adobe arch to frame a pasture where her horses nuzzle grama grass, high as their knees.

"But maybe he was referring to something else in Corinthians?"

"'Look not to Isaiah but to Corinthians for passage home,'" answers Sybil. "He's Isaiah, the rock from which the boys think they've been hewn, and he's not giving them a cent, because they think wrong. Of course, they couldn't look to Corinthians, either, because he was dead weeks before the cable was sent, but that was beside the point Cyrus was trying to make."

"She's dead and gone, but I don't think it's fair to accuse her of *that*."

"She was desperate and probably depressed, but she didn't do it in blind desperation, no, I don't think she was like that. I never knew her, and Myles only knew her when she was old, but I think I can make a case that she was clever and calculating, because she had to be, and manipulative, too, because she had to be. Had to be that way all her life. She took a huge chance, but she took it with her eyes wide open, I would bet on that. You said it isn't fair, but add this to the telegram: The summer starts off with my great-grandparents living together, it ends with them living apart, and in between, Cyrus writes to a lawyer about a divorce and Lockwood commits suicide. Then there's the last chapter in 1908, the year Cyrus died. Elizabeth had to go to court to get a share of his estate. He had cut her *and his sons* out of his will. Why the boys?"

"You're not saying he was the father of *all three*? I just can't picture that. Lockwood and her, and in those days."

"Too prim and proper for carrying on like that? Yes, maybe. But in another sense, those days had everything to do with what happened, okay, with what I *think* happened. To start with Nathaniel. Lockwood was just shy of nineteen at the time, Elizabeth just shy of twenty-three. You saw what a knockout she was, you can feel the heat coming off her in a photograph. Imagine what effect a woman like that would have had on a healthy nineteen-year-old boy, even if she is his father's wife. The two of them spent days together, locked up alone on islands in the bays of Maine. When Cyrus was home, you can bet that he bedded his young wife, every chance he got—breeding his mare, never knowing it was him who was dried up inside, not her, him all along."

"From what? Where do you come up with that diagnosis? He already fathered a son, so doesn't that suggest that it wasn't him? That neither of them was sterile, that her not conceiving was just the luck of the draw?"

"It's in his logbooks. In 'seventy-six he made a note that he'd caught the mumps and had to turn *Main Chance* over to his first mate while he recovered. I researched this. Before there was any such thing as mumps vaccine, the disease was a cause of sterility in men. Not as much as gonorrhea, but it was up there."

"All right. So go ahead."

"The house was small, and no matter how Victorian and decorous Cyrus and Elizabeth tried to be, Lockwood must have heard them making love and that must have tormented him. Then, Cyrus went off on the trip that was supposed to last two weeks but turned into six. Again, Lockwood and Elizabeth are alone. Two weeks pass, then three, and no word from Cyrus. There was the fear that he had been lost, but for Elizabeth there would be another fear. That he was with someone else or looking for someone else, a new broodmare. Now, let's imagine this, not for the fun of it, but because it's plausible. There is a dance in town, Lockwood and Elizabeth go to it to get out of the house, the Empress and the heir apparent. They drink a little punch, maybe they even dance together. Inhibitions are loosened, but Elizabeth's mind is working clearly. Lockwood looks like Cyrus, he's young, virile, and she needs to know, is it her or is it Cyrus? And, more than anything, she needs a baby. We can assume she must have felt some sexual tension from Lockwood, and I would guess that also put the idea of seducing him into her head. But how was she to do it? I mean, she must have been terrified by herself, she probably could not believe that she had such audacity. But I can picture her playing on his desires and his sympathies. That could have been when she told him that he was illegitmate, and learning that he'd been lied to all his life could have undermined whatever loyalties he felt toward his father. She tells Lockwood that she's afraid his father will leave her if she dosen't give him a baby. She starts to cry. Lockwood goes to comfort her, there is an embrace that starts off platonically but doesn't end that way. She's older, cleverer, she's in control, but I would imagine the whole thing had been very difficult for her. She was doing something reprehensible to live. Like a prostitute. And for Lockwood? It could well have been his first time, and everything that implies. He would have fallen in love. Anyway, he would have thought it was love. Can't tell the difference between heart and glands at that age. Afterward? She tutors Lockwood on how to act from now on, how to never give the least little hint that something is amiss, even though, in matters like this, Cyrus is thick as a plank, a human ironclad. This is a woman, don't forget, who knew how to live a lie. Myles told me that his father told him that there was always a strange distance between Elizabeth and Lockwood, they were at arms' length. It could be I'm all wet and nothing ever went on between them, but if I am right, then that distance, that coolness Eliot saw might have been a ruse. It was part of the camouflage.

"Okay," Sybil continues, "Lockwood left the family to go to sea right after Nathaniel was born, and Elizabeth encouraged him to go. That's nothing I made up, that's fact, also from Myles, and it would make sense for her to encourage him. Maybe she even suggested it. She might have been a good teacher in the art of dissembling, but I don't think the straight-from-the-shoulder sailor boy would have been an apt pupil. Having him around the house all the time would have been too risky, and too great a strain on them both. And there might have been this, too: Elizabeth was afraid of her emotions. Lockwood wasn't like his father, a steam-bent oak rib, but young and malleable. She might have taught him tenderness, which I don't think she got from *Capitano Furioso* until he was older and mellowed, and then it was probably a kind of patriarchal, condescending tenderness. Lockwood went to sea but came back, from time to time, and during those returns, when his father was away, assignations were arranged. I suppose Elizabeth would have been good at arranging them. I suppose she would have been good at anything having to do with concealment and secrecy, the girl with black blood who had lived all her life in a white world and maybe sometimes convinced herself that Pardon's blood was the only blood in her. There would have been these assignations, like I said, and Eliot came along and then my grandfather, and then it stopped after him. Cyrus did not have his five children, but did have his three sons, and maybe he was satisfied with that. I really don't know if things stopped between Elizabeth and Lockwood, or if it was only the bearing of children that stopped, either because nature made it so or because she started using whatever birth control there was for a woman at that time. Anyway, I'm pretty sure the reason a handsome man like Lockwood never found a girl was because he wasn't looking. Elizabeth captured him entirely. I'm not sure how much she allowed herself to feel for him, but she must have welcomed the tenderness, the not being plowed and harrowed and seeded, but loved. In time, she would have needed it as much as he needed her, and so maybe things did continue after it was no longer necessary for them to continue, and the only thing that stopped was more children. But I just don't know. You see, there's this—she did have an operation when she was about forty, and that's another fact. She mentioned, I mean alluded to, it, in a letter she wrote to Gertrude Williams. It's dated June 6, 1901. . . ." (Sybil reads aloud.) "'My dearest Gertrude, I am delighted to tell you that the procedure went smoothly and painlessly and without any complications. Dr. Simms was most understanding and kind and assures me that he will exercise the utmost discretion. I cannot thank you enough, my dear, dear friend, for recommending him to me (or was it me to him?). I feel a bit melancholy. This has been so difficult for me, and without you it would have been impossible. Dr. Matthews has looked in on me because I had a slight fever yesterday, but he tells me I'll be fine soon and back to Mingulay for the summer. He has been in contact with Dr. Simms, who told him he had performed a hysterectomy. How I wish that had not been necessary. Only a few years ago, it would not have been. I am so looking forward to seeing you at North Haven! . . .' What does that sound like to you?"

"Obvious, except for the one line," I say. "The one about something not being necessary a few years ago, that throws me off."

Sybil returns the letter to her folder. Above, the hawk wheels, though I'm not sure if it's the same hawk I saw earlier.

"I researched that, too. Abortions were legal in most states until the 1890s. That's when the moralists took over gynecology and passed the laws against it. But a lot of doctors continued to perform them."

"So, then it was still going on? After Lockwood came back from Florida, they picked up again where they left off? And whatever she had been using failed? But you said awhile back that Cyrus wanted, what was it? Five kids? That was his goal? So why would she—If this not-quite-incest with Lockwood was still going on, and she got pregnant, why not do what she'd done before? Have the baby and let Cyrus think it was his?"

"She might have had complications with the pregnancy. Elizabeth was pushing forty. Might have been something else. The timing. Cyrus was fifty-six, and fifty-six then wasn't like fifty-six now."

"Oh."

"Gertrude would have known who to go to. But I don't think Elizabeth would have told even her dear, dear friend who the other man was. She might not have told her there had been another man."

"So she, your great-grandmother, somehow or other arranged to see Lockwood when he was in New York?"

"I don't know. Hard to think of how she could have. Maybe he made secret trips to Boston, and she sneaked out of the house when Cyrus was off in Gloucester or somewhere else. I don't know. Like I said, I don't even know if it continued between them. This part gets real fuzzy."

"You don't know, Sybil, you don't really *know* if there ever was anything in the first place. And you haven't explained this—if there was something, how did Cyrus find out?"

"You're right," she says. "I haven't explained."

But now she tries. . . .

Cyrus's Testimony

The only plausible way for him to have found out would have been to hear it from Lockwood or Elizabeth herself, and Lockwood seems by far the more likely of the two. Sybil's imagination fails, it cannot show her what emotions had been felt by a man cuckolding his own father, a father he must have respected, if not loved, and yet resented at the same time, though he had no right to that resentment. And piled atop the resentment, the blocked affections that must have tormented him whenever he saw them, the sons of the father's son, his, *his*. My God, having to look upon them, even if it was only for a day or two, once a year at most, and all the while have to stifle what was in his heart and feign and dissemble, must have split him in two.

It would have happened when Lockwood appeared at Mingulay to beg his father for money once again. They would have gone into the library, that same room with its view of lawn and sea and island where, in Sybil's re-creating, Nathaniel had seen Lockwood drunkenly pissing on the desk, muttering "Liquidation!" Lockwood would have argued that he had learned his lesson and taken his medicine and done all the manly things, and that there was now no point in denying him that relief from debt which Cyrus could grant with a signature. The harsh laws of the sea did not prevail here, this wasn't a case of a man recklessly sailing into uncharted waters or carrying more sail than the wind would allow. Lockwood had not done anything foolish, but had only failed, while trying his damnedest not to. He was the son of a millionaire, and he was living in a boardinghouse on the New York waterfront, for Christ's sake, and through no fault of his own. "It's not that it isn't fair, Father," Lockwood might have said, "it's that it isn't *right*." Yet Cyrus turned him down, perhaps remembering that he had been reduced to poverty once through no fault of his own, had been shown the door by his father, and had walked out of it with never a look back or a cry for help, but had, by dint of unswerving effort and risk and vision, restored his fortunes and reclaimed what should have been his by heritage. Why should Lockwood do any less? Why should Lockwood, having been helped once and told to expect no more, now expect more?

Now, in Sybil's re-creation, comes the moment when Lockwood parts, like an overstressed shroud—*ping*—but on the inside only. On the outside, he achieves that level of anger he has seen so often in his father—not the flares of temper that made him *Capitano Furioso* but the subzero calm of an offended sense of justice and right. Lockwood sees himself as having nothing to lose, and that is his one advantange. Now he will take everything—everything, that is, but the money—from the father who had refused to marry his mother and had buried her in a pauper's grave, and had done her the further dishonor of never speaking her name again, and then had trod on her memory by lying to the son she'd borne him and died bearing. *Where is Mrs. Braithwaite, Father? . . . Oh, Boston, is it? . . . And what's she doing there? . . . A doctor, a female problem, you say? But you don't know anymore? . . . Well, I do, and I'll tell you. She's pregnant, and not by you. . . .* A long silence ensues, Cyrus advancing on his son, his coldness now matching Lockwood's and the contest to see which glacier shatters the other. . . . And then Lockwood, surprised that in his despair he has the strength to look into that unyielding face, without yielding himself: *Not by you, and it's never been by you, you're all thunder and no lightning, old man. Never by you, but you can see yourself in them, can't you? How would you explain that? That's something else you didn't know, but I reckon you do now. . . .*

Maybe it had happened like that, maybe in some other way, and with some other words.

The story of what came afterward requires less speculation. It has been passed down through the generations, and the source was the source of all secret scandals in upper-class families in those times—the help. Whispers overheard in the kitchen, in the hall, in the carriage house, whispers telling of how Moira had heard a shout in the library, and ran downstairs to see Cyrus dragging Lockwood by the collar across the floor, Lockwood's nose and mouth bloodied, how she watched the father throw the son out the front door, and then kick him in the ribs, there on the lawn of the great house that was monument to all he had achieved, and how Gideon and Dailey pulled him off and held him back, Cyrus shouting, *Get him out of here! Put him in the carriage and get him out of here before I kill him!*

They had seen and heard, but none of them—Moira the maid, Dailey the driver, Gideon the caretaker—had the temerity to ask Cyrus what had provoked him; and when the boys returned from the boatyard that evening, the help all knew what was expected of them. *It would be best if you leave your father alone tonight. Lockwood was here earlier in the day, and they had a dispute. He's quite upset. . . . What about? . . . He didn't tell us, and we think it would be smart if you don't ask him.*

So Nathaniel, Eliot, and Sybil's grandfather did not speak to their father that night, or see him. Like the help, they also knew what was expected of them, and in the morning said nothing to him until he addressed them. By that time, he gave all the appearances of having calmed down, but of course it wasn't calm; it must have been, Sybil theorizes, a kind of numbness brought on by fury, grief, disbelief, and revulsion of such depth and intensity as to cancel each other out. The betrayal! The betrayal! From the wife to whom he had given so much, from the son he could have cast aside but did not, even at the sacrifice of all that should have been his. The shock was not emotional but metaphysical, such as might be felt by a devout priest who comes upon irrefutable proof that God does not exist. Cyrus was, in short, insane, but not in his mind—in his soul. That species of madness is the kind that commonly results in mass domestic slaughters, and as Sybil looks back far into the past, through the prism of fact and imagination, her wonder is that Cyrus did not take his L. C. Smith and shoot the sons who were not his and the son who was, and the treasonous wife, and then himself. Instead, he sat and brooded for days, and, the rational brain thinking within the deranged soul, he decided on what he had to do. Had to do, perhaps, to prevent himself from picking up the gun and cleansing his polluted house in the blood of the guilty and the innocent alike.

Sybil stops talking and looks up into the square of blemishless blue, from which the hawk has flown. Now there is only empty, annihilating sky.

"All right," I say. "He had a plan, of sorts. A muddled plan, but a plan. The divorce was part of it, but he never went through with that. Right?"

"Right. His lawyer advised him against it." She fishes another paper out of another folder. "This was in a file in my great-grandfather's business stuff, and maybe it's what convinces me that I'm right in all this. I'll go chronologically. Here's what probably happened after Cyrus sent the boys away—that was on June 11, by the logbook. He took the train to Boston, saw the lawyer, and laid out the case, and then, that day, maybe the next, maybe the day after, confronted Elizabeth. I don't picture a violent scene, for some reason, I picture him telling her what he's found out in this spooky, icy way. He hates her so much he's beyond hate. Before she has a chance to say one word, he says that he's divorcing her, never wants to see her again, or hear her name, or have anything to do with her. He tells her that he's sent the boys to sea, and maybe even says he doesn't give a damn if they ever come back. Her precious boys, the issue of her unspeakable treachery. Now, it's her turn to be shocked, and terrified, and in a panic she writes to Lockwood, and tells him what Cyrus is going to do and that the scandal will be horrendous, that she can never forgive him for opening his mouth. Lockwood reads the letter, he's full of guilt, shame, and who knows what else. He broods for several days, and then the train platform.

"The sad thing," Sybil goes on, "is that the lawyer sent the letter talking Cyrus out of it only the day before Lockwood did himself in. June 21, 1901." (She reads aloud again.) "'Dear Mr. Braithwaite,' et cetera, blah, blah blah . . . 'After discussing your case with my partner, I must urge you to reconsider. . . . To proceed with this action, you would need to identify the correspondent. . . . You must be aware of the perils such a course would entail. Confidentiality can be promised, but cannot be guaranteed. You are a prominent man. Were the yellow press to get wind of this, if you'll excuse the phrase, it would create a sensation that would reach far beyond Boston. . . . I assure you that I am prepared to assist you in working out an arrangement that would give you a measure of satisfaction while avoiding all possibility of scandal. . . .' And that's it," Sybil concludes. "All that I have. Evidence, witnesses, motive."

"But I have to tell you, I'm not convinced beyond a reasonable doubt."

"Well, we're not in court, are we? And all these people are gone and it doesn't make much difference now, does it?"

"It must to you."

"I'm here. I am who I am and what I am, no matter what went on almost a hundred years ago."

"But it's still your family. They're in you. So tell me, if you really think this is what happened way back then, do you hate your family now?"

"Myles said it. You have to hate the sin but love the sinner."

"There are a lot of sinners to love in this story. How about the boys? Do you suppose they found out and kept it to themselves?"

"Nathaniel may have, although I don't see how. Maybe that's why he dropped out of Andover and joined the marines only a couple of months after he got home. Turned his back on everything . . . but . . . no, I don't think he found out, either. He probably enlisted looking for a chance to prove himself. I think the boys were innocent. If there was a conspiracy of silence, it was those two, Cyrus and Elizabeth."

She turns to look over her shoulder at the horse pasture in the near distance, and in the middle distance at the San Rafael valley, dipping then rising to foothills tiered beneath the snow-rimmed Huachucas and the ranges of Sonora in the far distance.

"But do you?" I ask.

"What?"

"Hate the sin but love the sinner? Or do you hate the sinners, too? Do you hate your family?"

Sybil rubs her teeth with the knuckle of her thumb and looks at her papers, at a photograph of Nathaniel, Eliot, and Andrew when they were young, at the mildewed log of the voyage that ended their boyhoods, but I sense that she is not imagining them as they were then.

She is remembering Eliot and her grandfather as she knew them in her own early years: Eliot tall and slender and half bald, fond of jokes, a tenor in the church choir, a retired textile executive; an old man who had amused her as a child by picking up pencils and coins with his limber big toe. Andrew, two inches shorter, with Cyrus's gray-blue eyes and hair still thick but gone pure white, retired from the mathematics department at MIT to work as a consultant for the Massachusetts State Economics Board in the 1950s, when he battled industrialists and labor unions alike to lay the foundation for what became the electronics research corridor along Route 128, a scholarly man in whom cool rationalism cohabited with a street fighter's toughness (when he was in his early fifties, he had run down an adolescent purse snatcher in a North Boston alley and snatched the purse back, saying, "I'll take that, young man").

She does not remember Nathaniel. No one in her family does. No one in the family, dead or living, saw him after he left for the marines, except in a photograph he mailed home in 1902. It shows him in a khaki uniform and campaign hat, a Krag slung over one shoulder, the opposite shoulder leaning against a tree somewhere in the Philippines, where he died of malaria in the autumn of that year.

"No," she answers, finally. "I don't hate them. Absolutely not."

ACKNOWLEDGMENTS

Particular gratitude goes to my late father-in-law, John P. Ware, who planted the seed in my head several years ago, but who should not be held responsible for the tree that grew out of it. Special thanks to Capt. Andrew Burton and the crews of S / V *Tudy* and S / V *Caribe* for introducing a shore-hugger to blue-water sailing; to Herb Matthews, for lessons in celestial navigation; to Bruce Kirby, for checking the manuscript for technical errors. All mistakes in terminology, sailing tactics, etc., are my fault, not his. Thanks also to Capt. Bill Schwicker, for providing nautical lore about the Florida Keys and the Bahamas; to Mike Monroe and "Captain Finnbar," for relating to me, one night years ago in Key West, their experiences in Hurricane Allen aboard the ketch *The Island Princess;* to Mary Perkins and Capt. Reef Perkins, for information on wrecking and salvaging; and to my wife, Leslie Ware, for teaching me how to hand, reef, and steer, and especially for her invaluable suggestions and editing of countless rough drafts.

I am also indebted to a small library of books, but especially to the following:

Richard Meade Bach, *The Young Wrecker of the Florida Reef.* Lee and Shepard, 1865.

Graham Blackburn, *The Overlook Illustrated Dictionary of Nautical Terms.* Overlook Press, 1981.

Roger F. Duncan, *Coastal Maine: A Maritime History.* W. W. Norton, 1992.

Roger F. Duncan and John P. Ware, *The Cruising Guide to the New England Coast.* G. P. Putnam & Sons, 1990.

Barbara H. Erkkila, *Hammers on Stone: The History of Cape Ann Granite.* Peter Smith Books, 1987.

Joseph E. Garland, *Gloucester on the Wind*. Arcadia Publishing, 1995.

Tria Giovan, *Cuba: The Elusive Island*. Harry N. Abrams, Inc., 1996.

Harry Johnson and Fredrick S. Lightfoot, *Maritime New York in Nineteenth Century Photographs*. Dover Publications, Inc., 1980.

Richard Maury, *The Saga of Cimba*. Harcourt Brace & Co., 1939.

Charles B. McLane, *Blue Hill Bay: Islands of the Maine Coast*. The Kennebec River Press, Inc., 1985.

James A. Michener and John Kings, *Six Days in Havana*. University of Texas Press, 1989.

Farley Mowat, *The Serpent's Coil*. McClelland & Stewart Ltd., 1980.

Joseph M. Murphy, *Santeria: African Spirits in America*. Beacon Press, 1993.

Henry M. Plummer, *The Boy, Me and the Cat*. Commonwealth Press, 1961 (from a self-published manuscript by Mr. Plummer, dated 1912).

Rear-Admiral H. F. Pullen, *Atlantic Schooners*. Brunswick Press, 1967.

Birse Shepard, *Lore of the Wreckers*. Beacon Press, 1961.

Peter H. Spectre, *A Passage in Time*. W. W. Norton, 1991.

Stan Windhorn and Wright Langley, *Yesterday's Key West*. Langley Press, 1973.

And thanks to the editors of Time-Life Books for *The Fabulous Century: Volume One: 1900–1910,* and Judy Crichton and the WGBH Educational Foundation for *America 1900,* Henry Holt & Co., 1998.

A NOTE ABOUT THE AUTHOR

Philip Caputo was raised in the Chicago suburbs. After college, he served with the marines for three years, including sixteen months in Vietnam, and then spent six years as a foreign correspondent for the Chicago *Tribune*. He was held hostage in Beirut in 1973, learning only upon release of his shared 1972 Pulitzer Prize for reporting on election fraud in Chicago. Two years later, he was wounded in Beirut, and, during his convalescence, completed the manuscript for *A Rumor of War,* a Vietnam memoir that was published while Caputo was in Moscow, back on assignment for the *Tribune*. In 1977, he left the paper and turned to novels, of which he has written four, as well as another memoir (*Means of Escape*) and a collection of three novellas (*Exiles*). He lives in Connecticut with his wife, Leslie Blanchard Ware.

A NOTE ON THE TYPE

The text of this book was set in Sabon, a typeface designed by Jan Tschichold (1902–1974), the well-known German typographer. Because it was designed in Frankfurt, Sabon was named for the famous Frankfurt type founder Jacques Sabon, who died in 1580 while manager of the Egenolff foundry. Based loosely on the original designs of Claude Garamond (c. 1480–1561), Sabon is unique in that it was explicitly designed for hot-metal composition on both the Monotype and Linotype machines as well as for film composition.

Composed by Stratford Publishing Services,
Brattleboro, Vermont

Printed and bound by Quebecor Printing,
Fairfield, Pennsylvania

Maps by Mark Stein

Typography and binding design
by Dorothy S. Baker

Caputo, Philip.
The voyage

FIC CAP

RSN=00060345

NO 1 5 '99

Delafield Public Library
Delafield, WI 53018

DELAFIELD PUBLIC LIBRARY

3 0646 00103 5843